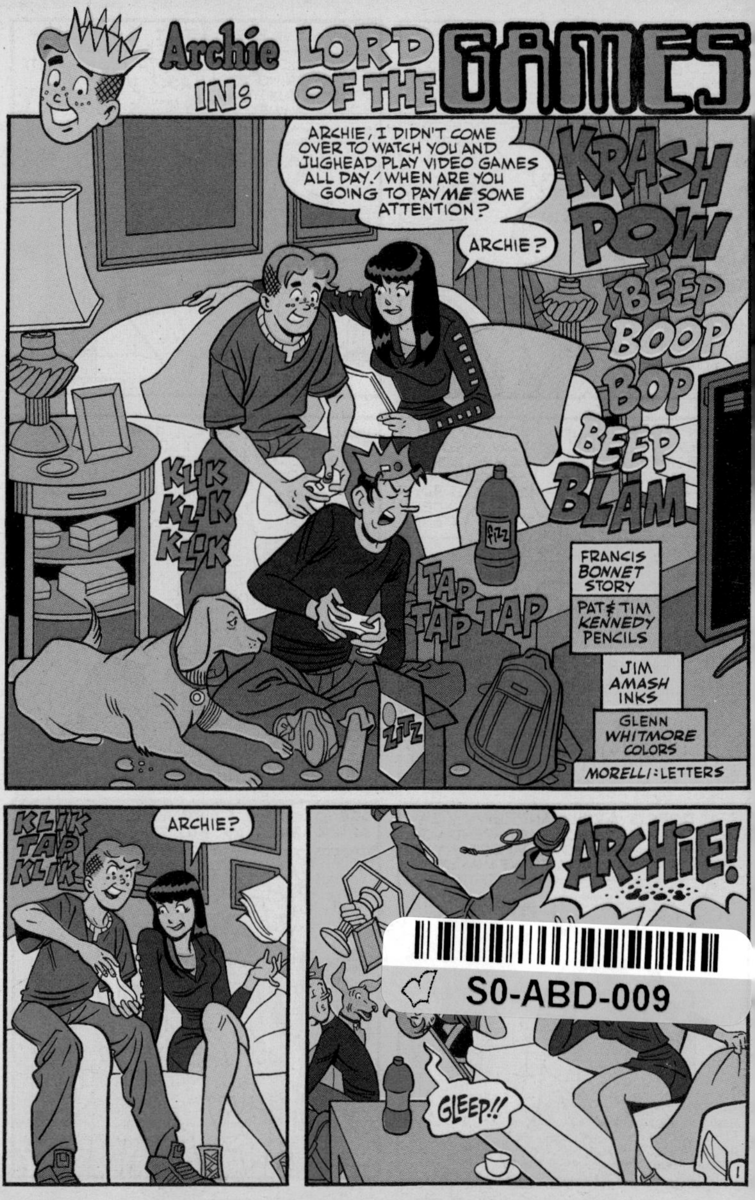
Archie IN: LORD OF THE GAMES
ARCHIE, I DIDN'T COME OVER TO WATCH YOU AND JUGHEAD PLAY VIDEO GAMES ALL DAY! WHEN ARE YOU GOING TO PAY ME SOME ATTENTION?
ARCHIE?
KRASH POW BEEP BOOP BOP BEEP BLAM
KLIK KLIK KLIK
TAP TAP TAP
FIZZ
ZITZ
FRANCIS BONNET STORY
PAT & TIM KENNEDY PENCILS
JIM AMASH INKS
GLENN WHITMORE COLORS
MORELLI: LETTERS
KLIK TAP KLIK
ARCHIE?
ARCHIE!
GLEEP!!
1

Panel 1:
Betty: EVER SINCE YOU GOT THAT SILLY *VIDEO GAME*, I'VE BARELY *SEEN* YOU!
Jughead: SORRY, RONNIE, BUT *FORKNITE* ISN'T SILLY! IT'S ONE OF THE BEST GAMES *EVER* MADE!
Archie: IT'S SO GOOD THAT I ONLY STOP FOR A SNACK EVERY *TEN* MINUTES INSTEAD OF *FIVE!*

Panel 2:
Archie: I KNOW I'VE BEEN BUSY WITH FORKNITE, BUT IT'S NOT LIKE I'M IGNORING YOU! DIDN'T I JUST TAKE YOU TO *DINNER?!*
Veronica: THAT WAS A *MONTH* AGO!
Archie: Hmm...NOW THAT YOU MENTION IT, *DINNER* SOUNDS GOOD...

Panel 3:
Veronica: I DON'T UNDERSTAND WHY YOU THINK THAT GAME IS *SO GREAT!* YOUR CHARACTER JUST RUNS AROUND BLOWING UP EVERYTHING THAT MOVES!
Archie: YOU DON'T PLAY VIDEO GAMES, RONNIE, YOU COULDN'T *POSSIBLY UNDERSTAND!* THAT'S *EXACTLY* WHY IT'S *SO GREAT!*

Panel 4:
Veronica: WELL, MAYBE I SHOULD TRY THE GAME AND *JUDGE* FOR MYSELF!
Archie: YOU COULD TRY, BUT JUG AND I ARE *MASTER-LEVEL* PLAYERS. NO OFFENSE, BUT WE'D MOP THE FLOOR WITH YOU IN THIS GAME!
Jughead: LIKE THAT TEN YEAR OLD KID DID TO *US* YESTERDAY?

Panel 5:

Veronica: THAT *DOES IT*, ARCHIE ANDREWS!! I'M GOING TO SHOW YOU THAT SPENDING TIME WITH ME IS MORE IMPORTANT THAN THAT SILLY GAME ONE WAY OR ANOTHER!!

Panel 6:
Jughead: ARE YOU GOING AFTER HER?
Archie: I PROBABLY *SHOULD*, BUT I'M A LITTLE *FRIGHTENED* RIGHT NOW!
SLAM

2

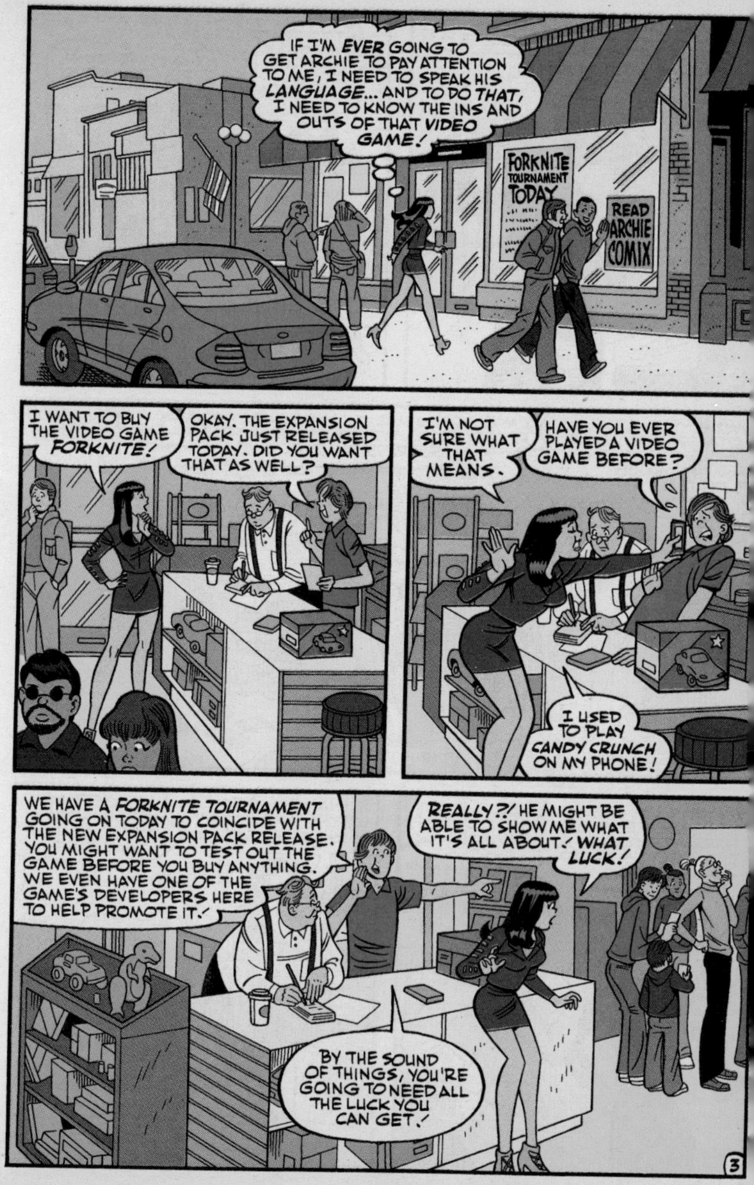
IF I'M EVER GOING TO GET ARCHIE TO PAY ATTENTION TO ME, I NEED TO SPEAK HIS LANGUAGE... AND TO DO THAT, I NEED TO KNOW THE INS AND OUTS OF THAT VIDEO GAME!
FORKNITE TOURNAMENT TODAY
READ ARCHIE COMIX
I WANT TO BUY THE VIDEO GAME FORKNITE!
OKAY. THE EXPANSION PACK JUST RELEASED TODAY. DID YOU WANT THAT AS WELL?
I'M NOT SURE WHAT THAT MEANS.
HAVE YOU EVER PLAYED A VIDEO GAME BEFORE?
I USED TO PLAY CANDY CRUNCH ON MY PHONE!
WE HAVE A FORKNITE TOURNAMENT GOING ON TODAY TO COINCIDE WITH THE NEW EXPANSION PACK RELEASE. YOU MIGHT WANT TO TEST OUT THE GAME BEFORE YOU BUY ANYTHING. WE EVEN HAVE ONE OF THE GAME'S DEVELOPERS HERE TO HELP PROMOTE IT.
REALLY?! HE MIGHT BE ABLE TO SHOW ME WHAT IT'S ALL ABOUT! WHAT LUCK!
BY THE SOUND OF THINGS, YOU'RE GOING TO NEED ALL THE LUCK YOU CAN GET!

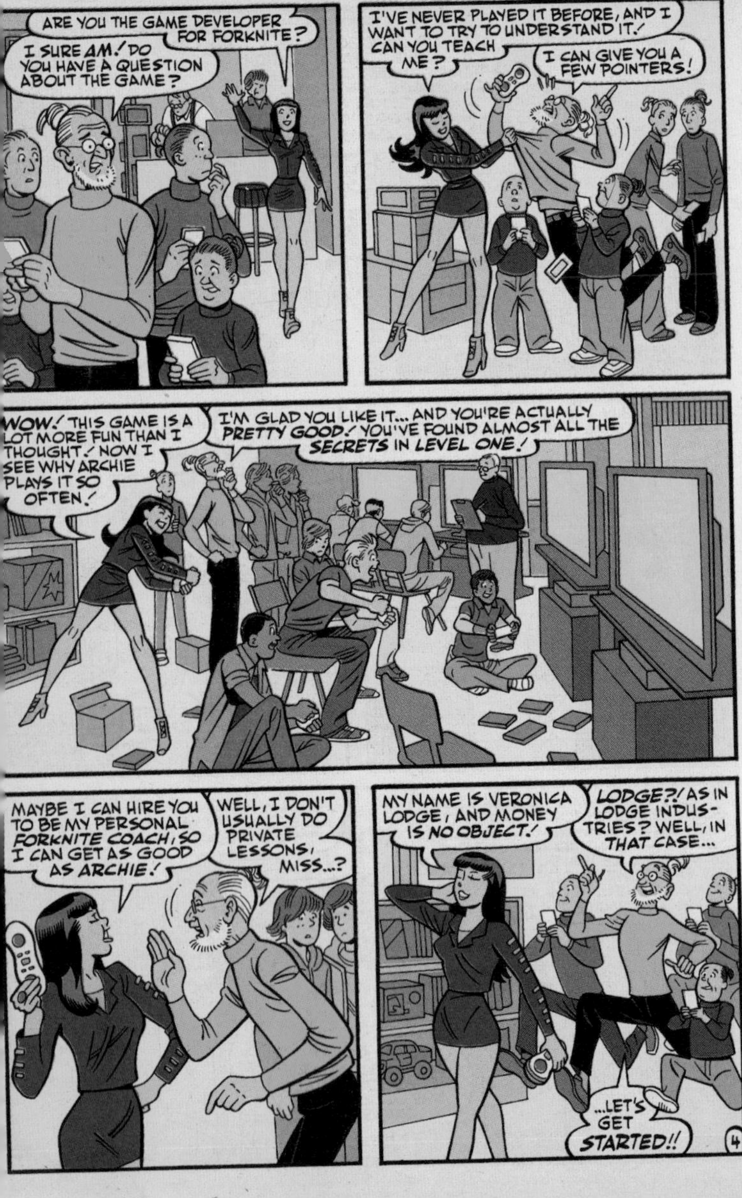
ARE YOU THE GAME DEVELOPER FOR FORKNITE?
I SURE AM! DO YOU HAVE A QUESTION ABOUT THE GAME?
I'VE NEVER PLAYED IT BEFORE, AND I WANT TO TRY TO UNDERSTAND IT! CAN YOU TEACH ME?
I CAN GIVE YOU A FEW POINTERS!
WOW! THIS GAME IS A LOT MORE FUN THAN I THOUGHT! NOW I SEE WHY ARCHIE PLAYS IT SO OFTEN!
I'M GLAD YOU LIKE IT... AND YOU'RE ACTUALLY PRETTY GOOD! YOU'VE FOUND ALMOST ALL THE SECRETS IN LEVEL ONE!
MAYBE I CAN HIRE YOU TO BE MY PERSONAL FORKNITE COACH, SO I CAN GET AS GOOD AS ARCHIE!
WELL, I DON'T USUALLY DO PRIVATE LESSONS, MISS...?
MY NAME IS VERONICA LODGE, AND MONEY IS NO OBJECT!
LODGE?! AS IN LODGE INDUSTRIES? WELL, IN THAT CASE...
...LET'S GET STARTED!!
4

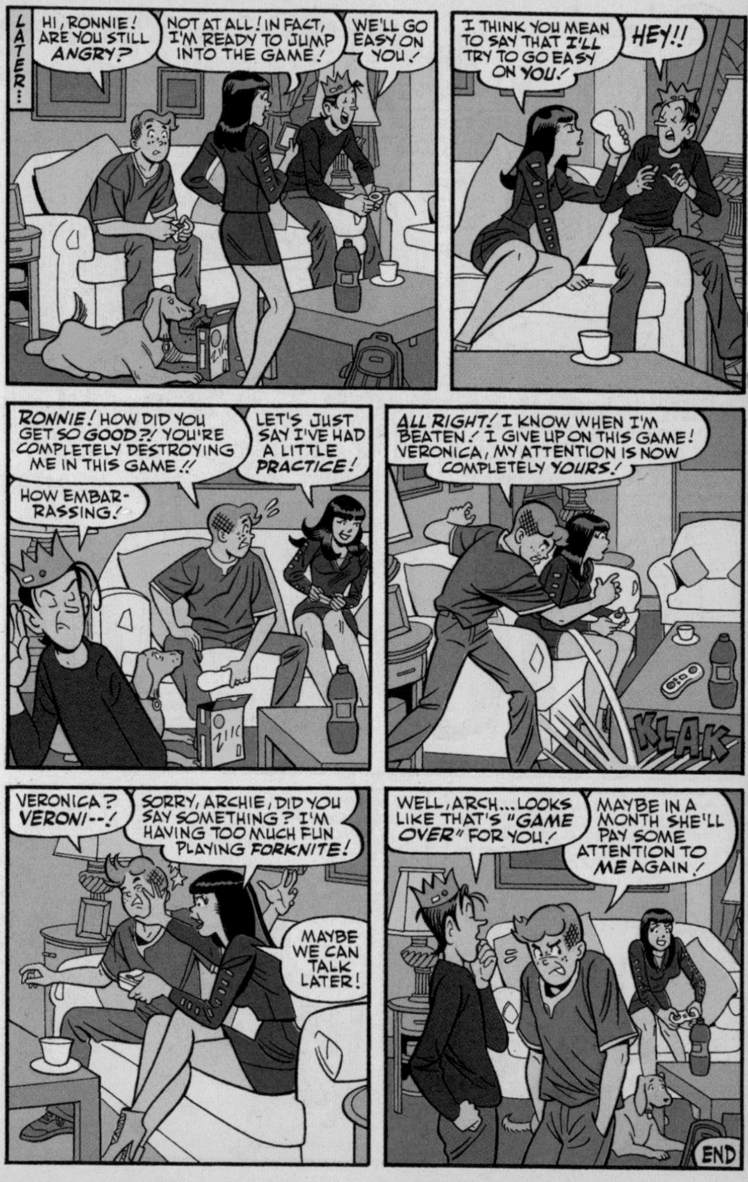
LATER...
HI, RONNIE! ARE YOU STILL ANGRY?
NOT AT ALL! IN FACT, I'M READY TO JUMP INTO THE GAME!
WE'LL GO EASY ON YOU!
I THINK YOU MEAN TO SAY THAT I'LL TRY TO GO EASY ON YOU!
HEY!!
RONNIE! HOW DID YOU GET SO GOOD?! YOU'RE COMPLETELY DESTROYING ME IN THIS GAME!!
LET'S JUST SAY I'VE HAD A LITTLE PRACTICE!
HOW EMBARRASSING!
ALL RIGHT! I KNOW WHEN I'M BEATEN! I GIVE UP ON THIS GAME! VERONICA, MY ATTENTION IS NOW COMPLETELY YOURS!
KLAK
VERONICA? VERONI--!
SORRY, ARCHIE, DID YOU SAY SOMETHING? I'M HAVING TOO MUCH FUN PLAYING FORKNITE!
MAYBE WE CAN TALK LATER!
WELL, ARCH... LOOKS LIKE THAT'S "GAME OVER" FOR YOU!
MAYBE IN A MONTH SHE'LL PAY SOME ATTENTION TO ME AGAIN!
END

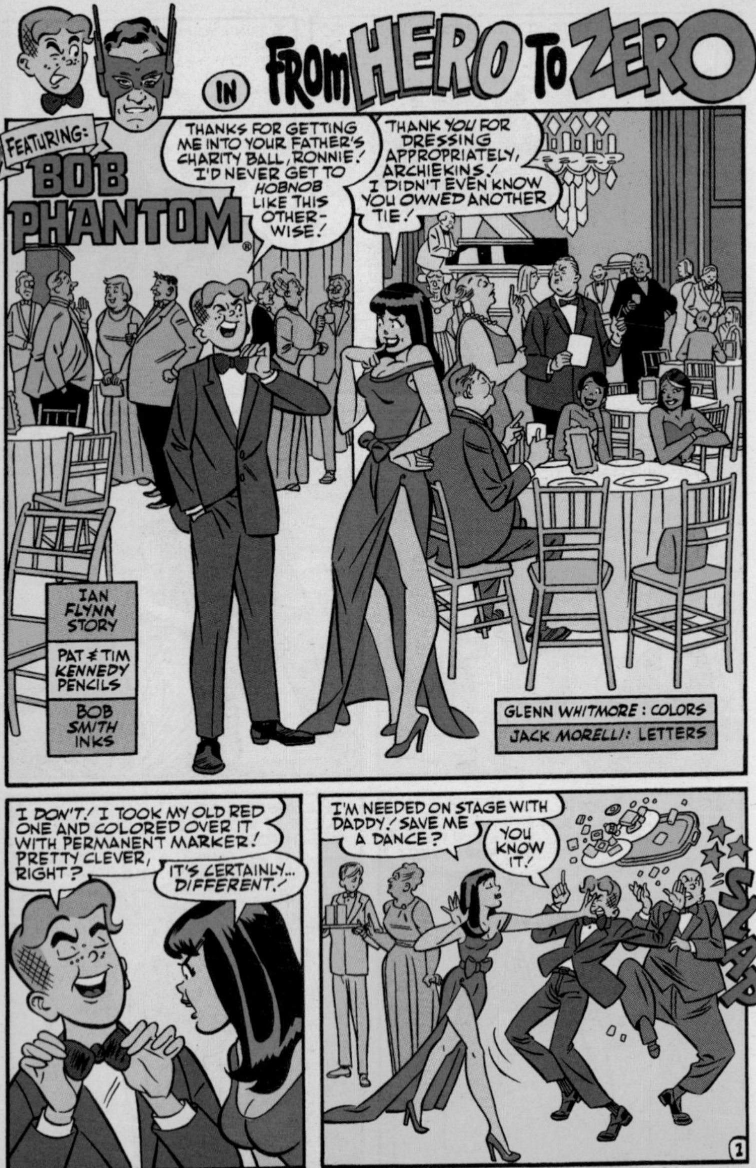
IN
FROM HERO TO ZERO
FEATURING: BOB PHANTOM®
THANKS FOR GETTING ME INTO YOUR FATHER'S CHARITY BALL, RONNIE! I'D NEVER GET TO HOBNOB LIKE THIS OTHERWISE!
THANK YOU FOR DRESSING APPROPRIATELY, ARCHIEKINS! I DIDN'T EVEN KNOW YOU OWNED ANOTHER TIE!
IAN FLYNN STORY
PAT & TIM KENNEDY PENCILS
BOB SMITH INKS
GLENN WHITMORE : COLORS
JACK MORELLI: LETTERS
I DON'T! I TOOK MY OLD RED ONE AND COLORED OVER IT WITH PERMANENT MARKER! PRETTY CLEVER, RIGHT?
IT'S CERTAINLY... DIFFERENT!
I'M NEEDED ON STAGE WITH DADDY! SAVE ME A DANCE?
YOU KNOW IT!
SLAP
1

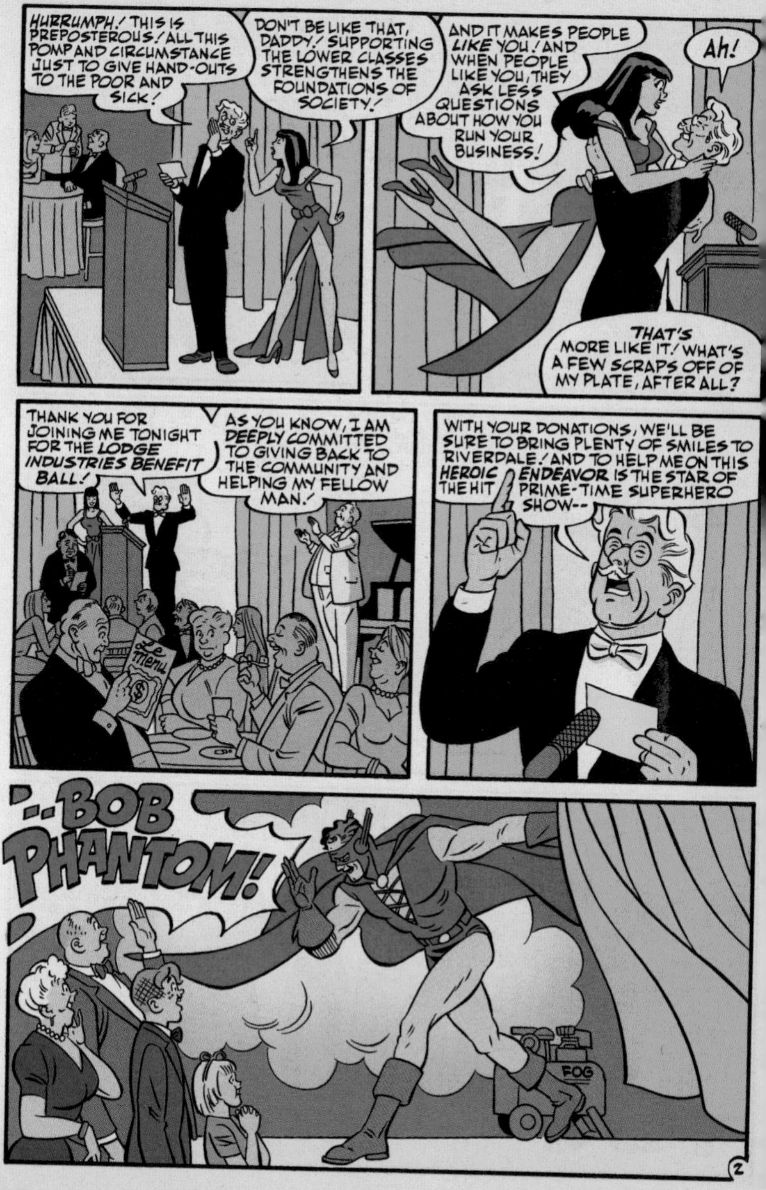
HURRUMPH! THIS IS PREPOSTEROUS! ALL THIS POMP AND CIRCUMSTANCE JUST TO GIVE HAND-OUTS TO THE POOR AND SICK!
DON'T BE LIKE THAT, DADDY! SUPPORTING THE LOWER CLASSES STRENGTHENS THE FOUNDATIONS OF SOCIETY!
AND IT MAKES PEOPLE LIKE YOU! AND WHEN PEOPLE LIKE YOU, THEY ASK LESS QUESTIONS ABOUT HOW YOU RUN YOUR BUSINESS!
Ah!
THAT'S MORE LIKE IT! WHAT'S A FEW SCRAPS OFF OF MY PLATE, AFTER ALL?
THANK YOU FOR JOINING ME TONIGHT FOR THE LODGE INDUSTRIES BENEFIT BALL!
AS YOU KNOW, I AM DEEPLY COMMITTED TO GIVING BACK TO THE COMMUNITY AND HELPING MY FELLOW MAN!
Le Menu
WITH YOUR DONATIONS, WE'LL BE SURE TO BRING PLENTY OF SMILES TO RIVERDALE! AND TO HELP ME ON THIS HEROIC ENDEAVOR IS THE STAR OF THE HIT PRIME-TIME SUPERHERO SHOW--
--BOB PHANTOM!
FOG

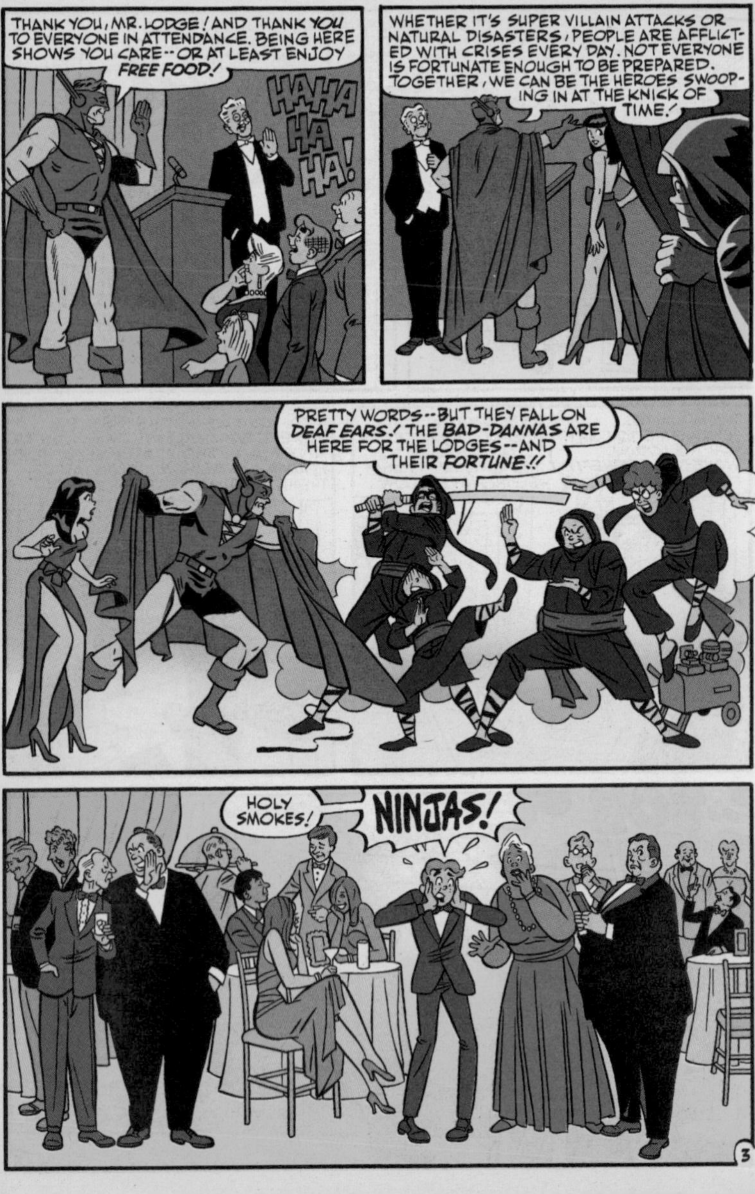
THANK YOU, MR. LODGE! AND THANK YOU TO EVERYONE IN ATTENDANCE. BEING HERE SHOWS YOU CARE-- OR AT LEAST ENJOY FREE FOOD!
HAHAHA HA HA!
WHETHER IT'S SUPER VILLAIN ATTACKS OR NATURAL DISASTERS, PEOPLE ARE AFFLICTED WITH CRISES EVERY DAY. NOT EVERYONE IS FORTUNATE ENOUGH TO BE PREPARED. TOGETHER, WE CAN BE THE HEROES SWOOPING IN AT THE KNICK OF TIME!
PRETTY WORDS--BUT THEY FALL ON DEAF EARS! THE BAD-DANNAS ARE HERE FOR THE LODGES--AND THEIR FORTUNE!!
HOLY SMOKES!
NINJAS!
3

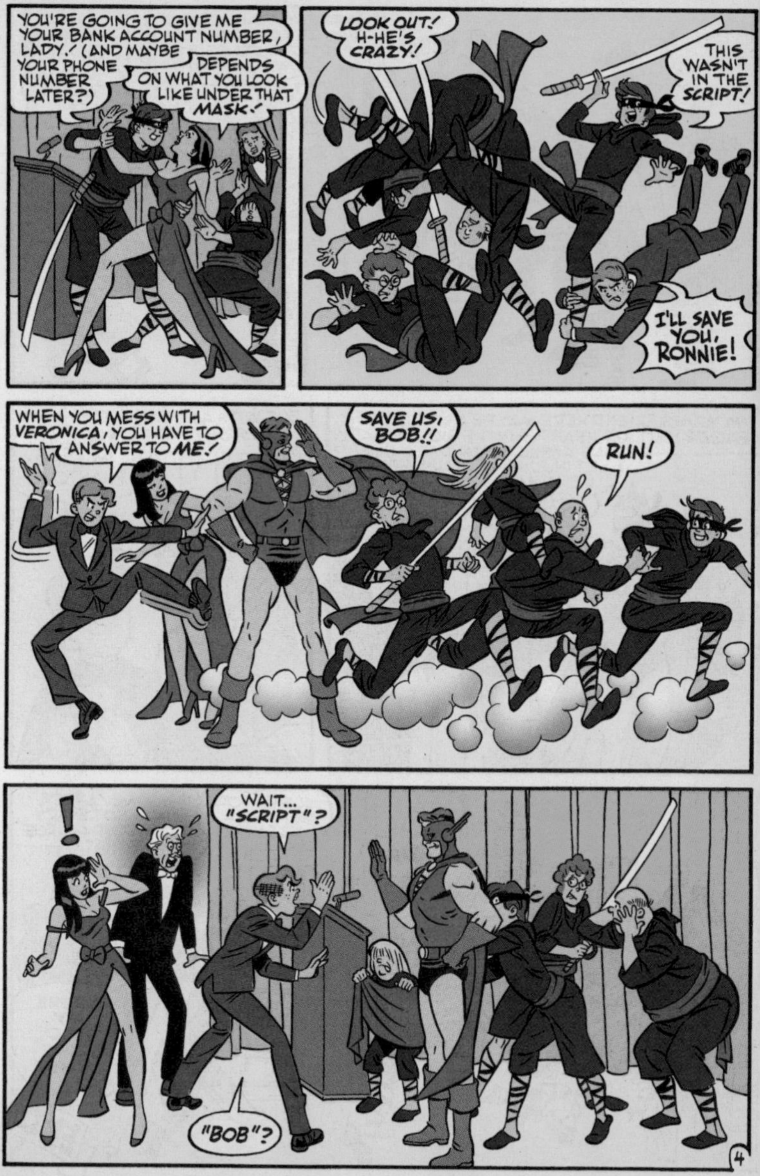

YOU'RE GOING TO GIVE ME YOUR BANK ACCOUNT NUMBER, LADY! (AND MAYBE YOUR PHONE NUMBER LATER?)
DEPENDS ON WHAT YOU LOOK LIKE UNDER THAT MASK!
LOOK OUT! H-HE'S CRAZY!
THIS WASN'T IN THE SCRIPT!
I'LL SAVE YOU, RONNIE!
WHEN YOU MESS WITH VERONICA, YOU HAVE TO ANSWER TO ME!
SAVE US, BOB!!
RUN!
!
WAIT... "SCRIPT"?
"BOB"?
4

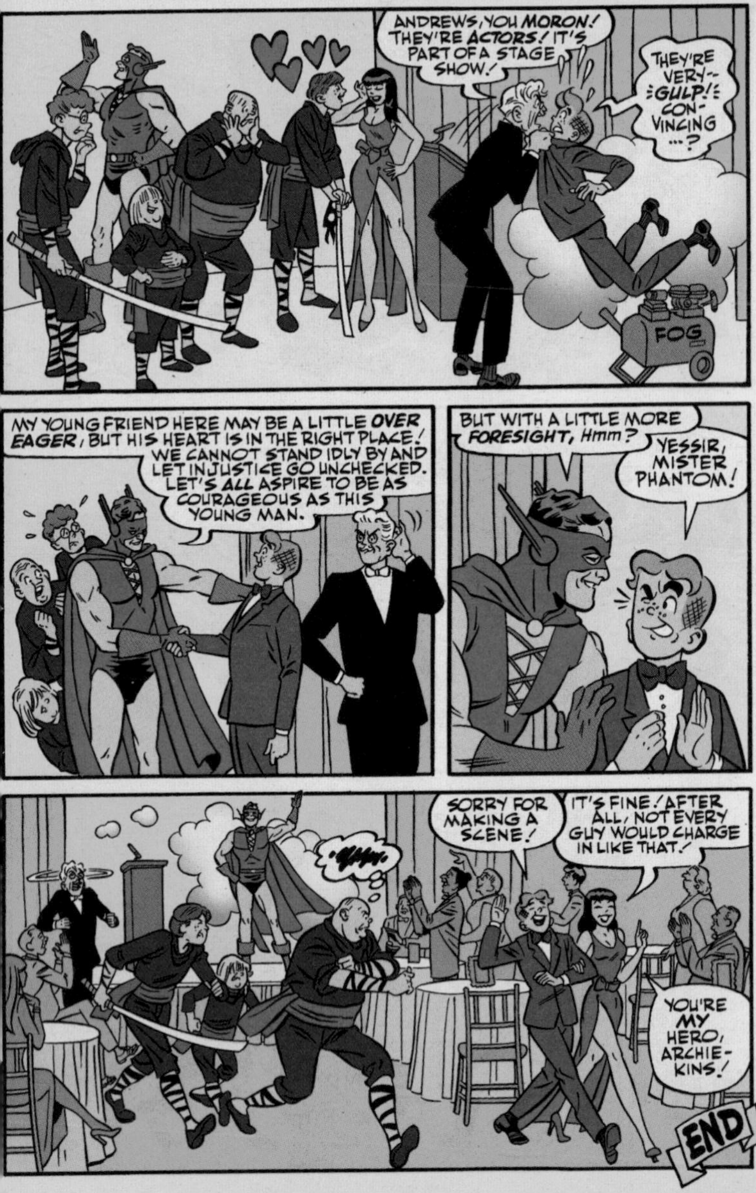
ANDREWS, YOU MORON! THEY'RE ACTORS! IT'S PART OF A STAGE SHOW!
THEY'RE VERY-- GULP! CONVINCING ...?
FOG
MY YOUNG FRIEND HERE MAY BE A LITTLE OVER EAGER, BUT HIS HEART IS IN THE RIGHT PLACE! WE CANNOT STAND IDLY BY AND LET INJUSTICE GO UNCHECKED. LET'S ALL ASPIRE TO BE AS COURAGEOUS AS THIS YOUNG MAN.
BUT WITH A LITTLE MORE FORESIGHT, Hmm?
YESSIR, MISTER PHANTOM!
SORRY FOR MAKING A SCENE!
IT'S FINE! AFTER ALL, NOT EVERY GUY WOULD CHARGE IN LIKE THAT!
YOU'RE MY HERO, ARCHIE-KINS!
END

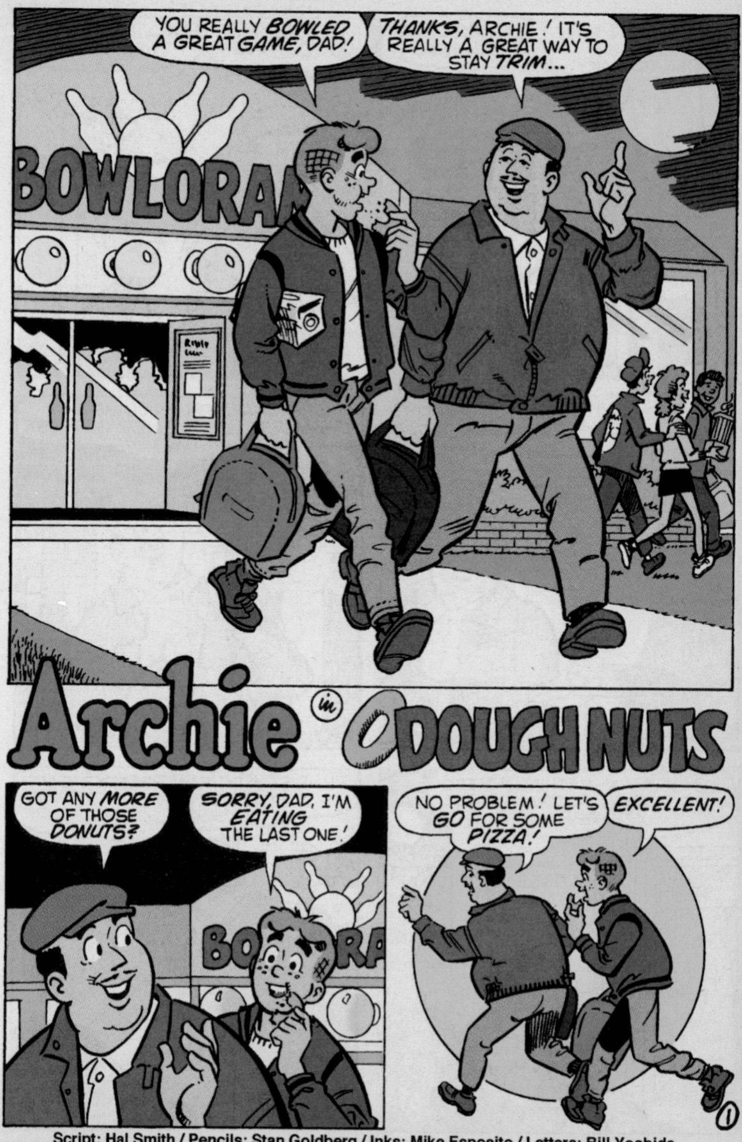
YOU REALLY BOWLED A GREAT GAME, DAD!
THANKS, ARCHIE! IT'S REALLY A GREAT WAY TO STAY TRIM...
BOWLORAM
Archie in DOUGHNUTS
GOT ANY MORE OF THOSE DONUTS?
SORRY, DAD, I'M EATING THE LAST ONE!
NO PROBLEM! LET'S GO FOR SOME PIZZA!
EXCELLENT!
1

Script: Hal Smith / Pencils: Stan Goldberg / Inks: Mike Esposito / Letters: Bill Yoshida

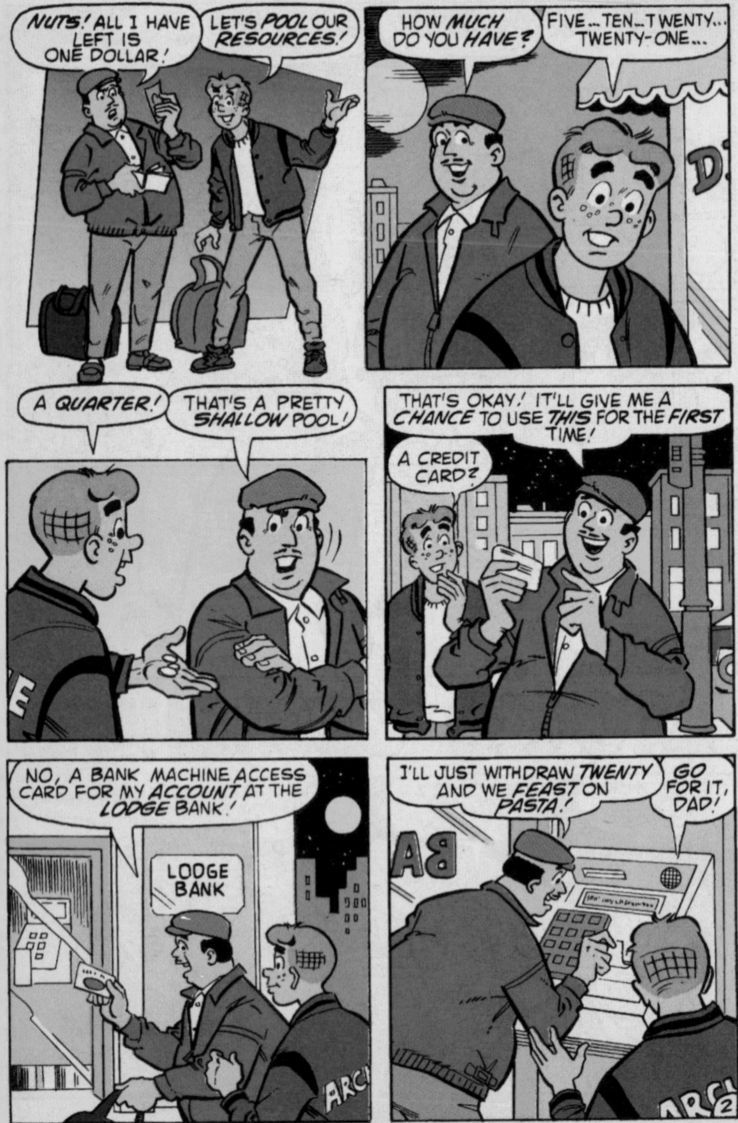
NUTS! ALL I HAVE LEFT IS ONE DOLLAR!
LET'S POOL OUR RESOURCES!
HOW MUCH DO YOU HAVE?
FIVE... TEN... TWENTY... TWENTY-ONE...
A QUARTER!
THAT'S A PRETTY SHALLOW POOL!
THAT'S OKAY! IT'LL GIVE ME A CHANCE TO USE THIS FOR THE FIRST TIME!
A CREDIT CARD?
NO, A BANK MACHINE ACCESS CARD FOR MY ACCOUNT AT THE LODGE BANK!
LODGE BANK
I'LL JUST WITHDRAW TWENTY AND WE FEAST ON PASTA!
GO FOR IT, DAD!
2

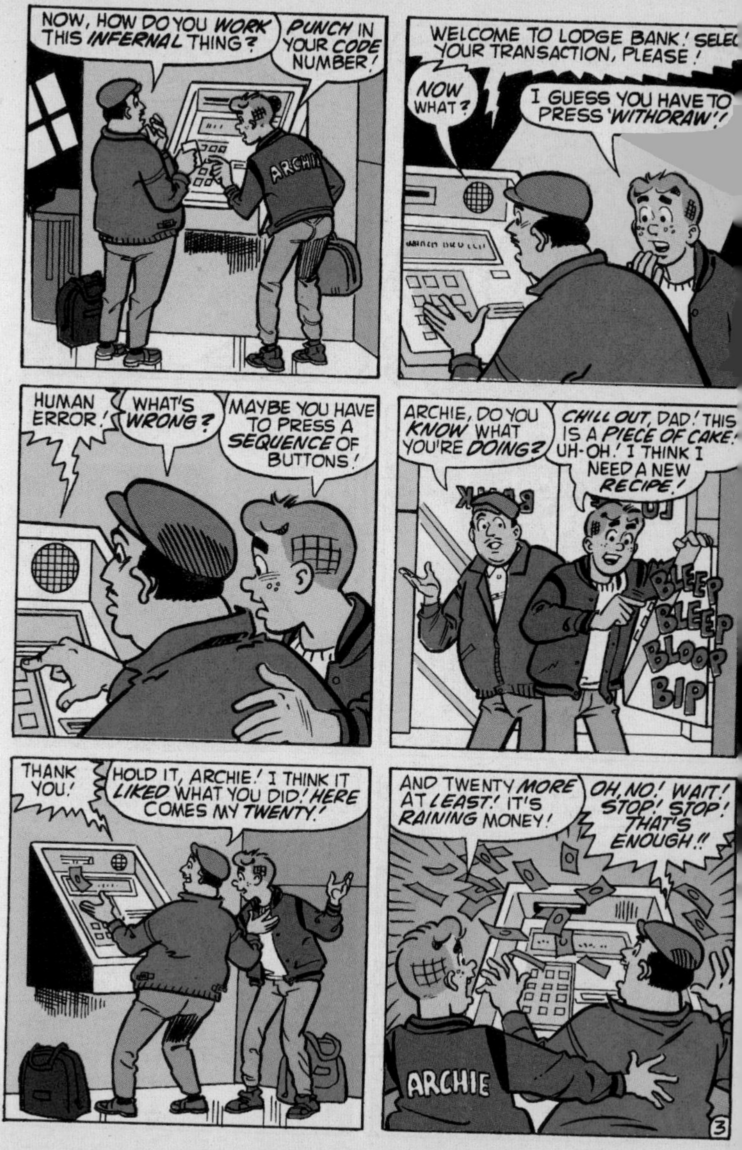
NOW, HOW DO YOU WORK THIS INFERNAL THING?
PUNCH IN YOUR CODE NUMBER!
ARCHIE
WELCOME TO LODGE BANK! SELEC YOUR TRANSACTION, PLEASE!
NOW WHAT?
I GUESS YOU HAVE TO PRESS 'WITHDRAW'!
HUMAN ERROR!
WHAT'S WRONG?
MAYBE YOU HAVE TO PRESS A SEQUENCE OF BUTTONS!
ARCHIE, DO YOU KNOW WHAT YOU'RE DOING?
CHILL OUT, DAD! THIS IS A PIECE OF CAKE! UH-OH! I THINK I NEED A NEW RECIPE!
BLEEP BLEEP BLOOP BIP
THANK YOU!
HOLD IT, ARCHIE! I THINK IT LIKED WHAT YOU DID! HERE COMES MY TWENTY!
AND TWENTY MORE AT LEAST! IT'S RAINING MONEY!
OH, NO! WAIT! STOP! STOP! THAT'S ENOUGH!!
ARCHIE
3

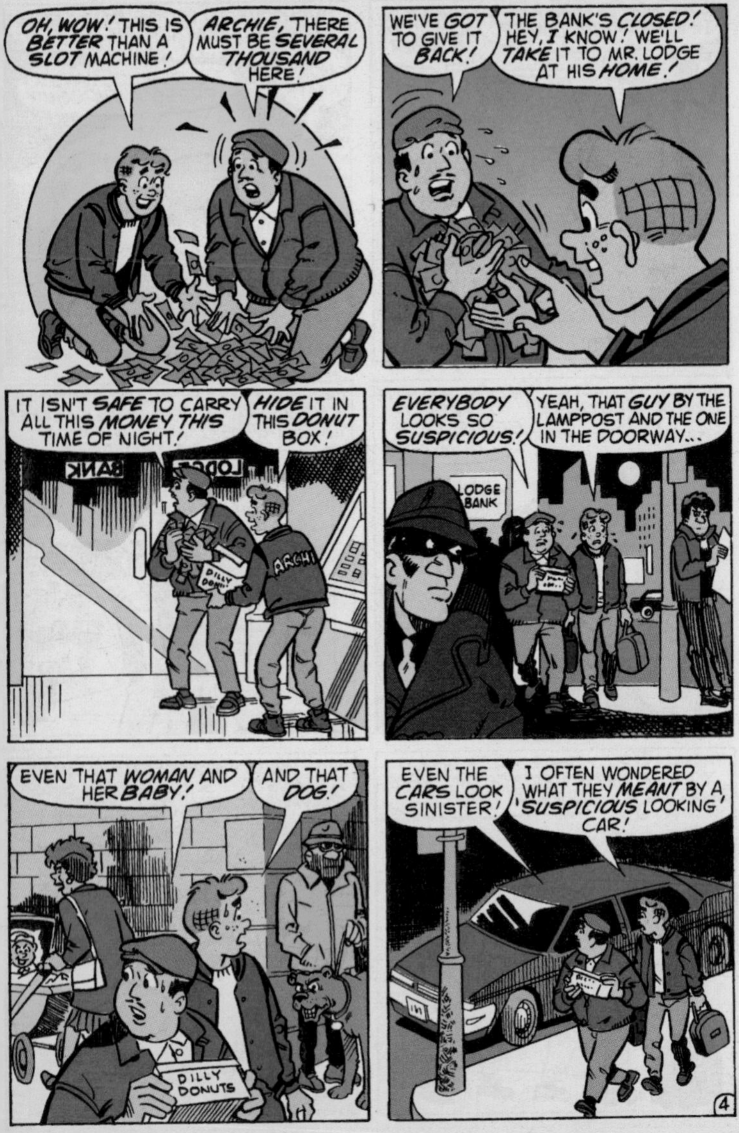

OH, WOW! THIS IS BETTER THAN A SLOT MACHINE!
ARCHIE, THERE MUST BE SEVERAL THOUSAND HERE!
WE'VE GOT TO GIVE IT BACK!
THE BANK'S CLOSED! HEY, I KNOW! WE'LL TAKE IT TO MR. LODGE AT HIS HOME!
IT ISN'T SAFE TO CARRY ALL THIS MONEY THIS TIME OF NIGHT!
HIDE IT IN THIS DONUT BOX!
DILLY DONUTS
ARCHI
EVERYBODY LOOKS SO SUSPICIOUS!
YEAH, THAT GUY BY THE LAMPPOST AND THE ONE IN THE DOORWAY...
LODGE BANK
EVEN THAT WOMAN AND HER BABY!
AND THAT DOG!
DILLY DONUTS
EVEN THE CARS LOOK SINISTER!
I OFTEN WONDERED WHAT THEY MEANT BY A 'SUSPICIOUS LOOKING' CAR!

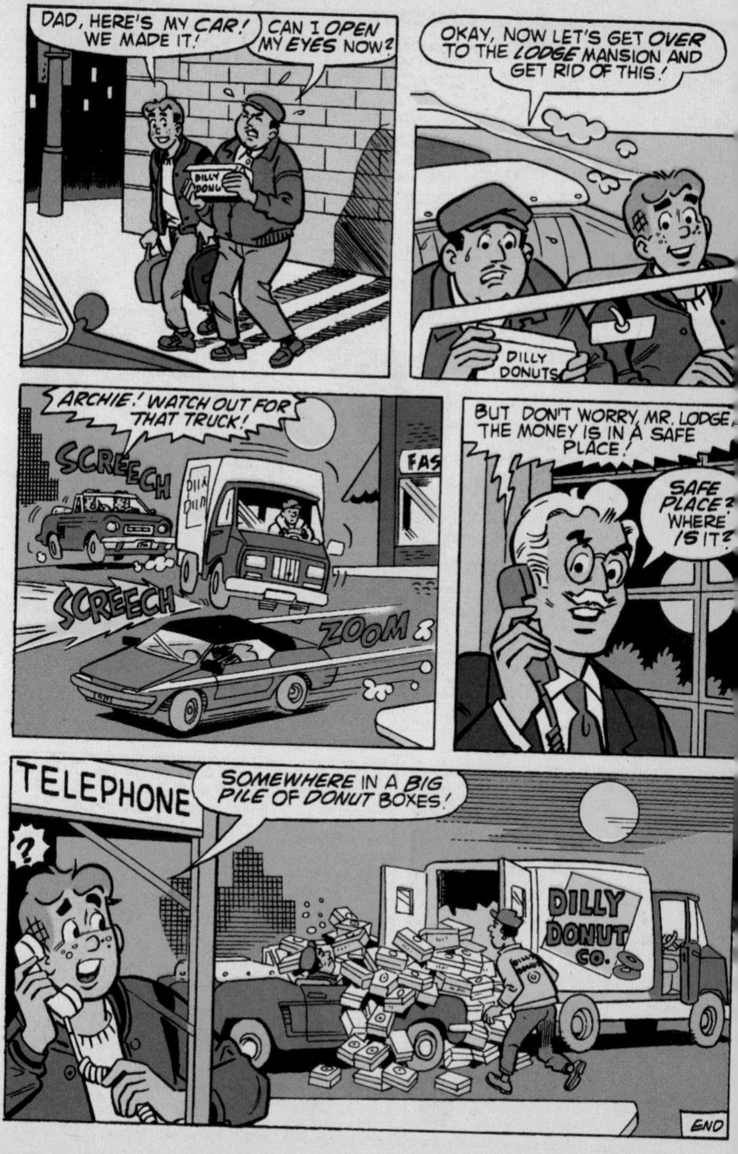
DAD, HERE'S MY *CAR*! WE MADE IT!
CAN I *OPEN* MY *EYES* NOW?
DILLY DONU
OKAY, NOW LET'S GET *OVER* TO THE *LODGE* MANSION AND GET RID OF THIS!
DILLY DONUTS
ARCHIE! WATCH OUT FOR THAT TRUCK!
SCREECH
SCREECH
ZOOM
BUT DON'T WORRY, MR. LODGE, THE MONEY IS IN A SAFE PLACE!
SAFE PLACE? WHERE *IS* IT?
TELEPHONE
SOMEWHERE IN A *BIG PILE* OF *DONUT* BOXES!
?
DILLY DONUT CO.
END

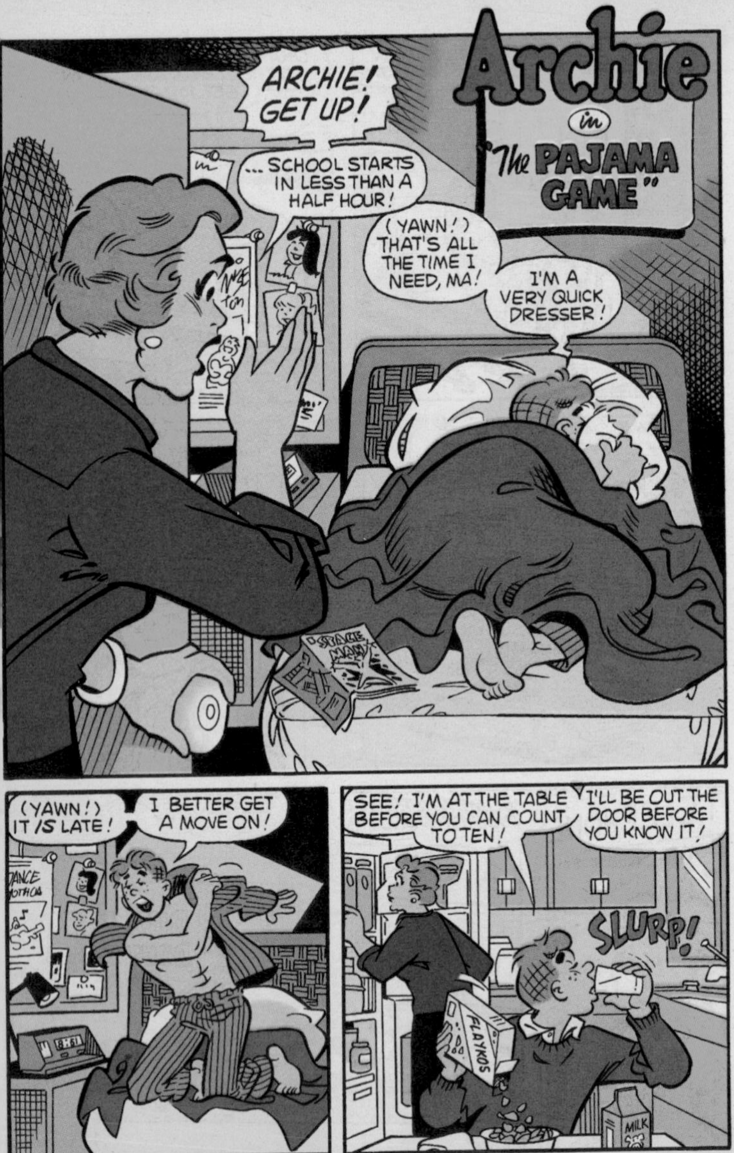
Archie
in
"The PAJAMA GAME"
ARCHIE! GET UP!
... SCHOOL STARTS IN LESS THAN A HALF HOUR!
(YAWN!) THAT'S ALL THE TIME I NEED, MA!
I'M A VERY QUICK DRESSER!
STACE MAN
(YAWN!) IT IS LATE!
I BETTER GET A MOVE ON!
DANCE
SEE! I'M AT THE TABLE BEFORE YOU CAN COUNT TO TEN!
I'LL BE OUT THE DOOR BEFORE YOU KNOW IT!
SLURP!
FLAYKOS
MILK

Script: George Gladir / Pencils: Stan Goldberg / Inks: Bob Smith / Letters: Bill Yoshida

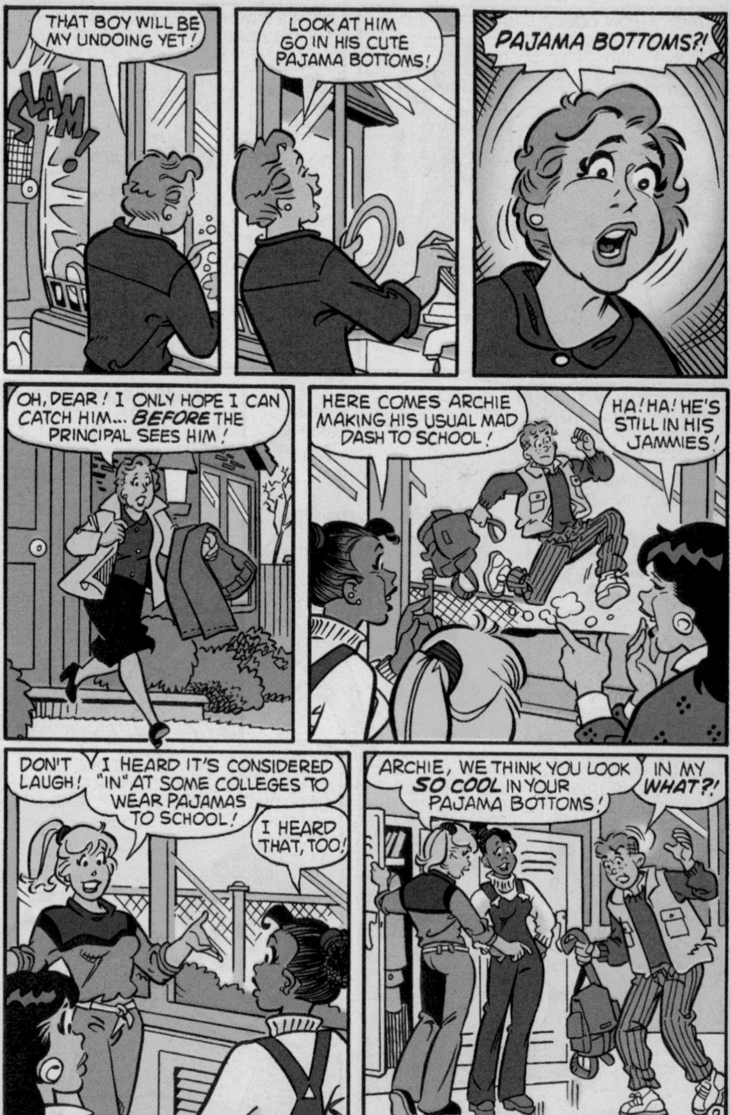

THAT BOY WILL BE MY UNDOING YET!
SLAM!
LOOK AT HIM GO IN HIS CUTE PAJAMA BOTTOMS!
PAJAMA BOTTOMS?!
OH, DEAR! I ONLY HOPE I CAN CATCH HIM... BEFORE THE PRINCIPAL SEES HIM!
HERE COMES ARCHIE MAKING HIS USUAL MAD DASH TO SCHOOL!
HA! HA! HE'S STILL IN HIS JAMMIES!
DON'T LAUGH!
I HEARD IT'S CONSIDERED "IN" AT SOME COLLEGES TO WEAR PAJAMAS TO SCHOOL!
I HEARD THAT, TOO!
ARCHIE, WE THINK YOU LOOK SO COOL IN YOUR PAJAMA BOTTOMS!
IN MY WHAT?!
2

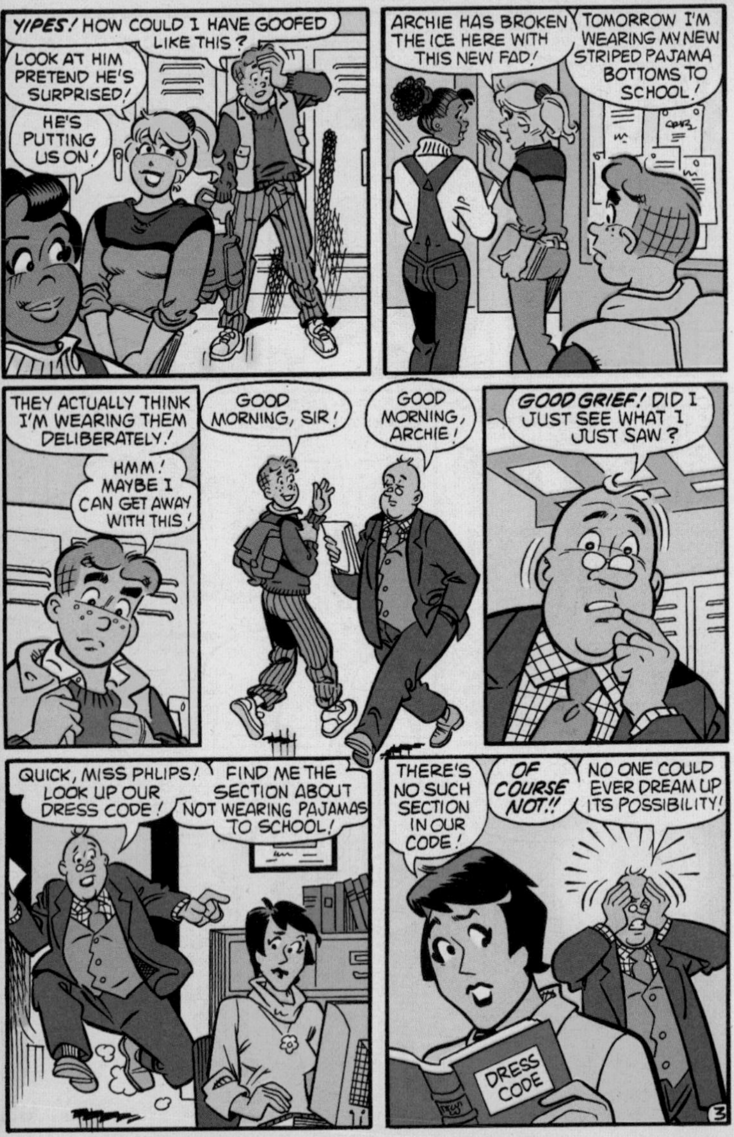
YIPES! HOW COULD I HAVE GOOFED LIKE THIS?
LOOK AT HIM PRETEND HE'S SURPRISED!
HE'S PUTTING US ON!
ARCHIE HAS BROKEN THE ICE HERE WITH THIS NEW FAD!
TOMORROW I'M WEARING MY NEW STRIPED PAJAMA BOTTOMS TO SCHOOL!
THEY ACTUALLY THINK I'M WEARING THEM DELIBERATELY!
HMM! MAYBE I CAN GET AWAY WITH THIS!
GOOD MORNING, SIR!
GOOD MORNING, ARCHIE!
GOOD GRIEF! DID I JUST SEE WHAT I JUST SAW?
QUICK, MISS PHLIPS! LOOK UP OUR DRESS CODE!
FIND ME THE SECTION ABOUT NOT WEARING PAJAMAS TO SCHOOL!
THERE'S NO SUCH SECTION IN OUR CODE!
OF COURSE NOT!!
NO ONE COULD EVER DREAM UP ITS POSSIBILITY!
DRESS CODE
3

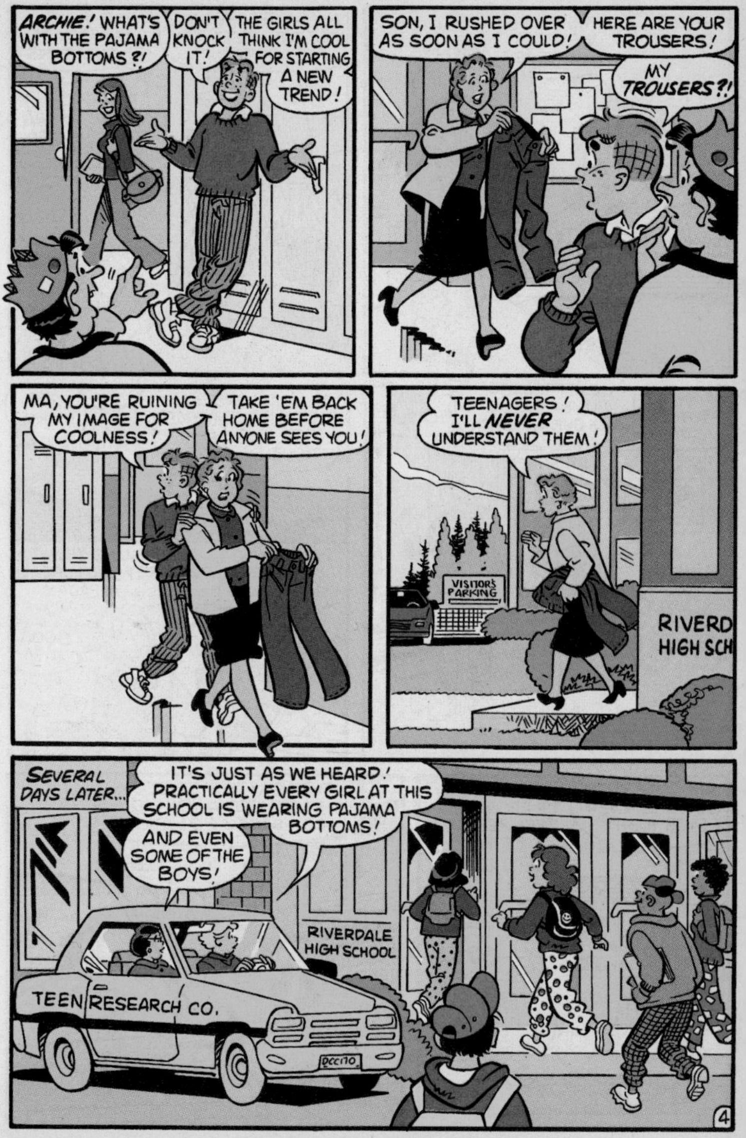
ARCHIE! WHAT'S WITH THE PAJAMA BOTTOMS?!
DON'T KNOCK IT!
THE GIRLS ALL THINK I'M COOL FOR STARTING A NEW TREND!
SON, I RUSHED OVER AS SOON AS I COULD!
HERE ARE YOUR TROUSERS!
MY TROUSERS?!
MA, YOU'RE RUINING MY IMAGE FOR COOLNESS!
TAKE 'EM BACK HOME BEFORE ANYONE SEES YOU!
TEENAGERS! I'LL NEVER UNDERSTAND THEM!
VISITORS PARKING
RIVERD
HIGH SCH
SEVERAL DAYS LATER...
IT'S JUST AS WE HEARD! PRACTICALLY EVERY GIRL AT THIS SCHOOL IS WEARING PAJAMA BOTTOMS!
AND EVEN SOME OF THE BOYS!
RIVERDALE HIGH SCHOOL
TEEN RESEARCH CO.
4

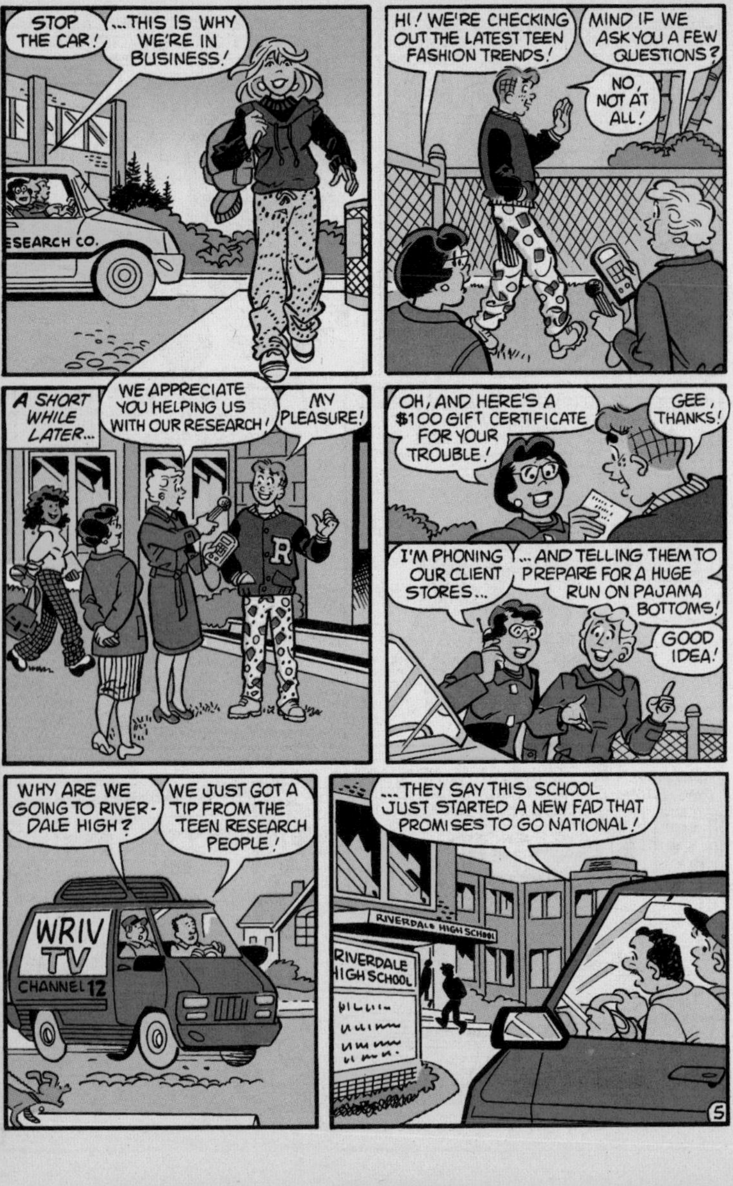

STOP THE CAR!
...THIS IS WHY WE'RE IN BUSINESS!
ESEARCH CO.
HI! WE'RE CHECKING OUT THE LATEST TEEN FASHION TRENDS!
MIND IF WE ASK YOU A FEW QUESTIONS?
NO, NOT AT ALL!
A SHORT WHILE LATER...
WE APPRECIATE YOU HELPING US WITH OUR RESEARCH!
MY PLEASURE!
R
OH, AND HERE'S A $100 GIFT CERTIFICATE FOR YOUR TROUBLE!
GEE, THANKS!
I'M PHONING OUR CLIENT STORES...
...AND TELLING THEM TO PREPARE FOR A HUGE RUN ON PAJAMA BOTTOMS!
GOOD IDEA!
WHY ARE WE GOING TO RIVERDALE HIGH?
WE JUST GOT A TIP FROM THE TEEN RESEARCH PEOPLE!
WRIV TV CHANNEL 12
...THEY SAY THIS SCHOOL JUST STARTED A NEW FAD THAT PROMISES TO GO NATIONAL!
RIVERDALE HIGH SCHOOL
RIVERDALE HIGH SCHOOL

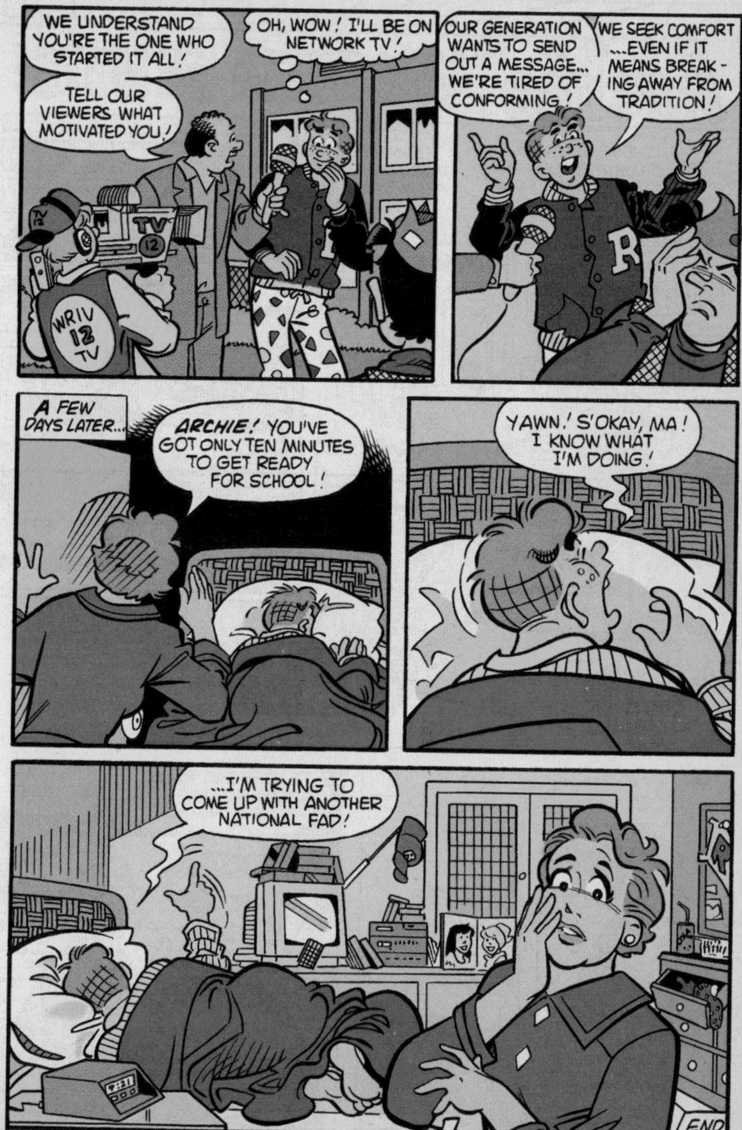
WE UNDERSTAND YOU'RE THE ONE WHO STARTED IT ALL!
TELL OUR VIEWERS WHAT MOTIVATED YOU!
OH, WOW! I'LL BE ON NETWORK TV!
TV 12
WRIV 12 TV
OUR GENERATION WANTS TO SEND OUT A MESSAGE... WE'RE TIRED OF CONFORMING!
WE SEEK COMFORT ...EVEN IF IT MEANS BREAKING AWAY FROM TRADITION!
A FEW DAYS LATER...
ARCHIE! YOU'VE GOT ONLY TEN MINUTES TO GET READY FOR SCHOOL!
YAWN! S'OKAY, MA! I KNOW WHAT I'M DOING!
...I'M TRYING TO COME UP WITH ANOTHER NATIONAL FAD!
END

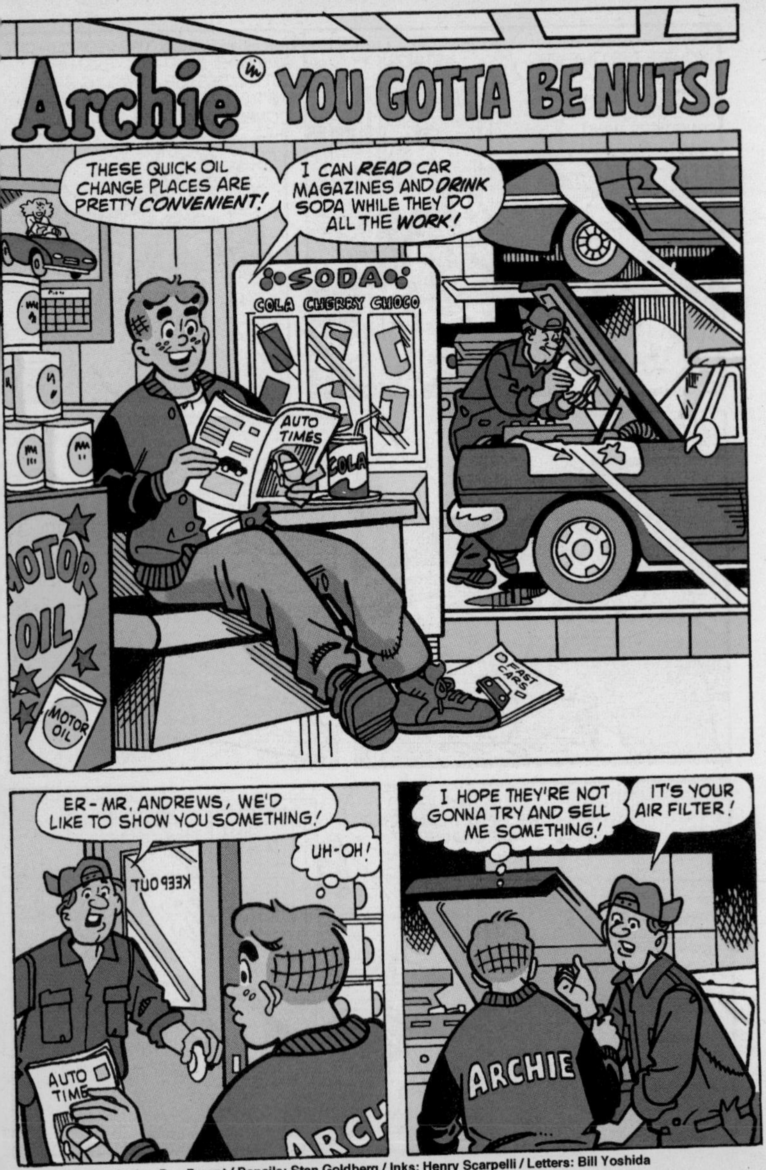
Archie in YOU GOTTA BE NUTS!
THESE QUICK OIL CHANGE PLACES ARE PRETTY CONVENIENT!
I CAN READ CAR MAGAZINES AND DRINK SODA WHILE THEY DO ALL THE WORK!
SODA
COLA CHERRY CHOCO
AUTO TIMES
COLA
MOTOR OIL
MOTOR OIL
FAST CARS
ER- MR. ANDREWS, WE'D LIKE TO SHOW YOU SOMETHING!
UH-OH!
KEEP OUT
AUTO TIME
I HOPE THEY'RE NOT GONNA TRY AND SELL ME SOMETHING!
IT'S YOUR AIR FILTER!
ARCHIE

Script: Dan Parent / Pencils: Stan Goldberg / Inks: Henry Scarpelli / Letters: Bill Yoshida

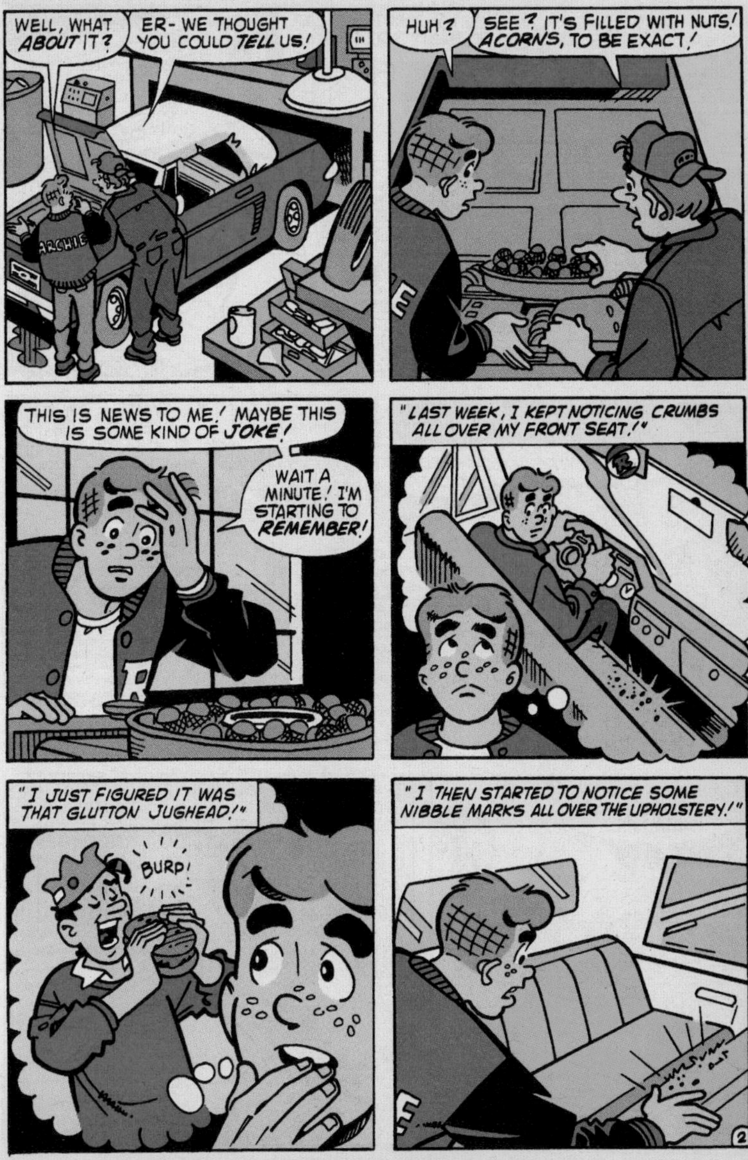
WELL, WHAT ABOUT IT?
ER- WE THOUGHT YOU COULD TELL US!
HUH?
SEE? IT'S FILLED WITH NUTS! ACORNS, TO BE EXACT!
THIS IS NEWS TO ME! MAYBE THIS IS SOME KIND OF JOKE!
WAIT A MINUTE! I'M STARTING TO REMEMBER!
"LAST WEEK, I KEPT NOTICING CRUMBS ALL OVER MY FRONT SEAT!"
"I JUST FIGURED IT WAS THAT GLUTTON JUGHEAD!"
BURP!
"I THEN STARTED TO NOTICE SOME NIBBLE MARKS ALL OVER THE UPHOLSTERY!"
2

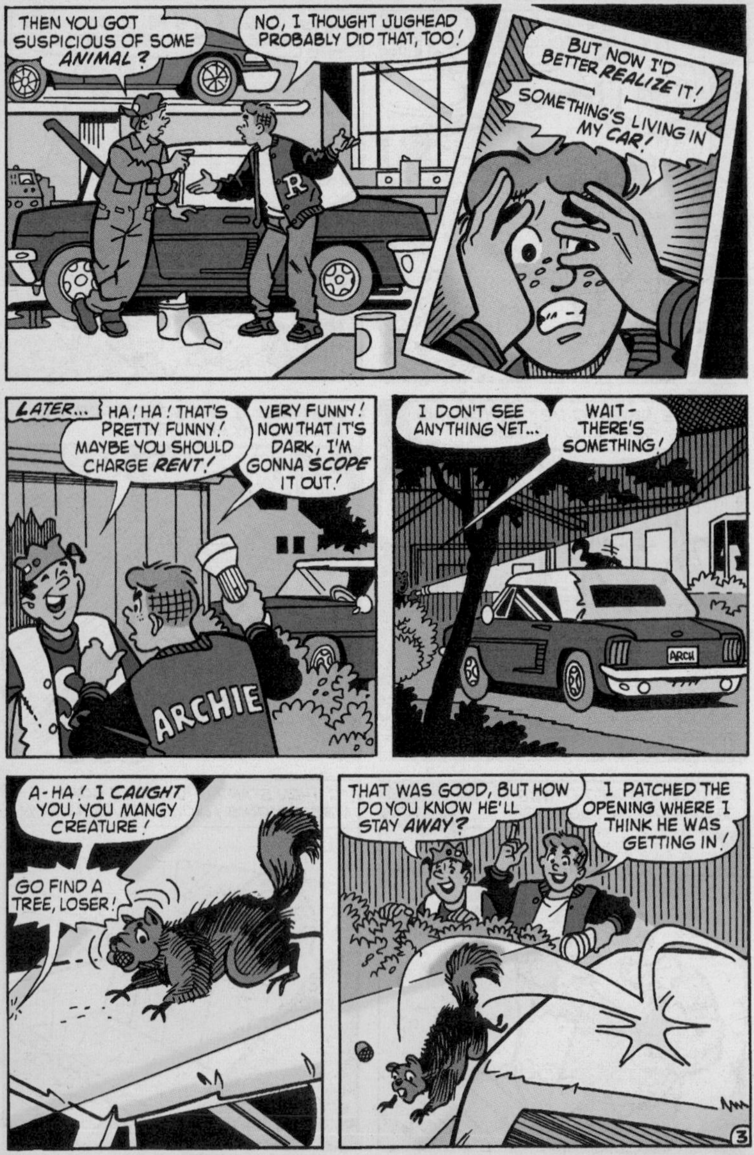

THEN YOU GOT SUSPICIOUS OF SOME ANIMAL?
NO, I THOUGHT JUGHEAD PROBABLY DID THAT, TOO!
BUT NOW I'D BETTER REALIZE IT!
SOMETHING'S LIVING IN MY CAR!
LATER...
HA! HA! THAT'S PRETTY FUNNY! MAYBE YOU SHOULD CHARGE RENT!
VERY FUNNY! NOW THAT IT'S DARK, I'M GONNA SCOPE IT OUT!
ARCHIE
I DON'T SEE ANYTHING YET...
WAIT- THERE'S SOMETHING!
ARCH
A-HA! I CAUGHT YOU, YOU MANGY CREATURE!
GO FIND A TREE, LOSER!
THAT WAS GOOD, BUT HOW DO YOU KNOW HE'LL STAY AWAY?
I PATCHED THE OPENING WHERE I THINK HE WAS GETTING IN!
3

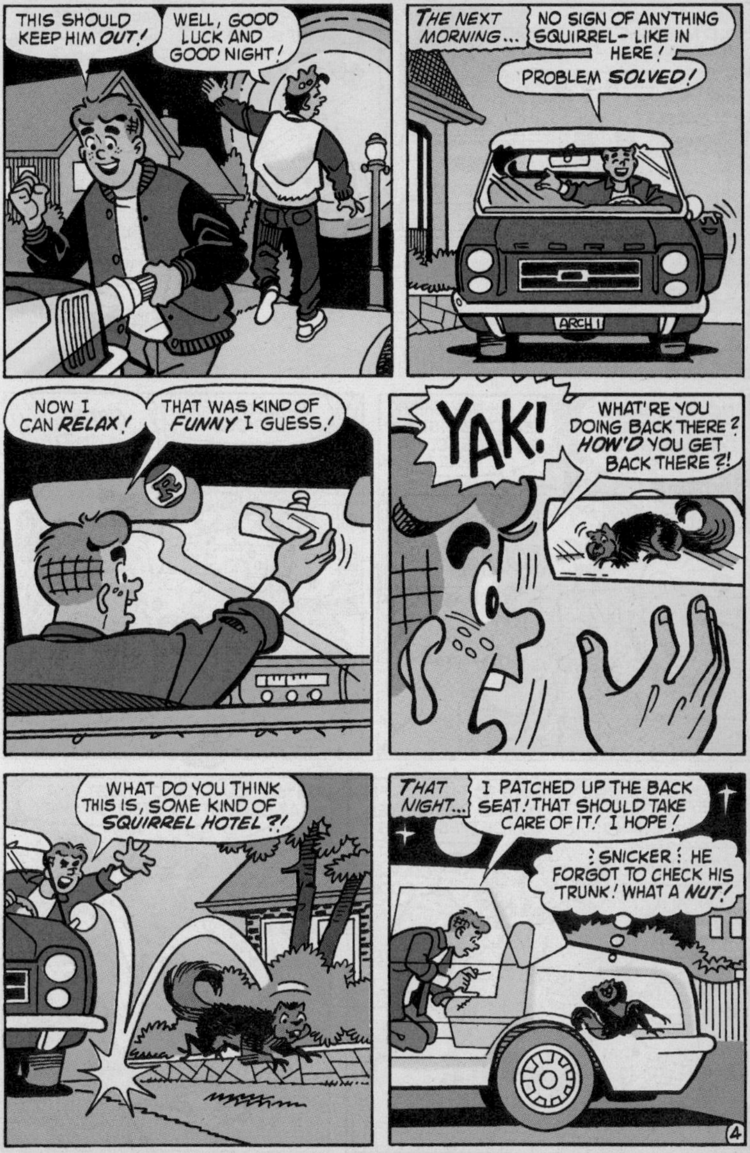
THIS SHOULD KEEP HIM *OUT*!
WELL, GOOD LUCK AND GOOD NIGHT!
THE NEXT MORNING...
NO SIGN OF ANYTHING SQUIRREL- LIKE IN HERE!
PROBLEM **SOLVED**!
ARCH 1
NOW I CAN **RELAX**!
THAT WAS KIND OF ***FUNNY*** I GUESS!
YAK!
WHAT'RE YOU DOING BACK THERE? ***HOW'D*** YOU GET BACK THERE?!
WHAT DO YOU THINK THIS IS, SOME KIND OF ***SQUIRREL HOTEL***?!
THAT NIGHT...
I PATCHED UP THE BACK SEAT! THAT SHOULD TAKE CARE OF IT! I HOPE!
:SNICKER: HE FORGOT TO CHECK HIS TRUNK! WHAT A ***NUT***!

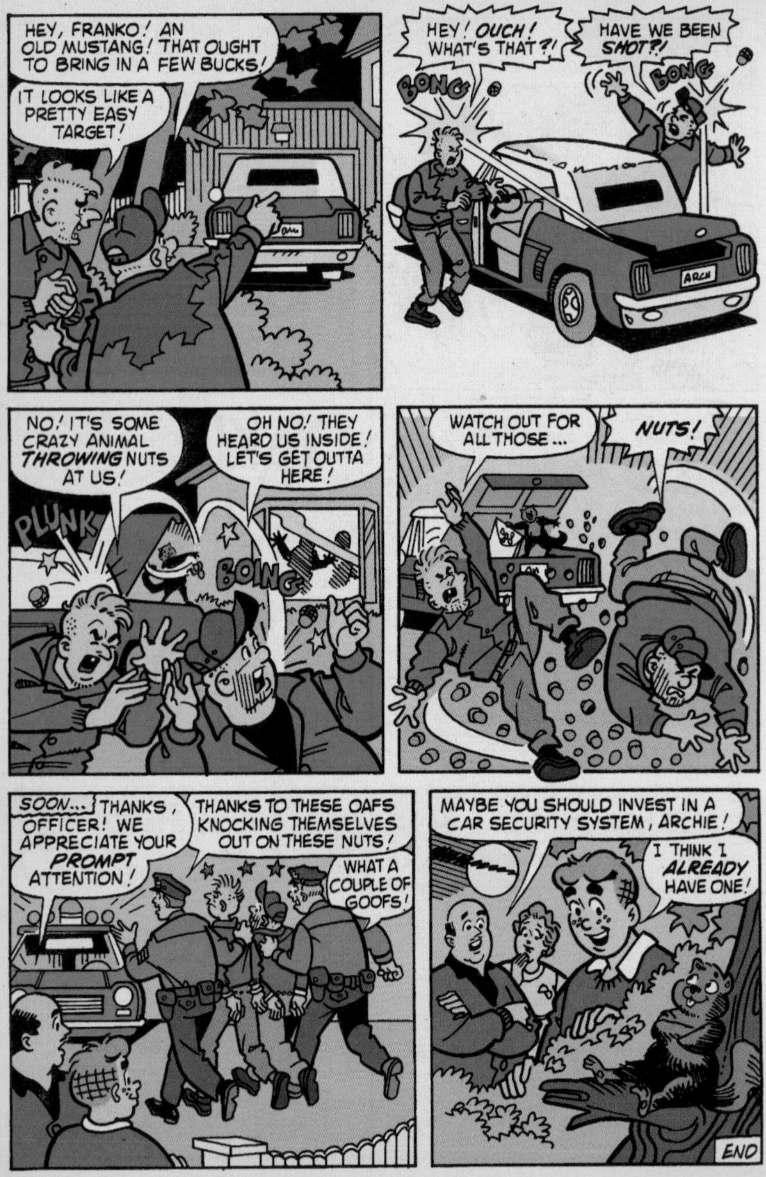
HEY, FRANKO! AN OLD MUSTANG! THAT OUGHT TO BRING IN A FEW BUCKS!
IT LOOKS LIKE A PRETTY EASY TARGET!
HEY! OUCH! WHAT'S THAT?!
HAVE WE BEEN SHOT?!
BONG
BONG
ARCH
NO! IT'S SOME CRAZY ANIMAL THROWING NUTS AT US!
OH NO! THEY HEARD US INSIDE! LET'S GET OUTTA HERE!
PLUNK
BOING
WATCH OUT FOR ALL THOSE...
NUTS!
SOON...
THANKS, OFFICER! WE APPRECIATE YOUR PROMPT ATTENTION!
THANKS TO THESE OAFS KNOCKING THEMSELVES OUT ON THESE NUTS!
WHAT A COUPLE OF GOOFS!
MAYBE YOU SHOULD INVEST IN A CAR SECURITY SYSTEM, ARCHIE!
I THINK I ALREADY HAVE ONE!
END

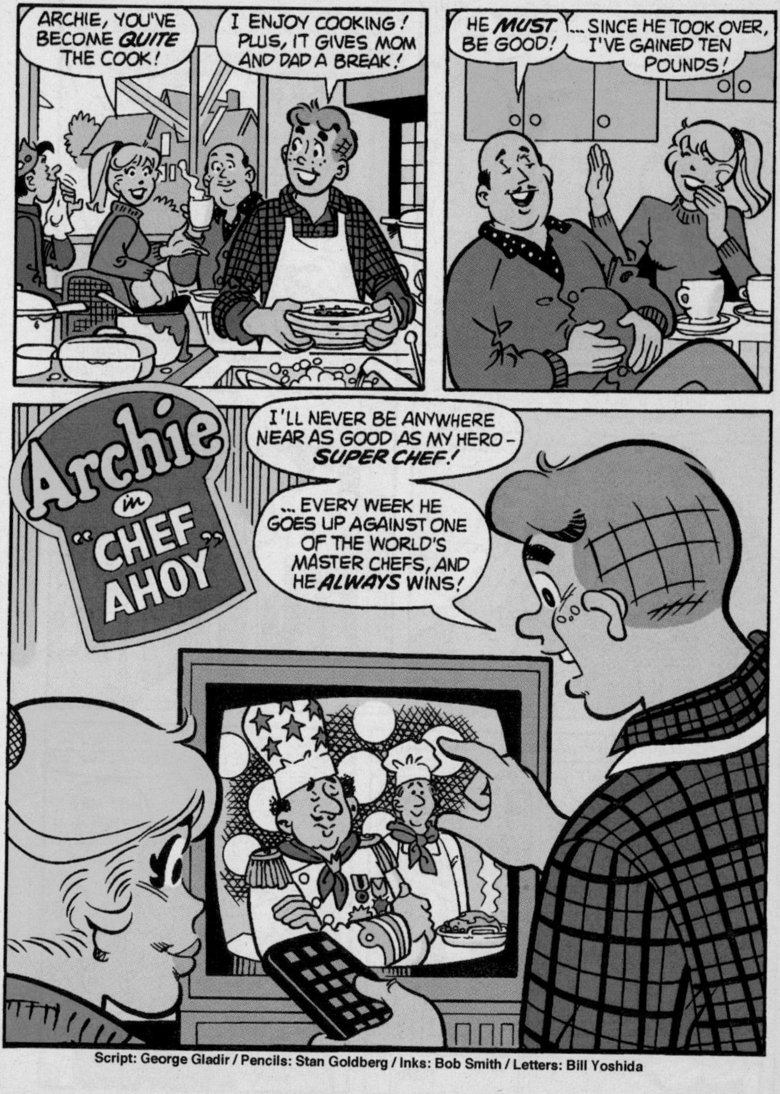
ARCHIE, YOU'VE BECOME QUITE THE COOK!
I ENJOY COOKING! PLUS, IT GIVES MOM AND DAD A BREAK!
HE MUST BE GOOD!
...SINCE HE TOOK OVER, I'VE GAINED TEN POUNDS!
Archie in "CHEF AHOY"
I'LL NEVER BE ANYWHERE NEAR AS GOOD AS MY HERO - SUPER CHEF!
...EVERY WEEK HE GOES UP AGAINST ONE OF THE WORLD'S MASTER CHEFS, AND HE ALWAYS WINS!

Script: George Gladir / Pencils: Stan Goldberg / Inks: Bob Smith / Letters: Bill Yoshida

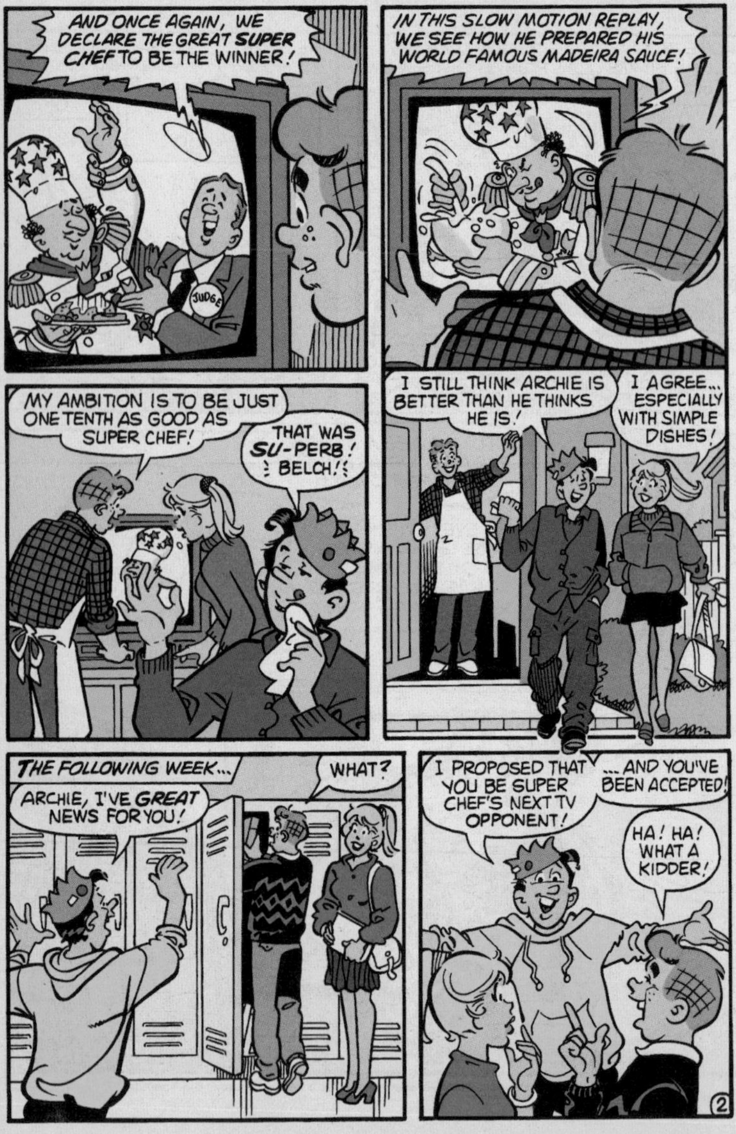
AND ONCE AGAIN, WE DECLARE THE GREAT SUPER CHEF TO BE THE WINNER!
JUDGE
IN THIS SLOW MOTION REPLAY, WE SEE HOW HE PREPARED HIS WORLD FAMOUS MADEIRA SAUCE!
MY AMBITION IS TO BE JUST ONE TENTH AS GOOD AS SUPER CHEF!
THAT WAS SU-PERB! BELCH!
I STILL THINK ARCHIE IS BETTER THAN HE THINKS HE IS!
I AGREE... ESPECIALLY WITH SIMPLE DISHES!
THE FOLLOWING WEEK...
ARCHIE, I'VE GREAT NEWS FOR YOU!
WHAT?
I PROPOSED THAT YOU BE SUPER CHEF'S NEXT TV OPPONENT!
... AND YOU'VE BEEN ACCEPTED!
HA! HA! WHAT A KIDDER!
2

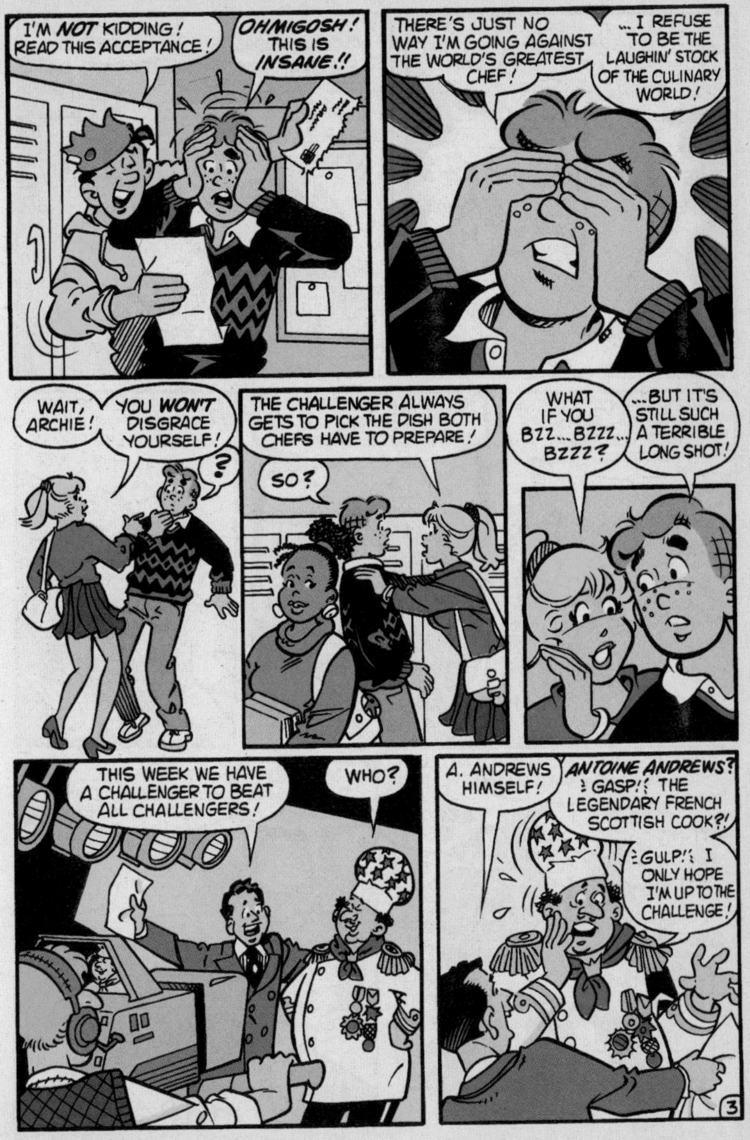
I'M NOT KIDDING! READ THIS ACCEPTANCE!
OHMIGOSH! THIS IS INSANE!!
THERE'S JUST NO WAY I'M GOING AGAINST THE WORLD'S GREATEST CHEF!
... I REFUSE TO BE THE LAUGHIN' STOCK OF THE CULINARY WORLD!
WAIT, ARCHIE!
YOU WON'T DISGRACE YOURSELF!
?
THE CHALLENGER ALWAYS GETS TO PICK THE DISH BOTH CHEFS HAVE TO PREPARE!
SO?
WHAT IF YOU BZZ... BZZZ... BZZZ?
...BUT IT'S STILL SUCH A TERRIBLE LONG SHOT!
THIS WEEK WE HAVE A CHALLENGER TO BEAT ALL CHALLENGERS!
WHO?
A. ANDREWS HIMSELF!
ANTOINE ANDREWS? GASP! THE LEGENDARY FRENCH SCOTTISH COOK?!
GULP! I ONLY HOPE I'M UP TO THE CHALLENGE!
3

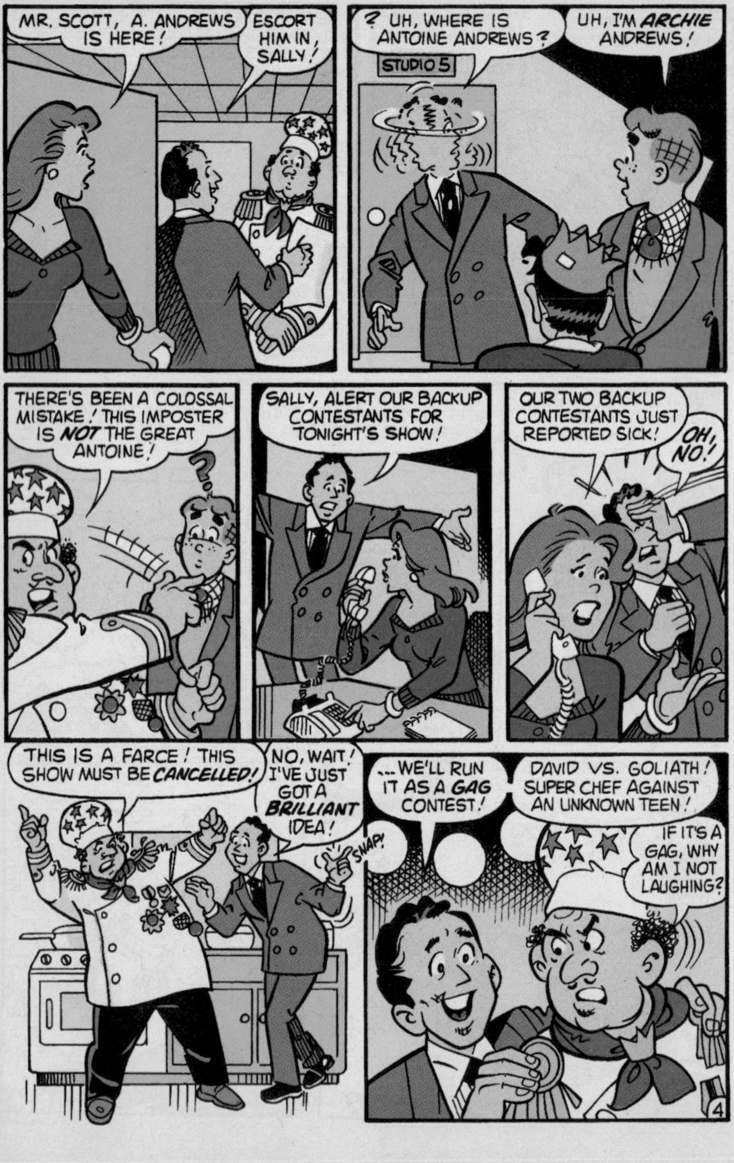
MR. SCOTT, A. ANDREWS IS HERE!
ESCORT HIM IN, SALLY!
? UH, WHERE IS ANTOINE ANDREWS?
UH, I'M ARCHIE ANDREWS!
STUDIO 5
THERE'S BEEN A COLOSSAL MISTAKE! THIS IMPOSTER IS NOT THE GREAT ANTOINE!
SALLY, ALERT OUR BACKUP CONTESTANTS FOR TONIGHT'S SHOW!
OUR TWO BACKUP CONTESTANTS JUST REPORTED SICK!
OH, NO!
THIS IS A FARCE! THIS SHOW MUST BE CANCELLED!
NO, WAIT! I'VE JUST GOT A BRILLIANT IDEA!
SNAP!
...WE'LL RUN IT AS A GAG CONTEST!
DAVID VS. GOLIATH! SUPER CHEF AGAINST AN UNKNOWN TEEN!
IF IT'S A GAG, WHY AM I NOT LAUGHING?
4

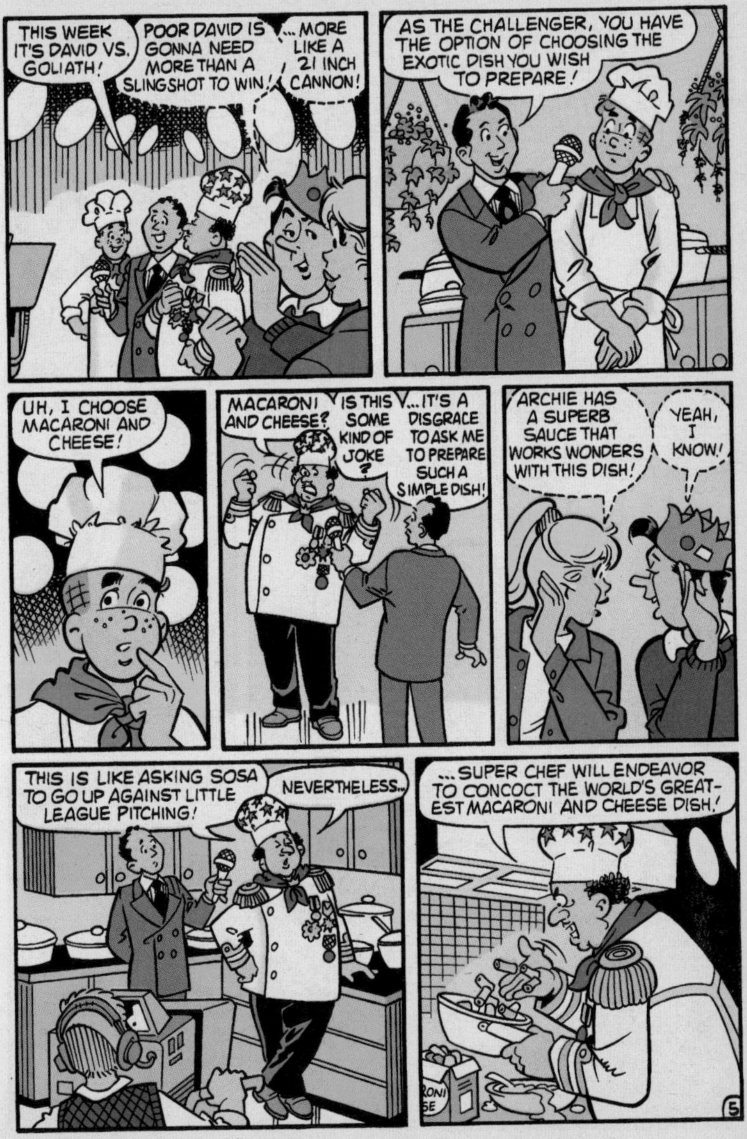
THIS WEEK IT'S DAVID VS. GOLIATH!
POOR DAVID IS GONNA NEED MORE THAN A SLINGSHOT TO WIN!
...MORE LIKE A 21 INCH CANNON!
AS THE CHALLENGER, YOU HAVE THE OPTION OF CHOOSING THE EXOTIC DISH YOU WISH TO PREPARE!
UH, I CHOOSE MACARONI AND CHEESE!
MACARONI AND CHEESE?
IS THIS SOME KIND OF JOKE?
...IT'S A DISGRACE TO ASK ME TO PREPARE SUCH A SIMPLE DISH!
ARCHIE HAS A SUPERB SAUCE THAT WORKS WONDERS WITH THIS DISH!
YEAH, I KNOW!
THIS IS LIKE ASKING SOSA TO GO UP AGAINST LITTLE LEAGUE PITCHING!
NEVERTHELESS...
...SUPER CHEF WILL ENDEAVOR TO CONCOCT THE WORLD'S GREAT-EST MACARONI AND CHEESE DISH!
5

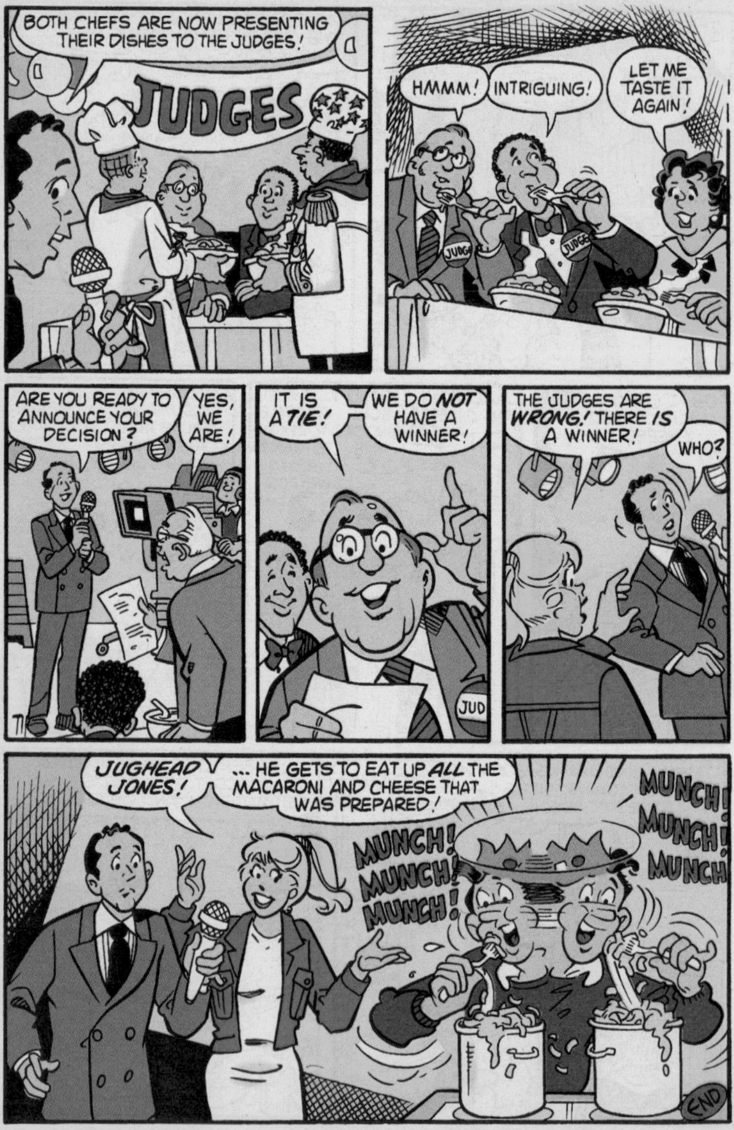
BOTH CHEFS ARE NOW PRESENTING THEIR DISHES TO THE JUDGES!
JUDGES
HMMM!
INTRIGUING!
LET ME TASTE IT AGAIN!
ARE YOU READY TO ANNOUNCE YOUR DECISION?
YES, WE ARE!
IT IS A TIE!
WE DO NOT HAVE A WINNER!
THE JUDGES ARE WRONG! THERE IS A WINNER!
WHO?
JUGHEAD JONES!
... HE GETS TO EAT UP ALL THE MACARONI AND CHEESE THAT WAS PREPARED!
MUNCH! MUNCH! MUNCH!
MUNCH! MUNCH! MUNCH
END

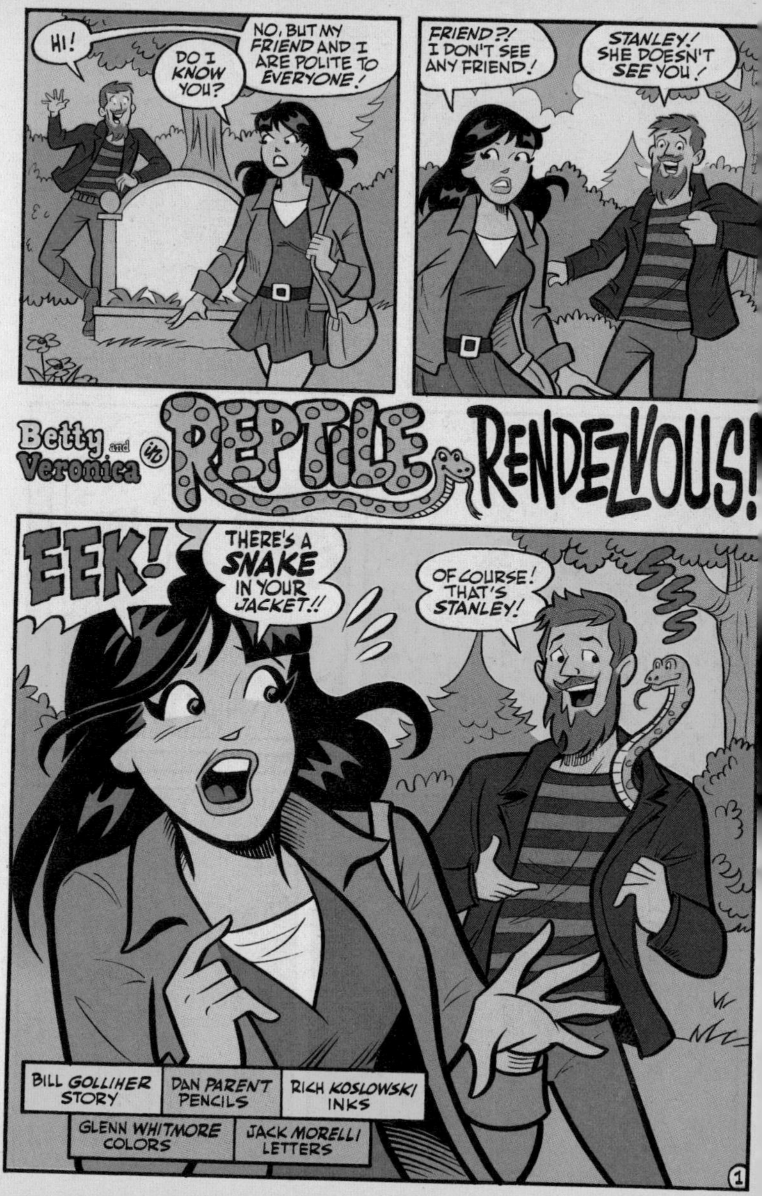
HI!
DO I KNOW YOU?
NO, BUT MY FRIEND AND I ARE POLITE TO EVERYONE!
FRIEND?! I DON'T SEE ANY FRIEND!
STANLEY! SHE DOESN'T SEE YOU!
Betty and Veronica in REPTILE RENDEZVOUS!
EEK!
THERE'S A SNAKE IN YOUR JACKET!!
OF COURSE! THAT'S STANLEY!
SSS
BILL GOLLIHER STORY
DAN PARENT PENCILS
RICH KOSLOWSKI INKS
GLENN WHITMORE COLORS
JACK MORELLI LETTERS

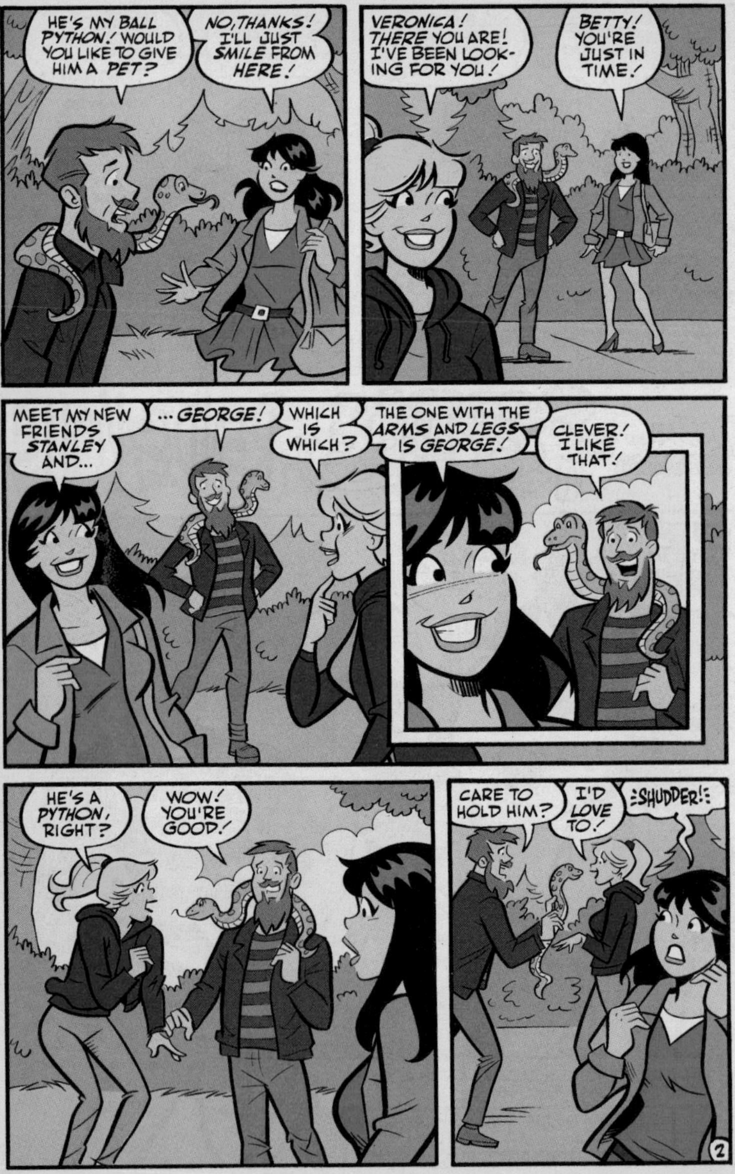
HE'S MY BALL PYTHON! WOULD YOU LIKE TO GIVE HIM A PET?
NO, THANKS! I'LL JUST SMILE FROM HERE!
VERONICA! THERE YOU ARE! I'VE BEEN LOOKING FOR YOU!
BETTY! YOU'RE JUST IN TIME!
MEET MY NEW FRIENDS STANLEY AND...
...GEORGE!
WHICH IS WHICH?
THE ONE WITH THE ARMS AND LEGS IS GEORGE!
CLEVER! I LIKE THAT!
HE'S A PYTHON, RIGHT?
WOW! YOU'RE GOOD!
CARE TO HOLD HIM?
I'D LOVE TO!
SHUDDER!
2

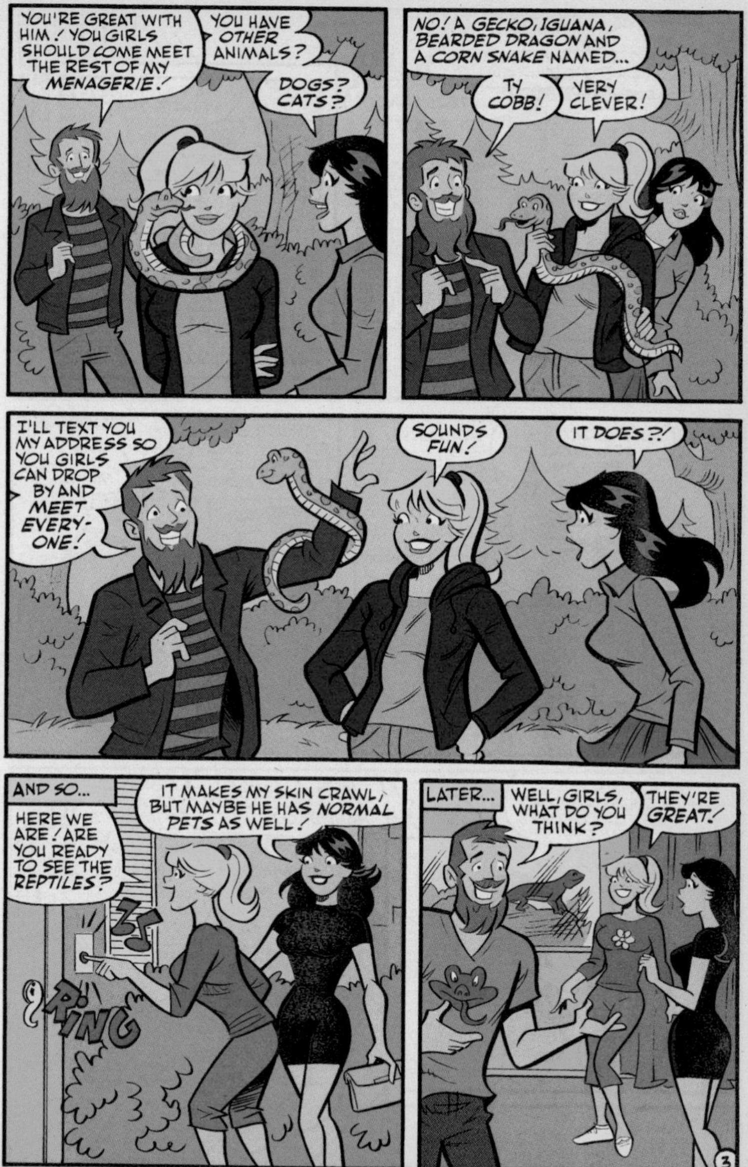
YOU'RE GREAT WITH HIM! YOU GIRLS SHOULD COME MEET THE REST OF MY MENAGERIE!
YOU HAVE OTHER ANIMALS?
DOGS? CATS?
NO! A GECKO, IGUANA, BEARDED DRAGON AND A CORN SNAKE NAMED...
TY COBB!
VERY CLEVER!
I'LL TEXT YOU MY ADDRESS SO YOU GIRLS CAN DROP BY AND MEET EVERY-ONE!
SOUNDS FUN!
IT DOES?!
AND SO...
HERE WE ARE! ARE YOU READY TO SEE THE REPTILES?
IT MAKES MY SKIN CRAWL, BUT MAYBE HE HAS NORMAL PETS AS WELL!
RING
LATER...
WELL, GIRLS, WHAT DO YOU THINK?
THEY'RE GREAT!
3

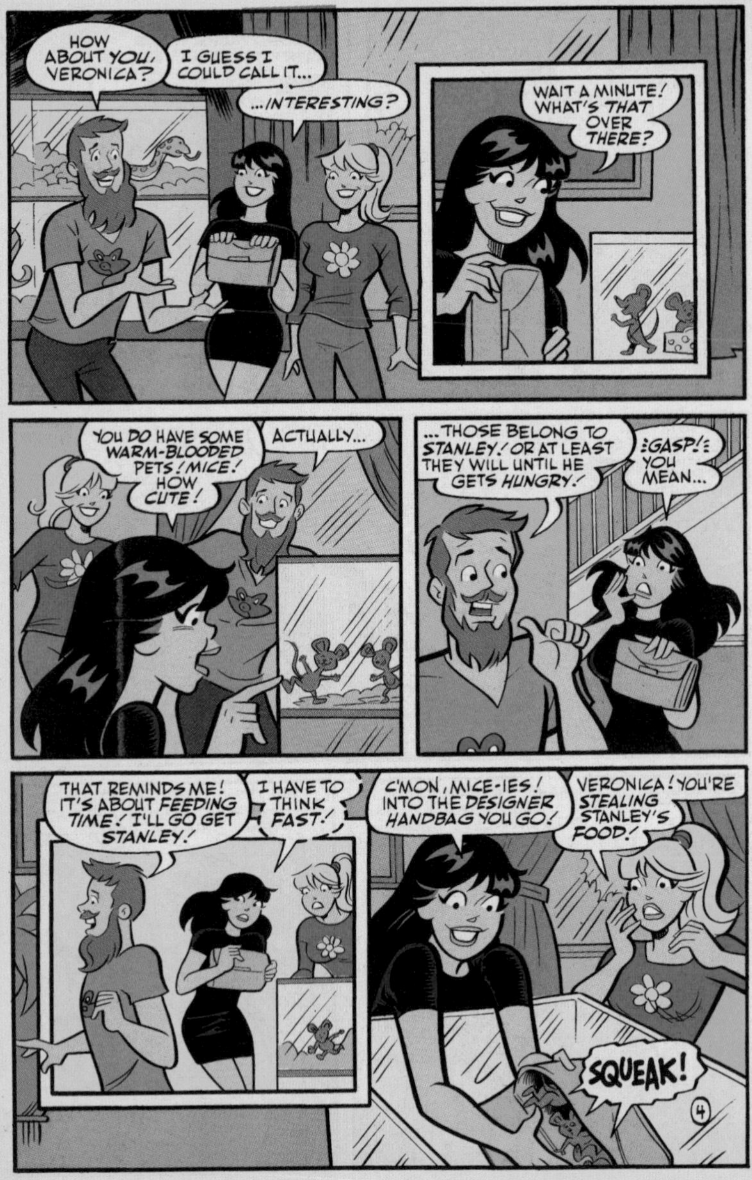
HOW ABOUT YOU, VERONICA?
I GUESS I COULD CALL IT...
...INTERESTING?
WAIT A MINUTE! WHAT'S THAT OVER THERE?
YOU DO HAVE SOME WARM-BLOODED PETS! MICE! HOW CUTE!
ACTUALLY...
...THOSE BELONG TO STANLEY! OR AT LEAST THEY WILL UNTIL HE GETS HUNGRY!
GASP! YOU MEAN...
THAT REMINDS ME! IT'S ABOUT FEEDING TIME! I'LL GO GET STANLEY!
I HAVE TO THINK FAST!
C'MON, MICE-IES! INTO THE DESIGNER HANDBAG YOU GO!
VERONICA! YOU'RE STEALING STANLEY'S FOOD!
SQUEAK!
4

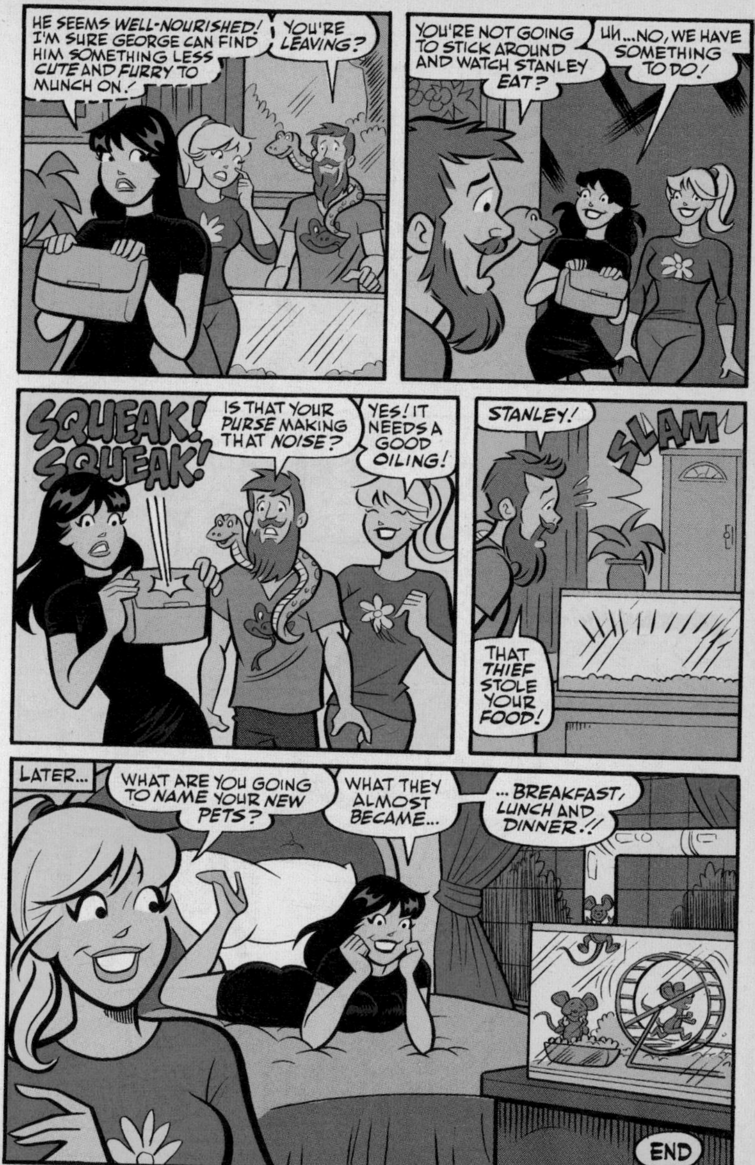
HE SEEMS WELL-NOURISHED! I'M SURE GEORGE CAN FIND HIM SOMETHING LESS CUTE AND FURRY TO MUNCH ON.!
YOU'RE LEAVING?
YOU'RE NOT GOING TO STICK AROUND AND WATCH STANLEY EAT?
UH...NO, WE HAVE SOMETHING TO DO!
SQUEAK! SQUEAK!
IS THAT YOUR PURSE MAKING THAT NOISE?
YES! IT NEEDS A GOOD OILING!
STANLEY!
SLAM
THAT THIEF STOLE YOUR FOOD!
LATER...
WHAT ARE YOU GOING TO NAME YOUR NEW PETS?
WHAT THEY ALMOST BECAME...
...BREAKFAST, LUNCH AND DINNER.!!
END

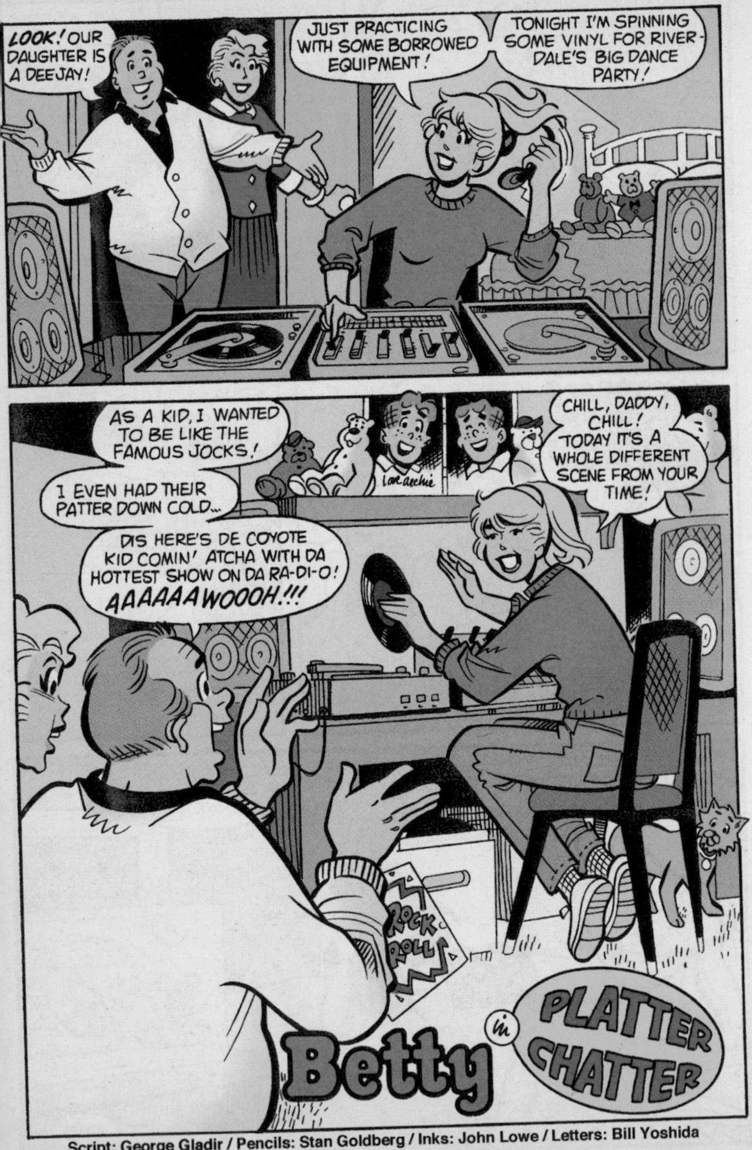
LOOK! OUR DAUGHTER IS A DEEJAY!
JUST PRACTICING WITH SOME BORROWED EQUIPMENT!
TONIGHT I'M SPINNING SOME VINYL FOR RIVER-DALE'S BIG DANCE PARTY!
AS A KID, I WANTED TO BE LIKE THE FAMOUS JOCKS!
I EVEN HAD THEIR PATTER DOWN COLD...
DIS HERE'S DE COYOTE KID COMIN' ATCHA WITH DA HOTTEST SHOW ON DA RA-DI-O! AAAAAAWOOOH!!!
CHILL, DADDY, CHILL! TODAY IT'S A WHOLE DIFFERENT SCENE FROM YOUR TIME!
Betty in PLATTER CHATTER

Script: George Gladir / Pencils: Stan Goldberg / Inks: John Lowe / Letters: Bill Yoshida

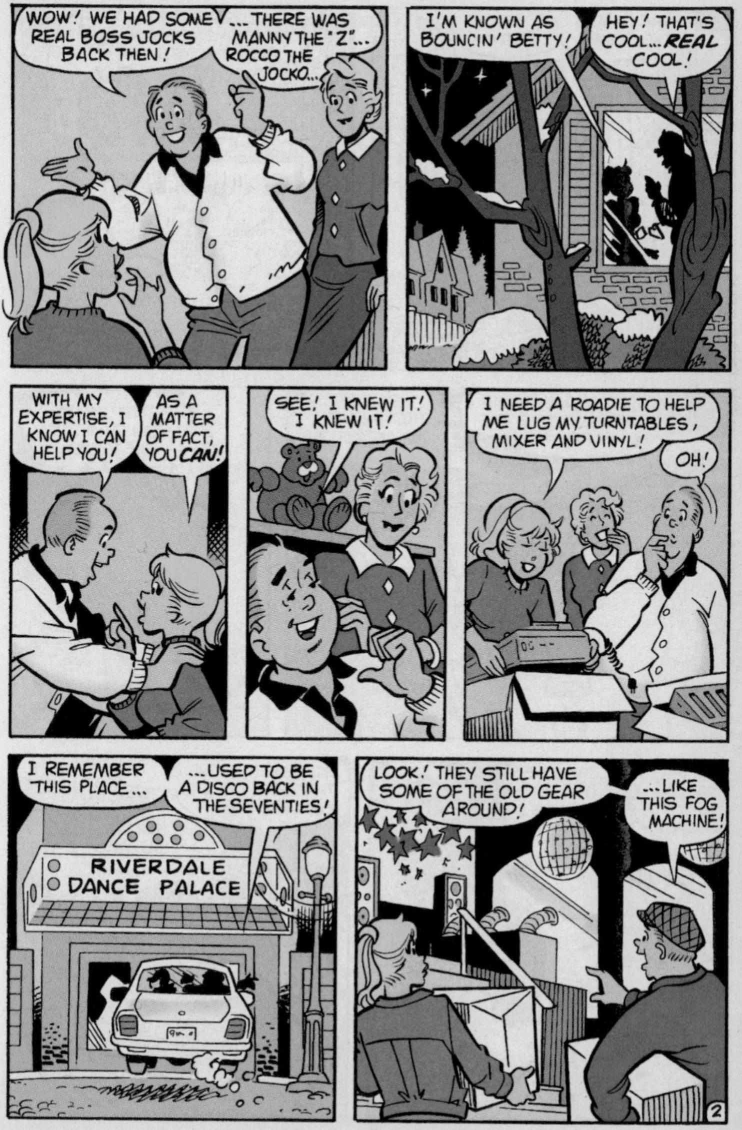
WOW! WE HAD SOME REAL BOSS JOCKS BACK THEN!
...THERE WAS MANNY THE "Z"... ROCCO THE JOCKO...
I'M KNOWN AS BOUNCIN' BETTY!
HEY! THAT'S COOL... REAL COOL!
WITH MY EXPERTISE, I KNOW I CAN HELP YOU!
AS A MATTER OF FACT, YOU CAN!
SEE! I KNEW IT! I KNEW IT!
I NEED A ROADIE TO HELP ME LUG MY TURNTABLES, MIXER AND VINYL!
OH!
I REMEMBER THIS PLACE...
...USED TO BE A DISCO BACK IN THE SEVENTIES!
RIVERDALE DANCE PALACE
LOOK! THEY STILL HAVE SOME OF THE OLD GEAR AROUND!
...LIKE THIS FOG MACHINE!
2

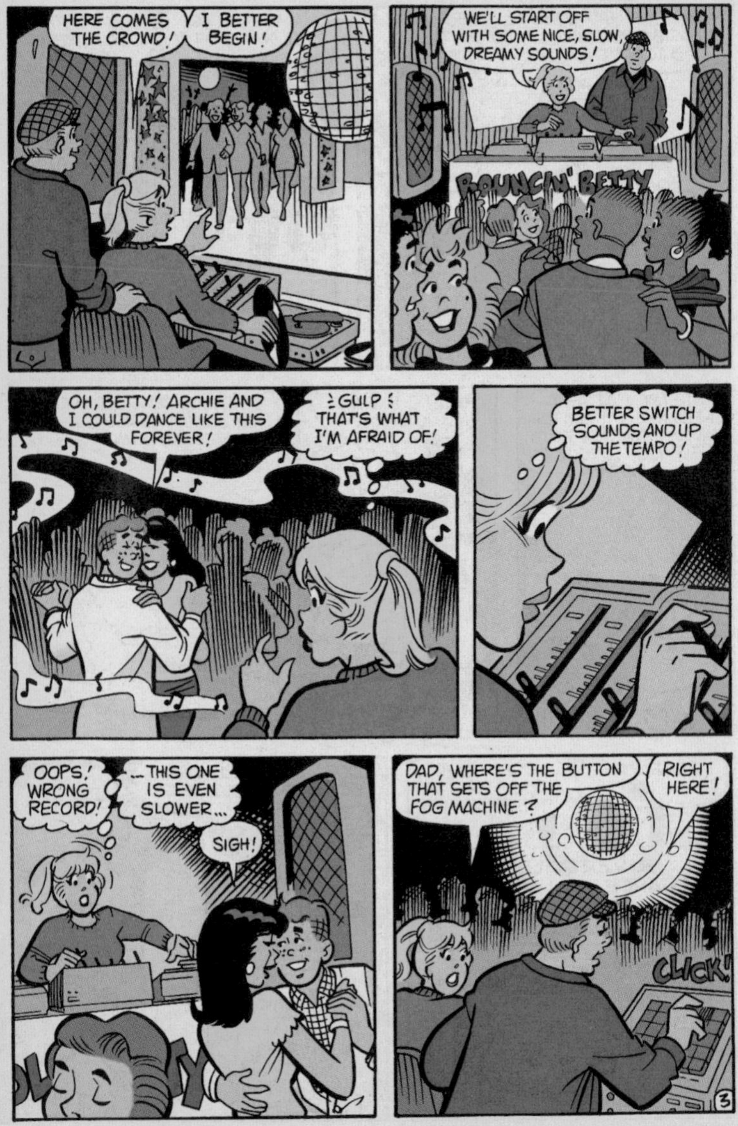
HERE COMES THE CROWD!
I BETTER BEGIN!
WE'LL START OFF WITH SOME NICE, SLOW, DREAMY SOUNDS!
BOUNCIN' BETTY
OH, BETTY! ARCHIE AND I COULD DANCE LIKE THIS FOREVER!
GULP THAT'S WHAT I'M AFRAID OF!
BETTER SWITCH SOUNDS AND UP THE TEMPO!
OOPS! WRONG RECORD!
...THIS ONE IS EVEN SLOWER...
SIGH!
DAD, WHERE'S THE BUTTON THAT SETS OFF THE FOG MACHINE?
RIGHT HERE!
CLICK!

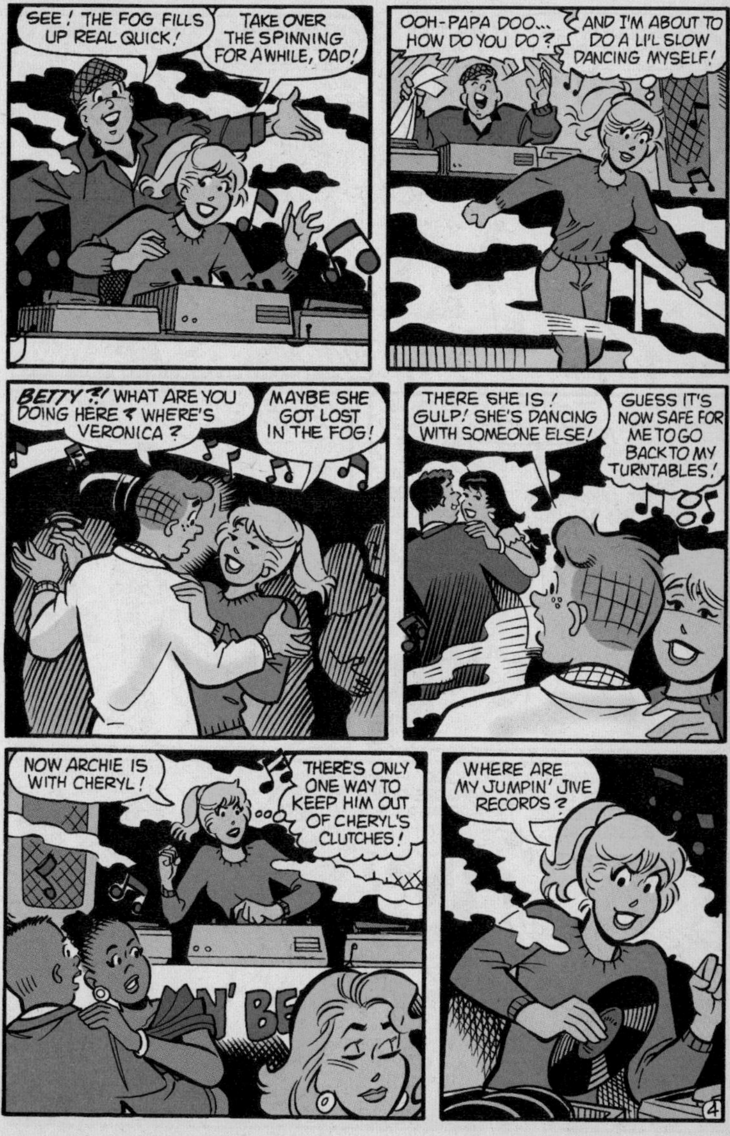
SEE! THE FOG FILLS UP REAL QUICK!
TAKE OVER THE SPINNING FOR AWHILE, DAD!
OOH-PAPA DOO... HOW DO YOU DO?
AND I'M ABOUT TO DO A LI'L SLOW DANCING MYSELF!
BETTY?! WHAT ARE YOU DOING HERE? WHERE'S VERONICA?
MAYBE SHE GOT LOST IN THE FOG!
THERE SHE IS! GULP! SHE'S DANCING WITH SOMEONE ELSE!
GUESS IT'S NOW SAFE FOR ME TO GO BACK TO MY TURNTABLES!
NOW ARCHIE IS WITH CHERYL!
THERE'S ONLY ONE WAY TO KEEP HIM OUT OF CHERYL'S CLUTCHES!
WHERE ARE MY JUMPIN' JIVE RECORDS?
4

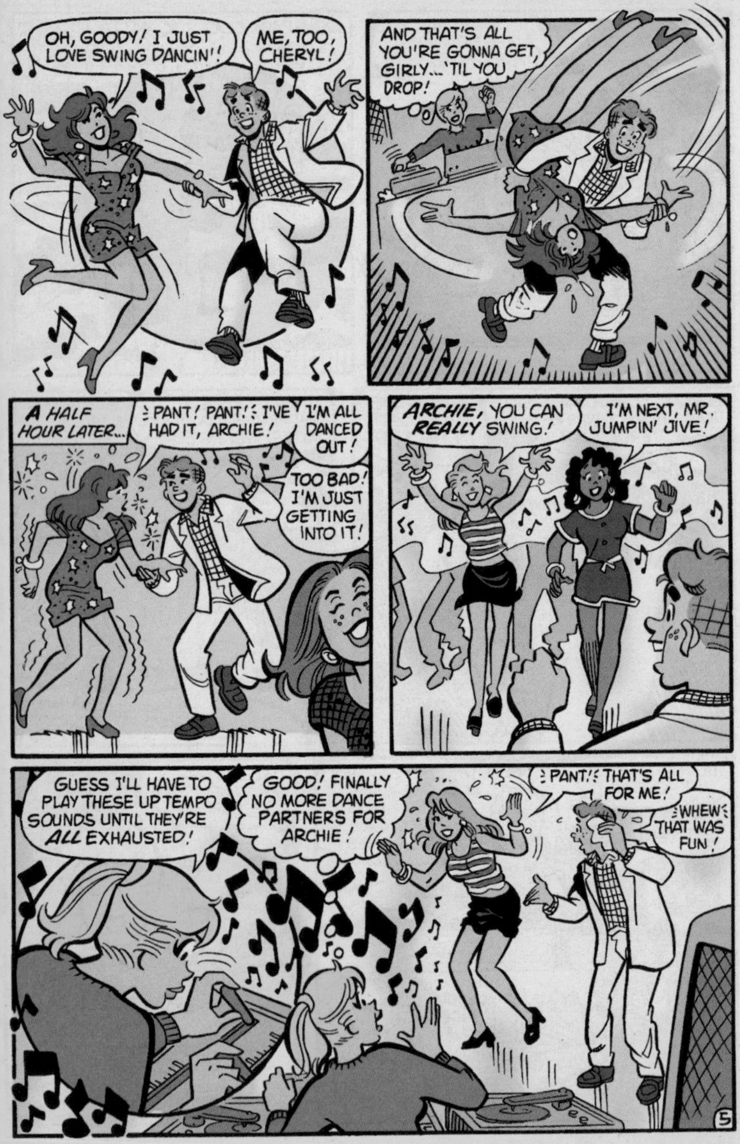
OH, GOODY! I JUST LOVE SWING DANCIN'!
ME, TOO, CHERYL!
AND THAT'S ALL YOU'RE GONNA GET, GIRLY...'TIL YOU DROP!
A HALF HOUR LATER...
PANT! PANT! I'VE HAD IT, ARCHIE!
I'M ALL DANCED OUT!
TOO BAD! I'M JUST GETTING INTO IT!
ARCHIE, YOU CAN REALLY SWING!
I'M NEXT, MR. JUMPIN' JIVE!
GUESS I'LL HAVE TO PLAY THESE UPTEMPO SOUNDS UNTIL THEY'RE ALL EXHAUSTED!
GOOD! FINALLY NO MORE DANCE PARTNERS FOR ARCHIE!
PANT! THAT'S ALL FOR ME!
WHEW! THAT WAS FUN!
5

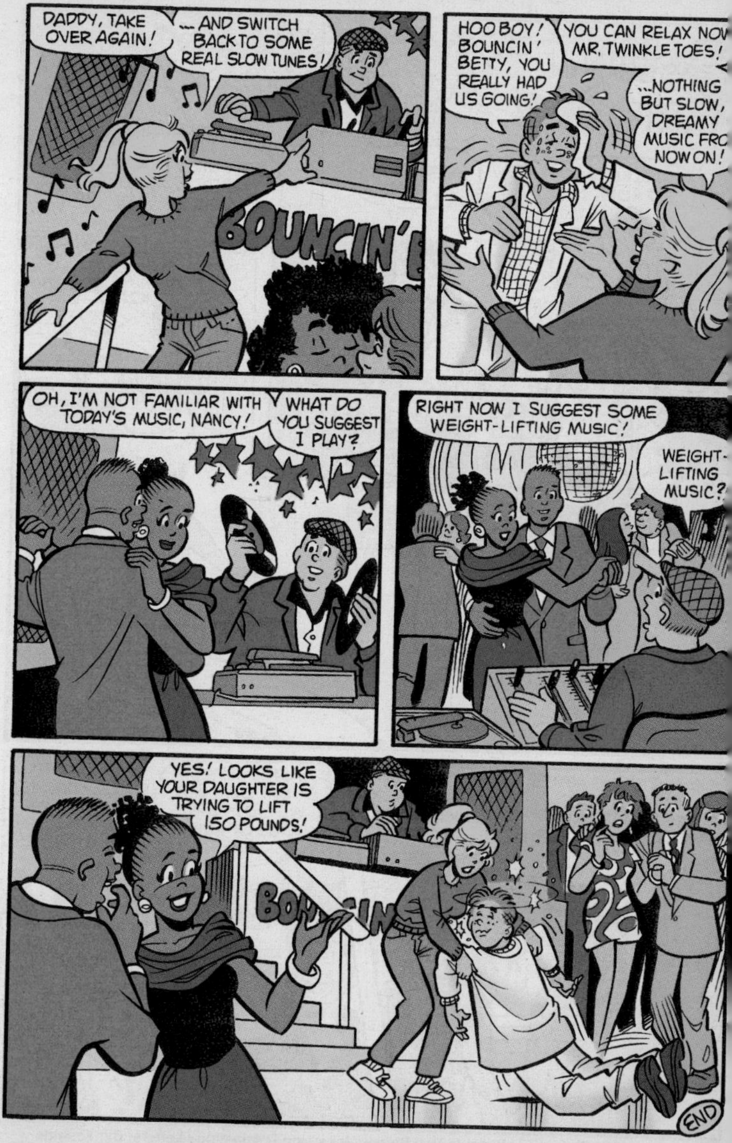
DADDY, TAKE OVER AGAIN!
...AND SWITCH BACK TO SOME REAL SLOW TUNES!
BOUNCIN' B
HOO BOY! BOUNCIN' BETTY, YOU REALLY HAD US GOING!
YOU CAN RELAX NOW MR. TWINKLE TOES!
...NOTHING BUT SLOW, DREAMY MUSIC FRO NOW ON!
OH, I'M NOT FAMILIAR WITH TODAY'S MUSIC, NANCY!
WHAT DO YOU SUGGEST I PLAY?
RIGHT NOW I SUGGEST SOME WEIGHT-LIFTING MUSIC!
WEIGHT-LIFTING MUSIC?
YES! LOOKS LIKE YOUR DAUGHTER IS TRYING TO LIFT 150 POUNDS!
END

Betty and Veronica in *Nameless Game!*

Betty: ARCHIE WAS *SO* FUNNY AT THE PARTY!

Veronica: HE'S ALWAYS A RIOT!

Nancy: SHEESH! ALL YOU TWO TALK ABOUT IS ARCHIE! SEE YA LATER!

SALE

Veronica: GEE... I DON'T AGREE WITH NANCY, BUT I GUESS WE DO TALK ABOUT ARCHIE QUITE OFTEN!

Betty: HIS NAME DOES COME UP IN OUR CONVERSATIONS A LOT!

Betty: ARCHIE IS A GREAT GUY, BUT WE BOTH HAVE TONS OF OTHER INTERESTS!

Veronica: TRUE! WHY SHOULD ARCHIE'S NAME ALWAYS BE ON THE TIPS OF OUR TONGUES?

Script: Mike Pellowski / Pencils: Dan Parent / Inks: Jon D'Agostino / Letters: Bill Yoshida

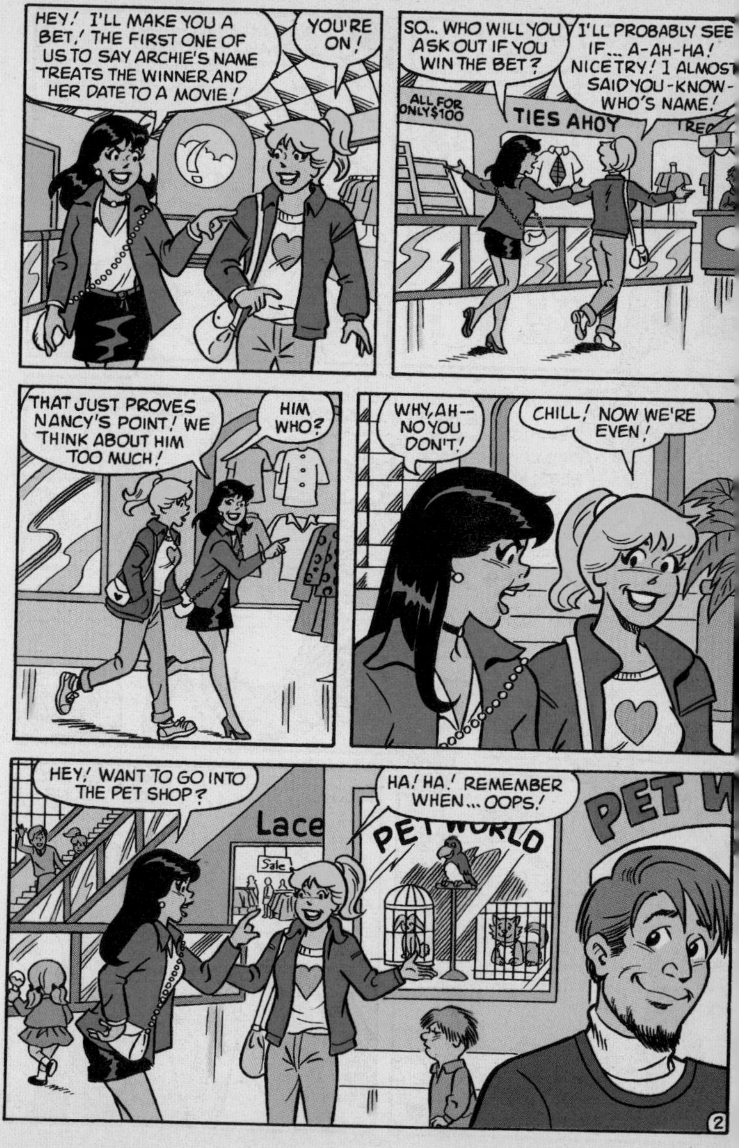
HEY! I'LL MAKE YOU A BET! THE FIRST ONE OF US TO SAY ARCHIE'S NAME TREATS THE WINNER AND HER DATE TO A MOVIE!
YOU'RE ON!
SO... WHO WILL YOU ASK OUT IF YOU WIN THE BET?
I'LL PROBABLY SEE IF... A-AH-HA! NICE TRY! I ALMOST SAID YOU-KNOW-WHO'S NAME!
ALL FOR ONLY $100
TIES AHOY
THAT JUST PROVES NANCY'S POINT! WE THINK ABOUT HIM TOO MUCH!
HIM WHO?
WHY, AH-- NO YOU DON'T!
CHILL! NOW WE'RE EVEN!
HEY! WANT TO GO INTO THE PET SHOP?
HA! HA! REMEMBER WHEN... OOPS!
Lace
Sale
PET WORLD
2

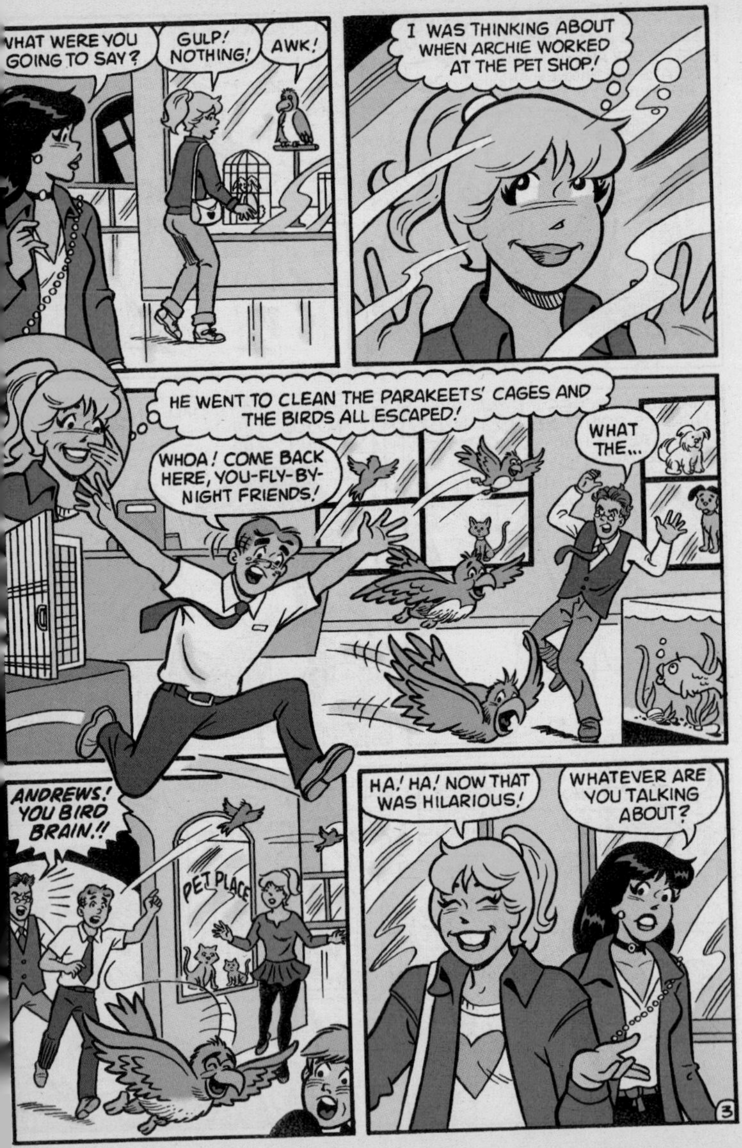
WHAT WERE YOU GOING TO SAY?
GULP! NOTHING!
AWK!
I WAS THINKING ABOUT WHEN ARCHIE WORKED AT THE PET SHOP!
HE WENT TO CLEAN THE PARAKEETS' CAGES AND THE BIRDS ALL ESCAPED!
WHOA! COME BACK HERE, YOU-FLY-BY-NIGHT FRIENDS!
WHAT THE...
ANDREWS! YOU BIRD BRAIN!!
PET PLACE
HA! HA! NOW THAT WAS HILARIOUS!
WHATEVER ARE YOU TALKING ABOUT?
3

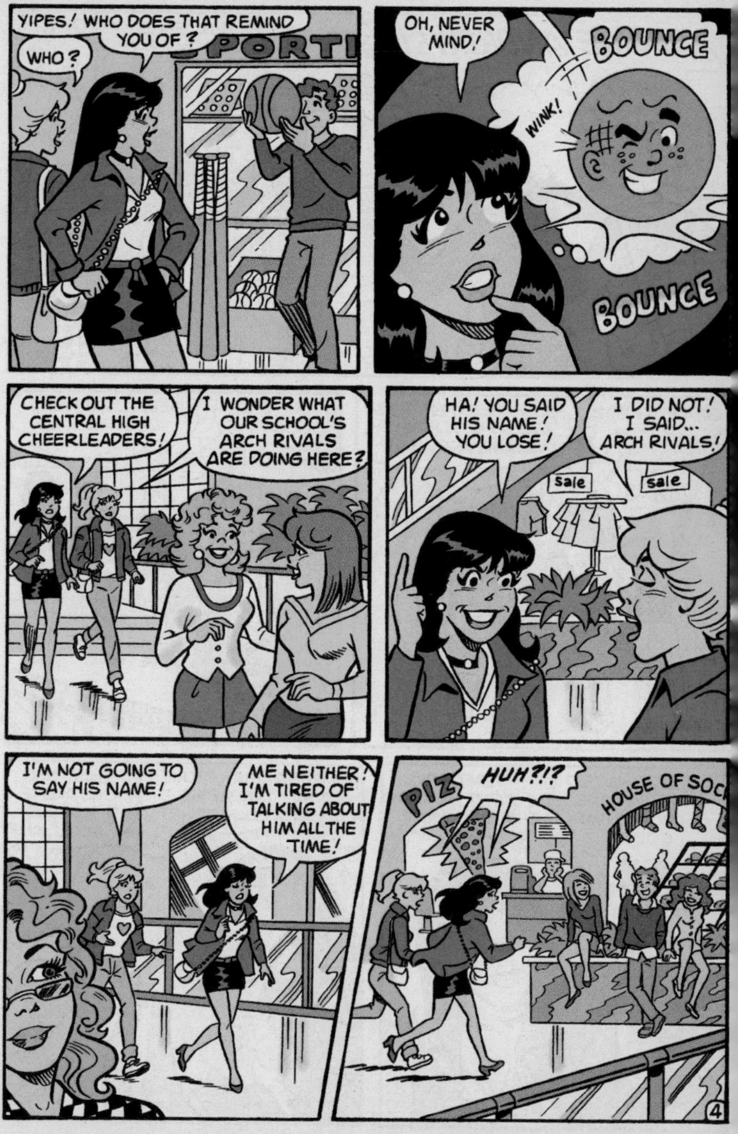
YIPES! WHO DOES THAT REMIND YOU OF?
WHO?
OH, NEVER MIND!
BOUNCE
WINK!
BOUNCE
CHECK OUT THE CENTRAL HIGH CHEERLEADERS!
I WONDER WHAT OUR SCHOOL'S ARCH RIVALS ARE DOING HERE?
HA! YOU SAID HIS NAME! YOU LOSE!
I DID NOT! I SAID... ARCH RIVALS!
Sale
Sale
I'M NOT GOING TO SAY HIS NAME!
ME NEITHER! I'M TIRED OF TALKING ABOUT HIM ALL THE TIME!
HUH?!?
HOUSE OF SOC
4

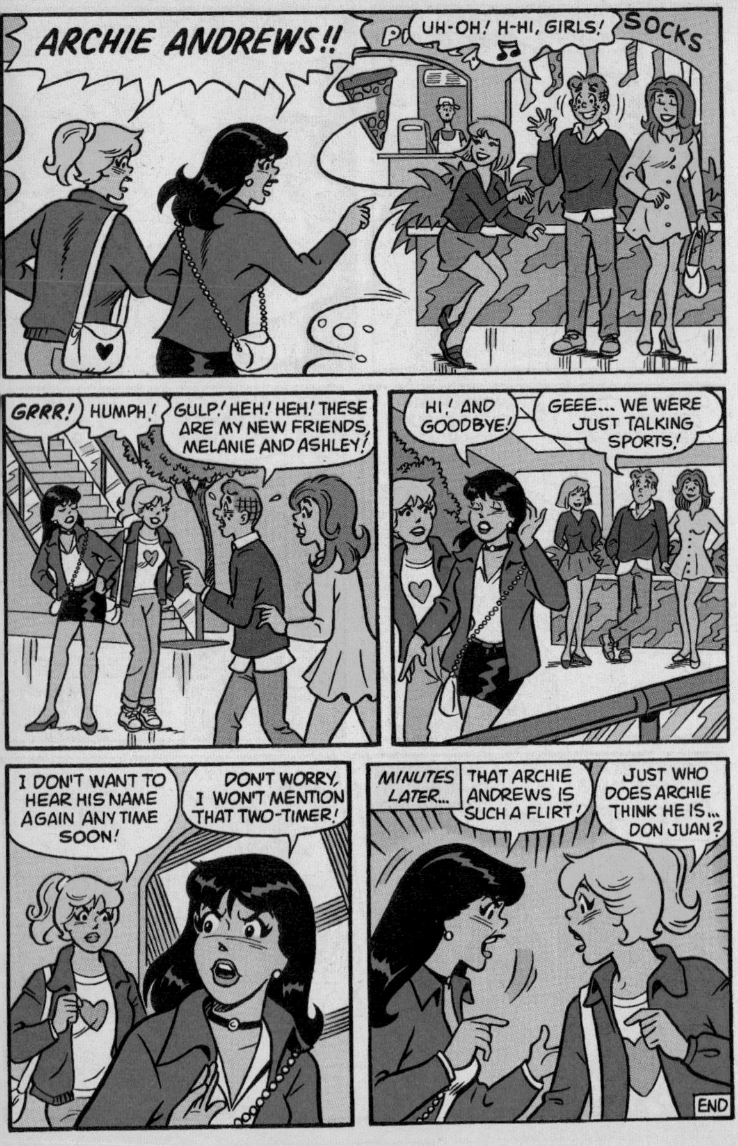

ARCHIE ANDREWS!!
UH-OH! H-HI, GIRLS!
SOCKS
GRRR!
HUMPH!
GULP! HEH! HEH! THESE ARE MY NEW FRIENDS, MELANIE AND ASHLEY!
HI! AND GOODBYE!
GEEE... WE WERE JUST TALKING SPORTS!
I DON'T WANT TO HEAR HIS NAME AGAIN ANY TIME SOON!
DON'T WORRY, I WON'T MENTION THAT TWO-TIMER!
MINUTES LATER...
THAT ARCHIE ANDREWS IS SUCH A FLIRT!
JUST WHO DOES ARCHIE THINK HE IS... DON JUAN?
END

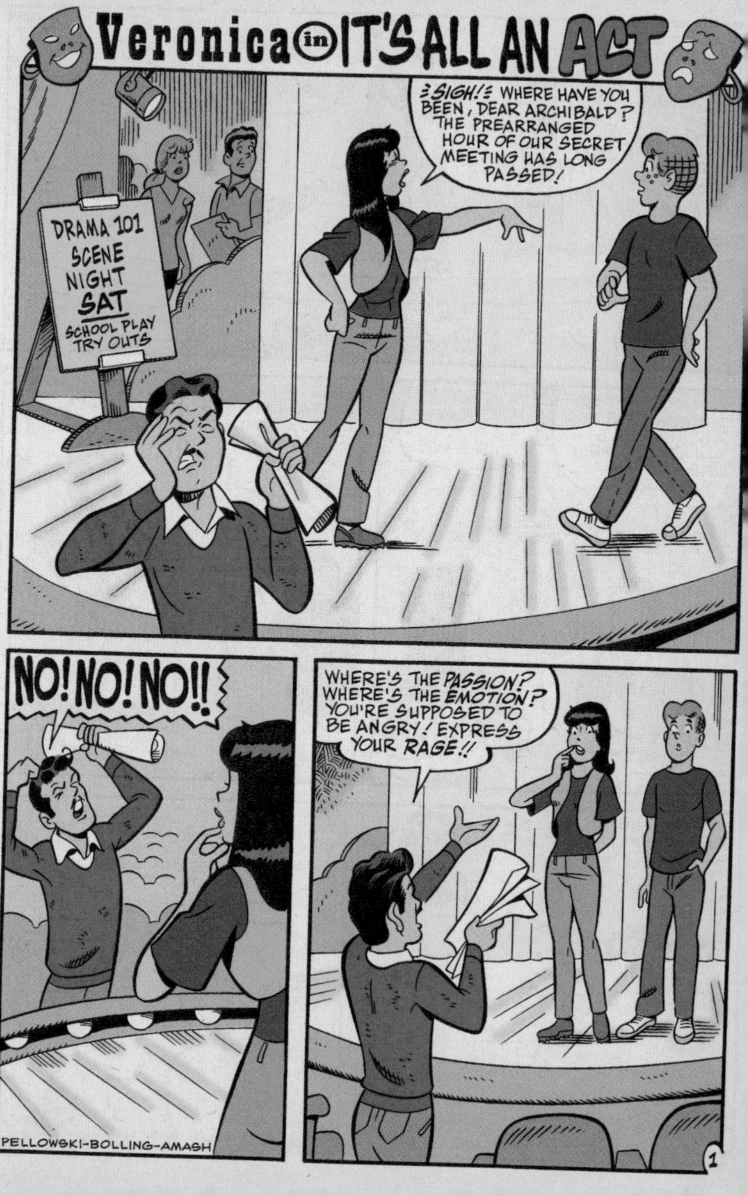
Veronica in IT'S ALL AN ACT
DRAMA 101 SCENE NIGHT SAT
SCHOOL PLAY TRY OUTS
SIGH! WHERE HAVE YOU BEEN, DEAR ARCHIBALD? THE PREARRANGED HOUR OF OUR SECRET MEETING HAS LONG PASSED!
NO! NO! NO!!
WHERE'S THE PASSION? WHERE'S THE EMOTION? YOU'RE SUPPOSED TO BE ANGRY! EXPRESS YOUR RAGE!!
PELLOWSKI-BOLLING-AMASH
1

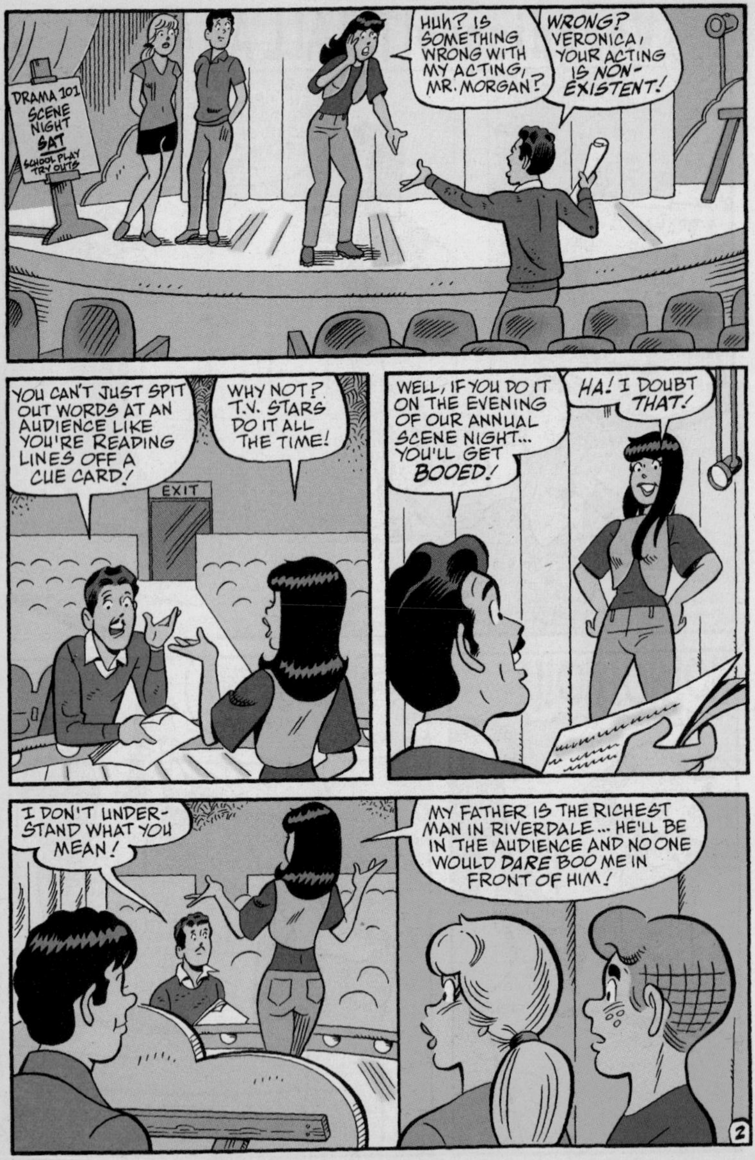
DRAMA 101 SCENE NIGHT SAT
SCHOOL PLAY TRY OUTS
HUH? IS SOMETHING WRONG WITH MY ACTING, MR. MORGAN?
WRONG? VERONICA, YOUR ACTING IS NON-EXISTENT!
YOU CAN'T JUST SPIT OUT WORDS AT AN AUDIENCE LIKE YOU'RE READING LINES OFF A CUE CARD!
WHY NOT? T.V. STARS DO IT ALL THE TIME!
EXIT
WELL, IF YOU DO IT ON THE EVENING OF OUR ANNUAL SCENE NIGHT... YOU'LL GET BOOED!
HA! I DOUBT THAT!
I DON'T UNDER-STAND WHAT YOU MEAN!
MY FATHER IS THE RICHEST MAN IN RIVERDALE... HE'LL BE IN THE AUDIENCE AND NO ONE WOULD DARE BOO ME IN FRONT OF HIM!
2

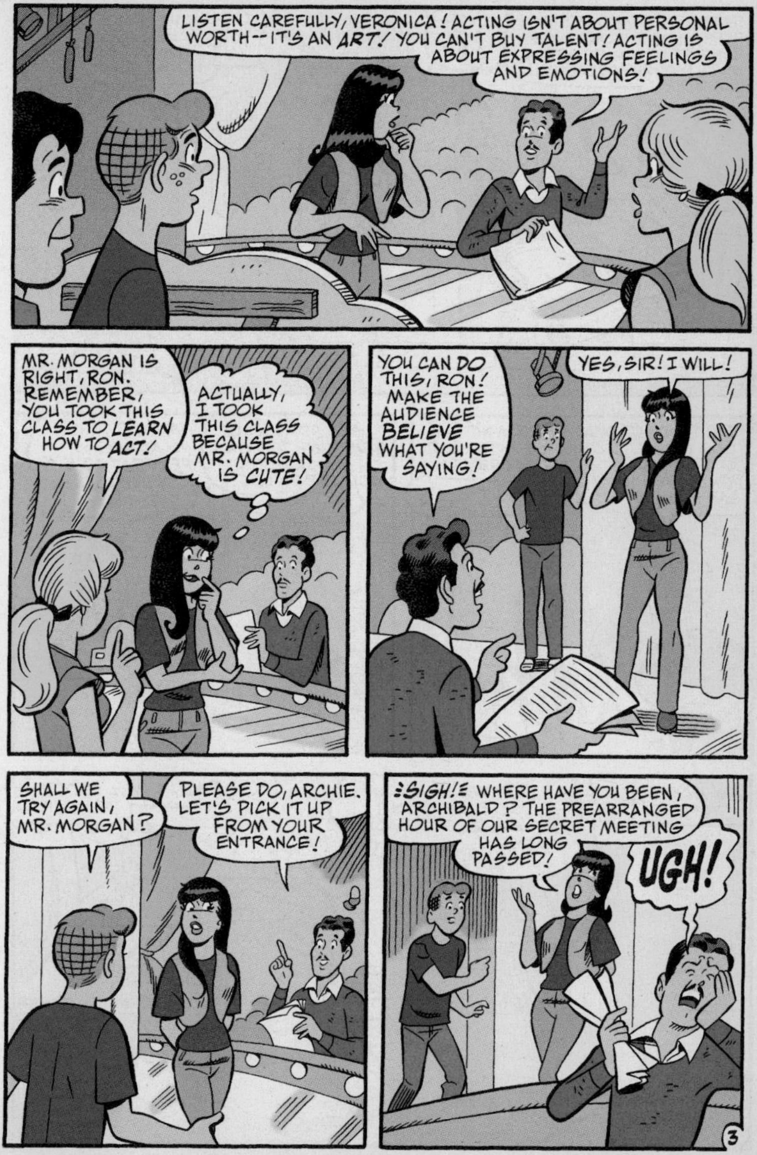
LISTEN CAREFULLY, VERONICA! ACTING ISN'T ABOUT PERSONAL WORTH-- IT'S AN ART! YOU CAN'T BUY TALENT! ACTING IS ABOUT EXPRESSING FEELINGS AND EMOTIONS!
MR. MORGAN IS RIGHT, RON. REMEMBER, YOU TOOK THIS CLASS TO LEARN HOW TO ACT!
ACTUALLY, I TOOK THIS CLASS BECAUSE MR. MORGAN IS CUTE!
YOU CAN DO THIS, RON! MAKE THE AUDIENCE BELIEVE WHAT YOU'RE SAYING!
YES, SIR! I WILL!
SHALL WE TRY AGAIN, MR. MORGAN?
PLEASE DO, ARCHIE. LET'S PICK IT UP FROM YOUR ENTRANCE!
SIGH! WHERE HAVE YOU BEEN, ARCHIBALD? THE PREARRANGED HOUR OF OUR SECRET MEETING HAS LONG PASSED!
UGH!
3

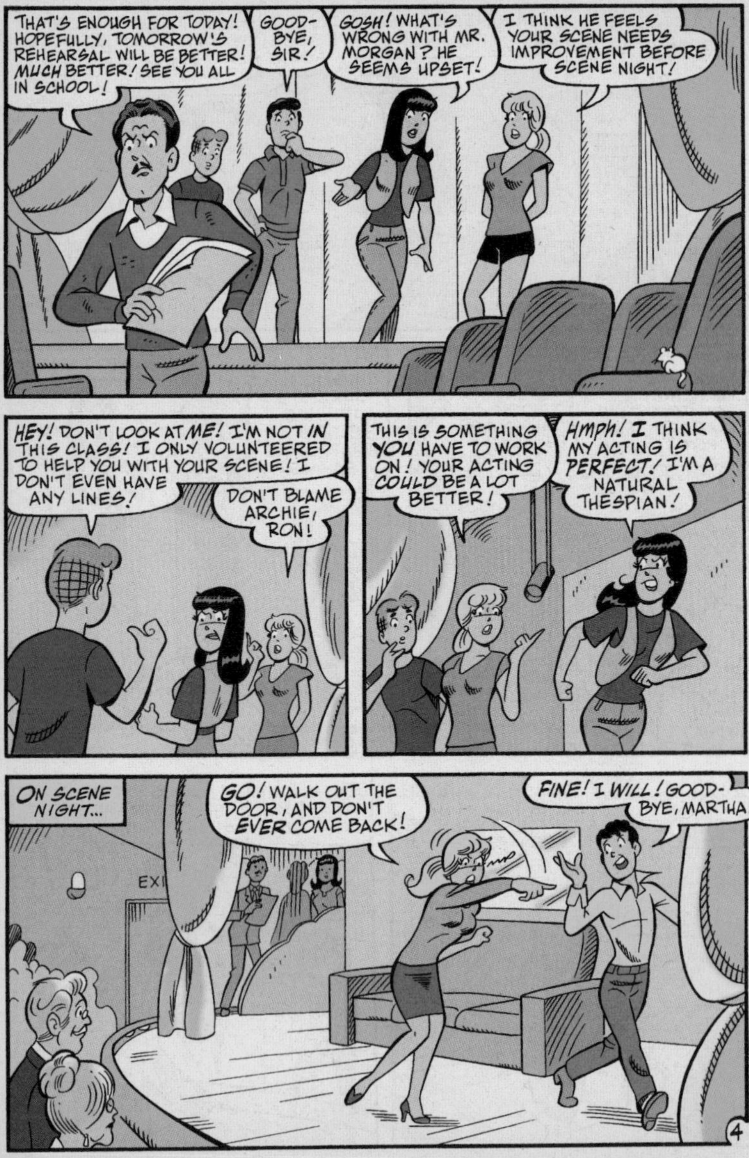
THAT'S ENOUGH FOR TODAY! HOPEFULLY, TOMORROW'S REHEARSAL WILL BE BETTER! MUCH BETTER! SEE YOU ALL IN SCHOOL!
GOOD-BYE, SIR!
GOSH! WHAT'S WRONG WITH MR. MORGAN? HE SEEMS UPSET!
I THINK HE FEELS YOUR SCENE NEEDS IMPROVEMENT BEFORE SCENE NIGHT!
HEY! DON'T LOOK AT ME! I'M NOT IN THIS CLASS! I ONLY VOLUNTEERED TO HELP YOU WITH YOUR SCENE! I DON'T EVEN HAVE ANY LINES!
DON'T BLAME ARCHIE, RON!
THIS IS SOMETHING YOU HAVE TO WORK ON! YOUR ACTING COULD BE A LOT BETTER!
Hmph! I THINK MY ACTING IS PERFECT! I'M A NATURAL THESPIAN!
ON SCENE NIGHT...
GO! WALK OUT THE DOOR, AND DON'T EVER COME BACK!
FINE! I WILL! GOOD-BYE, MARTHA!
EXI
4

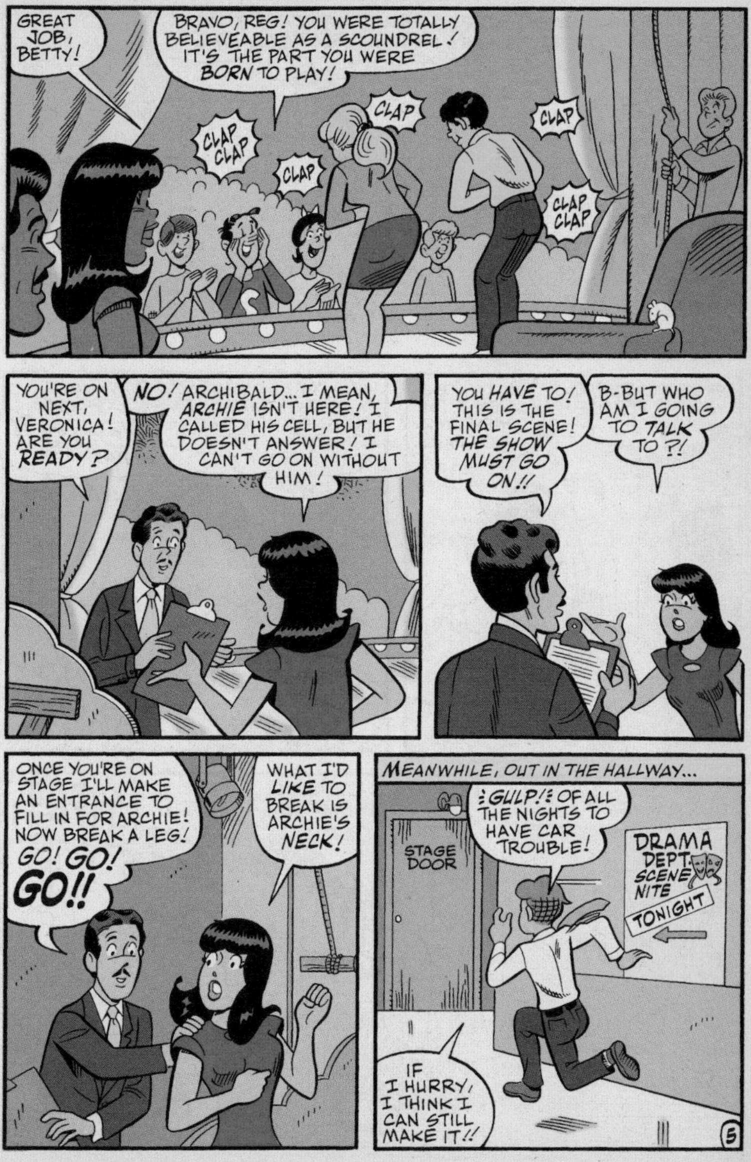
GREAT JOB, BETTY!
BRAVO, REG! YOU WERE TOTALLY BELIEVEABLE AS A SCOUNDREL! IT'S THE PART YOU WERE BORN TO PLAY!
CLAP CLAP
CLAP
CLAP
CLAP
CLAP CLAP
YOU'RE ON NEXT, VERONICA! ARE YOU READY?
NO! ARCHIBALD... I MEAN, ARCHIE ISN'T HERE! I CALLED HIS CELL, BUT HE DOESN'T ANSWER! I CAN'T GO ON WITHOUT HIM!
YOU HAVE TO! THIS IS THE FINAL SCENE! THE SHOW MUST GO ON!!
B-BUT WHO AM I GOING TO TALK TO?!
ONCE YOU'RE ON STAGE I'LL MAKE AN ENTRANCE TO FILL IN FOR ARCHIE! NOW BREAK A LEG! GO! GO! GO!!
WHAT I'D LIKE TO BREAK IS ARCHIE'S NECK!
MEANWHILE, OUT IN THE HALLWAY...
STAGE DOOR
:GULP!: OF ALL THE NIGHTS TO HAVE CAR TROUBLE!
DRAMA DEPT. SCENE NITE
TONIGHT
IF I HURRY, I THINK I CAN STILL MAKE IT!!
5

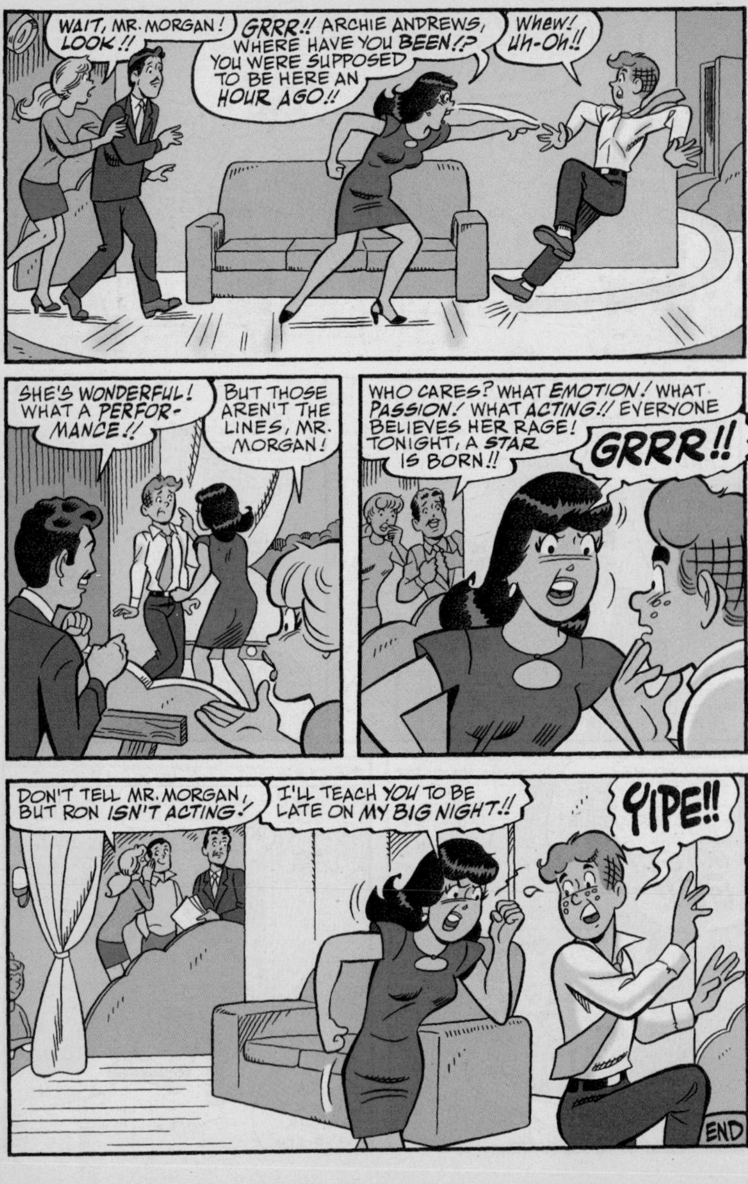
WAIT, MR. MORGAN! LOOK!!
GRRR!! ARCHIE ANDREWS, WHERE HAVE YOU BEEN!? YOU WERE SUPPOSED TO BE HERE AN HOUR AGO!!
Whew! Uh-Oh!!
SHE'S WONDERFUL! WHAT A PERFOR-MANCE!!
BUT THOSE AREN'T THE LINES, MR. MORGAN!
WHO CARES? WHAT EMOTION! WHAT PASSION! WHAT ACTING!! EVERYONE BELIEVES HER RAGE! TONIGHT, A STAR IS BORN!!
GRRR!!
DON'T TELL MR. MORGAN, BUT RON ISN'T ACTING!
I'LL TEACH YOU TO BE LATE ON MY BIG NIGHT!!
YIPE!!
END

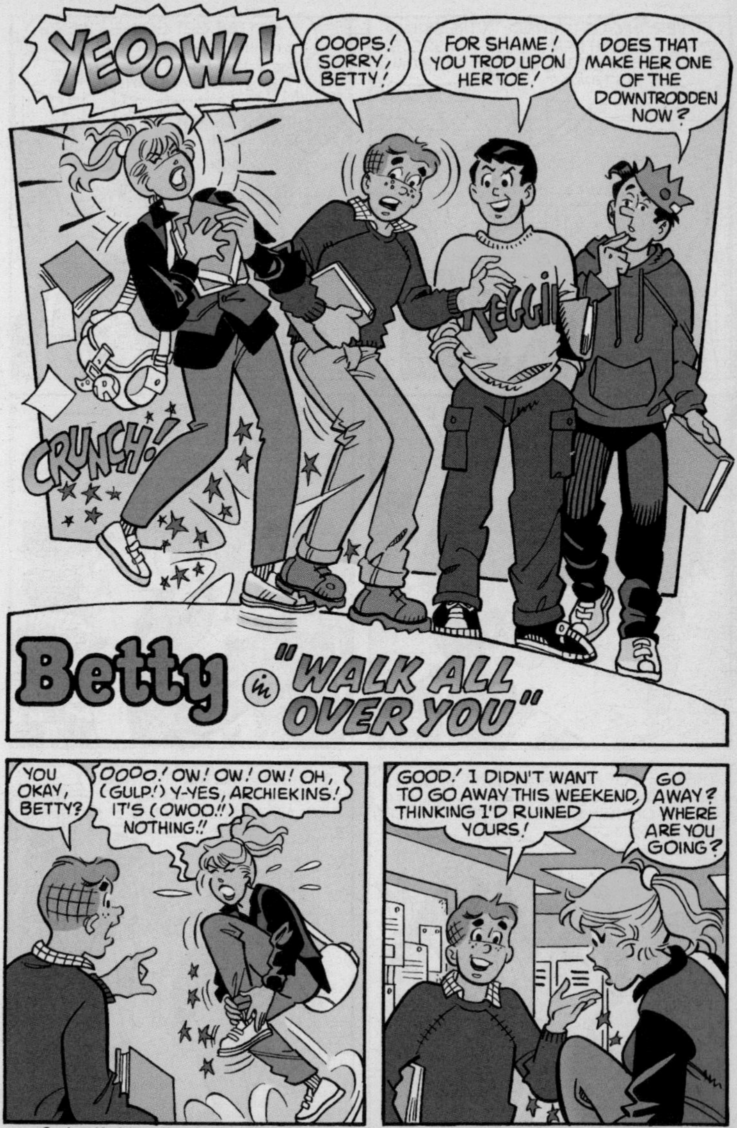
YEOOWL!
OOOPS! SORRY, BETTY!
FOR SHAME! YOU TROD UPON HER TOE!
DOES THAT MAKE HER ONE OF THE DOWNTRODDEN NOW?
CRUNCH!
REGGIE
Betty in "WALK ALL OVER YOU"
YOU OKAY, BETTY?
OOOO! OW! OW! OW! OH, (GULP!) Y-YES, ARCHIEKINS! IT'S (OWOO!!) NOTHING!!
GOOD! I DIDN'T WANT TO GO AWAY THIS WEEKEND, THINKING I'D RUINED YOURS!
GO AWAY? WHERE ARE YOU GOING?

Script: Kathleen Webb / Pencils: Stan Goldberg / Inks: John Lowe / Letters: Bill Yoshida

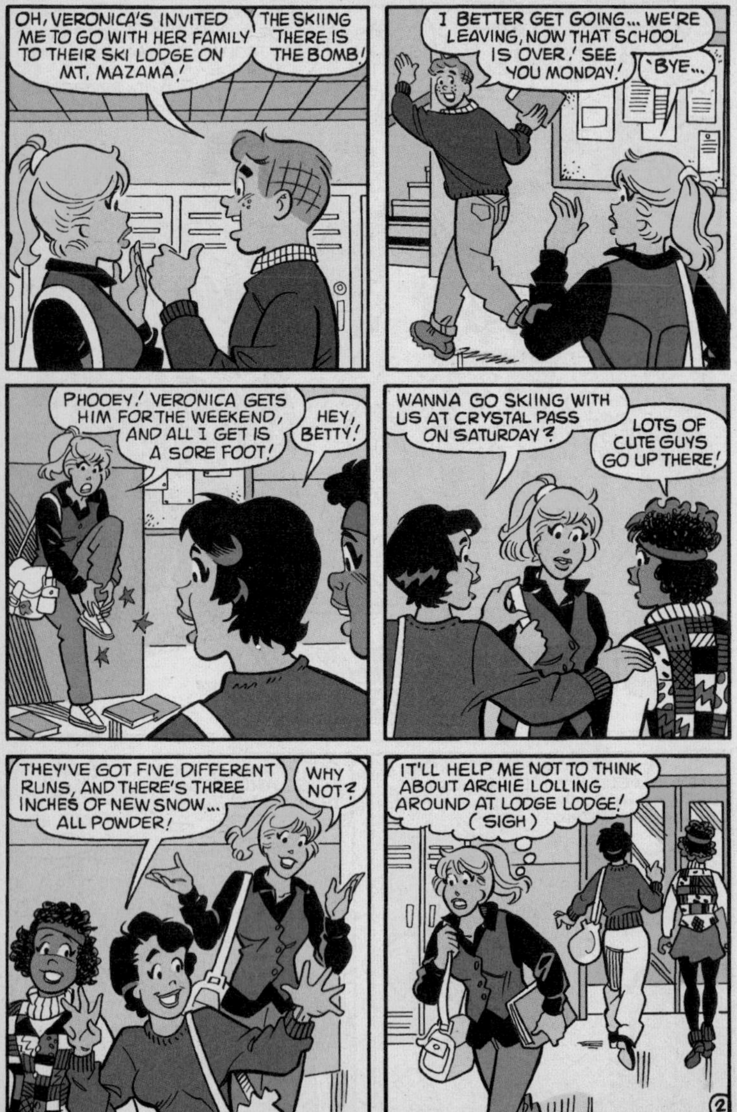
OH, VERONICA'S INVITED ME TO GO WITH HER FAMILY TO THEIR SKI LODGE ON MT. MAZAMA!
THE SKIING THERE IS THE BOMB!
I BETTER GET GOING... WE'RE LEAVING, NOW THAT SCHOOL IS OVER! SEE YOU MONDAY!
`BYE...
PHOOEY! VERONICA GETS HIM FOR THE WEEKEND, AND ALL I GET IS A SORE FOOT!
HEY, BETTY!
WANNA GO SKIING WITH US AT CRYSTAL PASS ON SATURDAY?
LOTS OF CUTE GUYS GO UP THERE!
THEY'VE GOT FIVE DIFFERENT RUNS, AND THERE'S THREE INCHES OF NEW SNOW... ALL POWDER!
WHY NOT?
IT'LL HELP ME NOT TO THINK ABOUT ARCHIE LOLLING AROUND AT LODGE LODGE! (SIGH)
2

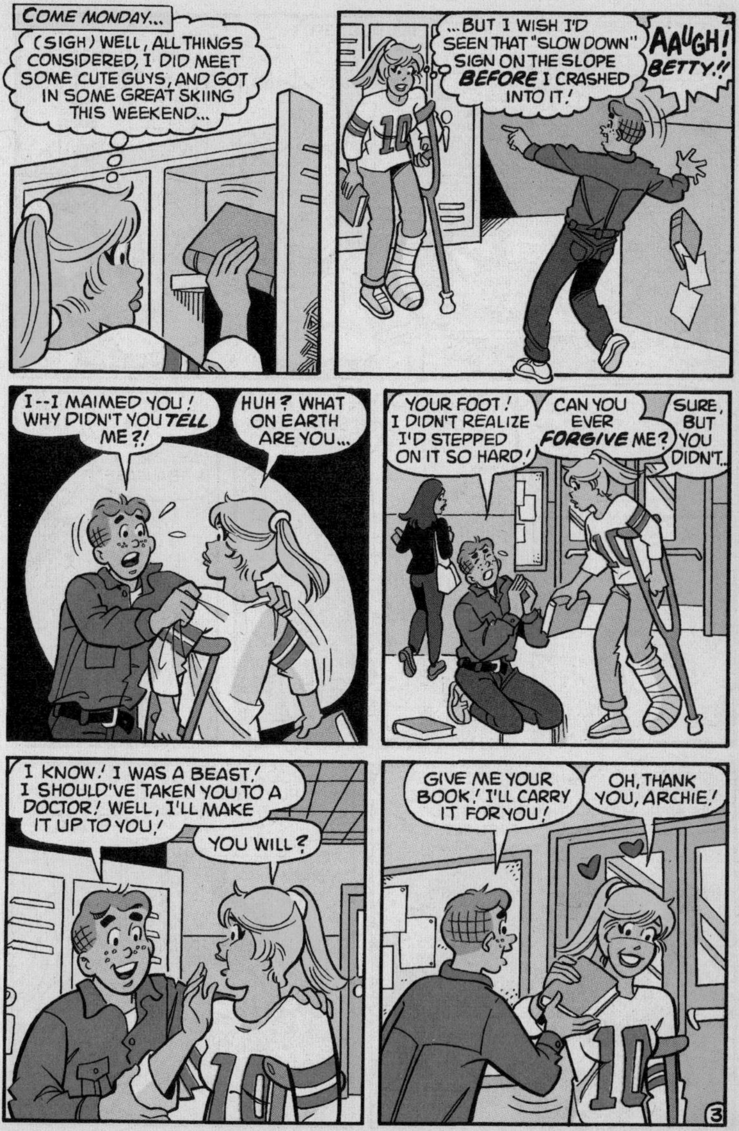

COME MONDAY...
(SIGH) WELL, ALL THINGS CONSIDERED, I DID MEET SOME CUTE GUYS, AND GOT IN SOME GREAT SKIING THIS WEEKEND...
...BUT I WISH I'D SEEN THAT "SLOW DOWN" SIGN ON THE SLOPE BEFORE I CRASHED INTO IT!
AAUGH! BETTY!!
I--I MAIMED YOU! WHY DIDN'T YOU TELL ME?!
HUH? WHAT ON EARTH ARE YOU...
YOUR FOOT! I DIDN'T REALIZE I'D STEPPED ON IT SO HARD!
CAN YOU EVER FORGIVE ME?
SURE, BUT YOU DIDN'T...
I KNOW! I WAS A BEAST! I SHOULD'VE TAKEN YOU TO A DOCTOR! WELL, I'LL MAKE IT UP TO YOU!
YOU WILL?
GIVE ME YOUR BOOK! I'LL CARRY IT FOR YOU!
OH, THANK YOU, ARCHIE!
3

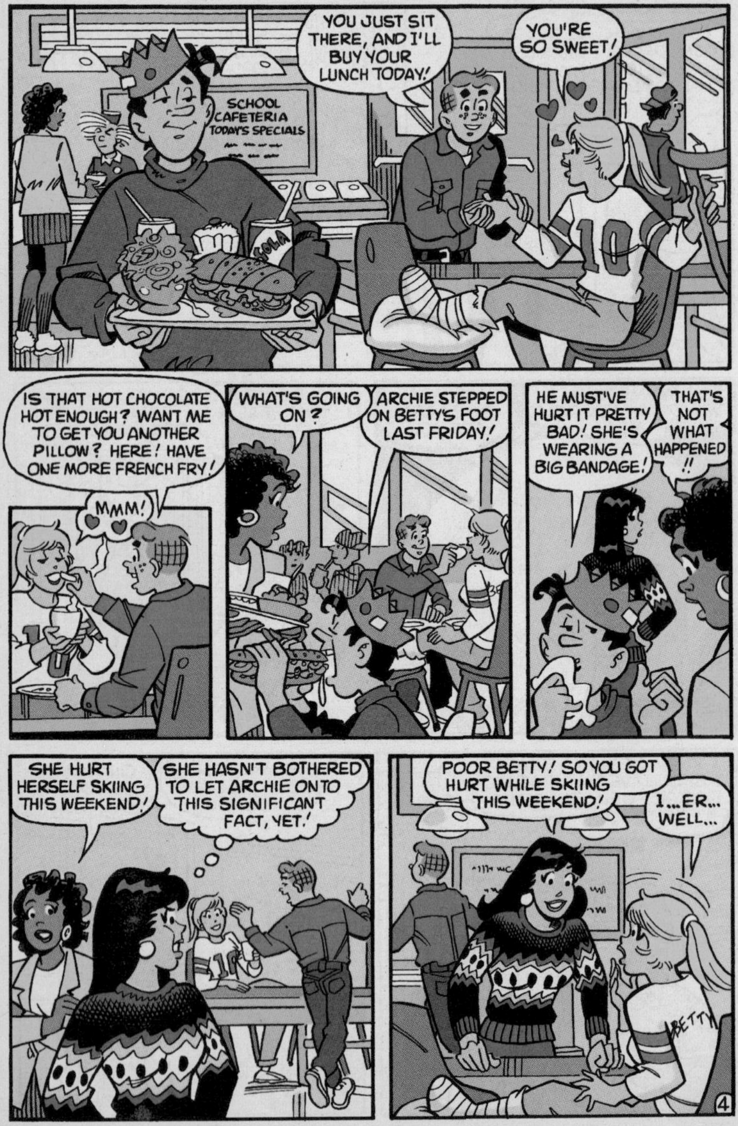

SCHOOL CAFETERIA TODAY'S SPECIALS
YOU JUST SIT THERE, AND I'LL BUY YOUR LUNCH TODAY!
YOU'RE SO SWEET!
IS THAT HOT CHOCOLATE HOT ENOUGH? WANT ME TO GET YOU ANOTHER PILLOW? HERE! HAVE ONE MORE FRENCH FRY!
MMM!
WHAT'S GOING ON?
ARCHIE STEPPED ON BETTY'S FOOT LAST FRIDAY!
HE MUST'VE HURT IT PRETTY BAD! SHE'S WEARING A BIG BANDAGE!
THAT'S NOT WHAT HAPPENED!!
SHE HURT HERSELF SKIING THIS WEEKEND!
SHE HASN'T BOTHERED TO LET ARCHIE ON TO THIS SIGNIFICANT FACT, YET!
POOR BETTY! SO YOU GOT HURT WHILE SKIING THIS WEEKEND!
I...ER... WELL...
BETTY
4

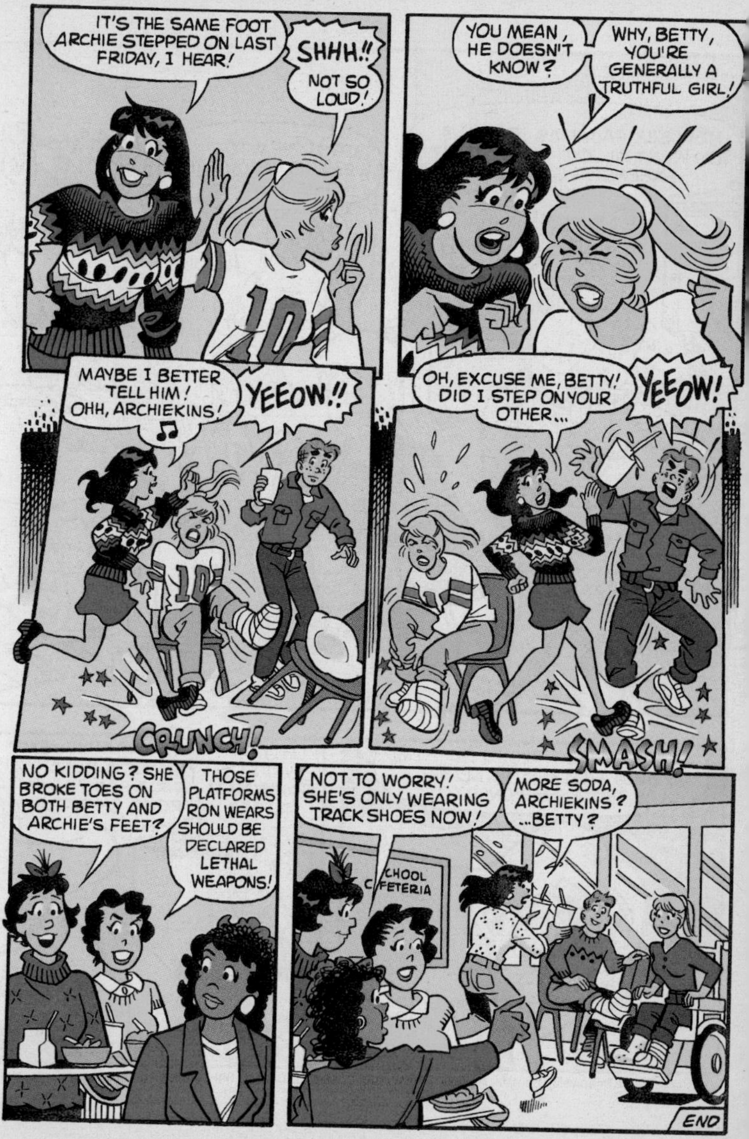
IT'S THE SAME FOOT ARCHIE STEPPED ON LAST FRIDAY, I HEAR!
SHHH!! NOT SO LOUD!
YOU MEAN, HE DOESN'T KNOW?
WHY, BETTY, YOU'RE GENERALLY A TRUTHFUL GIRL!
MAYBE I BETTER TELL HIM! OHH, ARCHIEKINS! ♫
YEEOW!!
CRUNCH!
OH, EXCUSE ME, BETTY! DID I STEP ON YOUR OTHER...
YEEOW!
SMASH!
NO KIDDING? SHE BROKE TOES ON BOTH BETTY AND ARCHIE'S FEET?
THOSE PLATFORMS RON WEARS SHOULD BE DECLARED LETHAL WEAPONS!
NOT TO WORRY! SHE'S ONLY WEARING TRACK SHOES NOW!
MORE SODA, ARCHIEKINS? ...BETTY?
CHOOL C FETERIA
END

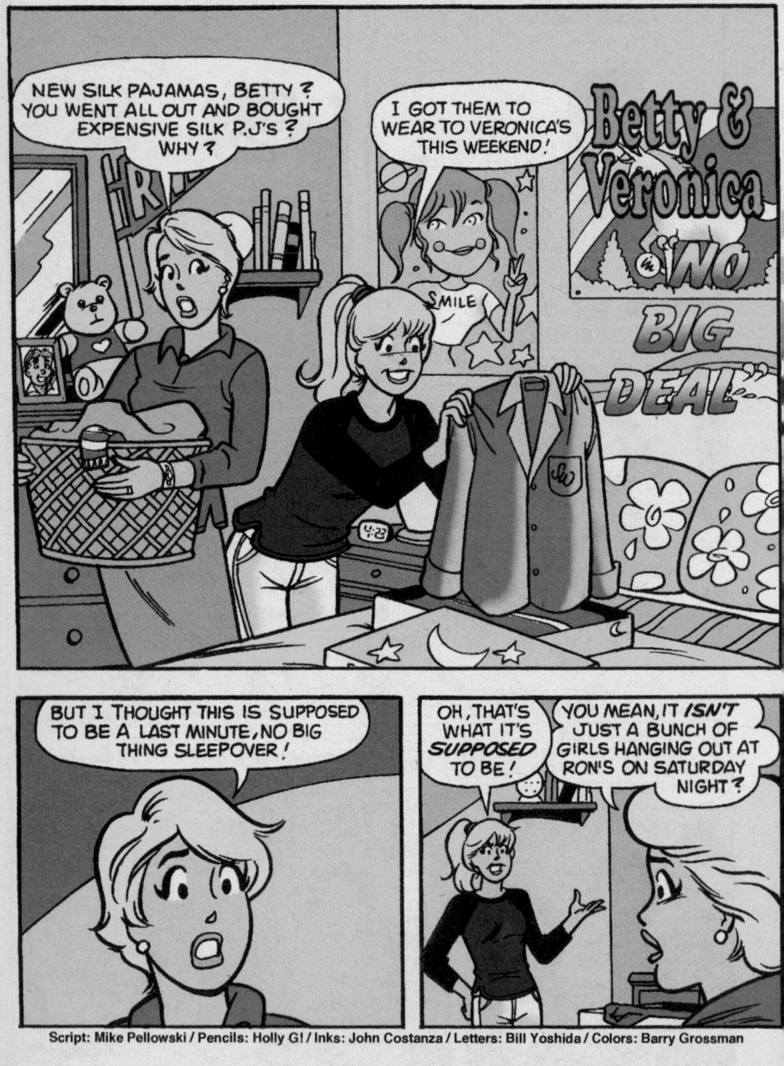
NEW SILK PAJAMAS, BETTY? YOU WENT ALL OUT AND BOUGHT EXPENSIVE SILK P.J'S? WHY?
I GOT THEM TO WEAR TO VERONICA'S THIS WEEKEND!
Betty & Veronica
in "NO BIG DEAL"
SMILE
BUT I THOUGHT THIS IS SUPPOSED TO BE A LAST MINUTE, NO BIG THING SLEEPOVER!
OH, THAT'S WHAT IT'S SUPPOSED TO BE!
YOU MEAN, IT ISN'T JUST A BUNCH OF GIRLS HANGING OUT AT RON'S ON SATURDAY NIGHT?

Script: Mike Pellowski / Pencils: Holly G! / Inks: John Costanza / Letters: Bill Yoshida / Colors: Barry Grossman

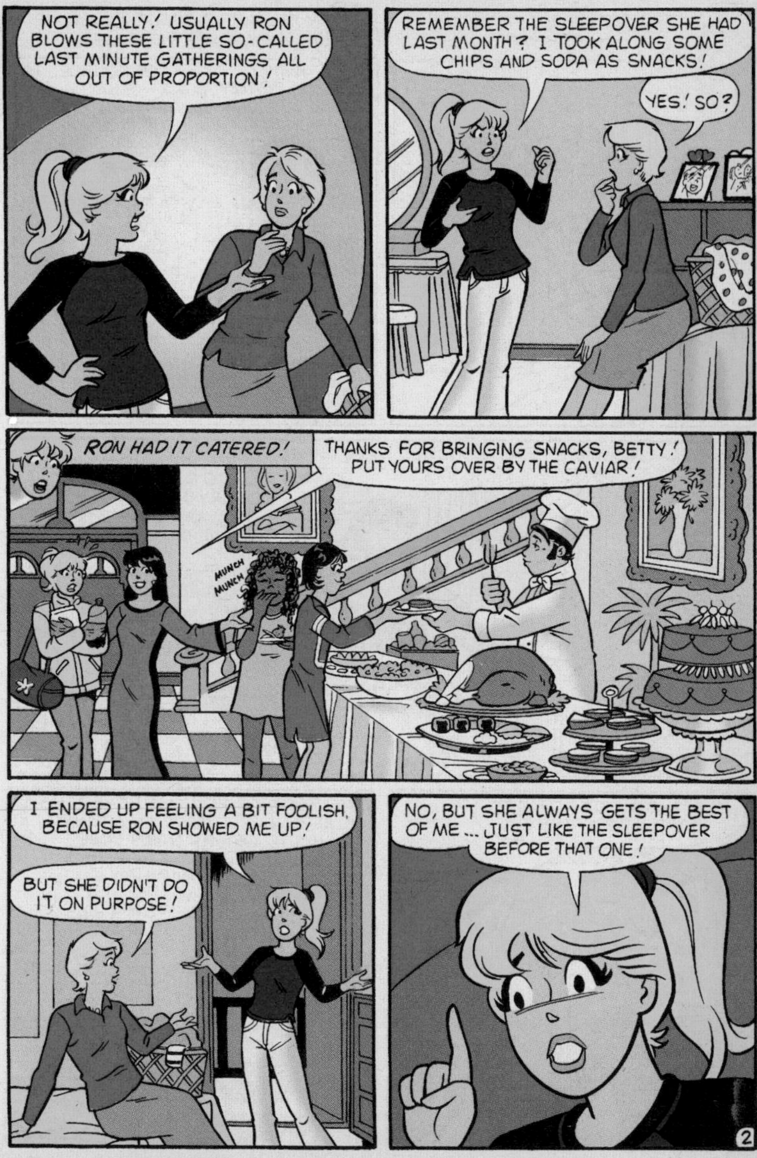
NOT REALLY! USUALLY RON BLOWS THESE LITTLE SO-CALLED LAST MINUTE GATHERINGS ALL OUT OF PROPORTION!
REMEMBER THE SLEEPOVER SHE HAD LAST MONTH? I TOOK ALONG SOME CHIPS AND SODA AS SNACKS!
YES! SO?
RON HAD IT CATERED!
THANKS FOR BRINGING SNACKS, BETTY! PUT YOURS OVER BY THE CAVIAR!
MUNCH MUNCH
I ENDED UP FEELING A BIT FOOLISH, BECAUSE RON SHOWED ME UP!
BUT SHE DIDN'T DO IT ON PURPOSE!
NO, BUT SHE ALWAYS GETS THE BEST OF ME ... JUST LIKE THE SLEEPOVER BEFORE THAT ONE!
2

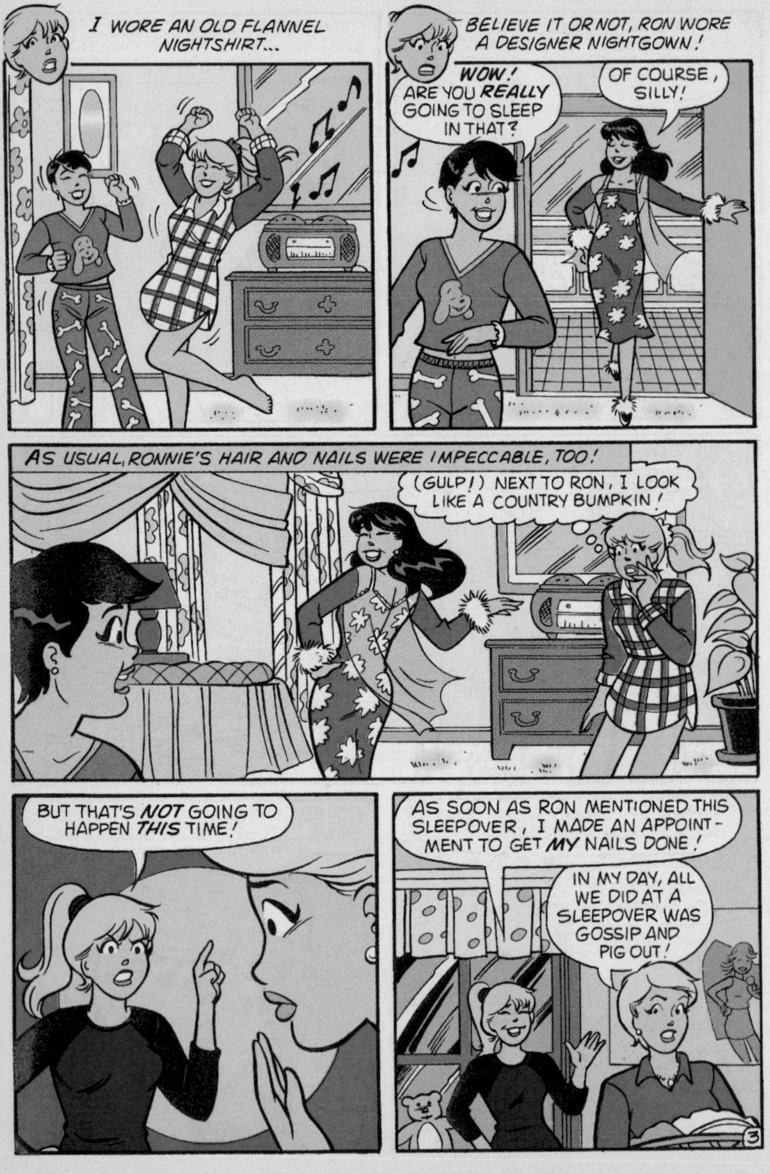

I WORE AN OLD FLANNEL NIGHTSHIRT...
BELIEVE IT OR NOT, RON WORE A DESIGNER NIGHTGOWN!
WOW! ARE YOU REALLY GOING TO SLEEP IN THAT?
OF COURSE, SILLY!
AS USUAL, RONNIE'S HAIR AND NAILS WERE IMPECCABLE, TOO!
(GULP!) NEXT TO RON, I LOOK LIKE A COUNTRY BUMPKIN!
BUT THAT'S NOT GOING TO HAPPEN THIS TIME!
AS SOON AS RON MENTIONED THIS SLEEPOVER, I MADE AN APPOINT-MENT TO GET MY NAILS DONE!
IN MY DAY, ALL WE DID AT A SLEEPOVER WAS GOSSIP AND PIG OUT!
3

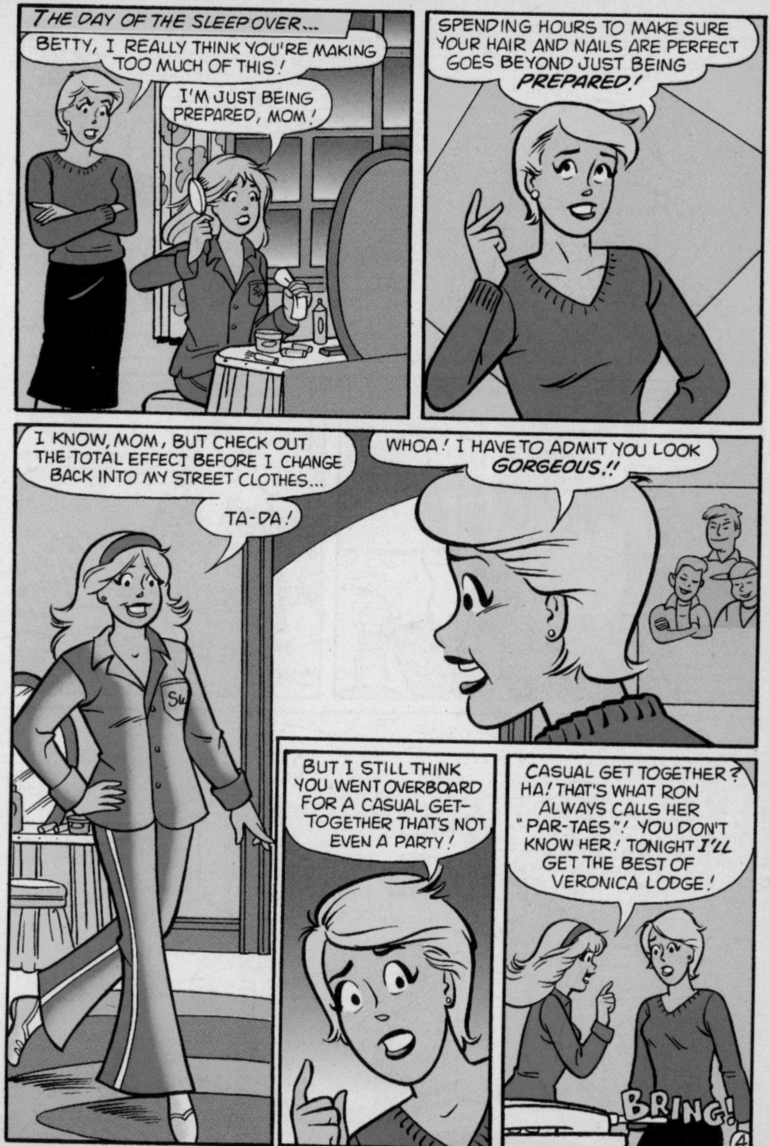
THE DAY OF THE SLEEPOVER...
BETTY, I REALLY THINK YOU'RE MAKING TOO MUCH OF THIS!
I'M JUST BEING PREPARED, MOM!
SPENDING HOURS TO MAKE SURE YOUR HAIR AND NAILS ARE PERFECT GOES BEYOND JUST BEING PREPARED!
I KNOW, MOM, BUT CHECK OUT THE TOTAL EFFECT BEFORE I CHANGE BACK INTO MY STREET CLOTHES...
TA-DA!
WHOA! I HAVE TO ADMIT YOU LOOK GORGEOUS!!
BUT I STILL THINK YOU WENT OVERBOARD FOR A CASUAL GET-TOGETHER THAT'S NOT EVEN A PARTY!
CASUAL GET TOGETHER? HA! THAT'S WHAT RON ALWAYS CALLS HER "PAR-TAES"! YOU DON'T KNOW HER! TONIGHT I'LL GET THE BEST OF VERONICA LODGE!
BRING!
4

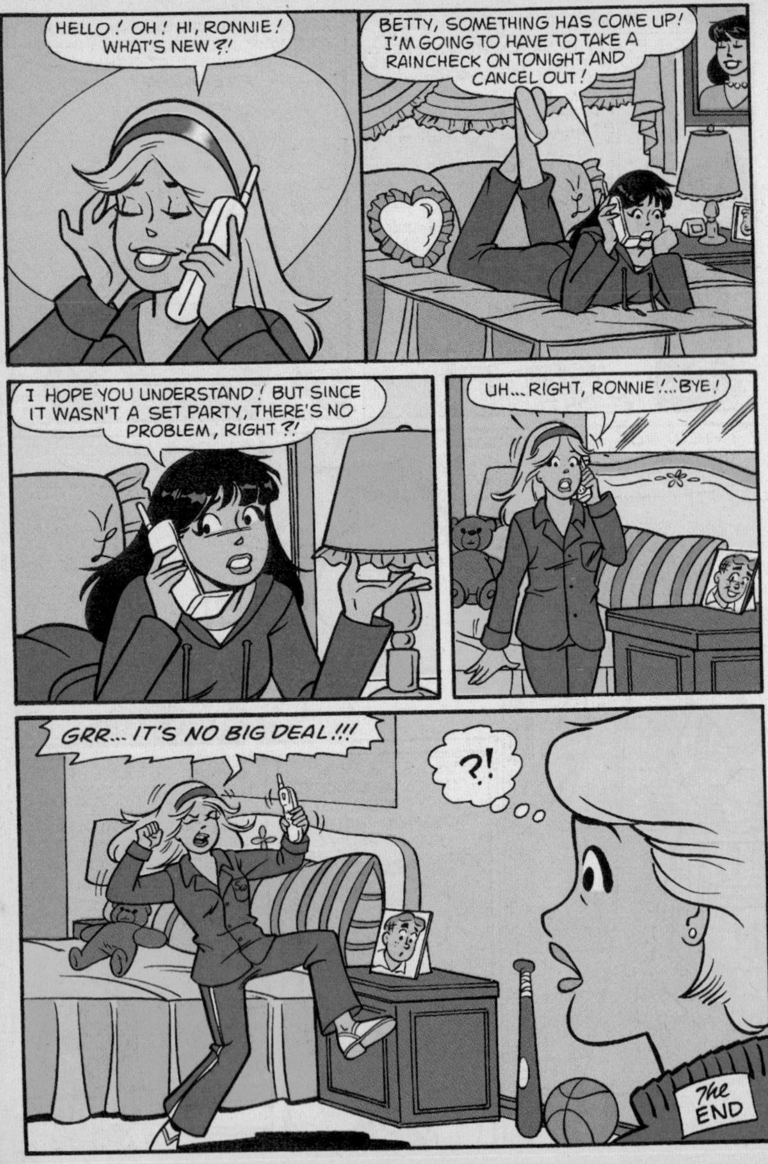
HELLO! OH! HI, RONNIE! WHAT'S NEW?!
BETTY, SOMETHING HAS COME UP! I'M GOING TO HAVE TO TAKE A RAINCHECK ON TONIGHT AND CANCEL OUT!
I HOPE YOU UNDERSTAND! BUT SINCE IT WASN'T A SET PARTY, THERE'S NO PROBLEM, RIGHT?!
UH... RIGHT, RONNIE!...BYE!
GRR... IT'S NO BIG DEAL!!!
?!
The END

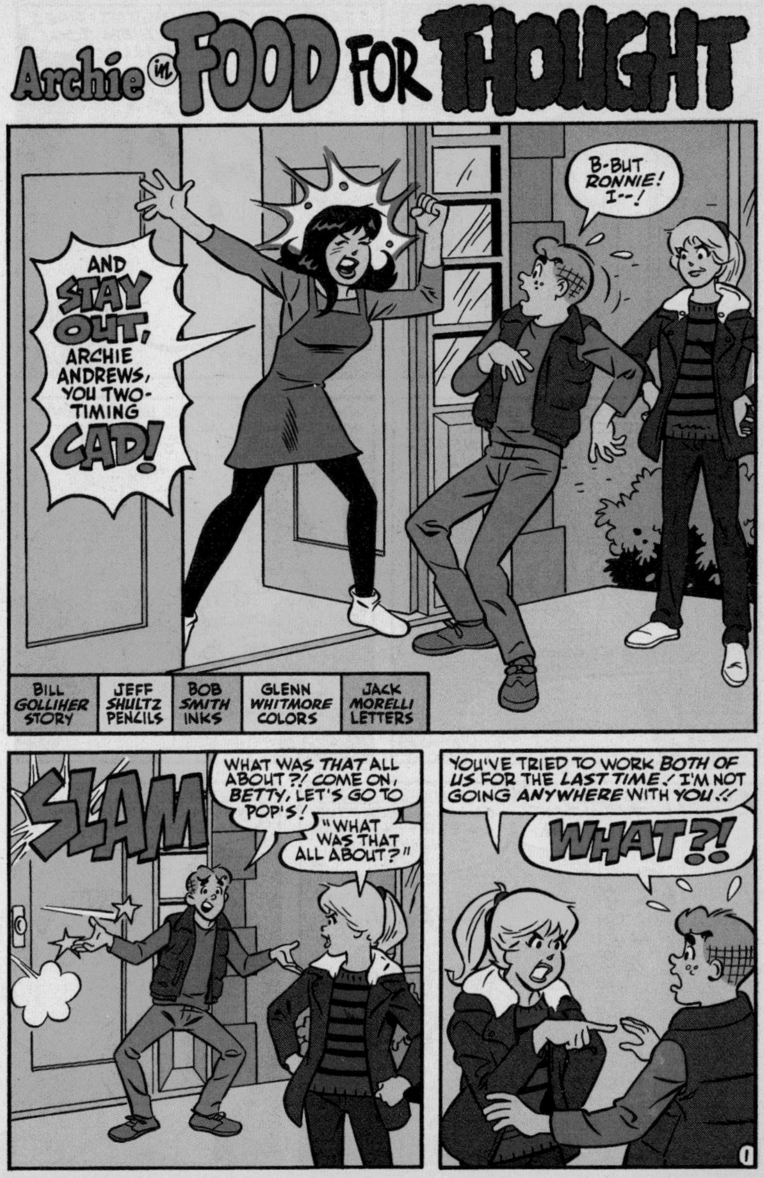
Archie in FOOD FOR THOUGHT
AND STAY OUT, ARCHIE ANDREWS, YOU TWO-TIMING CAD!
B-BUT RONNIE! I--!
BILL GOLLIHER STORY
JEFF SHULTZ PENCILS
BOB SMITH INKS
GLENN WHITMORE COLORS
JACK MORELLI LETTERS
SLAM
WHAT WAS THAT ALL ABOUT?! COME ON, BETTY, LET'S GO TO POP'S!
"WHAT WAS THAT ALL ABOUT?"
YOU'VE TRIED TO WORK BOTH OF US FOR THE LAST TIME! I'M NOT GOING ANYWHERE WITH YOU!!
WHAT?!
0

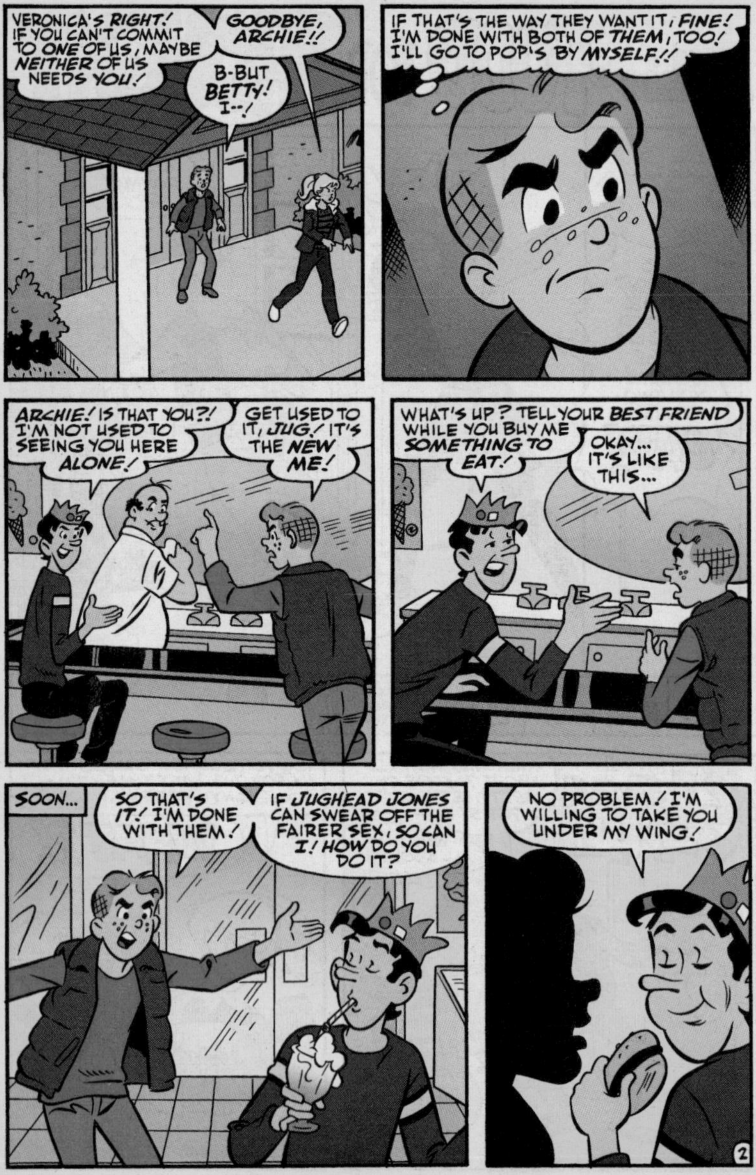

VERONICA'S RIGHT! IF YOU CAN'T COMMIT TO ONE OF US, MAYBE NEITHER OF US NEEDS YOU!
GOODBYE, ARCHIE!!
B-BUT BETTY! I--!
IF THAT'S THE WAY THEY WANT IT, FINE! I'M DONE WITH BOTH OF THEM, TOO! I'LL GO TO POP'S BY MYSELF!!
ARCHIE! IS THAT YOU?! I'M NOT USED TO SEEING YOU HERE ALONE!
GET USED TO IT, JUG! IT'S THE NEW ME!
WHAT'S UP? TELL YOUR BEST FRIEND WHILE YOU BUY ME SOMETHING TO EAT!
OKAY... IT'S LIKE THIS...
SOON...
SO THAT'S IT! I'M DONE WITH THEM!
IF JUGHEAD JONES CAN SWEAR OFF THE FAIRER SEX, SO CAN I! HOW DO YOU DO IT?
NO PROBLEM! I'M WILLING TO TAKE YOU UNDER MY WING!
2

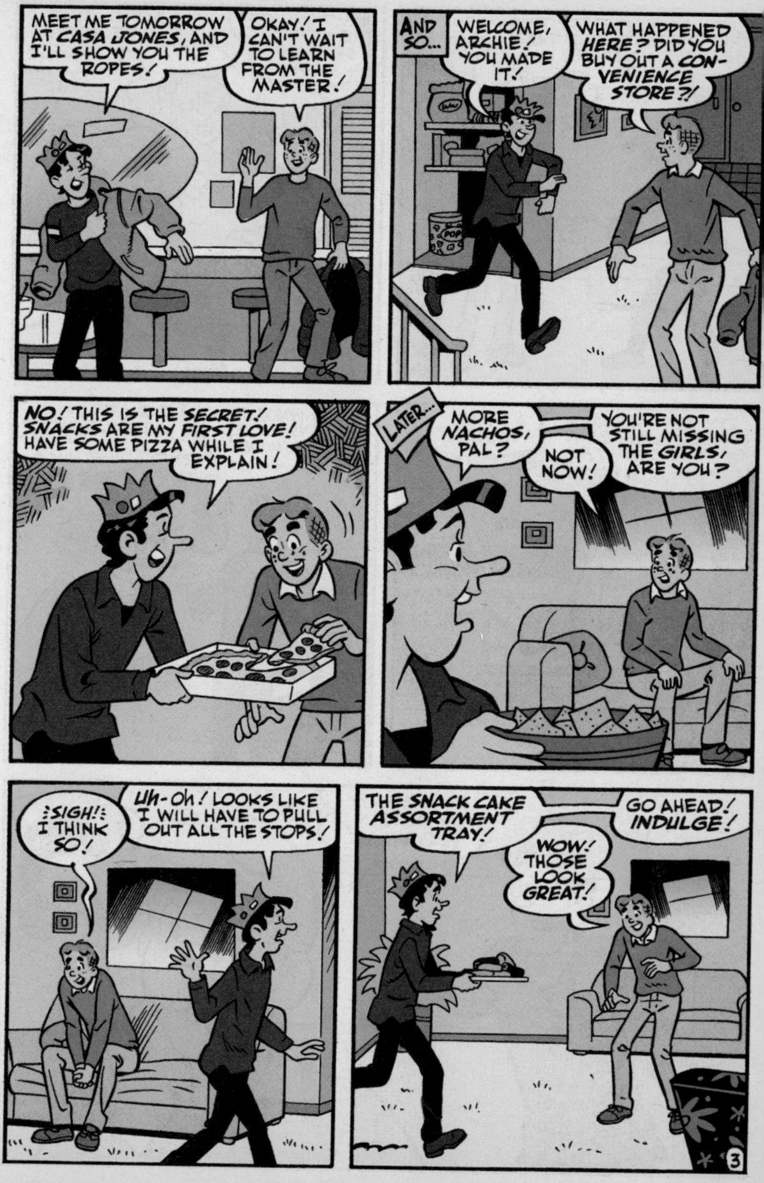
MEET ME TOMORROW AT CASA JONES, AND I'LL SHOW YOU THE ROPES!
OKAY! I CAN'T WAIT TO LEARN FROM THE MASTER!
AND SO...
WELCOME, ARCHIE! YOU MADE IT!
WHAT HAPPENED HERE? DID YOU BUY OUT A CONVENIENCE STORE?!
NO! THIS IS THE SECRET! SNACKS ARE MY FIRST LOVE! HAVE SOME PIZZA WHILE I EXPLAIN!
LATER...
MORE NACHOS, PAL?
NOT NOW!
YOU'RE NOT STILL MISSING THE GIRLS, ARE YOU?
SIGH! I THINK SO!
UH-OH! LOOKS LIKE I WILL HAVE TO PULL OUT ALL THE STOPS!
THE SNACK CAKE ASSORTMENT TRAY!
GO AHEAD! INDULGE!
WOW! THOSE LOOK GREAT!
3

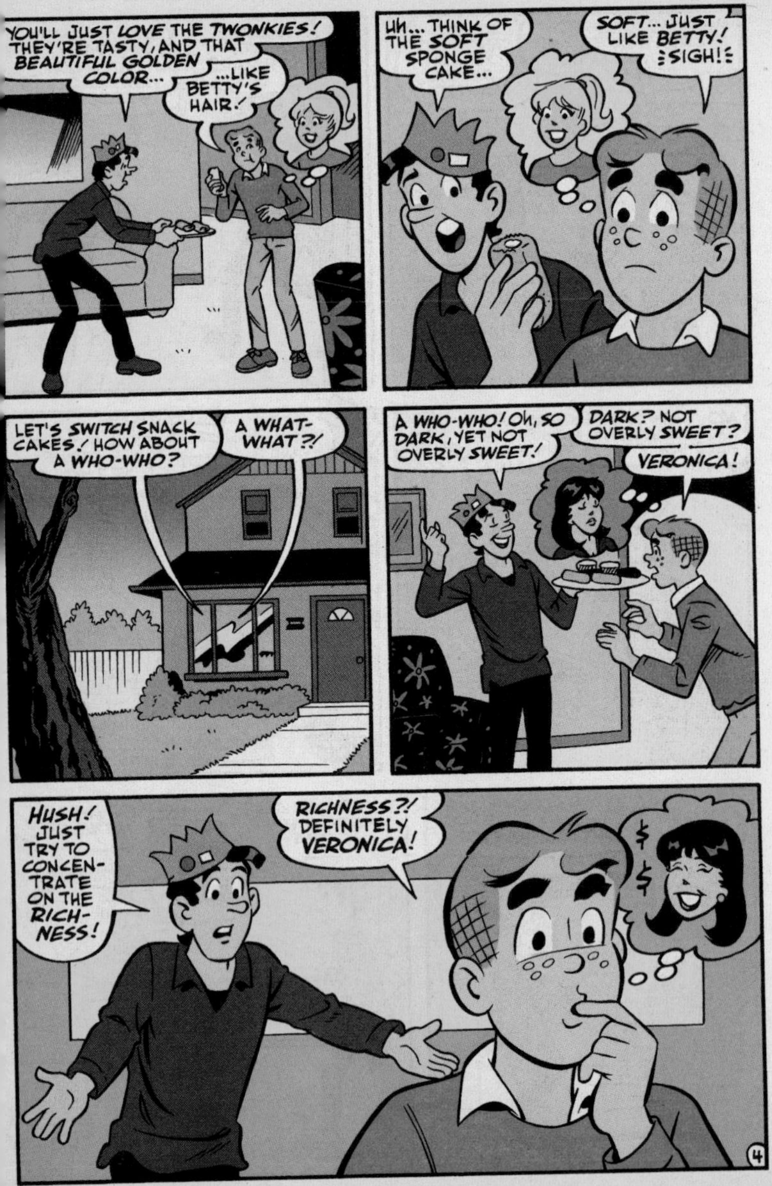
YOU'LL JUST LOVE THE TWONKIES! THEY'RE TASTY, AND THAT BEAUTIFUL GOLDEN COLOR...
...LIKE BETTY'S HAIR!
UH... THINK OF THE SOFT SPONGE CAKE...
SOFT... JUST LIKE BETTY! SIGH!
LET'S SWITCH SNACK CAKES! HOW ABOUT A WHO-WHO?
A WHAT-WHAT?!
A WHO-WHO! OH, SO DARK, YET NOT OVERLY SWEET!
DARK? NOT OVERLY SWEET?
VERONICA!
HUSH! JUST TRY TO CONCEN-TRATE ON THE RICH-NESS!
RICHNESS?! DEFINITELY VERONICA!
4

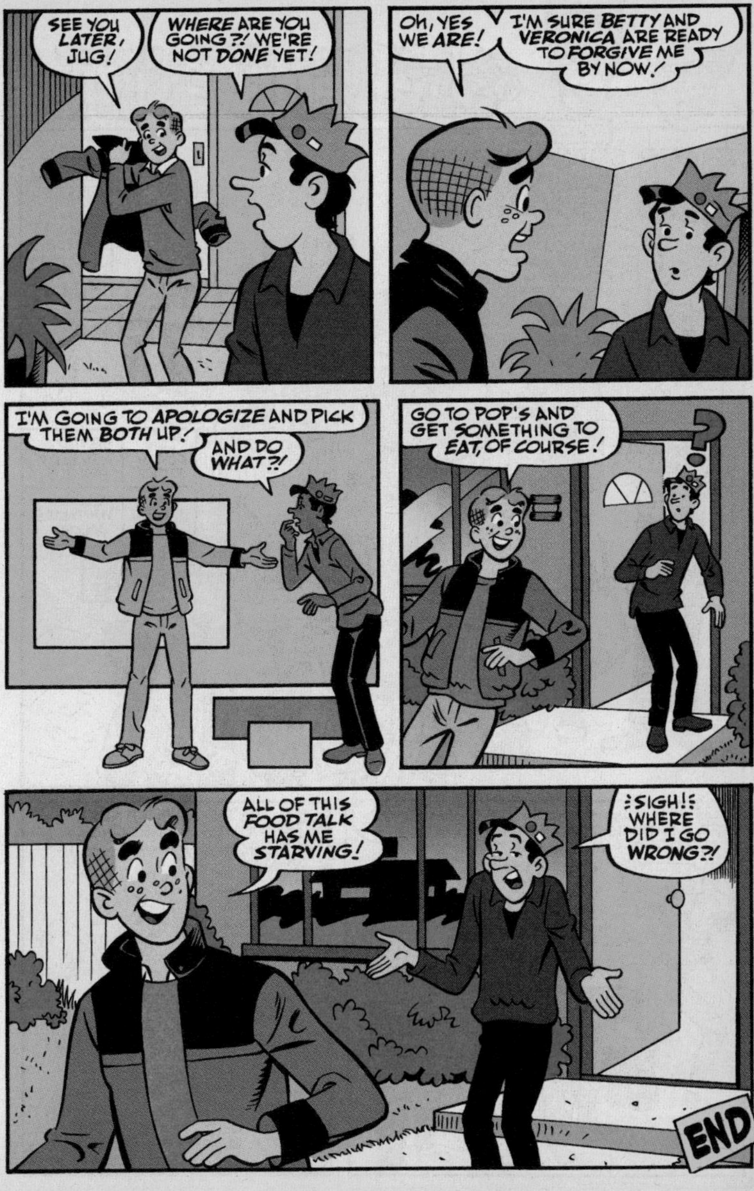
SEE YOU LATER, JUG!
WHERE ARE YOU GOING?! WE'RE NOT DONE YET!
Oh, YES WE ARE!
I'M SURE BETTY AND VERONICA ARE READY TO FORGIVE ME BY NOW!
I'M GOING TO APOLOGIZE AND PICK THEM BOTH UP!
AND DO WHAT?!
GO TO POP'S AND GET SOMETHING TO EAT, OF COURSE!
ALL OF THIS FOOD TALK HAS ME STARVING!
SIGH! WHERE DID I GO WRONG?!
END

(IN) SECRET IDENTITY

FEATURING BOB PHANTOM®

RIVERDALE COMIC EXPO PRESENTS BOB PHANTO...

EXIT

WOULD YOU *RELAX*? WE MADE IT INTO LINE, ARCH!

LINE ENDS HERE

YEAH, BUT IT GOES *FOREVER*! AND BOB PHANTOM IS DUE FOR A PANEL IN A FEW MINUTES!

IAN FLYNN STORY	BROTHERS KENNEDY PENCILS
JIM AMASH INKS	GLENN WHITMORE COLORS
JACK MORELLI LETTERS	

BOB PHANTOM IS A *HUGE STAR*! HIS SUPER-HERO SHOW IS THE ONLY THING I WATCH! I *NEED* THIS AUTOGRAPH!

AUGH! WE'RE OUT OF TIME! WE'RE GOING TO MISS HIM!

WE'RE NEXT IN LINE. *CHILL.*

1

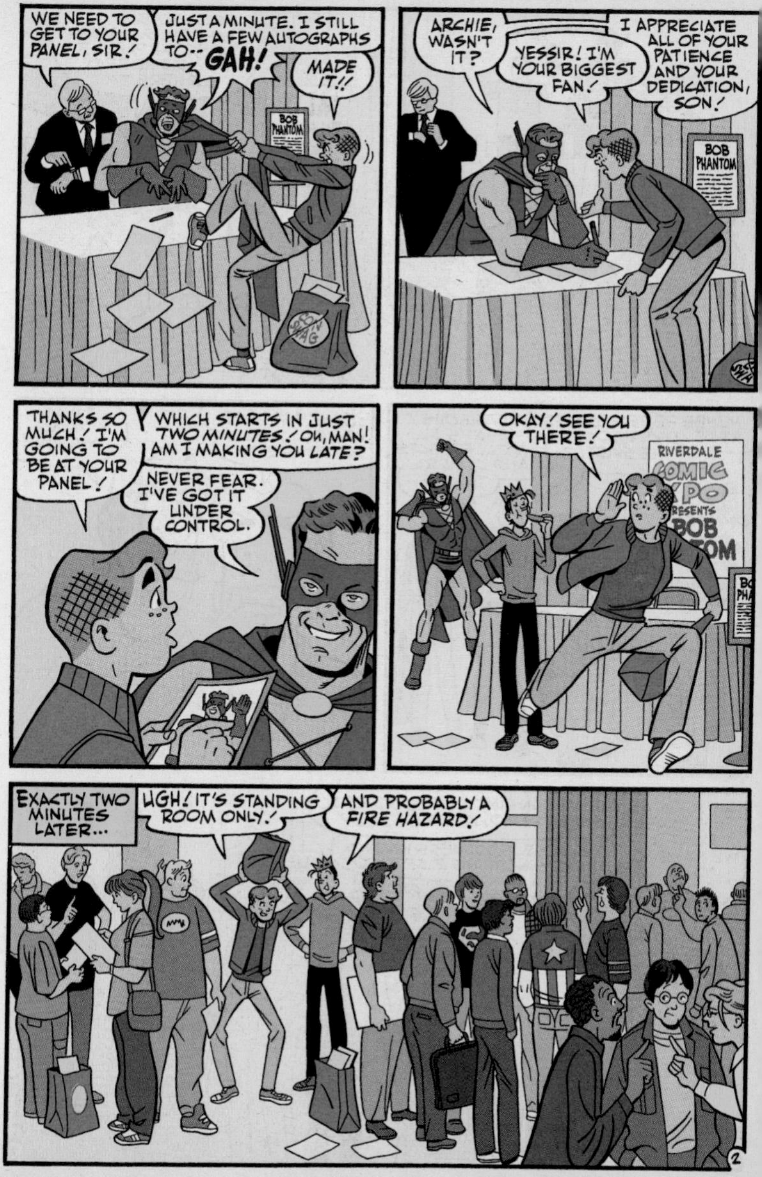
WE NEED TO GET TO YOUR PANEL, SIR!
JUST A MINUTE. I STILL HAVE A FEW AUTOGRAPHS TO-- GAH!
MADE IT!!
BOB PHANTOM
ARCHIE, WASN'T IT?
YESSIR! I'M YOUR BIGGEST FAN!
I APPRECIATE ALL OF YOUR PATIENCE AND YOUR DEDICATION, SON!
BOB PHANTOM
THANKS SO MUCH! I'M GOING TO BE AT YOUR PANEL!
WHICH STARTS IN JUST TWO MINUTES! OH, MAN! AM I MAKING YOU LATE?
NEVER FEAR. I'VE GOT IT UNDER CONTROL.
OKAY! SEE YOU THERE!
RIVERDALE COMIC XPO RESENTS BOB OM
EXACTLY TWO MINUTES LATER...
UGH! IT'S STANDING ROOM ONLY!
AND PROBABLY A FIRE HAZARD!

HOLD ON! BOB PHANTOM IS ALREADY DOING THE PANEL?! HOW DID HE BEAT US HERE?!!

MLJ PRESENTS: BOB PHANTOM

MAYBE HE *TELEPORTED* HERE, LIKE HE DOES IN THE SHOW?

RIDICULOUS! THAT'S ALL SPECIAL EFFECTS AND CAMERA TRICKS...

:GASP!: UNLESS HE *REALLY IS* A SUPER HERO!

I WAS *KIDDING,* Y'KNOW!

AS SOON AS THIS PANEL IS OVER, WE HAVE TO *TAIL* HIM!

IF WE CAN FIND OUT HE'S A REAL *SUPER HERO,* IT'LL BE *HUGE!*

BECAUSE GOODNESS KNOWS THERE'S NOTHING *ELSE* TO DO AT A CON...

MLJ PRESENTS: BOB PHANTOM

COMICS

3

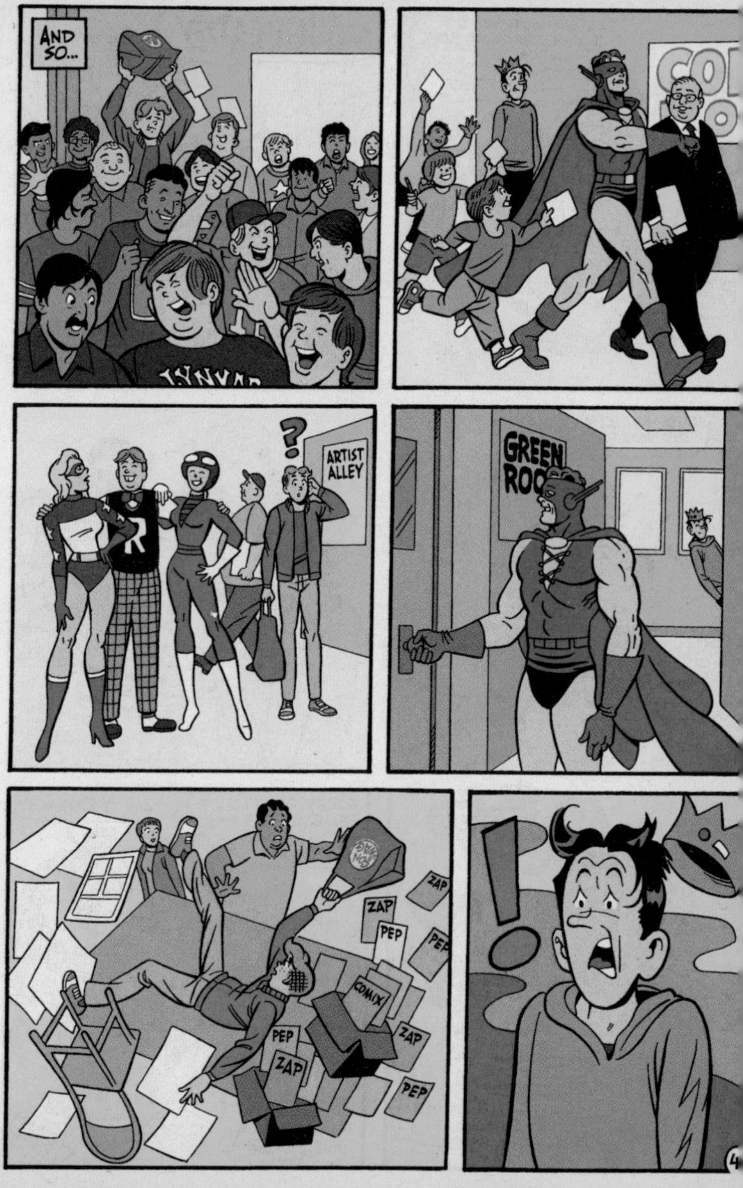
AND SO...
?
ARTIST ALLEY
GREEN
ROO
ZAP
PEP
PEP
COMIX
PEP
ZAP
ZAP
PEP

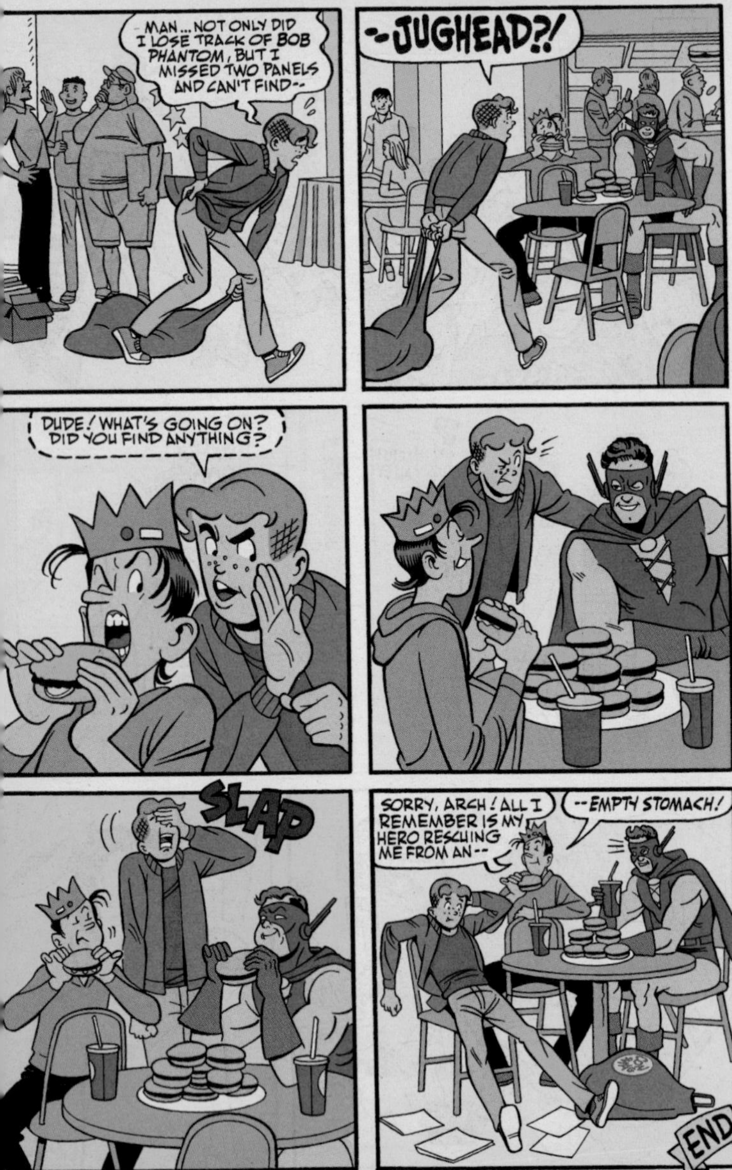
MAN... NOT ONLY DID I LOSE TRACK OF BOB PHANTOM, BUT I MISSED TWO PANELS AND CAN'T FIND--
--JUGHEAD?!
DUDE! WHAT'S GOING ON? DID YOU FIND ANYTHING?
SLAP
SORRY, ARCH! ALL I REMEMBER IS MY HERO RESCUING ME FROM AN--
--EMPTY STOMACH!
END

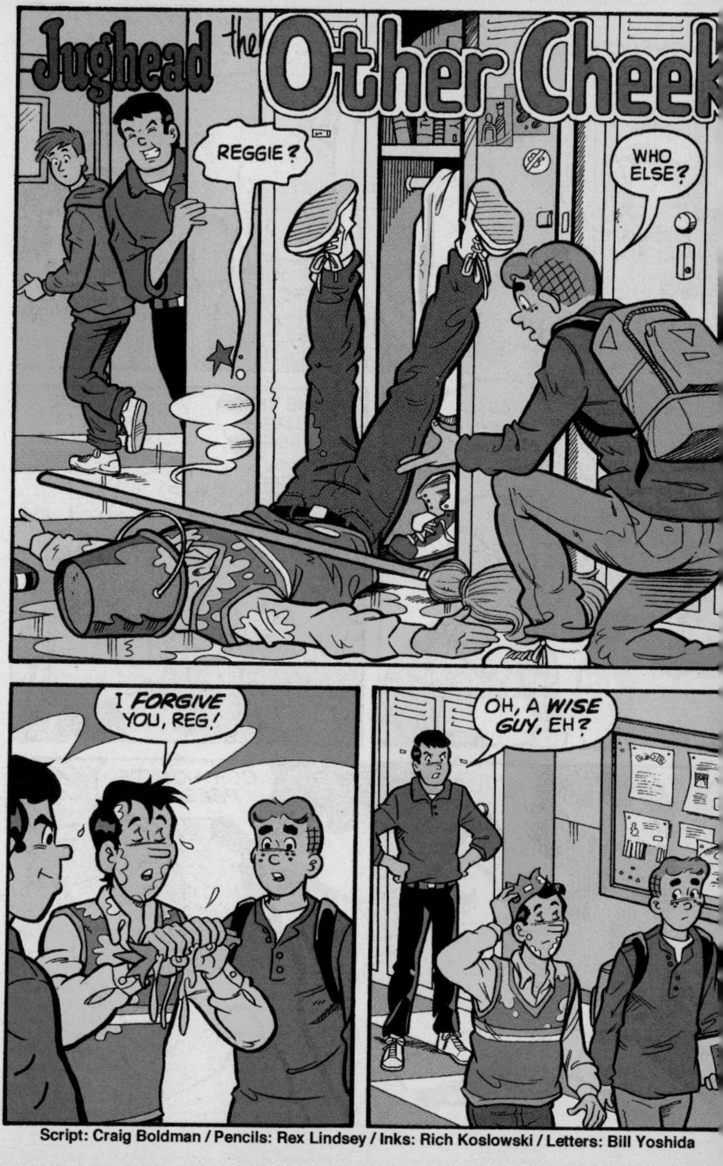
Jughead
the Other Cheek
REGGIE?
WHO ELSE?
I FORGIVE YOU, REG!
OH, A WISE GUY, EH?

Script: Craig Boldman / Pencils: Rex Lindsey / Inks: Rich Koslowski / Letters: Bill Yoshida

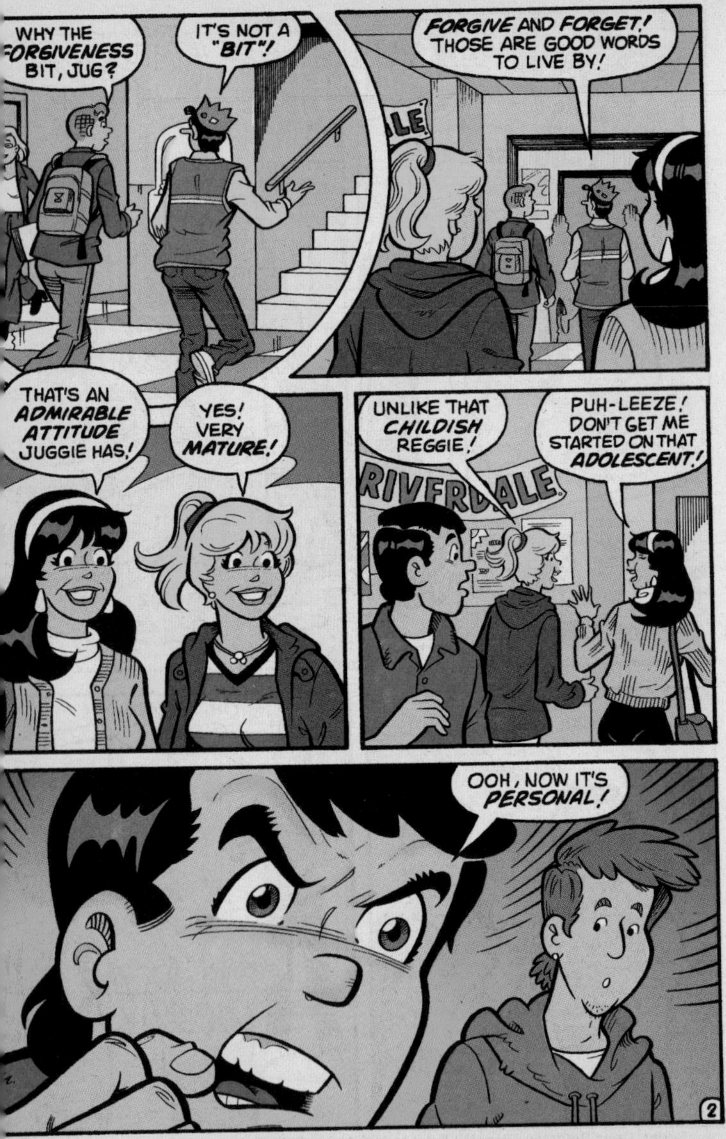
WHY THE FORGIVENESS BIT, JUG?
IT'S NOT A "BIT"!
FORGIVE AND FORGET! THOSE ARE GOOD WORDS TO LIVE BY!
ALE
THAT'S AN ADMIRABLE ATTITUDE JUGGIE HAS!
YES! VERY MATURE!
UNLIKE THAT CHILDISH REGGIE!
PUH-LEEZE! DON'T GET ME STARTED ON THAT ADOLESCENT!
RIVERDALE
OOH, NOW IT'S PERSONAL!
2

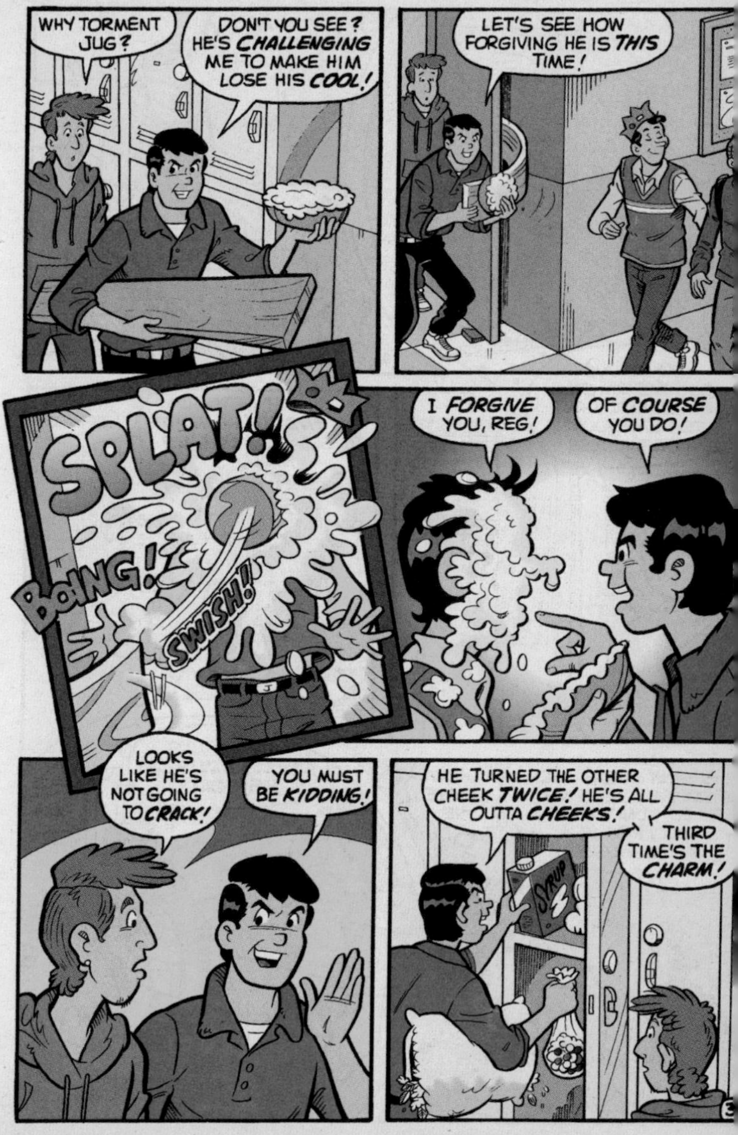
WHY TORMENT JUG?
DON'T YOU SEE? HE'S CHALLENGING ME TO MAKE HIM LOSE HIS COOL!
LET'S SEE HOW FORGIVING HE IS THIS TIME!
SPLAT!
BOING!
SWISH!
I FORGIVE YOU, REG!
OF COURSE YOU DO!
LOOKS LIKE HE'S NOT GOING TO CRACK!
YOU MUST BE KIDDING!
HE TURNED THE OTHER CHEEK TWICE! HE'S ALL OUTTA CHEEKS!
THIRD TIME'S THE CHARM!
SYRUP

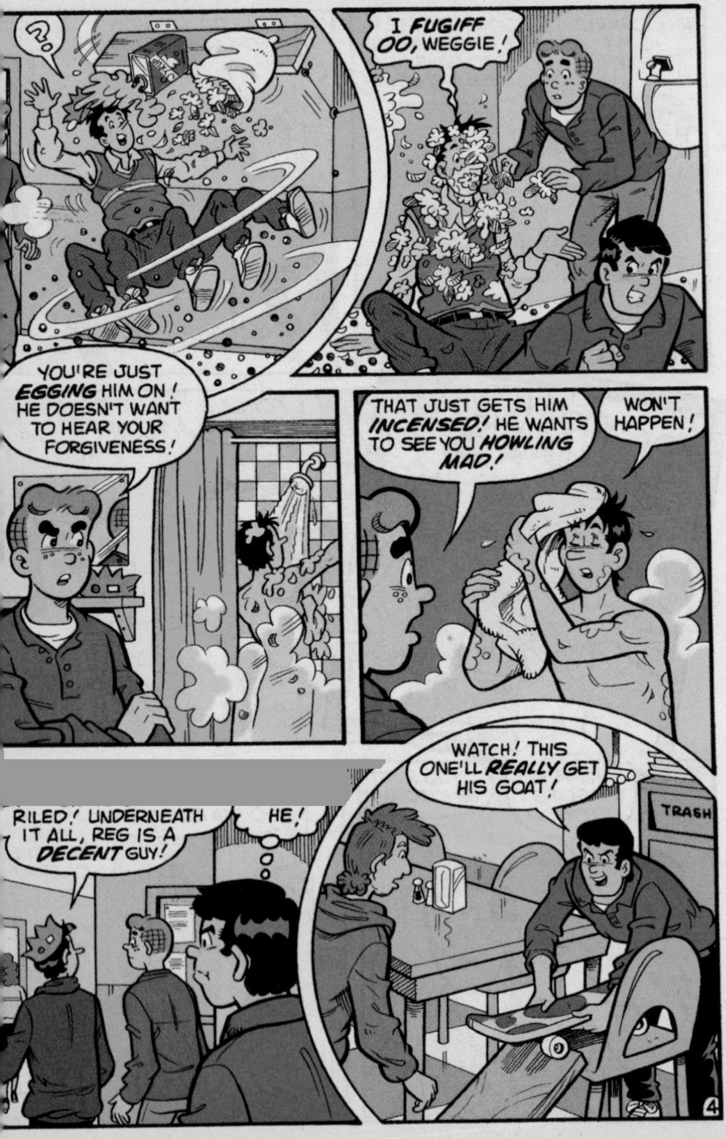
?
I FUGIFF OO, WEGGIE!
YOU'RE JUST EGGING HIM ON! HE DOESN'T WANT TO HEAR YOUR FORGIVENESS!
THAT JUST GETS HIM INCENSED! HE WANTS TO SEE YOU HOWLING MAD!
WON'T HAPPEN!
RILED! UNDERNEATH IT ALL, REG IS A DECENT GUY!
HE!
WATCH! THIS ONE'LL REALLY GET HIS GOAT!
TRASH
4

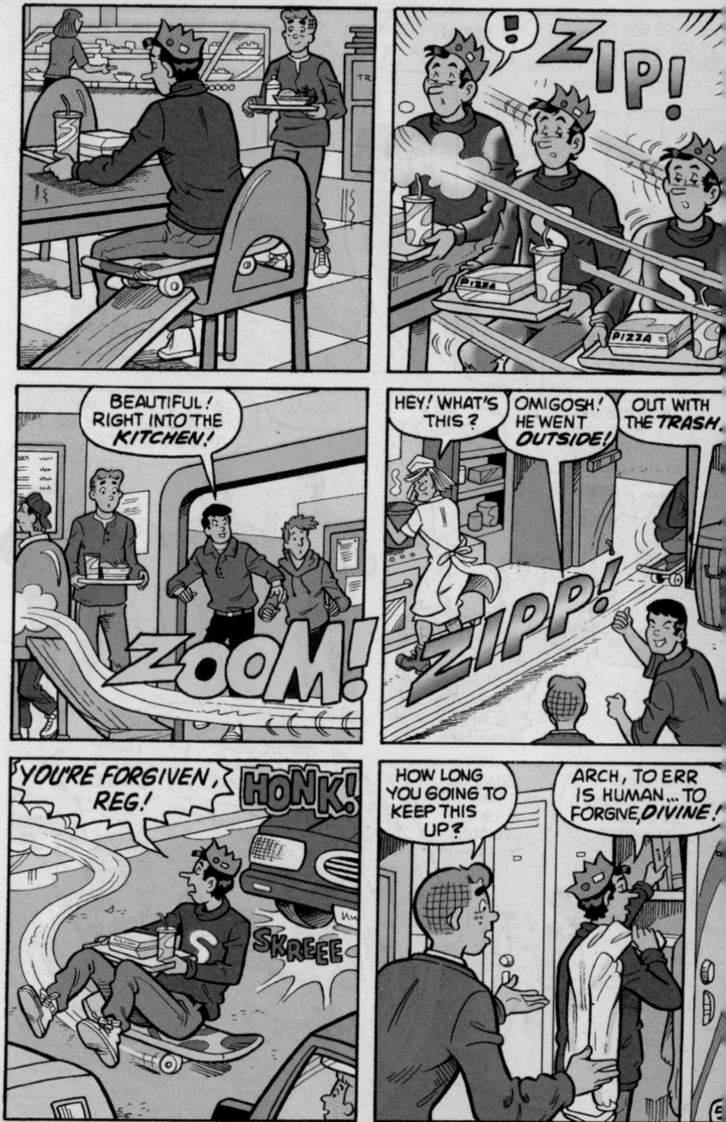
!
ZIP!
PIZZA
PIZZA
BEAUTIFUL! RIGHT INTO THE KITCHEN!
ZOOM!
HEY! WHAT'S THIS?
OMIGOSH! HE WENT OUTSIDE!
OUT WITH THE TRASH.
ZIPP!
YOU'RE FORGIVEN, REG!
HONK!
SKREEEE
HOW LONG YOU GOING TO KEEP THIS UP?
ARCH, TO ERR IS HUMAN... TO FORGIVE, DIVINE!
5

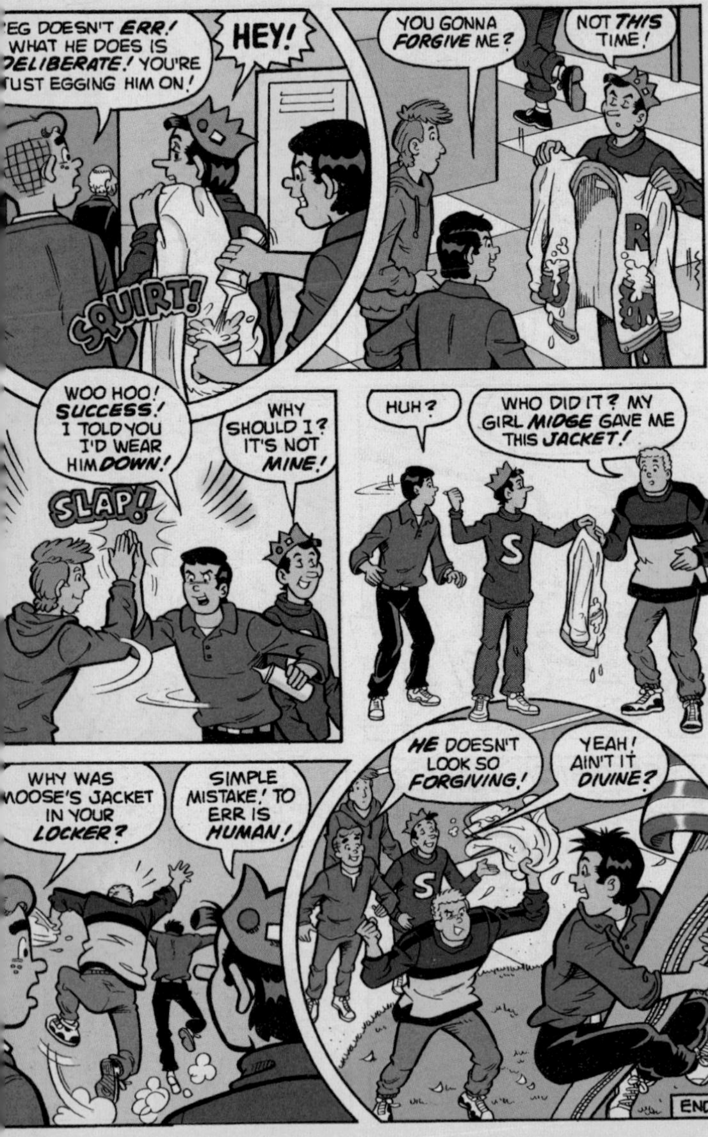
EG DOESN'T ERR! WHAT HE DOES IS ELIBERATE! YOU'RE UST EGGING HIM ON!
HEY!
SQUIRT!
YOU GONNA FORGIVE ME?
NOT THIS TIME!
WOO HOO! SUCCESS! I TOLD YOU I'D WEAR HIM DOWN!
WHY SHOULD I? IT'S NOT MINE!
SLAP!
HUH?
WHO DID IT? MY GIRL MIDGE GAVE ME THIS JACKET!
WHY WAS OOSE'S JACKET IN YOUR LOCKER?
SIMPLE MISTAKE! TO ERR IS HUMAN!
HE DOESN'T LOOK SO FORGIVING!
YEAH! AIN'T IT DIVINE?
END

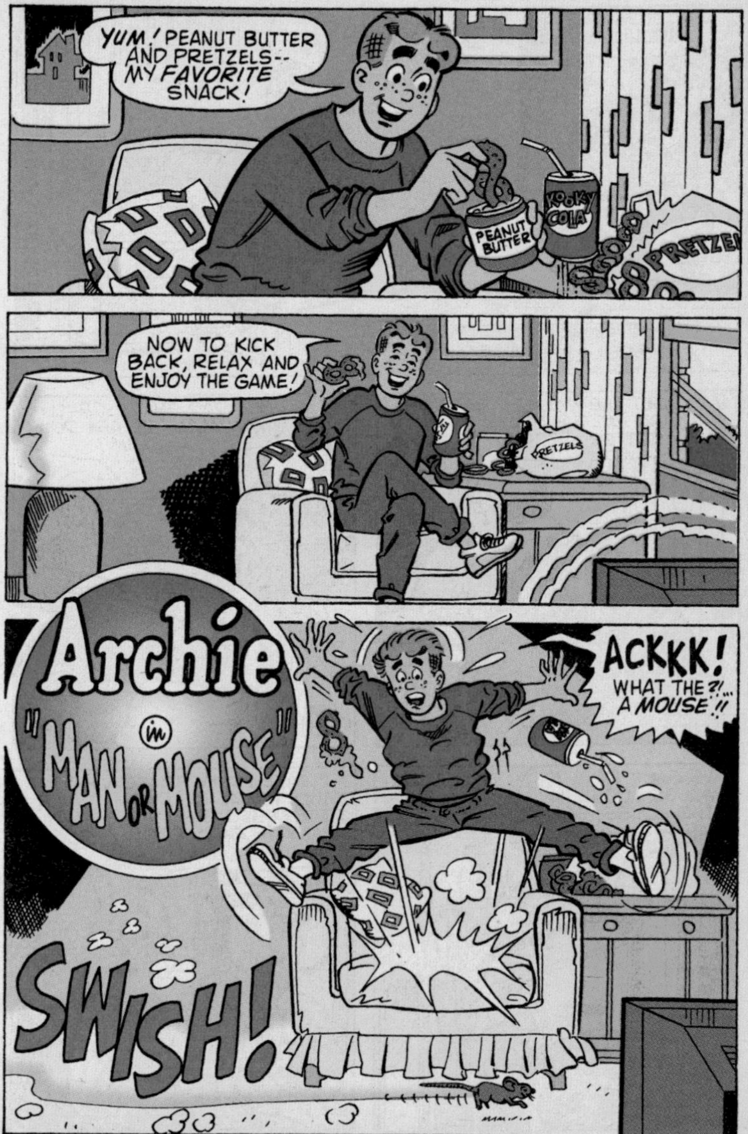
YUM! PEANUT BUTTER AND PRETZELS-- MY FAVORITE SNACK!
PEANUT BUTTER
KOOKY COLA
PRETZELS
NOW TO KICK BACK, RELAX AND ENJOY THE GAME!
PRETZELS
Archie
in
"MAN OR MOUSE"
ACKKK!
WHAT THE ?!... A MOUSE!!
SWISH!

Script: Paul Castiglia / Pencils: Henry Scarpelli / Inks: Mike Esposito / Letters: Bill Yoshida

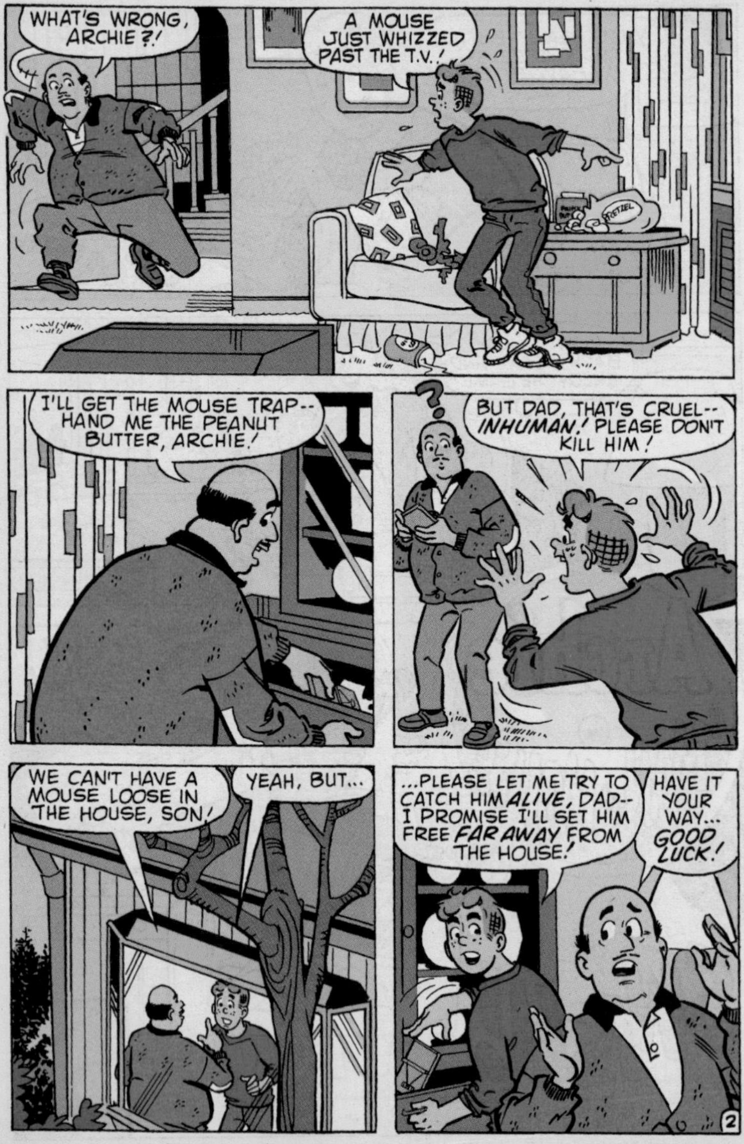
WHAT'S WRONG, ARCHIE ?!
A MOUSE JUST WHIZZED PAST THE T.V.!
I'LL GET THE MOUSE TRAP-- HAND ME THE PEANUT BUTTER, ARCHIE!
?
BUT DAD, THAT'S CRUEL-- INHUMAN! PLEASE DON'T KILL HIM!
WE CAN'T HAVE A MOUSE LOOSE IN THE HOUSE, SON!
YEAH, BUT...
...PLEASE LET ME TRY TO CATCH HIM ALIVE, DAD-- I PROMISE I'LL SET HIM FREE FAR AWAY FROM THE HOUSE!
HAVE IT YOUR WAY... GOOD LUCK!
2

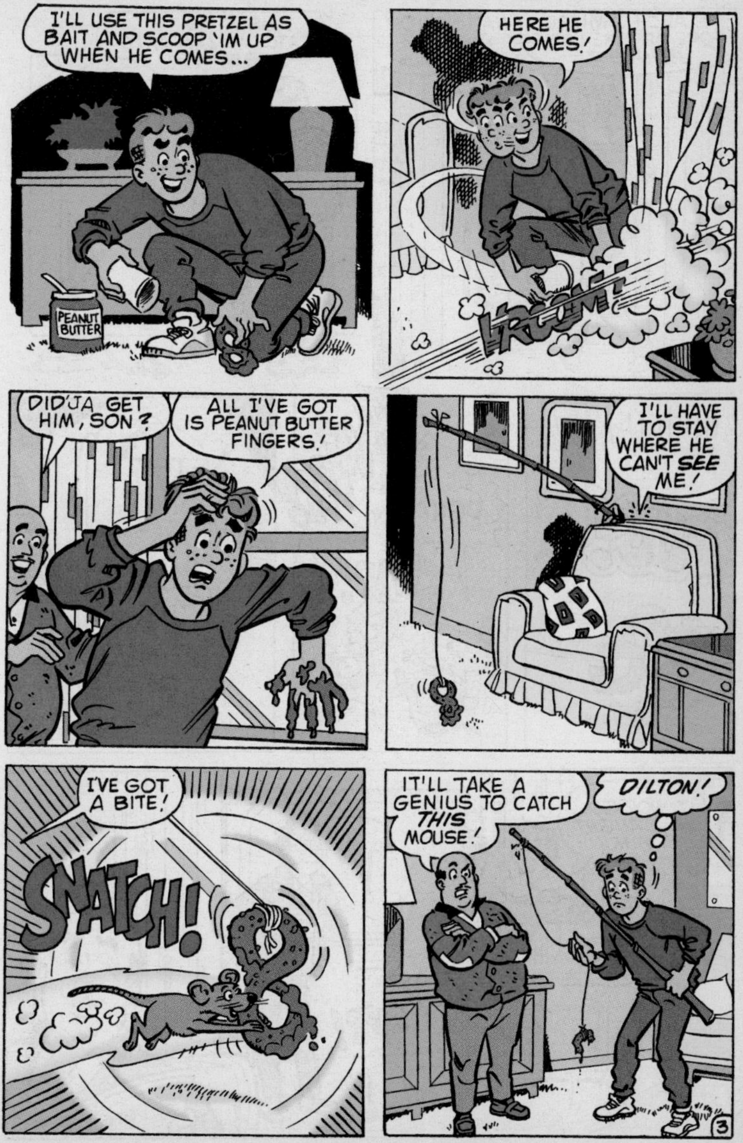
I'LL USE THIS PRETZEL AS BAIT AND SCOOP 'IM UP WHEN HE COMES...
PEANUT BUTTER
HERE HE COMES!
VROOM!
DID'JA GET HIM, SON?
ALL I'VE GOT IS PEANUT BUTTER FINGERS!
I'LL HAVE TO STAY WHERE HE CAN'T SEE ME!
I'VE GOT A BITE!
SNATCH!
IT'LL TAKE A GENIUS TO CATCH THIS MOUSE!
DILTON!
3

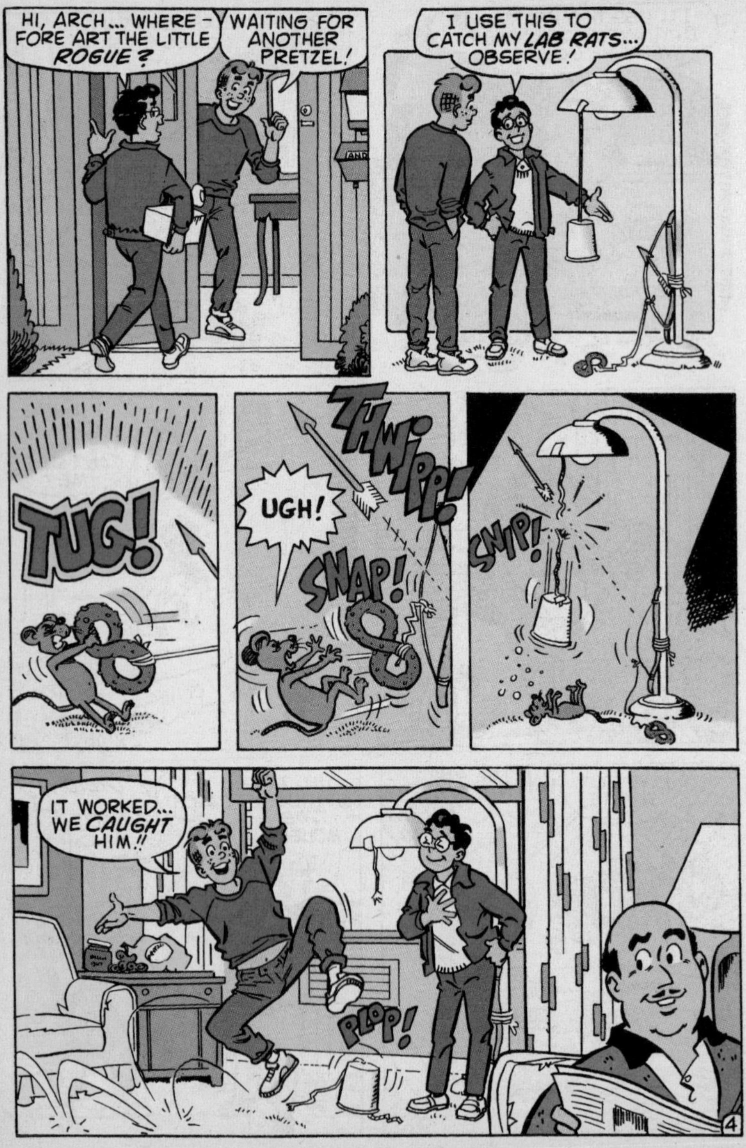
HI, ARCH... WHERE-FORE ART THE LITTLE ROGUE?
WAITING FOR ANOTHER PRETZEL!
I USE THIS TO CATCH MY LAB RATS... OBSERVE!
TUG!
THWIPP!
UGH!
SNAP!
SNIP!
IT WORKED... WE CAUGHT HIM!!
PLOP!
4

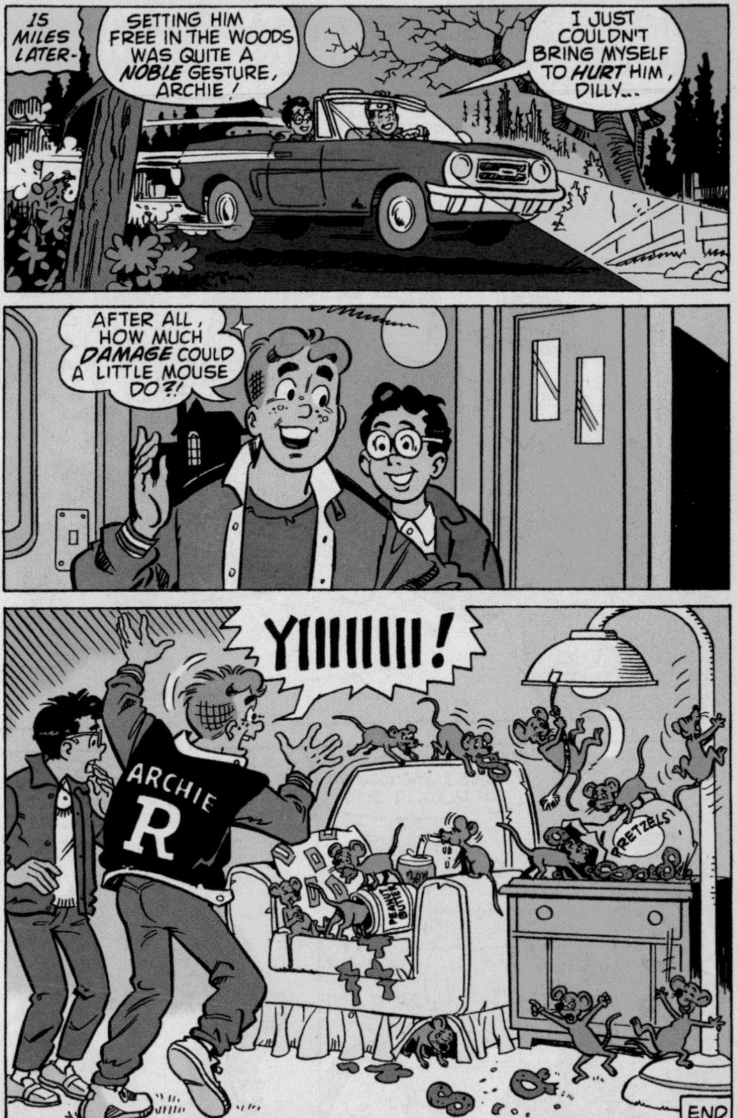

15 MILES LATER-
SETTING HIM FREE IN THE WOODS WAS QUITE A NOBLE GESTURE, ARCHIE!
I JUST COULDN'T BRING MYSELF TO HURT HIM, DILLY...
AFTER ALL, HOW MUCH DAMAGE COULD A LITTLE MOUSE DO?!
YIIIIIIII!
ARCHIE
R
PRETZELS
PEANUT BUTTER
END

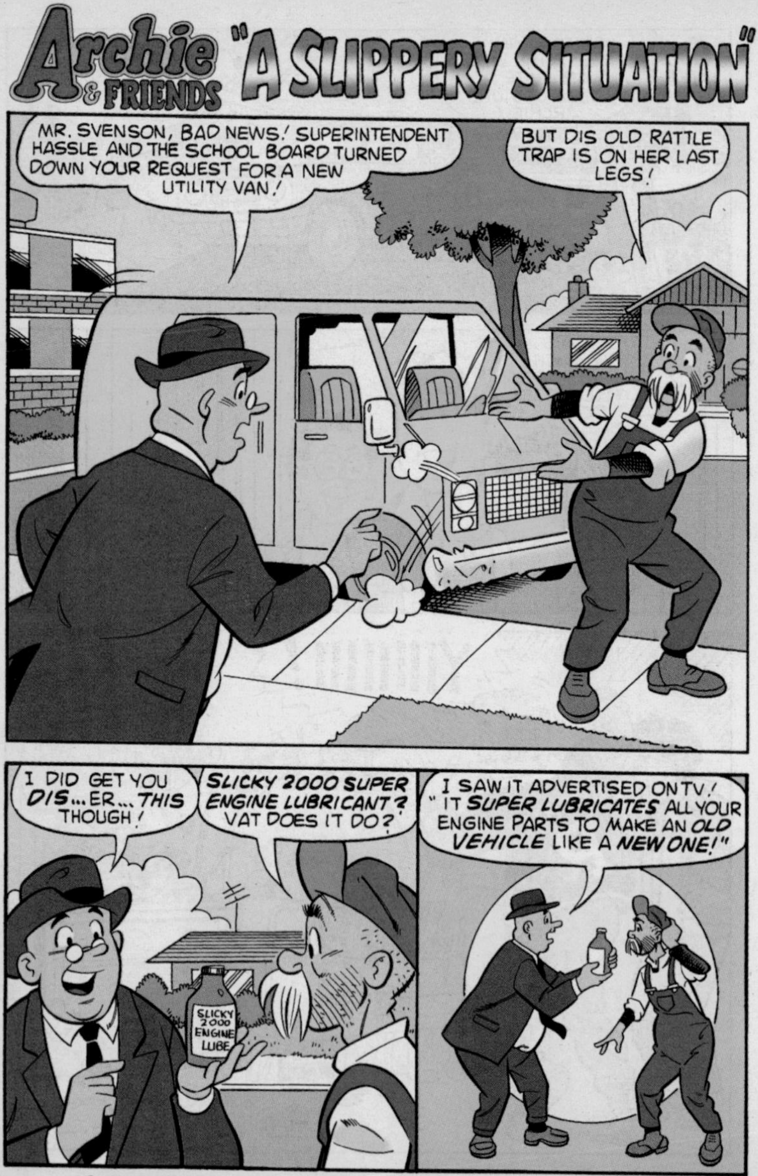
Archie & FRIENDS
"A SLIPPERY SITUATION"
MR. SVENSON, BAD NEWS! SUPERINTENDENT HASSLE AND THE SCHOOL BOARD TURNED DOWN YOUR REQUEST FOR A NEW UTILITY VAN!
BUT DIS OLD RATTLE TRAP IS ON HER LAST LEGS!
I DID GET YOU DIS...ER... THIS THOUGH!
SLICKY 2000 SUPER ENGINE LUBRICANT? VAT DOES IT DO?
SLICKY 2000 ENGINE LUBE
I SAW IT ADVERTISED ON TV! "IT SUPER LUBRICATES ALL YOUR ENGINE PARTS TO MAKE AN OLD VEHICLE LIKE A NEW ONE!"

Script: Bill Golliher / Pencils: Jeff Shultz / Inks: John Lowe / Letters: Bill Yoshida

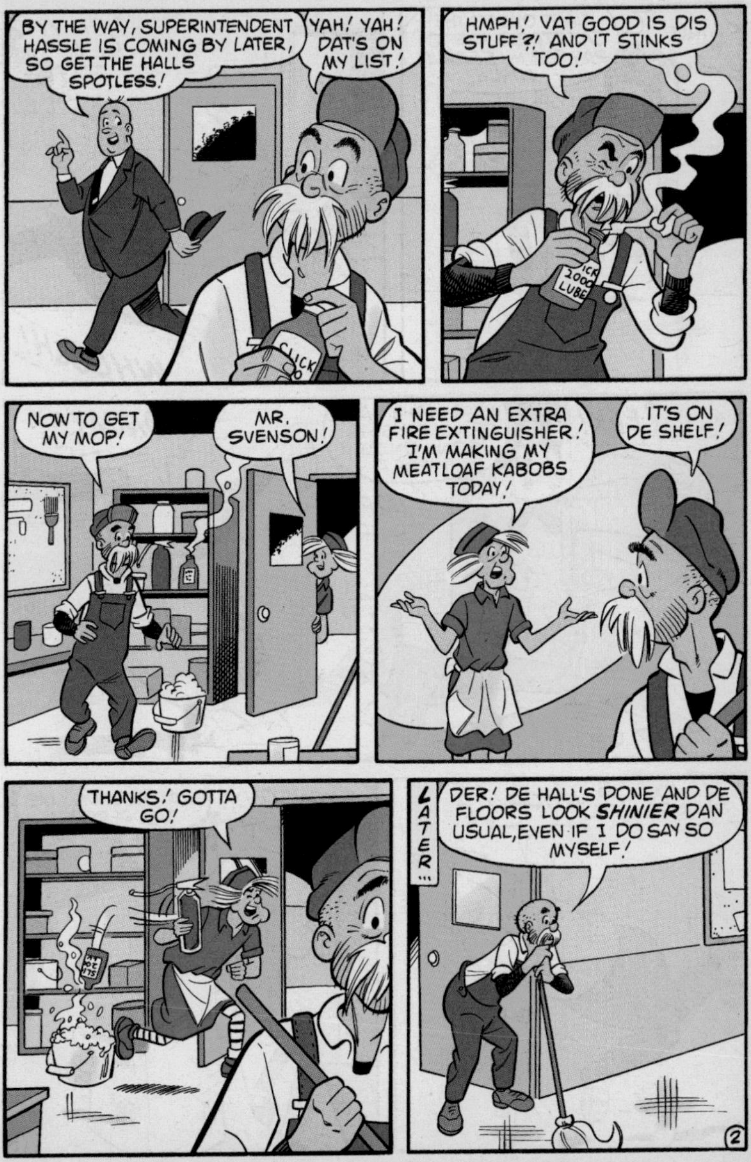
BY THE WAY, SUPERINTENDENT HASSLE IS COMING BY LATER, SO GET THE HALLS SPOTLESS!
YAH! YAH! DAT'S ON MY LIST!
HMPH! VAT GOOD IS DIS STUFF?! AND IT STINKS TOO!
NOW TO GET MY MOP!
MR. SVENSON!
I NEED AN EXTRA FIRE EXTINGUISHER! I'M MAKING MY MEATLOAF KABOBS TODAY!
IT'S ON DE SHELF!
THANKS! GOTTA GO!
LATER...
DER! DE HALL'S DONE AND DE FLOORS LOOK SHINIER DAN USUAL, EVEN IF I DO SAY SO MYSELF!
2

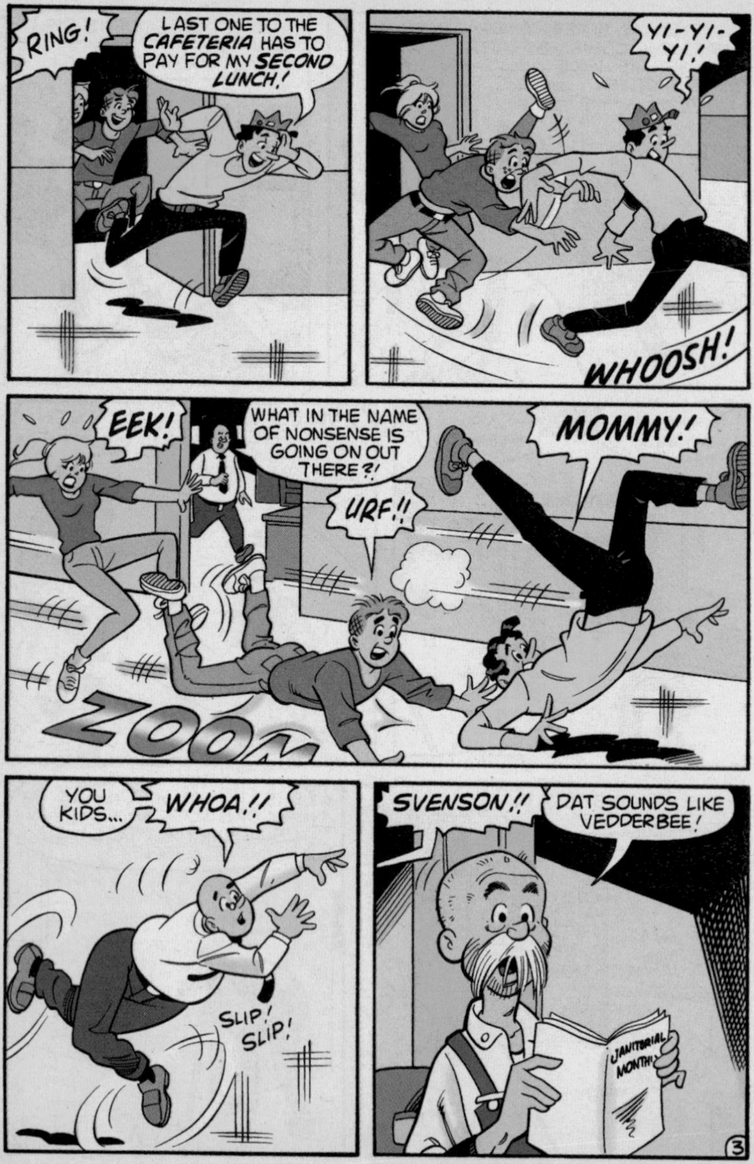
RING!
LAST ONE TO THE CAFETERIA HAS TO PAY FOR MY SECOND LUNCH!
YI-YI-YI!
WHOOSH!
EEK!
WHAT IN THE NAME OF NONSENSE IS GOING ON OUT THERE?!
MOMMY!
URF!!
ZOOM
YOU KIDS...
WHOA!!
SLIP! SLIP!
SVENSON!!
DAT SOUNDS LIKE VEDDERBEE!
JANITORIAL MONTHLY
3

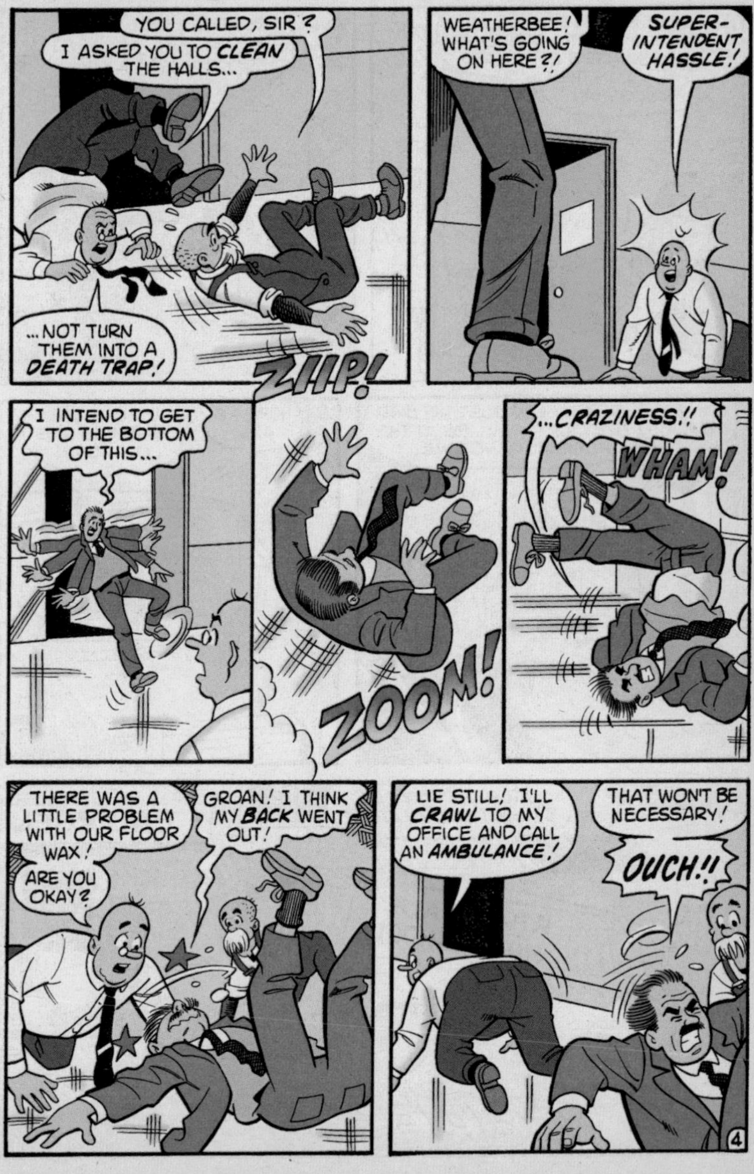
YOU CALLED, SIR?
I ASKED YOU TO CLEAN THE HALLS...
...NOT TURN THEM INTO A DEATH TRAP!
ZIIP!
WEATHERBEE! WHAT'S GOING ON HERE?!
SUPER-INTENDENT HASSLE!
I INTEND TO GET TO THE BOTTOM OF THIS...
ZOOM!
...CRAZINESS!!
WHAM!
THERE WAS A LITTLE PROBLEM WITH OUR FLOOR WAX!
ARE YOU OKAY?
GROAN! I THINK MY BACK WENT OUT!
LIE STILL! I'LL CRAWL TO MY OFFICE AND CALL AN AMBULANCE!
THAT WON'T BE NECESSARY!
OUCH!!
4

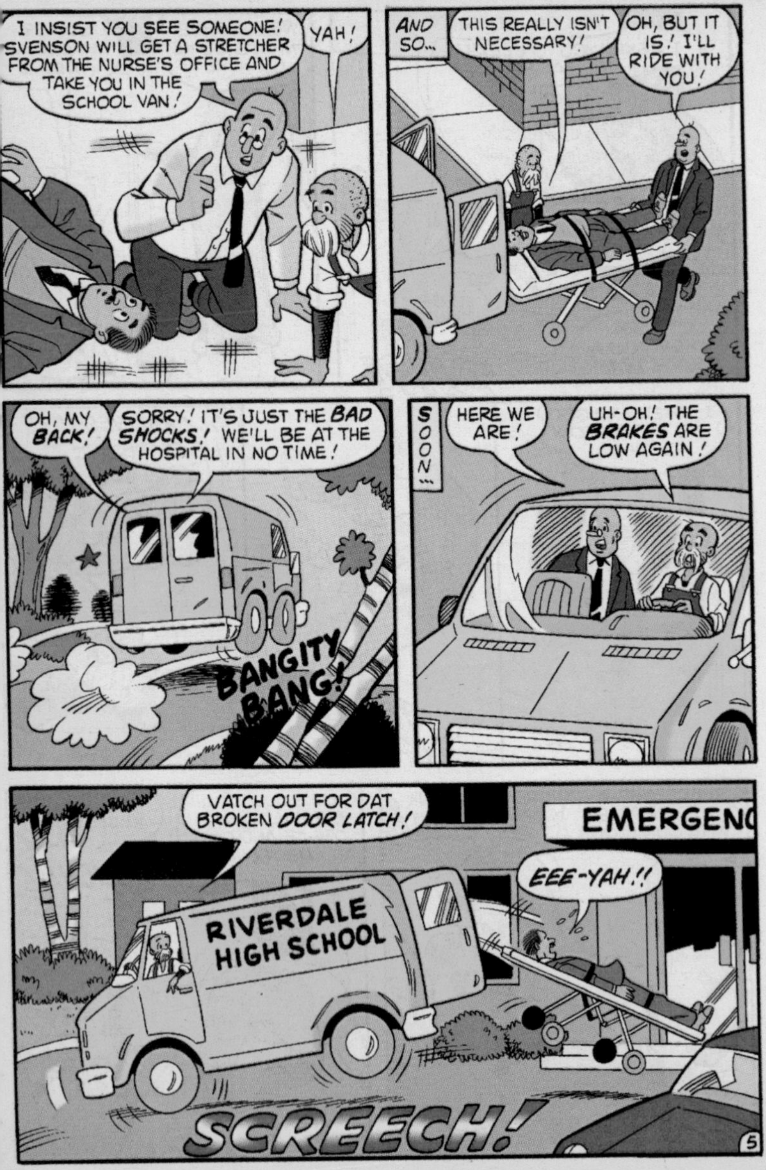
I INSIST YOU SEE SOMEONE! SVENSON WILL GET A STRETCHER FROM THE NURSE'S OFFICE AND TAKE YOU IN THE SCHOOL VAN!
YAH!
AND SO...
THIS REALLY ISN'T NECESSARY!
OH, BUT IT IS! I'LL RIDE WITH YOU!
OH, MY BACK!
SORRY! IT'S JUST THE BAD SHOCKS! WE'LL BE AT THE HOSPITAL IN NO TIME!
BANGITY BANG!
SOON...
HERE WE ARE!
UH-OH! THE BRAKES ARE LOW AGAIN!
VATCH OUT FOR DAT BROKEN DOOR LATCH!
EMERGENC
RIVERDALE HIGH SCHOOL
EEE-YAH!!
SCREECH!
5

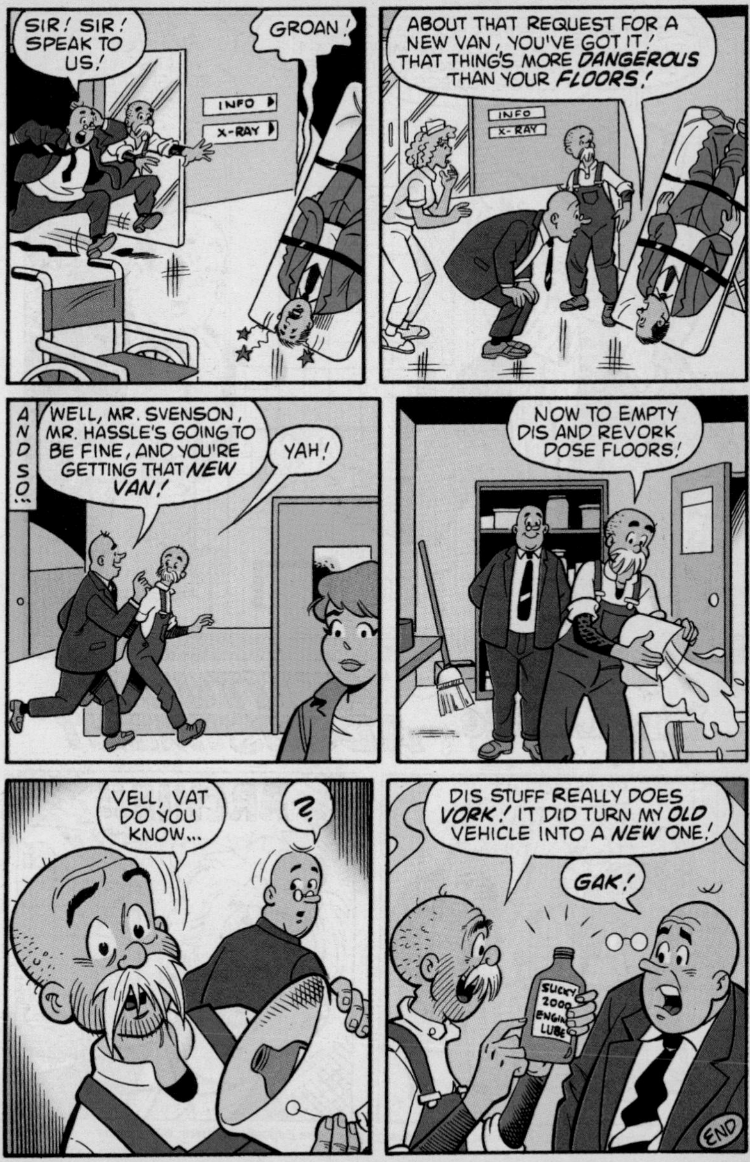
SIR! SIR! SPEAK TO US!
GROAN!
ABOUT THAT REQUEST FOR A NEW VAN, YOU'VE GOT IT! THAT THING'S MORE DANGEROUS THAN YOUR FLOORS!
INFO
X-RAY
AND SO...
WELL, MR. SVENSON, MR. HASSLE'S GOING TO BE FINE, AND YOU'RE GETTING THAT NEW VAN!
YAH!
NOW TO EMPTY DIS AND REVORK DOSE FLOORS!
VELL, VAT DO YOU KNOW...
?
DIS STUFF REALLY DOES VORK! IT DID TURN MY OLD VEHICLE INTO A NEW ONE!
GAK!
SLICKY 2000 ENGINE LUBE
END

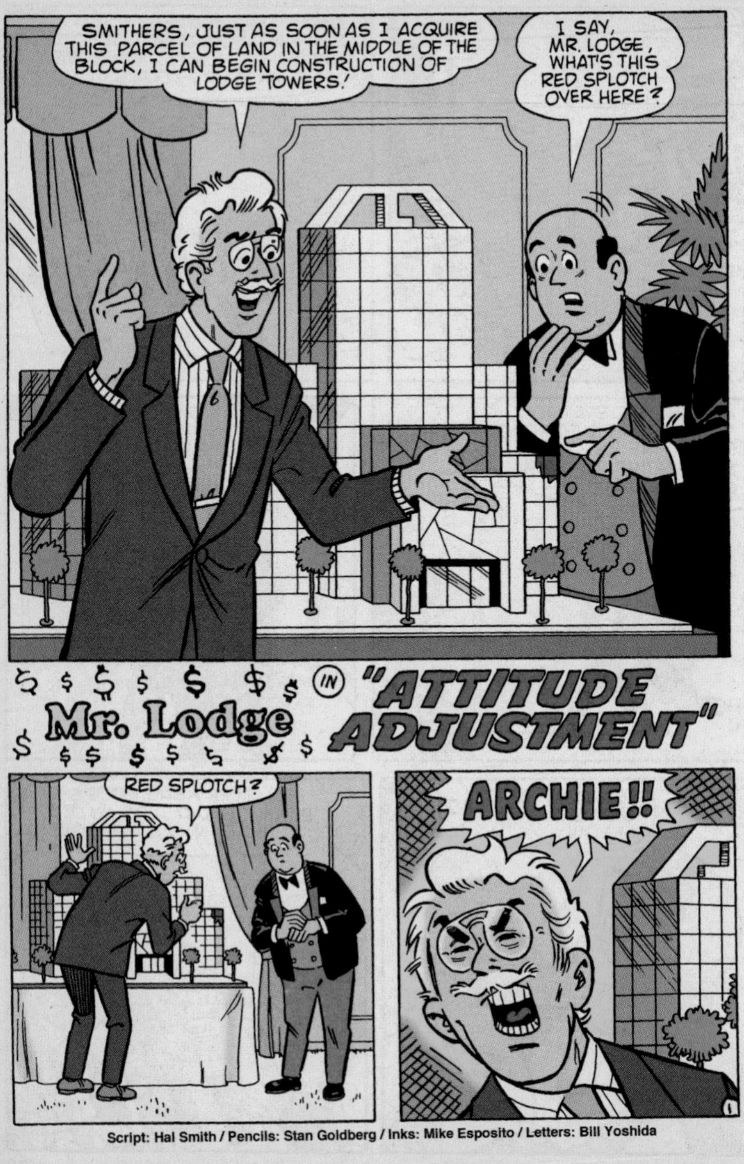
SMITHERS, JUST AS SOON AS I ACQUIRE THIS PARCEL OF LAND IN THE MIDDLE OF THE BLOCK, I CAN BEGIN CONSTRUCTION OF LODGE TOWERS!
I SAY, MR. LODGE, WHAT'S THIS RED SPLOTCH OVER HERE?
Mr. Lodge IN "ATTITUDE ADJUSTMENT"
RED SPLOTCH?
ARCHIE!!
1

Script: Hal Smith / Pencils: Stan Goldberg / Inks: Mike Esposito / Letters: Bill Yoshida

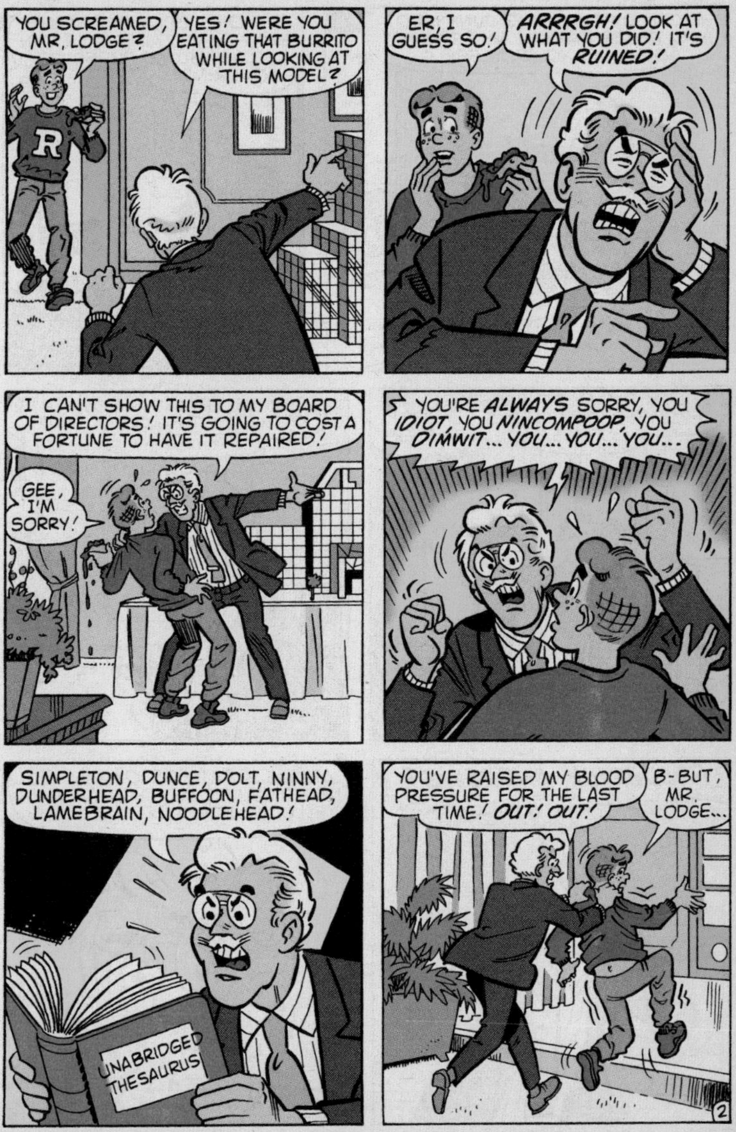

YOU SCREAMED, MR. LODGE?
YES! WERE YOU EATING THAT BURRITO WHILE LOOKING AT THIS MODEL?
ER, I GUESS SO!
ARRRGH! LOOK AT WHAT YOU DID! IT'S RUINED!
I CAN'T SHOW THIS TO MY BOARD OF DIRECTORS! IT'S GOING TO COST A FORTUNE TO HAVE IT REPAIRED!
GEE, I'M SORRY!
YOU'RE ALWAYS SORRY, YOU IDIOT, YOU NINCOMPOOP, YOU DIMWIT... YOU... YOU... YOU...
SIMPLETON, DUNCE, DOLT, NINNY, DUNDERHEAD, BUFFOON, FATHEAD, LAMEBRAIN, NOODLEHEAD!
UNABRIDGED THESAURUS
YOU'VE RAISED MY BLOOD PRESSURE FOR THE LAST TIME! OUT! OUT!
B-BUT, MR. LODGE...

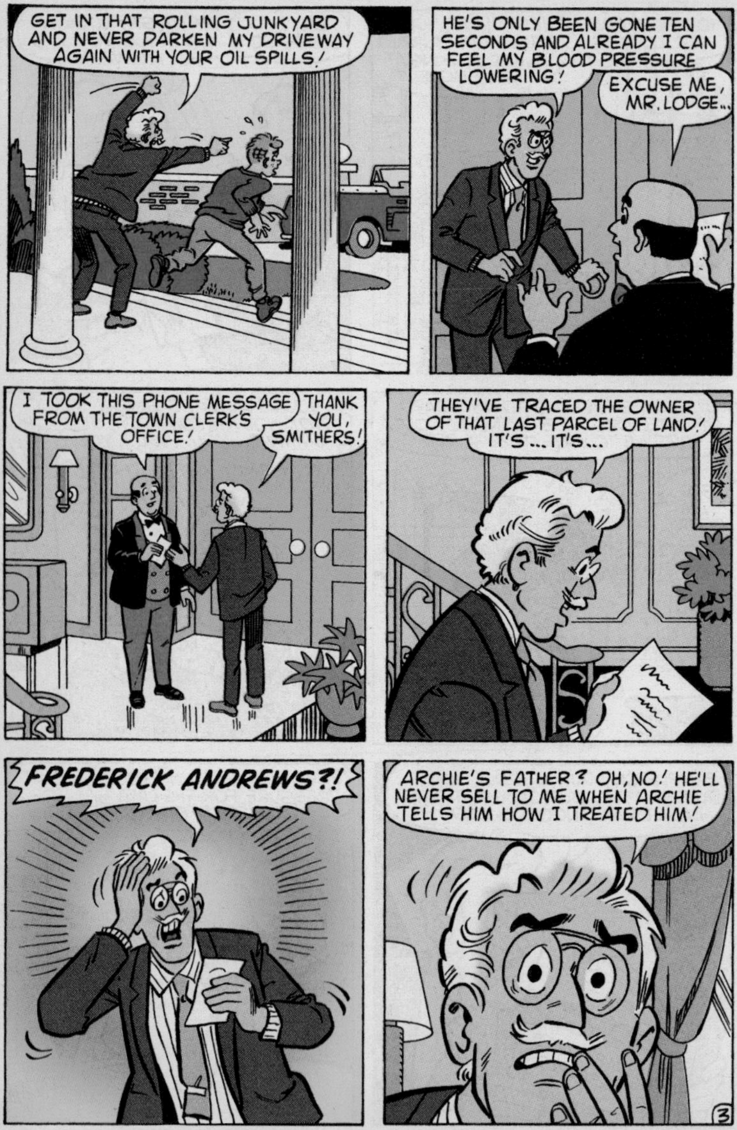
GET IN THAT ROLLING JUNKYARD AND NEVER DARKEN MY DRIVEWAY AGAIN WITH YOUR OIL SPILLS!
HE'S ONLY BEEN GONE TEN SECONDS AND ALREADY I CAN FEEL MY BLOOD PRESSURE LOWERING!
EXCUSE ME, MR. LODGE...
I TOOK THIS PHONE MESSAGE FROM THE TOWN CLERK'S OFFICE!
THANK YOU, SMITHERS!
THEY'VE TRACED THE OWNER OF THAT LAST PARCEL OF LAND! IT'S ... IT'S ...
FREDERICK ANDREWS?!
ARCHIE'S FATHER? OH, NO! HE'LL NEVER SELL TO ME WHEN ARCHIE TELLS HIM HOW I TREATED HIM!
3

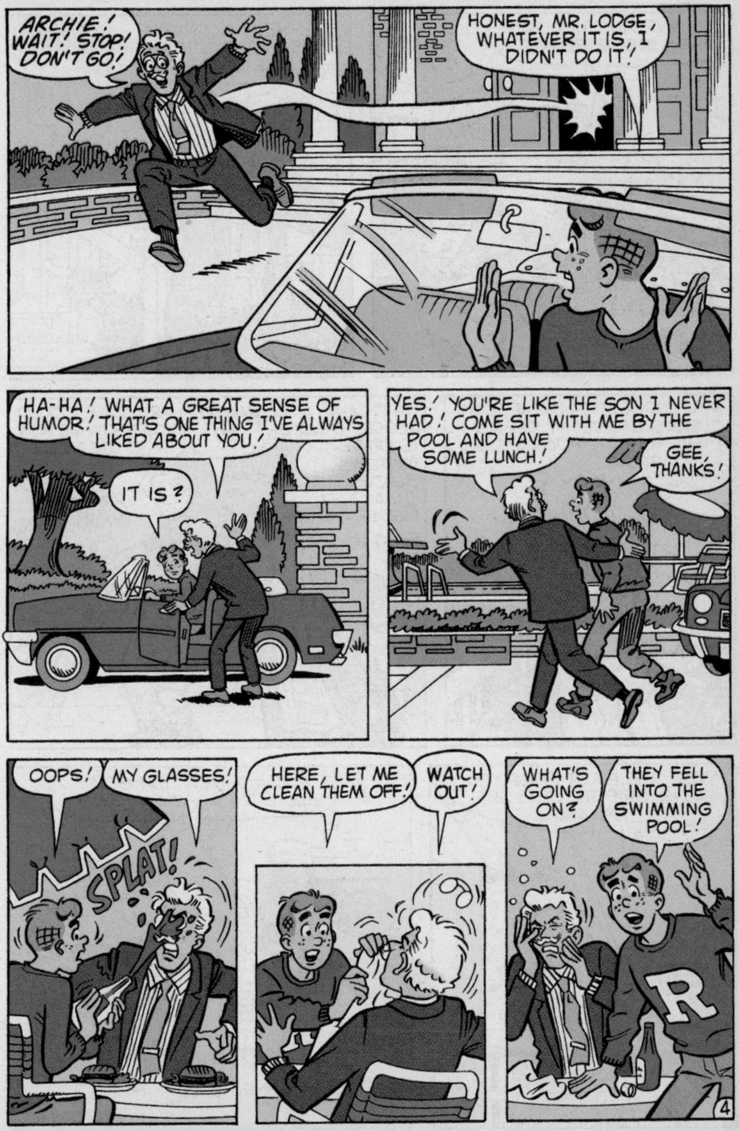
ARCHIE! WAIT! STOP! DON'T GO!
HONEST, MR. LODGE, WHATEVER IT IS, I DIDN'T DO IT!
HA-HA! WHAT A GREAT SENSE OF HUMOR! THAT'S ONE THING I'VE ALWAYS LIKED ABOUT YOU!
IT IS?
YES! YOU'RE LIKE THE SON I NEVER HAD! COME SIT WITH ME BY THE POOL AND HAVE SOME LUNCH!
GEE, THANKS!
OOPS!
MY GLASSES!
SPLAT!
HERE, LET ME CLEAN THEM OFF!
WATCH OUT!
WHAT'S GOING ON?
THEY FELL INTO THE SWIMMING POOL!

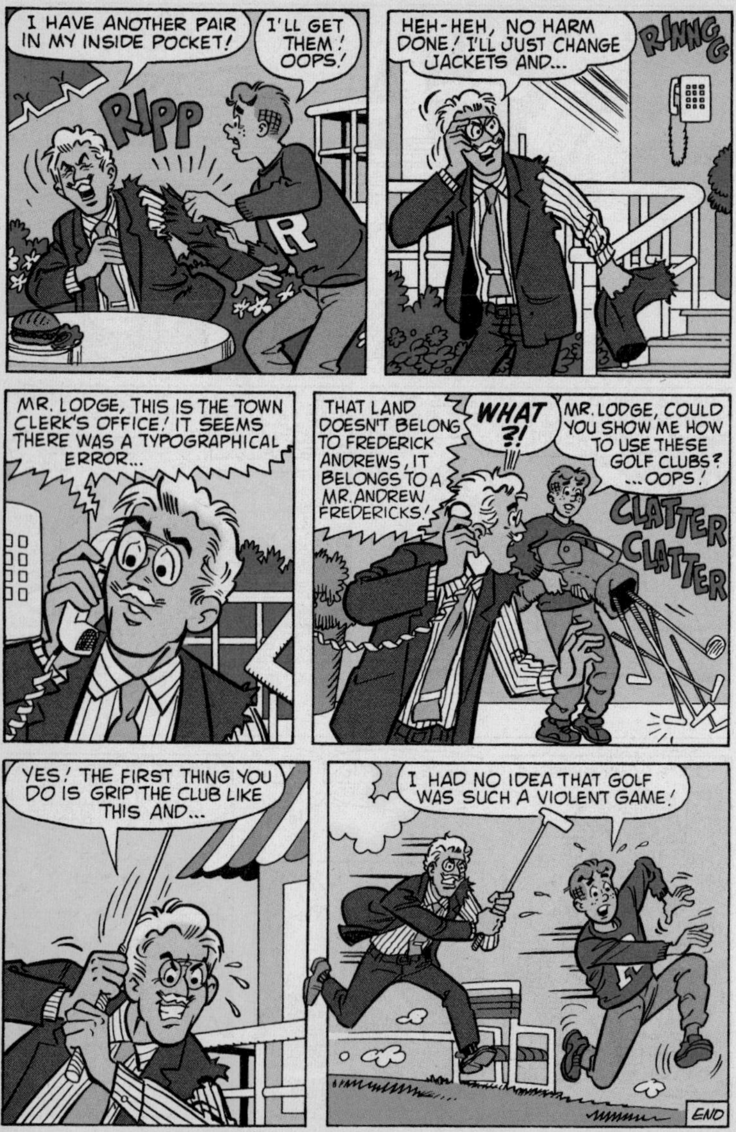
I HAVE ANOTHER PAIR IN MY INSIDE POCKET!
I'LL GET THEM! OOPS!
RIPP
HEH-HEH, NO HARM DONE! I'LL JUST CHANGE JACKETS AND...
RINNGG
MR. LODGE, THIS IS THE TOWN CLERK'S OFFICE! IT SEEMS THERE WAS A TYPOGRAPHICAL ERROR...
THAT LAND DOESN'T BELONG TO FREDERICK ANDREWS, IT BELONGS TO A MR. ANDREW FREDERICKS!
WHAT?!
MR. LODGE, COULD YOU SHOW ME HOW TO USE THESE GOLF CLUBS? ...OOPS!
CLATTER CLATTER
YES! THE FIRST THING YOU DO IS GRIP THE CLUB LIKE THIS AND...
I HAD NO IDEA THAT GOLF WAS SUCH A VIOLENT GAME!
END

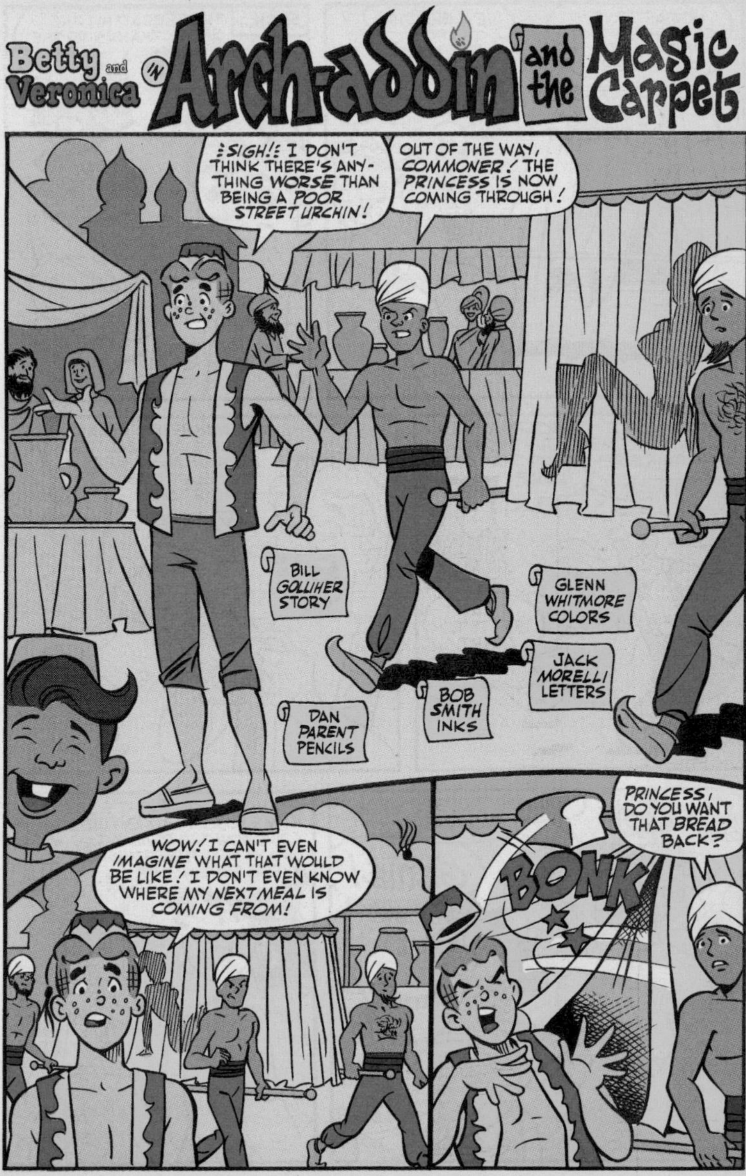
Betty and Veronica in Arch-addin and the Magic Carpet
:SIGH!: I DON'T THINK THERE'S ANY-THING WORSE THAN BEING A POOR STREET URCHIN!
OUT OF THE WAY, COMMONER! THE PRINCESS IS NOW COMING THROUGH!
BILL GOLLIHER STORY
GLENN WHITMORE COLORS
JACK MORELLI LETTERS
BOB SMITH INKS
DAN PARENT PENCILS
WOW! I CAN'T EVEN IMAGINE WHAT THAT WOULD BE LIKE! I DON'T EVEN KNOW WHERE MY NEXT MEAL IS COMING FROM!
PRINCESS, DO YOU WANT THAT BREAD BACK?
BONK

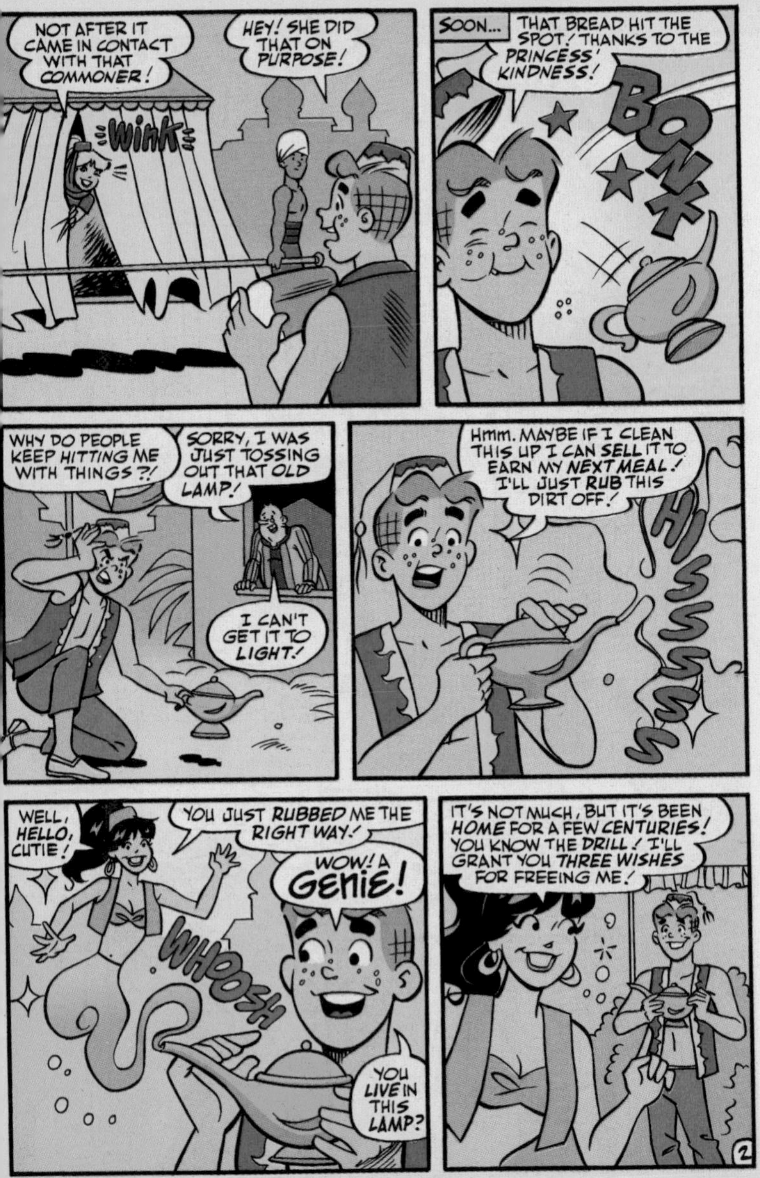
NOT AFTER IT CAME IN CONTACT WITH THAT COMMONER!
WINK
HEY! SHE DID THAT ON PURPOSE!
SOON...
THAT BREAD HIT THE SPOT! THANKS TO THE PRINCESS' KINDNESS!
BONK
WHY DO PEOPLE KEEP HITTING ME WITH THINGS?!
SORRY, I WAS JUST TOSSING OUT THAT OLD LAMP!
I CAN'T GET IT TO LIGHT!
Hmm. MAYBE IF I CLEAN THIS UP I CAN SELL IT TO EARN MY NEXT MEAL! I'LL JUST RUB THIS DIRT OFF!
HISSSSSS
WELL, HELLO, CUTIE!
YOU JUST RUBBED ME THE RIGHT WAY!
WOW! A GENIE!
WHOOSH
YOU LIVE IN THIS LAMP?
IT'S NOT MUCH, BUT IT'S BEEN HOME FOR A FEW CENTURIES! YOU KNOW THE DRILL! I'LL GRANT YOU THREE WISHES FOR FREEING ME!
2

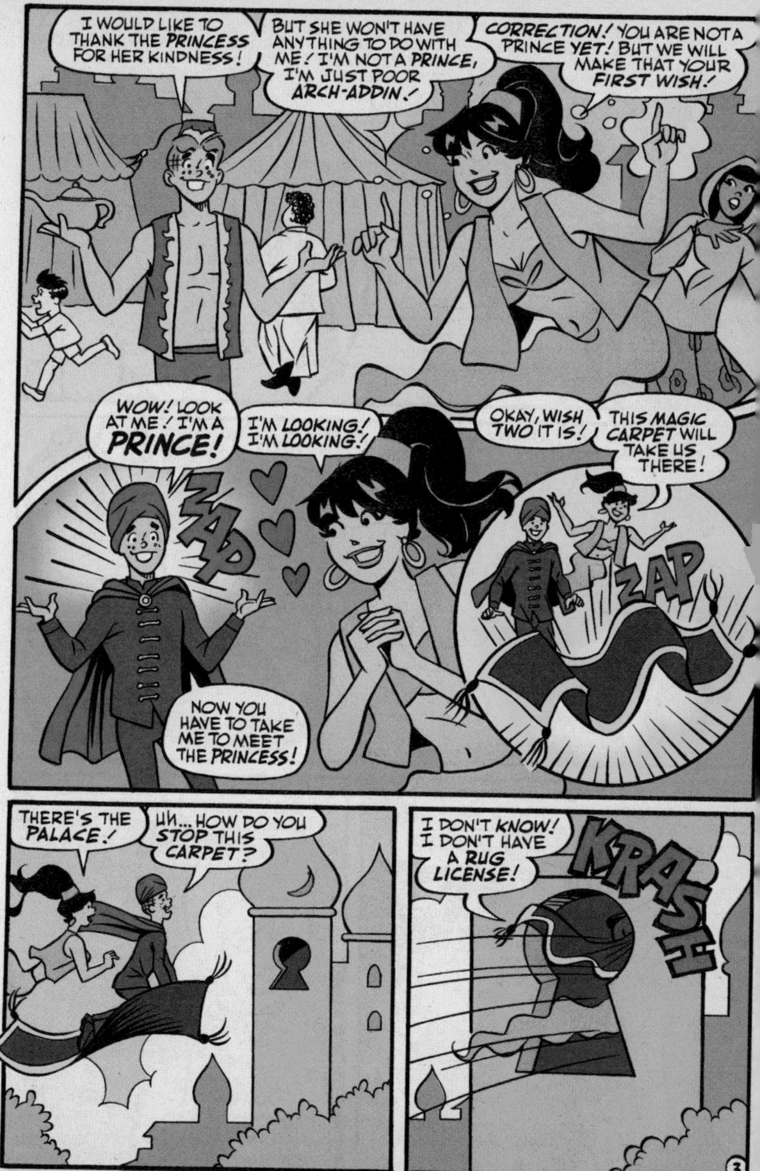
I WOULD LIKE TO THANK THE PRINCESS FOR HER KINDNESS!
BUT SHE WON'T HAVE ANYTHING TO DO WITH ME! I'M NOT A PRINCE, I'M JUST POOR ARCH-ADDIN!
CORRECTION! YOU ARE NOT A PRINCE YET! BUT WE WILL MAKE THAT YOUR FIRST WISH!
WOW! LOOK AT ME! I'M A PRINCE!
I'M LOOKING! I'M LOOKING!
ZAP
NOW YOU HAVE TO TAKE ME TO MEET THE PRINCESS!
OKAY, WISH TWO IT IS!
THIS MAGIC CARPET WILL TAKE US THERE!
ZAP
THERE'S THE PALACE!
UH... HOW DO YOU STOP THIS CARPET?
I DON'T KNOW! I DON'T HAVE A RUG LICENSE!
KRASH

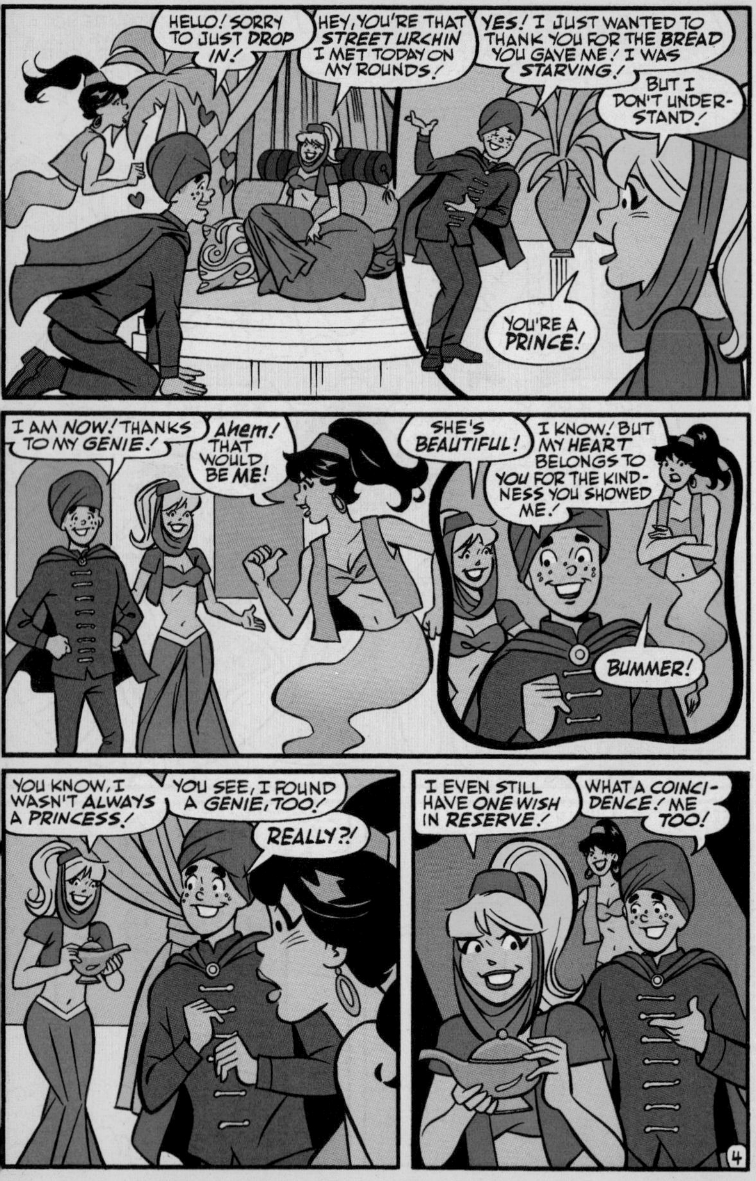
HELLO! SORRY TO JUST DROP IN!
HEY, YOU'RE THAT STREET URCHIN I MET TODAY ON MY ROUNDS!
YES! I JUST WANTED TO THANK YOU FOR THE BREAD YOU GAVE ME! I WAS STARVING!
BUT I DON'T UNDERSTAND!
YOU'RE A PRINCE!
I AM NOW! THANKS TO MY GENIE!
Ahem! THAT WOULD BE ME!
SHE'S BEAUTIFUL!
I KNOW! BUT MY HEART BELONGS TO YOU FOR THE KINDNESS YOU SHOWED ME!
BUMMER!
YOU KNOW, I WASN'T ALWAYS A PRINCESS!
YOU SEE, I FOUND A GENIE, TOO!
REALLY?!
I EVEN STILL HAVE ONE WISH IN RESERVE!
WHAT A COINCIDENCE! ME TOO!
4

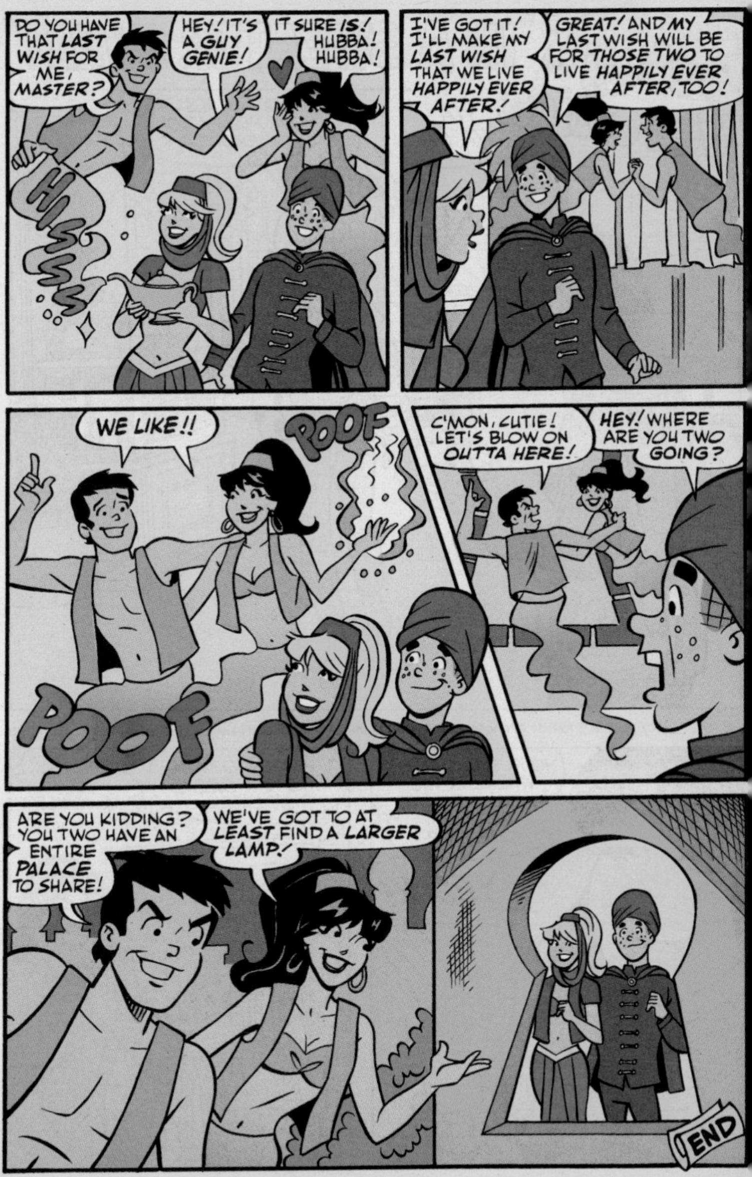
DO YOU HAVE THAT LAST WISH FOR ME, MASTER?
HEY! IT'S A GUY GENIE!
IT SURE IS! HUBBA! HUBBA!
HISSSS
I'VE GOT IT! I'LL MAKE MY LAST WISH THAT WE LIVE HAPPILY EVER AFTER!
GREAT! AND MY LAST WISH WILL BE FOR THOSE TWO TO LIVE HAPPILY EVER AFTER, TOO!
WE LIKE!!
POOF
POOF
C'MON, CUTIE! LET'S BLOW ON OUTTA HERE!
HEY! WHERE ARE YOU TWO GOING?
ARE YOU KIDDING? YOU TWO HAVE AN ENTIRE PALACE TO SHARE!
WE'VE GOT TO AT LEAST FIND A LARGER LAMP!
END

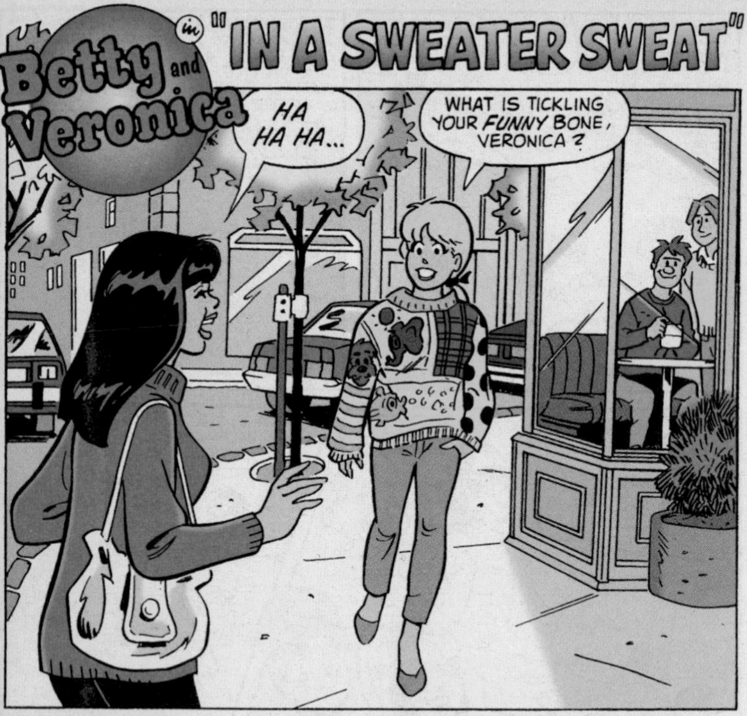
Betty and Veronica in
"IN A SWEATER SWEAT"
HA HA HA...
WHAT IS TICKLING YOUR *FUNNY* BONE, VERONICA?

Script: Joe Edwards / Pencils: Dan DeCarlo / Inks: Alison Flood / Letters: Bill Yoshida

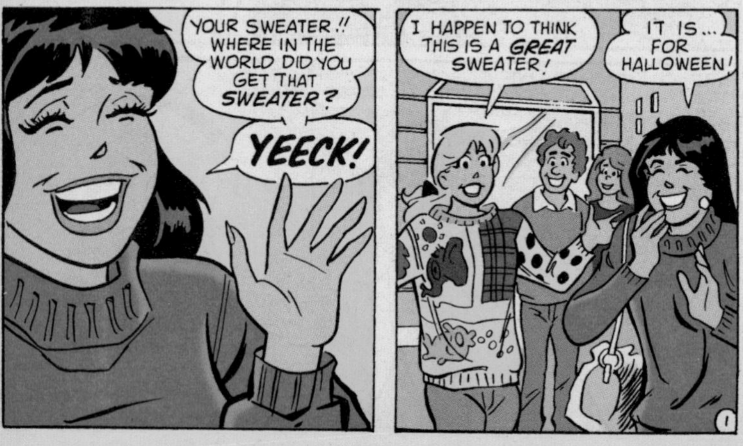
YOUR SWEATER!! WHERE IN THE WORLD DID YOU GET THAT *SWEATER*?
YEECK!
I HAPPEN TO THINK THIS IS A *GREAT* SWEATER!
IT IS... FOR HALLOWEEN!

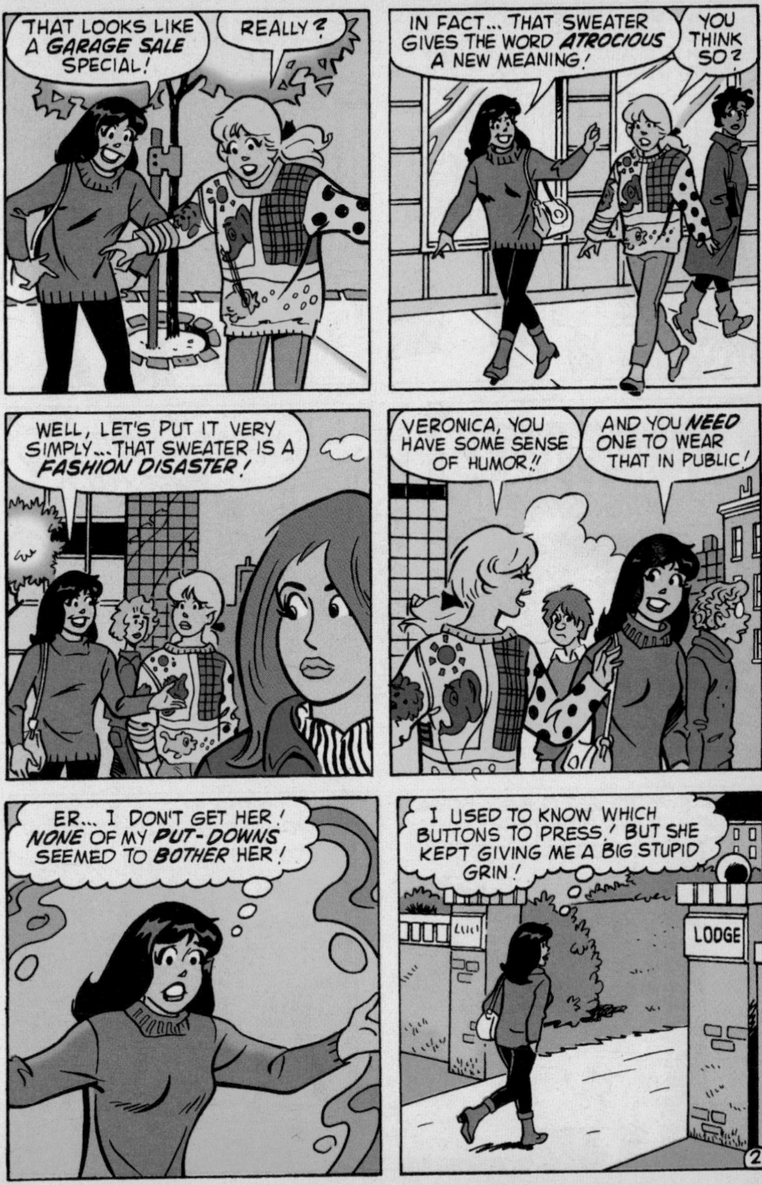

THAT LOOKS LIKE A GARAGE SALE SPECIAL!
REALLY?
IN FACT... THAT SWEATER GIVES THE WORD ATROCIOUS A NEW MEANING!
YOU THINK SO?
WELL, LET'S PUT IT VERY SIMPLY... THAT SWEATER IS A FASHION DISASTER!
VERONICA, YOU HAVE SOME SENSE OF HUMOR!!
AND YOU NEED ONE TO WEAR THAT IN PUBLIC!
ER... I DON'T GET HER! NONE OF MY PUT-DOWNS SEEMED TO BOTHER HER!
I USED TO KNOW WHICH BUTTONS TO PRESS! BUT SHE KEPT GIVING ME A BIG STUPID GRIN!
LODGE
2

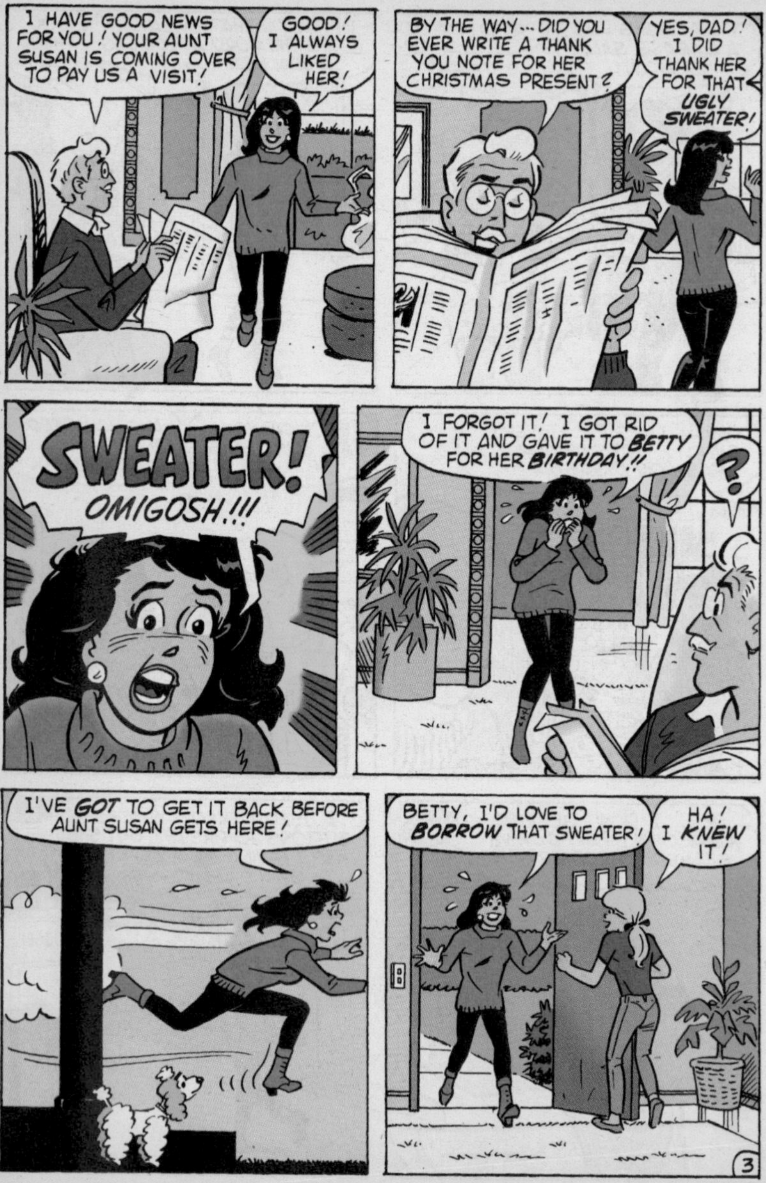
I HAVE GOOD NEWS FOR YOU! YOUR AUNT SUSAN IS COMING OVER TO PAY US A VISIT!
GOOD! I ALWAYS LIKED HER!
BY THE WAY... DID YOU EVER WRITE A THANK YOU NOTE FOR HER CHRISTMAS PRESENT?
YES, DAD! I DID THANK HER FOR THAT UGLY SWEATER!
SWEATER! OMIGOSH!!!
I FORGOT IT! I GOT RID OF IT AND GAVE IT TO BETTY FOR HER BIRTHDAY!!
?
I'VE GOT TO GET IT BACK BEFORE AUNT SUSAN GETS HERE!
BETTY, I'D LOVE TO BORROW THAT SWEATER!
HA! I KNEW IT!
3

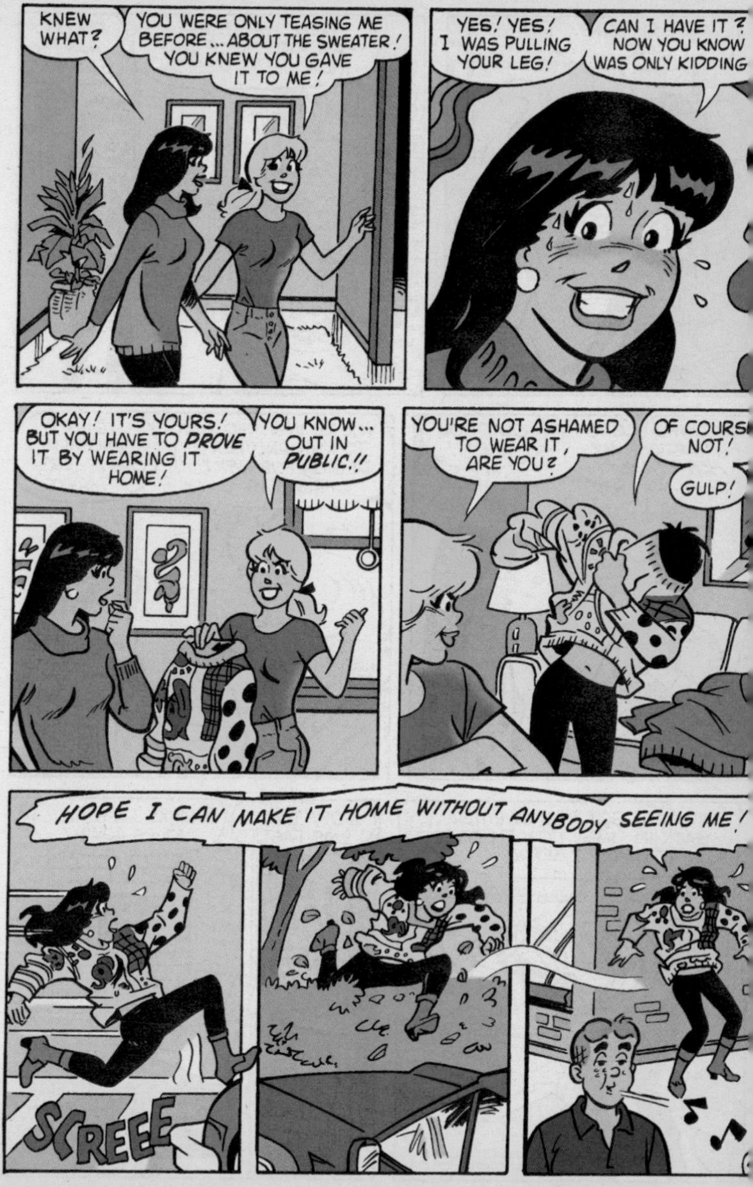
KNEW WHAT?
YOU WERE ONLY TEASING ME BEFORE... ABOUT THE SWEATER! YOU KNEW YOU GAVE IT TO ME!
YES! YES! I WAS PULLING YOUR LEG!
CAN I HAVE IT? NOW YOU KNOW WAS ONLY KIDDING
OKAY! IT'S YOURS! BUT YOU HAVE TO PROVE IT BY WEARING IT HOME!
YOU KNOW... OUT IN PUBLIC!!
YOU'RE NOT ASHAMED TO WEAR IT, ARE YOU?
OF COURS NOT!
GULP!
HOPE I CAN MAKE IT HOME WITHOUT ANYBODY SEEING ME!
SCREEE

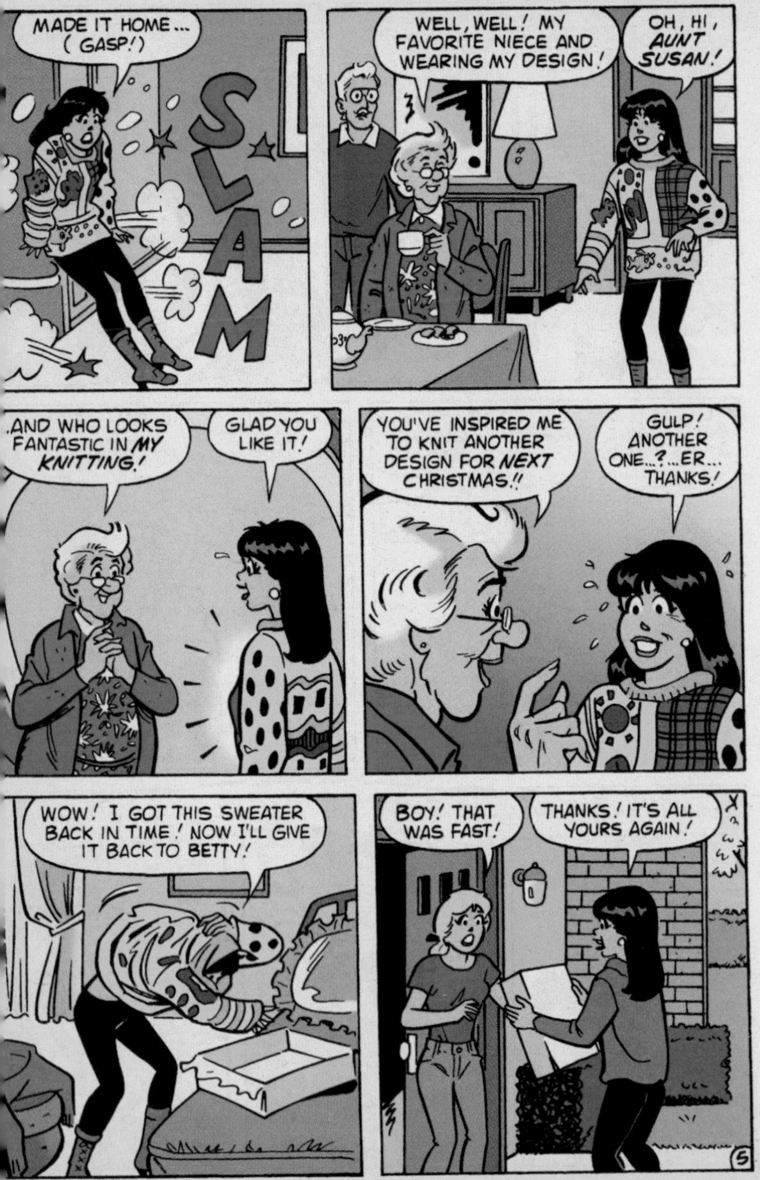
MADE IT HOME... (GASP!)
SLAM
WELL, WELL! MY FAVORITE NIECE AND WEARING MY DESIGN!
OH, HI, AUNT SUSAN!
.AND WHO LOOKS FANTASTIC IN MY KNITTING!
GLAD YOU LIKE IT!
YOU'VE INSPIRED ME TO KNIT ANOTHER DESIGN FOR NEXT CHRISTMAS!!
GULP! ANOTHER ONE...?...ER... THANKS!
WOW! I GOT THIS SWEATER BACK IN TIME! NOW I'LL GIVE IT BACK TO BETTY!
BOY! THAT WAS FAST!
THANKS! IT'S ALL YOURS AGAIN!
5

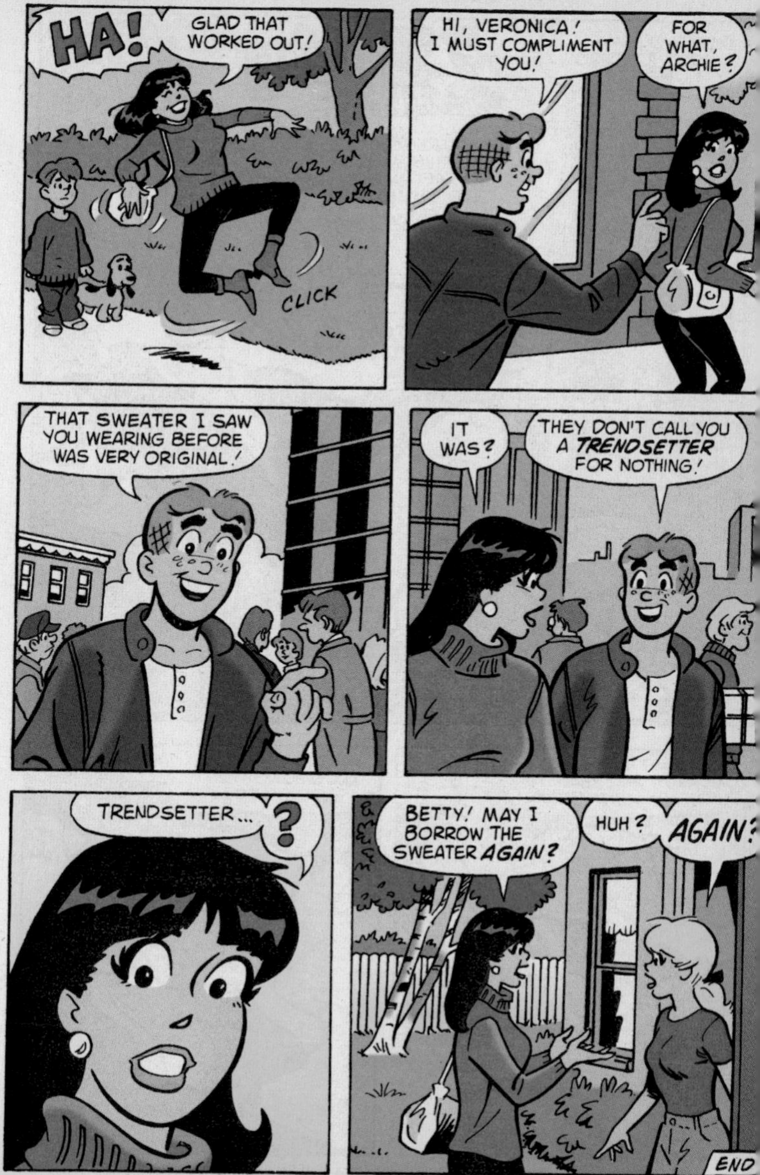

HA!
GLAD THAT WORKED OUT!
CLICK
HI, VERONICA! I MUST COMPLIMENT YOU!
FOR WHAT, ARCHIE?
THAT SWEATER I SAW YOU WEARING BEFORE WAS VERY ORIGINAL!
IT WAS?
THEY DON'T CALL YOU A TRENDSETTER FOR NOTHING!
TRENDSETTER...?
BETTY! MAY I BORROW THE SWEATER AGAIN?
HUH?
AGAIN?
END

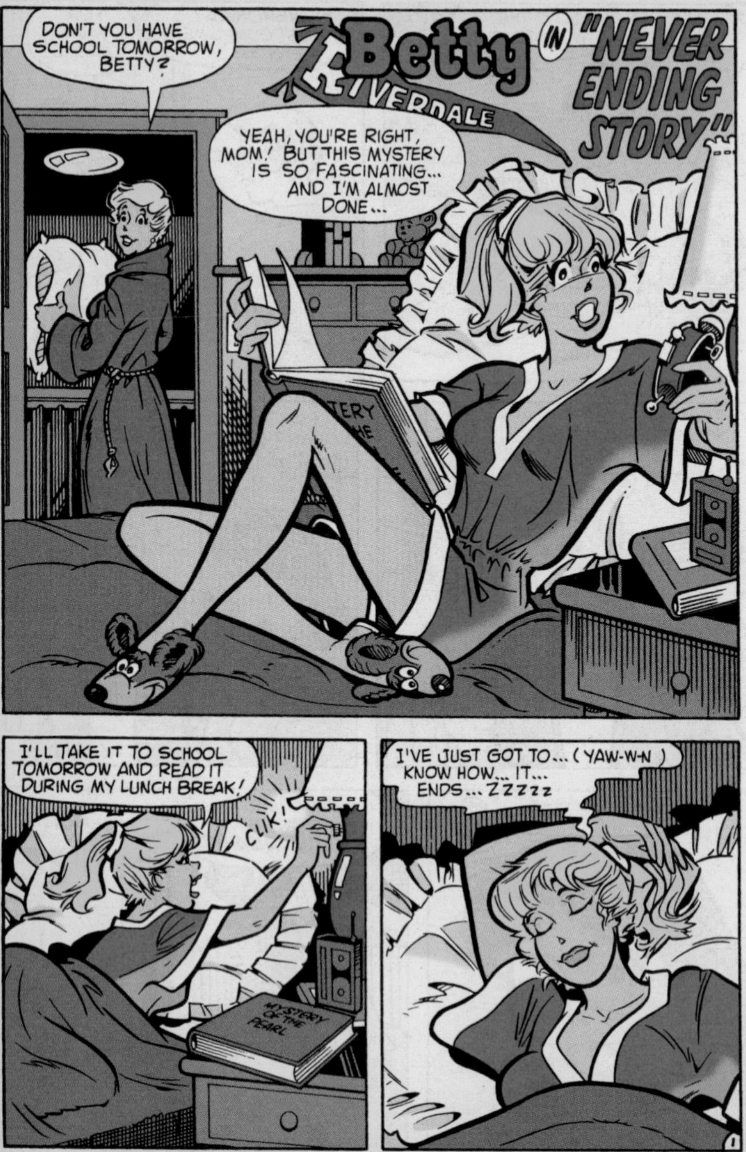
DON'T YOU HAVE SCHOOL TOMORROW, BETTY?
Betty IN "NEVER ENDING STORY"
RIVERDALE
YEAH, YOU'RE RIGHT, MOM! BUT THIS MYSTERY IS SO FASCINATING... AND I'M ALMOST DONE...
I'LL TAKE IT TO SCHOOL TOMORROW AND READ IT DURING MY LUNCH BREAK!
CLIK!
MYSTERY OF THE PEARL
I'VE JUST GOT TO... (YAW-W-N) KNOW HOW... IT... ENDS... Zzzzz
1

Script: Kathleen Webb / Pencils: Doug Crane / Inks: Ken Selig / Letters: Bill Yoshida

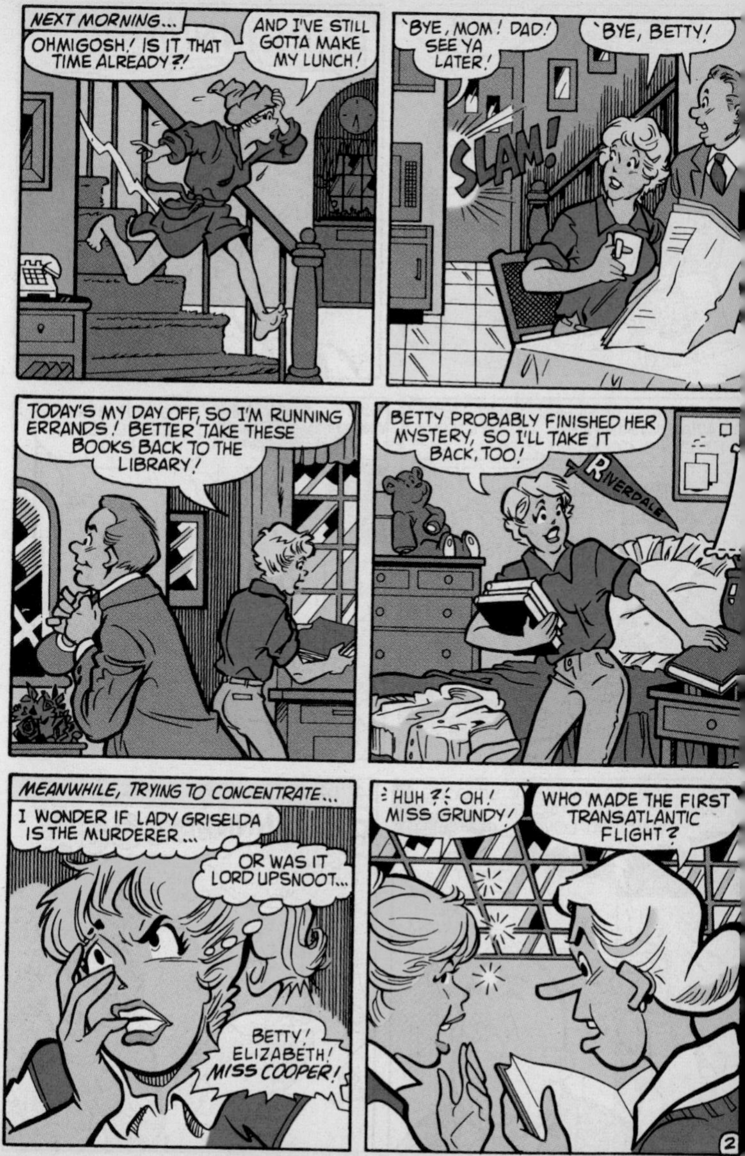
NEXT MORNING...
OHMIGOSH! IS IT THAT TIME ALREADY?!
AND I'VE STILL GOTTA MAKE MY LUNCH!
`BYE, MOM! DAD! SEE YA LATER!
`BYE, BETTY!
SLAM!
TODAY'S MY DAY OFF, SO I'M RUNNING ERRANDS! BETTER TAKE THESE BOOKS BACK TO THE LIBRARY!
BETTY PROBABLY FINISHED HER MYSTERY, SO I'LL TAKE IT BACK, TOO!
RIVERDALE
MEANWHILE, TRYING TO CONCENTRATE...
I WONDER IF LADY GRISELDA IS THE MURDERER...
OR WAS IT LORD UPSNOOT...
BETTY! ELIZABETH! MISS COOPER!
HUH?! OH! MISS GRUNDY!
WHO MADE THE FIRST TRANSATLANTIC FLIGHT?

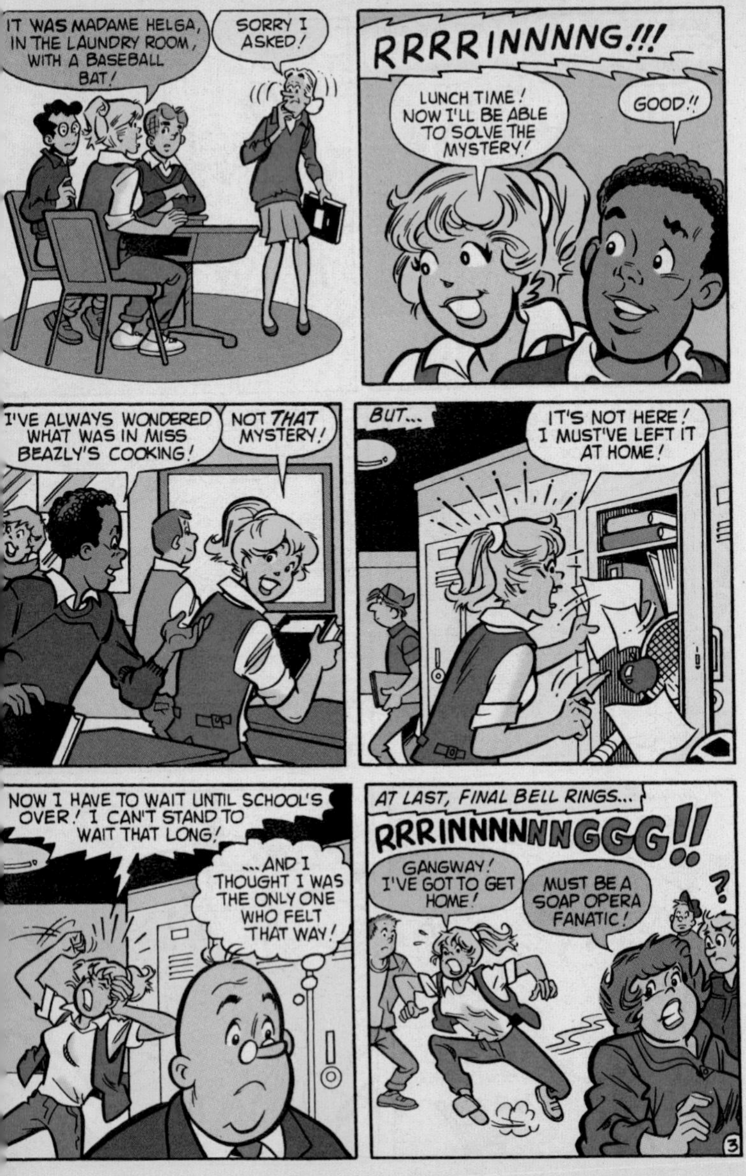
IT WAS MADAME HELGA, IN THE LAUNDRY ROOM, WITH A BASEBALL BAT!
SORRY I ASKED!
RRRRINNNNG!!!
LUNCH TIME! NOW I'LL BE ABLE TO SOLVE THE MYSTERY!
GOOD!!
I'VE ALWAYS WONDERED WHAT WAS IN MISS BEAZLY'S COOKING!
NOT THAT MYSTERY!
BUT...
IT'S NOT HERE! I MUST'VE LEFT IT AT HOME!
NOW I HAVE TO WAIT UNTIL SCHOOL'S OVER! I CAN'T STAND TO WAIT THAT LONG!
...AND I THOUGHT I WAS THE ONLY ONE WHO FELT THAT WAY!
AT LAST, FINAL BELL RINGS...
RRRINNNNNNGGG!!
GANGWAY! I'VE GOT TO GET HOME!
MUST BE A SOAP OPERA FANATIC!
?
3

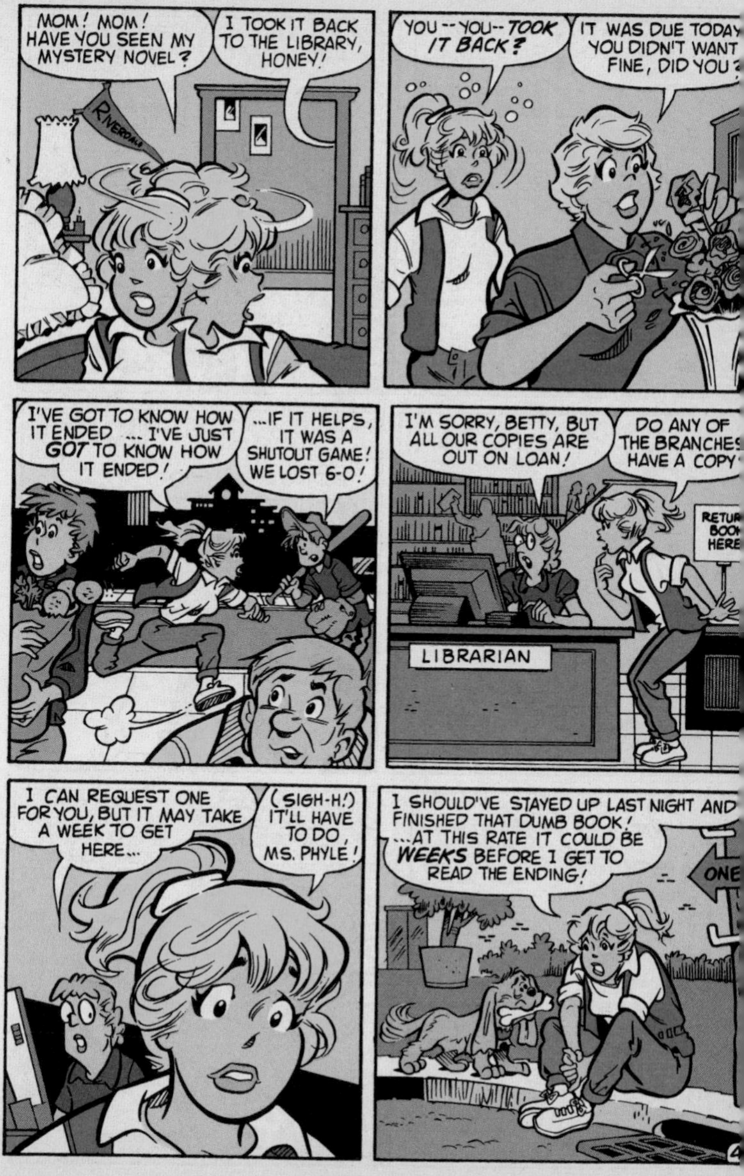

MOM! MOM! HAVE YOU SEEN MY MYSTERY NOVEL?
I TOOK IT BACK TO THE LIBRARY, HONEY!
RIVERDALE
YOU -- YOU -- TOOK IT BACK?
IT WAS DUE TODAY YOU DIDN'T WANT FINE, DID YOU?
I'VE GOT TO KNOW HOW IT ENDED ... I'VE JUST GOT TO KNOW HOW IT ENDED!
...IF IT HELPS, IT WAS A SHUTOUT GAME! WE LOST 6-0!
I'M SORRY, BETTY, BUT ALL OUR COPIES ARE OUT ON LOAN!
DO ANY OF THE BRANCHES HAVE A COPY
LIBRARIAN
I CAN REQUEST ONE FOR YOU, BUT IT MAY TAKE A WEEK TO GET HERE...
(SIGH-H!) IT'LL HAVE TO DO, MS. PHYLE!
I SHOULD'VE STAYED UP LAST NIGHT AND FINISHED THAT DUMB BOOK! ...AT THIS RATE IT COULD BE WEEKS BEFORE I GET TO READ THE ENDING!

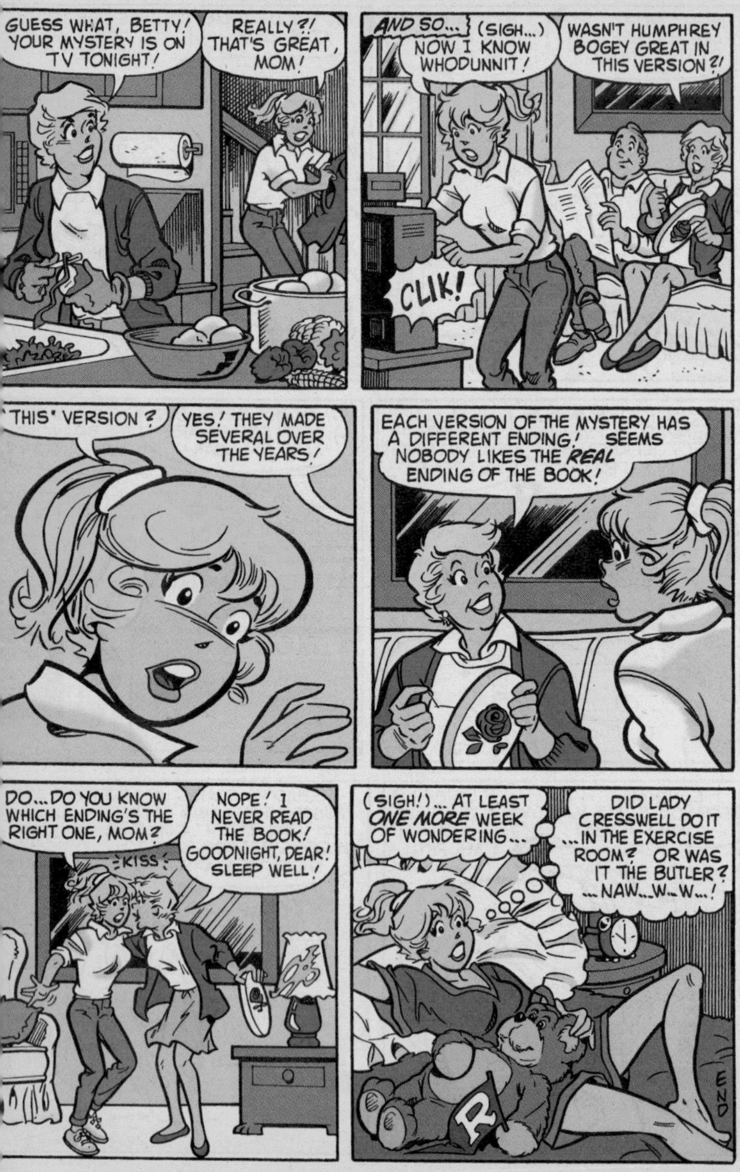
GUESS WHAT, BETTY! YOUR MYSTERY IS ON TV TONIGHT!
REALLY?! THAT'S GREAT, MOM!
AND SO...
(SIGH...) NOW I KNOW WHODUNNIT!
WASN'T HUMPHREY BOGEY GREAT IN THIS VERSION?!
CLIK!
"THIS" VERSION?
YES! THEY MADE SEVERAL OVER THE YEARS!
EACH VERSION OF THE MYSTERY HAS A DIFFERENT ENDING! SEEMS NOBODY LIKES THE REAL ENDING OF THE BOOK!
DO...DO YOU KNOW WHICH ENDING'S THE RIGHT ONE, MOM?
KISS
NOPE! I NEVER READ THE BOOK! GOODNIGHT, DEAR! SLEEP WELL!
(SIGH!)... AT LEAST ONE MORE WEEK OF WONDERING...
DID LADY CRESSWELL DO IT ...IN THE EXERCISE ROOM? OR WAS IT THE BUTLER? ...NAW...W...W...!
R
END

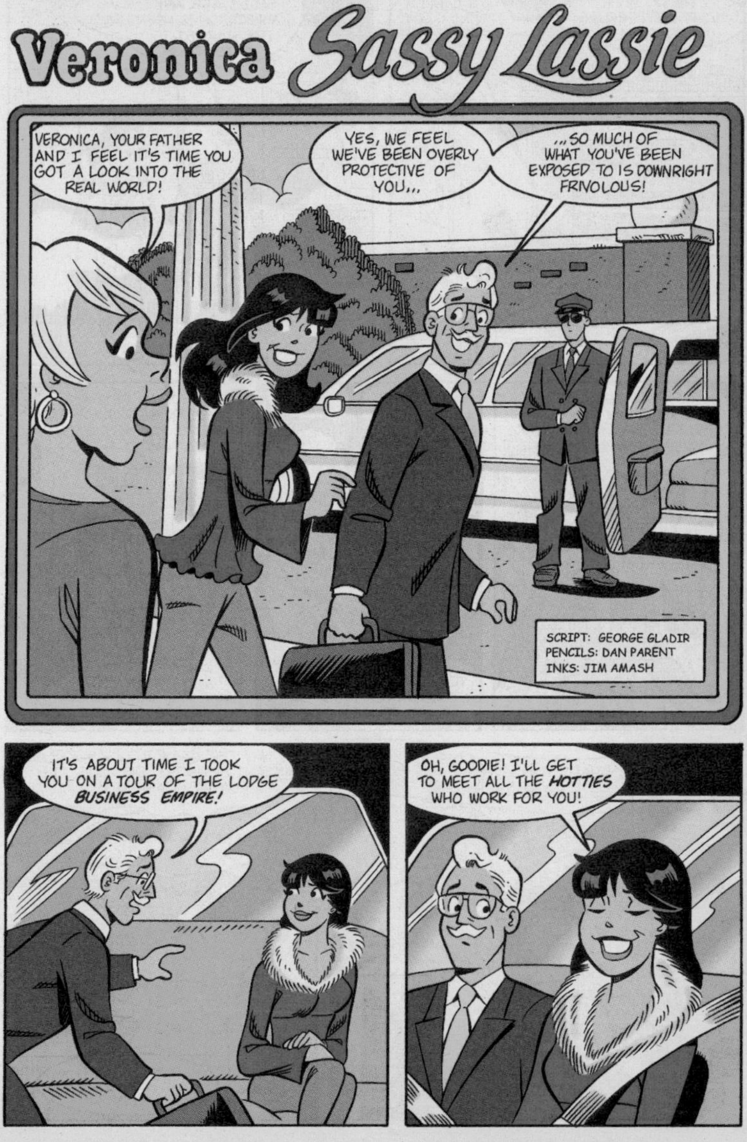
Veronica Sassy Lassie
VERONICA, YOUR FATHER AND I FEEL IT'S TIME YOU GOT A LOOK INTO THE REAL WORLD!
YES, WE FEEL WE'VE BEEN OVERLY PROTECTIVE OF YOU...
...SO MUCH OF WHAT YOU'VE BEEN EXPOSED TO IS DOWNRIGHT FRIVOLOUS!
SCRIPT: GEORGE GLADIR
PENCILS: DAN PARENT
INKS: JIM AMASH
IT'S ABOUT TIME I TOOK YOU ON A TOUR OF THE LODGE BUSINESS EMPIRE!
OH, GOODIE! I'LL GET TO MEET ALL THE HOTTIES WHO WORK FOR YOU!

FIRST, WE'LL TOUR OUR PERFUME DIVISION...

...IT'S BEEN HAVING A LOT OF PROBLEMS LATELY!

LODGE INDUSTRIES

SALES ARE *WAY* DOWN... COMPETITION IS KEEN ...AND THE MARKET IS *SATURATED!*

IF ONLY THERE WAS SOME WAY TO STIMULATE SALES AND EXPAND OUR MARKET!

MAY I MAKE A SUGGESTION?

HA! HA!

YES, YOU'RE FREE TO DO *ANYTHING* YOUR HEART DESIRES!

MANY OF MY FRIENDS COMPLAIN THEIR BOYFRIENDS AREN'T PAYING ENOUGH ATTENTION TO THEM...

...BECAUSE THE BOYS ARE SO *ABSORBED* IN VIDEO GAMES!

" WHAT IF A GIRL HAD A SPECIAL DEVICE THAT COULD DISPENSE HER BRAND OF PERFUME ON HIS GAME SETUP?"

SQUIRT!

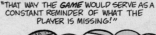

"THAT WAY THE *GAME* WOULD SERVE AS A CONSTANT REMINDER OF WHAT THE PLAYER IS MISSING!"

GEE! I WONDER WHAT CAROL IS DOING...

SN*FF*

530   75

...I BETTER GIVE HER A CALL RIGHT NOW!

2

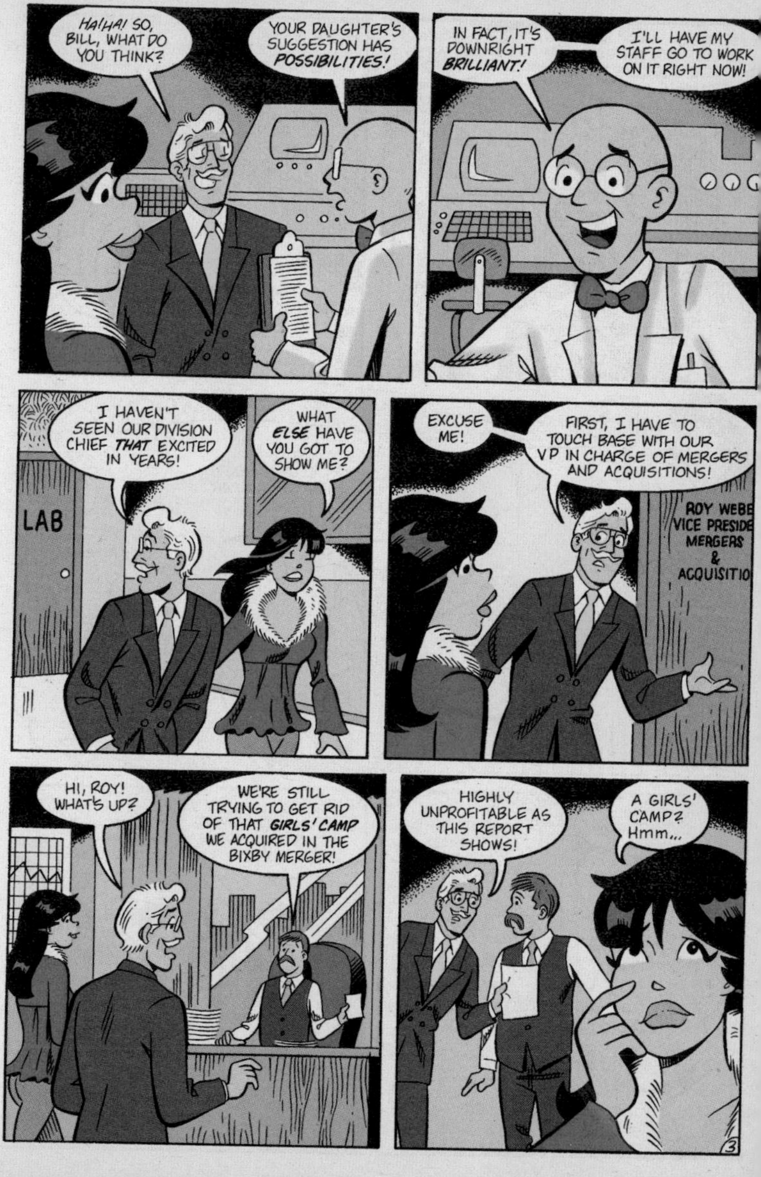
HA! HA! SO, BILL, WHAT DO YOU THINK?
YOUR DAUGHTER'S SUGGESTION HAS POSSIBILITIES!
IN FACT, IT'S DOWNRIGHT BRILLIANT!
I'LL HAVE MY STAFF GO TO WORK ON IT RIGHT NOW!
I HAVEN'T SEEN OUR DIVISION CHIEF THAT EXCITED IN YEARS!
WHAT ELSE HAVE YOU GOT TO SHOW ME?
LAB
EXCUSE ME!
FIRST, I HAVE TO TOUCH BASE WITH OUR VP IN CHARGE OF MERGERS AND ACQUISITIONS!
ROY WEBE
VICE PRESIDE
MERGERS
&
ACQUISITIO
HI, ROY! WHAT'S UP?
WE'RE STILL TRYING TO GET RID OF THAT GIRLS' CAMP WE ACQUIRED IN THE BIXBY MERGER!
HIGHLY UNPROFITABLE AS THIS REPORT SHOWS!
A GIRLS' CAMP? Hmm...

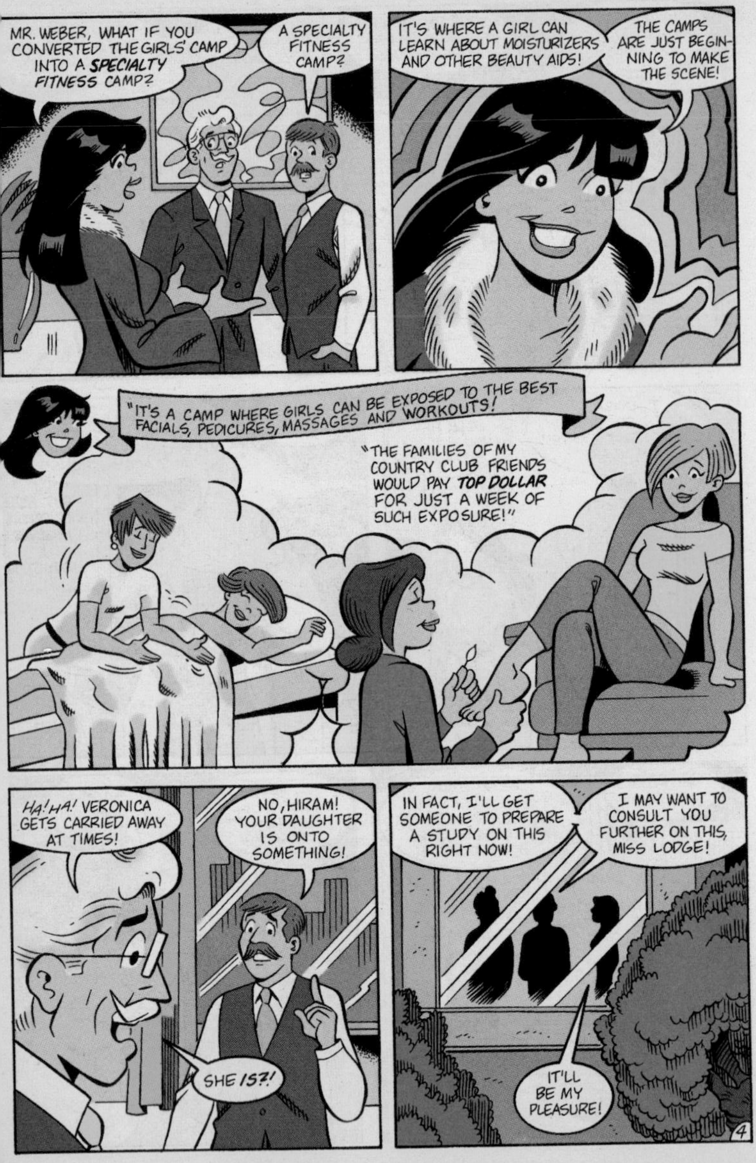

MR. WEBER, WHAT IF YOU CONVERTED THE GIRLS' CAMP INTO A **SPECIALTY FITNESS** CAMP?
A SPECIALTY FITNESS CAMP?
IT'S WHERE A GIRL CAN LEARN ABOUT MOISTURIZERS AND OTHER BEAUTY AIDS!
THE CAMPS ARE JUST BEGINNING TO MAKE THE SCENE!
"IT'S A CAMP WHERE GIRLS CAN BE EXPOSED TO THE BEST FACIALS, PEDICURES, MASSAGES AND WORKOUTS!
"THE FAMILIES OF MY COUNTRY CLUB FRIENDS WOULD PAY **TOP DOLLAR** FOR JUST A WEEK OF SUCH EXPOSURE!"
HA! HA! VERONICA GETS CARRIED AWAY AT TIMES!
NO, HIRAM! YOUR DAUGHTER IS ONTO SOMETHING!
SHE *IS?!*
IN FACT, I'LL GET SOMEONE TO PREPARE A STUDY ON THIS RIGHT NOW!
I MAY WANT TO CONSULT YOU FURTHER ON THIS, MISS LODGE!
IT'LL BE MY PLEASURE!
4

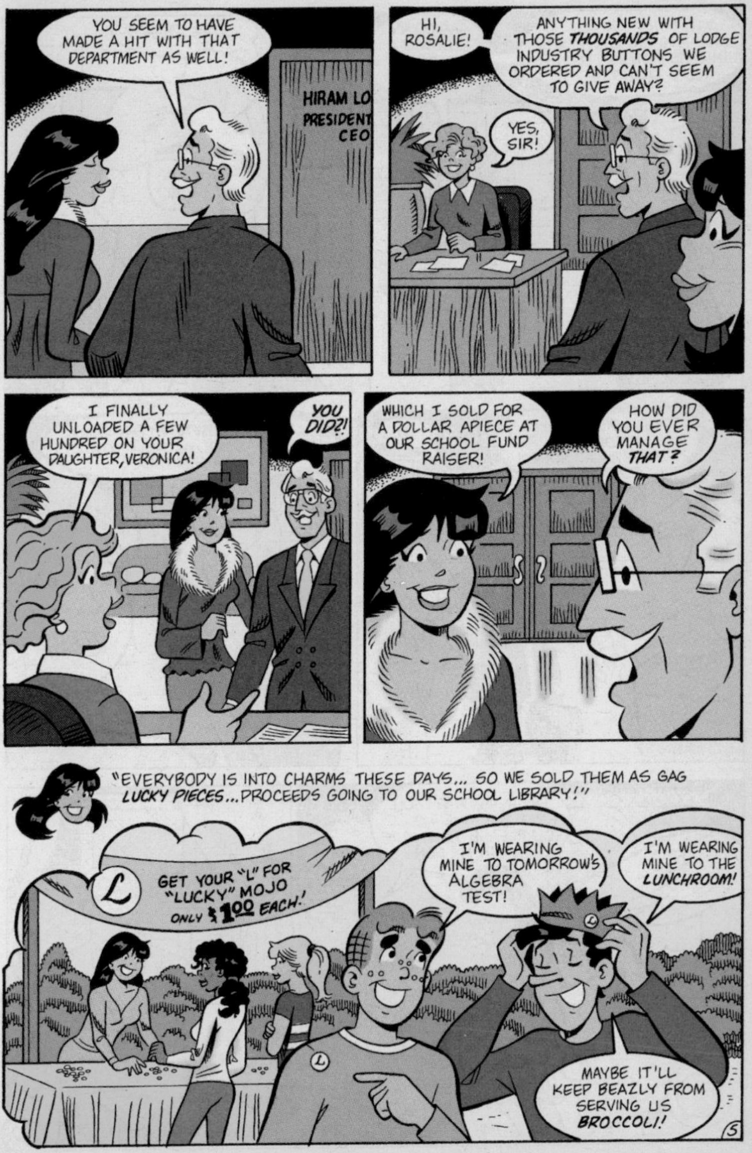
YOU SEEM TO HAVE MADE A HIT WITH THAT DEPARTMENT AS WELL!
HIRAM LO
PRESIDENT
CEO
HI, ROSALIE!
ANYTHING NEW WITH THOSE THOUSANDS OF LODGE INDUSTRY BUTTONS WE ORDERED AND CAN'T SEEM TO GIVE AWAY?
YES, SIR!
I FINALLY UNLOADED A FEW HUNDRED ON YOUR DAUGHTER, VERONICA!
YOU DID?!
WHICH I SOLD FOR A DOLLAR APIECE AT OUR SCHOOL FUND RAISER!
HOW DID YOU EVER MANAGE THAT?
"EVERYBODY IS INTO CHARMS THESE DAYS... SO WE SOLD THEM AS GAG LUCKY PIECES...PROCEEDS GOING TO OUR SCHOOL LIBRARY!"
GET YOUR "L" FOR "LUCKY" MOJO ONLY $1.00 EACH!
I'M WEARING MINE TO TOMORROW'S ALGEBRA TEST!
I'M WEARING MINE TO THE LUNCHROOM!
MAYBE IT'LL KEEP BEAZLY FROM SERVING US BROCCOLI!
5

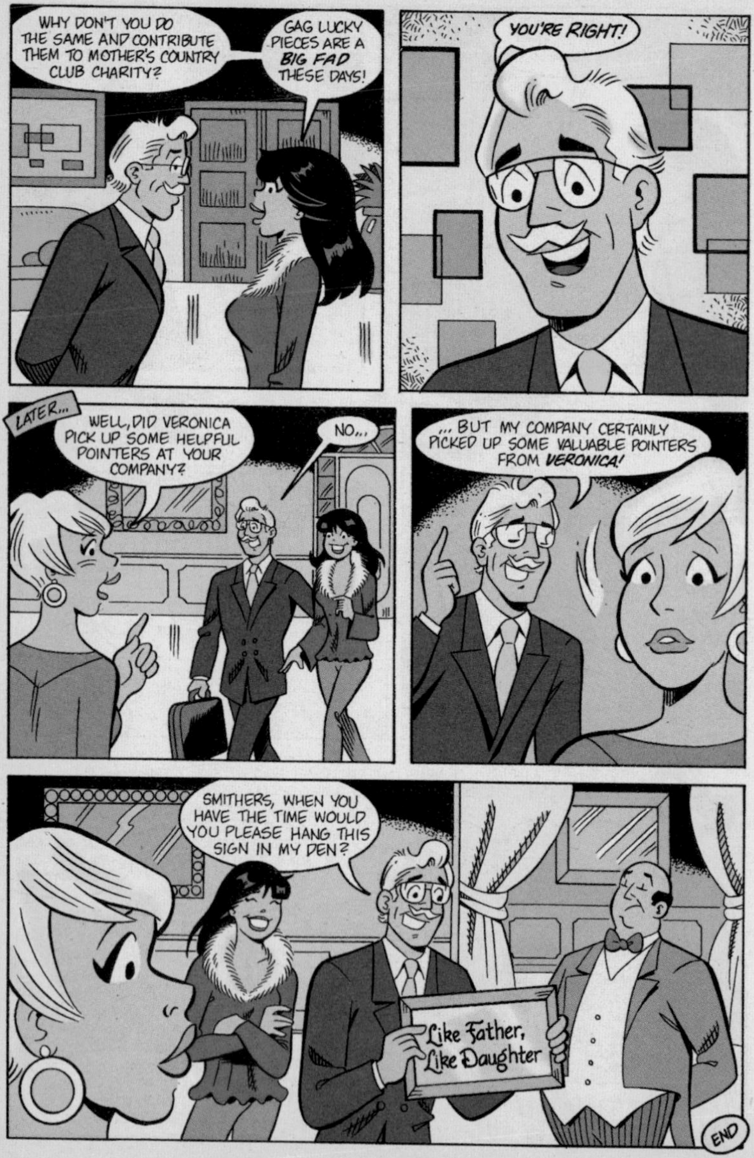
WHY DON'T YOU DO THE SAME AND CONTRIBUTE THEM TO MOTHER'S COUNTRY CLUB CHARITY?
GAG LUCKY PIECES ARE A BIG FAD THESE DAYS!
YOU'RE RIGHT!
LATER...
WELL, DID VERONICA PICK UP SOME HELPFUL POINTERS AT YOUR COMPANY?
NO...
...BUT MY COMPANY CERTAINLY PICKED UP SOME VALUABLE POINTERS FROM VERONICA!
SMITHERS, WHEN YOU HAVE THE TIME WOULD YOU PLEASE HANG THIS SIGN IN MY DEN?
Like Father, Like Daughter
END

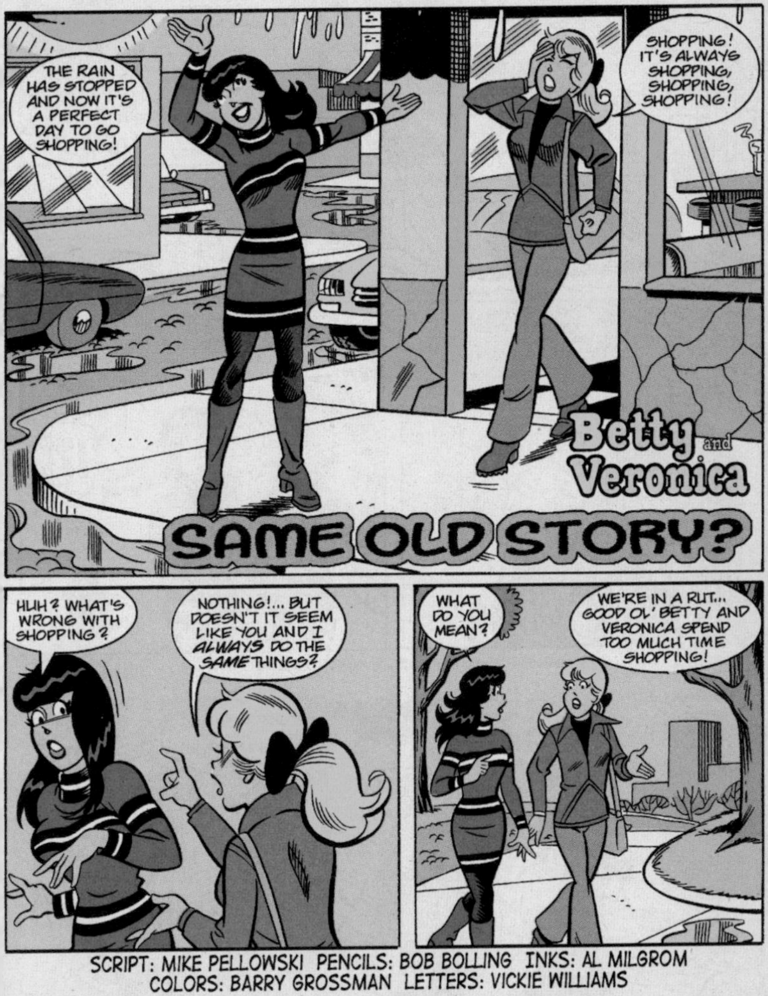
THE RAIN HAS STOPPED AND NOW IT'S A PERFECT DAY TO GO SHOPPING!
SHOPPING! IT'S ALWAYS SHOPPING, SHOPPING, SHOPPING!
Betty and Veronica
SAME OLD STORY?
HUH? WHAT'S WRONG WITH SHOPPING?
NOTHING!... BUT DOESN'T IT SEEM LIKE YOU AND I ALWAYS DO THE SAME THINGS?
WHAT DO YOU MEAN?
WE'RE IN A RUT... GOOD OL' BETTY AND VERONICA SPEND TOO MUCH TIME SHOPPING!

SCRIPT: MIKE PELLOWSKI PENCILS: BOB BOLLING INKS: AL MILGROM
COLORS: BARRY GROSSMAN LETTERS: VICKIE WILLIAMS

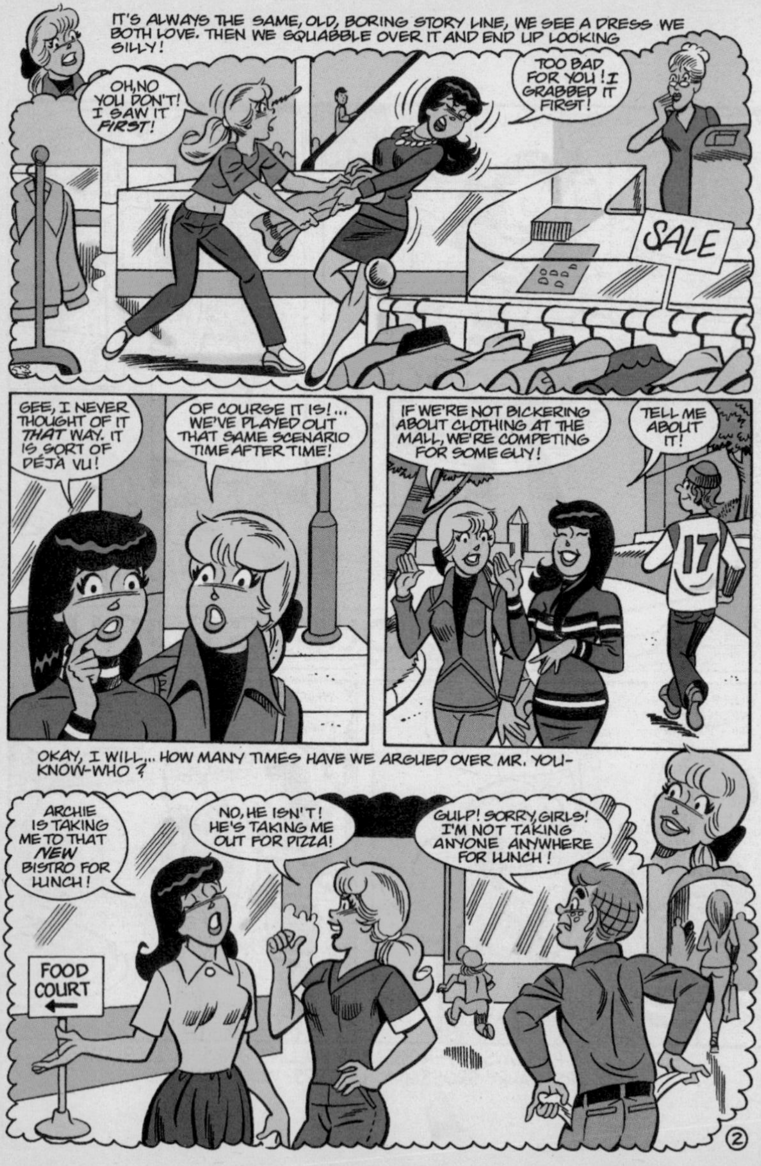
IT'S ALWAYS THE SAME, OLD, BORING STORY LINE, WE SEE A DRESS WE BOTH LOVE. THEN WE SQUABBLE OVER IT AND END UP LOOKING SILLY!
OH, NO YOU DON'T! I SAW IT FIRST!
TOO BAD FOR YOU! I GRABBED IT FIRST!
SALE
GEE, I NEVER THOUGHT OF IT THAT WAY. IT IS SORT OF DÉJÀ VU!
OF COURSE IT IS!... WE'VE PLAYED OUT THAT SAME SCENARIO TIME AFTER TIME!
IF WE'RE NOT BICKERING ABOUT CLOTHING AT THE MALL, WE'RE COMPETING FOR SOME GUY!
TELL ME ABOUT IT!
17
OKAY, I WILL... HOW MANY TIMES HAVE WE ARGUED OVER MR. YOU-KNOW-WHO?
ARCHIE IS TAKING ME TO THAT NEW BISTRO FOR LUNCH!
NO, HE ISN'T! HE'S TAKING ME OUT FOR PIZZA!
GULP! SORRY, GIRLS! I'M NOT TAKING ANYONE ANYWHERE FOR LUNCH!
FOOD COURT

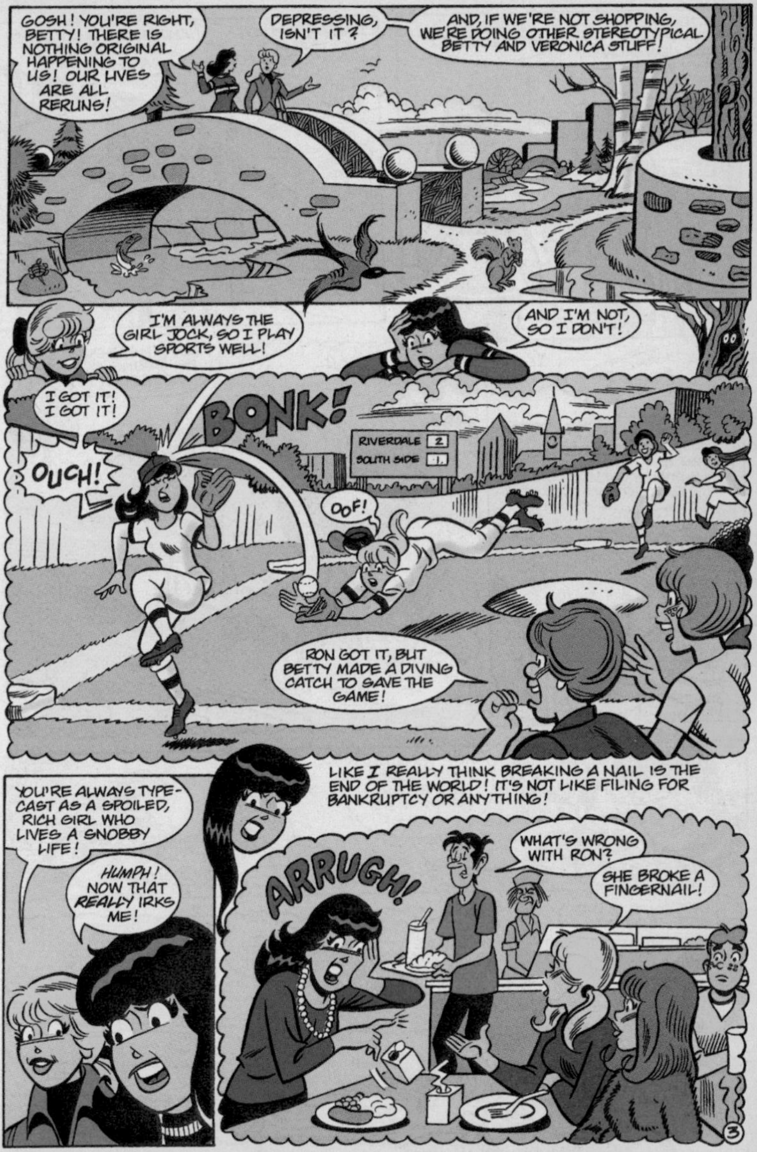
GOSH! YOU'RE RIGHT, BETTY! THERE IS NOTHING ORIGINAL HAPPENING TO US! OUR LIVES ARE ALL RERUNS!
DEPRESSING, ISN'T IT?
AND, IF WE'RE NOT SHOPPING, WE'RE DOING OTHER STEREOTYPICAL BETTY AND VERONICA STUFF!
I'M ALWAYS THE GIRL JOCK, SO I PLAY SPORTS WELL!
AND I'M NOT, SO I DON'T!
I GOT IT! I GOT IT!
BONK!
OUCH!
RIVERDALE 2
SOUTH SIDE 1
OOF!
RON GOT IT, BUT BETTY MADE A DIVING CATCH TO SAVE THE GAME!
YOU'RE ALWAYS TYPE-CAST AS A SPOILED, RICH GIRL WHO LIVES A SNOBBY LIFE!
HUMPH! NOW THAT REALLY IRKS ME!
LIKE I REALLY THINK BREAKING A NAIL IS THE END OF THE WORLD! IT'S NOT LIKE FILING FOR BANKRUPTCY OR ANYTHING!
ARRUGH!
WHAT'S WRONG WITH RON?
SHE BROKE A FINGERNAIL!
3

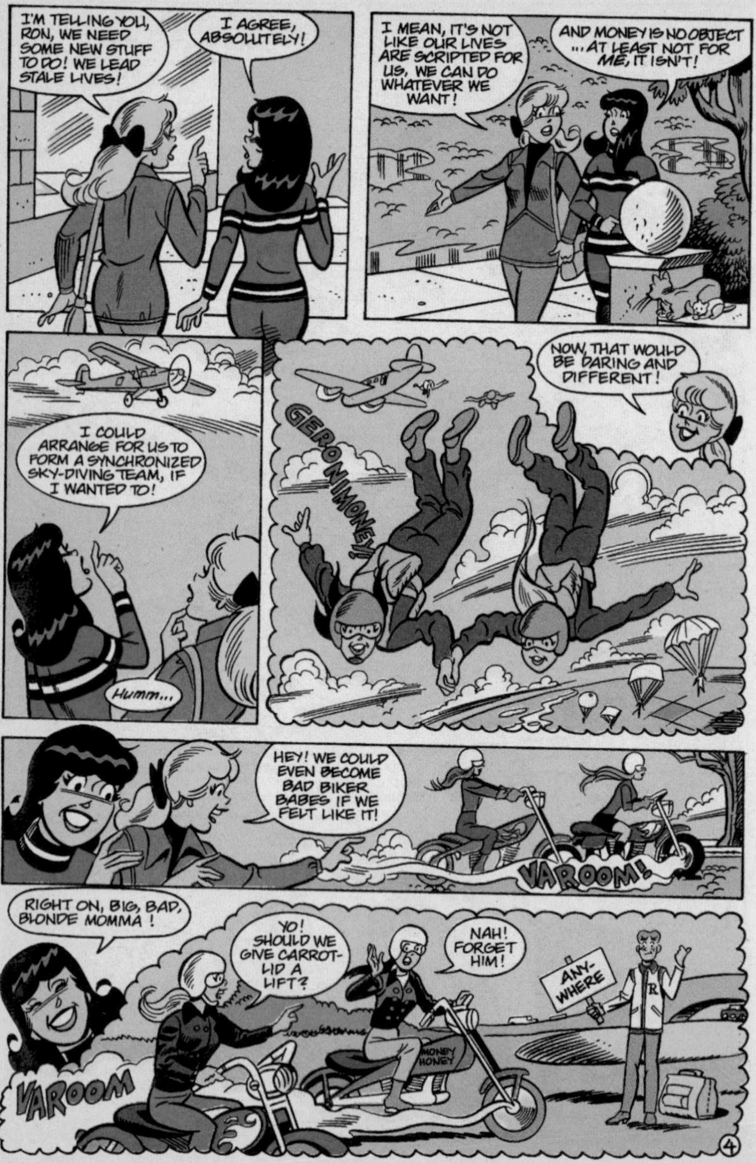

I'M TELLING YOU, RON, WE NEED SOME NEW STUFF TO DO! WE LEAD STALE LIVES!
I AGREE, ABSOLUTELY!
I MEAN, IT'S NOT LIKE OUR LIVES ARE SCRIPTED FOR US, WE CAN DO WHATEVER WE WANT!
AND MONEY IS NO OBJECT ...AT LEAST NOT FOR ME, IT ISN'T!
I COULD ARRANGE FOR US TO FORM A SYNCHRONIZED SKY-DIVING TEAM, IF I WANTED TO!
Humm...
GERONIMONEY!!
NOW, THAT WOULD BE DARING AND DIFFERENT!
HEY! WE COULD EVEN BECOME BAD BIKER BABES IF WE FELT LIKE IT!
VAROOM!
RIGHT ON, BIG, BAD, BLONDE MOMMA!
YO! SHOULD WE GIVE CARROT-LID A LIFT?
NAH! FORGET HIM!
ANY-WHERE
MONEY HONEY
VAROOM

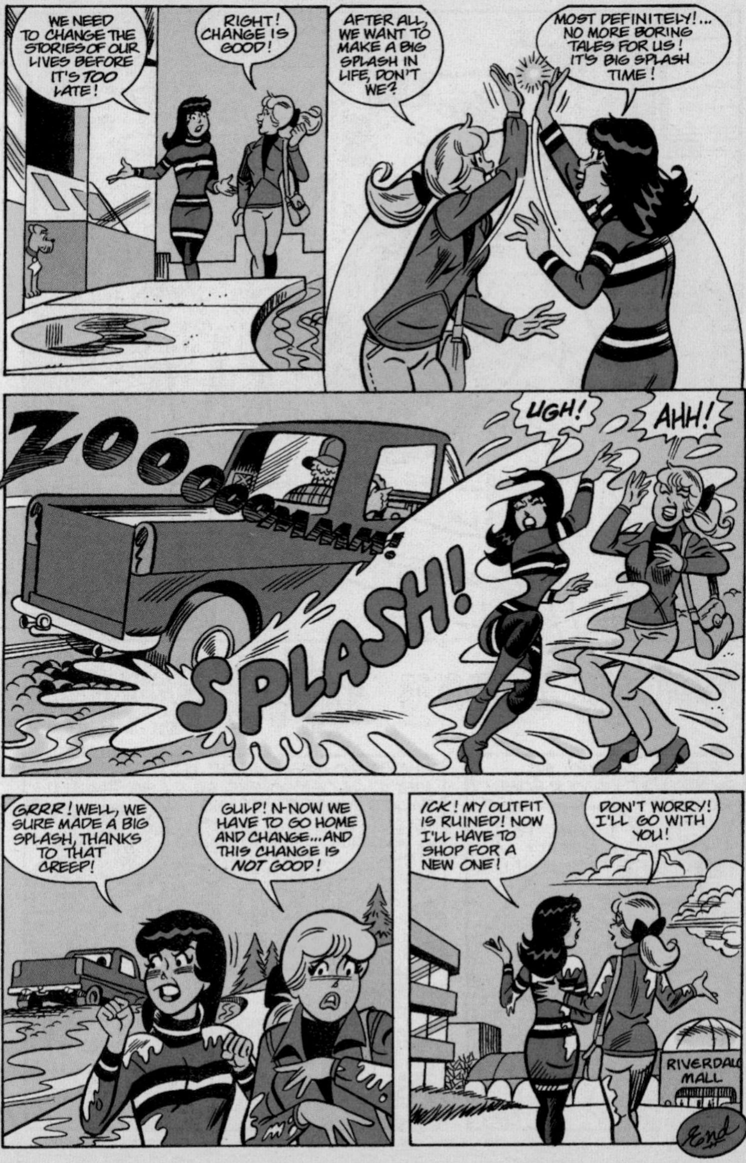
WE NEED TO CHANGE THE STORIES OF OUR LIVES BEFORE IT'S TOO LATE!
RIGHT! CHANGE IS GOOD!
AFTER ALL, WE WANT TO MAKE A BIG SPLASH IN LIFE, DON'T WE?
MOST DEFINITELY!... NO MORE BORING TALES FOR US! IT'S BIG SPLASH TIME!
ZOOOOOOMMM!
UGH!
AHH!
SPLASH!
GRRR! WELL, WE SURE MADE A BIG SPLASH, THANKS TO THAT CREEP!
GULP! N-NOW WE HAVE TO GO HOME AND CHANGE...AND THIS CHANGE IS NOT GOOD!
ICK! MY OUTFIT IS RUINED! NOW I'LL HAVE TO SHOP FOR A NEW ONE!
DON'T WORRY! I'LL GO WITH YOU!
RIVERDALE MALL
End

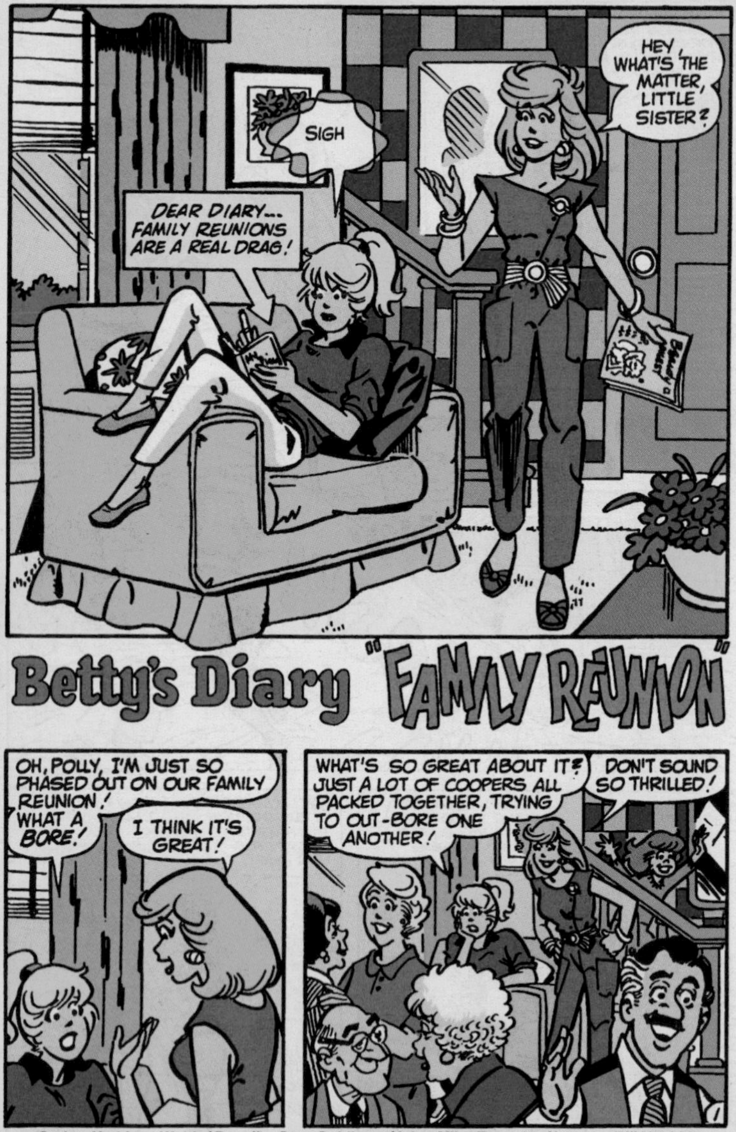
SIGH
HEY, WHAT'S THE MATTER, LITTLE SISTER?
DEAR DIARY... FAMILY REUNIONS ARE A REAL DRAG!
Betty's Diary "FAMILY REUNION"
OH, POLLY, I'M JUST SO PHASED OUT ON OUR FAMILY REUNION! WHAT A BORE!
I THINK IT'S GREAT!
WHAT'S SO GREAT ABOUT IT? JUST A LOT OF COOPERS ALL PACKED TOGETHER, TRYING TO OUT-BORE ONE ANOTHER!
DON'T SOUND SO THRILLED!
1

Script: Kathleen Webb / Pencils: Stan Goldberg / Inks: Mike Esposito / Letters: Bill Yoshida

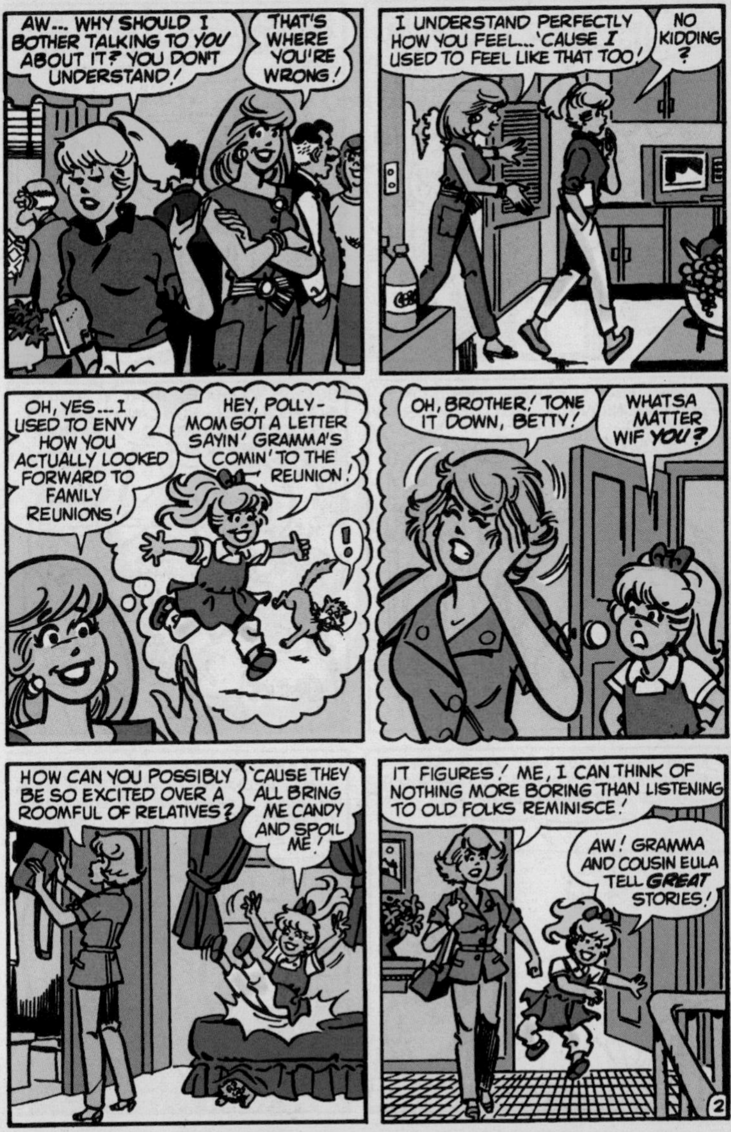
AW... WHY SHOULD I BOTHER TALKING TO YOU ABOUT IT? YOU DON'T UNDERSTAND!
THAT'S WHERE YOU'RE WRONG!
I UNDERSTAND PERFECTLY HOW YOU FEEL...'CAUSE I USED TO FEEL LIKE THAT TOO!
NO KIDDING?
OH, YES... I USED TO ENVY HOW YOU ACTUALLY LOOKED FORWARD TO FAMILY REUNIONS!
HEY, POLLY- MOM GOT A LETTER SAYIN' GRAMMA'S COMIN' TO THE REUNION!
!
OH, BROTHER! TONE IT DOWN, BETTY!
WHATSA MATTER WIF YOU?
HOW CAN YOU POSSIBLY BE SO EXCITED OVER A ROOMFUL OF RELATIVES?
'CAUSE THEY ALL BRING ME CANDY AND SPOIL ME!
IT FIGURES! ME, I CAN THINK OF NOTHING MORE BORING THAN LISTENING TO OLD FOLKS REMINISCE!
AW! GRAMMA AND COUSIN EULA TELL GREAT STORIES!
2

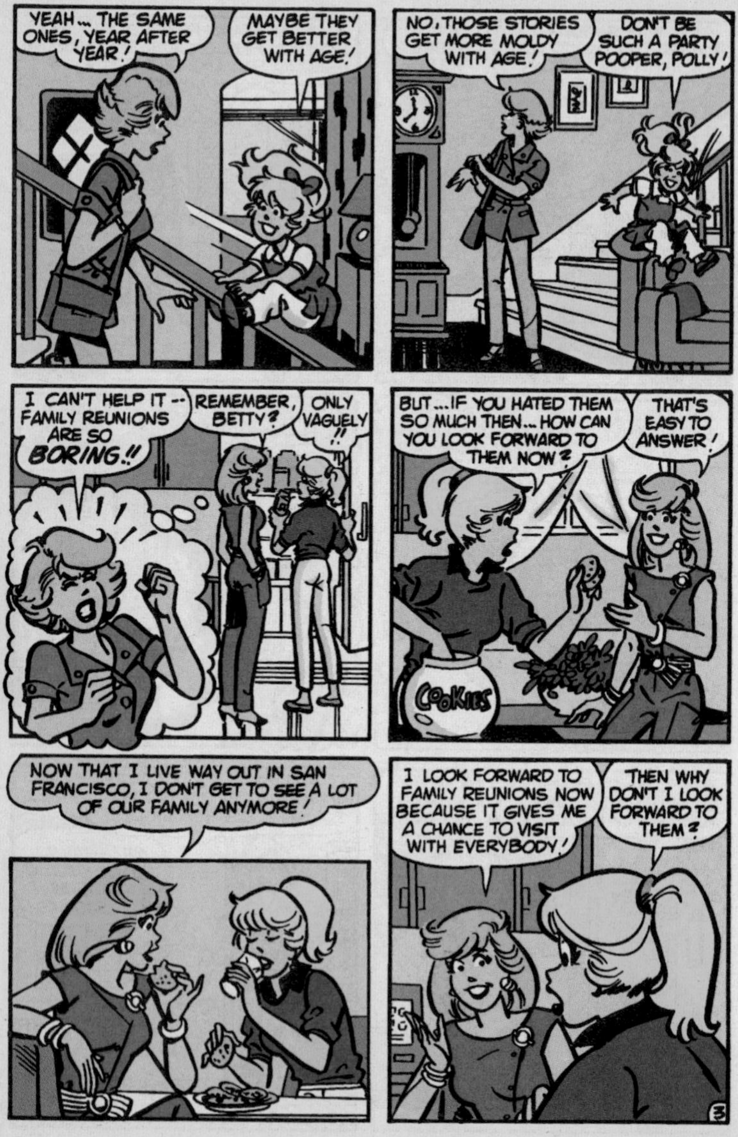

YEAH... THE SAME ONES, YEAR AFTER YEAR!
MAYBE THEY GET BETTER WITH AGE!
NO, THOSE STORIES GET MORE MOLDY WITH AGE!
DON'T BE SUCH A PARTY POOPER, POLLY!
I CAN'T HELP IT -- FAMILY REUNIONS ARE SO BORING!!
REMEMBER, BETTY?
ONLY VAGUELY!!
BUT...IF YOU HATED THEM SO MUCH THEN... HOW CAN YOU LOOK FORWARD TO THEM NOW?
THAT'S EASY TO ANSWER!
COOKIES
NOW THAT I LIVE WAY OUT IN SAN FRANCISCO, I DON'T GET TO SEE A LOT OF OUR FAMILY ANYMORE!
I LOOK FORWARD TO FAMILY REUNIONS NOW BECAUSE IT GIVES ME A CHANCE TO VISIT WITH EVERYBODY!
THEN WHY DON'T I LOOK FORWARD TO THEM?
3

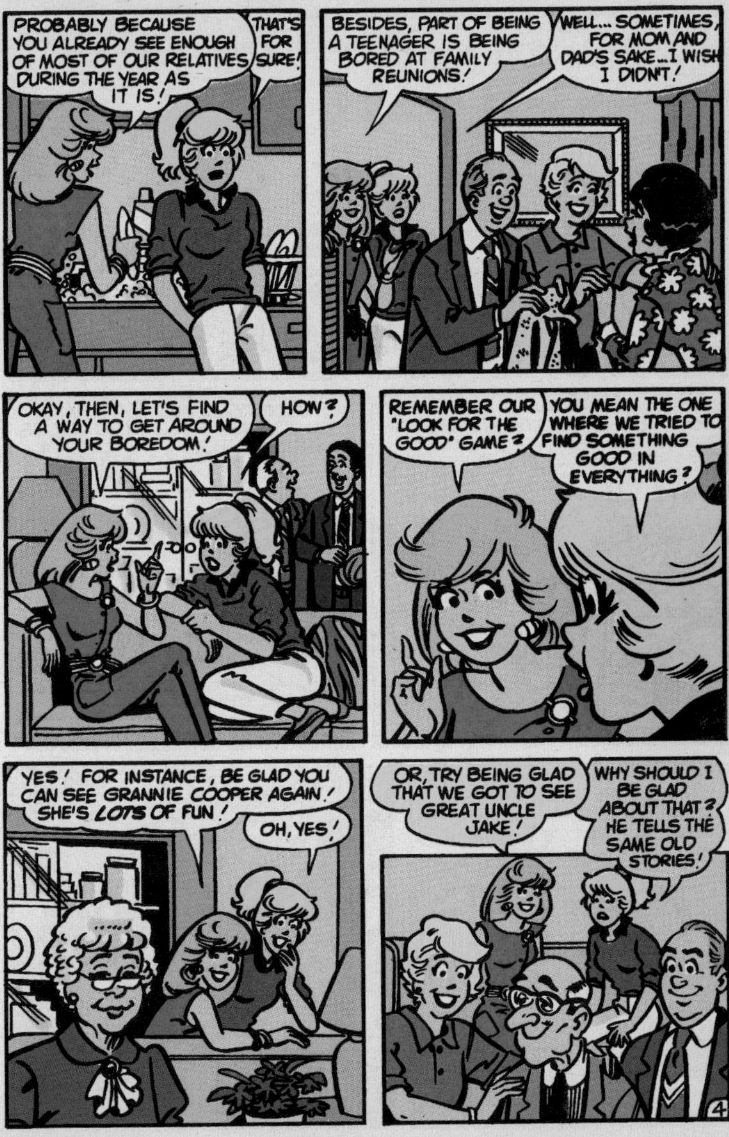
PROBABLY BECAUSE YOU ALREADY SEE ENOUGH OF MOST OF OUR RELATIVES DURING THE YEAR AS IT IS!
THAT'S FOR SURE!
BESIDES, PART OF BEING A TEENAGER IS BEING BORED AT FAMILY REUNIONS!
WELL... SOMETIMES, FOR MOM AND DAD'S SAKE...I WISH I DIDN'T!
OKAY, THEN, LET'S FIND A WAY TO GET AROUND YOUR BOREDOM!
HOW?
REMEMBER OUR "LOOK FOR THE GOOD" GAME?
YOU MEAN THE ONE WHERE WE TRIED TO FIND SOMETHING GOOD IN EVERYTHING?
YES! FOR INSTANCE, BE GLAD YOU CAN SEE GRANNIE COOPER AGAIN! SHE'S LOTS OF FUN!
OH, YES!
OR, TRY BEING GLAD THAT WE GOT TO SEE GREAT UNCLE JAKE!
WHY SHOULD I BE GLAD ABOUT THAT? HE TELLS THE SAME OLD STORIES!
4

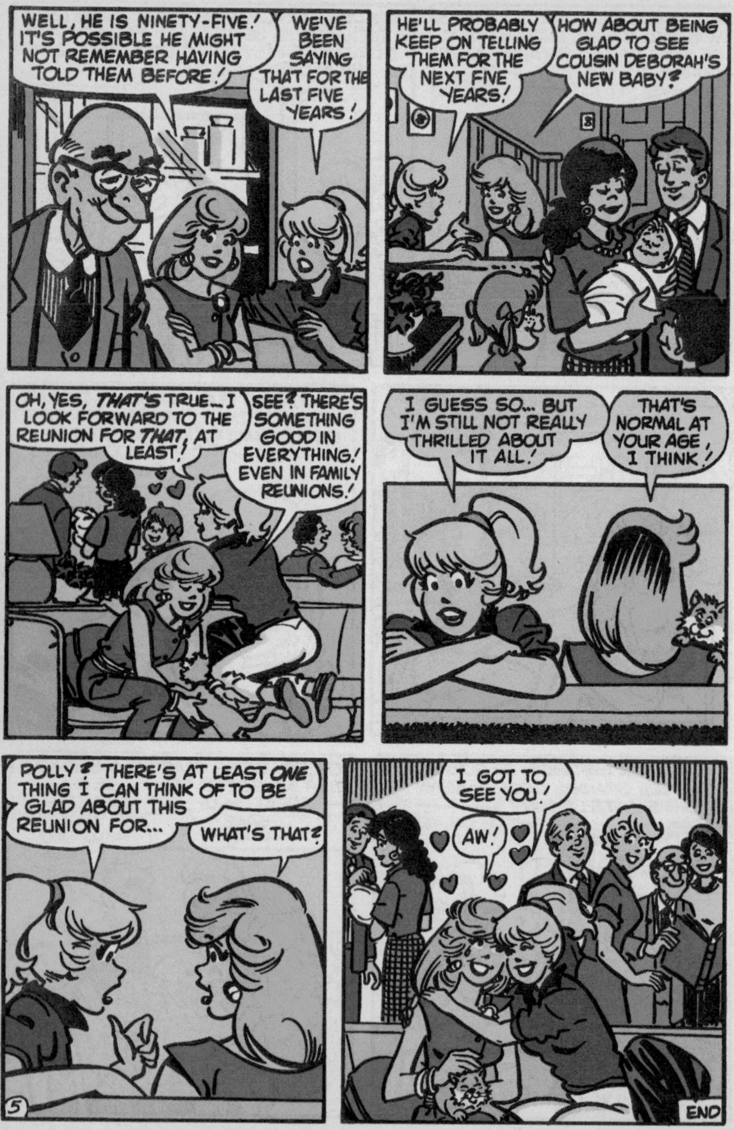
WELL, HE IS NINETY-FIVE! IT'S POSSIBLE HE MIGHT NOT REMEMBER HAVING TOLD THEM BEFORE!
WE'VE BEEN SAYING THAT FOR THE LAST FIVE YEARS!
HE'LL PROBABLY KEEP ON TELLING THEM FOR THE NEXT FIVE YEARS!
HOW ABOUT BEING GLAD TO SEE COUSIN DEBORAH'S NEW BABY?
OH, YES, THAT'S TRUE... I LOOK FORWARD TO THE REUNION FOR THAT, AT LEAST!
SEE? THERE'S SOMETHING GOOD IN EVERYTHING! EVEN IN FAMILY REUNIONS!
I GUESS SO... BUT I'M STILL NOT REALLY THRILLED ABOUT IT ALL!
THAT'S NORMAL AT YOUR AGE, I THINK!
POLLY? THERE'S AT LEAST ONE THING I CAN THINK OF TO BE GLAD ABOUT THIS REUNION FOR...
WHAT'S THAT?
5
I GOT TO SEE YOU!
AW!
END

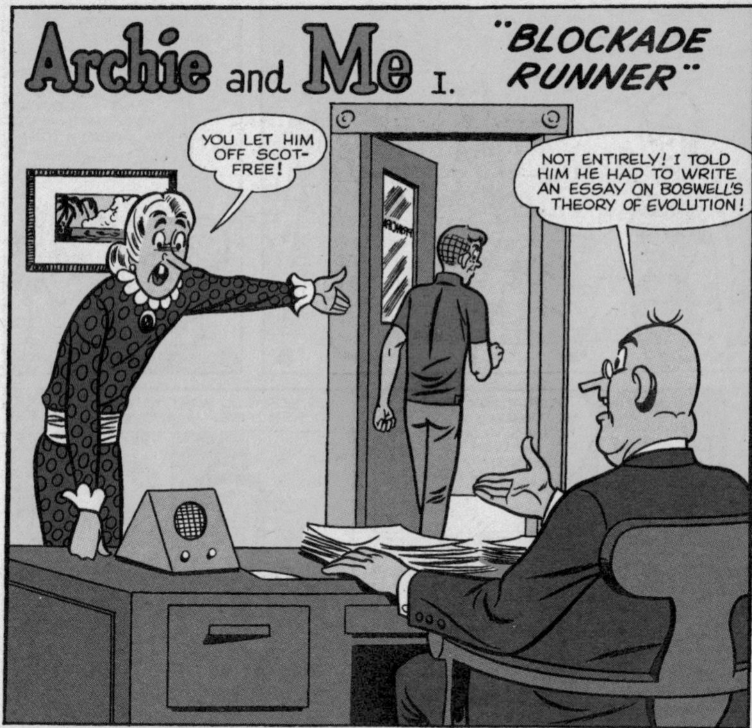
Archie and Me I.
"BLOCKADE RUNNER"
YOU LET HIM OFF SCOT-FREE!
NOT ENTIRELY! I TOLD HIM HE HAD TO WRITE AN ESSAY ON BOSWELL'S THEORY OF EVOLUTION!

Script: Frank Doyle / Pencils: Bob Bolling / Inks & Letters: Mario Acquaviva

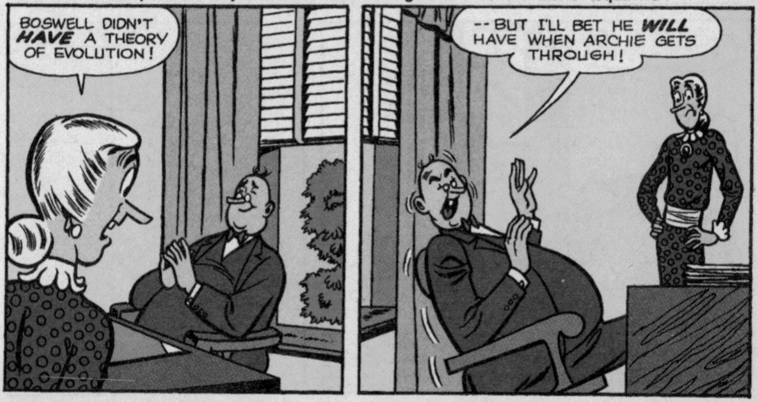
BOSWELL DIDN'T ***HAVE*** A THEORY OF EVOLUTION!
-- BUT I'LL BET HE ***WILL*** HAVE WHEN ARCHIE GETS THROUGH!

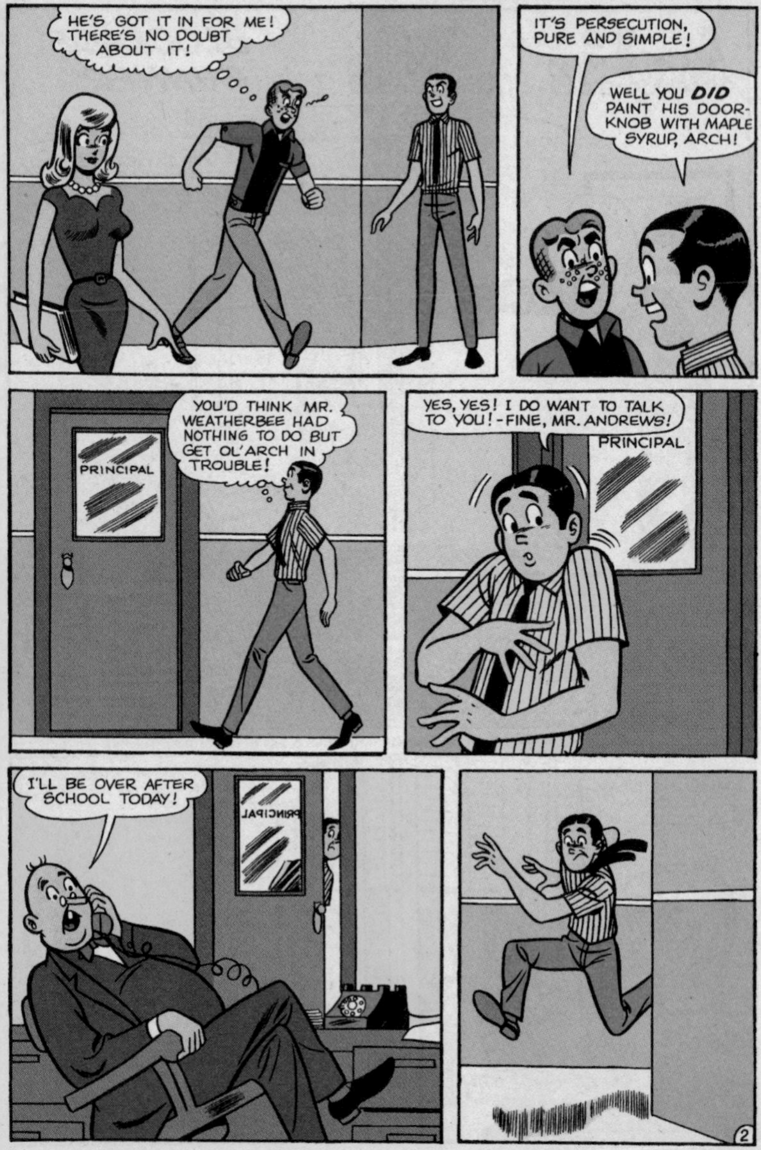
HE'S GOT IT IN FOR ME! THERE'S NO DOUBT ABOUT IT!
IT'S PERSECUTION, PURE AND SIMPLE!
WELL YOU DID PAINT HIS DOOR-KNOB WITH MAPLE SYRUP, ARCH!
YOU'D THINK MR. WEATHERBEE HAD NOTHING TO DO BUT GET OL' ARCH IN TROUBLE!
PRINCIPAL
YES, YES! I DO WANT TO TALK TO YOU! - FINE, MR. ANDREWS!
PRINCIPAL
I'LL BE OVER AFTER SCHOOL TODAY!
PRINCIPAL
2

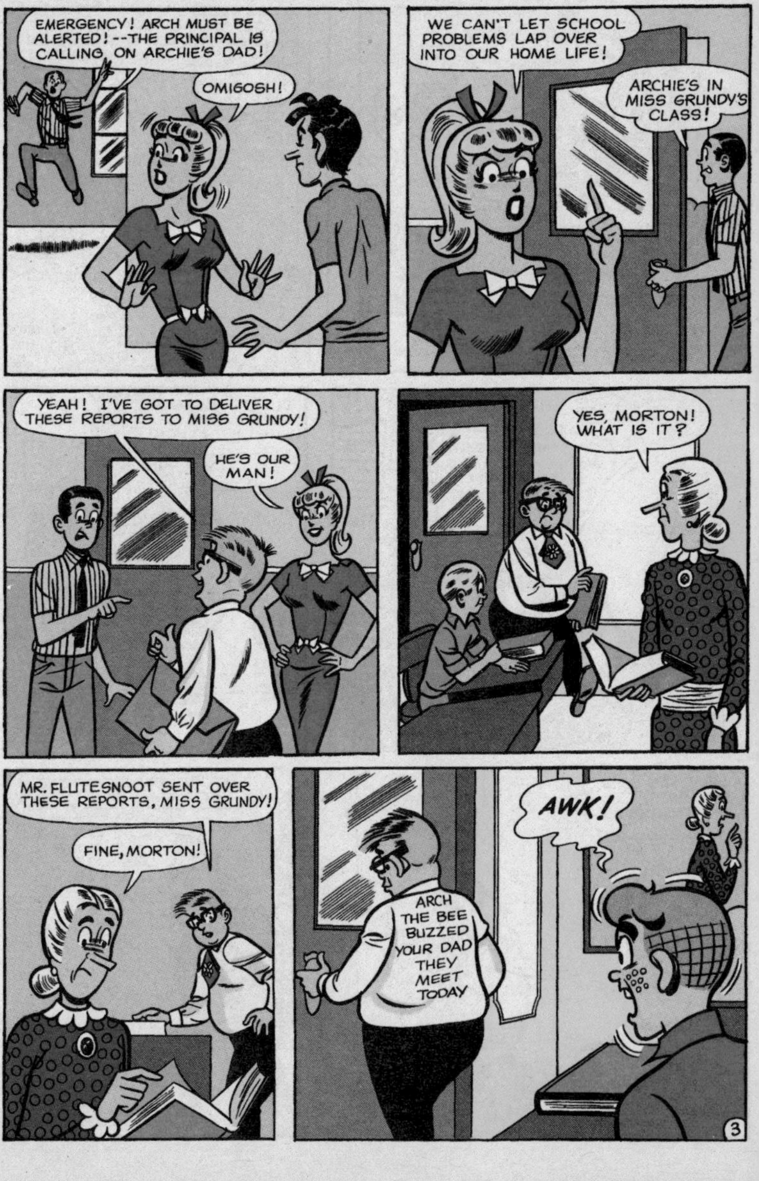
EMERGENCY! ARCH MUST BE ALERTED! --THE PRINCIPAL IS CALLING ON ARCHIE'S DAD!
OMIGOSH!
WE CAN'T LET SCHOOL PROBLEMS LAP OVER INTO OUR HOME LIFE!
ARCHIE'S IN MISS GRUNDY'S CLASS!
YEAH! I'VE GOT TO DELIVER THESE REPORTS TO MISS GRUNDY!
HE'S OUR MAN!
YES, MORTON! WHAT IS IT?
MR. FLUTESNOOT SENT OVER THESE REPORTS, MISS GRUNDY!
FINE, MORTON!
AWK!
ARCH THE BEE BUZZED YOUR DAD THEY MEET TODAY
3

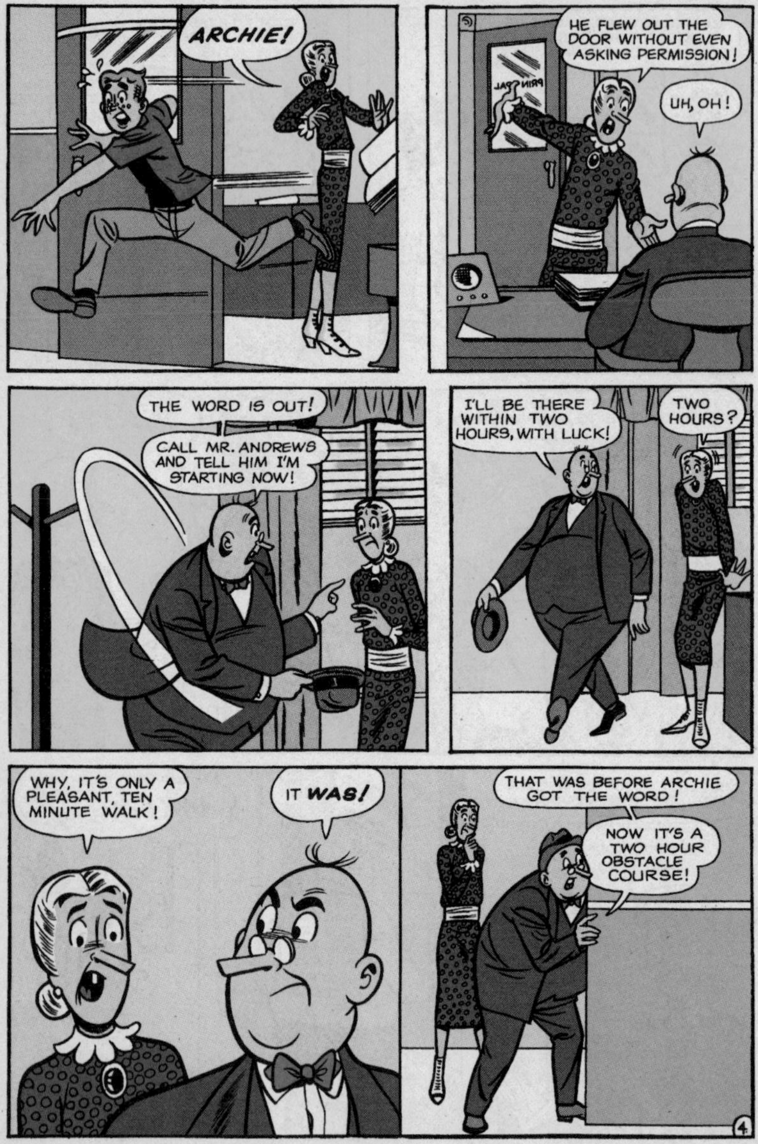
ARCHIE!
HE FLEW OUT THE DOOR WITHOUT EVEN ASKING PERMISSION!
UH, OH!
THE WORD IS OUT!
CALL MR. ANDREWS AND TELL HIM I'M STARTING NOW!
I'LL BE THERE WITHIN TWO HOURS, WITH LUCK!
TWO HOURS?
WHY, IT'S ONLY A PLEASANT, TEN MINUTE WALK!
IT WAS!
THAT WAS BEFORE ARCHIE GOT THE WORD!
NOW IT'S A TWO HOUR OBSTACLE COURSE!
4

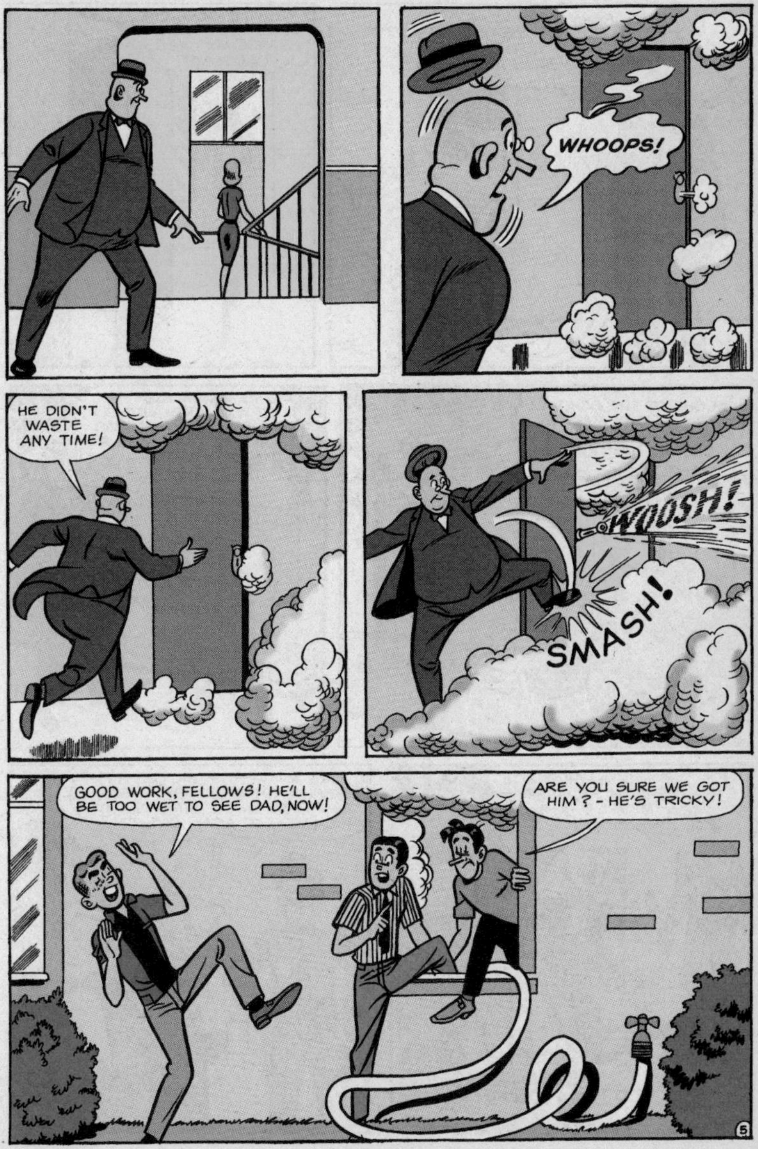
WHOOPS!
HE DIDN'T WASTE ANY TIME!
WOOSH!
SMASH!
GOOD WORK, FELLOWS! HE'LL BE TOO WET TO SEE DAD, NOW!
ARE YOU SURE WE GOT HIM? - HE'S TRICKY!
5

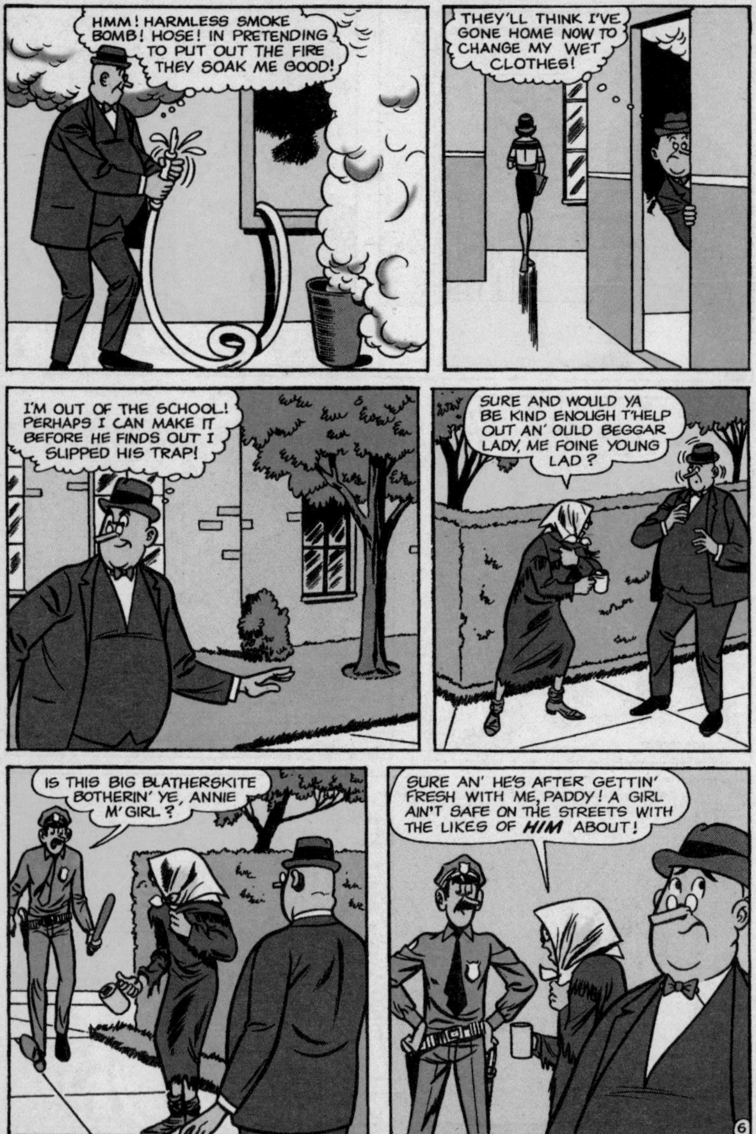
HMM! HARMLESS SMOKE BOMB! HOSE! IN PRETENDING TO PUT OUT THE FIRE THEY SOAK ME GOOD!
THEY'LL THINK I'VE GONE HOME NOW TO CHANGE MY WET CLOTHES!
I'M OUT OF THE SCHOOL! PERHAPS I CAN MAKE IT BEFORE HE FINDS OUT I SLIPPED HIS TRAP!
SURE AND WOULD YA BE KIND ENOUGH T'HELP OUT AN' OULD BEGGAR LADY, ME FOINE YOUNG LAD?
IS THIS BIG BLATHERSKITE BOTHERIN' YE, ANNIE M'GIRL?
SURE AN' HE'S AFTER GETTIN' FRESH WITH ME, PADDY! A GIRL AIN'T SAFE ON THE STREETS WITH THE LIKES OF HIM ABOUT!
6

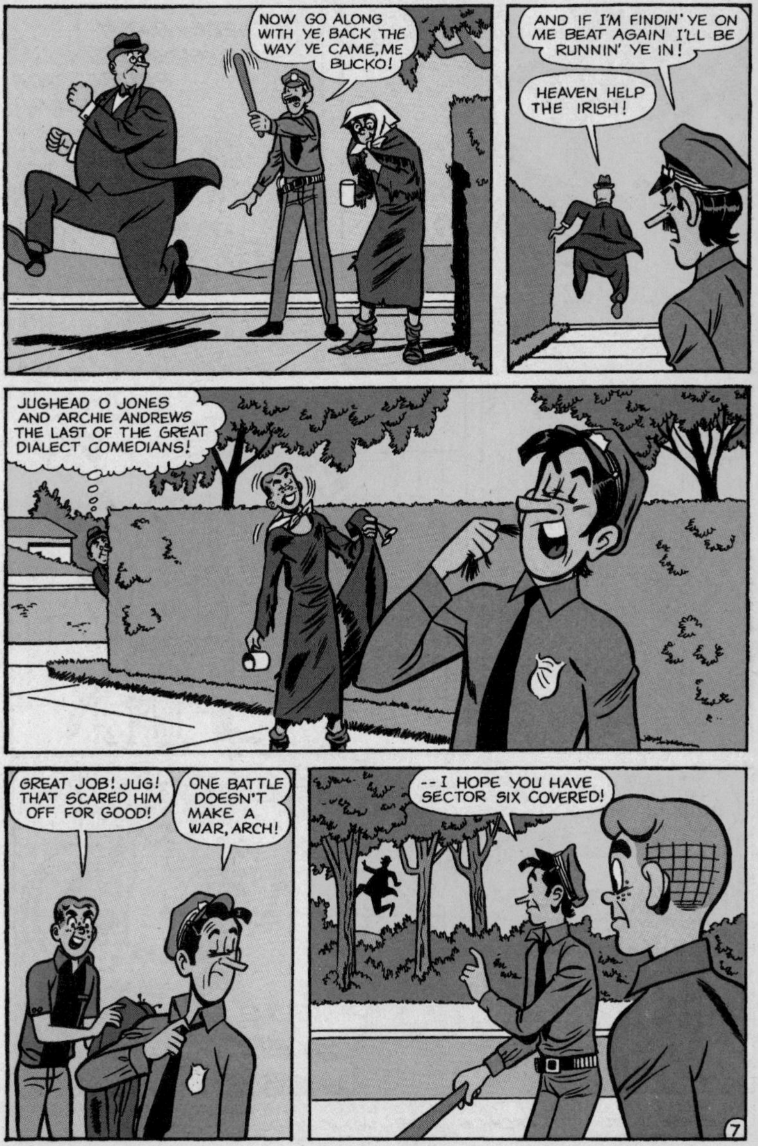
NOW GO ALONG WITH YE, BACK THE WAY YE CAME, ME BUCKO!
AND IF I'M FINDIN' YE ON ME BEAT AGAIN I'LL BE RUNNIN' YE IN!
HEAVEN HELP THE IRISH!
JUGHEAD O JONES AND ARCHIE ANDREWS THE LAST OF THE GREAT DIALECT COMEDIANS!
GREAT JOB! JUG! THAT SCARED HIM OFF FOR GOOD!
ONE BATTLE DOESN'T MAKE A WAR, ARCH!
-- I HOPE YOU HAVE SECTOR SIX COVERED!

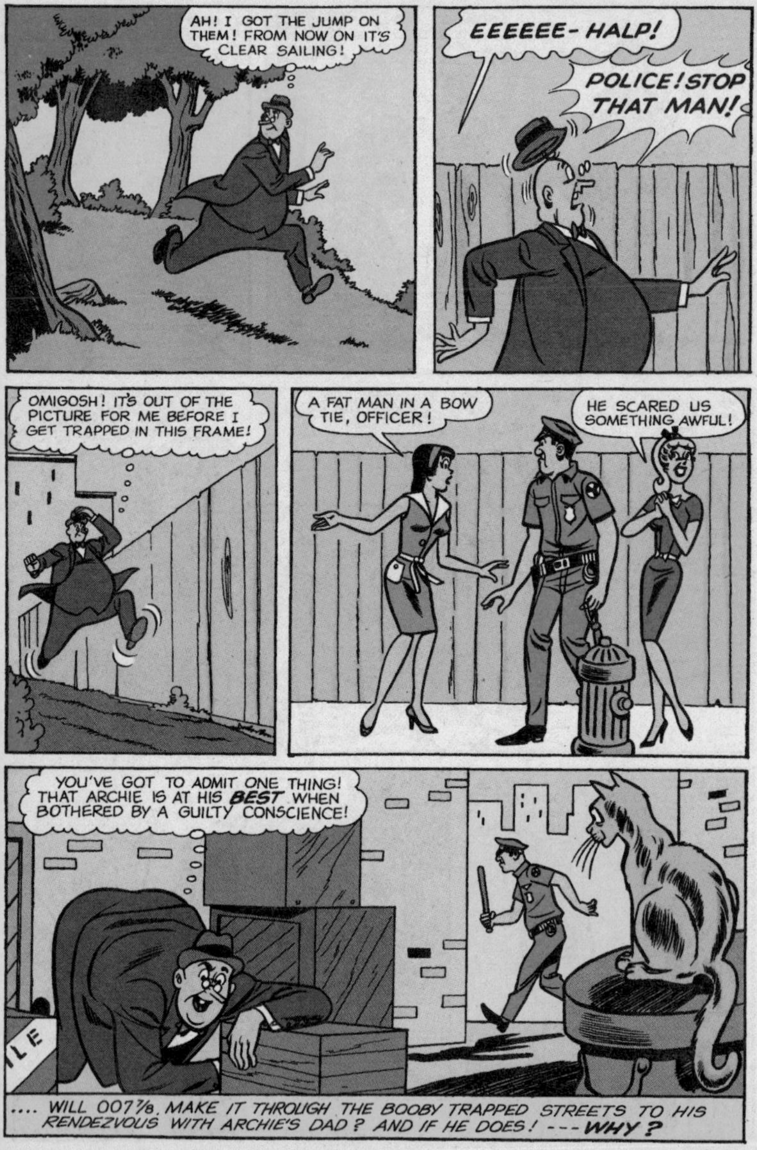
AH! I GOT THE JUMP ON THEM! FROM NOW ON IT'S CLEAR SAILING!
EEEEEE- HALP!
POLICE! STOP THAT MAN!
OMIGOSH! IT'S OUT OF THE PICTURE FOR ME BEFORE I GET TRAPPED IN THIS FRAME!
A FAT MAN IN A BOW TIE, OFFICER!
HE SCARED US SOMETHING AWFUL!
YOU'VE GOT TO ADMIT ONE THING! THAT ARCHIE IS AT HIS BEST WHEN BOTHERED BY A GUILTY CONSCIENCE!
.... WILL 007⅞, MAKE IT THROUGH THE BOOBY TRAPPED STREETS TO HIS RENDEZVOUS WITH ARCHIE'S DAD? AND IF HE DOES! ---WHY?

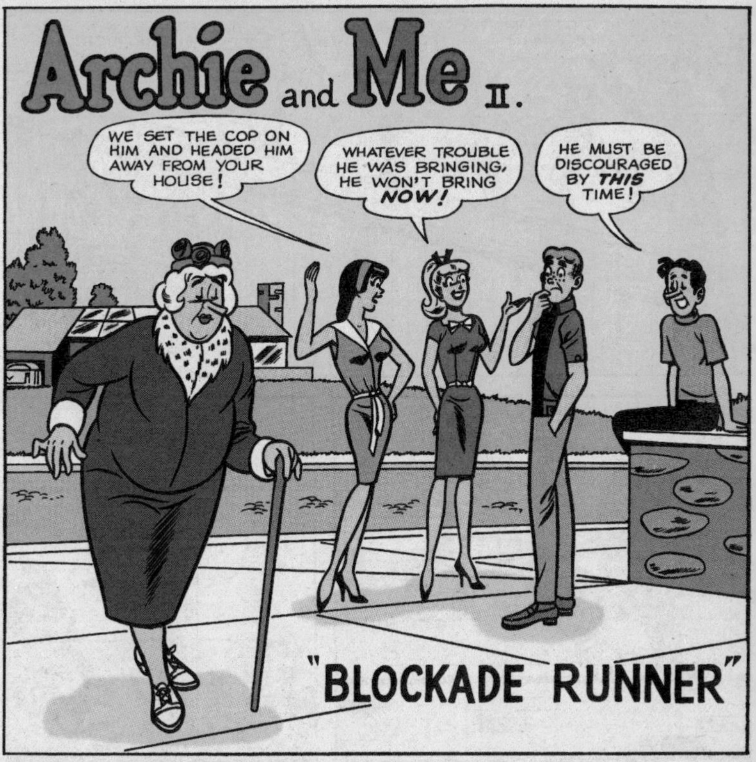
Archie and Me II.
WE SET THE COP ON HIM AND HEADED HIM AWAY FROM YOUR HOUSE!
WHATEVER TROUBLE HE WAS BRINGING, HE WON'T BRING NOW!
HE MUST BE DISCOURAGED BY THIS TIME!
"BLOCKADE RUNNER"

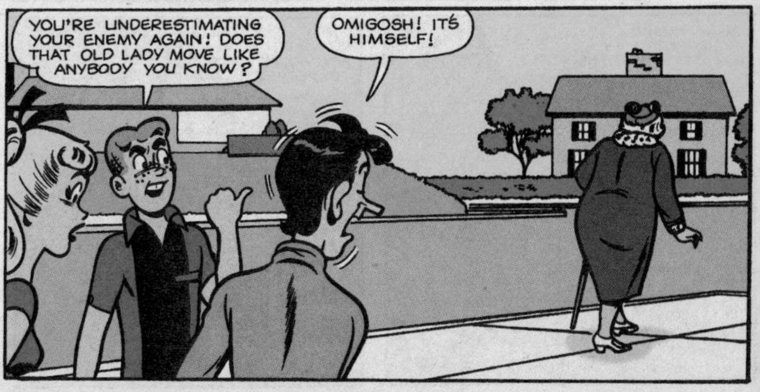
YOU'RE UNDERESTIMATING YOUR ENEMY AGAIN! DOES THAT OLD LADY MOVE LIKE ANYBODY YOU KNOW?
OMIGOSH! IT'S HIMSELF!

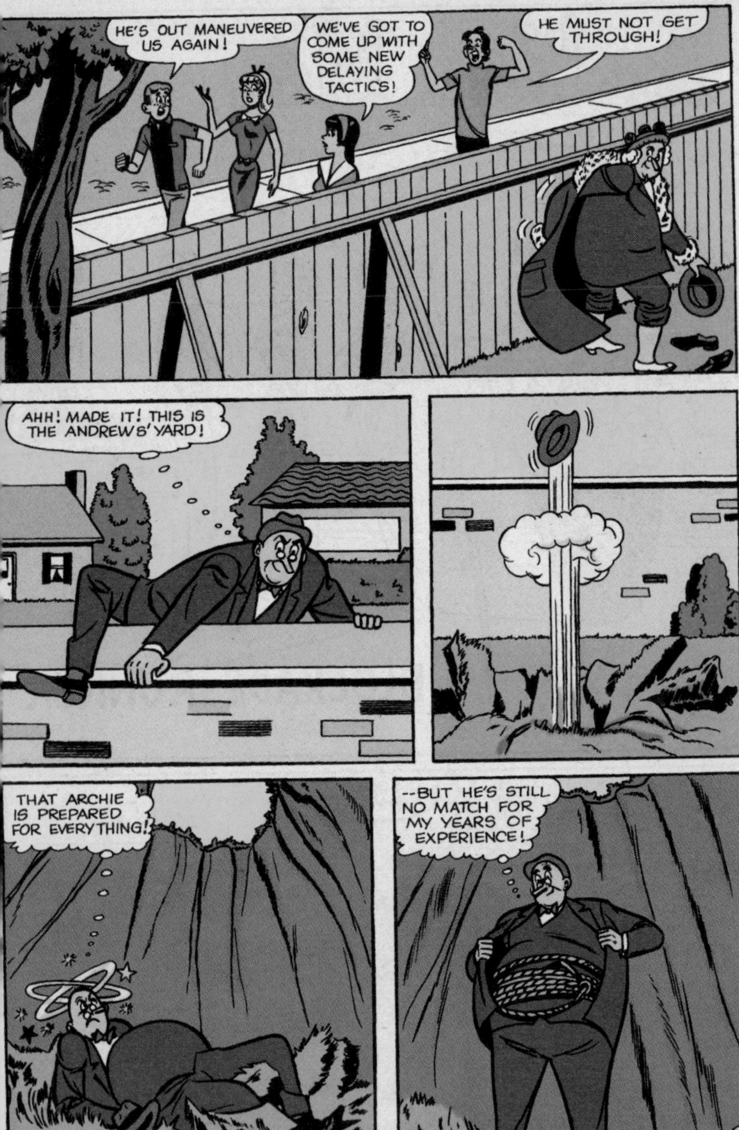
HE'S OUT MANEUVERED US AGAIN!
WE'VE GOT TO COME UP WITH SOME NEW DELAYING TACTICS!
HE MUST NOT GET THROUGH!
AHH! MADE IT! THIS IS THE ANDREWS' YARD!
THAT ARCHIE IS PREPARED FOR EVERYTHING!
--BUT HE'S STILL NO MATCH FOR MY YEARS OF EXPERIENCE!
2

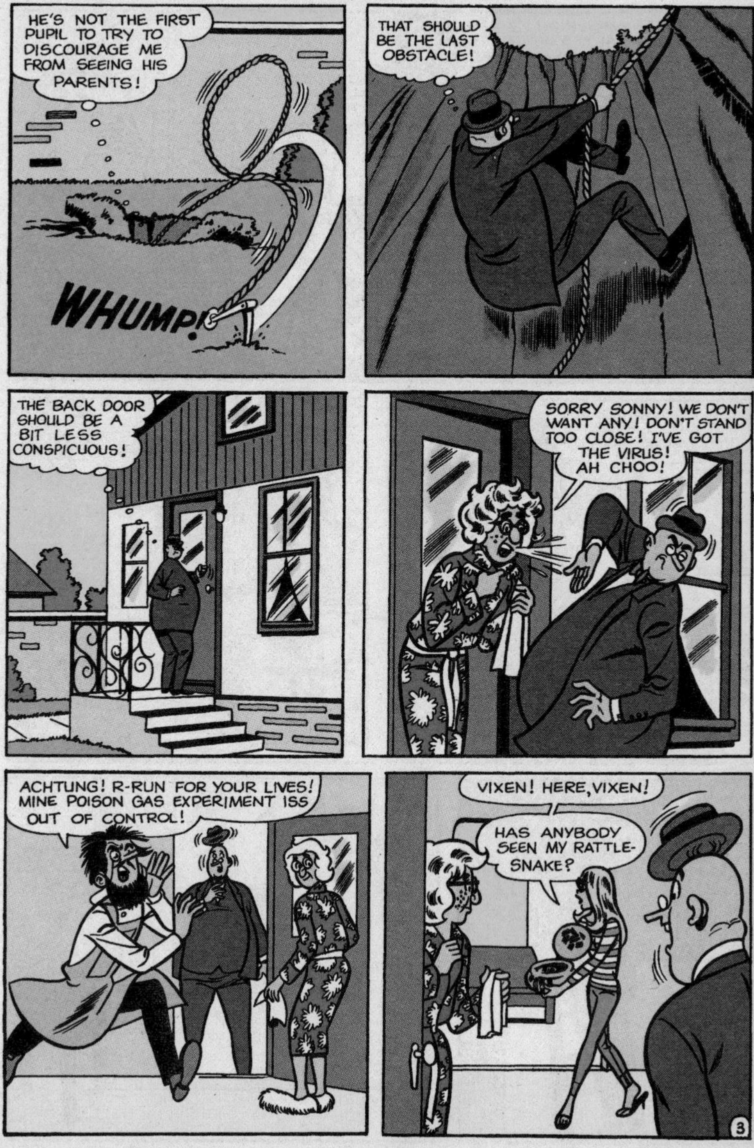
HE'S NOT THE FIRST PUPIL TO TRY TO DISCOURAGE ME FROM SEEING HIS PARENTS!
WHUMP!
THAT SHOULD BE THE LAST OBSTACLE!
THE BACK DOOR SHOULD BE A BIT LESS CONSPICUOUS!
SORRY SONNY! WE DON'T WANT ANY! DON'T STAND TOO CLOSE! I'VE GOT THE VIRUS! AH CHOO!
ACHTUNG! R-RUN FOR YOUR LIVES! MINE POISON GAS EXPERIMENT ISS OUT OF CONTROL!
VIXEN! HERE, VIXEN!
HAS ANYBODY SEEN MY RATTLE-SNAKE?
3

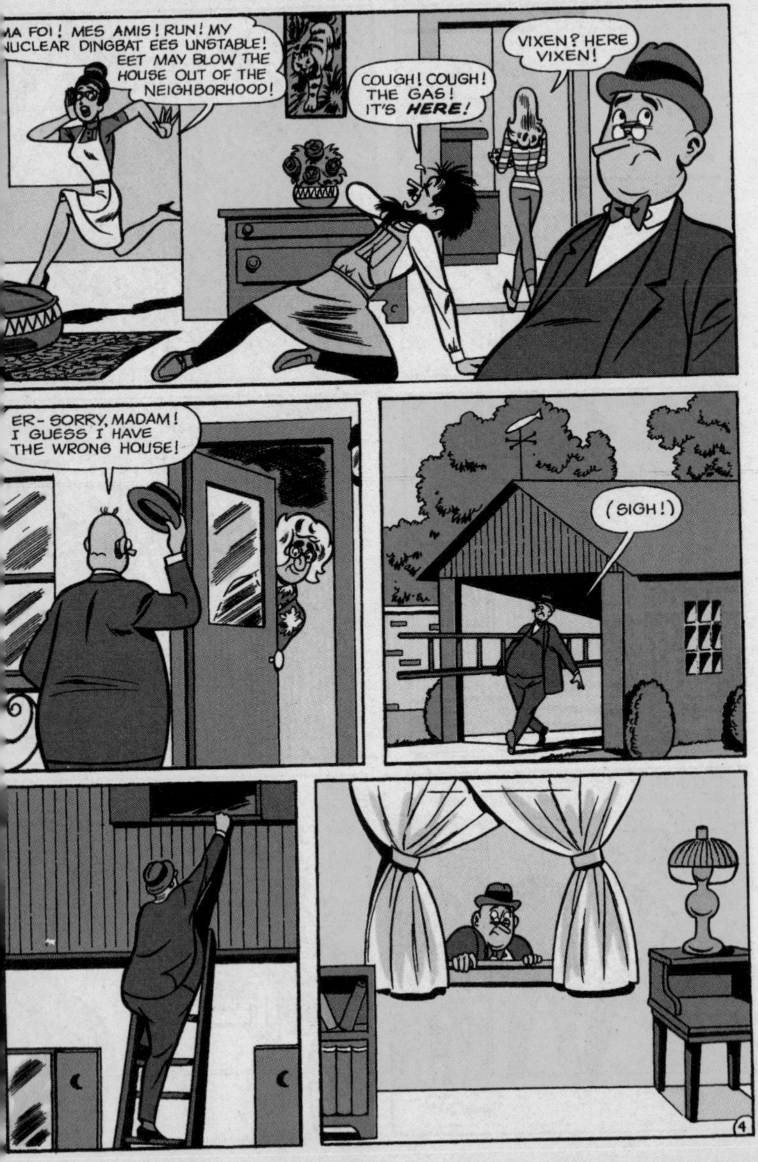
MA FOI! MES AMIS! RUN! MY NUCLEAR DINGBAT EES UNSTABLE! EET MAY BLOW THE HOUSE OUT OF THE NEIGHBORHOOD!
COUGH! COUGH! THE GAS! IT'S HERE!
VIXEN? HERE VIXEN!
ER- SORRY, MADAM! I GUESS I HAVE THE WRONG HOUSE!
(SIGH!)
4

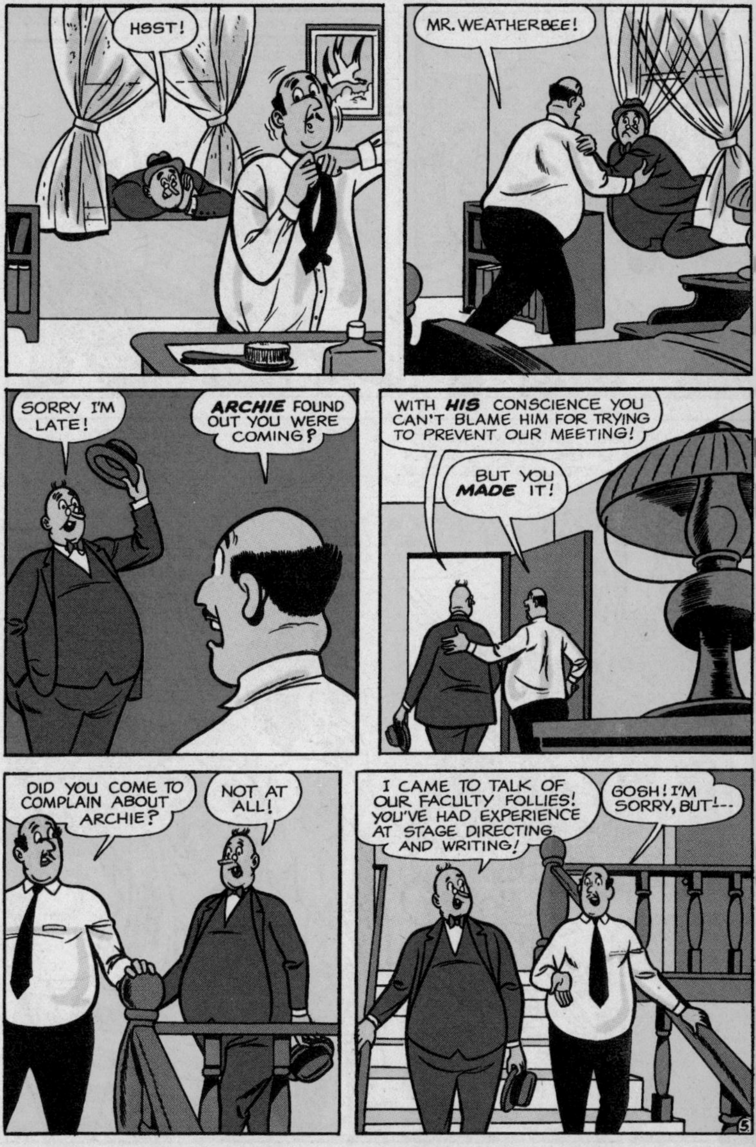
HSST!
MR. WEATHERBEE!
SORRY I'M LATE!
ARCHIE FOUND OUT YOU WERE COMING?
WITH HIS CONSCIENCE YOU CAN'T BLAME HIM FOR TRYING TO PREVENT OUR MEETING!
BUT YOU MADE IT!
DID YOU COME TO COMPLAIN ABOUT ARCHIE?
NOT AT ALL!
I CAME TO TALK OF OUR FACULTY FOLLIES! YOU'VE HAD EXPERIENCE AT STAGE DIRECTING AND WRITING!
GOSH! I'M SORRY, BUT!--
5

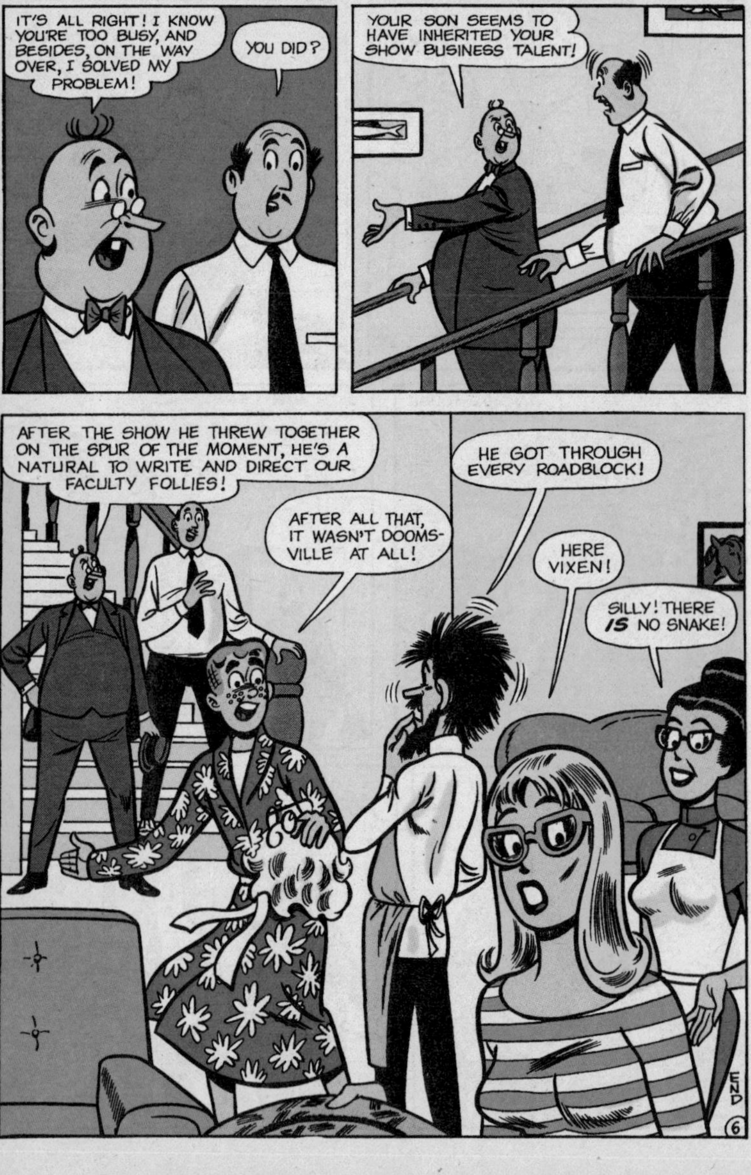
IT'S ALL RIGHT! I KNOW YOU'RE TOO BUSY, AND BESIDES, ON THE WAY OVER, I SOLVED MY PROBLEM!
YOU DID?
YOUR SON SEEMS TO HAVE INHERITED YOUR SHOW BUSINESS TALENT!
AFTER THE SHOW HE THREW TOGETHER ON THE SPUR OF THE MOMENT, HE'S A NATURAL TO WRITE AND DIRECT OUR FACULTY FOLLIES!
AFTER ALL THAT, IT WASN'T DOOMS-VILLE AT ALL!
HE GOT THROUGH EVERY ROADBLOCK!
HERE VIXEN!
SILLY! THERE *IS* NO SNAKE!
END
6

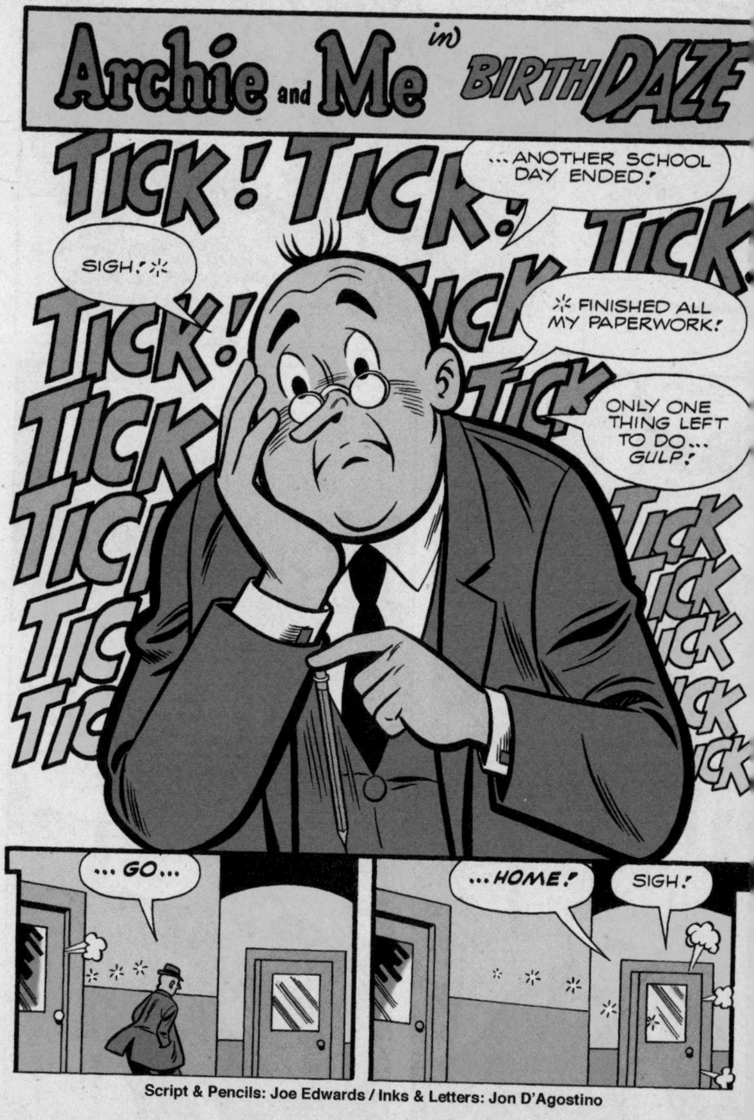
Archie and Me in BIRTH DAZE
TICK! TICK!
...ANOTHER SCHOOL DAY ENDED!
TICK
SIGH! ✳
TICK!
TICK
✳ FINISHED ALL MY PAPERWORK!
TICK
TICK
ONLY ONE THING LEFT TO DO... GULP!
... GO...
...HOME!
SIGH!

Script & Pencils: Joe Edwards / Inks & Letters: Jon D'Agostino

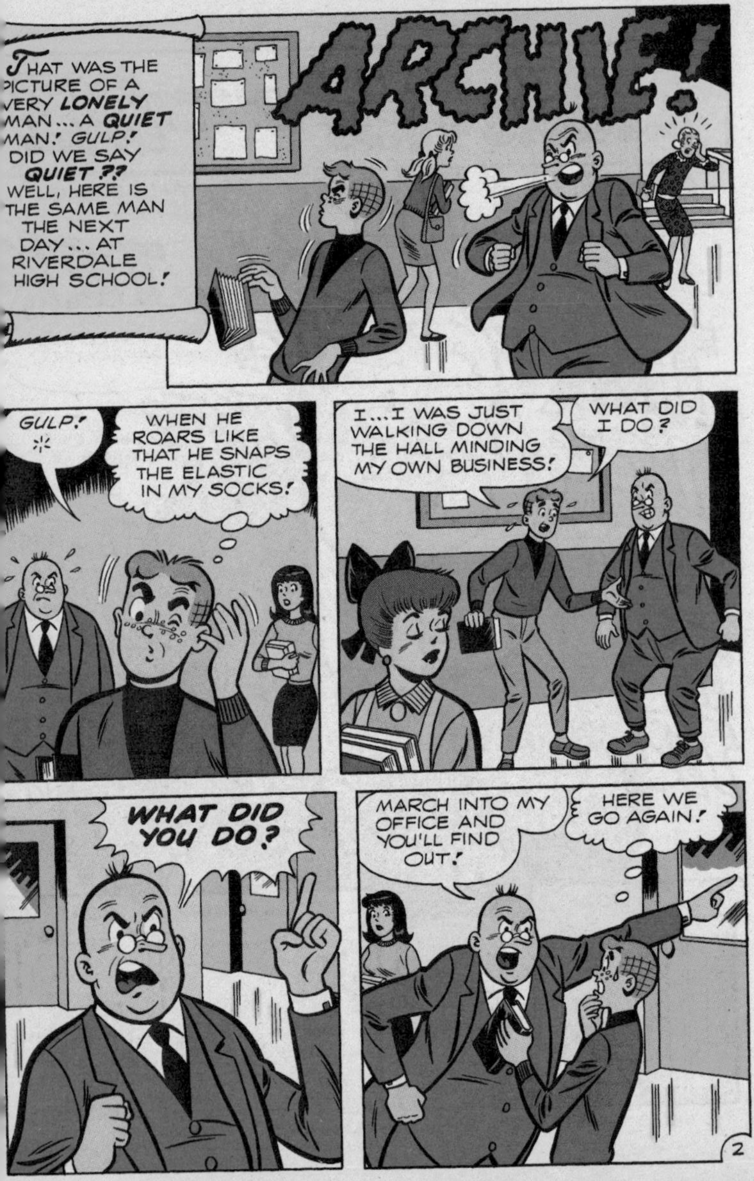

THAT WAS THE PICTURE OF A VERY LONELY MAN... A QUIET MAN! GULP! DID WE SAY QUIET ?? WELL, HERE IS THE SAME MAN THE NEXT DAY... AT RIVERDALE HIGH SCHOOL!
ARCHIE!
GULP!
WHEN HE ROARS LIKE THAT HE SNAPS THE ELASTIC IN MY SOCKS!
I...I WAS JUST WALKING DOWN THE HALL MINDING MY OWN BUSINESS!
WHAT DID I DO?
WHAT DID YOU DO?
MARCH INTO MY OFFICE AND YOU'LL FIND OUT!
HERE WE GO AGAIN!

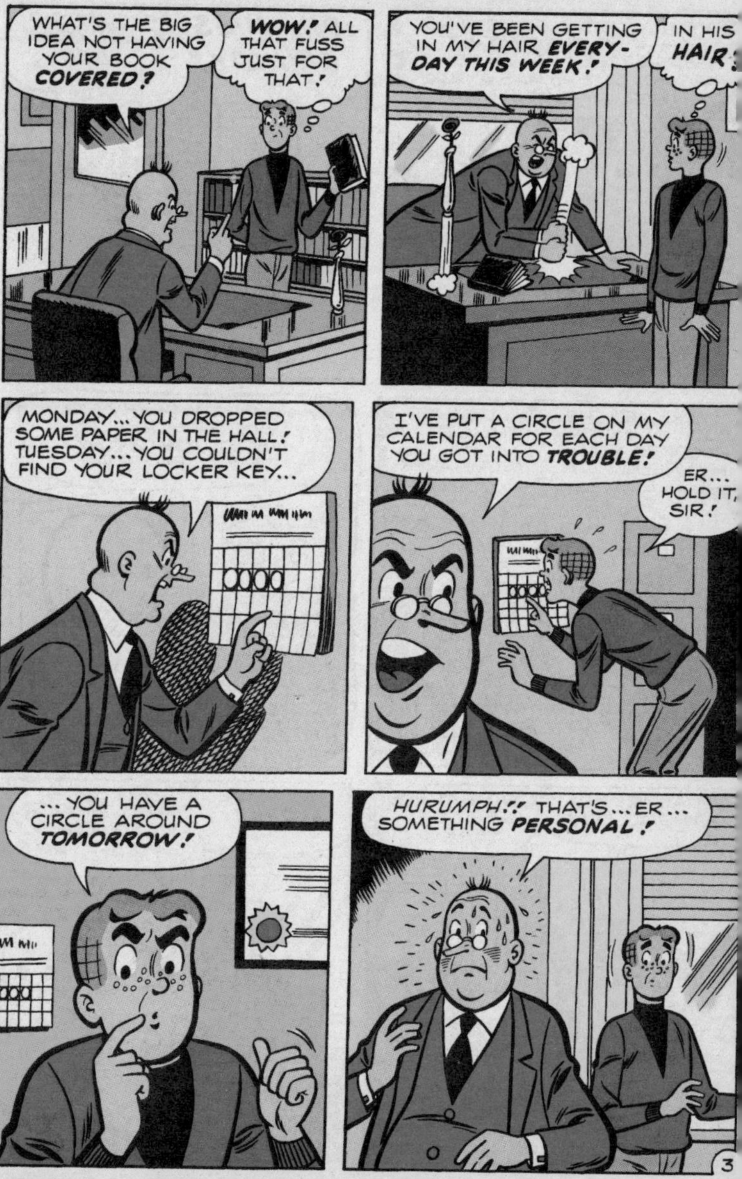
WHAT'S THE BIG IDEA NOT HAVING YOUR BOOK COVERED?
WOW! ALL THAT FUSS JUST FOR THAT!
YOU'VE BEEN GETTING IN MY HAIR EVERY-DAY THIS WEEK!
IN HIS HAIR
MONDAY... YOU DROPPED SOME PAPER IN THE HALL! TUESDAY... YOU COULDN'T FIND YOUR LOCKER KEY...
I'VE PUT A CIRCLE ON MY CALENDAR FOR EACH DAY YOU GOT INTO TROUBLE!
ER... HOLD IT, SIR!
... YOU HAVE A CIRCLE AROUND TOMORROW!
HURUMPH!! THAT'S... ER... SOMETHING PERSONAL!

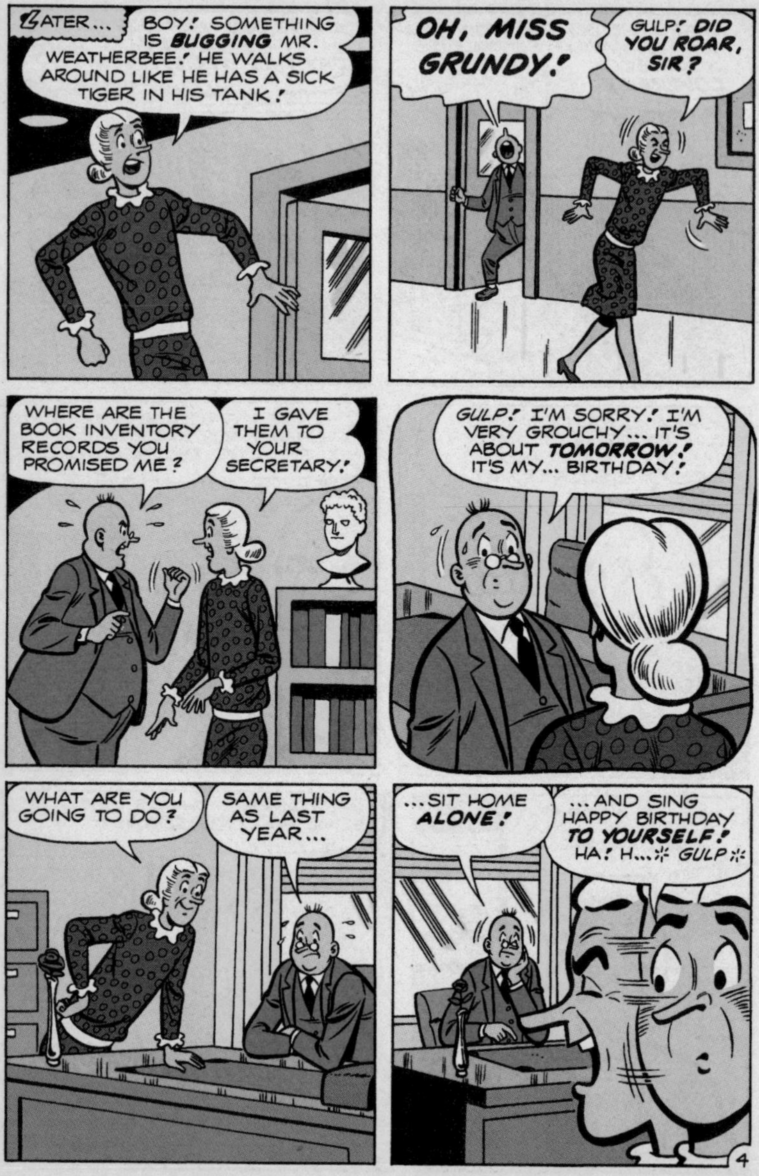
LATER...
BOY! SOMETHING IS BUGGING MR. WEATHERBEE! HE WALKS AROUND LIKE HE HAS A SICK TIGER IN HIS TANK!
OH, MISS GRUNDY!
GULP! DID YOU ROAR, SIR?
WHERE ARE THE BOOK INVENTORY RECORDS YOU PROMISED ME?
I GAVE THEM TO YOUR SECRETARY!
GULP! I'M SORRY! I'M VERY GROUCHY... IT'S ABOUT TOMORROW! IT'S MY... BIRTHDAY!
WHAT ARE YOU GOING TO DO?
SAME THING AS LAST YEAR...
...SIT HOME ALONE!
...AND SING HAPPY BIRTHDAY TO YOURSELF! HA! H... GULP
4

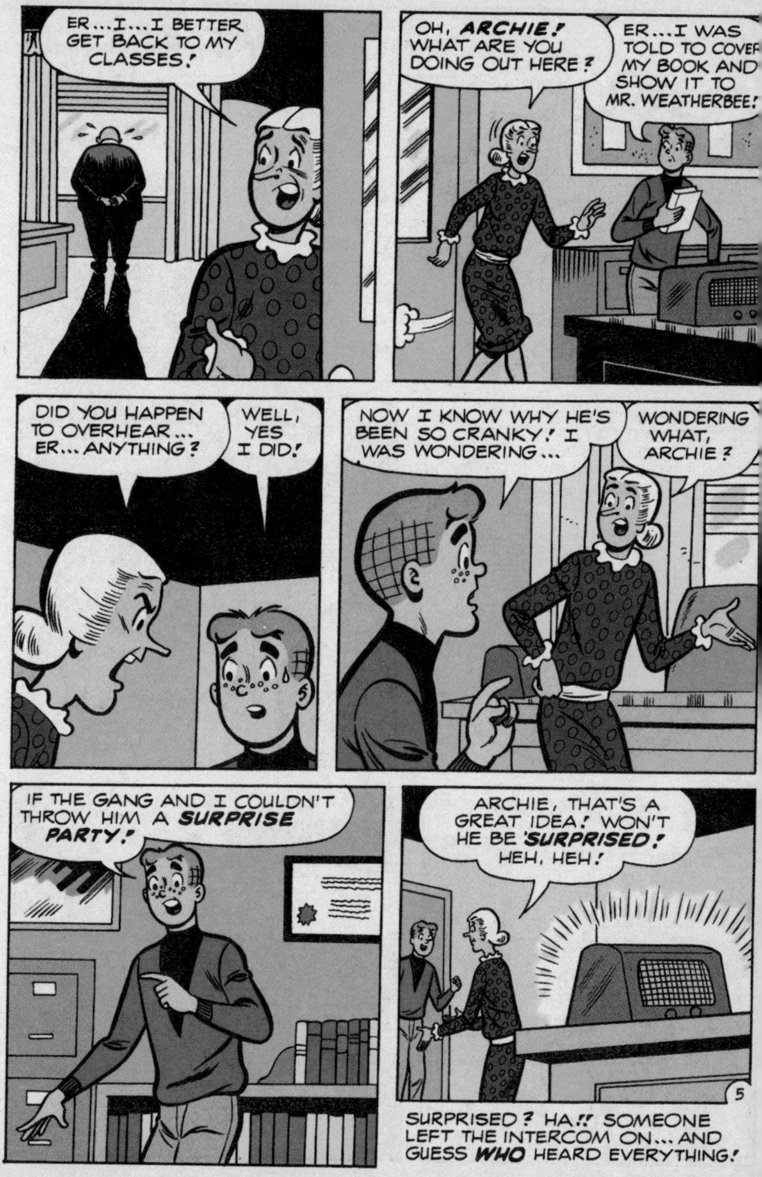
ER...I...I BETTER GET BACK TO MY CLASSES!
OH, ARCHIE! WHAT ARE YOU DOING OUT HERE?
ER...I WAS TOLD TO COVER MY BOOK AND SHOW IT TO MR. WEATHERBEE!
DID YOU HAPPEN TO OVERHEAR... ER... ANYTHING?
WELL, YES I DID!
NOW I KNOW WHY HE'S BEEN SO CRANKY! I WAS WONDERING...
WONDERING WHAT, ARCHIE?
IF THE GANG AND I COULDN'T THROW HIM A SURPRISE PARTY!
ARCHIE, THAT'S A GREAT IDEA! WON'T HE BE 'SURPRISED'! HEH, HEH!
5
SURPRISED? HA!! SOMEONE LEFT THE INTERCOM ON... AND GUESS WHO HEARD EVERYTHING!

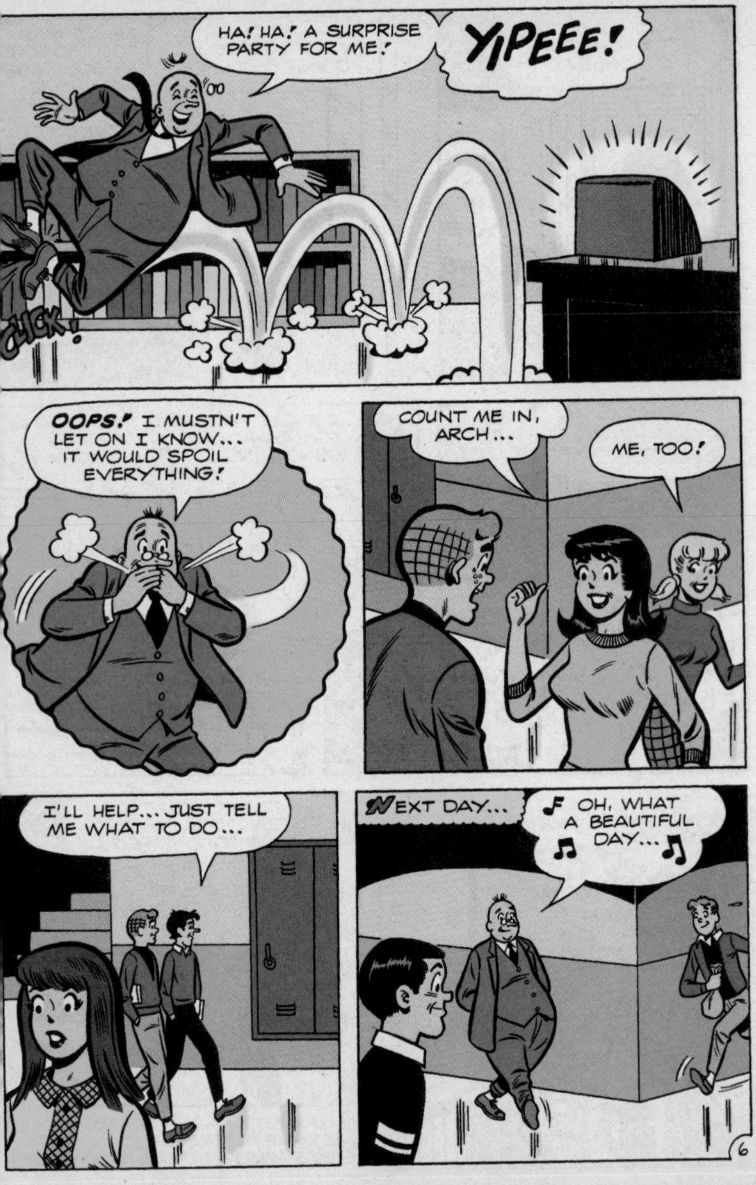

HA! HA! A SURPRISE PARTY FOR ME!
YIPEEE!
CLICK!
OOPS! I MUSTN'T LET ON I KNOW... IT WOULD SPOIL EVERYTHING!
COUNT ME IN, ARCH...
ME, TOO!
I'LL HELP... JUST TELL ME WHAT TO DO...
NEXT DAY...
OH, WHAT A BEAUTIFUL DAY...

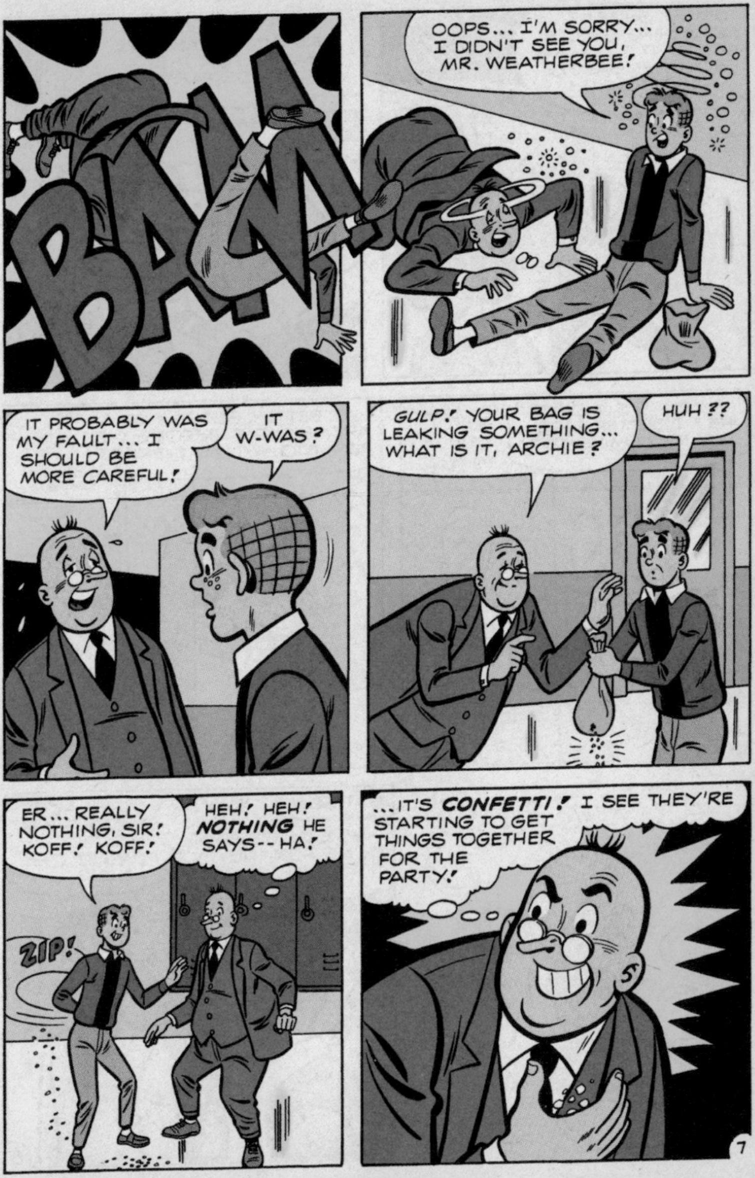
BAM
OOPS... I'M SORRY... I DIDN'T SEE YOU, MR. WEATHERBEE!
IT PROBABLY WAS MY FAULT... I SHOULD BE MORE CAREFUL!
IT W-WAS?
GULP! YOUR BAG IS LEAKING SOMETHING... WHAT IS IT, ARCHIE?
HUH??
ER... REALLY NOTHING, SIR! KOFF! KOFF!
HEH! HEH! NOTHING HE SAYS-- HA!
ZIP!
...IT'S CONFETTI! I SEE THEY'RE STARTING TO GET THINGS TOGETHER FOR THE PARTY!

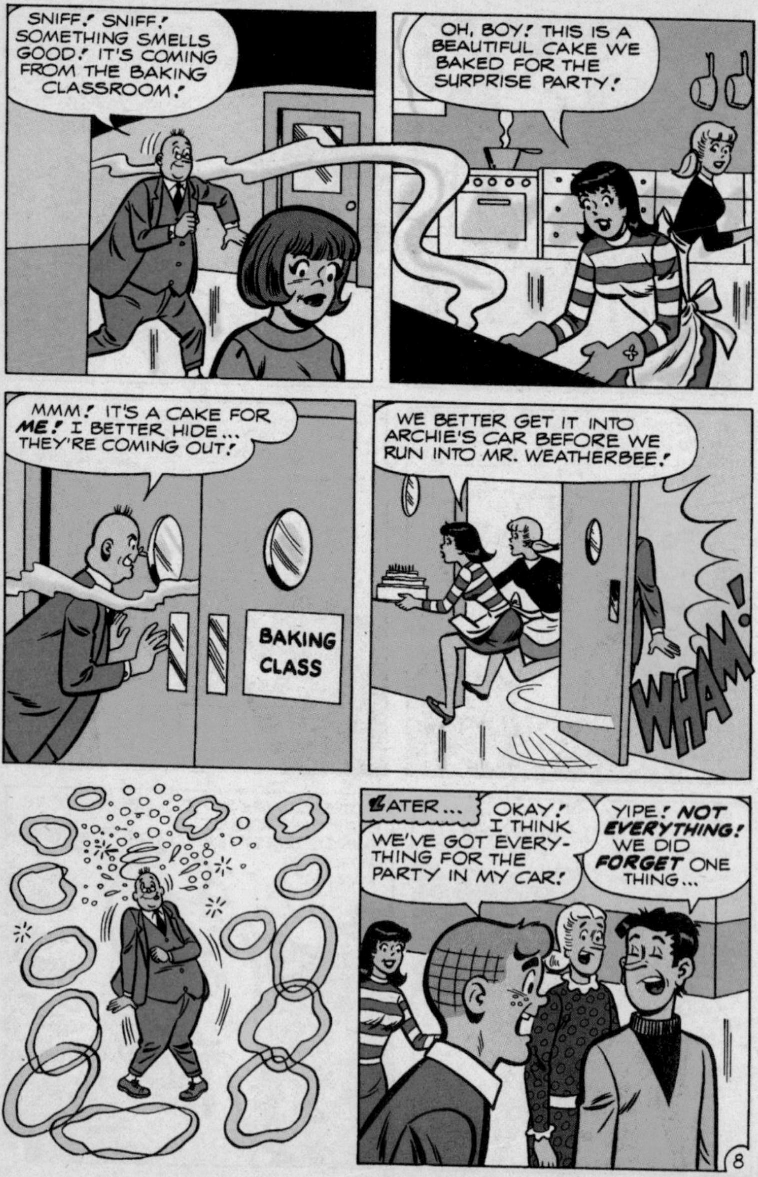
SNIFF! SNIFF! SOMETHING SMELLS GOOD! IT'S COMING FROM THE BAKING CLASSROOM!
OH, BOY! THIS IS A BEAUTIFUL CAKE WE BAKED FOR THE SURPRISE PARTY!
MMM! IT'S A CAKE FOR ME! I BETTER HIDE... THEY'RE COMING OUT!
BAKING CLASS
WE BETTER GET IT INTO ARCHIE'S CAR BEFORE WE RUN INTO MR. WEATHERBEE!
WHAM!
LATER...
OKAY! I THINK WE'VE GOT EVERYTHING FOR THE PARTY IN MY CAR!
YIPE! NOT EVERYTHING! WE DID FORGET ONE THING...

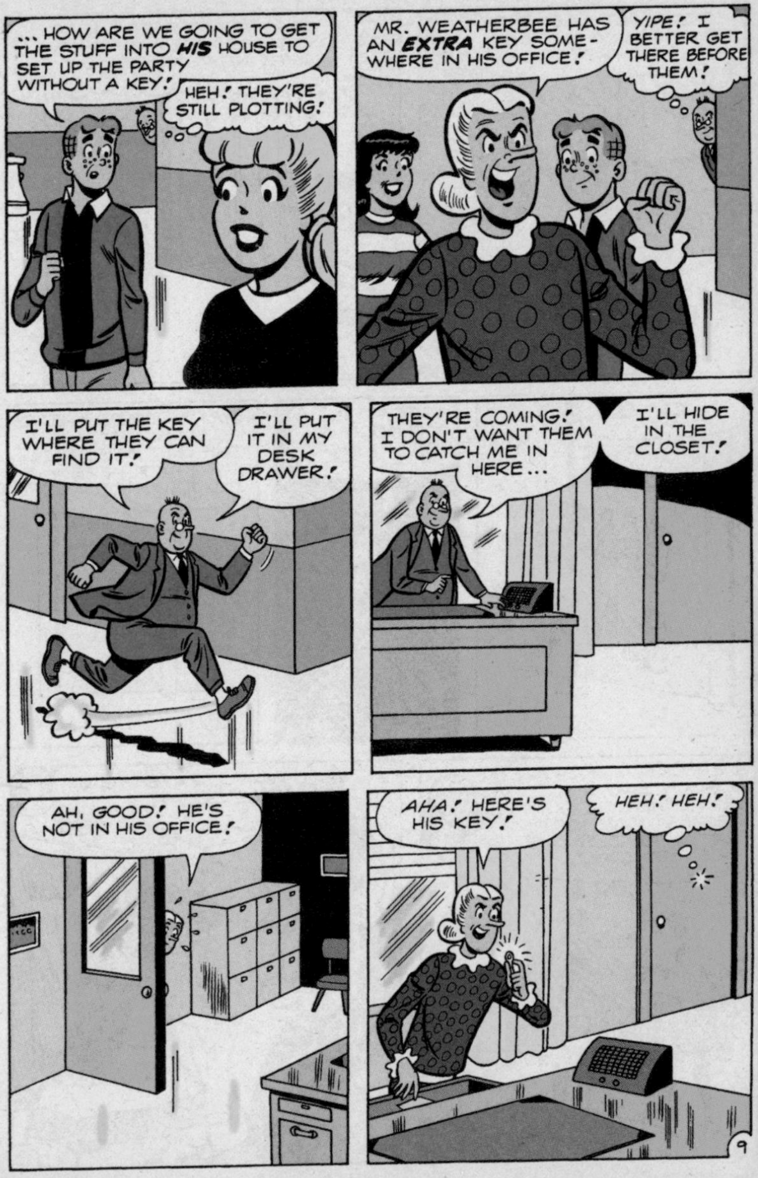

... HOW ARE WE GOING TO GET THE STUFF INTO HIS HOUSE TO SET UP THE PARTY WITHOUT A KEY!
HEH! THEY'RE STILL PLOTTING!
MR. WEATHERBEE HAS AN EXTRA KEY SOME-WHERE IN HIS OFFICE!
YIPE! I BETTER GET THERE BEFORE THEM!
I'LL PUT THE KEY WHERE THEY CAN FIND IT!
I'LL PUT IT IN MY DESK DRAWER!
THEY'RE COMING! I DON'T WANT THEM TO CATCH ME IN HERE...
I'LL HIDE IN THE CLOSET!
AH, GOOD! HE'S NOT IN HIS OFFICE!
AHA! HERE'S HIS KEY!
HEH! HEH!

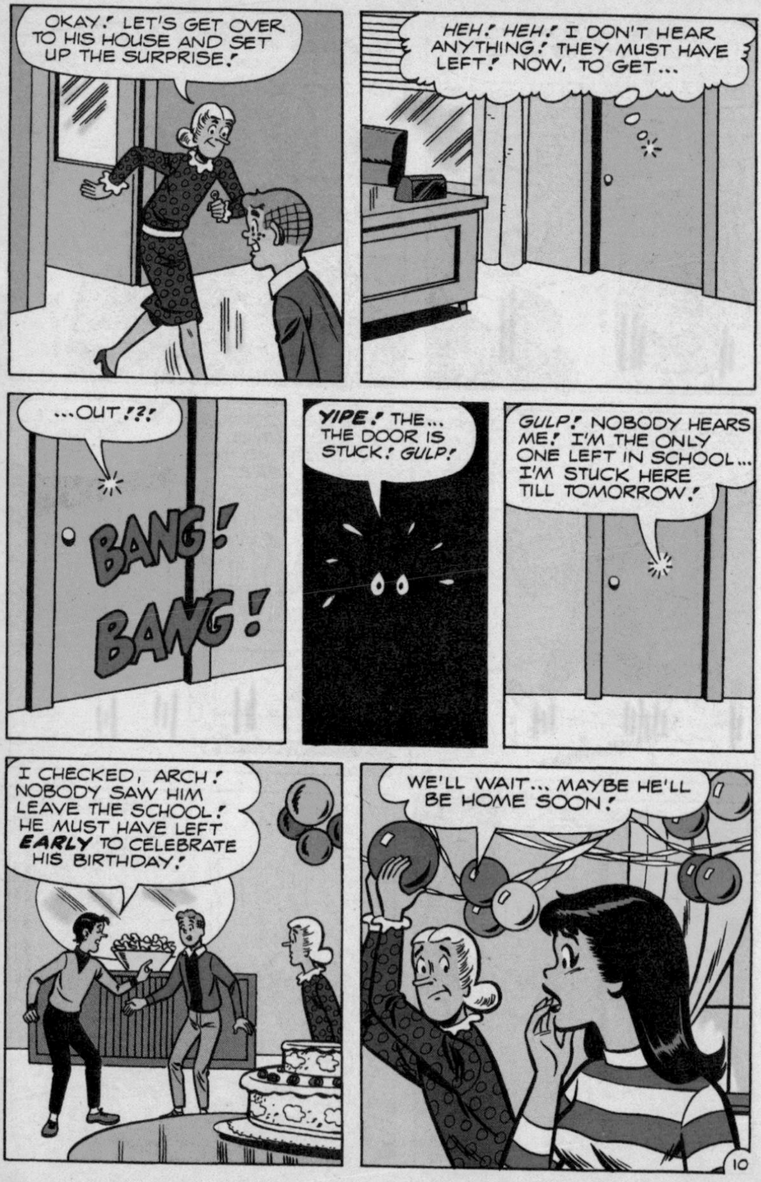
OKAY! LET'S GET OVER TO HIS HOUSE AND SET UP THE SURPRISE!
HEH! HEH! I DON'T HEAR ANYTHING! THEY MUST HAVE LEFT! NOW, TO GET...
...OUT!?!
BANG! BANG!
YIPE! THE... THE DOOR IS STUCK! GULP!
GULP! NOBODY HEARS ME! I'M THE ONLY ONE LEFT IN SCHOOL... I'M STUCK HERE TILL TOMORROW!
I CHECKED, ARCH! NOBODY SAW HIM LEAVE THE SCHOOL! HE MUST HAVE LEFT EARLY TO CELEBRATE HIS BIRTHDAY!
WE'LL WAIT... MAYBE HE'LL BE HOME SOON!
10

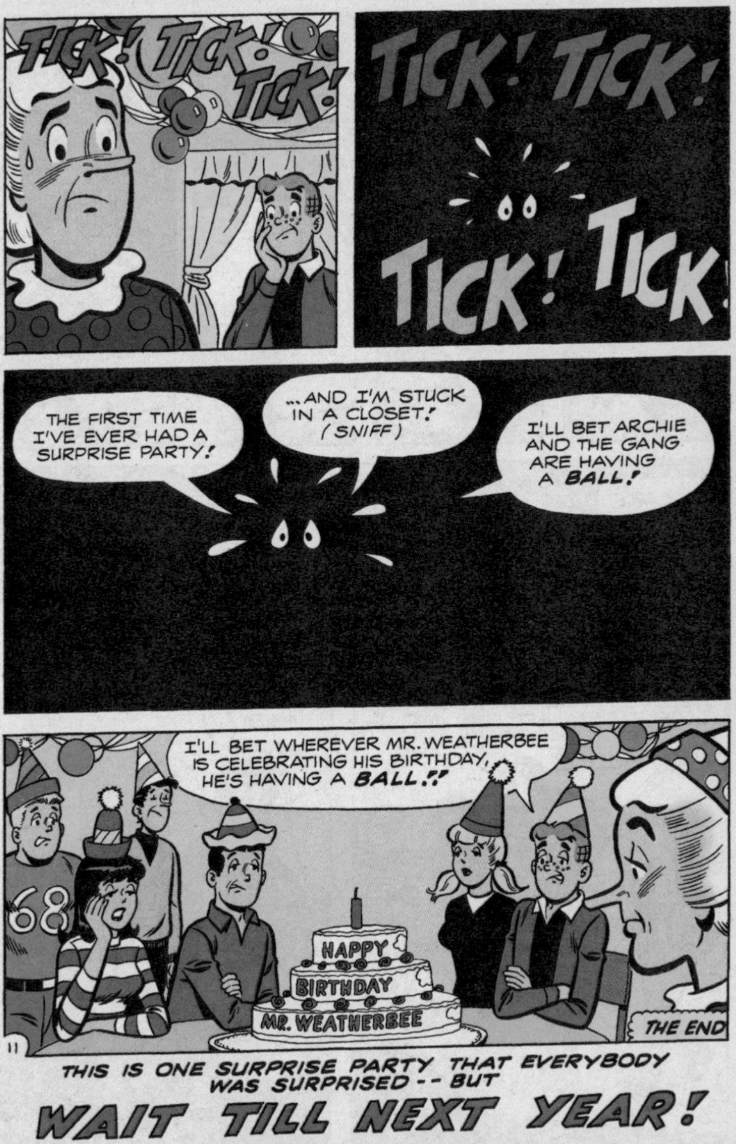
TICK! TICK! TICK!
TICK! TICK!
TICK! TICK!
THE FIRST TIME I'VE EVER HAD A SURPRISE PARTY!
...AND I'M STUCK IN A CLOSET! (SNIFF)
I'LL BET ARCHIE AND THE GANG ARE HAVING A BALL!
I'LL BET WHEREVER MR. WEATHERBEE IS CELEBRATING HIS BIRTHDAY, HE'S HAVING A BALL!?!
68
HAPPY BIRTHDAY MR. WEATHERBEE
THE END

THIS IS ONE SURPRISE PARTY THAT EVERYBODY WAS SURPRISED -- BUT

WAIT TILL NEXT YEAR!

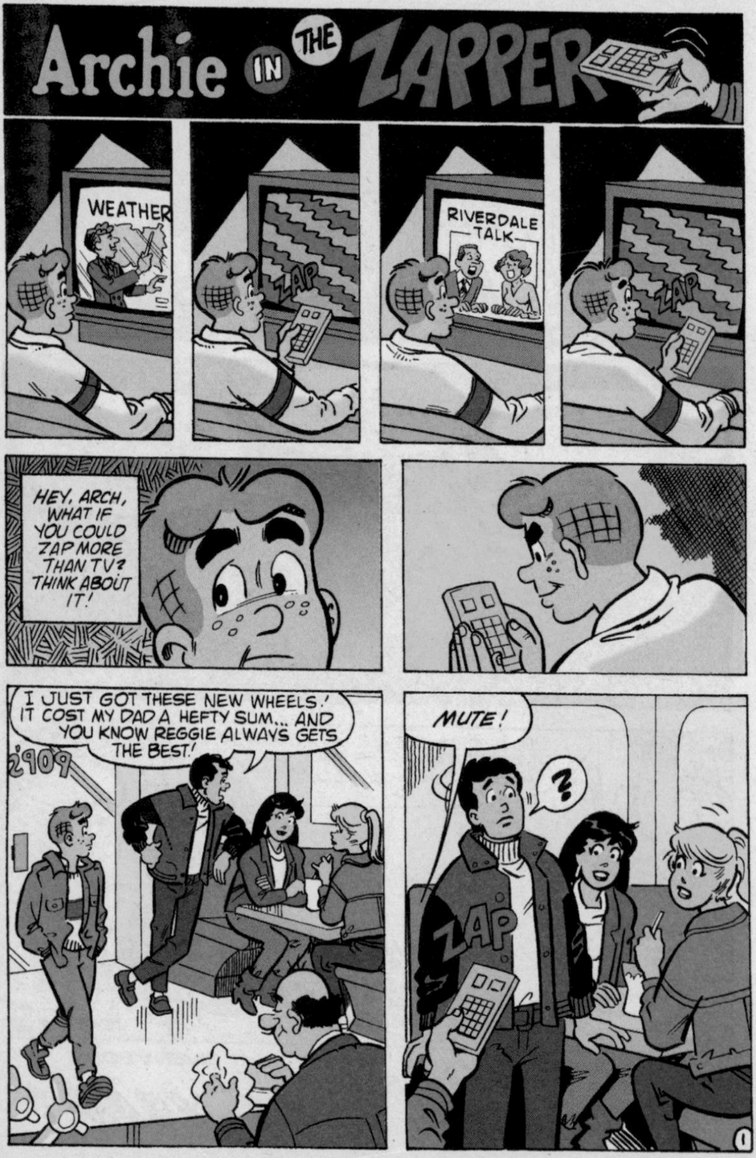
Archie IN THE ZAPPER
WEATHER
ZAP
RIVERDALE TALK
ZAP
HEY, ARCH, WHAT IF YOU COULD ZAP MORE THAN TV? THINK ABOUT IT!
I JUST GOT THESE NEW WHEELS! IT COST MY DAD A HEFTY SUM... AND YOU KNOW REGGIE ALWAYS GETS THE BEST!
POP'S
MUTE!
?
ZAP
1

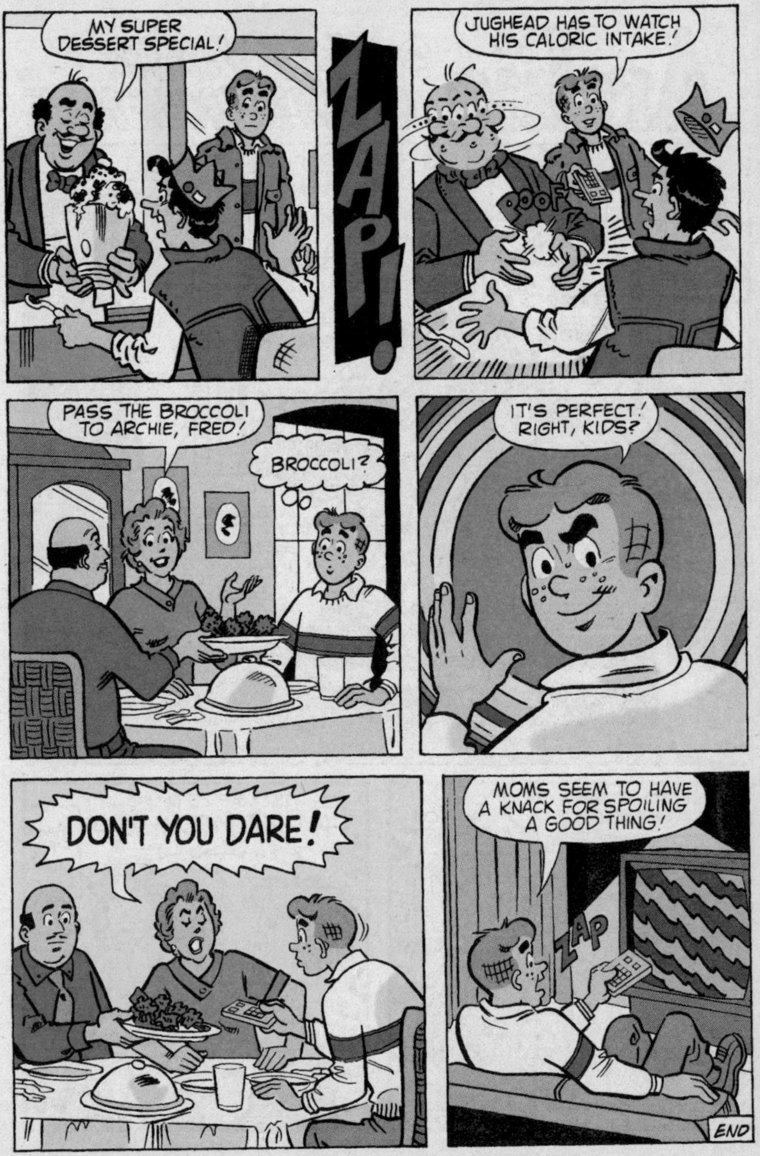
MY SUPER DESSERT SPECIAL!
ZAP!
JUGHEAD HAS TO WATCH HIS CALORIC INTAKE!
POOF
PASS THE BROCCOLI TO ARCHIE, FRED!
BROCCOLI?
IT'S PERFECT! RIGHT, KIDS?
DON'T YOU DARE!
MOMS SEEM TO HAVE A KNACK FOR SPOILING A GOOD THING!
ZAP
END

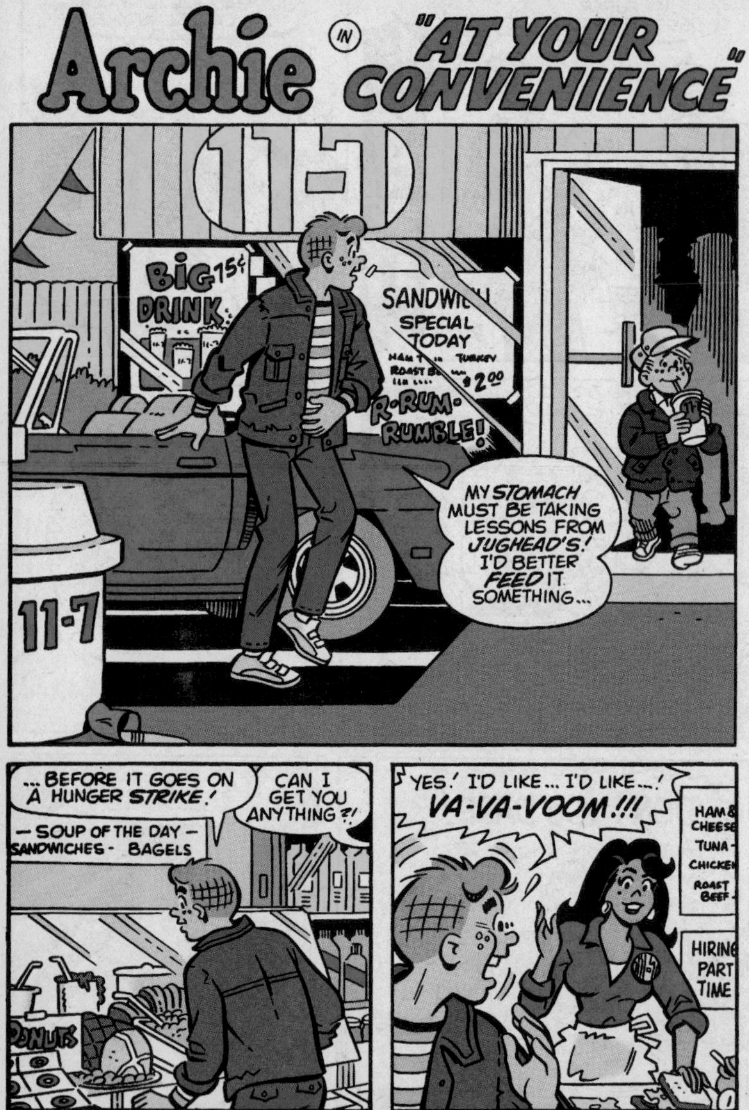
Archie IN "AT YOUR CONVENIENCE"
11-7
BIG 15¢ DRINK
SANDWI
SPECIAL TODAY
$2.00
R-RUM-RUMBLE!
MY STOMACH MUST BE TAKING LESSONS FROM JUGHEAD'S! I'D BETTER FEED IT SOMETHING...
11-7
... BEFORE IT GOES ON A HUNGER STRIKE!
CAN I GET YOU ANYTHING?!
— SOUP OF THE DAY — SANDWICHES - BAGELS
DONUTS
YES! I'D LIKE... I'D LIKE...! VA-VA-VOOM!!!
HAM & CHEESE
TUNA
CHICKEN
ROAST BEEF
HIRING PART TIME

Script: Rich Margopoulos / Pencils: Stan Goldberg / Inks: Rudy Lapick / Letters: Bill Yoshida

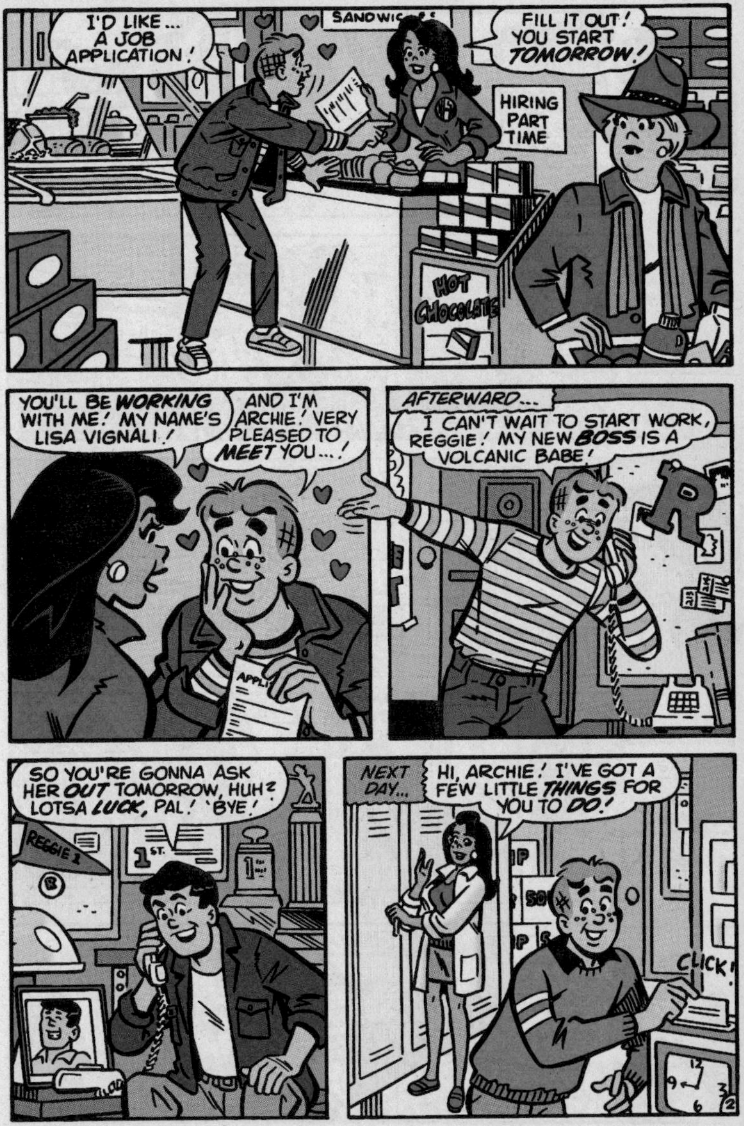

I'D LIKE... A JOB APPLICATION!
SANDWIC
FILL IT OUT! YOU START TOMORROW!
HIRING PART TIME
HOT CHOCOLATE
YOU'LL BE WORKING WITH ME! MY NAME'S LISA VIGNALI!
AND I'M ARCHIE! VERY PLEASED TO MEET YOU...!
APPLI
AFTERWARD...
I CAN'T WAIT TO START WORK, REGGIE! MY NEW BOSS IS A VOLCANIC BABE!
SO YOU'RE GONNA ASK HER OUT TOMORROW, HUH? LOTSA LUCK, PAL! 'BYE!
REGGIE 1
1ST.
NEXT DAY...
HI, ARCHIE! I'VE GOT A FEW LITTLE THINGS FOR YOU TO DO!
CLICK!
2

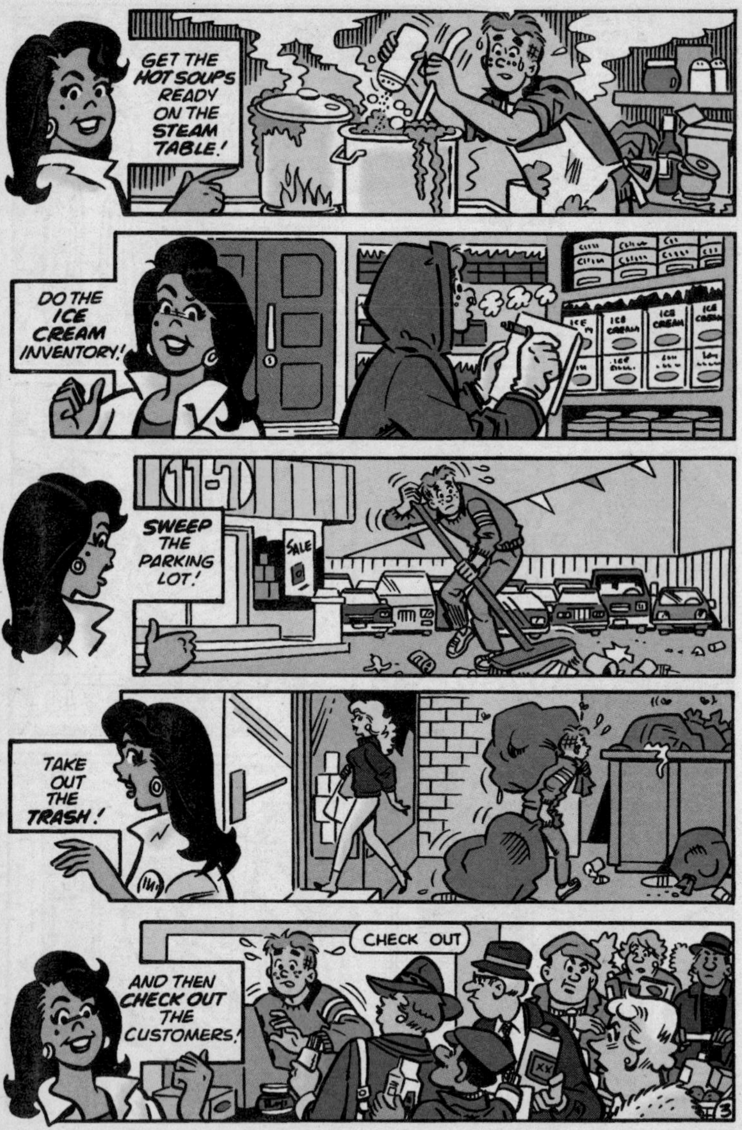
GET THE HOT SOUPS READY ON THE STEAM TABLE!
DO THE ICE CREAM INVENTORY!
ICE CREAM
SWEEP THE PARKING LOT!
SALE
TAKE OUT THE TRASH!
CHECK OUT
AND THEN CHECK OUT THE CUSTOMERS!

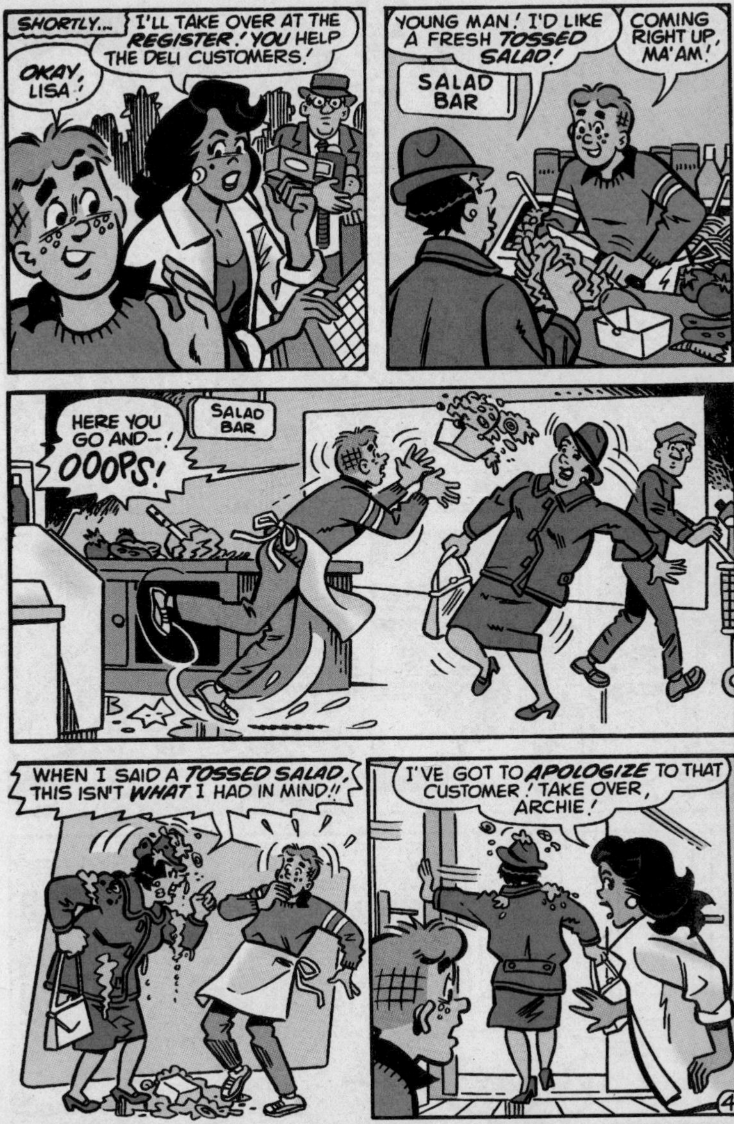

SHORTLY...
I'LL TAKE OVER AT THE REGISTER! YOU HELP THE DELI CUSTOMERS!
OKAY, LISA!
YOUNG MAN! I'D LIKE A FRESH TOSSED SALAD!
COMING RIGHT UP, MA'AM!
SALAD BAR
HERE YOU GO AND--!
OOOPS!
SALAD BAR
WHEN I SAID A TOSSED SALAD, THIS ISN'T WHAT I HAD IN MIND!!
I'VE GOT TO APOLOGIZE TO THAT CUSTOMER! TAKE OVER, ARCHIE!
4

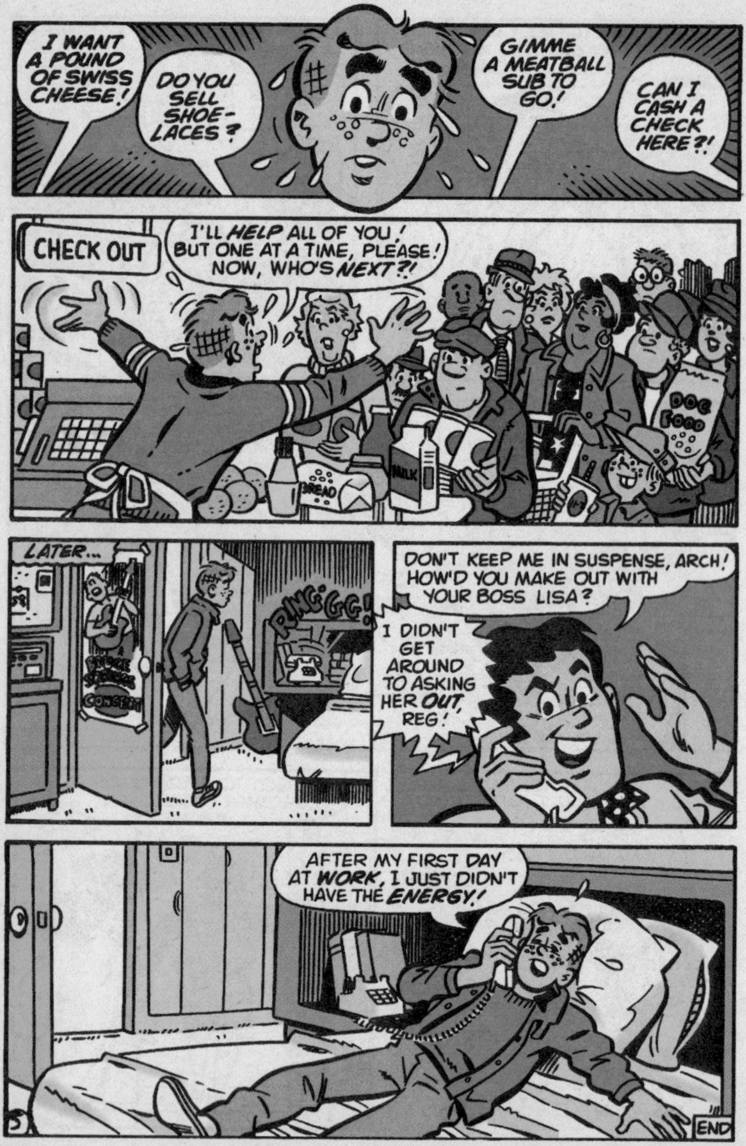
I WANT A POUND OF SWISS CHEESE!
DO YOU SELL SHOE-LACES?
GIMME A MEATBALL SUB TO GO!
CAN I CASH A CHECK HERE?!
CHECK OUT
I'LL HELP ALL OF YOU! BUT ONE AT A TIME, PLEASE! NOW, WHO'S NEXT?!
DOG FOOD
BREAD
MILK
LATER...
RING GG!
DON'T KEEP ME IN SUSPENSE, ARCH! HOW'D YOU MAKE OUT WITH YOUR BOSS LISA?
I DIDN'T GET AROUND TO ASKING HER OUT, REG!
AFTER MY FIRST DAY AT WORK, I JUST DIDN'T HAVE THE ENERGY!
END

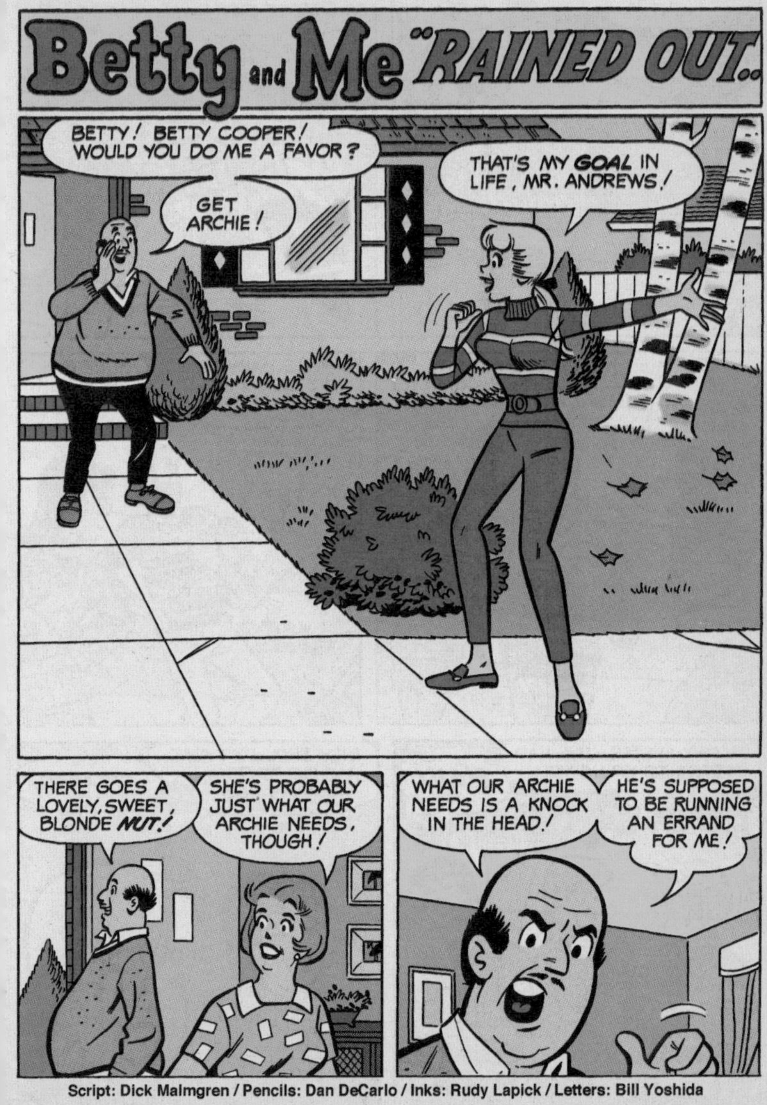
Betty and Me
"RAINED OUT.."
BETTY! BETTY COOPER! WOULD YOU DO ME A FAVOR?
GET ARCHIE!
THAT'S MY GOAL IN LIFE, MR. ANDREWS!
THERE GOES A LOVELY, SWEET, BLONDE NUT!
SHE'S PROBABLY JUST WHAT OUR ARCHIE NEEDS, THOUGH!
WHAT OUR ARCHIE NEEDS IS A KNOCK IN THE HEAD!
HE'S SUPPOSED TO BE RUNNING AN ERRAND FOR ME!

Script: Dick Malmgren / Pencils: Dan DeCarlo / Inks: Rudy Lapick / Letters: Bill Yoshida

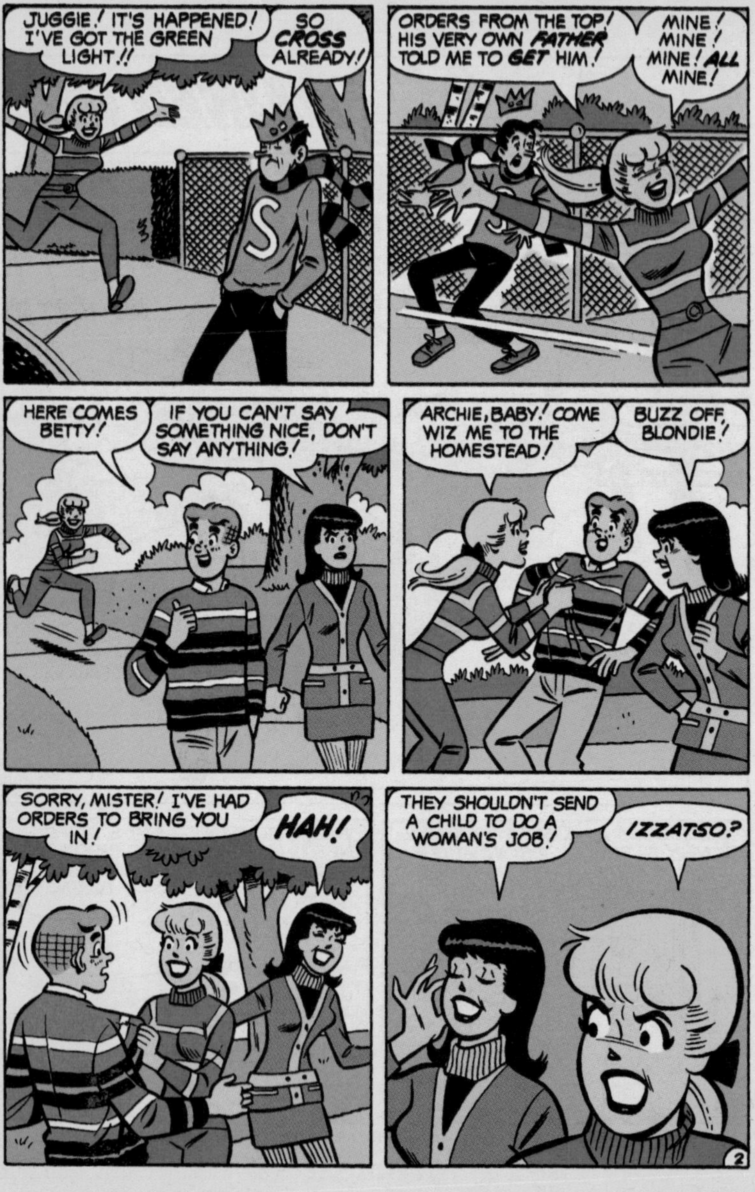
JUGGIE! IT'S HAPPENED! I'VE GOT THE GREEN LIGHT!!
SO CROSS ALREADY!
ORDERS FROM THE TOP! HIS VERY OWN FATHER TOLD ME TO GET HIM!
MINE! MINE! MINE! ALL MINE!
HERE COMES BETTY!
IF YOU CAN'T SAY SOMETHING NICE, DON'T SAY ANYTHING!
ARCHIE, BABY! COME WIZ ME TO THE HOMESTEAD!
BUZZ OFF, BLONDIE!
SORRY, MISTER! I'VE HAD ORDERS TO BRING YOU IN!
HAH!
THEY SHOULDN'T SEND A CHILD TO DO A WOMAN'S JOB!
IZZATSO?
2

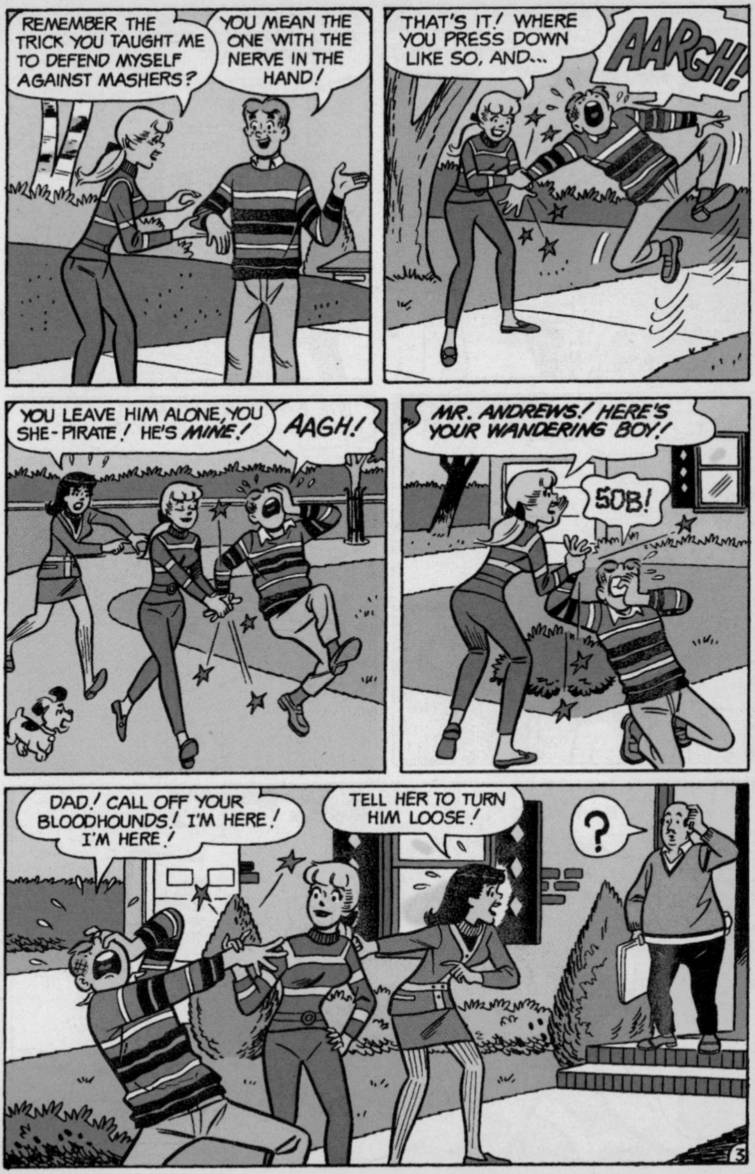
REMEMBER THE TRICK YOU TAUGHT ME TO DEFEND MYSELF AGAINST MASHERS?
YOU MEAN THE ONE WITH THE NERVE IN THE HAND!
THAT'S IT! WHERE YOU PRESS DOWN LIKE SO, AND...
AARGH!
YOU LEAVE HIM ALONE, YOU SHE-PIRATE! HE'S MINE!
AAGH!
MR. ANDREWS! HERE'S YOUR WANDERING BOY!
SOB!
DAD! CALL OFF YOUR BLOODHOUNDS! I'M HERE! I'M HERE!
TELL HER TO TURN HIM LOOSE!
?
3

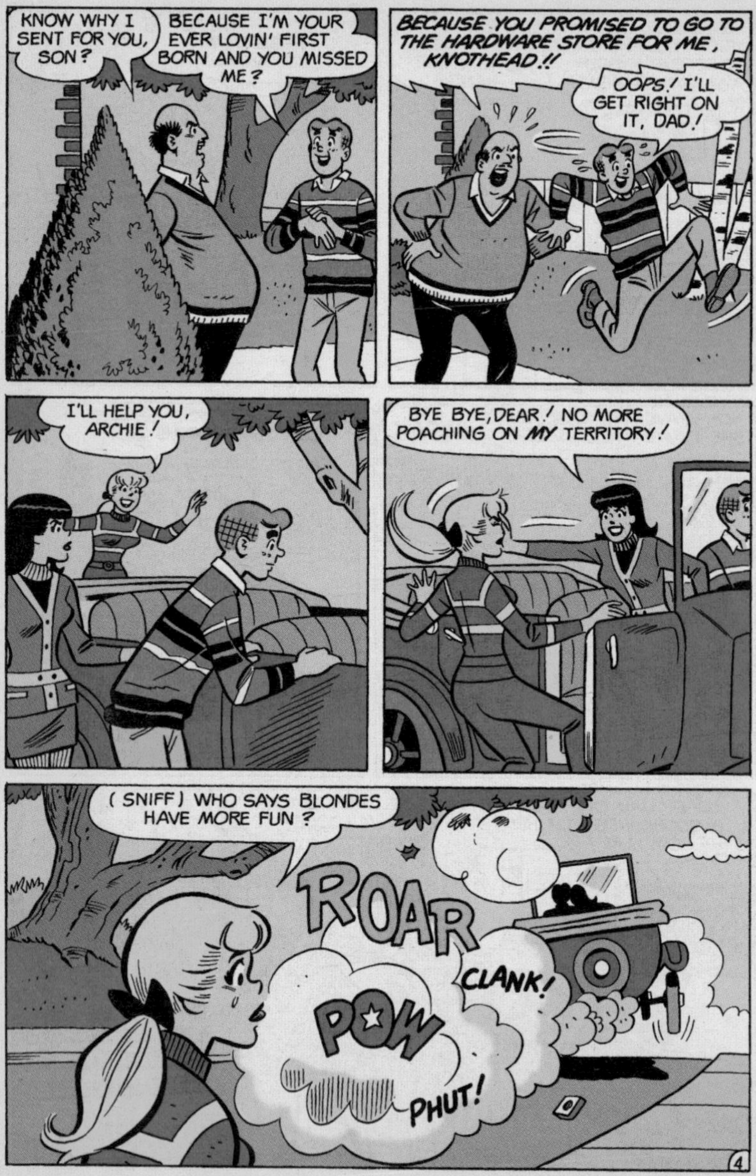
KNOW WHY I SENT FOR YOU, SON?
BECAUSE I'M YOUR EVER LOVIN' FIRST BORN AND YOU MISSED ME?
BECAUSE YOU PROMISED TO GO TO THE HARDWARE STORE FOR ME, KNOTHEAD!!
OOPS! I'LL GET RIGHT ON IT, DAD!
I'LL HELP YOU, ARCHIE!
BYE BYE, DEAR! NO MORE POACHING ON MY TERRITORY!
(SNIFF) WHO SAYS BLONDES HAVE MORE FUN?
ROAR
CLANK!
POW
PHUT!
4

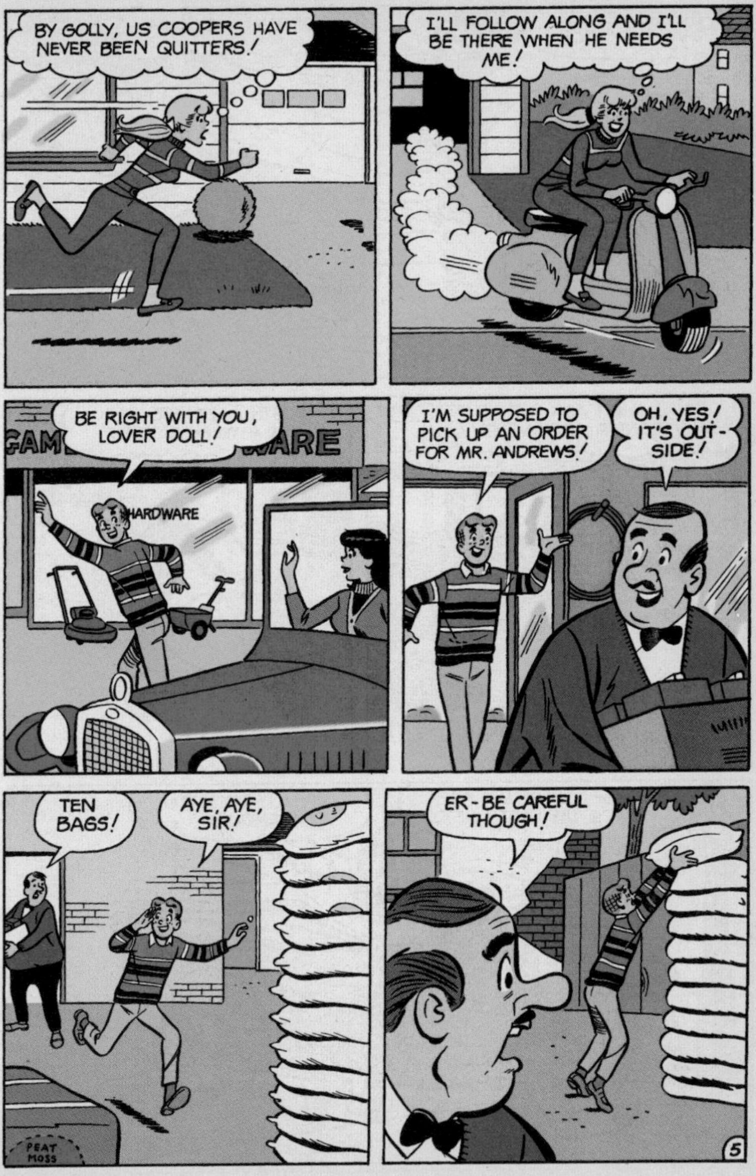
BY GOLLY, US COOPERS HAVE NEVER BEEN QUITTERS!
I'LL FOLLOW ALONG AND I'LL BE THERE WHEN HE NEEDS ME!
GAM
WARE
BE RIGHT WITH YOU, LOVER DOLL!
HARDWARE
I'M SUPPOSED TO PICK UP AN ORDER FOR MR. ANDREWS!
OH, YES! IT'S OUT-SIDE!
TEN BAGS!
AYE, AYE, SIR!
PEAT MOSS
ER-BE CAREFUL THOUGH!

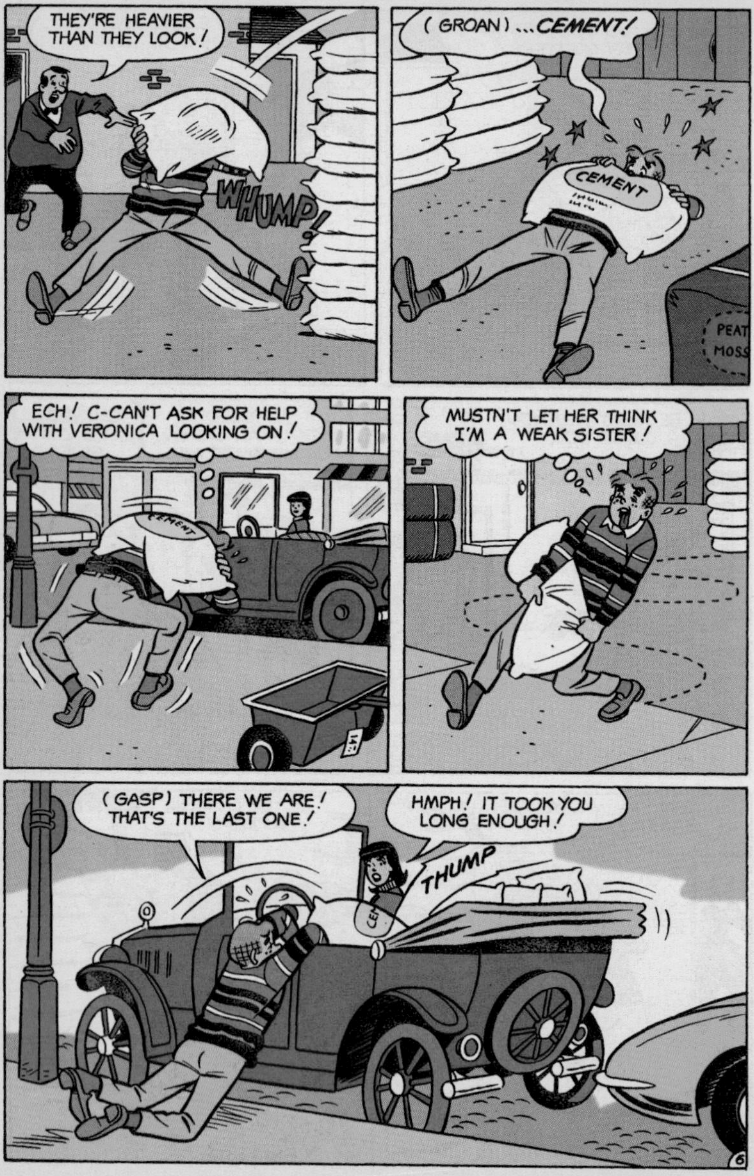
THEY'RE HEAVIER THAN THEY LOOK!
WHUMP!
(GROAN)...CEMENT!
CEMENT
PEAT MOSS
ECH! C-CAN'T ASK FOR HELP WITH VERONICA LOOKING ON!
CEMENT
MUSTN'T LET HER THINK I'M A WEAK SISTER!
(GASP) THERE WE ARE! THAT'S THE LAST ONE!
HMPH! IT TOOK YOU LONG ENOUGH!
THUMP

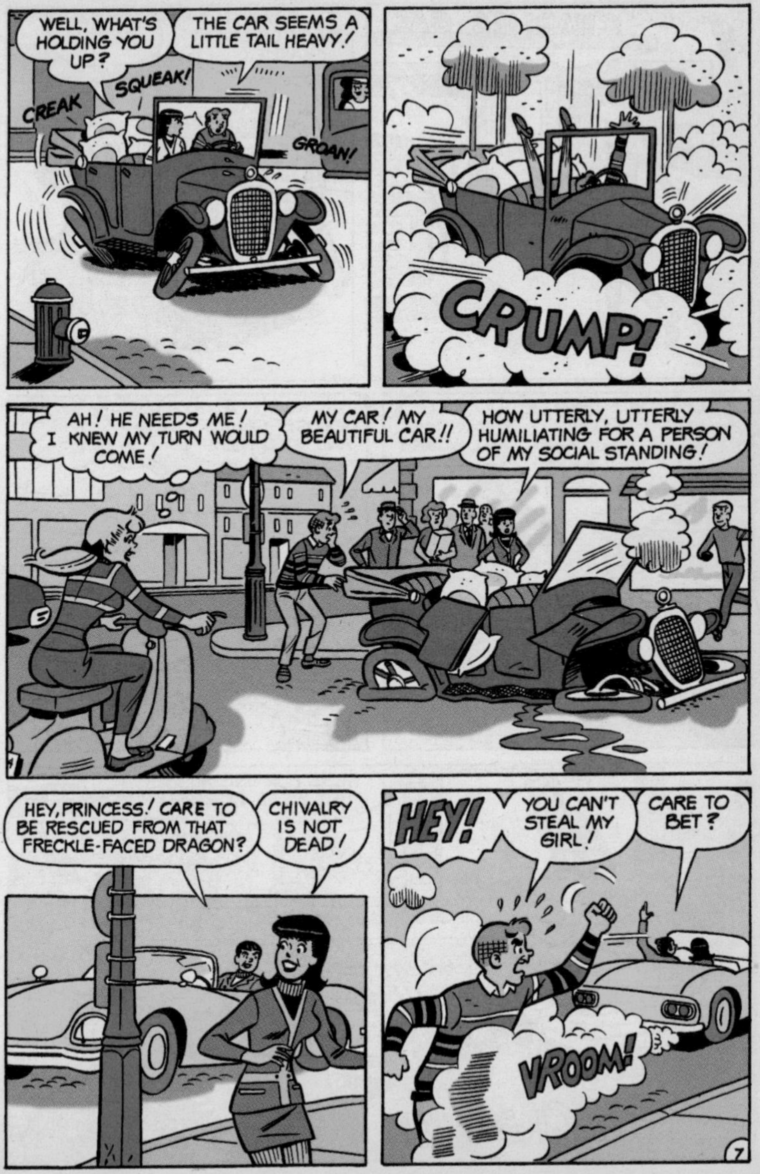

WELL, WHAT'S HOLDING YOU UP?
THE CAR SEEMS A LITTLE TAIL HEAVY!
SQUEAK!
CREAK
GROAN!
CRUMP!
AH! HE NEEDS ME! I KNEW MY TURN WOULD COME!
MY CAR! MY BEAUTIFUL CAR!!
HOW UTTERLY, UTTERLY HUMILIATING FOR A PERSON OF MY SOCIAL STANDING!
HEY, PRINCESS! CARE TO BE RESCUED FROM THAT FRECKLE-FACED DRAGON?
CHIVALRY IS NOT DEAD!
HEY!
YOU CAN'T STEAL MY GIRL!
CARE TO BET?
VROOM!

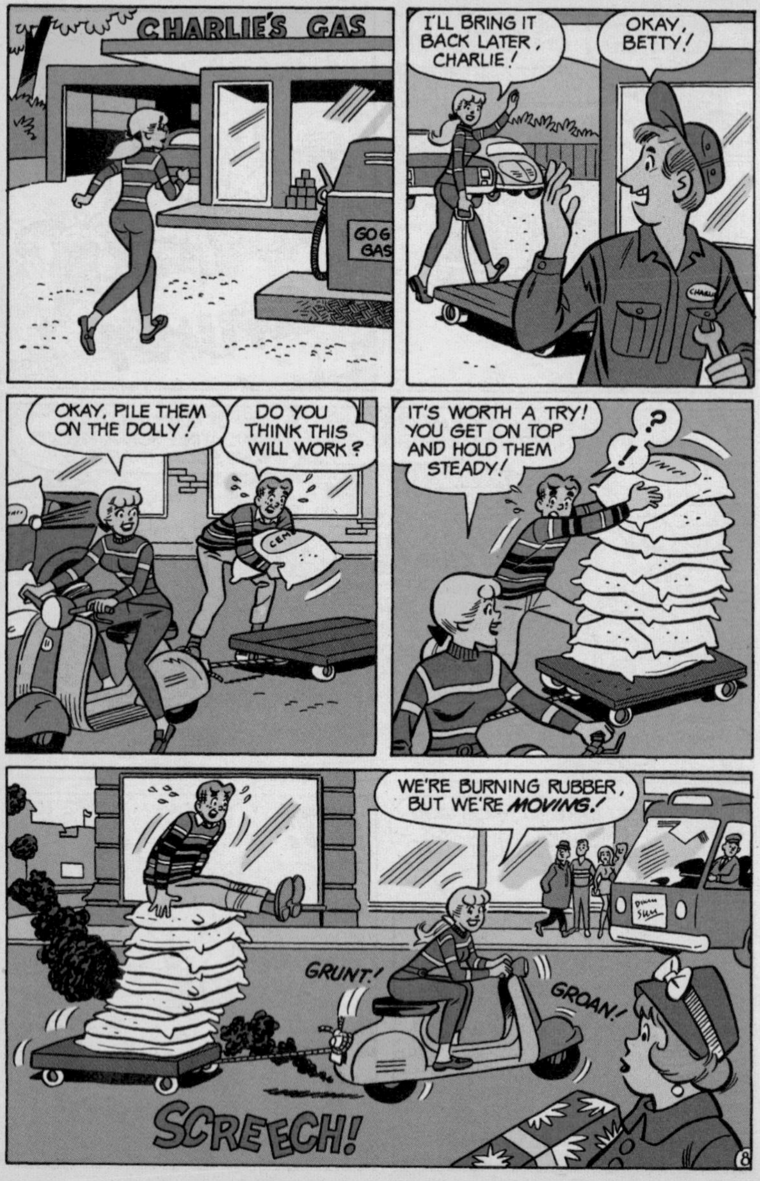
CHARLIE'S GAS
GO G GAS
I'LL BRING IT BACK LATER, CHARLIE!
OKAY, BETTY!
OKAY, PILE THEM ON THE DOLLY!
DO YOU THINK THIS WILL WORK?
IT'S WORTH A TRY! YOU GET ON TOP AND HOLD THEM STEADY!
?
!
WE'RE BURNING RUBBER, BUT WE'RE *MOVING*!
GRUNT!
GROAN!
SCREECH!

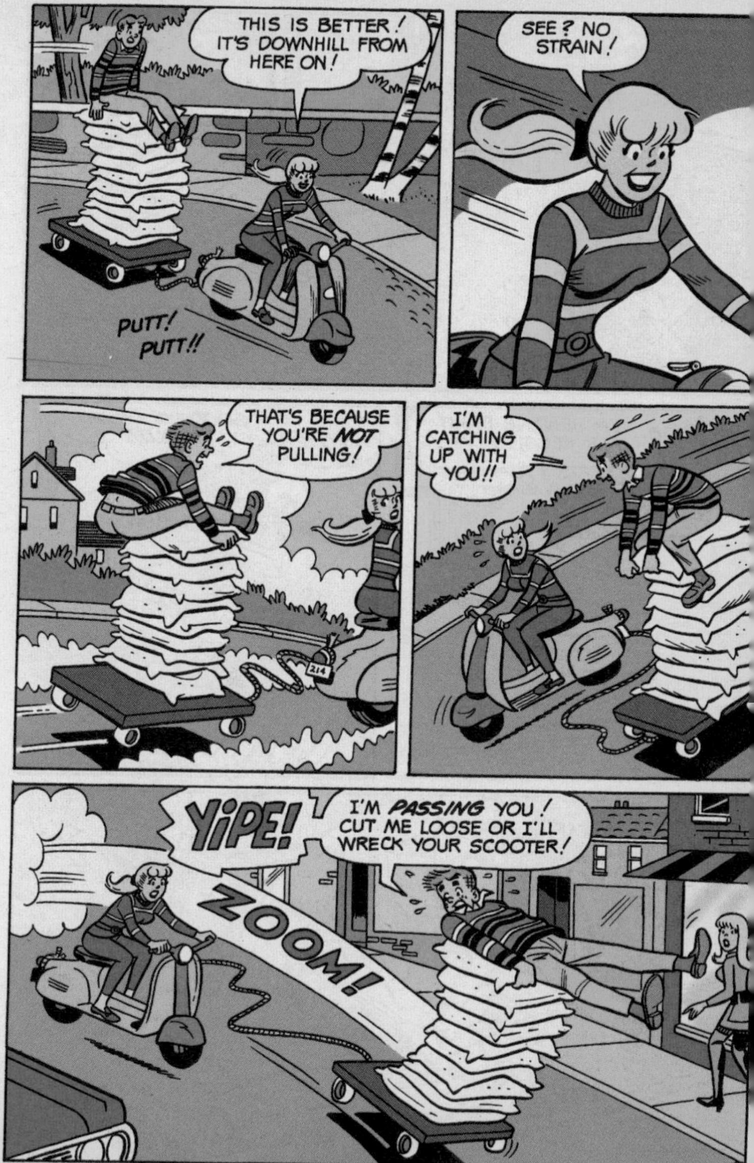
THIS IS BETTER! IT'S DOWNHILL FROM HERE ON!
PUTT! PUTT!!
SEE? NO STRAIN!
THAT'S BECAUSE YOU'RE NOT PULLING!
214
I'M CATCHING UP WITH YOU!!
YIPE!
I'M PASSING YOU! CUT ME LOOSE OR I'LL WRECK YOUR SCOOTER!
ZOOM!

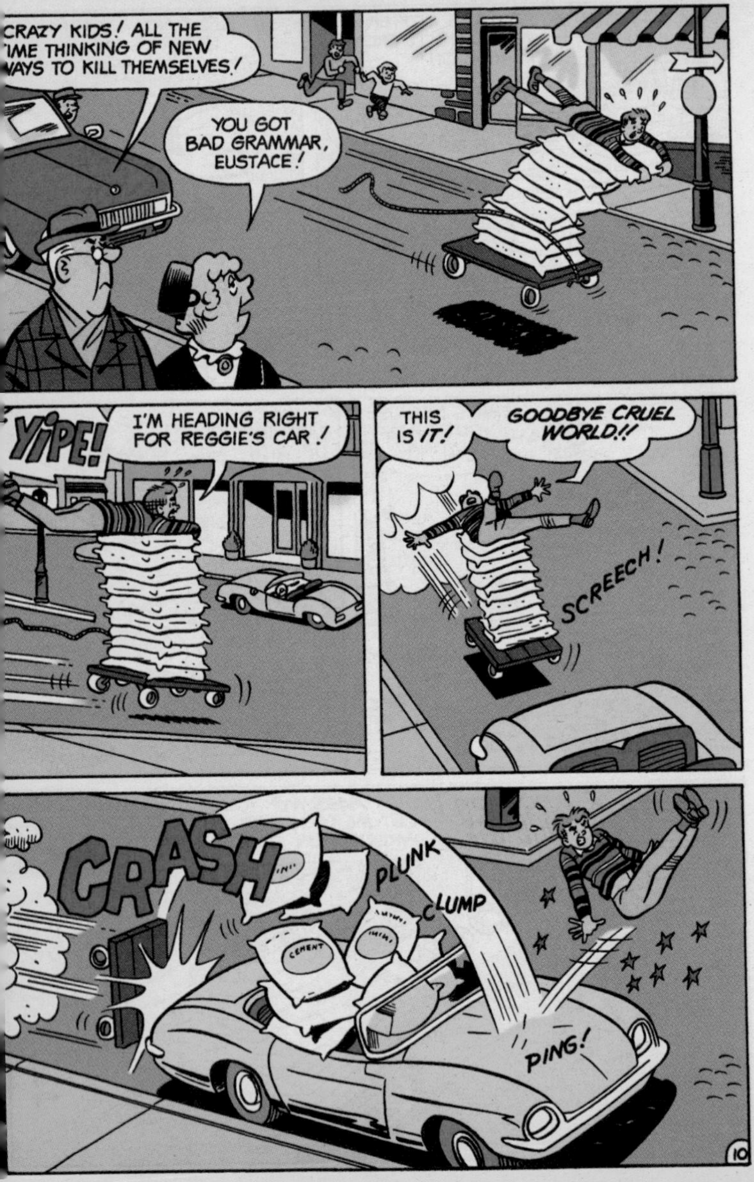
CRAZY KIDS! ALL THE TIME THINKING OF NEW WAYS TO KILL THEMSELVES!
YOU GOT BAD GRAMMAR, EUSTACE!
YIPE!
I'M HEADING RIGHT FOR REGGIE'S CAR!
THIS IS IT!
GOODBYE CRUEL WORLD!!
SCREECH!
CRASH
PLUNK
CLUMP
CEMENT
PING!
10

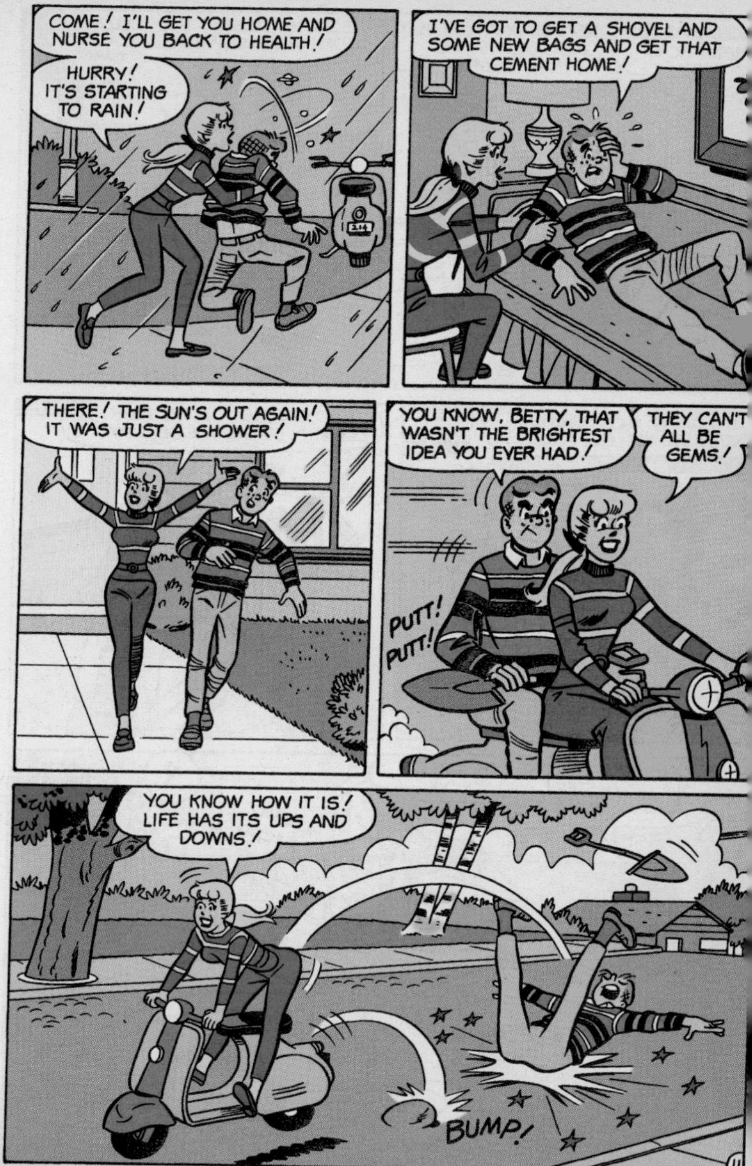
COME! I'LL GET YOU HOME AND NURSE YOU BACK TO HEALTH!
HURRY! IT'S STARTING TO RAIN!
I'VE GOT TO GET A SHOVEL AND SOME NEW BAGS AND GET THAT CEMENT HOME!
THERE! THE SUN'S OUT AGAIN! IT WAS JUST A SHOWER!
YOU KNOW, BETTY, THAT WASN'T THE BRIGHTEST IDEA YOU EVER HAD!
THEY CAN'T ALL BE GEMS!
PUTT! PUTT!
YOU KNOW HOW IT IS! LIFE HAS ITS UPS AND DOWNS!
BUMP!
11

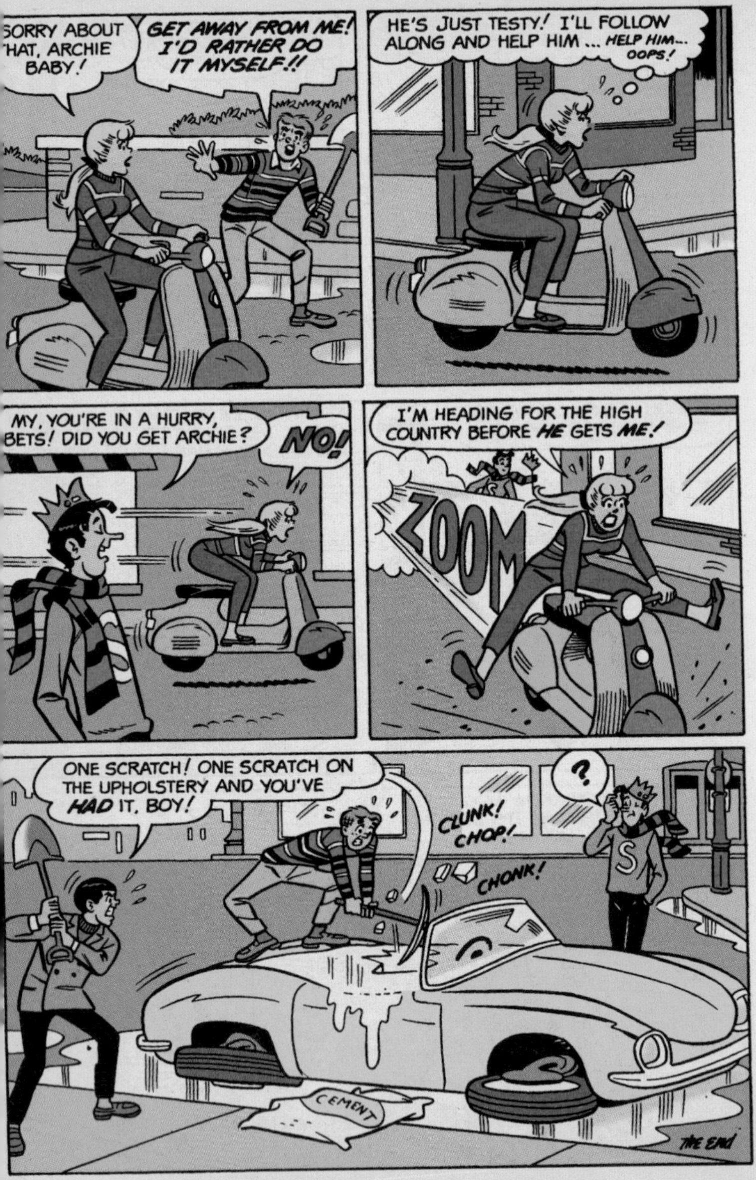
SORRY ABOUT THAT, ARCHIE BABY!
GET AWAY FROM ME! I'D RATHER DO IT MYSELF!!
HE'S JUST TESTY! I'LL FOLLOW ALONG AND HELP HIM ... HELP HIM... OOPS!
MY, YOU'RE IN A HURRY, BETS! DID YOU GET ARCHIE?
NO!
I'M HEADING FOR THE HIGH COUNTRY BEFORE HE GETS ME!
ZOOM
ONE SCRATCH! ONE SCRATCH ON THE UPHOLSTERY AND YOU'VE HAD IT, BOY!
?
CLUNK! CHOP!
CHONK!
CEMENT
THE END

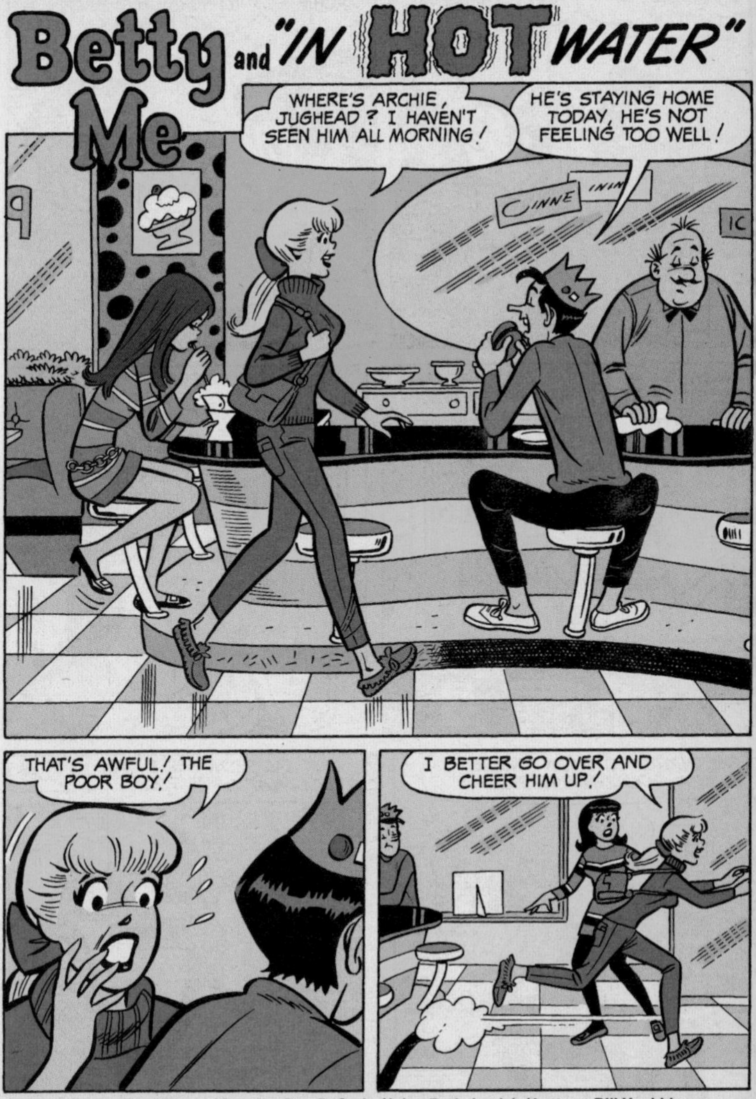
Betty and Me
"IN HOT WATER"
WHERE'S ARCHIE, JUGHEAD? I HAVEN'T SEEN HIM ALL MORNING!
HE'S STAYING HOME TODAY, HE'S NOT FEELING TOO WELL!
THAT'S AWFUL! THE POOR BOY!
I BETTER GO OVER AND CHEER HIM UP!

Script: Frank Doyle / Pencils: Dan DeCarlo / Inks: Rudy Lapick / Letters: Bill Yoshida

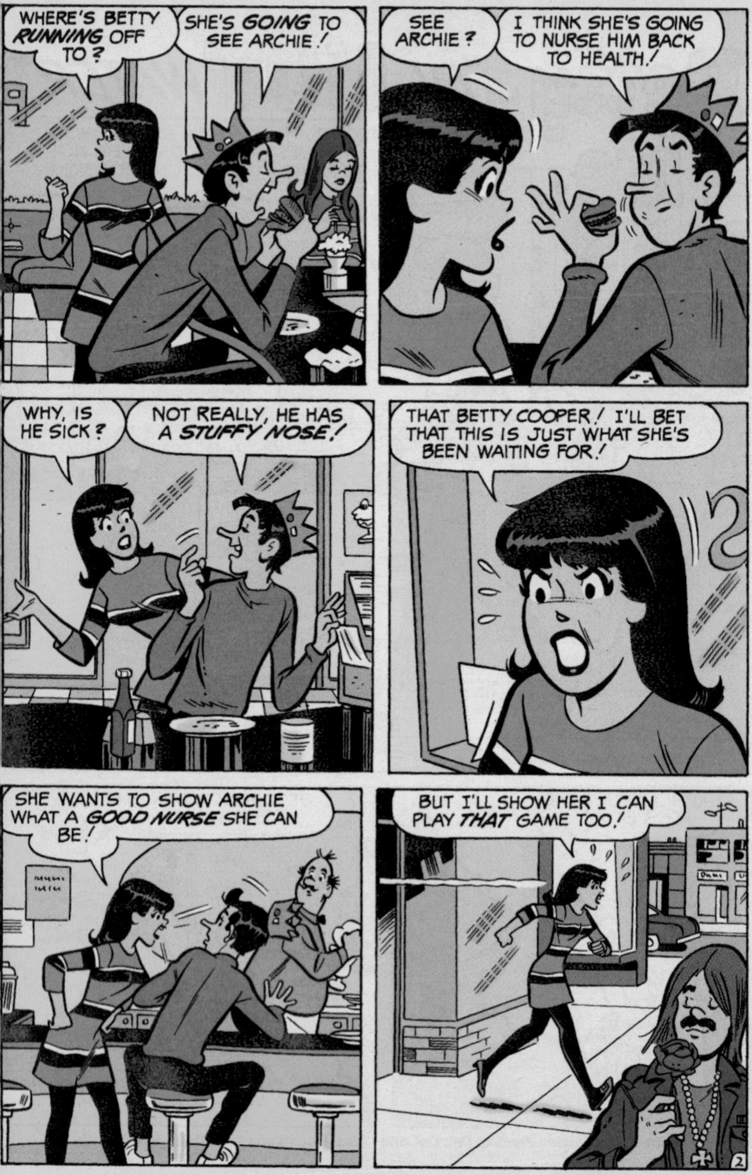
WHERE'S BETTY RUNNING OFF TO?
SHE'S GOING TO SEE ARCHIE!
SEE ARCHIE?
I THINK SHE'S GOING TO NURSE HIM BACK TO HEALTH!
WHY, IS HE SICK?
NOT REALLY, HE HAS A STUFFY NOSE!
THAT BETTY COOPER! I'LL BET THAT THIS IS JUST WHAT SHE'S BEEN WAITING FOR!
SHE WANTS TO SHOW ARCHIE WHAT A GOOD NURSE SHE CAN BE!
BUT I'LL SHOW HER I CAN PLAY THAT GAME TOO!
2

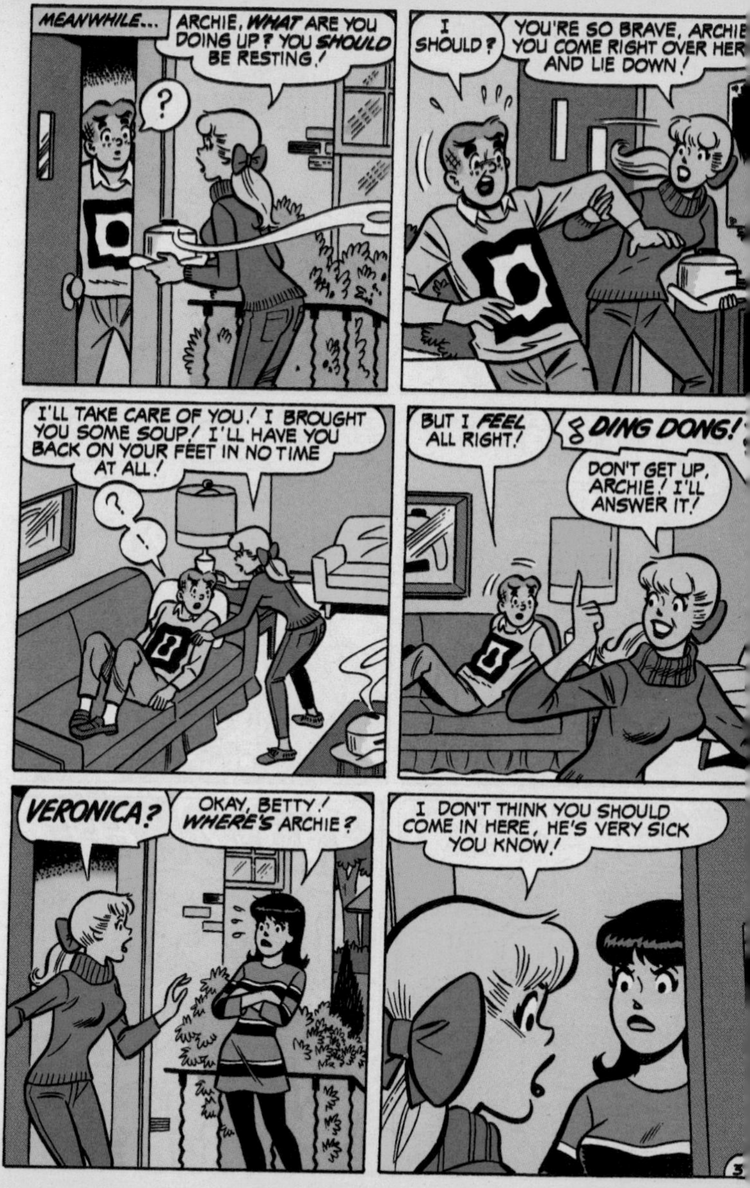
MEANWHILE...
ARCHIE, WHAT ARE YOU DOING UP? YOU SHOULD BE RESTING!
?
I SHOULD?
YOU'RE SO BRAVE, ARCHIE! YOU COME RIGHT OVER HERE AND LIE DOWN!
I'LL TAKE CARE OF YOU! I BROUGHT YOU SOME SOUP! I'LL HAVE YOU BACK ON YOUR FEET IN NO TIME AT ALL!
?
!
BUT I FEEL ALL RIGHT!
DING DONG!
DON'T GET UP, ARCHIE! I'LL ANSWER IT!
VERONICA?
OKAY, BETTY! WHERE'S ARCHIE?
I DON'T THINK YOU SHOULD COME IN HERE, HE'S VERY SICK YOU KNOW!
3

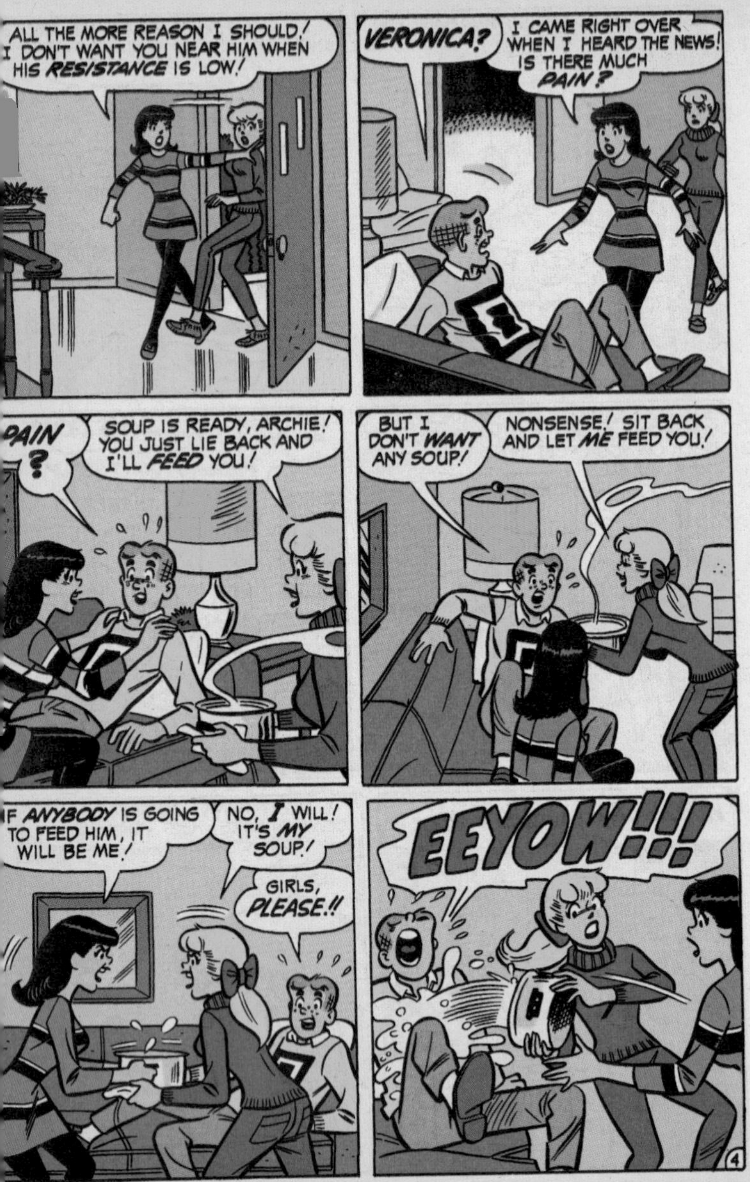
ALL THE MORE REASON I SHOULD! I DON'T WANT YOU NEAR HIM WHEN HIS RESISTANCE IS LOW!
VERONICA?
I CAME RIGHT OVER WHEN I HEARD THE NEWS! IS THERE MUCH PAIN?
PAIN ?
SOUP IS READY, ARCHIE! YOU JUST LIE BACK AND I'LL FEED YOU!
BUT I DON'T WANT ANY SOUP!
NONSENSE! SIT BACK AND LET ME FEED YOU!
IF ANYBODY IS GOING TO FEED HIM, IT WILL BE ME!
NO, I WILL! IT'S MY SOUP!
GIRLS, PLEASE.!!
EEYOW!!!

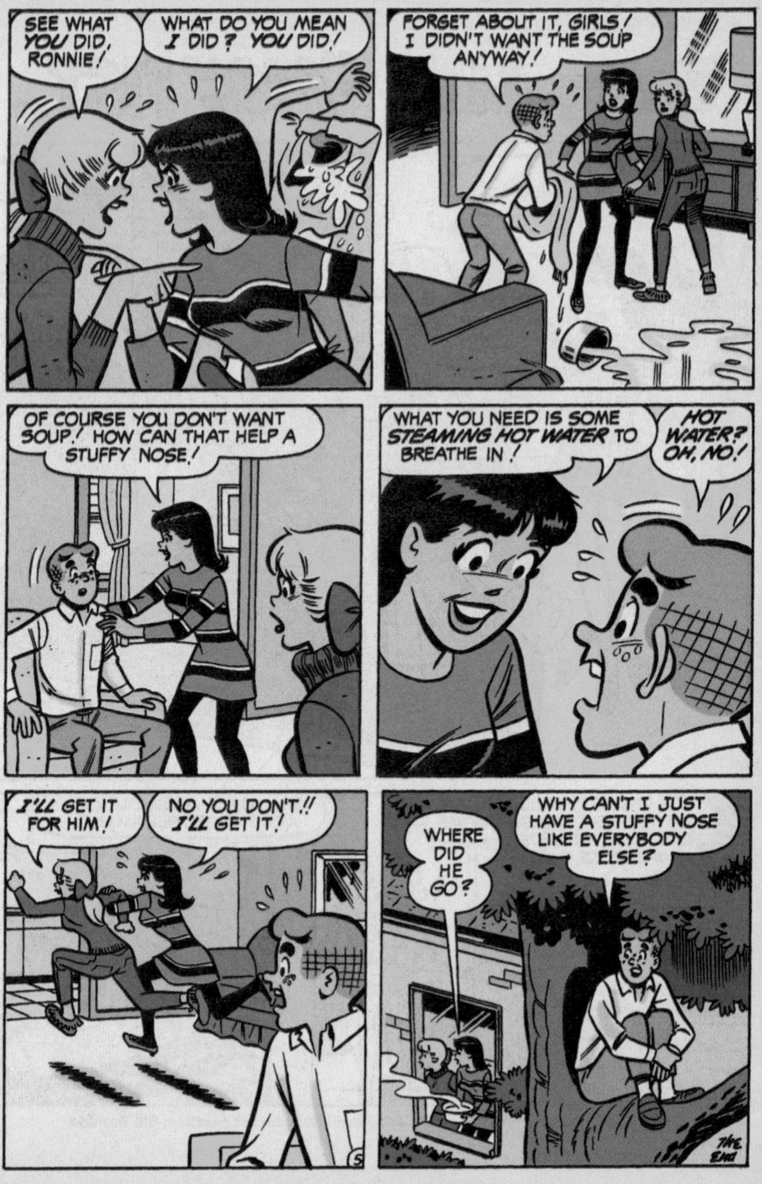
SEE WHAT YOU DID, RONNIE!
WHAT DO YOU MEAN I DID? YOU DID!
FORGET ABOUT IT, GIRLS! I DIDN'T WANT THE SOUP ANYWAY!
OF COURSE YOU DON'T WANT SOUP! HOW CAN THAT HELP A STUFFY NOSE!
WHAT YOU NEED IS SOME STEAMING HOT WATER TO BREATHE IN!
HOT WATER? OH, NO!
I'LL GET IT FOR HIM!
NO YOU DON'T!! I'LL GET IT!
WHERE DID HE GO?
WHY CAN'T I JUST HAVE A STUFFY NOSE LIKE EVERYBODY ELSE?
THE END

Betty and Me -in- The "IRON FIST"

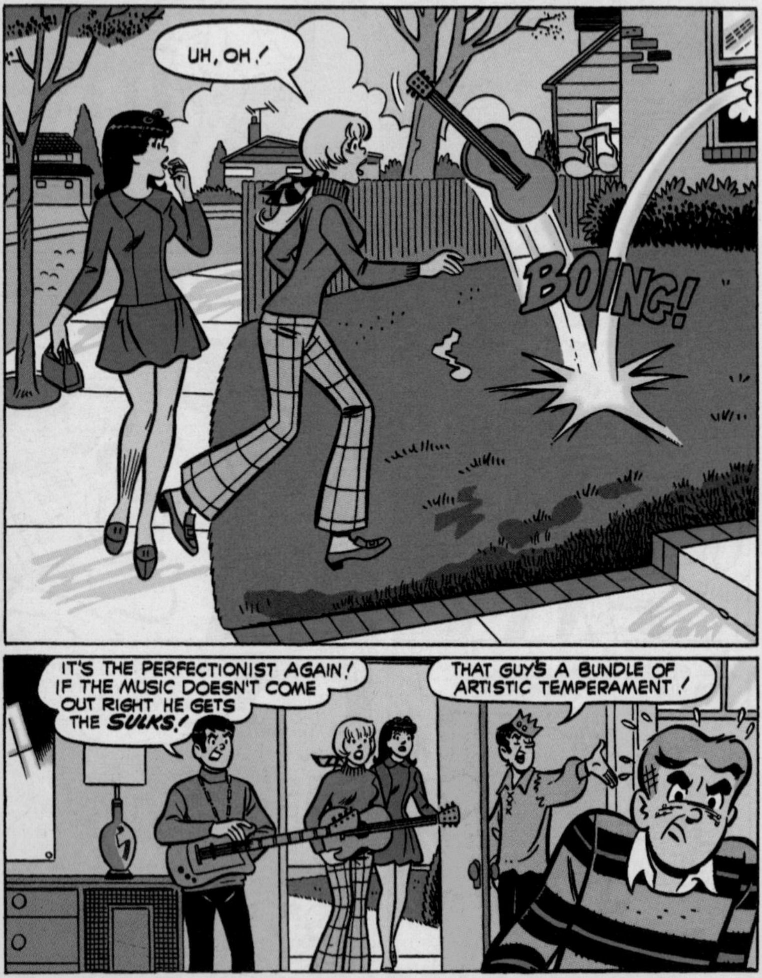
UH, OH!
BOING!
IT'S THE PERFECTIONIST AGAIN! IF THE MUSIC DOESN'T COME OUT RIGHT HE GETS THE SULKS!
THAT GUY'S A BUNDLE OF ARTISTIC TEMPERAMENT!

Script: Frank Doyle / Pencils: Dan DeCarlo / Inks: Rudy Lapick / Letters: Bill Yoshida

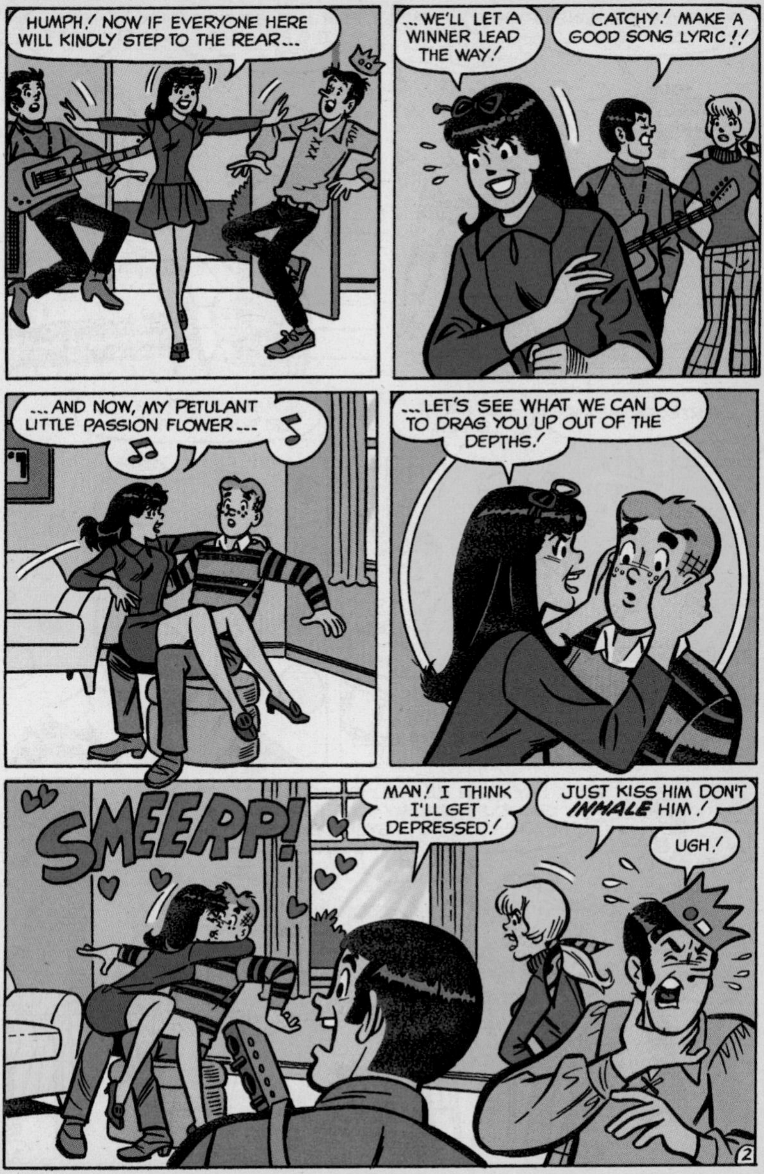
HUMPH! NOW IF EVERYONE HERE WILL KINDLY STEP TO THE REAR...
...WE'LL LET A WINNER LEAD THE WAY!
CATCHY! MAKE A GOOD SONG LYRIC!!
...AND NOW, MY PETULANT LITTLE PASSION FLOWER...
...LET'S SEE WHAT WE CAN DO TO DRAG YOU UP OUT OF THE DEPTHS!
SMEERP!
MAN! I THINK I'LL GET DEPRESSED!
JUST KISS HIM DON'T INHALE HIM!
UGH!
2

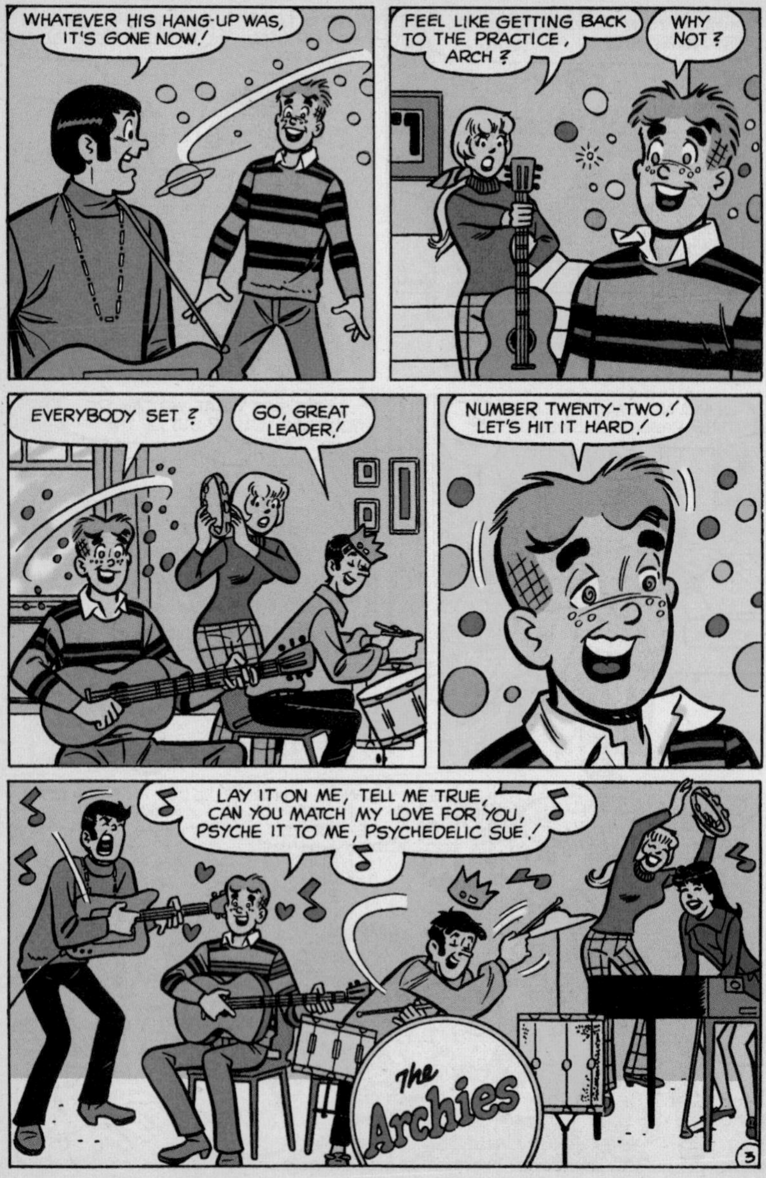
WHATEVER HIS HANG-UP WAS, IT'S GONE NOW!
FEEL LIKE GETTING BACK TO THE PRACTICE, ARCH?
WHY NOT?
EVERYBODY SET?
GO, GREAT LEADER!
NUMBER TWENTY-TWO! LET'S HIT IT HARD!
LAY IT ON ME, TELL ME TRUE, CAN YOU MATCH MY LOVE FOR YOU, PSYCHE IT TO ME, PSYCHEDELIC SUE!
The Archies
3

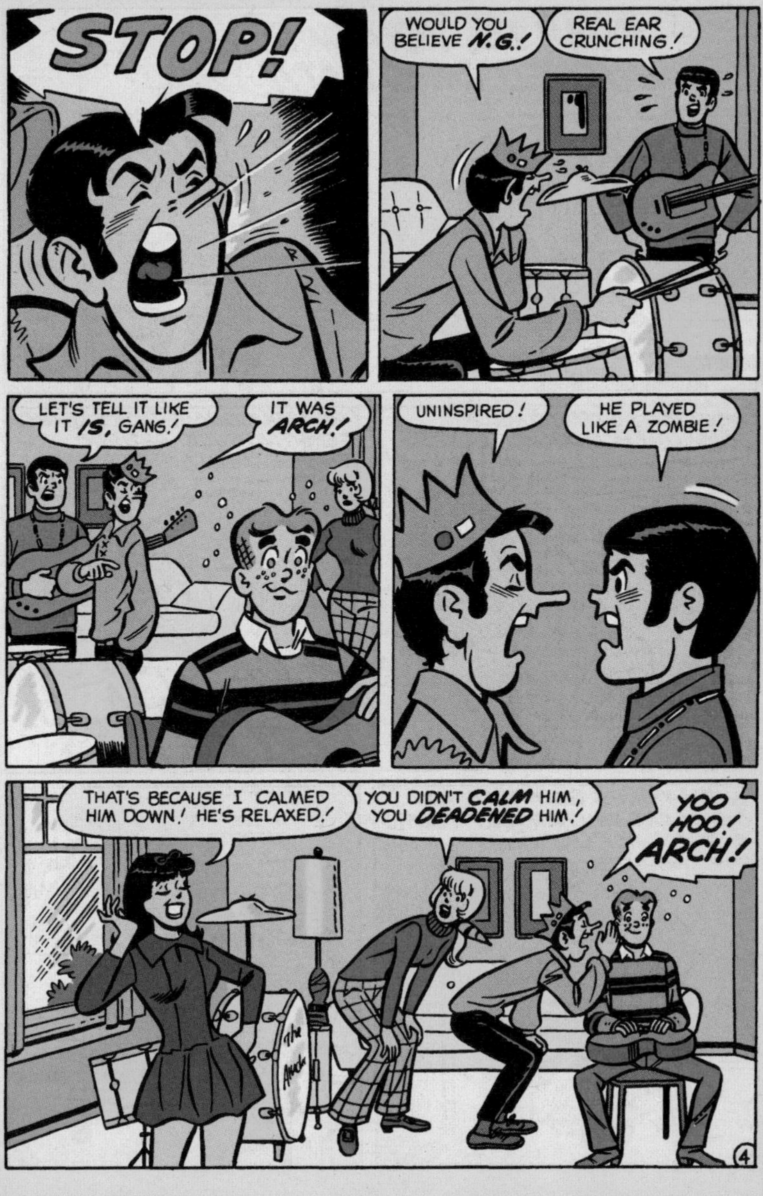
STOP!
WOULD YOU BELIEVE N.G.!
REAL EAR CRUNCHING!
LET'S TELL IT LIKE IT IS, GANG!
IT WAS ARCH!
UNINSPIRED!
HE PLAYED LIKE A ZOMBIE!
THAT'S BECAUSE I CALMED HIM DOWN! HE'S RELAXED!
YOU DIDN'T CALM HIM, YOU DEADENED HIM!
YOO HOO! ARCH!
4

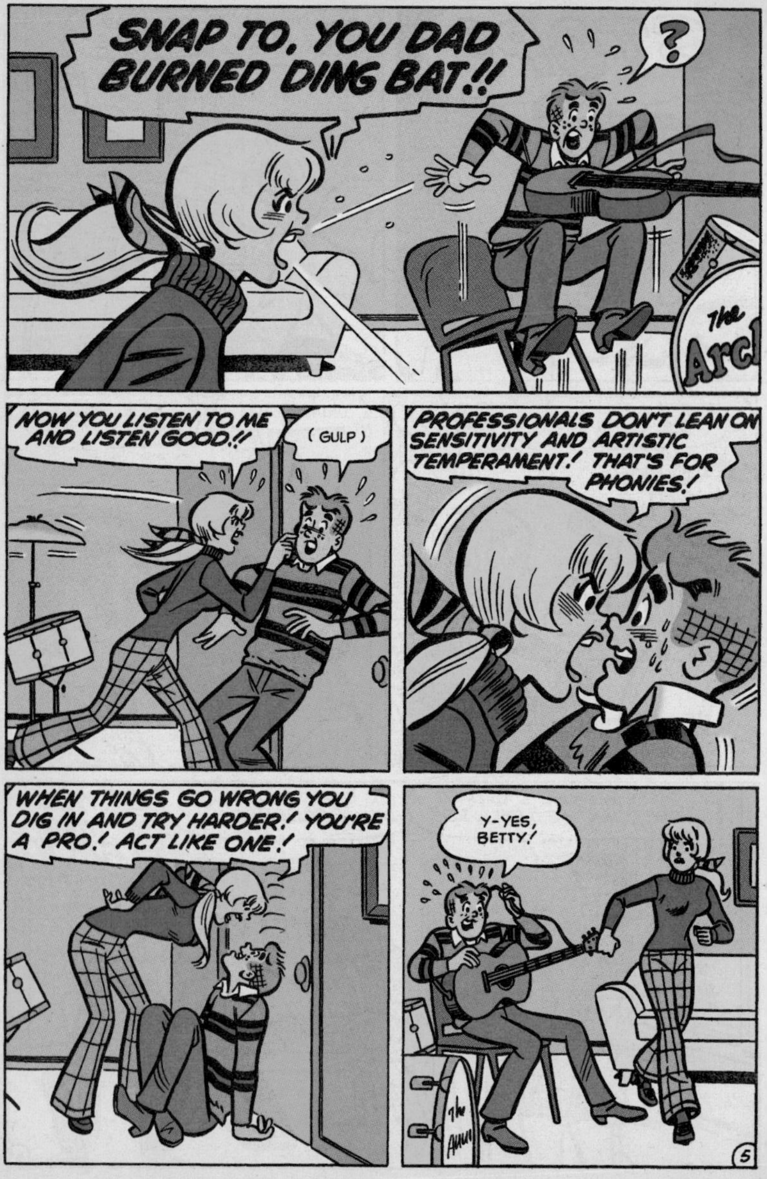
SNAP TO, YOU DAD BURNED DING BAT.!!
?
The Arch
NOW YOU LISTEN TO ME AND LISTEN GOOD.!!
(GULP)
PROFESSIONALS DON'T LEAN ON SENSITIVITY AND ARTISTIC TEMPERAMENT! THAT'S FOR PHONIES!
WHEN THINGS GO WRONG YOU DIG IN AND TRY HARDER! YOU'RE A PRO! ACT LIKE ONE!
Y-YES, BETTY!
5

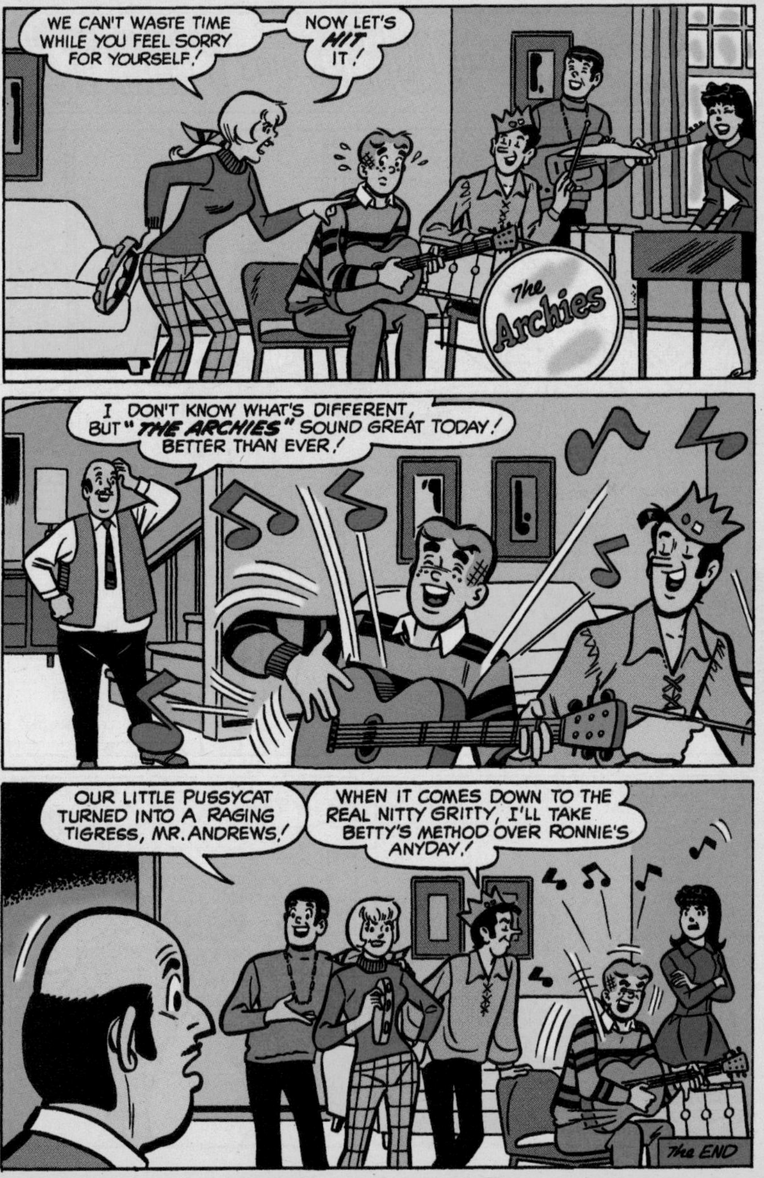
WE CAN'T WASTE TIME WHILE YOU FEEL SORRY FOR YOURSELF!
NOW LET'S HIT IT!
The Archies
I DON'T KNOW WHAT'S DIFFERENT, BUT "THE ARCHIES" SOUND GREAT TODAY! BETTER THAN EVER!
OUR LITTLE PUSSYCAT TURNED INTO A RAGING TIGRESS, MR. ANDREWS!
WHEN IT COMES DOWN TO THE REAL NITTY GRITTY, I'LL TAKE BETTY'S METHOD OVER RONNIE'S ANYDAY!
The END

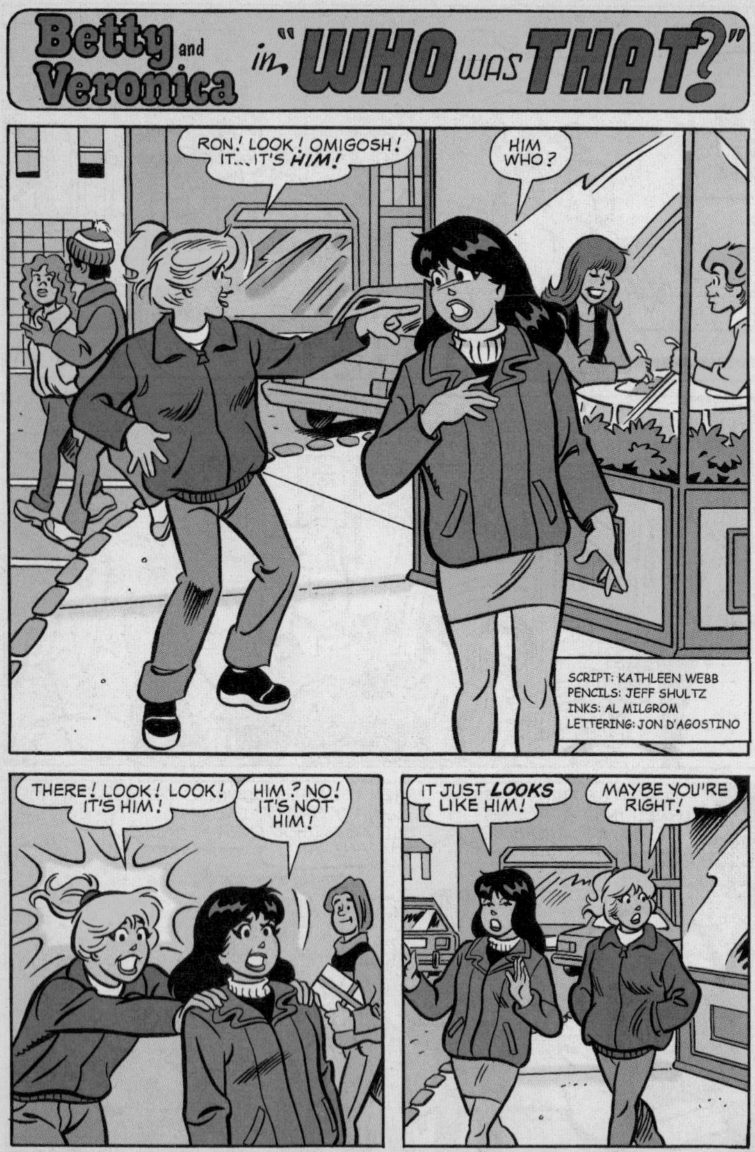
Betty and Veronica in "WHO WAS THAT?"
RON! LOOK! OMIGOSH! IT... IT'S HIM!
HIM WHO?
SCRIPT: KATHLEEN WEBB
PENCILS: JEFF SHULTZ
INKS: AL MILGROM
LETTERING: JON D'AGOSTINO
THERE! LOOK! LOOK! IT'S HIM!
HIM? NO! IT'S NOT HIM!
IT JUST LOOKS LIKE HIM!
MAYBE YOU'RE RIGHT!

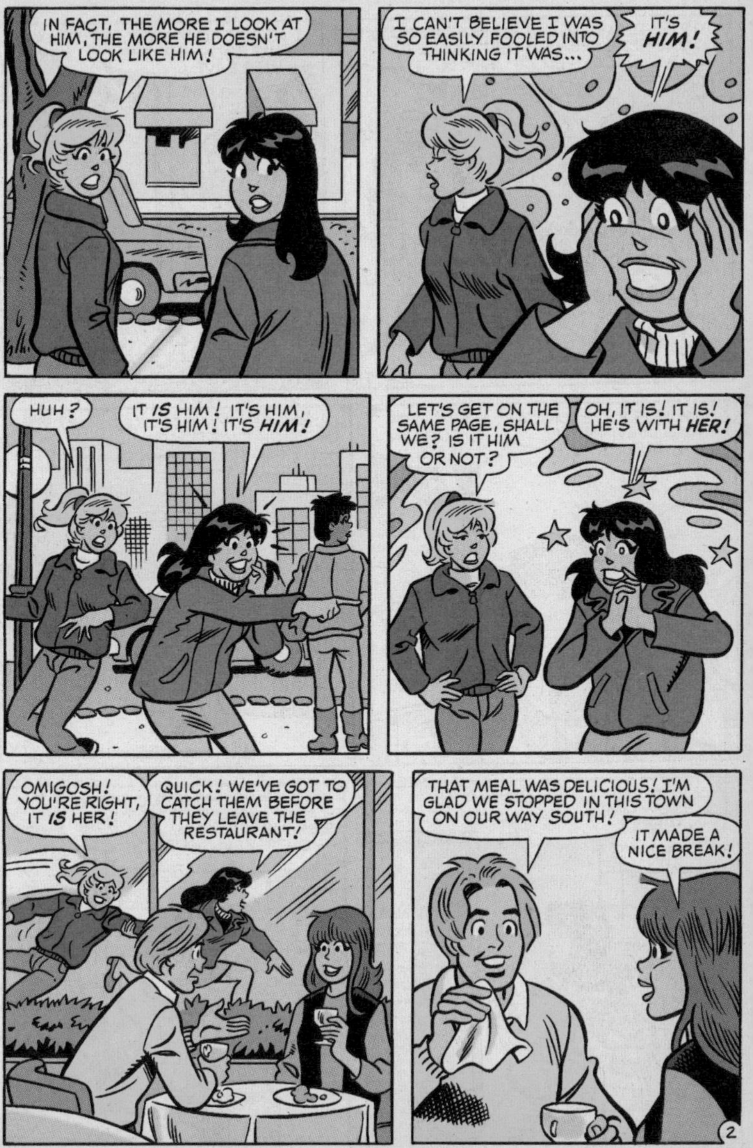

IN FACT, THE MORE I LOOK AT HIM, THE MORE HE DOESN'T LOOK LIKE HIM!
I CAN'T BELIEVE I WAS SO EASILY FOOLED INTO THINKING IT WAS...
IT'S HIM!
HUH?
IT IS HIM! IT'S HIM, IT'S HIM! IT'S HIM!
LET'S GET ON THE SAME PAGE, SHALL WE? IS IT HIM OR NOT?
OH, IT IS! IT IS! HE'S WITH HER!
OMIGOSH! YOU'RE RIGHT, IT IS HER!
QUICK! WE'VE GOT TO CATCH THEM BEFORE THEY LEAVE THE RESTAURANT!
THAT MEAL WAS DELICIOUS! I'M GLAD WE STOPPED IN THIS TOWN ON OUR WAY SOUTH!
IT MADE A NICE BREAK!
2

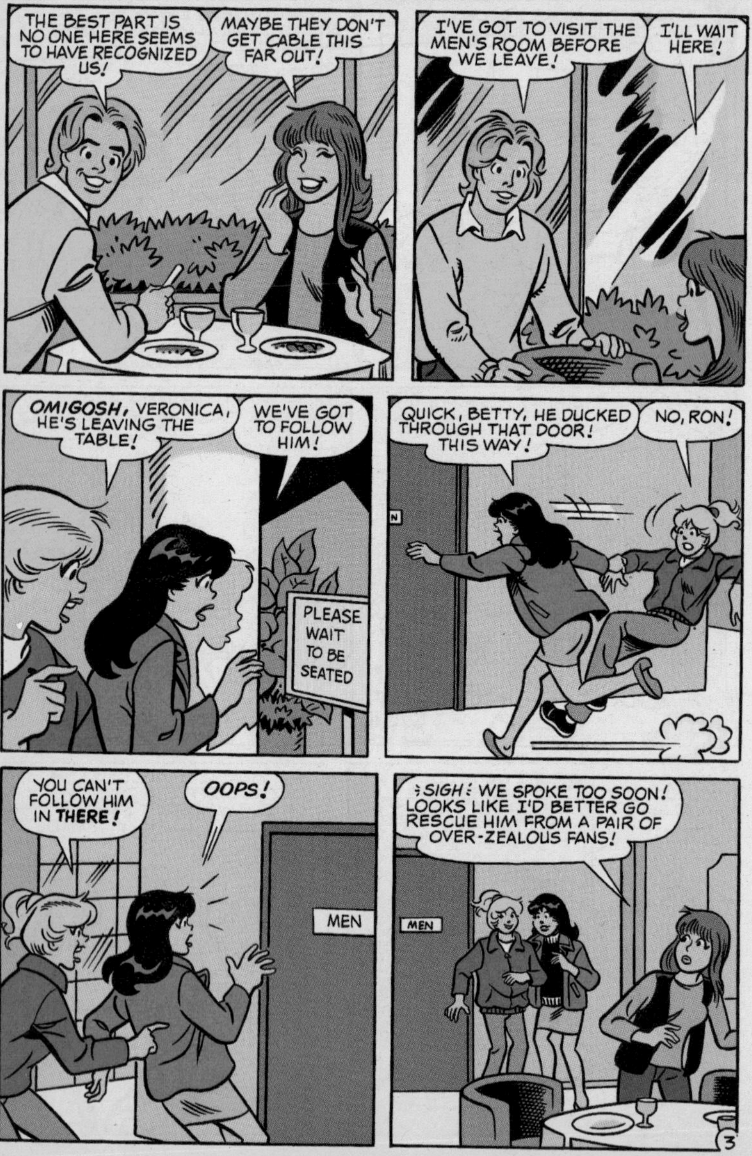
THE BEST PART IS NO ONE HERE SEEMS TO HAVE RECOGNIZED US!
MAYBE THEY DON'T GET CABLE THIS FAR OUT!
I'VE GOT TO VISIT THE MEN'S ROOM BEFORE WE LEAVE!
I'LL WAIT HERE!
OMIGOSH, VERONICA, HE'S LEAVING THE TABLE!
WE'VE GOT TO FOLLOW HIM!
PLEASE WAIT TO BE SEATED
QUICK, BETTY, HE DUCKED THROUGH THAT DOOR! THIS WAY!
NO, RON!
YOU CAN'T FOLLOW HIM IN THERE!
OOPS!
MEN
SIGH WE SPOKE TOO SOON! LOOKS LIKE I'D BETTER GO RESCUE HIM FROM A PAIR OF OVER-ZEALOUS FANS!
MEN

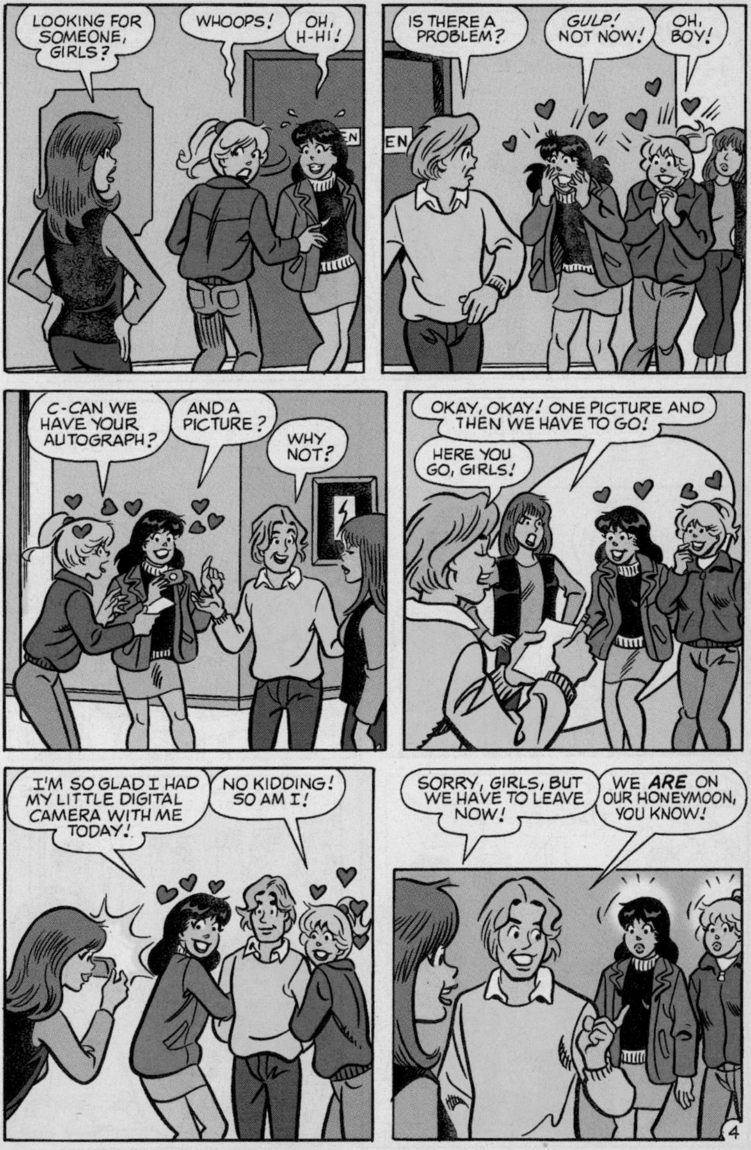
LOOKING FOR SOMEONE, GIRLS?
WHOOPS!
OH, H-HI!
EN
EN
IS THERE A PROBLEM?
GULP! NOT NOW!
OH, BOY!
C-CAN WE HAVE YOUR AUTOGRAPH?
AND A PICTURE?
WHY NOT?
OKAY, OKAY! ONE PICTURE AND THEN WE HAVE TO GO!
HERE YOU GO, GIRLS!
I'M SO GLAD I HAD MY LITTLE DIGITAL CAMERA WITH ME TODAY!
NO KIDDING! SO AM I!
SORRY, GIRLS, BUT WE HAVE TO LEAVE NOW!
WE ARE ON OUR HONEYMOON, YOU KNOW!

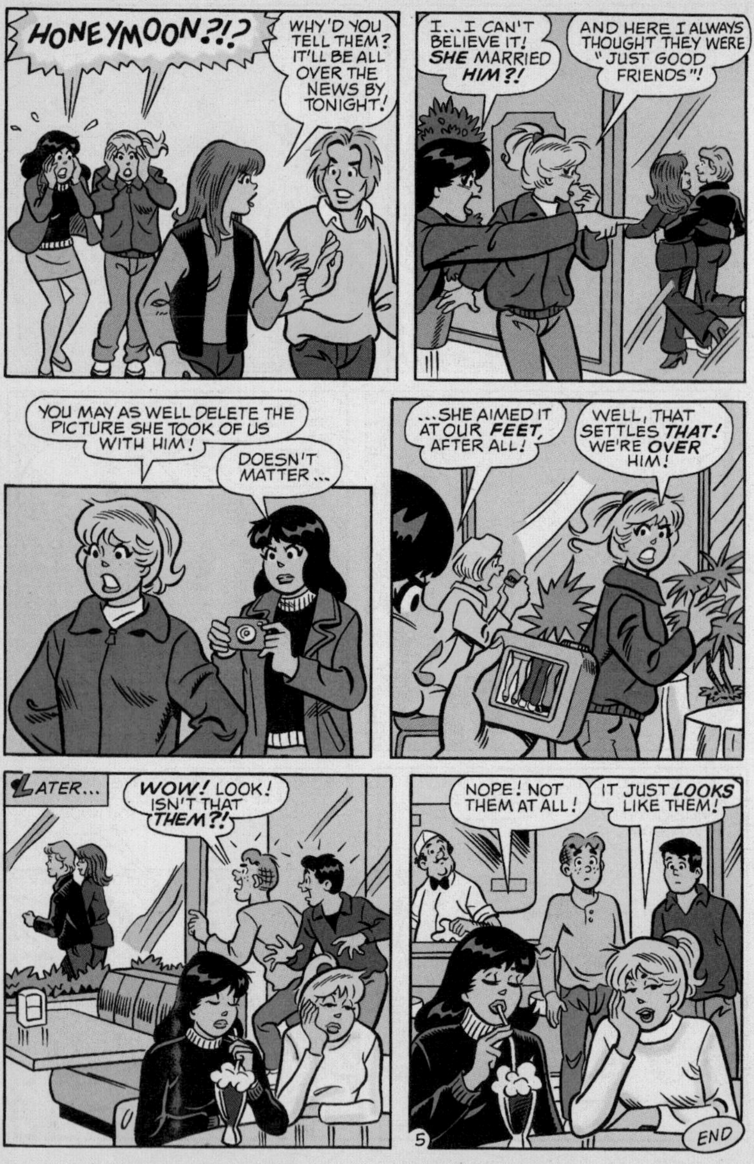
HONEYMOON?!?
WHY'D YOU TELL THEM? IT'LL BE ALL OVER THE NEWS BY TONIGHT!
I... I CAN'T BELIEVE IT! SHE MARRIED HIM?!
AND HERE I ALWAYS THOUGHT THEY WERE "JUST GOOD FRIENDS"!
YOU MAY AS WELL DELETE THE PICTURE SHE TOOK OF US WITH HIM!
DOESN'T MATTER...
...SHE AIMED IT AT OUR FEET, AFTER ALL!
WELL, THAT SETTLES THAT! WE'RE OVER HIM!
LATER...
WOW! LOOK! ISN'T THAT THEM?!
NOPE! NOT THEM AT ALL!
IT JUST LOOKS LIKE THEM!
5
END

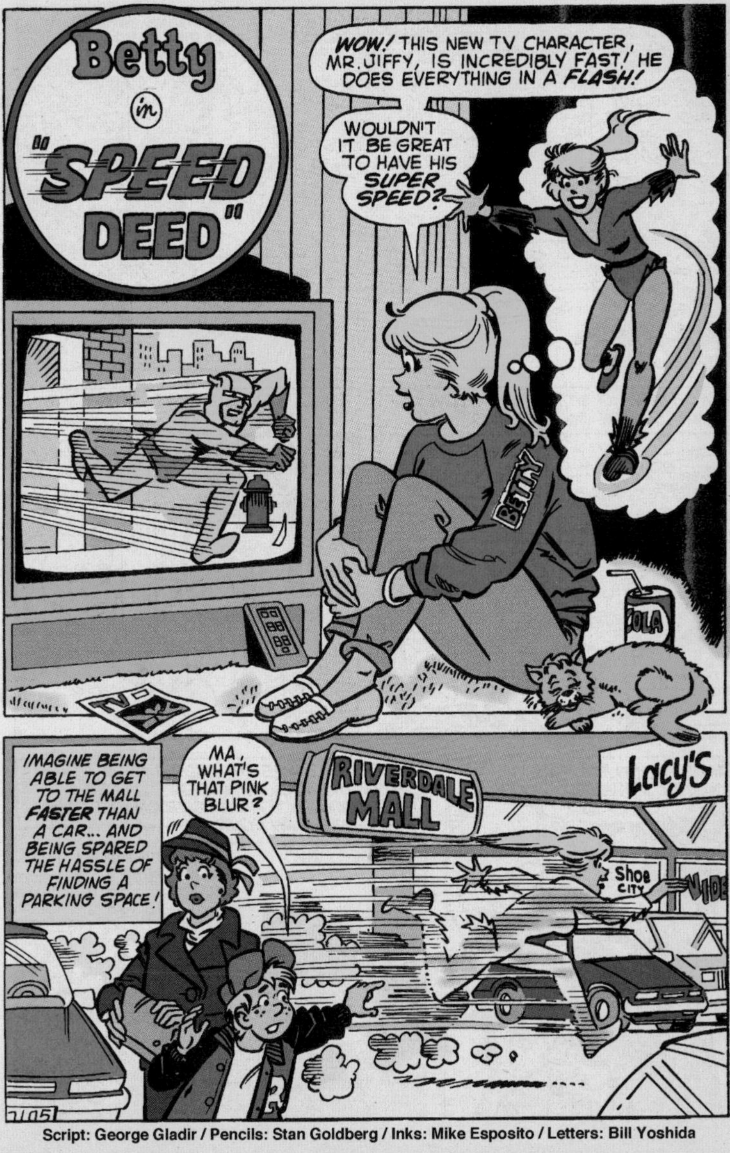
Betty
in
"SPEED DEED"
WOW! THIS NEW TV CHARACTER, MR. JIFFY, IS INCREDIBLY FAST! HE DOES EVERYTHING IN A FLASH!
WOULDN'T IT BE GREAT TO HAVE HIS SUPER SPEED?
BETTY
COLA
TV
IMAGINE BEING ABLE TO GET TO THE MALL FASTER THAN A CAR... AND BEING SPARED THE HASSLE OF FINDING A PARKING SPACE!
MA, WHAT'S THAT PINK BLUR?
RIVERDALE MALL
Lacy's
Shoe CITY

Script: George Gladir / Pencils: Stan Goldberg / Inks: Mike Esposito / Letters: Bill Yoshida

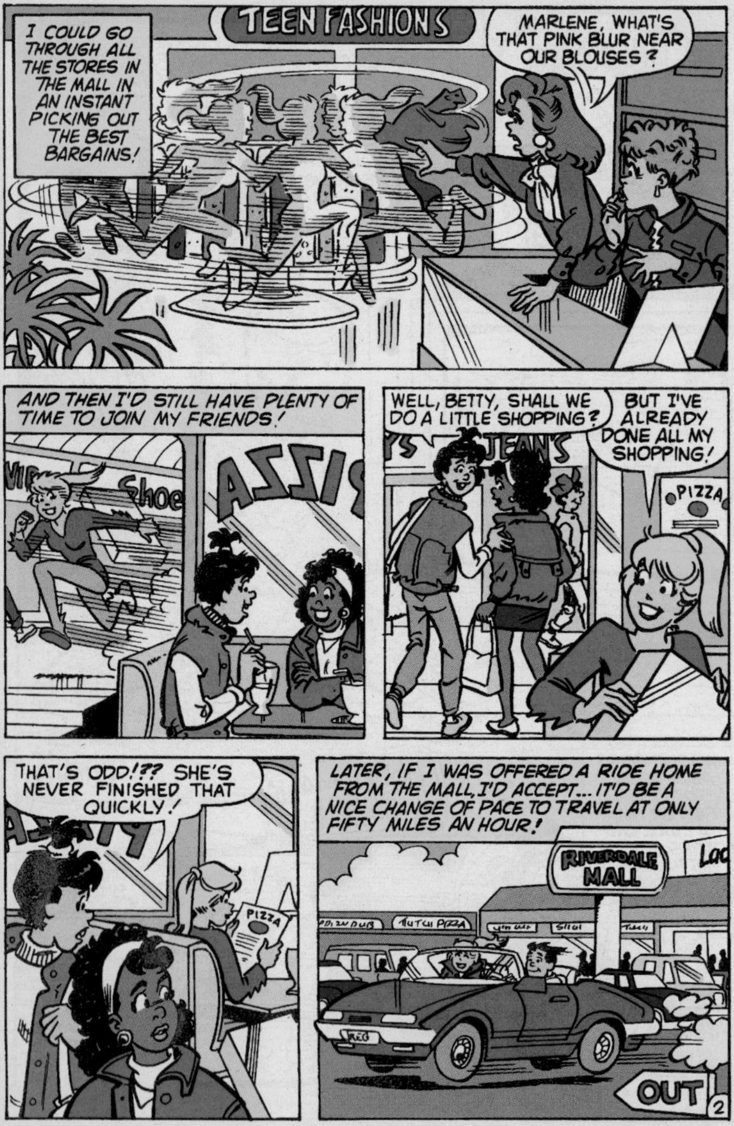

TEEN FASHIONS
I COULD GO THROUGH ALL THE STORES IN THE MALL IN AN INSTANT PICKING OUT THE BEST BARGAINS!
MARLENE, WHAT'S THAT PINK BLUR NEAR OUR BLOUSES?
AND THEN I'D STILL HAVE PLENTY OF TIME TO JOIN MY FRIENDS!
PIZZA
Shoe
WELL, BETTY, SHALL WE DO A LITTLE SHOPPING?
BUT I'VE ALREADY DONE ALL MY SHOPPING!
JEAN'S
PIZZA
THAT'S ODD!?? SHE'S NEVER FINISHED THAT QUICKLY!
PIZZA
LATER, IF I WAS OFFERED A RIDE HOME FROM THE MALL, I'D ACCEPT... IT'D BE A NICE CHANGE OF PACE TO TRAVEL AT ONLY FIFTY MILES AN HOUR!
RIVERDALE MALL
OUT
REG

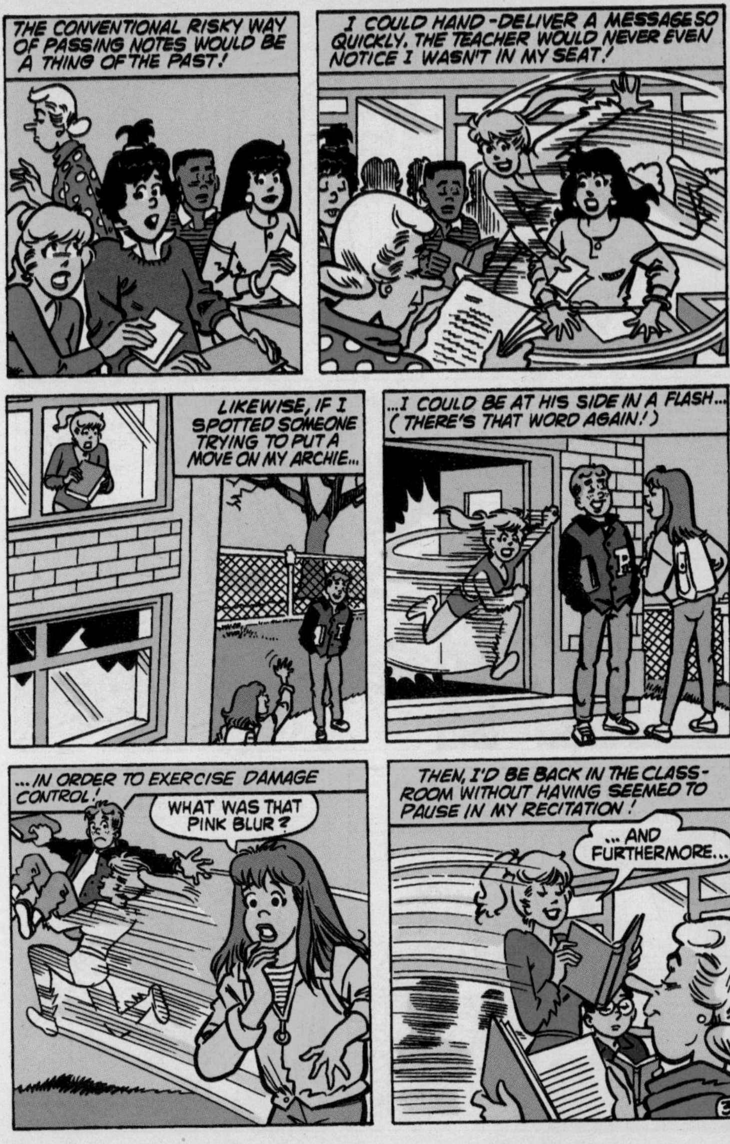
THE CONVENTIONAL RISKY WAY OF PASSING NOTES WOULD BE A THING OF THE PAST!
I COULD HAND-DELIVER A MESSAGE SO QUICKLY, THE TEACHER WOULD NEVER EVEN NOTICE I WASN'T IN MY SEAT!
LIKEWISE, IF I SPOTTED SOMEONE TRYING TO PUT A MOVE ON MY ARCHIE...
...I COULD BE AT HIS SIDE IN A FLASH... (THERE'S THAT WORD AGAIN!)
...IN ORDER TO EXERCISE DAMAGE CONTROL!
WHAT WAS THAT PINK BLUR?
THEN, I'D BE BACK IN THE CLASS-ROOM WITHOUT HAVING SEEMED TO PAUSE IN MY RECITATION!
... AND FURTHERMORE...
3

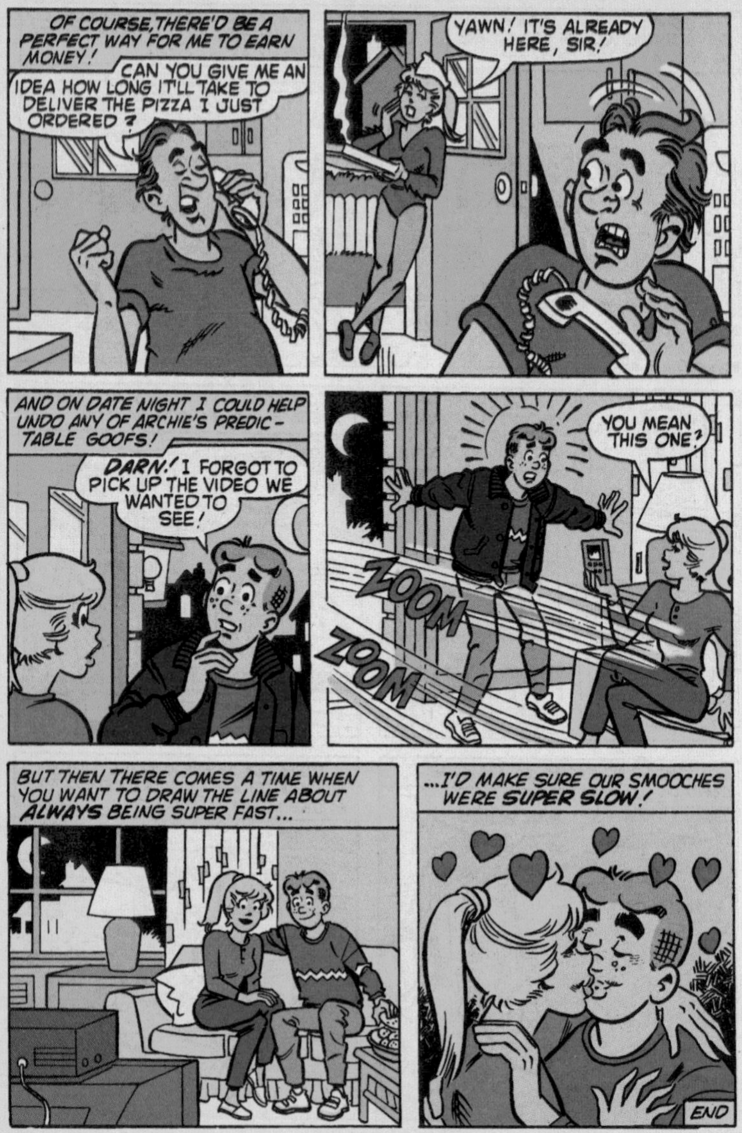

OF COURSE, THERE'D BE A PERFECT WAY FOR ME TO EARN MONEY!
CAN YOU GIVE ME AN IDEA HOW LONG IT'LL TAKE TO DELIVER THE PIZZA I JUST ORDERED?
YAWN! IT'S ALREADY HERE, SIR!
AND ON DATE NIGHT I COULD HELP UNDO ANY OF ARCHIE'S PREDIC-TABLE GOOFS!
DARN! I FORGOT TO PICK UP THE VIDEO WE WANTED TO SEE!
YOU MEAN THIS ONE?
ZOOM
ZOOM
BUT THEN THERE COMES A TIME WHEN YOU WANT TO DRAW THE LINE ABOUT ALWAYS BEING SUPER FAST...
...I'D MAKE SURE OUR SMOOCHES WERE SUPER SLOW!
END

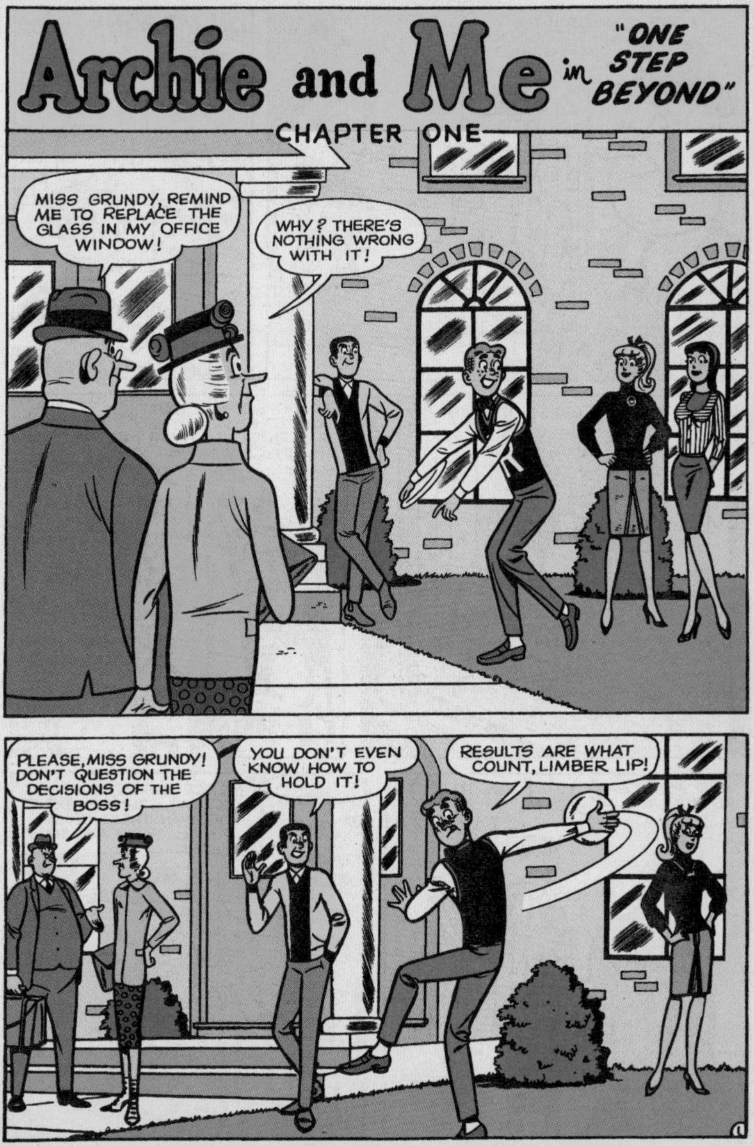
Archie and Me in "ONE STEP BEYOND"
CHAPTER ONE
MISS GRUNDY, REMIND ME TO REPLACE THE GLASS IN MY OFFICE WINDOW!
WHY? THERE'S NOTHING WRONG WITH IT!
PLEASE, MISS GRUNDY! DON'T QUESTION THE DECISIONS OF THE BOSS!
YOU DON'T EVEN KNOW HOW TO HOLD IT!
RESULTS ARE WHAT COUNT, LIMBER LIP!
1

Script: Frank Doyle / Pencils: Bob Bolling / Inks & Letters: Mario Acquaviva

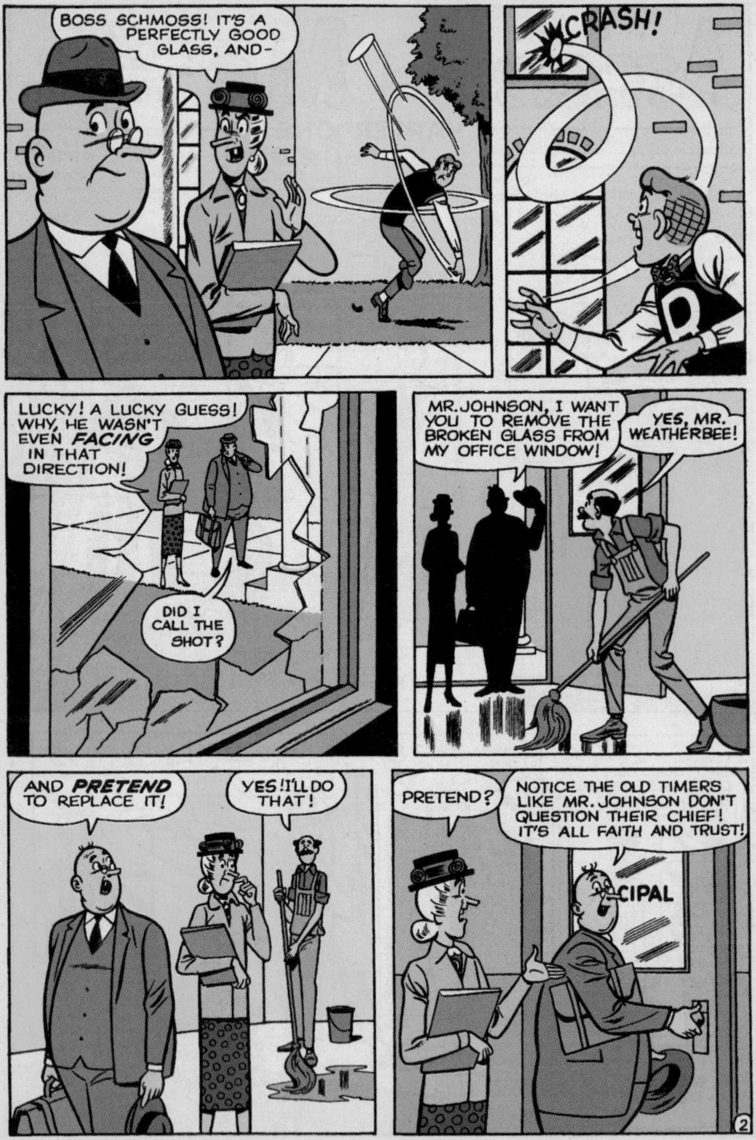
BOSS SCHMOSS! IT'S A PERFECTLY GOOD GLASS, AND-
CRASH!
LUCKY! A LUCKY GUESS! WHY, HE WASN'T EVEN FACING IN THAT DIRECTION!
DID I CALL THE SHOT?
MR. JOHNSON, I WANT YOU TO REMOVE THE BROKEN GLASS FROM MY OFFICE WINDOW!
YES, MR. WEATHERBEE!
AND PRETEND TO REPLACE IT!
YES! I'LL DO THAT!
PRETEND?
NOTICE THE OLD TIMERS LIKE MR. JOHNSON DON'T QUESTION THEIR CHIEF! IT'S ALL FAITH AND TRUST!
CIPAL
2

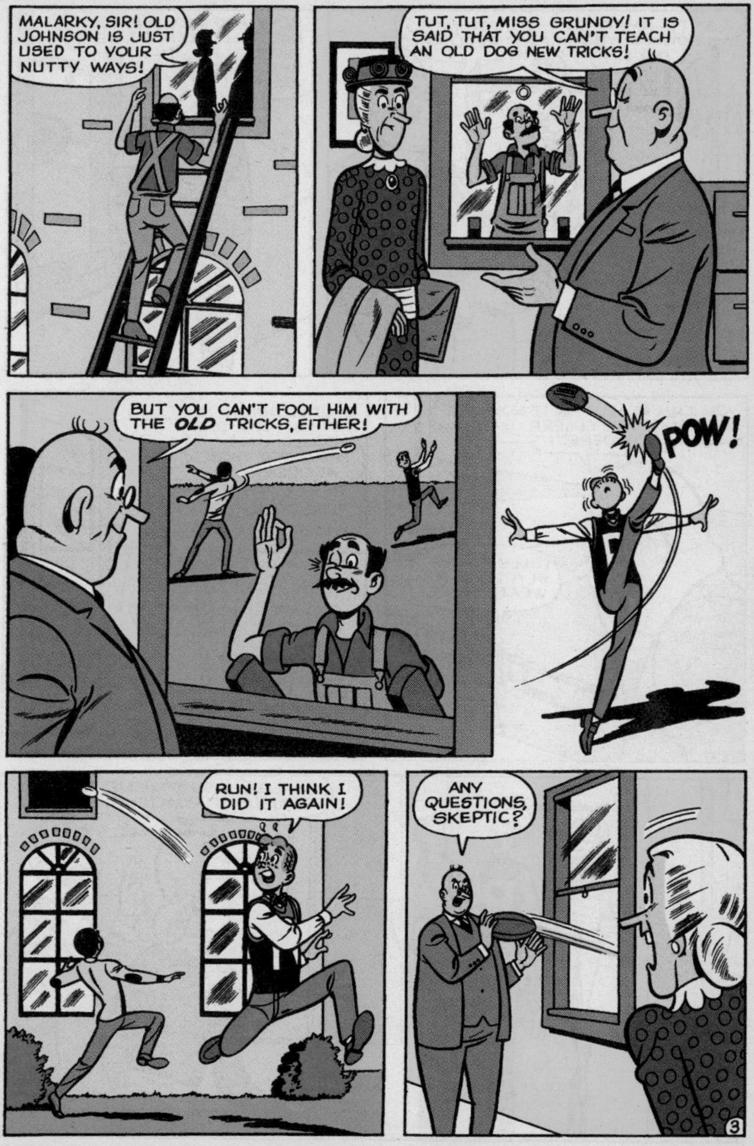
MALARKY, SIR! OLD JOHNSON IS JUST USED TO YOUR NUTTY WAYS!
TUT, TUT, MISS GRUNDY! IT IS SAID THAT YOU CAN'T TEACH AN OLD DOG NEW TRICKS!
BUT YOU CAN'T FOOL HIM WITH THE OLD TRICKS, EITHER!
POW!
RUN! I THINK I DID IT AGAIN!
ANY QUESTIONS, SKEPTIC?
3

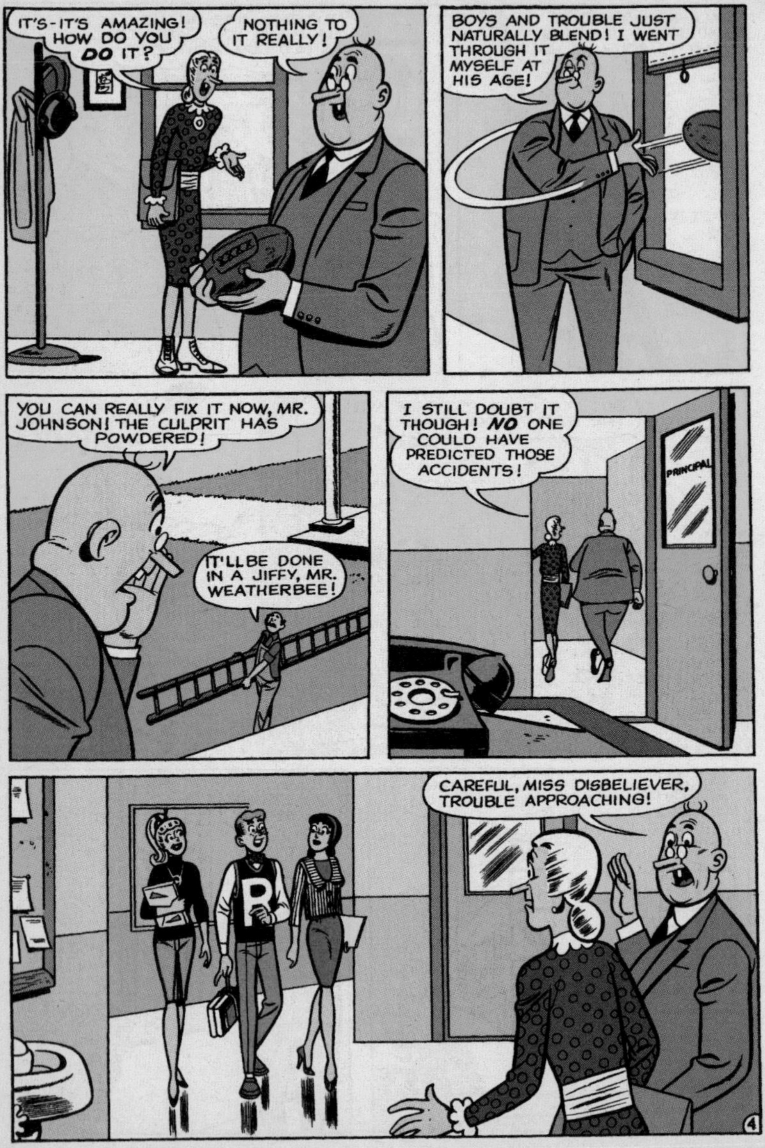

IT'S-IT'S AMAZING! HOW DO YOU DO IT?
NOTHING TO IT REALLY!
BOYS AND TROUBLE JUST NATURALLY BLEND! I WENT THROUGH IT MYSELF AT HIS AGE!
YOU CAN REALLY FIX IT NOW, MR. JOHNSON! THE CULPRIT HAS POWDERED!
IT'LL BE DONE IN A JIFFY, MR. WEATHERBEE!
I STILL DOUBT IT THOUGH! NO ONE COULD HAVE PREDICTED THOSE ACCIDENTS!
PRINCIPAL
CAREFUL, MISS DISBELIEVER, TROUBLE APPROACHING!
R
4

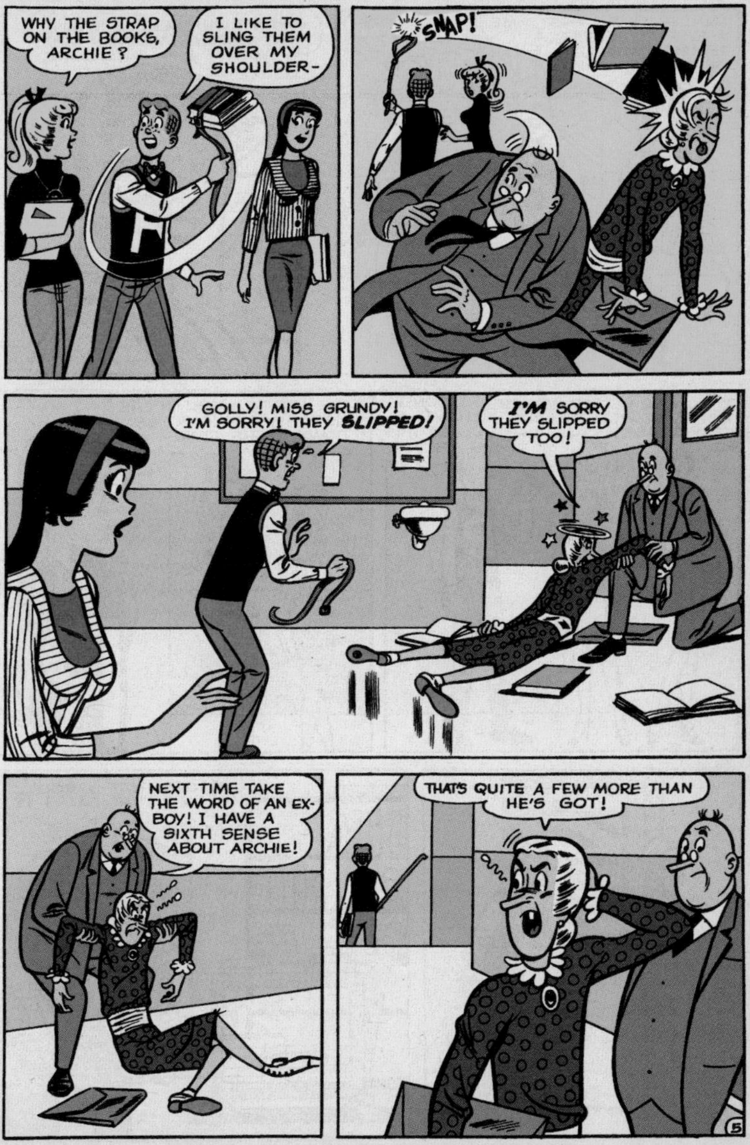
WHY THE STRAP ON THE BOOKS, ARCHIE ?
I LIKE TO SLING THEM OVER MY SHOULDER-
SNAP!
GOLLY! MISS GRUNDY! I'M SORRY! THEY SLIPPED!
I'M SORRY THEY SLIPPED TOO!
NEXT TIME TAKE THE WORD OF AN EX-BOY! I HAVE A SIXTH SENSE ABOUT ARCHIE!
THAT'S QUITE A FEW MORE THAN HE'S GOT!
5

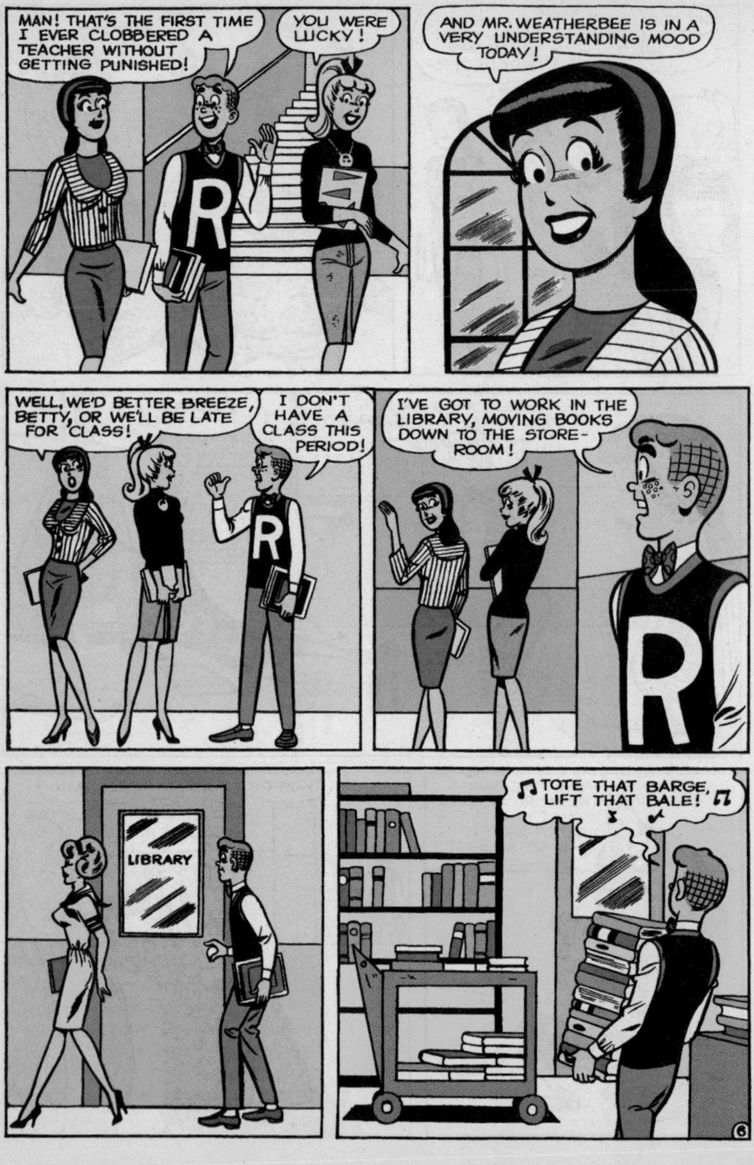

MAN! THAT'S THE FIRST TIME I EVER CLOBBERED A TEACHER WITHOUT GETTING PUNISHED!
YOU WERE LUCKY!
AND MR. WEATHERBEE IS IN A VERY UNDERSTANDING MOOD TODAY!
WELL, WE'D BETTER BREEZE, BETTY, OR WE'LL BE LATE FOR CLASS!
I DON'T HAVE A CLASS THIS PERIOD!
I'VE GOT TO WORK IN THE LIBRARY, MOVING BOOKS DOWN TO THE STORE-ROOM!
LIBRARY
TOTE THAT BARGE, LIFT THAT BALE!
6

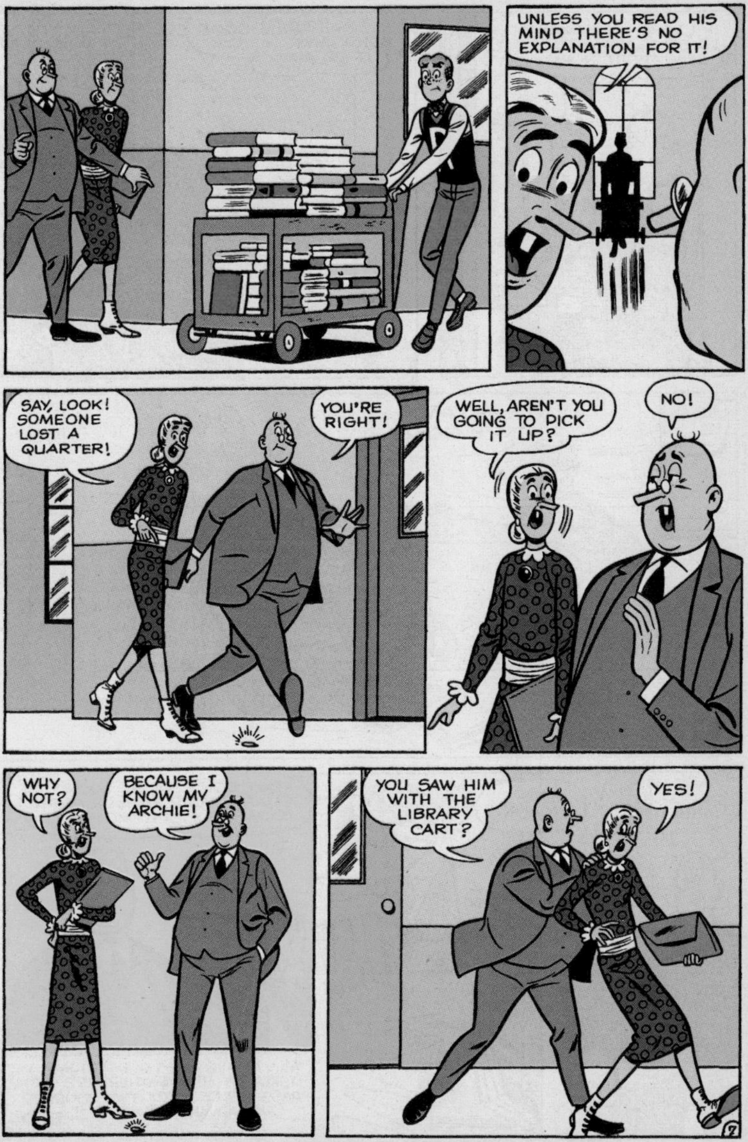

UNLESS YOU READ HIS MIND THERE'S NO EXPLANATION FOR IT!
SAY, LOOK! SOMEONE LOST A QUARTER!
YOU'RE RIGHT!
WELL, AREN'T YOU GOING TO PICK IT UP?
NO!
WHY NOT?
BECAUSE I KNOW MY ARCHIE!
YOU SAW HIM WITH THE LIBRARY CART?
YES!
7

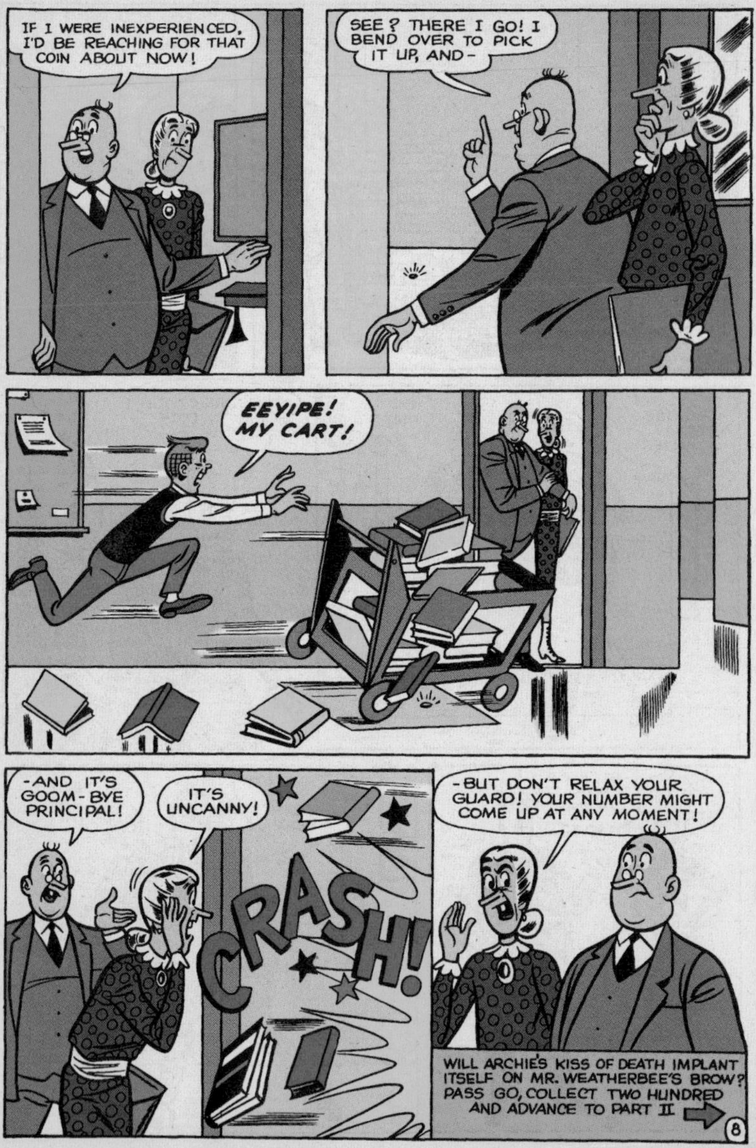
IF I WERE INEXPERIENCED, I'D BE REACHING FOR THAT COIN ABOUT NOW!
SEE? THERE I GO! I BEND OVER TO PICK IT UP, AND-
EEYIPE! MY CART!
-AND IT'S GOOM-BYE PRINCIPAL!
IT'S UNCANNY!
CRASH!
-BUT DON'T RELAX YOUR GUARD! YOUR NUMBER MIGHT COME UP AT ANY MOMENT!
WILL ARCHIE'S KISS OF DEATH IMPLANT ITSELF ON MR. WEATHERBEE'S BROW? PASS GO, COLLECT TWO HUNDRED AND ADVANCE TO PART II
8

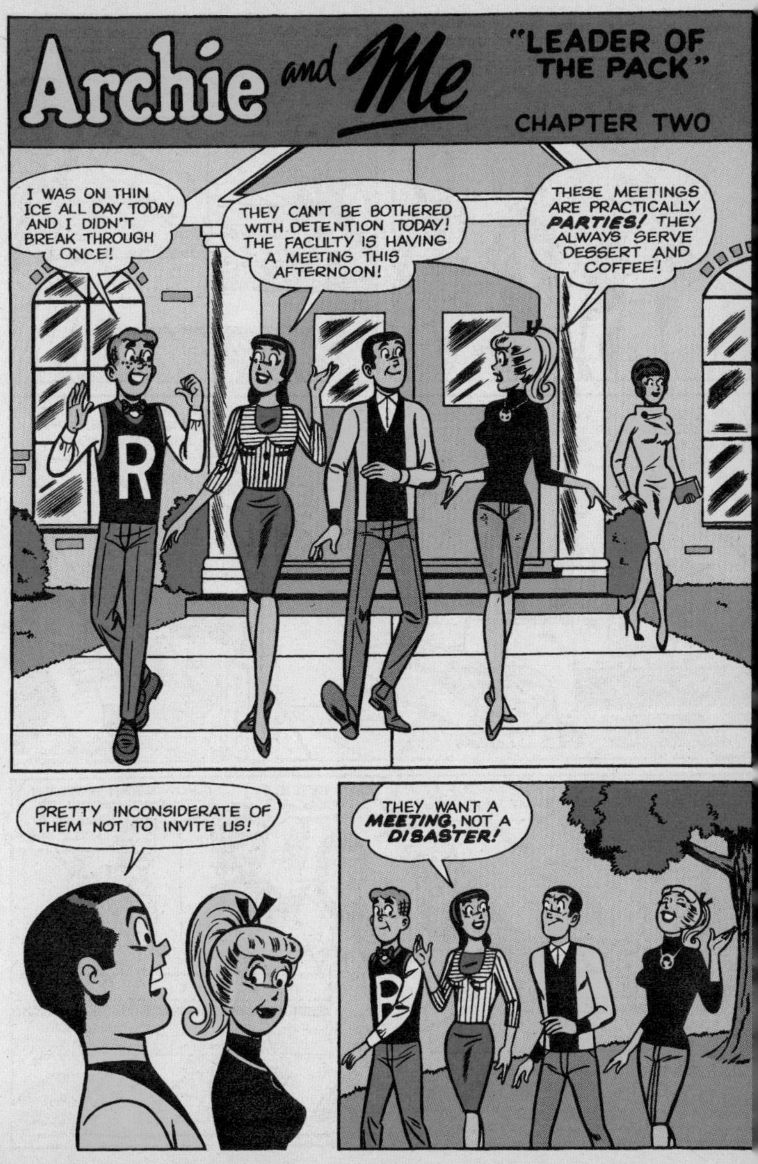
Archie and Me
"LEADER OF THE PACK"
CHAPTER TWO
I WAS ON THIN ICE ALL DAY TODAY AND I DIDN'T BREAK THROUGH ONCE!
THEY CAN'T BE BOTHERED WITH DETENTION TODAY! THE FACULTY IS HAVING A MEETING THIS AFTERNOON!
THESE MEETINGS ARE PRACTICALLY PARTIES! THEY ALWAYS SERVE DESSERT AND COFFEE!
PRETTY INCONSIDERATE OF THEM NOT TO INVITE US!
THEY WANT A MEETING, NOT A DISASTER!

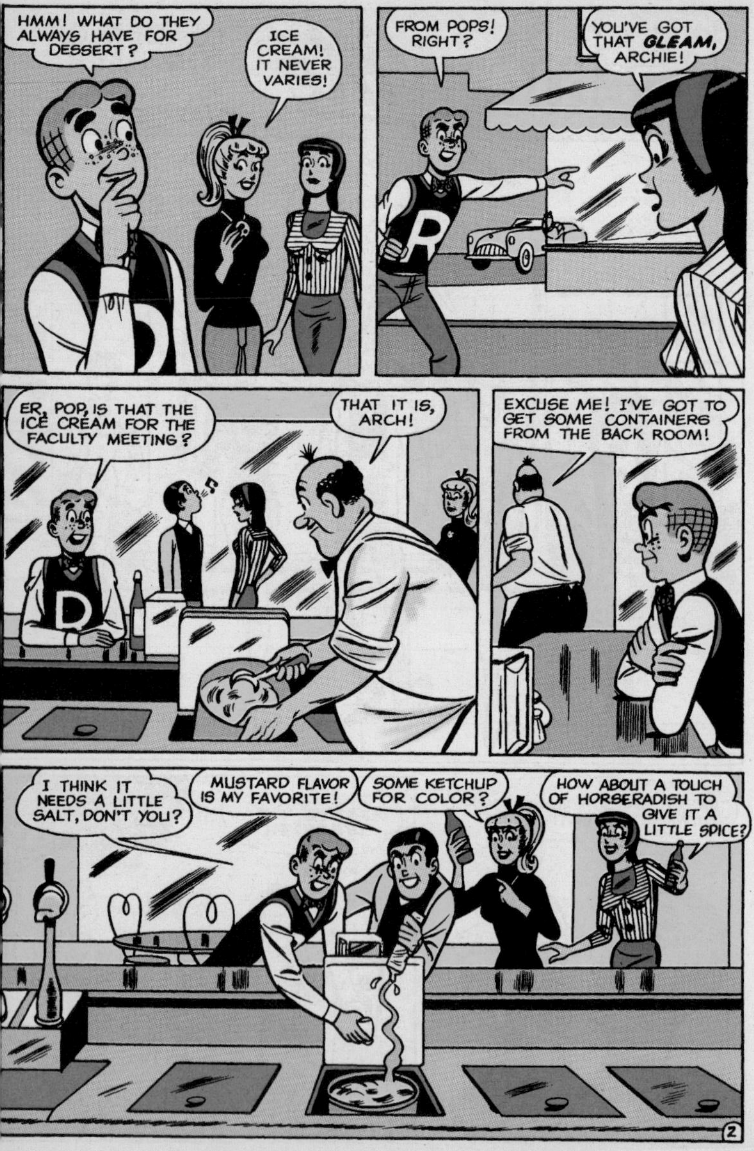
HMM! WHAT DO THEY ALWAYS HAVE FOR DESSERT?
ICE CREAM! IT NEVER VARIES!
FROM POPS! RIGHT?
YOU'VE GOT THAT GLEAM, ARCHIE!
ER, POP, IS THAT THE ICE CREAM FOR THE FACULTY MEETING?
THAT IT IS, ARCH!
EXCUSE ME! I'VE GOT TO GET SOME CONTAINERS FROM THE BACK ROOM!
I THINK IT NEEDS A LITTLE SALT, DON'T YOU?
MUSTARD FLAVOR IS MY FAVORITE!
SOME KETCHUP FOR COLOR?
HOW ABOUT A TOUCH OF HORSERADISH TO GIVE IT A LITTLE SPICE?
2

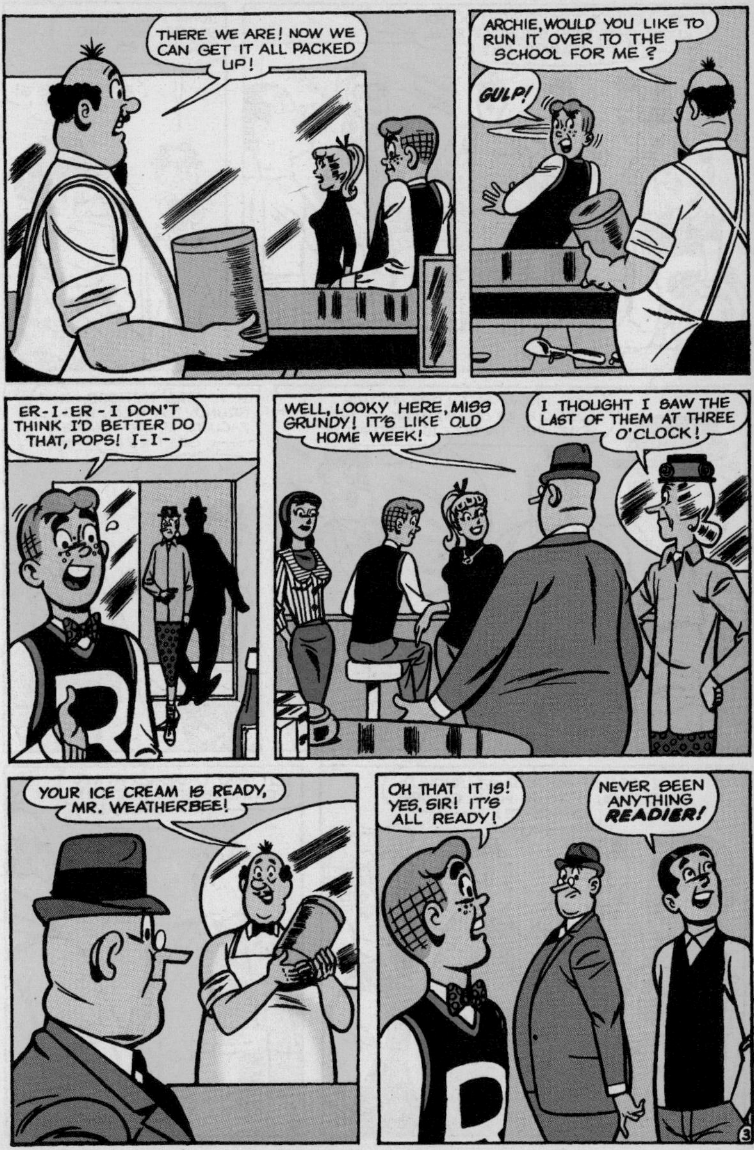
THERE WE ARE! NOW WE CAN GET IT ALL PACKED UP!
ARCHIE, WOULD YOU LIKE TO RUN IT OVER TO THE SCHOOL FOR ME?
GULP!
ER-I-ER-I DON'T THINK I'D BETTER DO THAT, POPS! I-I-
WELL, LOOKY HERE, MISS GRUNDY! IT'S LIKE OLD HOME WEEK!
I THOUGHT I SAW THE LAST OF THEM AT THREE O'CLOCK!
YOUR ICE CREAM IS READY, MR. WEATHERBEE!
OH THAT IT IS! YES, SIR! IT'S ALL READY!
NEVER SEEN ANYTHING READIER!
3

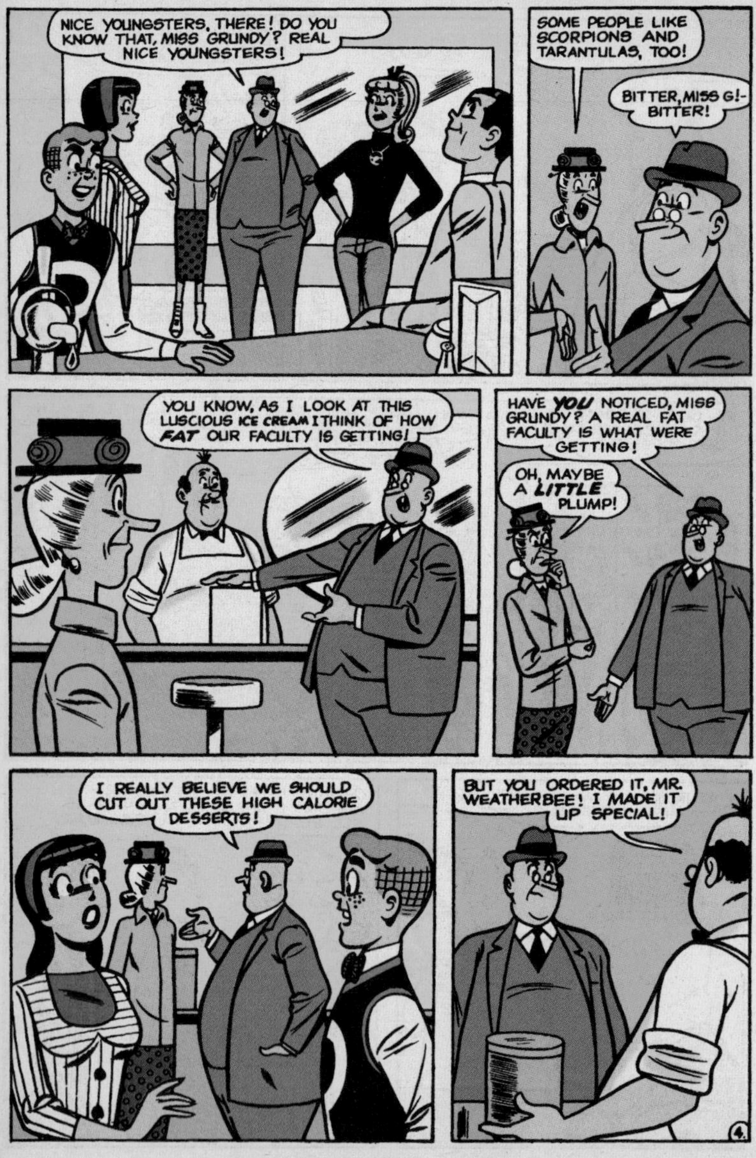
NICE YOUNGSTERS, THERE! DO YOU KNOW THAT, MISS GRUNDY? REAL NICE YOUNGSTERS!
SOME PEOPLE LIKE SCORPIONS AND TARANTULAS, TOO!
BITTER, MISS G!- BITTER!
YOU KNOW, AS I LOOK AT THIS LUSCIOUS ICE CREAM I THINK OF HOW FAT OUR FACULTY IS GETTING!
HAVE YOU NOTICED, MISS GRUNDY? A REAL FAT FACULTY IS WHAT WERE GETTING!
OH, MAYBE A LITTLE PLUMP!
I REALLY BELIEVE WE SHOULD CUT OUT THESE HIGH CALORIE DESSERTS!
BUT YOU ORDERED IT, MR. WEATHERBEE! I MADE IT UP SPECIAL!
4.

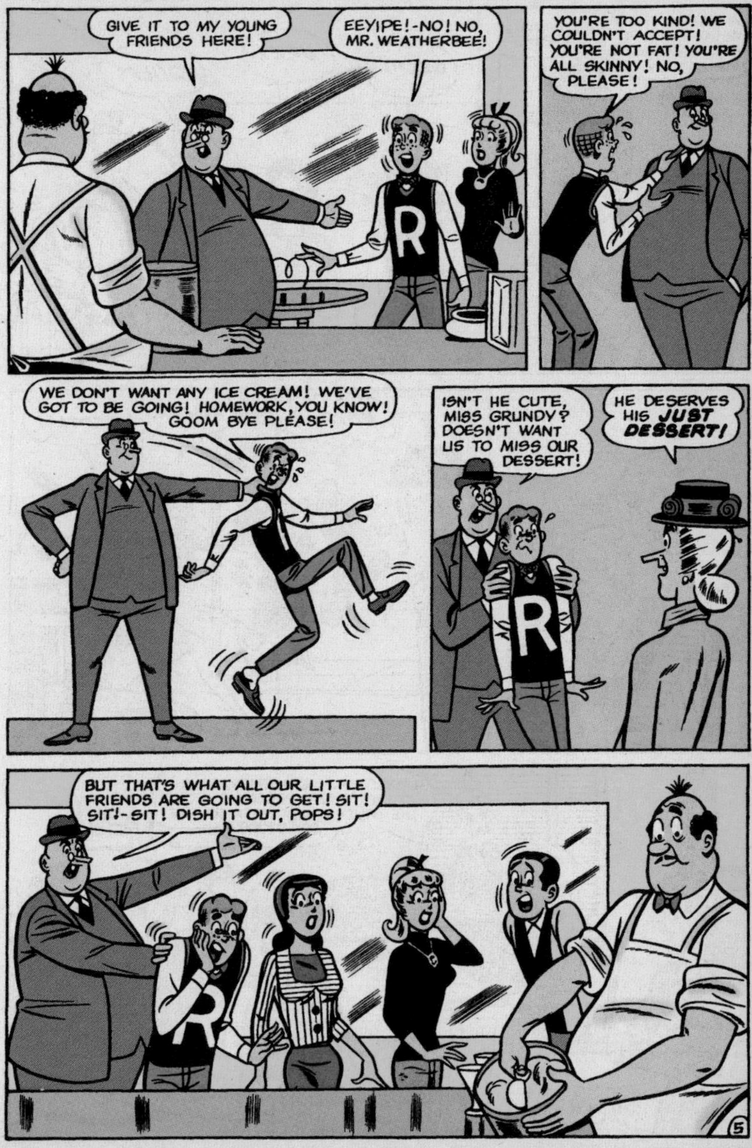

GIVE IT TO MY YOUNG FRIENDS HERE!
EEYIPE!-NO! NO, MR. WEATHERBEE!
YOU'RE TOO KIND! WE COULDN'T ACCEPT! YOU'RE NOT FAT! YOU'RE ALL SKINNY! NO, PLEASE!
WE DON'T WANT ANY ICE CREAM! WE'VE GOT TO BE GOING! HOMEWORK, YOU KNOW! GOOM BYE PLEASE!
ISN'T HE CUTE, MISS GRUNDY? DOESN'T WANT US TO MISS OUR DESSERT!
HE DESERVES HIS JUST DESSERT!
BUT THAT'S WHAT ALL OUR LITTLE FRIENDS ARE GOING TO GET! SIT! SIT!-SIT! DISH IT OUT, POPS!
5

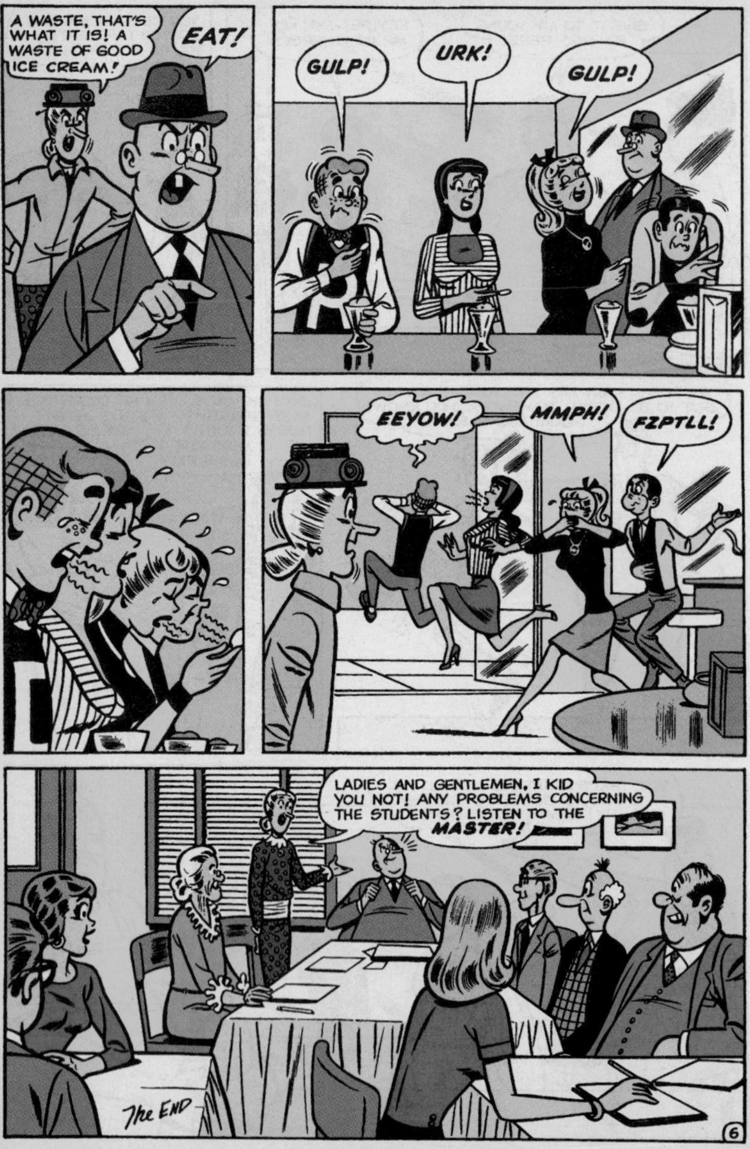
A WASTE, THAT'S WHAT IT IS! A WASTE OF GOOD ICE CREAM!
EAT!
GULP!
URK!
GULP!
EEYOW!
MMPH!
FZPTLL!
LADIES AND GENTLEMEN, I KID YOU NOT! ANY PROBLEMS CONCERNING THE STUDENTS? LISTEN TO THE MASTER!
The END
6

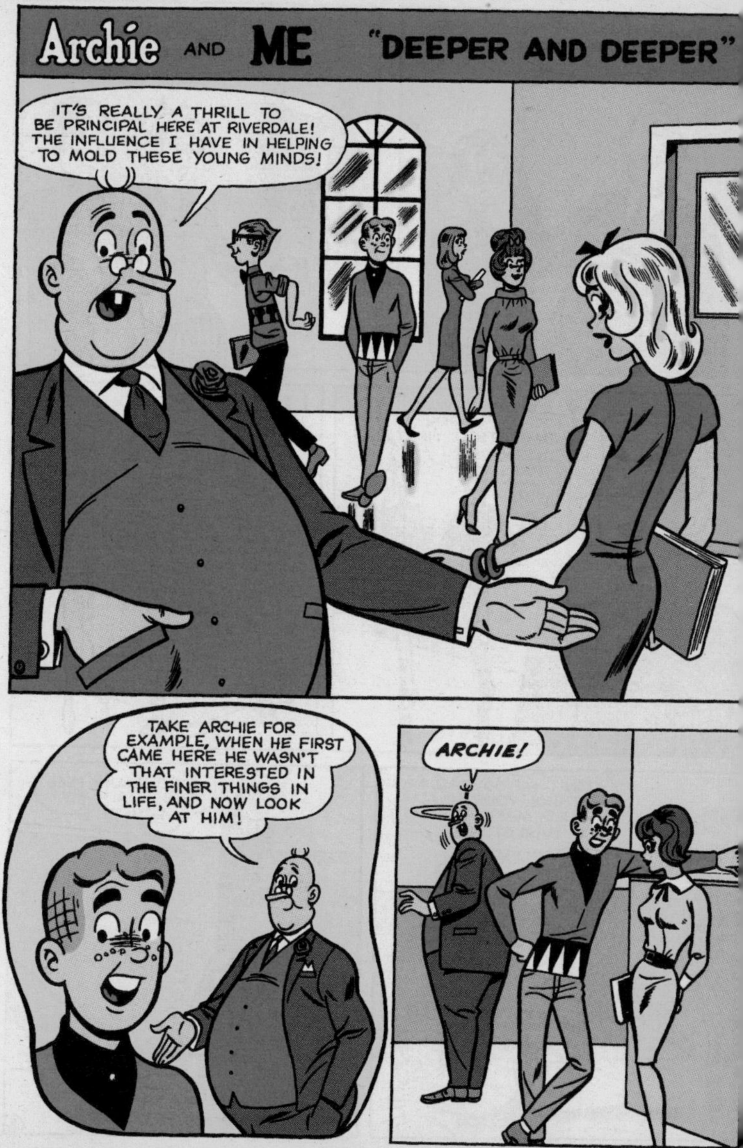
Archie AND ME "DEEPER AND DEEPER"
IT'S REALLY A THRILL TO BE PRINCIPAL HERE AT RIVERDALE! THE INFLUENCE I HAVE IN HELPING TO MOLD THESE YOUNG MINDS!
TAKE ARCHIE FOR EXAMPLE, WHEN HE FIRST CAME HERE HE WASN'T THAT INTERESTED IN THE FINER THINGS IN LIFE, AND NOW LOOK AT HIM!
ARCHIE!

Script & Pencils: Bob Bolling / Inks & Letters: Mario Acquaviva

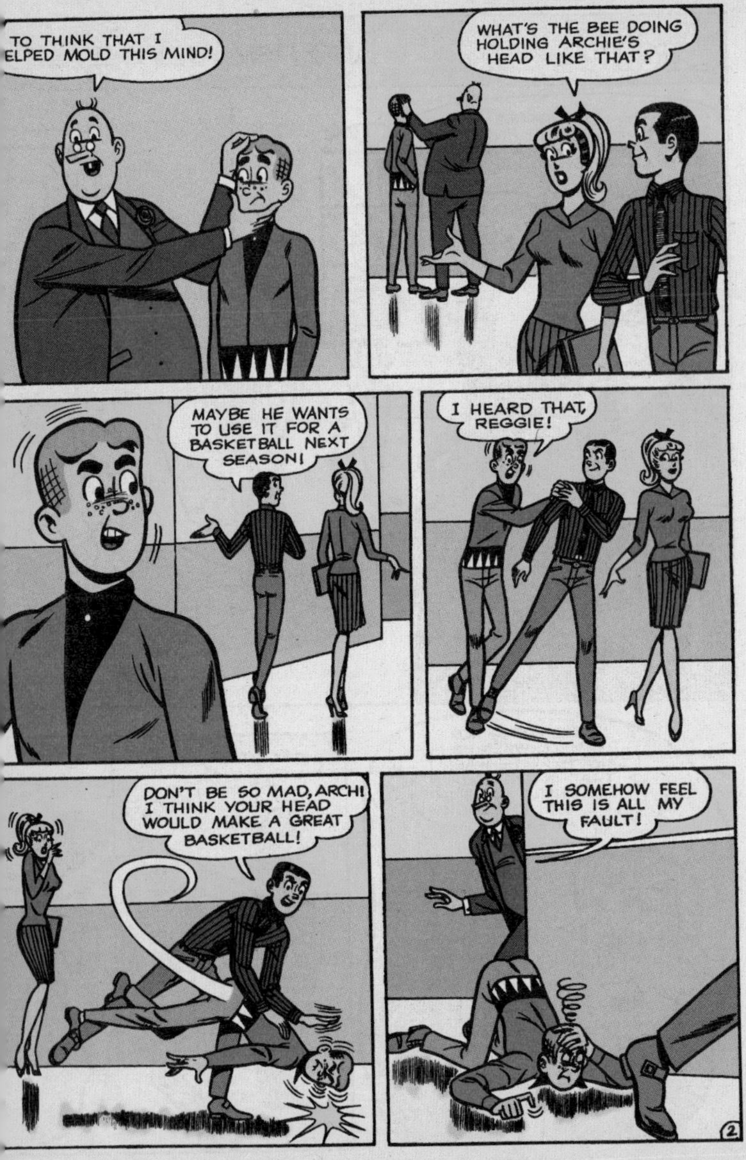

TO THINK THAT I
ELPED MOLD THIS MIND!
WHAT'S THE BEE DOING HOLDING ARCHIE'S HEAD LIKE THAT?
MAYBE HE WANTS TO USE IT FOR A BASKETBALL NEXT SEASON!
I HEARD THAT, REGGIE!
DON'T BE SO MAD, ARCH! I THINK YOUR HEAD WOULD MAKE A GREAT BASKETBALL!
I SOMEHOW FEEL THIS IS ALL MY FAULT!
2

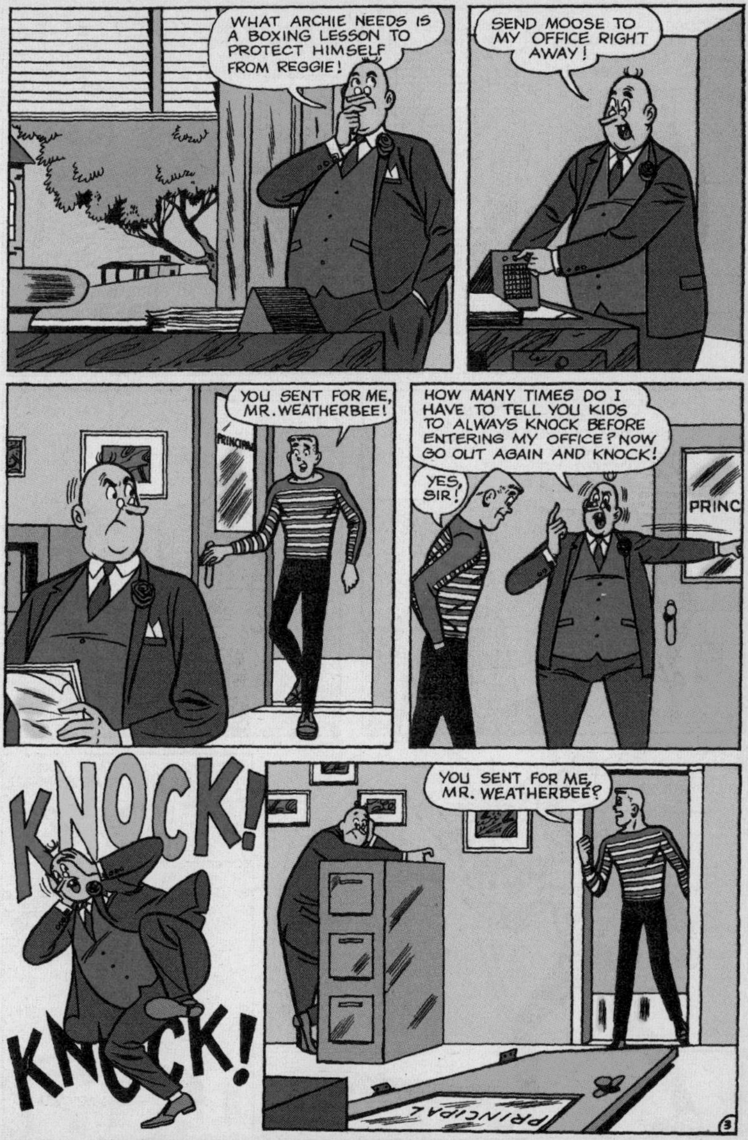
WHAT ARCHIE NEEDS IS A BOXING LESSON TO PROTECT HIMSELF FROM REGGIE!
SEND MOOSE TO MY OFFICE RIGHT AWAY!
YOU SENT FOR ME, MR. WEATHERBEE!
PRINCIPAL
HOW MANY TIMES DO I HAVE TO TELL YOU KIDS TO ALWAYS KNOCK BEFORE ENTERING MY OFFICE? NOW GO OUT AGAIN AND KNOCK!
YES, SIR!
PRINC
KNOCK!
KNOCK!
YOU SENT FOR ME, MR. WEATHERBEE?
PRINCIPAL
3

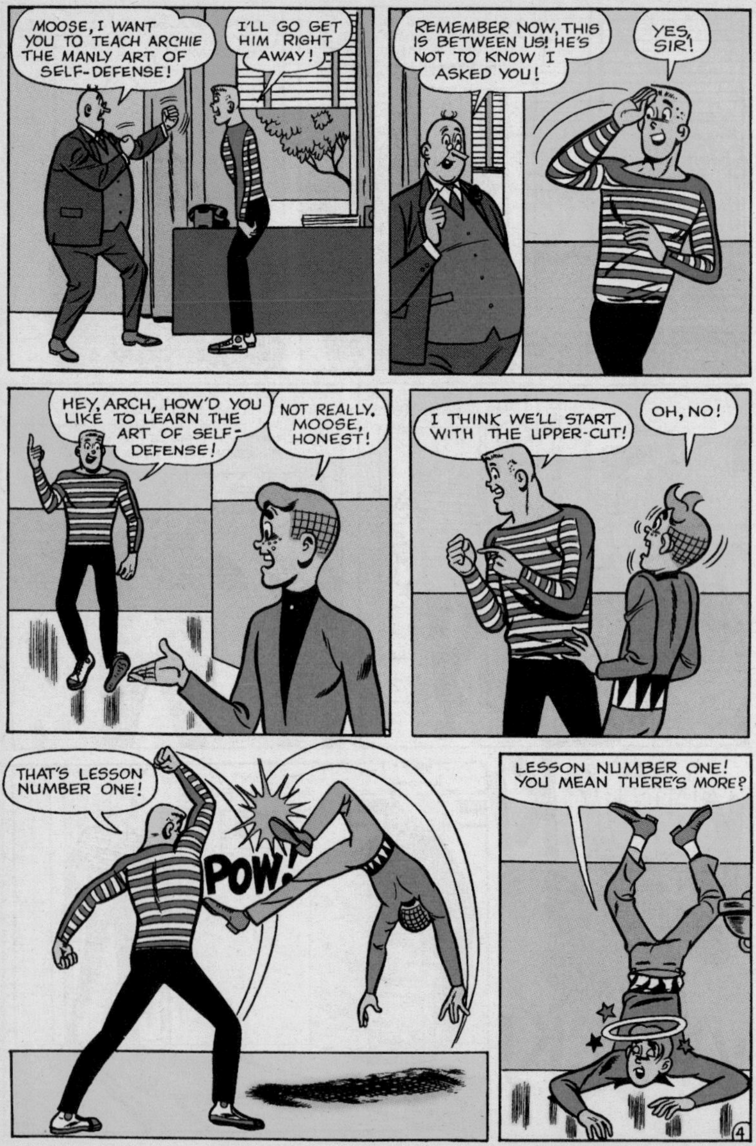
MOOSE, I WANT YOU TO TEACH ARCHIE THE MANLY ART OF SELF-DEFENSE!
I'LL GO GET HIM RIGHT AWAY!
REMEMBER NOW, THIS IS BETWEEN US! HE'S NOT TO KNOW I ASKED YOU!
YES, SIR!
HEY, ARCH, HOW'D YOU LIKE TO LEARN THE ART OF SELF-DEFENSE!
NOT REALLY, MOOSE, HONEST!
I THINK WE'LL START WITH THE UPPER-CUT!
OH, NO!
THAT'S LESSON NUMBER ONE!
POW!
LESSON NUMBER ONE! YOU MEAN THERE'S MORE?
4

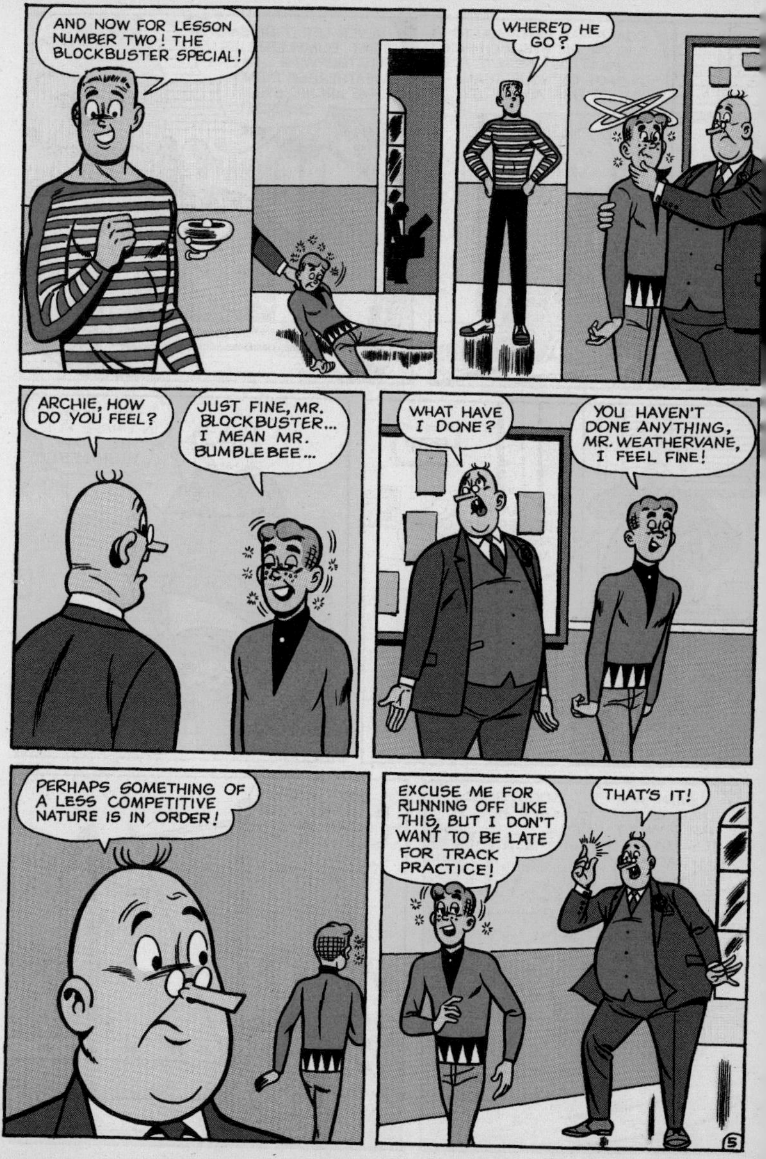

AND NOW FOR LESSON NUMBER TWO! THE BLOCKBUSTER SPECIAL!
WHERE'D HE GO?
ARCHIE, HOW DO YOU FEEL?
JUST FINE, MR. BLOCKBUSTER... I MEAN MR. BUMBLEBEE...
WHAT HAVE I DONE?
YOU HAVEN'T DONE ANYTHING, MR. WEATHERVANE, I FEEL FINE!
PERHAPS SOMETHING OF A LESS COMPETITIVE NATURE IS IN ORDER!
EXCUSE ME FOR RUNNING OFF LIKE THIS, BUT I DON'T WANT TO BE LATE FOR TRACK PRACTICE!
THAT'S IT!
5

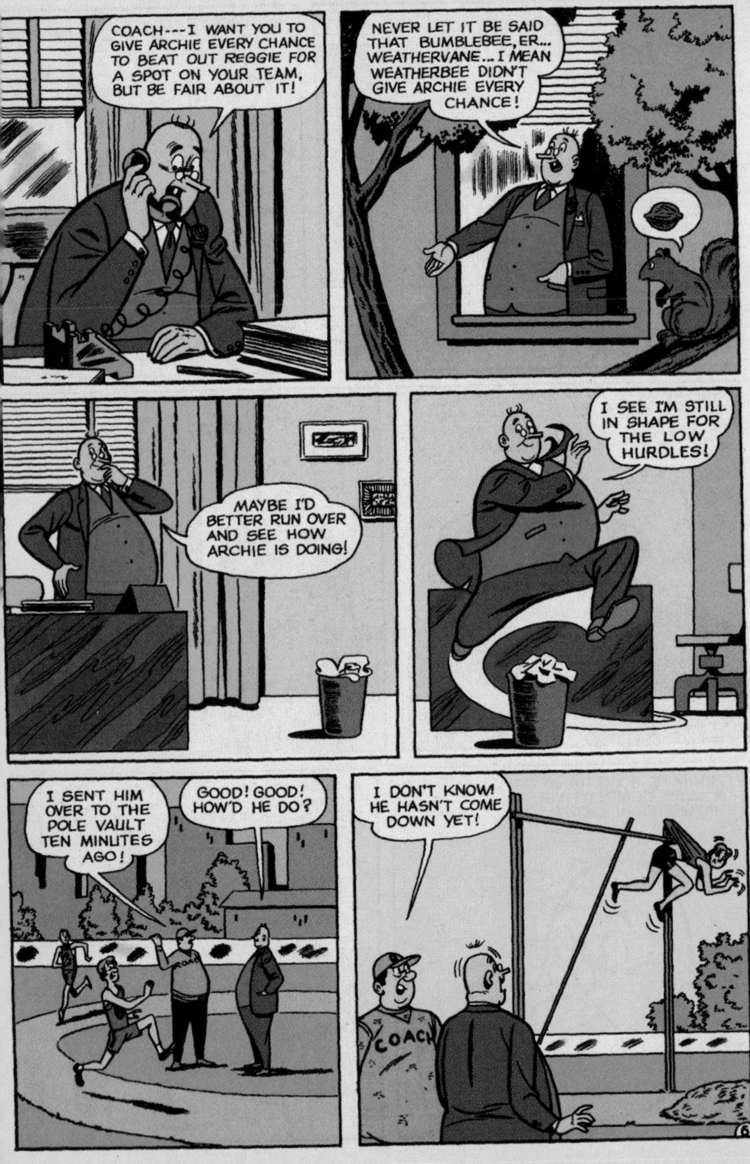
COACH---I WANT YOU TO GIVE ARCHIE EVERY CHANCE TO BEAT OUT REGGIE FOR A SPOT ON YOUR TEAM, BUT BE FAIR ABOUT IT!
NEVER LET IT BE SAID THAT BUMBLEBEE, ER... WEATHERVANE... I MEAN WEATHERBEE DIDN'T GIVE ARCHIE EVERY CHANCE!
MAYBE I'D BETTER RUN OVER AND SEE HOW ARCHIE IS DOING!
I SEE I'M STILL IN SHAPE FOR THE LOW HURDLES!
I SENT HIM OVER TO THE POLE VAULT TEN MINUTES AGO!
GOOD! GOOD! HOW'D HE DO?
I DON'T KNOW! HE HASN'T COME DOWN YET!
COACH
COACH
6

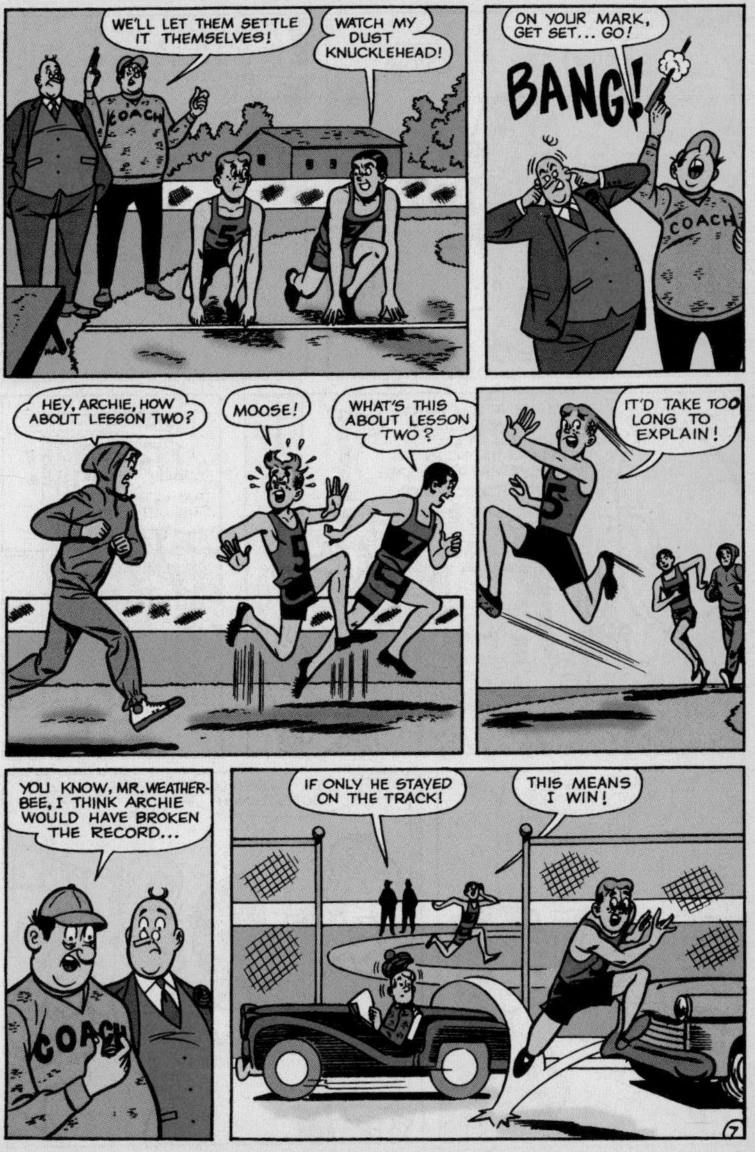
WE'LL LET THEM SETTLE IT THEMSELVES!
WATCH MY DUST KNUCKLEHEAD!
ON YOUR MARK, GET SET... GO!
BANG!
HEY, ARCHIE, HOW ABOUT LESSON TWO?
MOOSE!
WHAT'S THIS ABOUT LESSON TWO?
IT'D TAKE TOO LONG TO EXPLAIN!
YOU KNOW, MR. WEATHERBEE, I THINK ARCHIE WOULD HAVE BROKEN THE RECORD...
IF ONLY HE STAYED ON THE TRACK!
THIS MEANS I WIN!
COACH
7

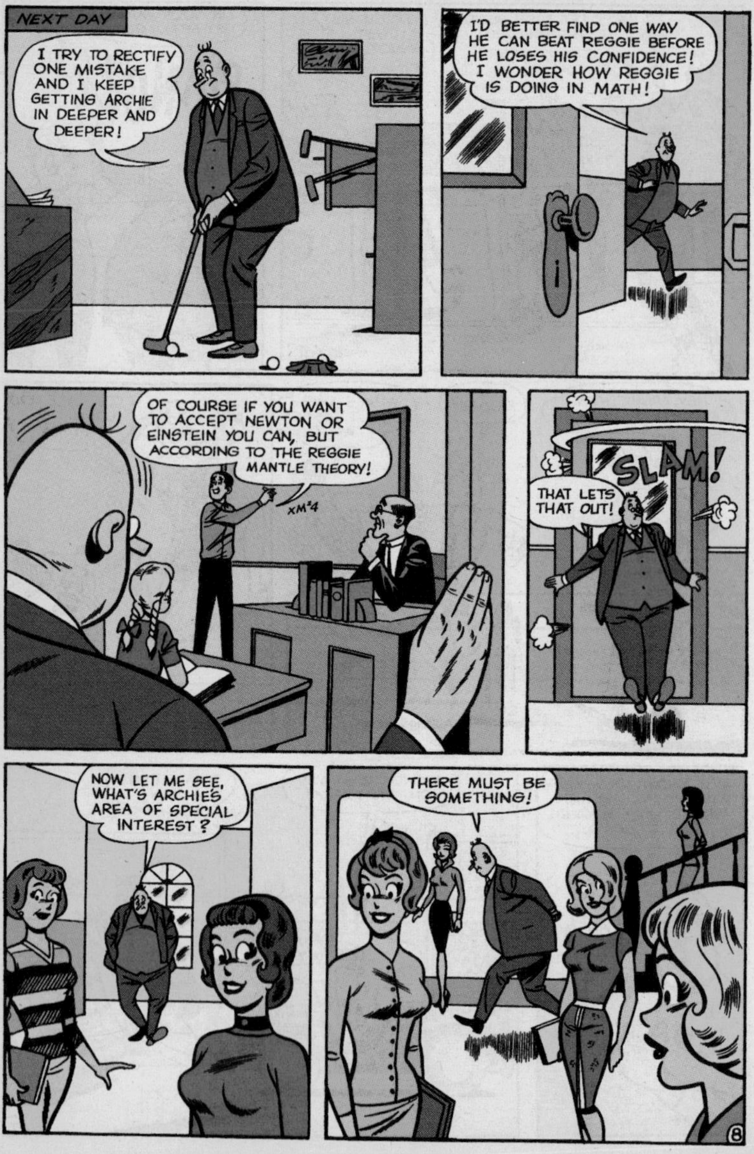
NEXT DAY
I TRY TO RECTIFY ONE MISTAKE AND I KEEP GETTING ARCHIE IN DEEPER AND DEEPER!
I'D BETTER FIND ONE WAY HE CAN BEAT REGGIE BEFORE HE LOSES HIS CONFIDENCE! I WONDER HOW REGGIE IS DOING IN MATH!
OF COURSE IF YOU WANT TO ACCEPT NEWTON OR EINSTEIN YOU CAN, BUT ACCORDING TO THE REGGIE MANTLE THEORY!
SLAM!
THAT LETS THAT OUT!
NOW LET ME SEE, WHAT'S ARCHIE'S AREA OF SPECIAL INTEREST?
THERE MUST BE SOMETHING!

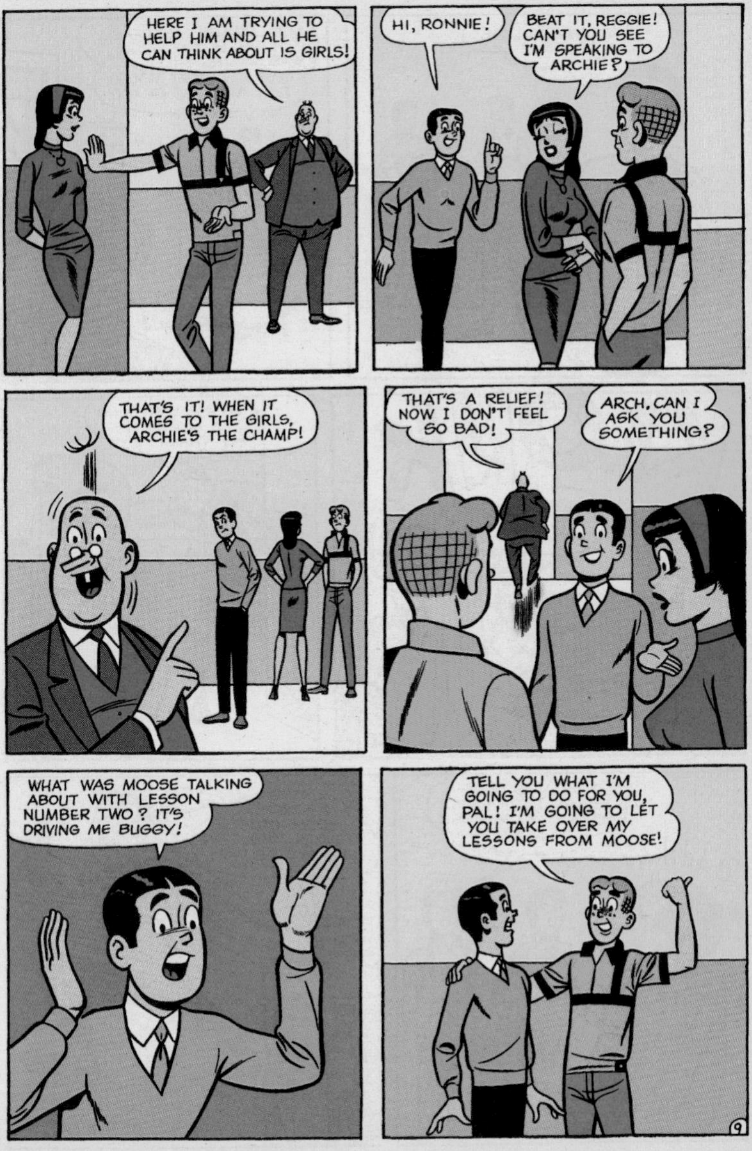
HERE I AM TRYING TO HELP HIM AND ALL HE CAN THINK ABOUT IS GIRLS!
HI, RONNIE!
BEAT IT, REGGIE! CAN'T YOU SEE I'M SPEAKING TO ARCHIE?
THAT'S IT! WHEN IT COMES TO THE GIRLS, ARCHIE'S THE CHAMP!
THAT'S A RELIEF! NOW I DON'T FEEL SO BAD!
ARCH, CAN I ASK YOU SOMETHING?
WHAT WAS MOOSE TALKING ABOUT WITH LESSON NUMBER TWO? IT'S DRIVING ME BUGGY!
TELL YOU WHAT I'M GOING TO DO FOR YOU, PAL! I'M GOING TO LET YOU TAKE OVER MY LESSONS FROM MOOSE!

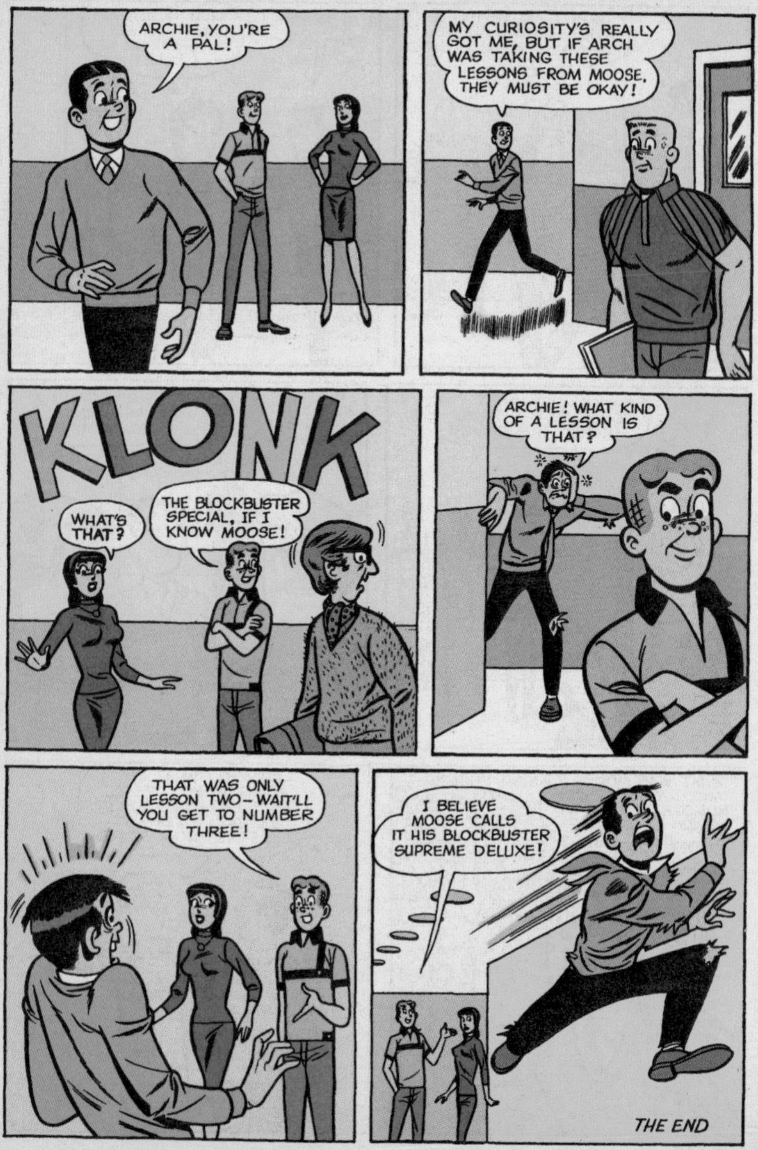
ARCHIE, YOU'RE A PAL!
MY CURIOSITY'S REALLY GOT ME, BUT IF ARCH WAS TAKING THESE LESSONS FROM MOOSE, THEY MUST BE OKAY!
KLONK
WHAT'S THAT?
THE BLOCKBUSTER SPECIAL, IF I KNOW MOOSE!
ARCHIE! WHAT KIND OF A LESSON IS THAT?
THAT WAS ONLY LESSON TWO-WAIT'LL YOU GET TO NUMBER THREE!
I BELIEVE MOOSE CALLS IT HIS BLOCKBUSTER SUPREME DELUXE!
THE END

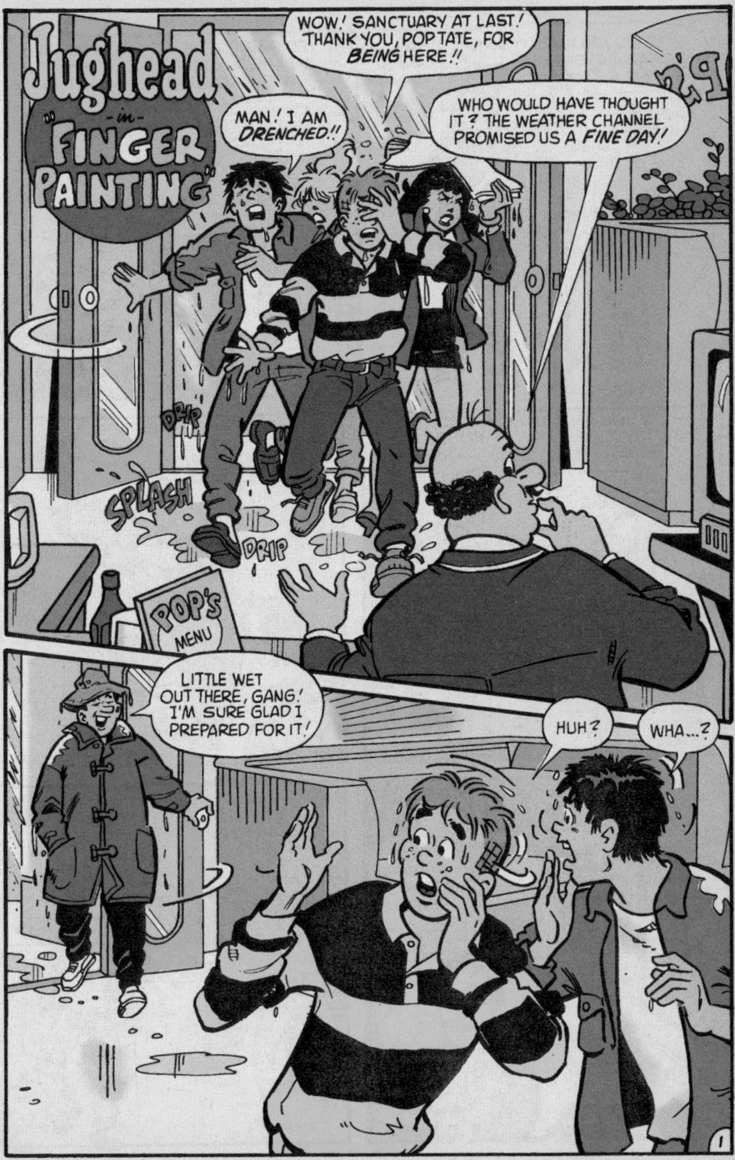
Jughead
-in-
"FINGER PAINTING"
WOW! SANCTUARY AT LAST! THANK YOU, POP TATE, FOR BEING HERE!!
MAN! I AM DRENCHED!!
WHO WOULD HAVE THOUGHT IT? THE WEATHER CHANNEL PROMISED US A FINE DAY!
DRIP
SPLASH
DRIP
POP'S MENU
LITTLE WET OUT THERE, GANG! I'M SURE GLAD I PREPARED FOR IT!
HUH?
WHA...?
1

Script: Frank Doyle / Pencils: Stan Goldberg / Inks: Mike Esposito / Letters: Bill Yoshida

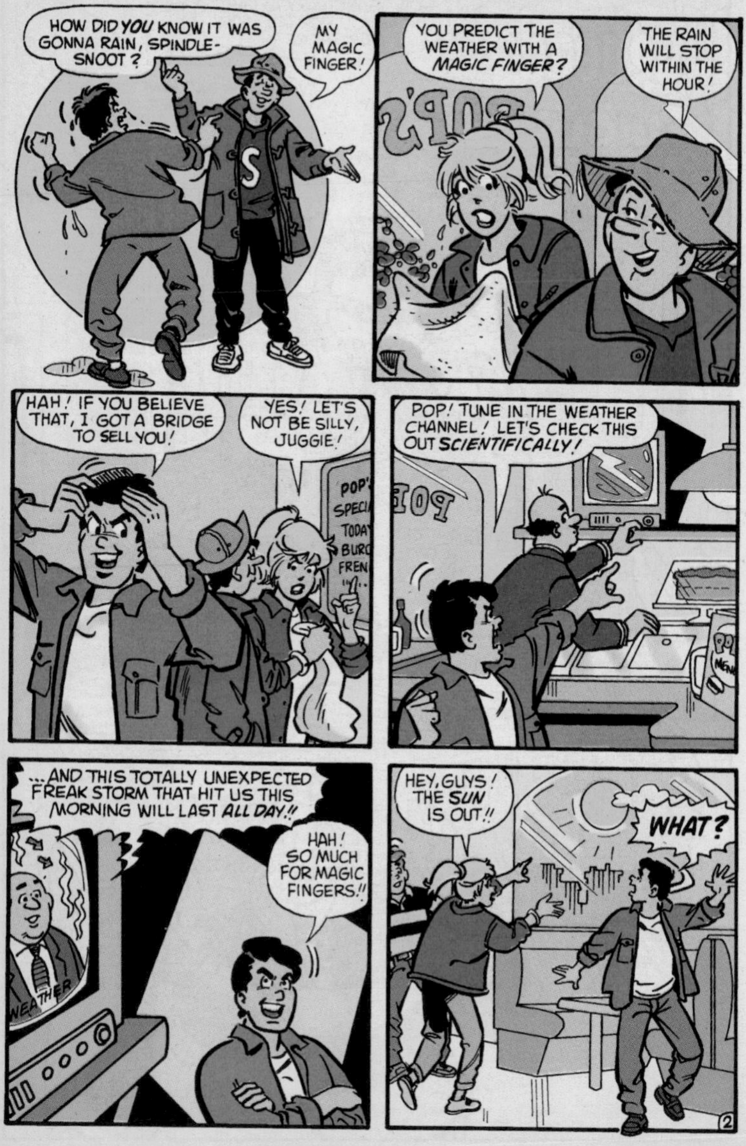
HOW DID YOU KNOW IT WAS GONNA RAIN, SPINDLE-SNOOT?
MY MAGIC FINGER!
YOU PREDICT THE WEATHER WITH A MAGIC FINGER?
THE RAIN WILL STOP WITHIN THE HOUR!
POP'S
HAH! IF YOU BELIEVE THAT, I GOT A BRIDGE TO SELL YOU!
YES! LET'S NOT BE SILLY, JUGGIE!
POP'S SPECI TODAY BURG FREN
POP! TUNE IN THE WEATHER CHANNEL! LET'S CHECK THIS OUT SCIENTIFICALLY!
...AND THIS TOTALLY UNEXPECTED FREAK STORM THAT HIT US THIS MORNING WILL LAST ALL DAY!!
HAH! SO MUCH FOR MAGIC FINGERS!!
WEATHER
HEY, GUYS! THE SUN IS OUT!!
WHAT?
2

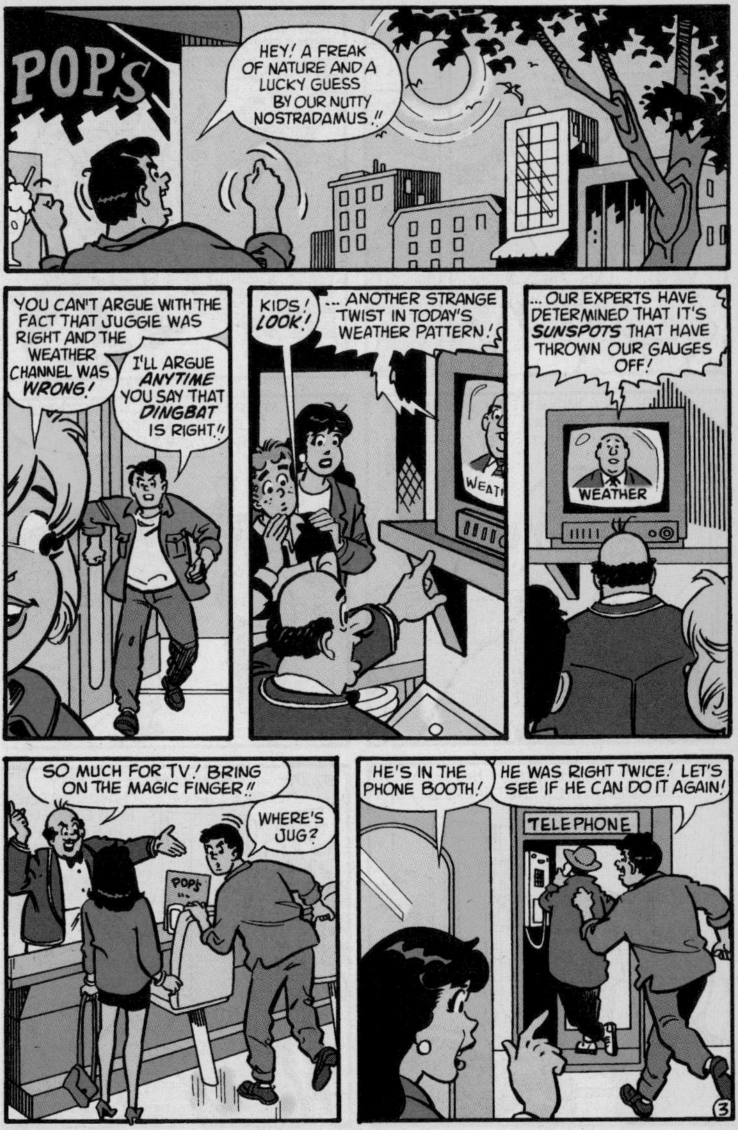
POP'S
HEY! A FREAK OF NATURE AND A LUCKY GUESS BY OUR NUTTY NOSTRADAMUS!!
YOU CAN'T ARGUE WITH THE FACT THAT JUGGIE WAS RIGHT AND THE WEATHER CHANNEL WAS WRONG!
I'LL ARGUE ANYTIME YOU SAY THAT DINGBAT IS RIGHT!!
KIDS! LOOK!
... ANOTHER STRANGE TWIST IN TODAY'S WEATHER PATTERN!
... OUR EXPERTS HAVE DETERMINED THAT IT'S SUNSPOTS THAT HAVE THROWN OUR GAUGES OFF!
WEATHER
SO MUCH FOR TV! BRING ON THE MAGIC FINGER!!
WHERE'S JUG?
HE'S IN THE PHONE BOOTH!
HE WAS RIGHT TWICE! LET'S SEE IF HE CAN DO IT AGAIN!
TELEPHONE
3

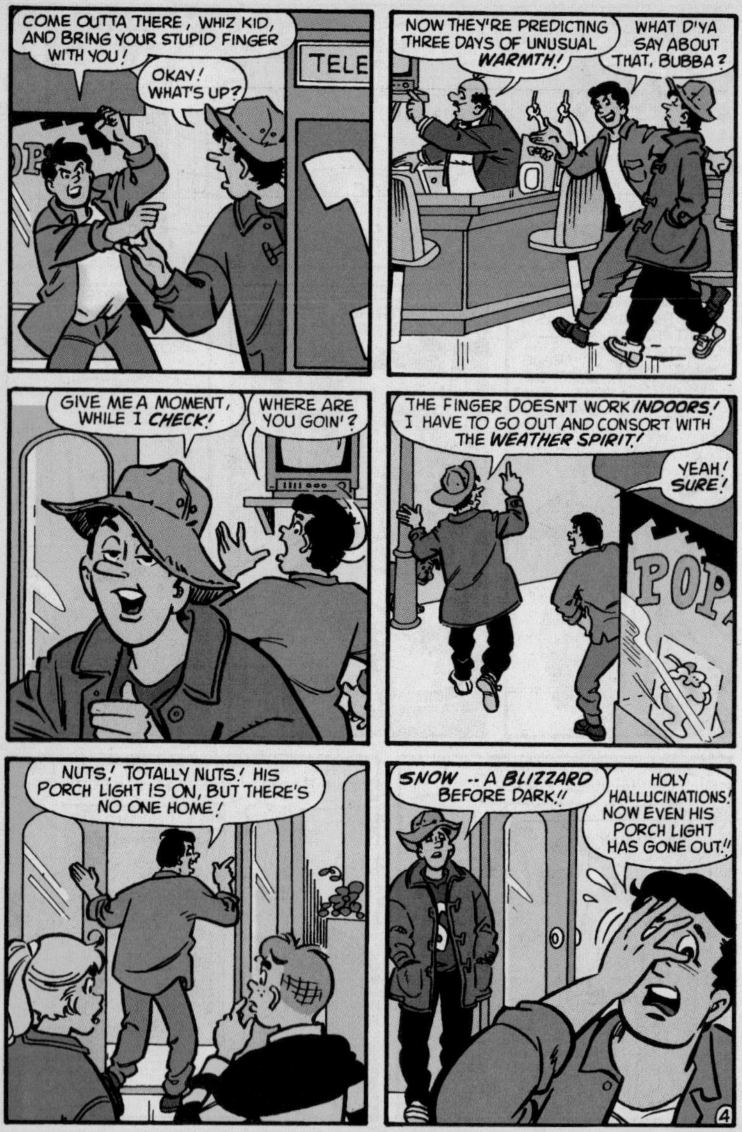
COME OUTTA THERE, WHIZ KID, AND BRING YOUR STUPID FINGER WITH YOU!
OKAY! WHAT'S UP?
TELE
NOW THEY'RE PREDICTING THREE DAYS OF UNUSUAL WARMTH!
WHAT D'YA SAY ABOUT THAT, BUBBA?
GIVE ME A MOMENT, WHILE I CHECK!
WHERE ARE YOU GOIN'?
THE FINGER DOESN'T WORK INDOORS! I HAVE TO GO OUT AND CONSORT WITH THE WEATHER SPIRIT!
YEAH! SURE!
POP
NUTS! TOTALLY NUTS! HIS PORCH LIGHT IS ON, BUT THERE'S NO ONE HOME!
SNOW -- A BLIZZARD BEFORE DARK!!
HOLY HALLUCINATIONS! NOW EVEN HIS PORCH LIGHT HAS GONE OUT!!
4

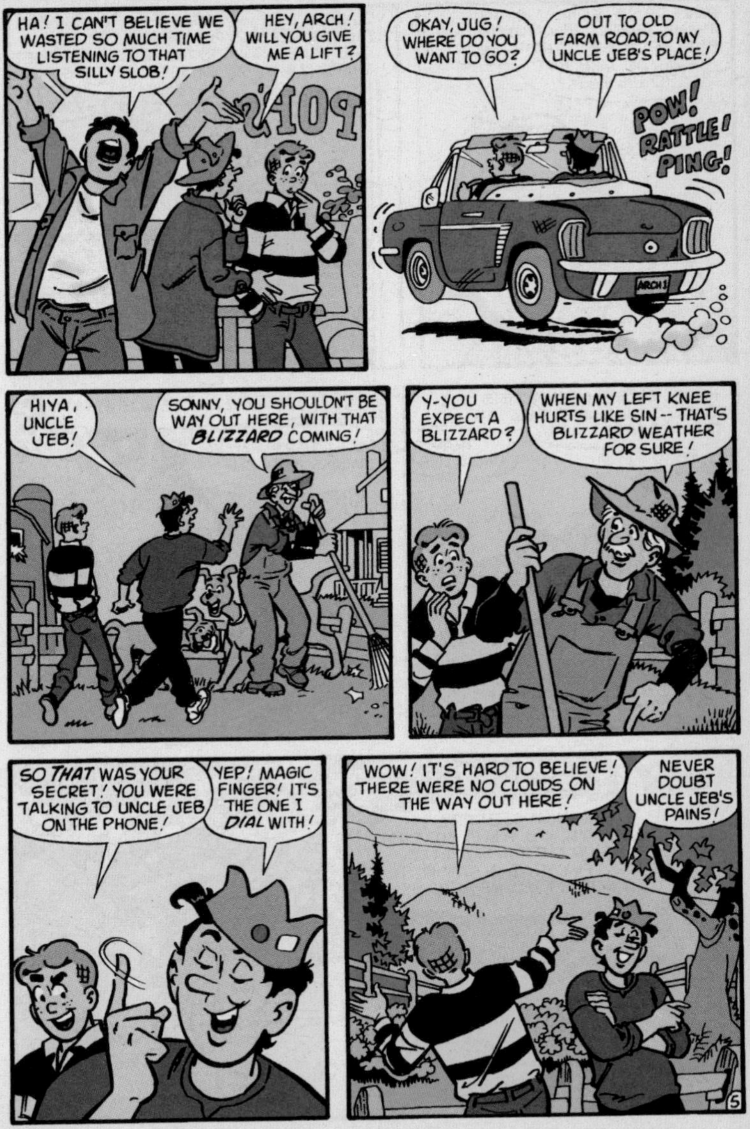
HA! I CAN'T BELIEVE WE WASTED SO MUCH TIME LISTENING TO THAT SILLY SLOB!
HEY, ARCH! WILL YOU GIVE ME A LIFT?
POP'S
OKAY, JUG! WHERE DO YOU WANT TO GO?
OUT TO OLD FARM ROAD, TO MY UNCLE JEB'S PLACE!
POW! RATTLE! PING!
ARCH 1
HIYA, UNCLE JEB!
SONNY, YOU SHOULDN'T BE WAY OUT HERE, WITH THAT BLIZZARD COMING!
Y-YOU EXPECT A BLIZZARD?
WHEN MY LEFT KNEE HURTS LIKE SIN -- THAT'S BLIZZARD WEATHER FOR SURE!
SO THAT WAS YOUR SECRET! YOU WERE TALKING TO UNCLE JEB ON THE PHONE!
YEP! MAGIC FINGER! IT'S THE ONE I DIAL WITH!
WOW! IT'S HARD TO BELIEVE! THERE WERE NO CLOUDS ON THE WAY OUT HERE!
NEVER DOUBT UNCLE JEB'S PAINS!
5

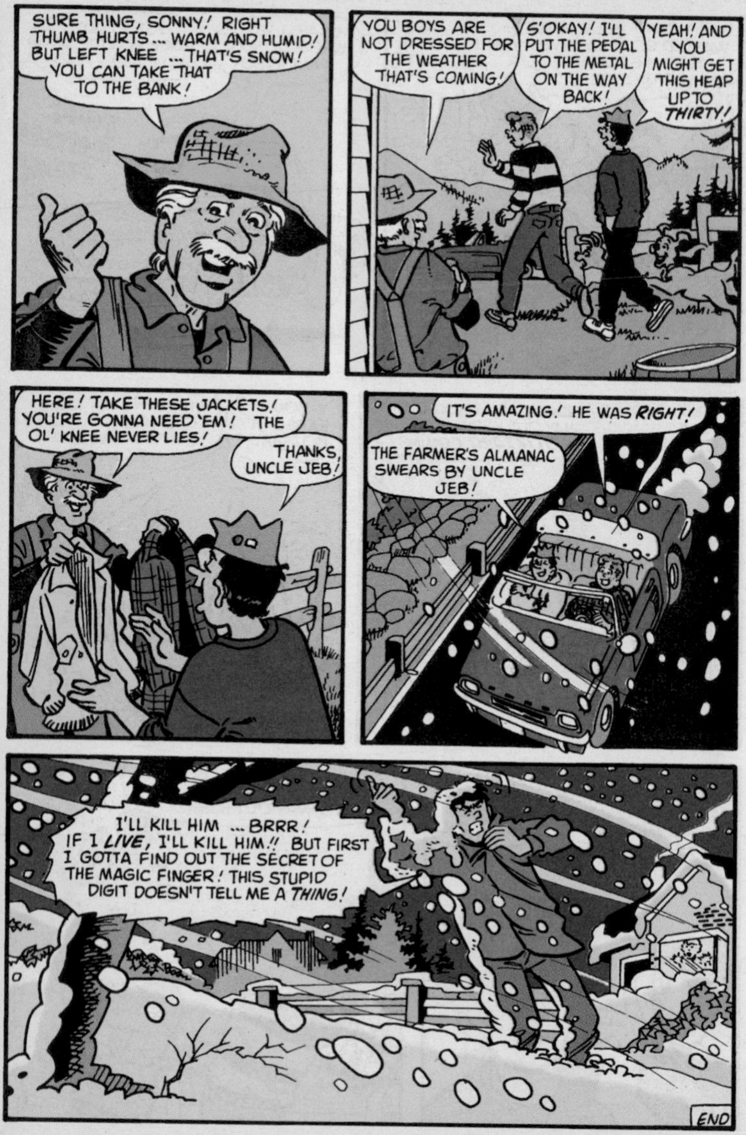
SURE THING, SONNY! RIGHT THUMB HURTS... WARM AND HUMID! BUT LEFT KNEE ...THAT'S SNOW! YOU CAN TAKE THAT TO THE BANK!
YOU BOYS ARE NOT DRESSED FOR THE WEATHER THAT'S COMING!
S'OKAY! I'LL PUT THE PEDAL TO THE METAL ON THE WAY BACK!
YEAH! AND YOU MIGHT GET THIS HEAP UP TO THIRTY!
HERE! TAKE THESE JACKETS! YOU'RE GONNA NEED 'EM! THE OL' KNEE NEVER LIES!
THANKS, UNCLE JEB!
IT'S AMAZING! HE WAS RIGHT!
THE FARMER'S ALMANAC SWEARS BY UNCLE JEB!
I'LL KILL HIM ... BRRR! IF I LIVE, I'LL KILL HIM!! BUT FIRST I GOTTA FIND OUT THE SECRET OF THE MAGIC FINGER! THIS STUPID DIGIT DOESN'T TELL ME A THING!
END

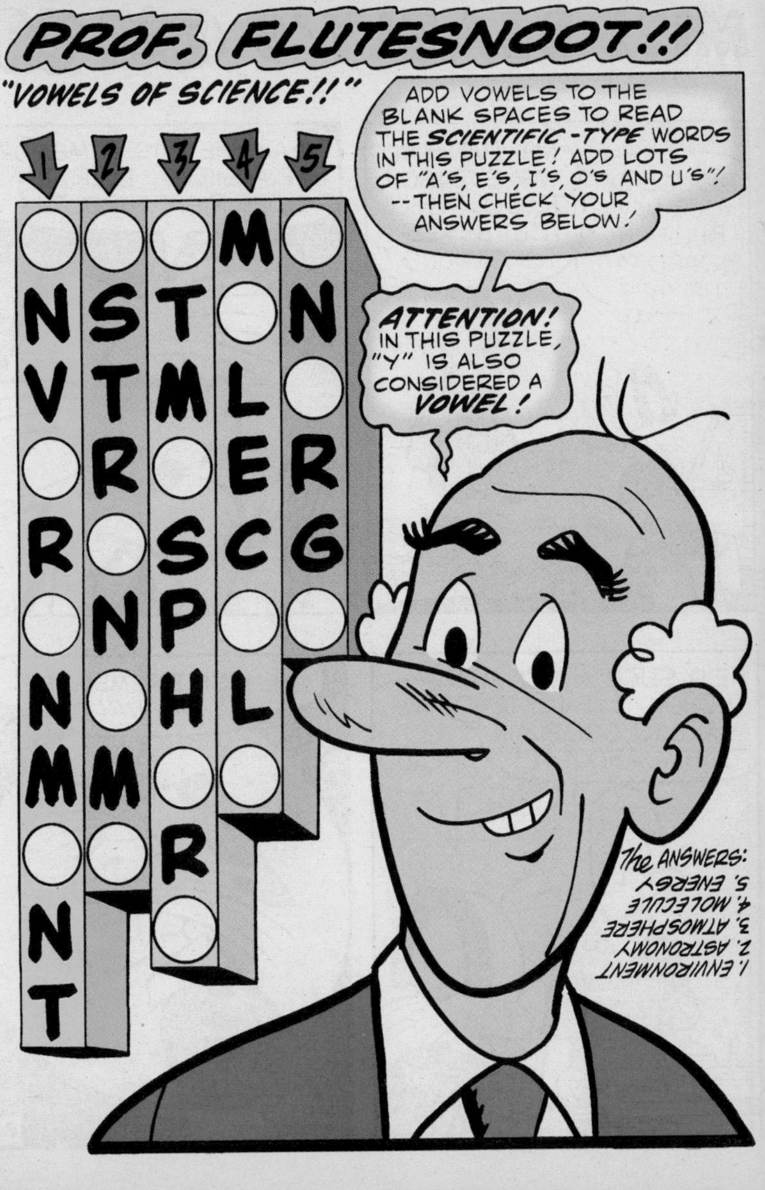
PROF. FLUTESNOOT!!
"VOWELS OF SCIENCE!!"
ADD VOWELS TO THE BLANK SPACES TO READ THE SCIENTIFIC-TYPE WORDS IN THIS PUZZLE! ADD LOTS OF "A'S, E'S, I'S, O'S AND U'S"! --THEN CHECK YOUR ANSWERS BELOW!
ATTENTION! IN THIS PUZZLE, "Y" IS ALSO CONSIDERED A VOWEL!
1 2 3 4 5
N V R N M N T
S T R N M
T M S P H R
M L E C L
N R G
The ANSWERS:
1. ENVIRONMENT
2. ASTRONOMY
3. ATMOSPHERE
4. MOLECULE
5. ENERGY

MISS BEAZLY'S GAG BA

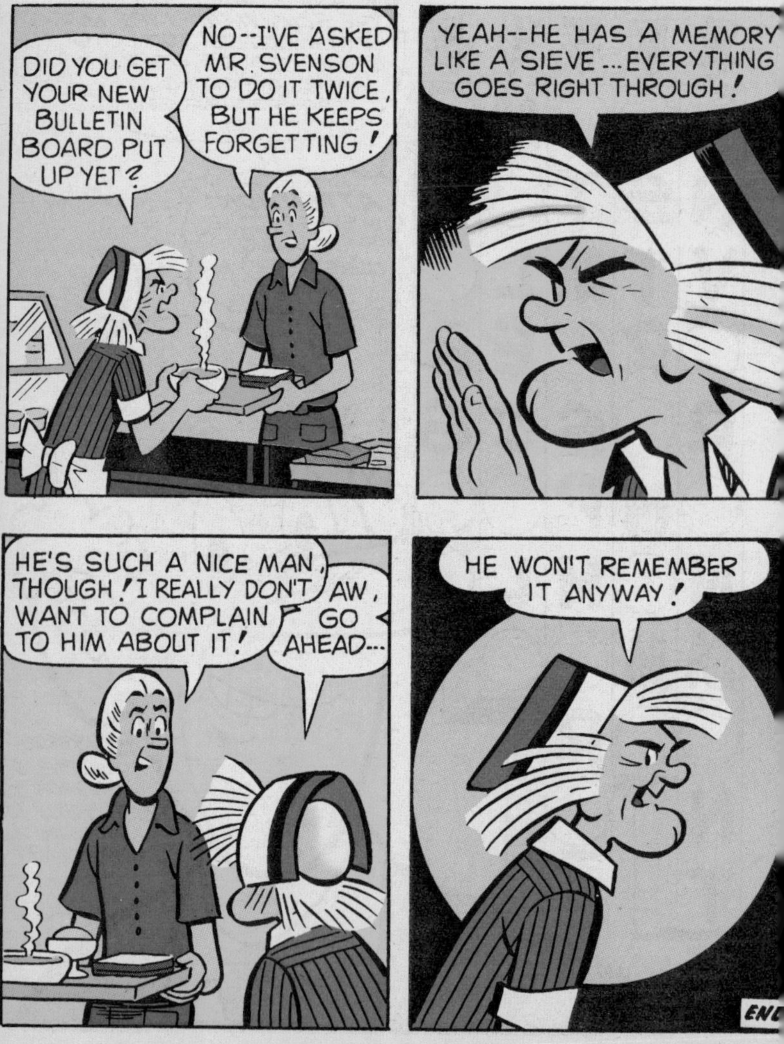
DID YOU GET YOUR NEW BULLETIN BOARD PUT UP YET?
NO--I'VE ASKED MR. SVENSON TO DO IT TWICE, BUT HE KEEPS FORGETTING!
YEAH--HE HAS A MEMORY LIKE A SIEVE...EVERYTHING GOES RIGHT THROUGH!
HE'S SUCH A NICE MAN, THOUGH! I REALLY DON'T WANT TO COMPLAIN TO HIM ABOUT IT!
AW, GO AHEAD...
HE WON'T REMEMBER IT ANYWAY!

Betty in "SECRET PALS"

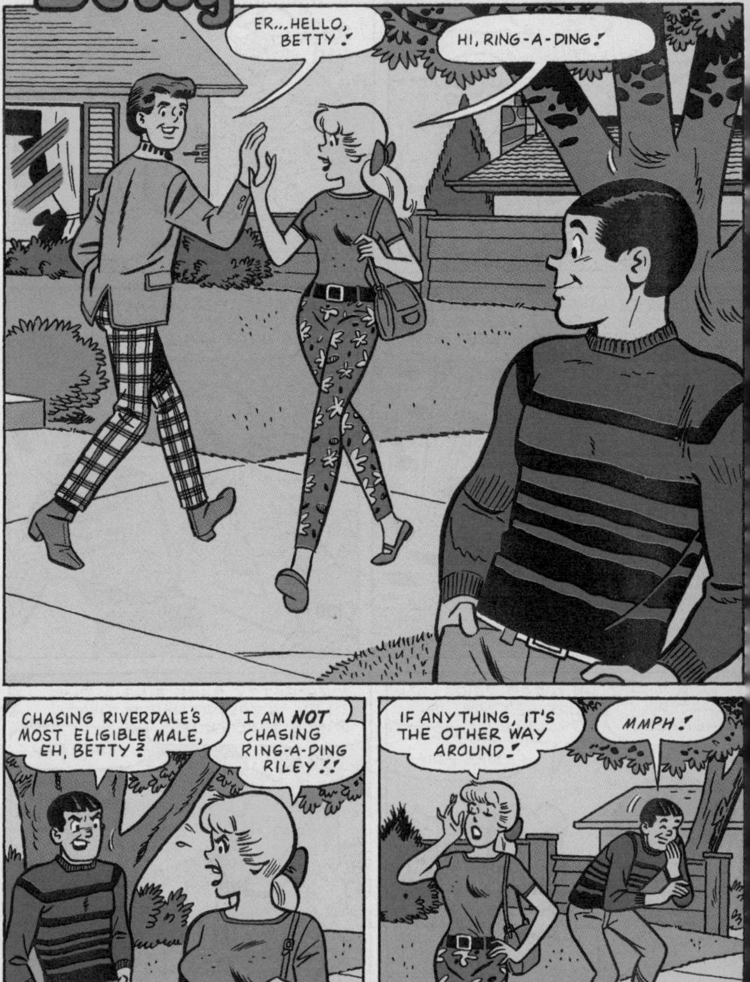
ER...HELLO, BETTY!
HI, RING-A-DING!
CHASING RIVERDALE'S MOST ELIGIBLE MALE, EH, BETTY?
I AM NOT CHASING RING-A-DING RILEY!!
IF ANYTHING, IT'S THE OTHER WAY AROUND!
MMPH!

Script: Frank Doyle / Pencils: Dan DeCarlo / Inks: Rudy Lapick / Letters: Vince DeCarlo

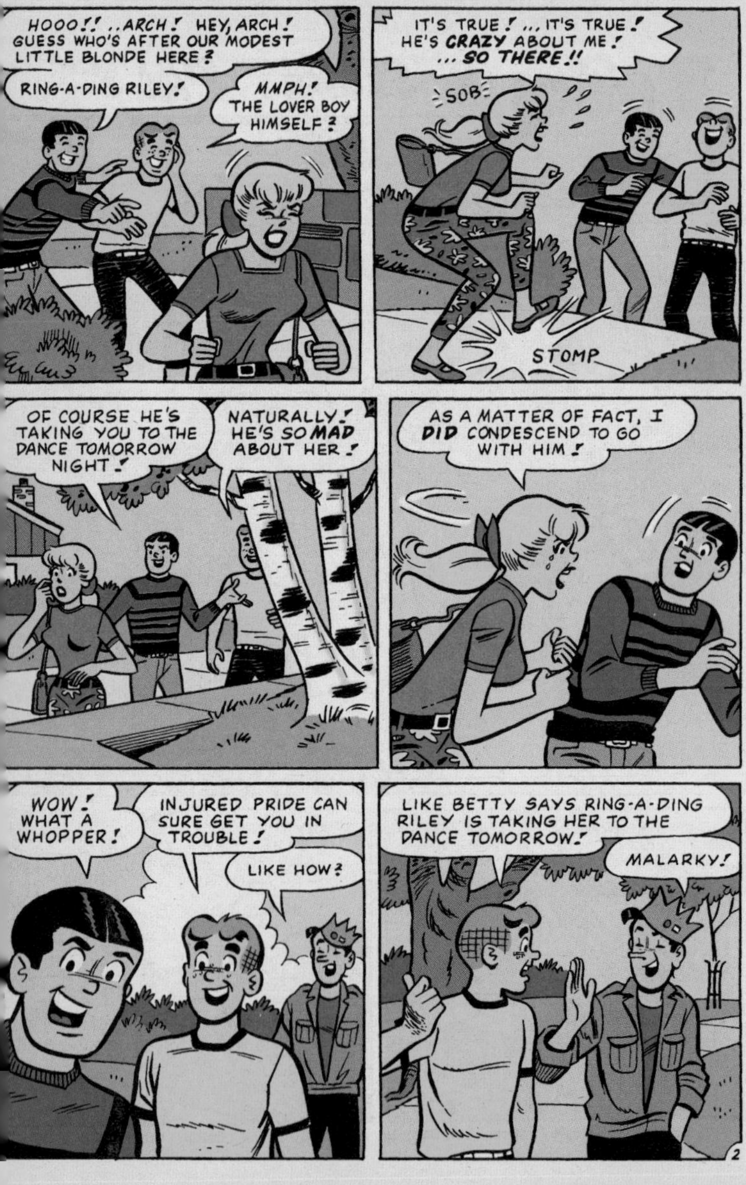

HOOO!! ..ARCH! HEY, ARCH! GUESS WHO'S AFTER OUR MODEST LITTLE BLONDE HERE?
RING-A-DING RILEY!
MMPH! THE LOVER BOY HIMSELF?
IT'S TRUE! ... IT'S TRUE! HE'S CRAZY ABOUT ME! ... SO THERE!!
SOB
STOMP
OF COURSE HE'S TAKING YOU TO THE DANCE TOMORROW NIGHT!
NATURALLY! HE'S SO MAD ABOUT HER!
AS A MATTER OF FACT, I DID CONDESCEND TO GO WITH HIM!
WOW! WHAT A WHOPPER!
INJURED PRIDE CAN SURE GET YOU IN TROUBLE!
LIKE HOW?
LIKE BETTY SAYS RING-A-DING RILEY IS TAKING HER TO THE DANCE TOMORROW!
MALARKY!

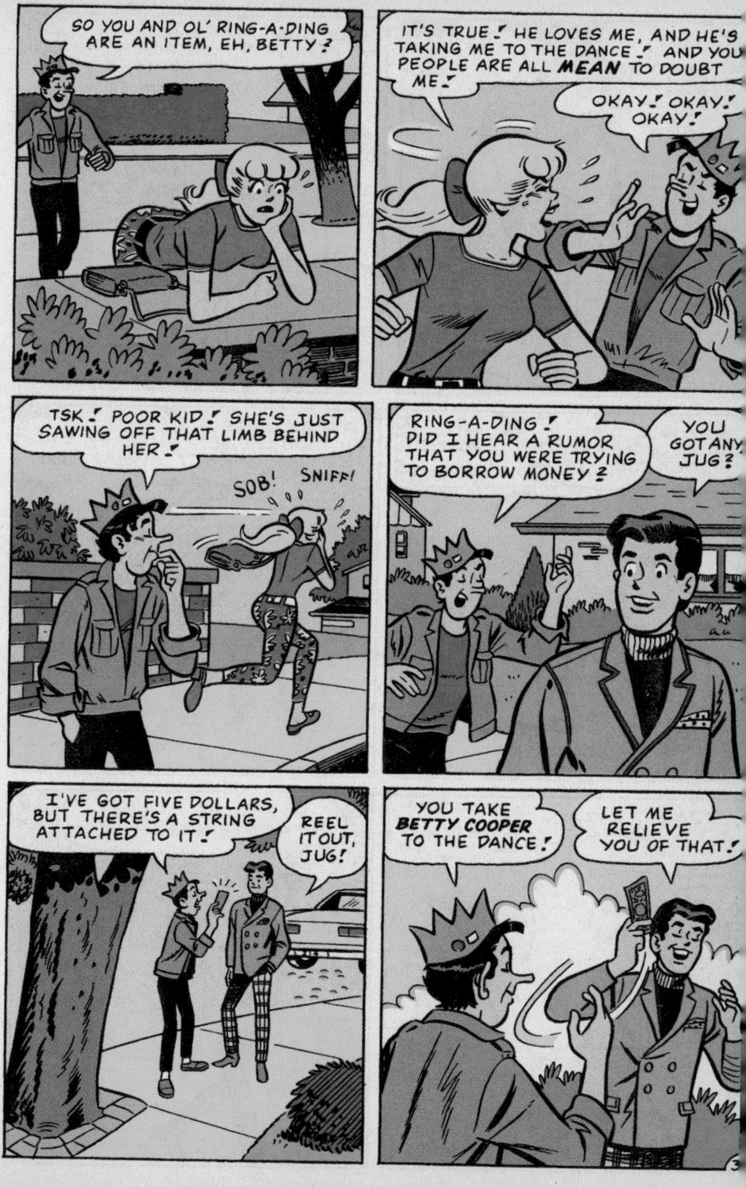
SO YOU AND OL' RING-A-DING ARE AN ITEM, EH, BETTY?
IT'S TRUE! HE LOVES ME, AND HE'S TAKING ME TO THE DANCE! AND YOU PEOPLE ARE ALL **MEAN** TO DOUBT ME!
OKAY! OKAY! OKAY!
TSK! POOR KID! SHE'S JUST SAWING OFF THAT LIMB BEHIND HER!
SOB! SNIFF!
RING-A-DING! DID I HEAR A RUMOR THAT YOU WERE TRYING TO BORROW MONEY?
YOU GOT ANY, JUG?
I'VE GOT FIVE DOLLARS, BUT THERE'S A STRING ATTACHED TO IT!
REEL IT OUT, JUG!
YOU TAKE **BETTY COOPER** TO THE DANCE!
LET ME RELIEVE YOU OF THAT!

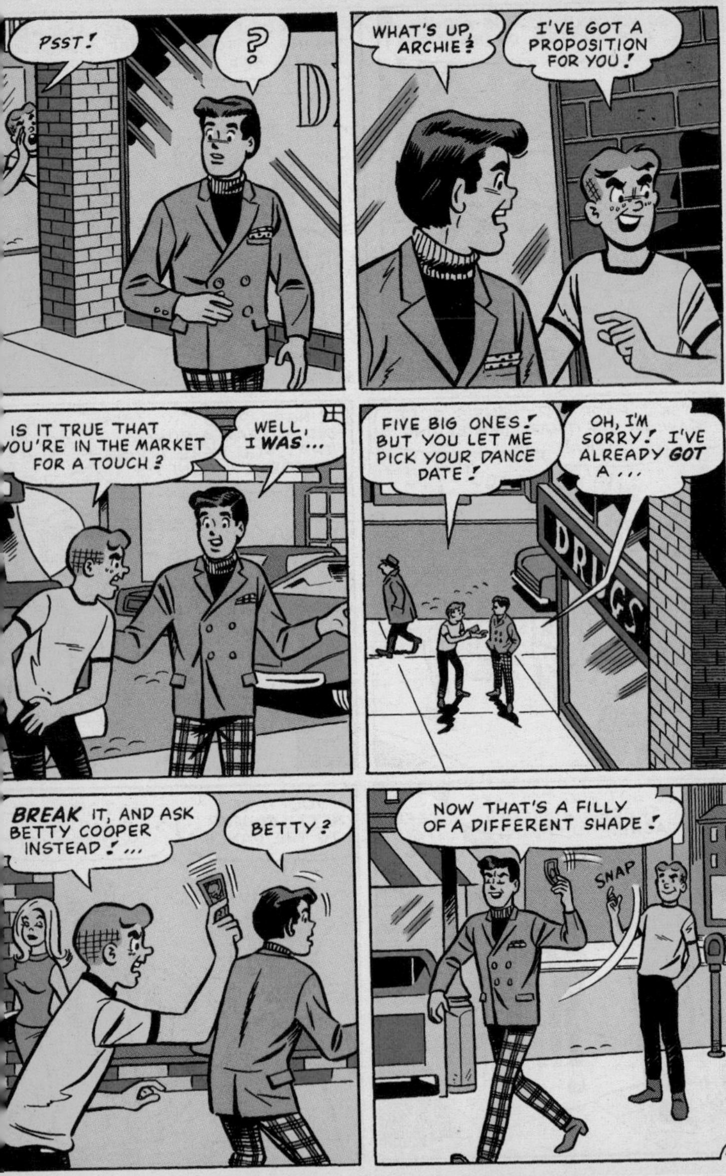
PSST!
?
WHAT'S UP, ARCHIE?
I'VE GOT A PROPOSITION FOR YOU!
IS IT TRUE THAT YOU'RE IN THE MARKET FOR A TOUCH?
WELL, I WAS...
FIVE BIG ONES! BUT YOU LET ME PICK YOUR DANCE DATE!
OH, I'M SORRY! I'VE ALREADY GOT A...
DRUGS
BREAK IT, AND ASK BETTY COOPER INSTEAD! ...
BETTY?
NOW THAT'S A FILLY OF A DIFFERENT SHADE!
SNAP
4

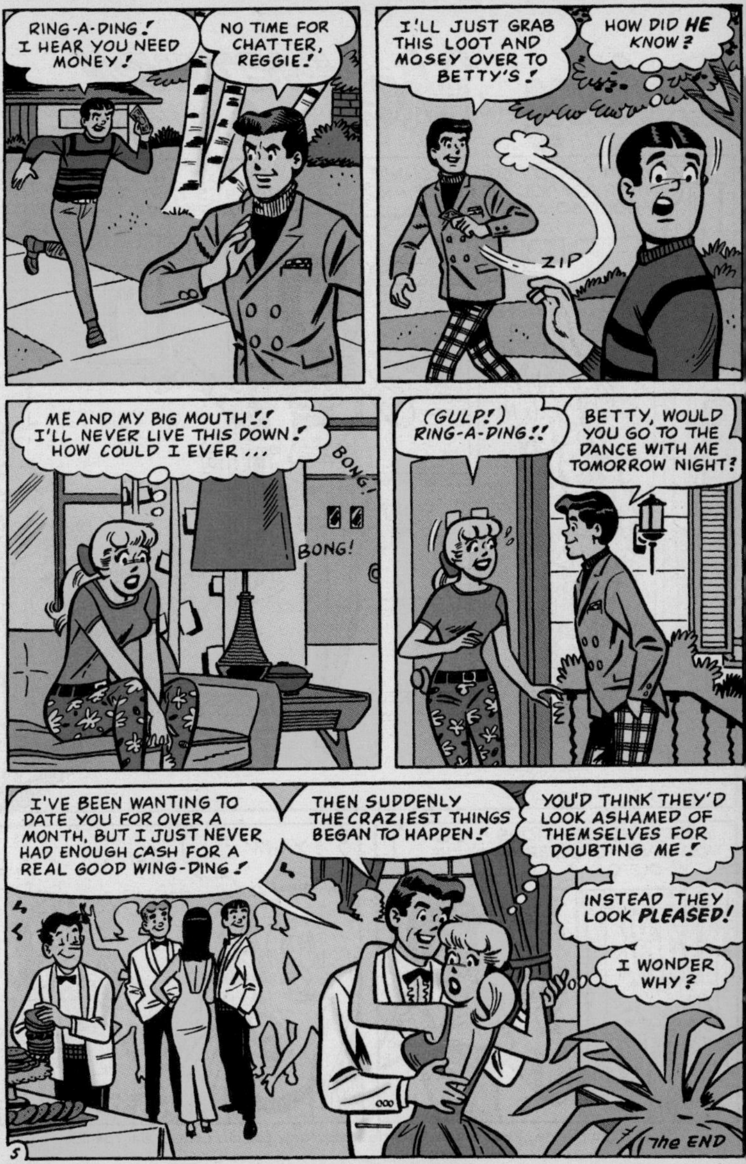
RING-A-DING! I HEAR YOU NEED MONEY!
NO TIME FOR CHATTER, REGGIE!
I'LL JUST GRAB THIS LOOT AND MOSEY OVER TO BETTY'S!
HOW DID HE KNOW?
ZIP
ME AND MY BIG MOUTH!! I'LL NEVER LIVE THIS DOWN! HOW COULD I EVER ...
BONG!
BONG!
(GULP!) RING-A-DING!!
BETTY, WOULD YOU GO TO THE DANCE WITH ME TOMORROW NIGHT?
I'VE BEEN WANTING TO DATE YOU FOR OVER A MONTH, BUT I JUST NEVER HAD ENOUGH CASH FOR A REAL GOOD WING-DING!
THEN SUDDENLY THE CRAZIEST THINGS BEGAN TO HAPPEN!
YOU'D THINK THEY'D LOOK ASHAMED OF THEMSELVES FOR DOUBTING ME!
INSTEAD THEY LOOK PLEASED!
I WONDER WHY?
The END
5

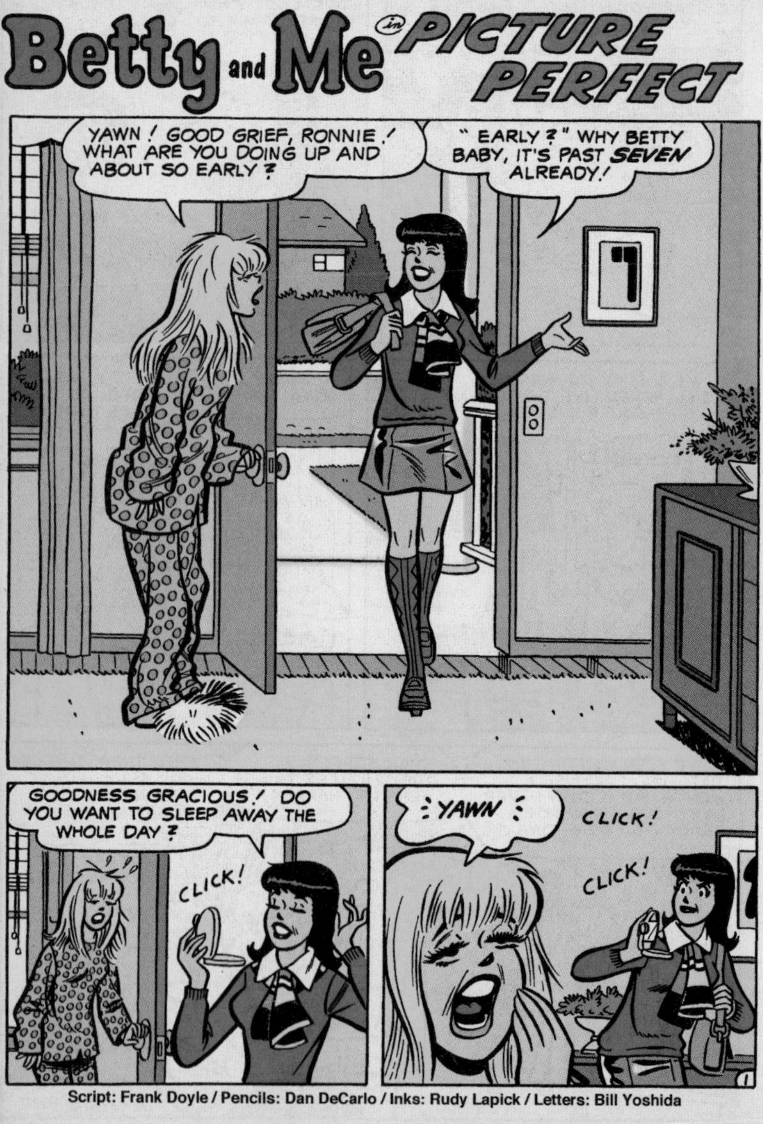
Betty and Me in PICTURE PERFECT
YAWN! GOOD GRIEF, RONNIE! WHAT ARE YOU DOING UP AND ABOUT SO EARLY?
"EARLY?" WHY BETTY BABY, IT'S PAST SEVEN ALREADY!
GOODNESS GRACIOUS! DO YOU WANT TO SLEEP AWAY THE WHOLE DAY?
CLICK!
YAWN
CLICK!
CLICK!
1

Script: Frank Doyle / Pencils: Dan DeCarlo / Inks: Rudy Lapick / Letters: Bill Yoshida

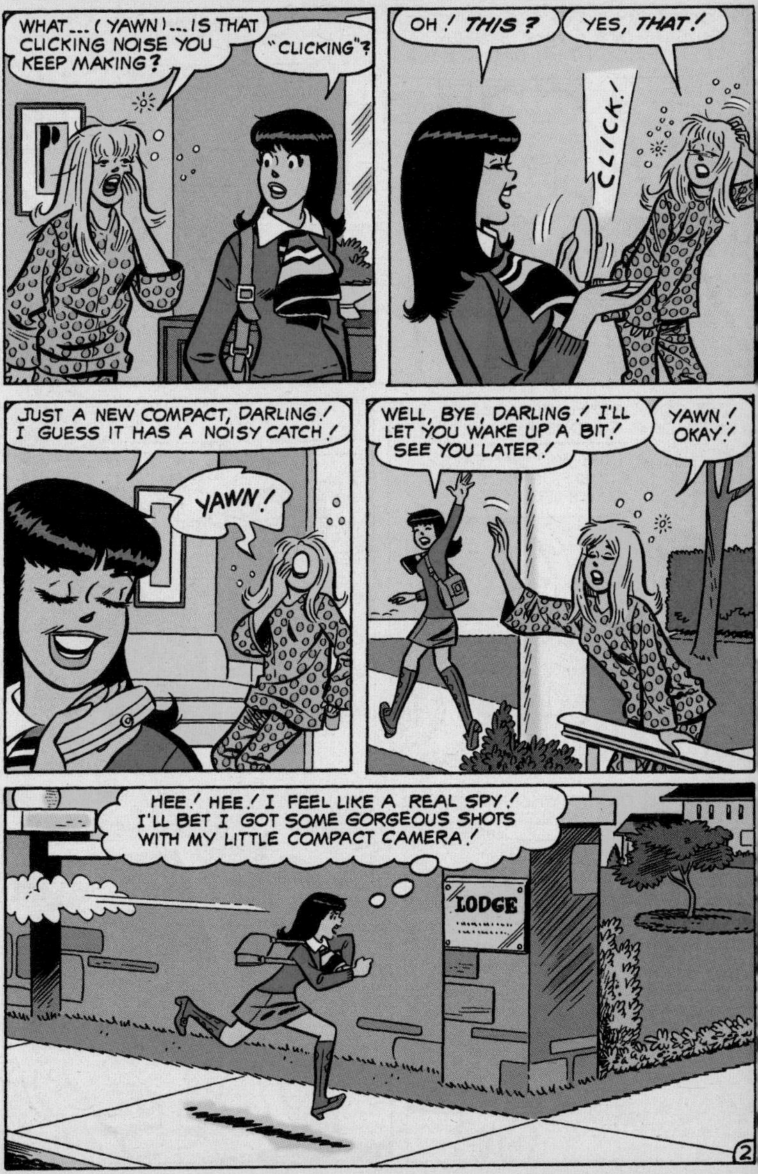

WHAT... (YAWN)... IS THAT CLICKING NOISE YOU KEEP MAKING?
"CLICKING"?
OH! THIS?
YES, THAT!
CLICK!
JUST A NEW COMPACT, DARLING! I GUESS IT HAS A NOISY CATCH!
YAWN!
WELL, BYE, DARLING! I'LL LET YOU WAKE UP A BIT! SEE YOU LATER!
YAWN! OKAY!
HEE! HEE! I FEEL LIKE A REAL SPY! I'LL BET I GOT SOME GORGEOUS SHOTS WITH MY LITTLE COMPACT CAMERA!
LODGE
2

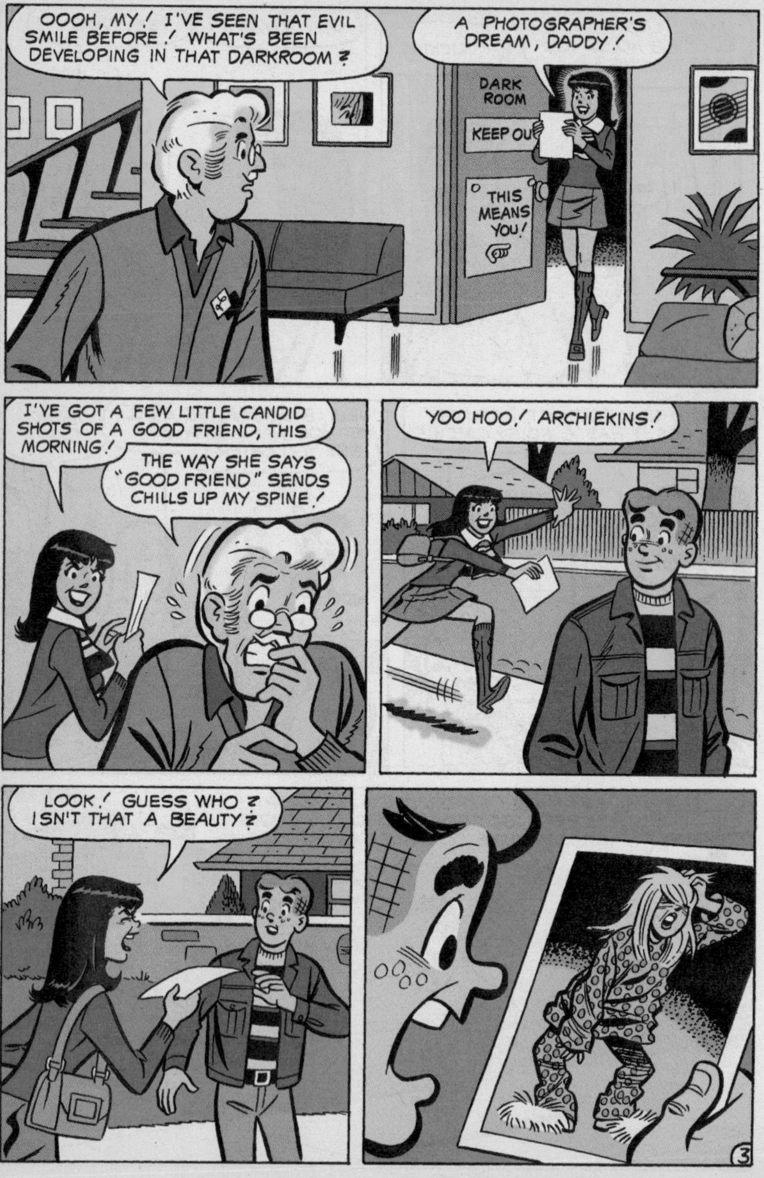
OOOH, MY! I'VE SEEN THAT EVIL SMILE BEFORE! WHAT'S BEEN DEVELOPING IN THAT DARKROOM?
A PHOTOGRAPHER'S DREAM, DADDY!
DARK ROOM
KEEP OU
THIS MEANS YOU!
I'VE GOT A FEW LITTLE CANDID SHOTS OF A GOOD FRIEND, THIS MORNING!
THE WAY SHE SAYS "GOOD FRIEND" SENDS CHILLS UP MY SPINE!
YOO HOO! ARCHIEKINS!
LOOK! GUESS WHO? ISN'T THAT A BEAUTY?
3

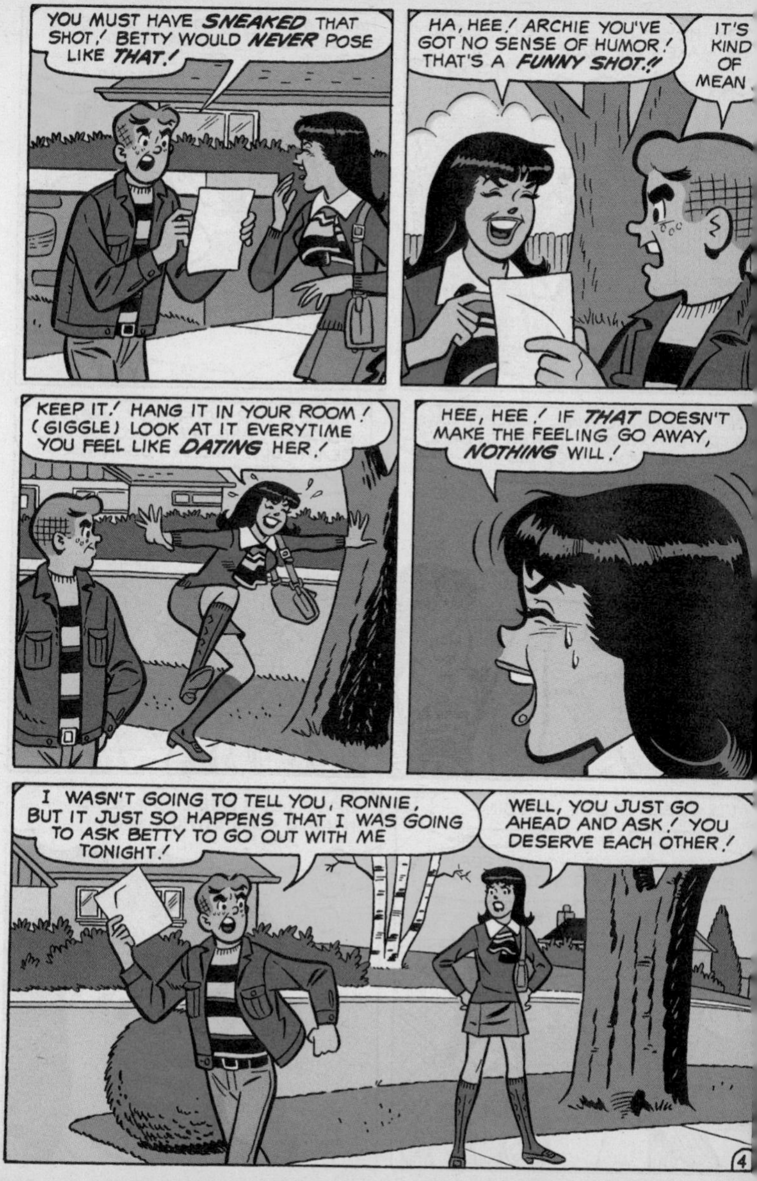

YOU MUST HAVE SNEAKED THAT SHOT! BETTY WOULD NEVER POSE LIKE THAT!
HA, HEE! ARCHIE YOU'VE GOT NO SENSE OF HUMOR! THAT'S A FUNNY SHOT!!
IT'S KIND OF MEAN
KEEP IT! HANG IT IN YOUR ROOM! (GIGGLE) LOOK AT IT EVERYTIME YOU FEEL LIKE DATING HER!
HEE, HEE! IF THAT DOESN'T MAKE THE FEELING GO AWAY, NOTHING WILL!
I WASN'T GOING TO TELL YOU, RONNIE, BUT IT JUST SO HAPPENS THAT I WAS GOING TO ASK BETTY TO GO OUT WITH ME TONIGHT!
WELL, YOU JUST GO AHEAD AND ASK! YOU DESERVE EACH OTHER!
4

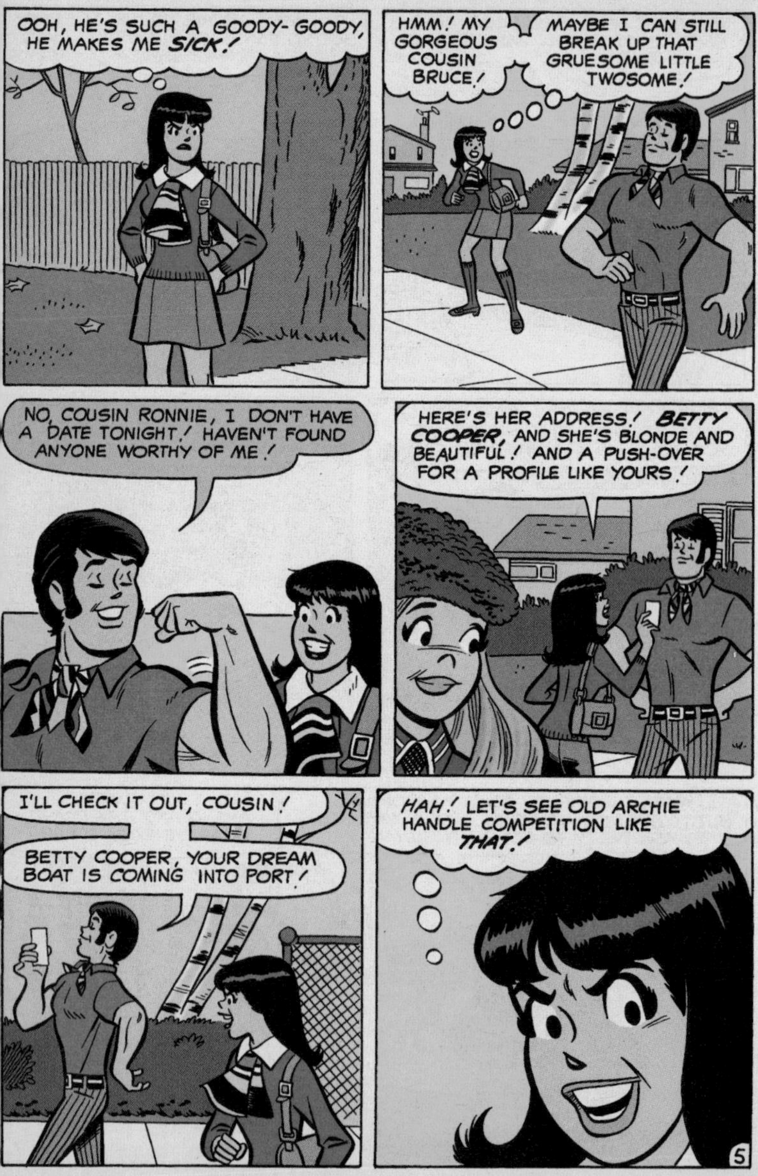
OOH, HE'S SUCH A GOODY-GOODY, HE MAKES ME SICK!
HMM! MY GORGEOUS COUSIN BRUCE!
MAYBE I CAN STILL BREAK UP THAT GRUESOME LITTLE TWOSOME!
NO, COUSIN RONNIE, I DON'T HAVE A DATE TONIGHT! HAVEN'T FOUND ANYONE WORTHY OF ME!
HERE'S HER ADDRESS! BETTY COOPER, AND SHE'S BLONDE AND BEAUTIFUL! AND A PUSH-OVER FOR A PROFILE LIKE YOURS!
I'LL CHECK IT OUT, COUSIN!
BETTY COOPER, YOUR DREAM BOAT IS COMING INTO PORT!
HAH! LET'S SEE OLD ARCHIE HANDLE COMPETITION LIKE THAT!
5

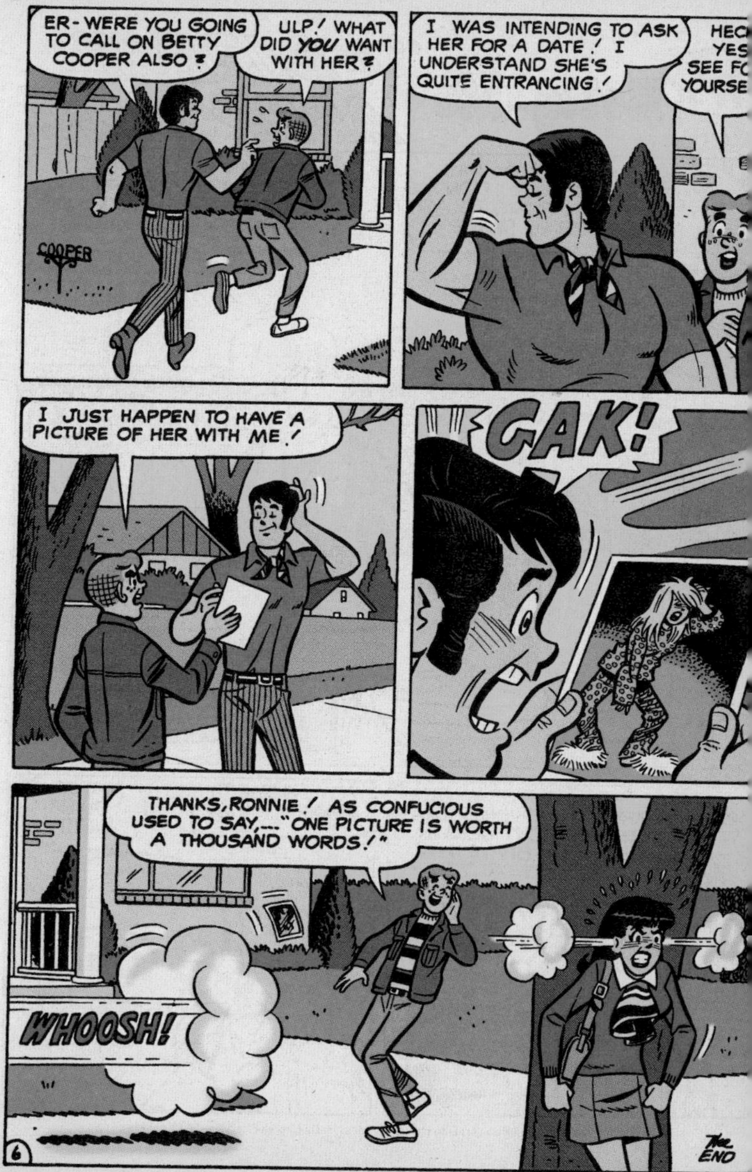

ER-WERE YOU GOING TO CALL ON BETTY COOPER ALSO ?
ULP! WHAT DID YOU WANT WITH HER?
COOPER
I WAS INTENDING TO ASK HER FOR A DATE! I UNDERSTAND SHE'S QUITE ENTRANCING!
I JUST HAPPEN TO HAVE A PICTURE OF HER WITH ME!
GAK!
THANKS, RONNIE! AS CONFUCIOUS USED TO SAY,..."ONE PICTURE IS WORTH A THOUSAND WORDS!"
WHOOSH!
6
THE END

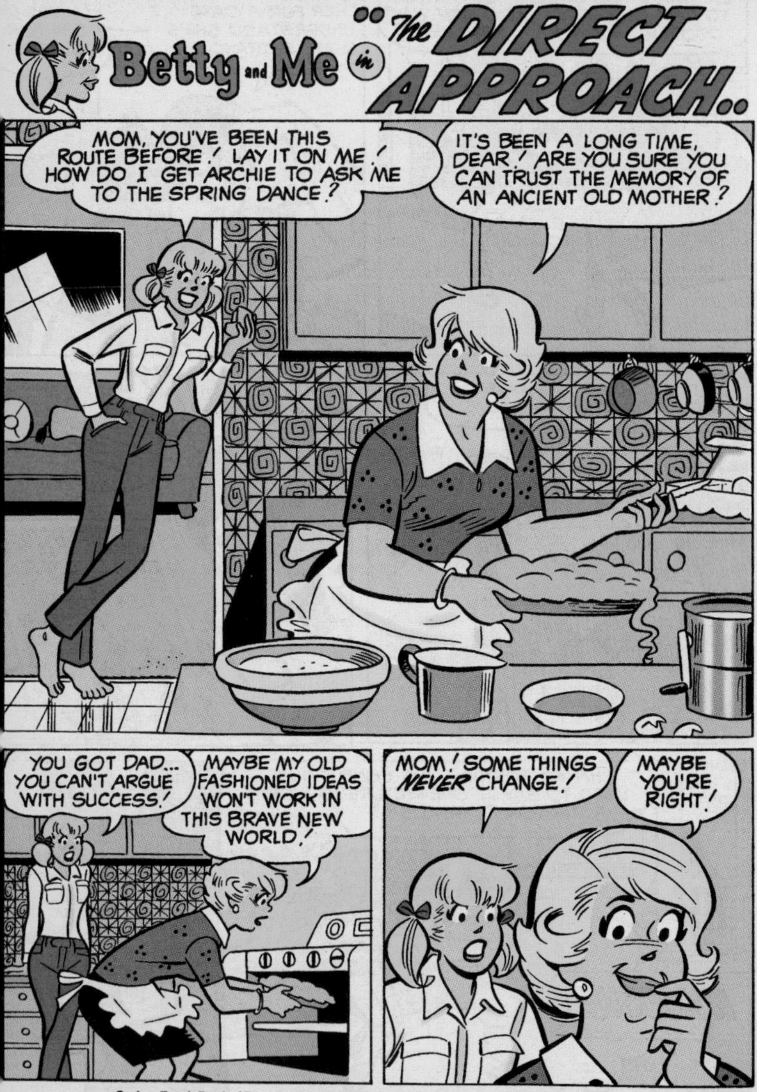
Betty and Me in
The DIRECT APPROACH..
MOM, YOU'VE BEEN THIS ROUTE BEFORE! LAY IT ON ME! HOW DO I GET ARCHIE TO ASK ME TO THE SPRING DANCE?
IT'S BEEN A LONG TIME, DEAR! ARE YOU SURE YOU CAN TRUST THE MEMORY OF AN ANCIENT OLD MOTHER?
YOU GOT DAD... YOU CAN'T ARGUE WITH SUCCESS!
MAYBE MY OLD FASHIONED IDEAS WON'T WORK IN THIS BRAVE NEW WORLD!
MOM! SOME THINGS NEVER CHANGE!
MAYBE YOU'RE RIGHT!
Script: Frank Doyle / Pencils: Dan DeCarlo / Inks: Rudy Lapick / Letters: Bill Yoshida

FEEDING!

"FEEDING"? FOOD IS THE ANSWER?

I WANT *ARCHIE*, NOT *JUGHEAD!*

NO! NOT ONLY *FOOD!*

FEED HIS VANITY, HIS EGO, *AND* HIS STOMACH!

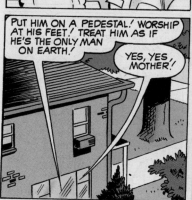

PUT HIM ON A PEDESTAL! WORSHIP AT HIS FEET! TREAT HIM AS IF HE'S THE ONLY *MAN* ON EARTH!

YES, YES MOTHER!

BUT WHAT CAN I DO THAT I DON'T DO *NOW*?

LAY IT ON A LITTLE THICKER!

AND SO, OPERATION OVERFEED SWINGS INTO ACTION!

"HANDSOME"? ME?

YOU'RE SO MODEST!

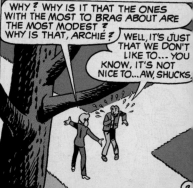

WHY? WHY IS IT THAT THE ONES WITH THE MOST TO BRAG ABOUT ARE THE MOST MODEST? WHY IS THAT, *ARCHIE*?

WELL, IT'S JUST THAT WE DON'T LIKE TO... YOU KNOW, IT'S NOT NICE TO... AW, SHUCKS.

2

LOOK AT OL' ARCH! SOMEBODY MUST HAVE PUMPED HIM FULL OF AIR!

WEARING HIS NOSE HIGH LIKE THAT, HE'S GONNA...

... TRIP OVER SOMETHING!

TRIP!

SMASH

AND SO IT CONTINUES THRU THE WEEK!

THIS OL' RAG?

IT ISN'T THE *AGE* THAT MATTERS DARLING!

IT'S... IT'S THE WAY YOU WEAR IT! YOU KNOW! WITH THAT CERTAIN *FLAIR!*

WELL, LIKE *YEAH!*

YOU'RE COMPARING THOSE REMNANTS WITH *MY* EXPENSIVE THREADS?

IT'S THE WAY I WEAR THEM THAT MAKES THE DIFFERENCE!

I'LL SAY IT DOES! THAT'S WHAT KEEPS THE CROWS OUT OF THE CORNFIELD!

SHEER JEALOUSLY!!

3

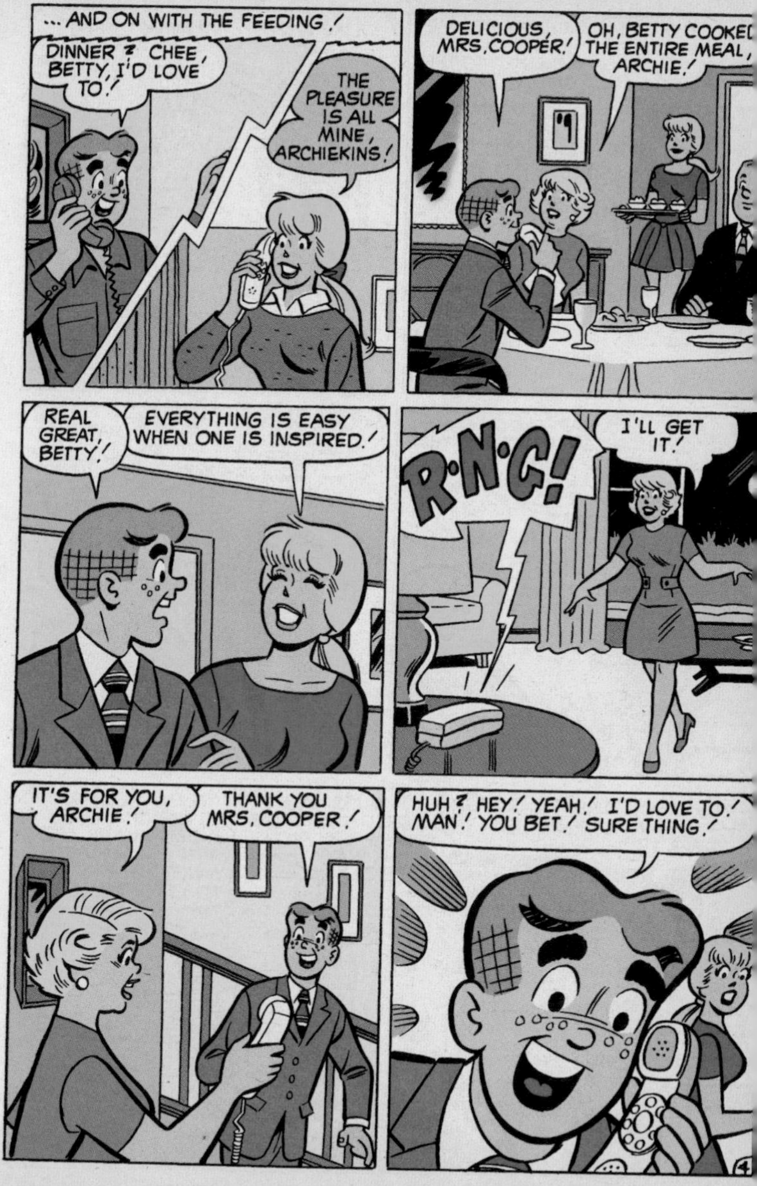

... AND ON WITH THE FEEDING!
DINNER? CHEE, BETTY, I'D LOVE TO!
THE PLEASURE IS ALL MINE, ARCHIEKINS!
DELICIOUS, MRS. COOPER!
OH, BETTY COOKED THE ENTIRE MEAL, ARCHIE!
REAL GREAT, BETTY!
EVERYTHING IS EASY WHEN ONE IS INSPIRED!
R-N-G!
I'LL GET IT!
IT'S FOR YOU, ARCHIE!
THANK YOU MRS. COOPER!
HUH? HEY! YEAH! I'D LOVE TO! MAN! YOU BET! SURE THING!
4

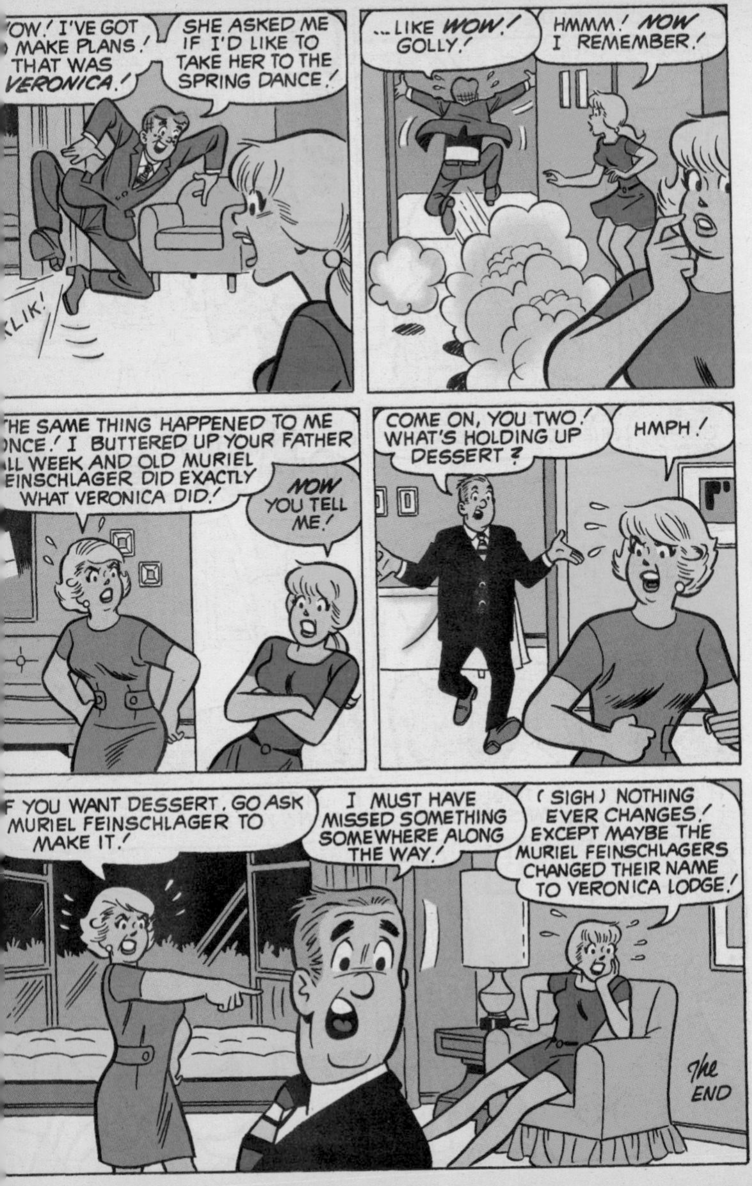
OW! I'VE GOT
MAKE PLANS! THAT WAS VERONICA!
SHE ASKED ME IF I'D LIKE TO TAKE HER TO THE SPRING DANCE!
KLIK!
...LIKE WOW! GOLLY!
HMMM! NOW I REMEMBER!
HE SAME THING HAPPENED TO ME NCE! I BUTTERED UP YOUR FATHER LL WEEK AND OLD MURIEL EINSCHLAGER DID EXACTLY WHAT VERONICA DID!
NOW YOU TELL ME!
COME ON, YOU TWO! WHAT'S HOLDING UP DESSERT?
HMPH!
F YOU WANT DESSERT, GO ASK MURIEL FEINSCHLAGER TO MAKE IT!
I MUST HAVE MISSED SOMETHING SOMEWHERE ALONG THE WAY!
(SIGH) NOTHING EVER CHANGES! EXCEPT MAYBE THE MURIEL FEINSCHLAGERS CHANGED THEIR NAME TO VERONICA LODGE!
The END

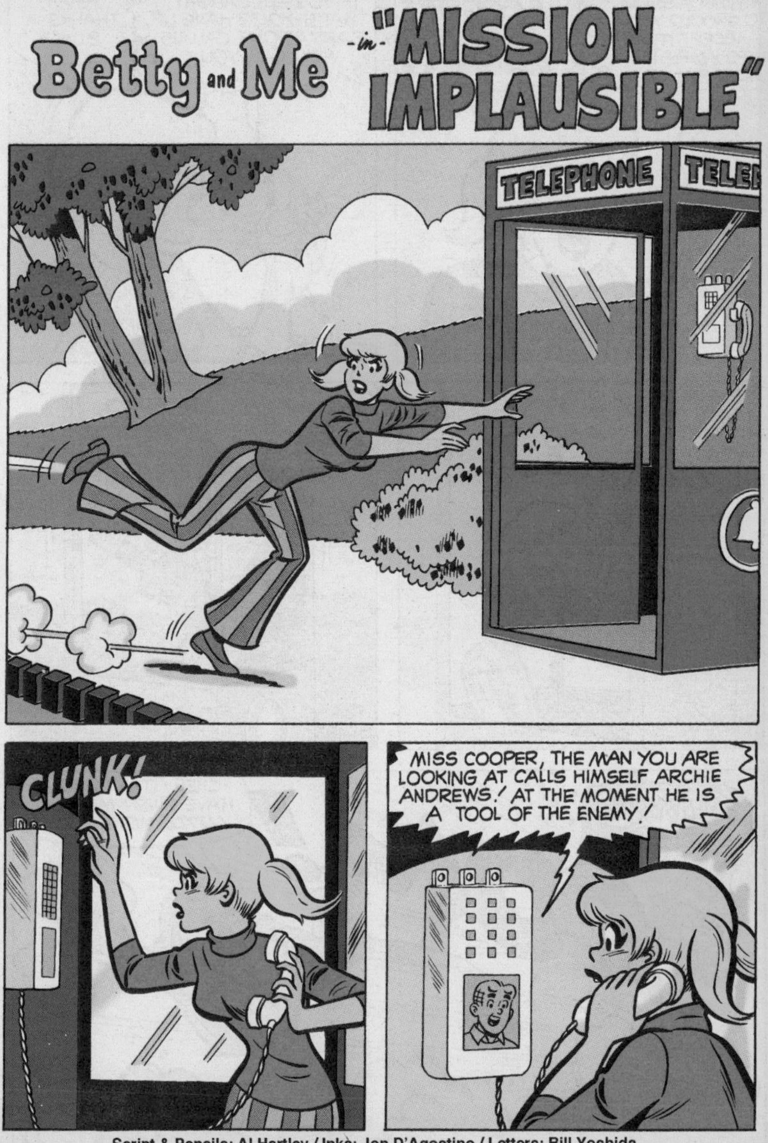
Betty and Me -in- "MISSION IMPLAUSIBLE"
TELEPHONE
CLUNK!
MISS COOPER, THE MAN YOU ARE LOOKING AT CALLS HIMSELF ARCHIE ANDREWS! AT THE MOMENT HE IS A TOOL OF THE ENEMY!

Script & Pencils: Al Hartley / Inks: Jon D'Agostino / Letters: Bill Yoshida

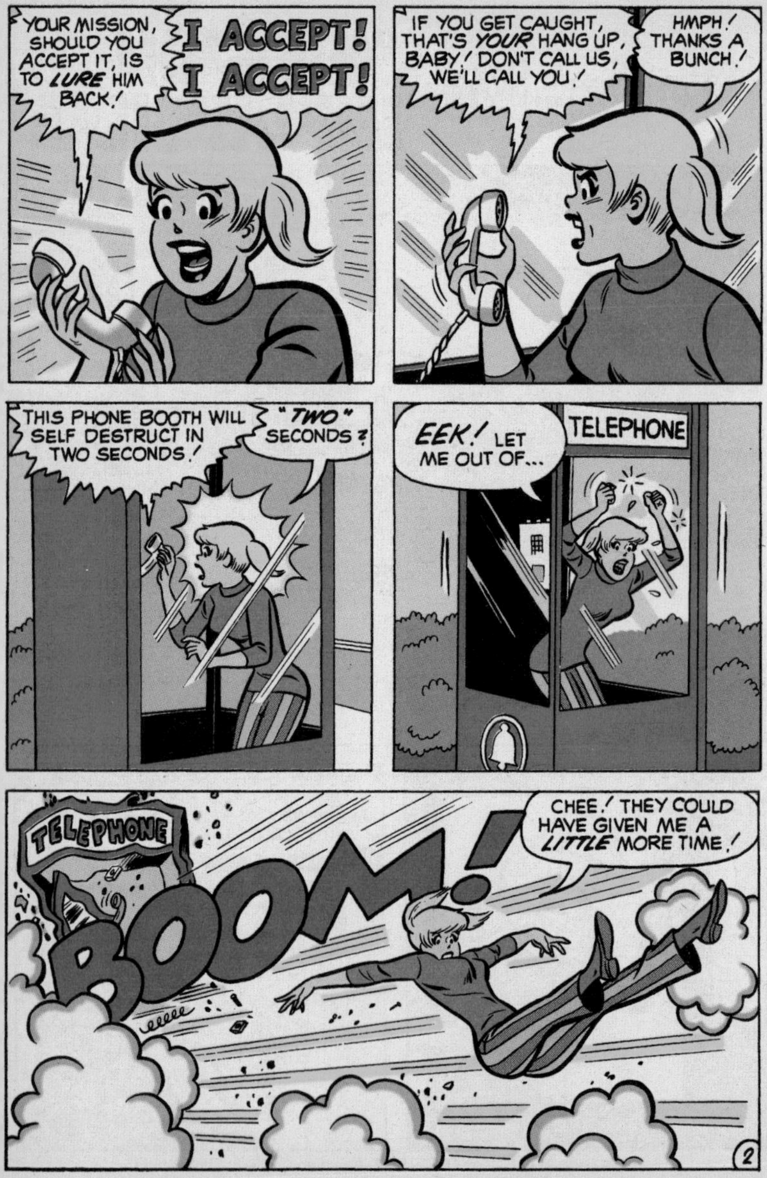
YOUR MISSION, SHOULD YOU ACCEPT IT, IS TO *LURE* HIM BACK!
I ACCEPT! I ACCEPT!
IF YOU GET CAUGHT, THAT'S *YOUR* HANG UP, BABY! DON'T CALL US, WE'LL CALL YOU!
HMPH! THANKS A BUNCH!
THIS PHONE BOOTH WILL SELF DESTRUCT IN TWO SECONDS!
"*TWO*" SECONDS?
EEK! LET ME OUT OF...
TELEPHONE
TELEPHONE
BOOM!
CHEE! THEY COULD HAVE GIVEN ME A *LITTLE* MORE TIME!

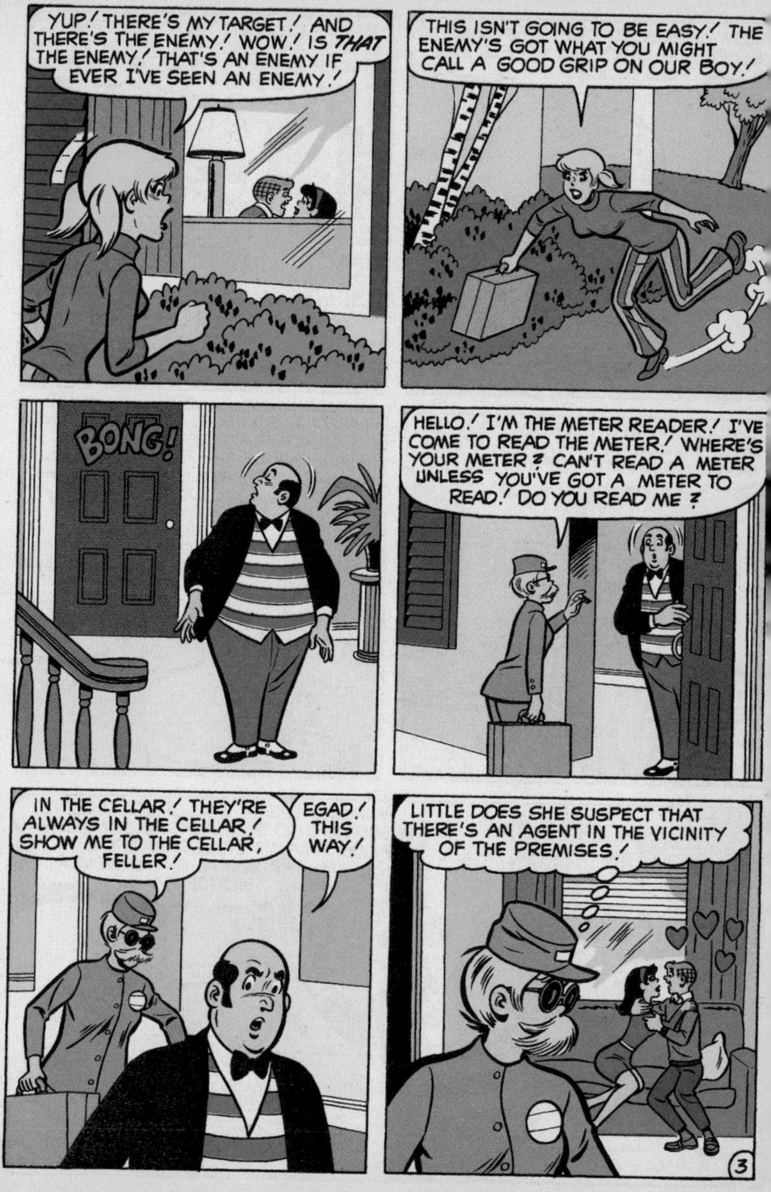
YUP! THERE'S MY TARGET! AND THERE'S THE ENEMY! WOW! IS THAT THE ENEMY! THAT'S AN ENEMY IF EVER I'VE SEEN AN ENEMY!
THIS ISN'T GOING TO BE EASY! THE ENEMY'S GOT WHAT YOU MIGHT CALL A GOOD GRIP ON OUR BOY!
BONG!
HELLO! I'M THE METER READER! I'VE COME TO READ THE METER! WHERE'S YOUR METER? CAN'T READ A METER UNLESS YOU'VE GOT A METER TO READ! DO YOU READ ME?
IN THE CELLAR! THEY'RE ALWAYS IN THE CELLAR! SHOW ME TO THE CELLAR, FELLER!
EGAD! THIS WAY!
LITTLE DOES SHE SUSPECT THAT THERE'S AN AGENT IN THE VICINITY OF THE PREMISES!
3

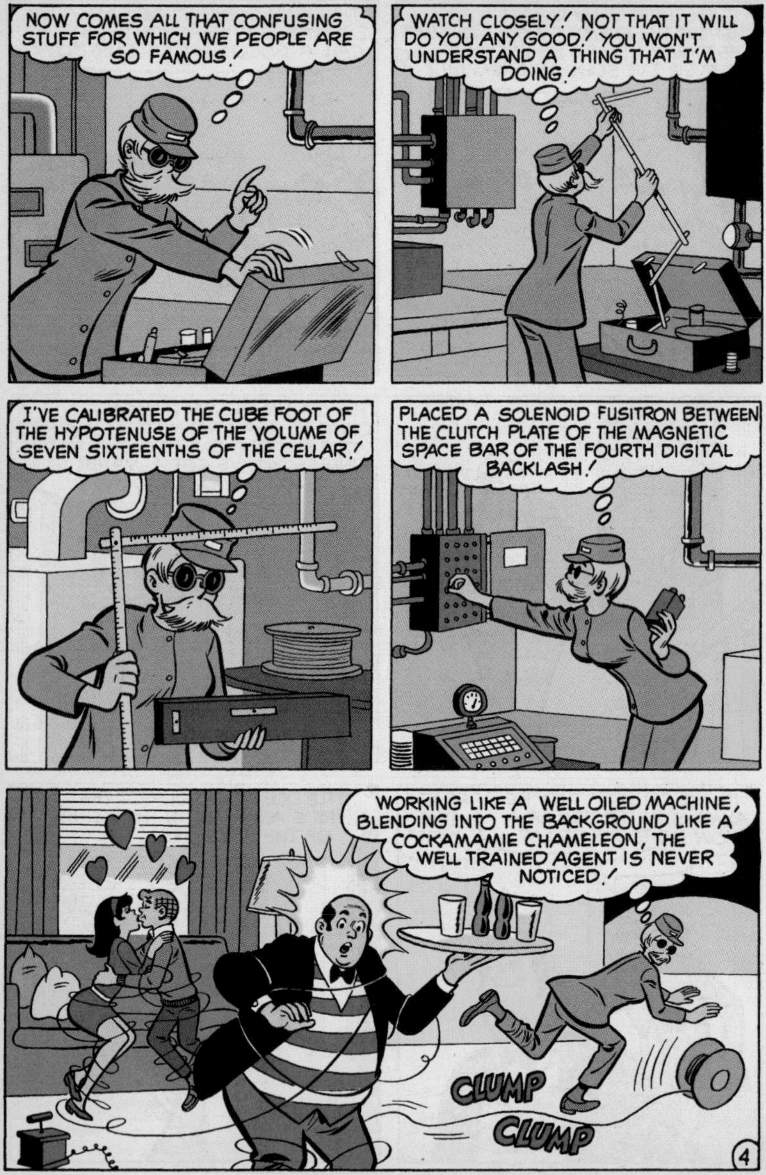
NOW COMES ALL THAT CONFUSING STUFF FOR WHICH WE PEOPLE ARE SO FAMOUS!
WATCH CLOSELY! NOT THAT IT WILL DO YOU ANY GOOD! YOU WON'T UNDERSTAND A THING THAT I'M DOING!
I'VE CALIBRATED THE CUBE FOOT OF THE HYPOTENUSE OF THE VOLUME OF SEVEN SIXTEENTHS OF THE CELLAR!
PLACED A SOLENOID FUSITRON BETWEEN THE CLUTCH PLATE OF THE MAGNETIC SPACE BAR OF THE FOURTH DIGITAL BACKLASH!
WORKING LIKE A WELL OILED MACHINE, BLENDING INTO THE BACKGROUND LIKE A COCKAMAMIE CHAMELEON, THE WELL TRAINED AGENT IS NEVER NOTICED!
CLUMP
CLUMP

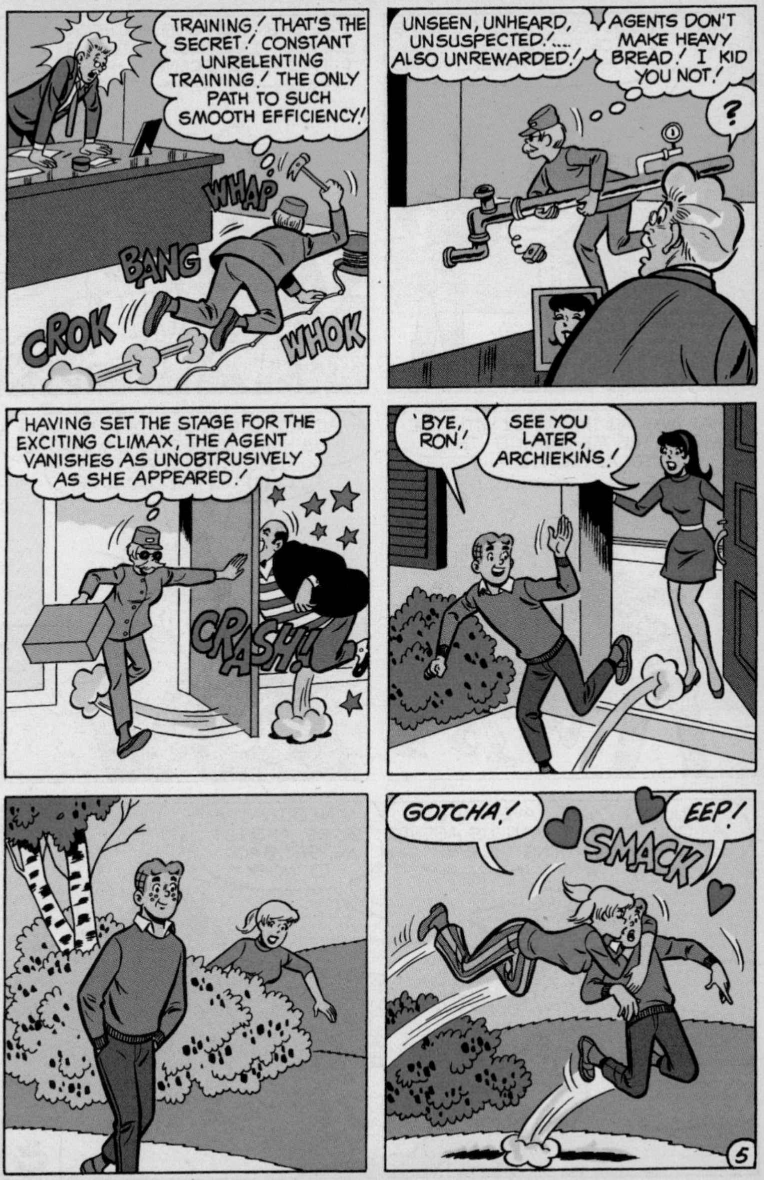
TRAINING! THAT'S THE SECRET! CONSTANT UNRELENTING TRAINING! THE ONLY PATH TO SUCH SMOOTH EFFICIENCY!
WHAP
BANG
CROK
WHOK
UNSEEN, UNHEARD, UNSUSPECTED!.... ALSO UNREWARDED!
AGENTS DON'T MAKE HEAVY BREAD! I KID YOU NOT!
?
HAVING SET THE STAGE FOR THE EXCITING CLIMAX, THE AGENT VANISHES AS UNOBTRUSIVELY AS SHE APPEARED!
CRASH!!
'BYE, RON!
SEE YOU LATER, ARCHIEKINS!
GOTCHA!
EEP!
SMACK

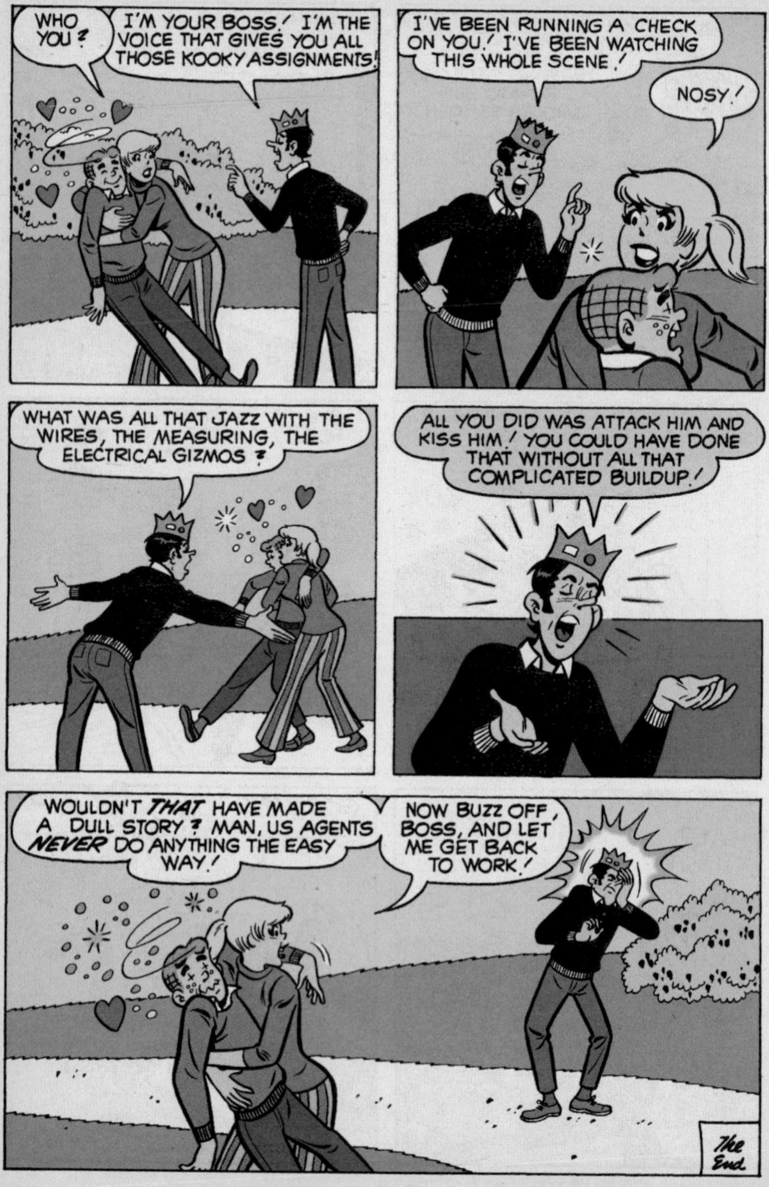
WHO YOU?
I'M YOUR BOSS! I'M THE VOICE THAT GIVES YOU ALL THOSE KOOKY ASSIGNMENTS!
I'VE BEEN RUNNING A CHECK ON YOU! I'VE BEEN WATCHING THIS WHOLE SCENE!
NOSY!
WHAT WAS ALL THAT JAZZ WITH THE WIRES, THE MEASURING, THE ELECTRICAL GIZMOS?
ALL YOU DID WAS ATTACK HIM AND KISS HIM! YOU COULD HAVE DONE THAT WITHOUT ALL THAT COMPLICATED BUILDUP!
WOULDN'T THAT HAVE MADE A DULL STORY? MAN, US AGENTS NEVER DO ANYTHING THE EASY WAY!
NOW BUZZ OFF, BOSS, AND LET ME GET BACK TO WORK!
The End

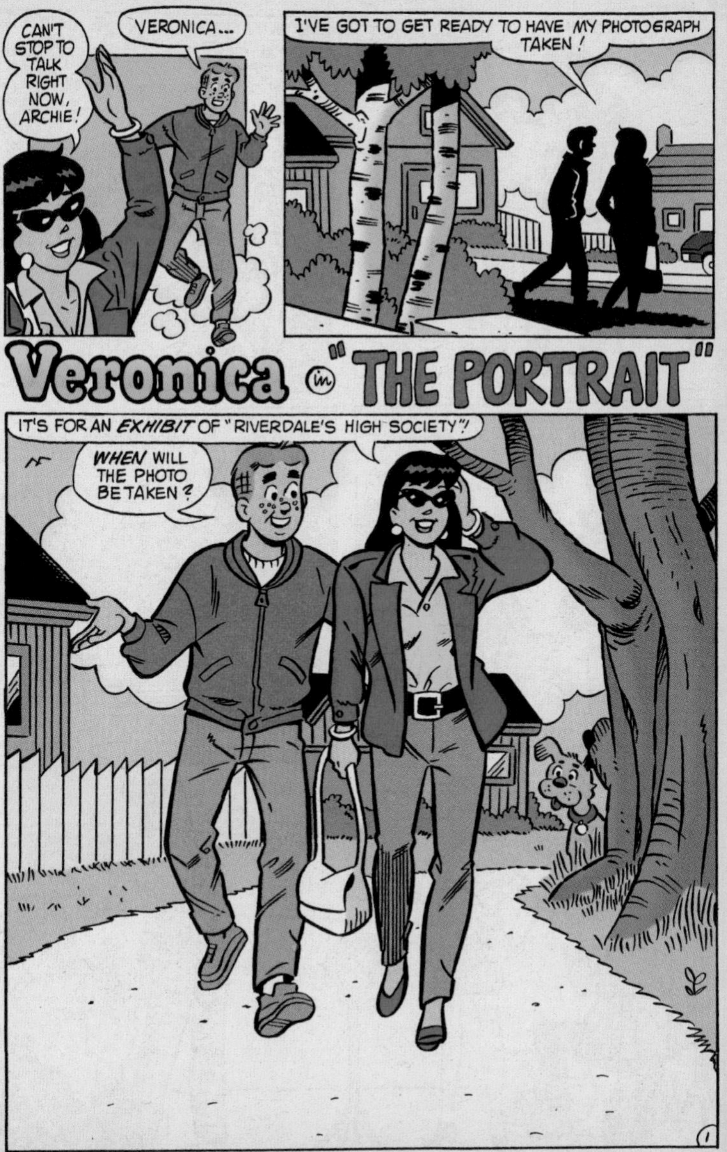
VERONICA...
CAN'T STOP TO TALK RIGHT NOW, ARCHIE!
I'VE GOT TO GET READY TO HAVE MY PHOTOGRAPH TAKEN!
Veronica in "THE PORTRAIT"
IT'S FOR AN EXHIBIT OF "RIVERDALE'S HIGH SOCIETY"!
WHEN WILL THE PHOTO BE TAKEN?
1

Script: Hal Smith / Pencils: Tim Kennedy / Inks: Rudy Lapick / Letters: Bill Yoshida

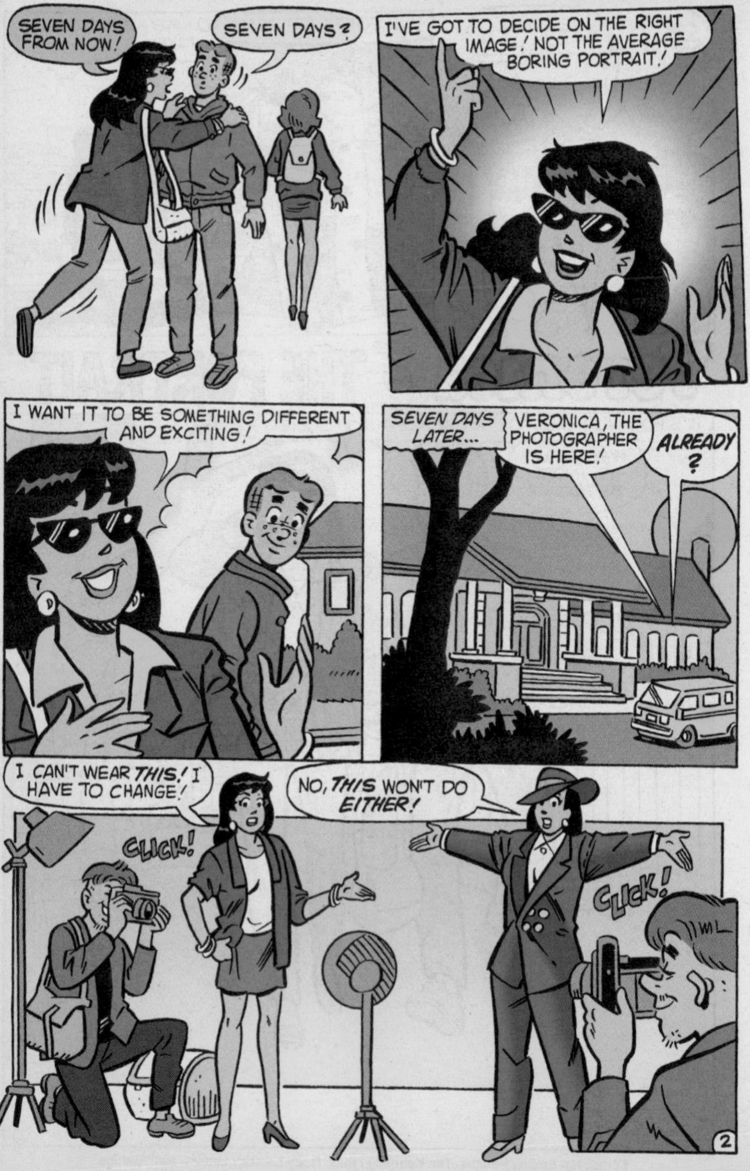
SEVEN DAYS FROM NOW!
SEVEN DAYS?
I'VE GOT TO DECIDE ON THE RIGHT IMAGE! NOT THE AVERAGE BORING PORTRAIT!
I WANT IT TO BE SOMETHING DIFFERENT AND EXCITING!
SEVEN DAYS LATER...
VERONICA, THE PHOTOGRAPHER IS HERE!
ALREADY?
I CAN'T WEAR THIS! I HAVE TO CHANGE!
CLICK!
NO, THIS WON'T DO EITHER!
CLICK!
2

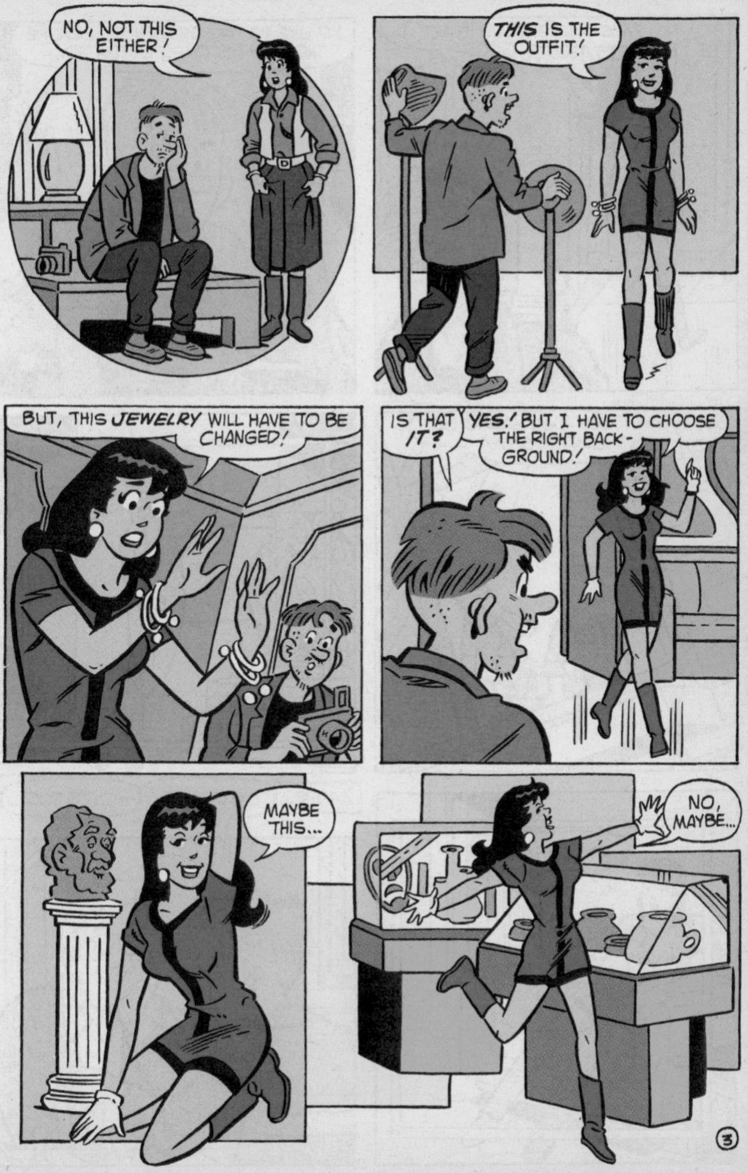
NO, NOT THIS EITHER!
THIS IS THE OUTFIT!
BUT, THIS JEWELRY WILL HAVE TO BE CHANGED!
IS THAT IT?
YES! BUT I HAVE TO CHOOSE THE RIGHT BACK-GROUND!
MAYBE THIS...
NO, MAYBE...

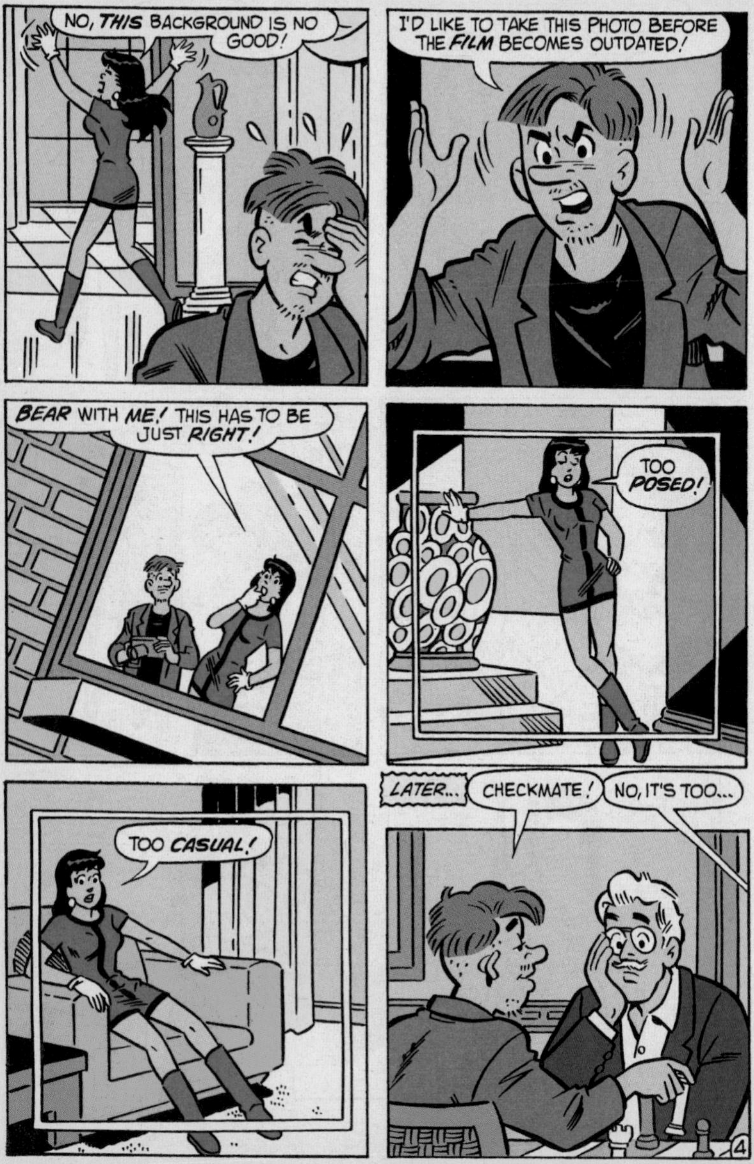
NO, THIS BACKGROUND IS NO GOOD!
I'D LIKE TO TAKE THIS PHOTO BEFORE THE FILM BECOMES OUTDATED!
BEAR WITH ME! THIS HAS TO BE JUST RIGHT!
TOO POSED!
TOO CASUAL!
LATER...
CHECKMATE!
NO, IT'S TOO...
4

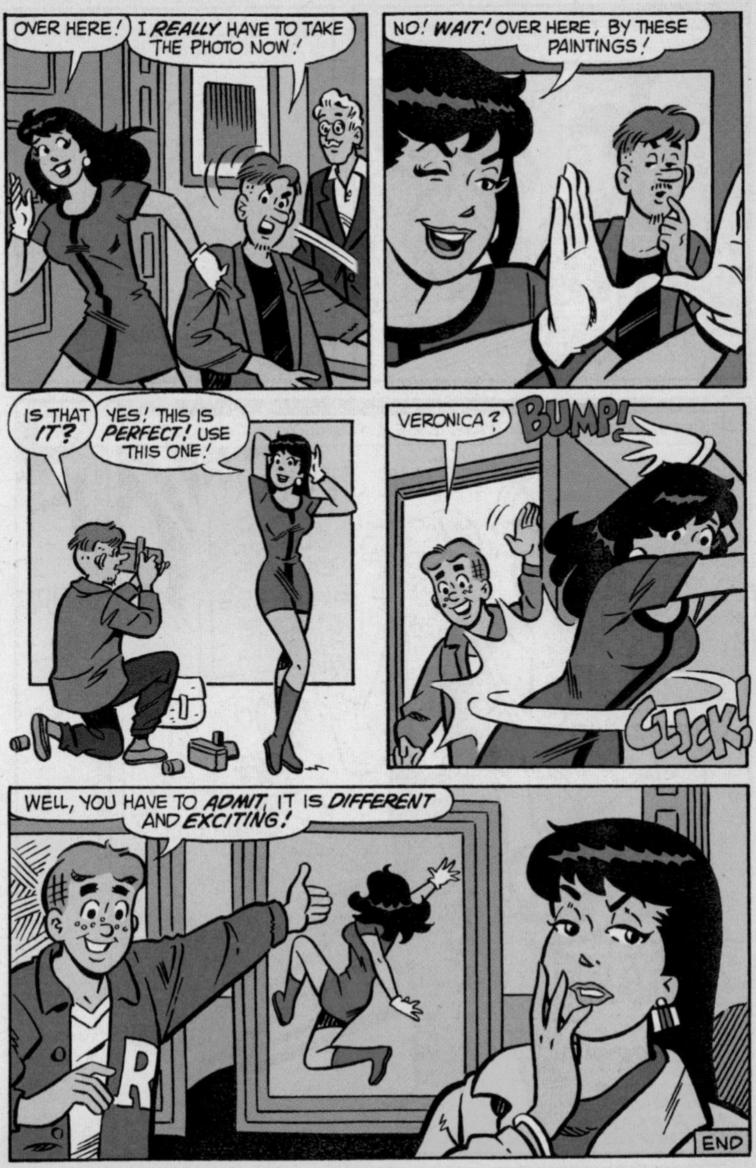
OVER HERE!
I REALLY HAVE TO TAKE THE PHOTO NOW!
NO! WAIT! OVER HERE, BY THESE PAINTINGS!
IS THAT IT?
YES! THIS IS PERFECT! USE THIS ONE!
VERONICA?
BUMP!
CLICK!
WELL, YOU HAVE TO ADMIT, IT IS DIFFERENT AND EXCITING!
END

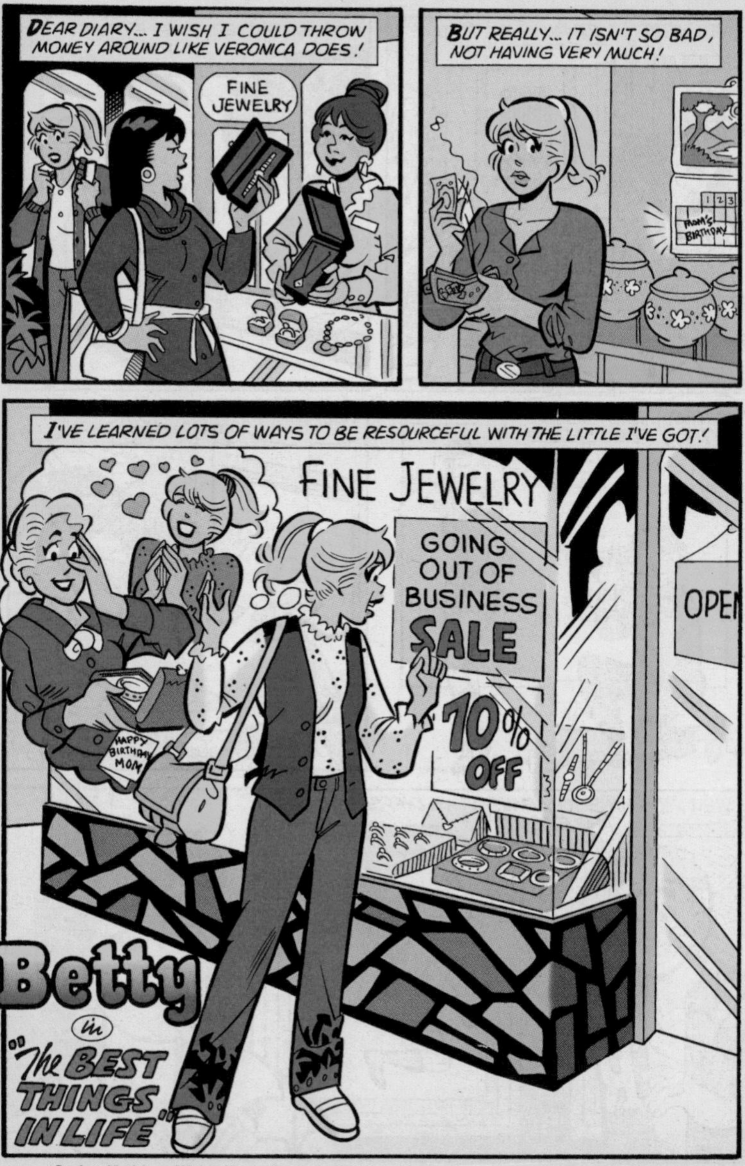
DEAR DIARY... I WISH I COULD THROW MONEY AROUND LIKE VERONICA DOES!
FINE JEWELRY
BUT REALLY... IT ISN'T SO BAD, NOT HAVING VERY MUCH!
MOM'S BIRTHDAY
I'VE LEARNED LOTS OF WAYS TO BE RESOURCEFUL WITH THE LITTLE I'VE GOT!
HAPPY BIRTHDAY MOM
FINE JEWELRY
GOING OUT OF BUSINESS SALE
10% OFF
OPEN
Betty
in
"The BEST THINGS IN LIFE"

Script: Kathleen Webb / Pencils: Stan Goldberg / Inks: John Lowe / Letters: Bill Yoshida

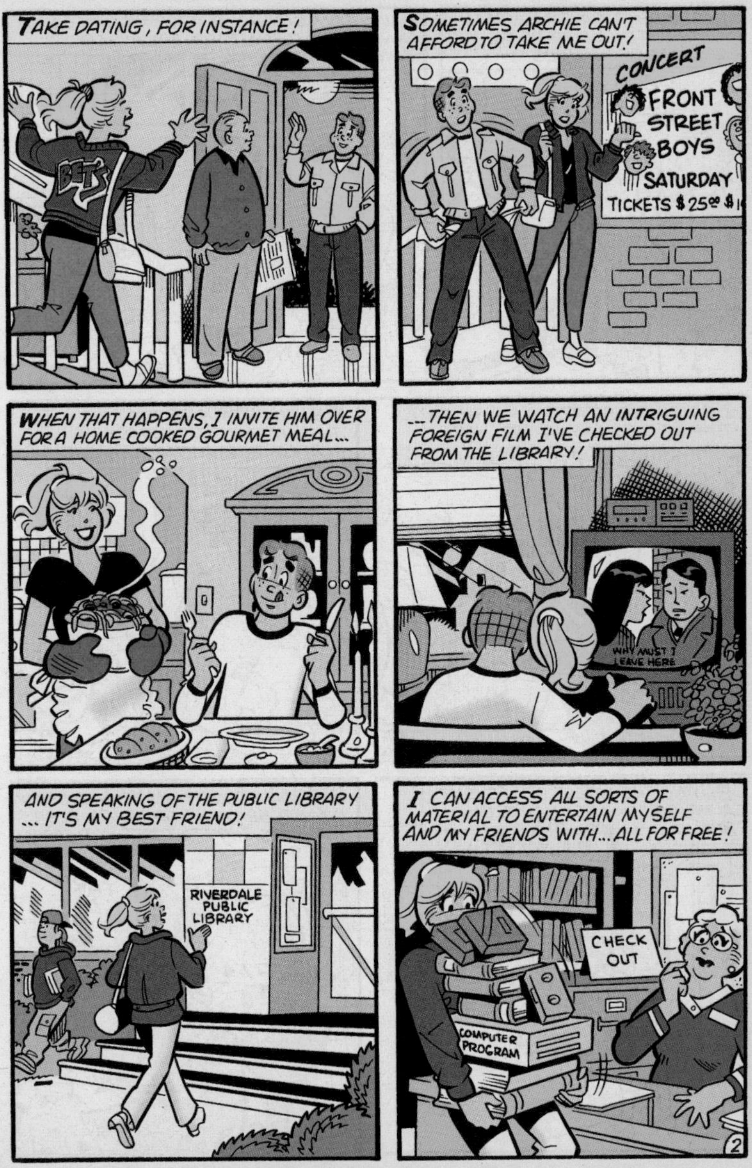
TAKE DATING, FOR INSTANCE!
SOMETIMES ARCHIE CAN'T AFFORD TO TAKE ME OUT!
CONCERT
FRONT STREET BOYS
SATURDAY
TICKETS $25.00
WHEN THAT HAPPENS, I INVITE HIM OVER FOR A HOME COOKED GOURMET MEAL...
...THEN WE WATCH AN INTRIGUING FOREIGN FILM I'VE CHECKED OUT FROM THE LIBRARY!
WHY MUST I LEAVE HERE
AND SPEAKING OF THE PUBLIC LIBRARY ... IT'S MY BEST FRIEND!
RIVERDALE PUBLIC LIBRARY
I CAN ACCESS ALL SORTS OF MATERIAL TO ENTERTAIN MYSELF AND MY FRIENDS WITH... ALL FOR FREE!
CHECK OUT
COMPUTER PROGRAM

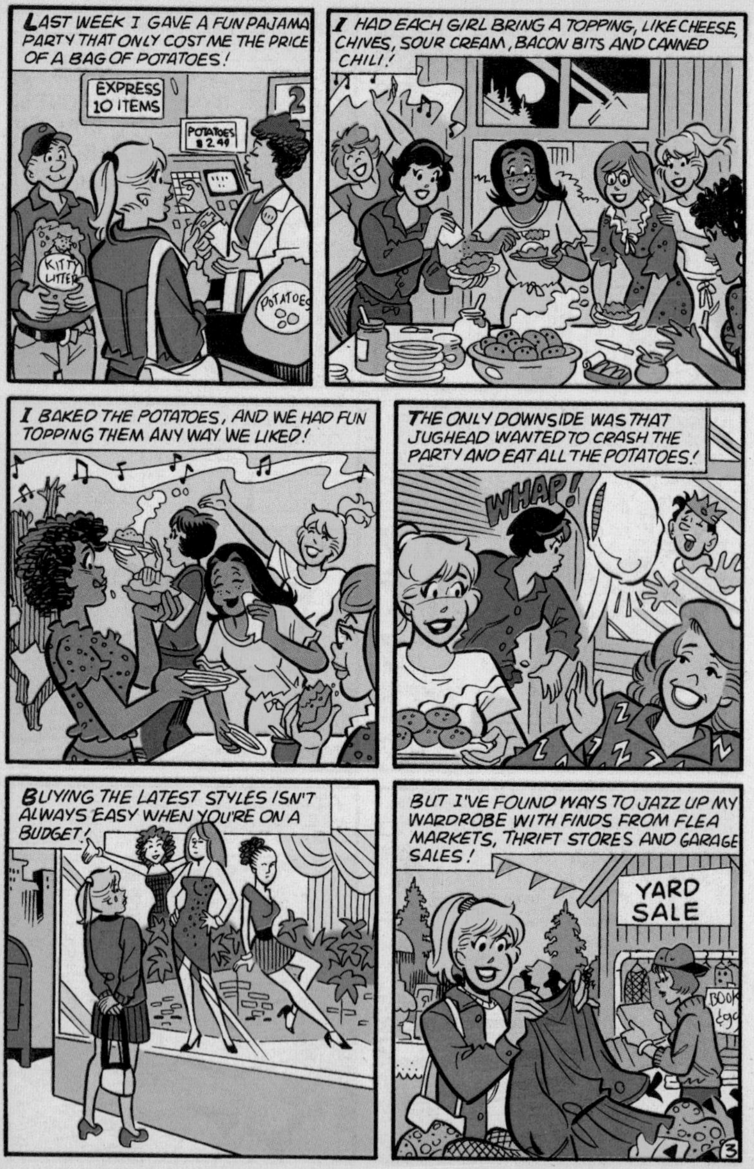
LAST WEEK I GAVE A FUN PAJAMA PARTY THAT ONLY COST ME THE PRICE OF A BAG OF POTATOES!
EXPRESS 10 ITEMS
2
POTATOES $2.49
KITTY LITTER
POTATOES
I HAD EACH GIRL BRING A TOPPING, LIKE CHEESE, CHIVES, SOUR CREAM, BACON BITS AND CANNED CHILI!
I BAKED THE POTATOES, AND WE HAD FUN TOPPING THEM ANY WAY WE LIKED!
THE ONLY DOWNSIDE WAS THAT JUGHEAD WANTED TO CRASH THE PARTY AND EAT ALL THE POTATOES!
WHAP!
BUYING THE LATEST STYLES ISN'T ALWAYS EASY WHEN YOU'RE ON A BUDGET!
BUT I'VE FOUND WAYS TO JAZZ UP MY WARDROBE WITH FINDS FROM FLEA MARKETS, THRIFT STORES AND GARAGE SALES!
YARD SALE
3

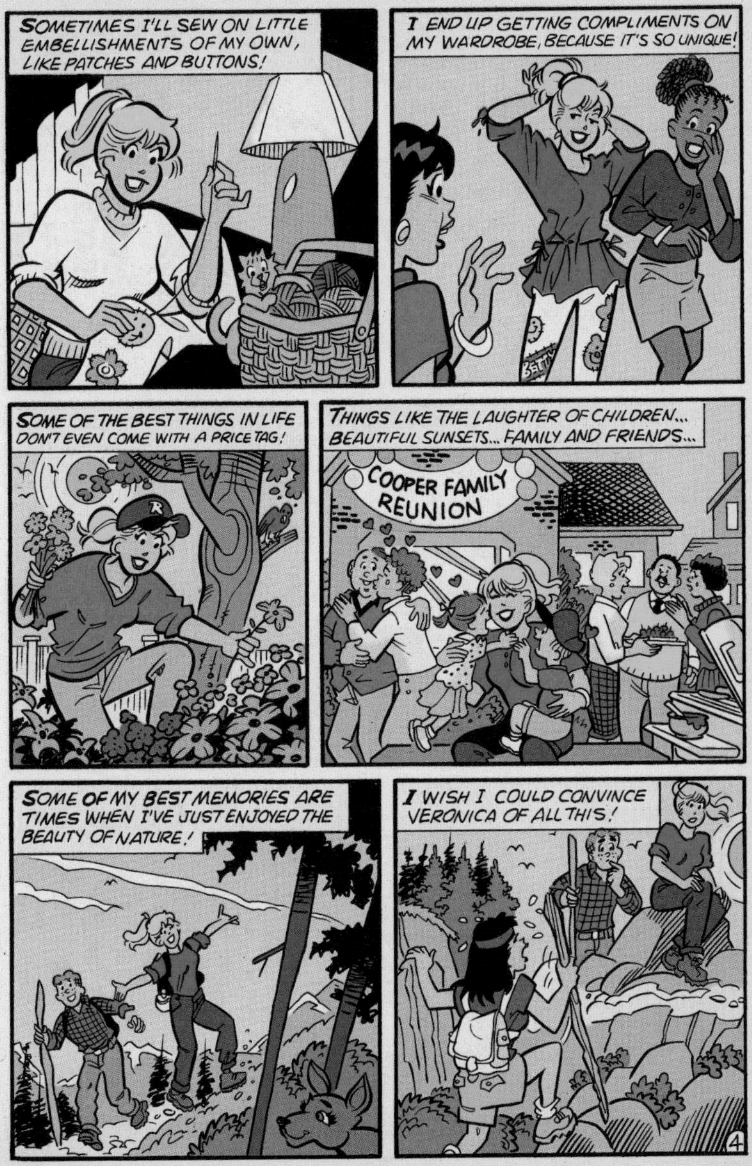
SOMETIMES I'LL SEW ON LITTLE EMBELLISHMENTS OF MY OWN, LIKE PATCHES AND BUTTONS!
I END UP GETTING COMPLIMENTS ON MY WARDROBE, BECAUSE IT'S SO UNIQUE!
BETTY
SOME OF THE BEST THINGS IN LIFE DON'T EVEN COME WITH A PRICE TAG!
THINGS LIKE THE LAUGHTER OF CHILDREN... BEAUTIFUL SUNSETS... FAMILY AND FRIENDS...
COOPER FAMILY REUNION
SOME OF MY BEST MEMORIES ARE TIMES WHEN I'VE JUST ENJOYED THE BEAUTY OF NATURE!
I WISH I COULD CONVINCE VERONICA OF ALL THIS!
4

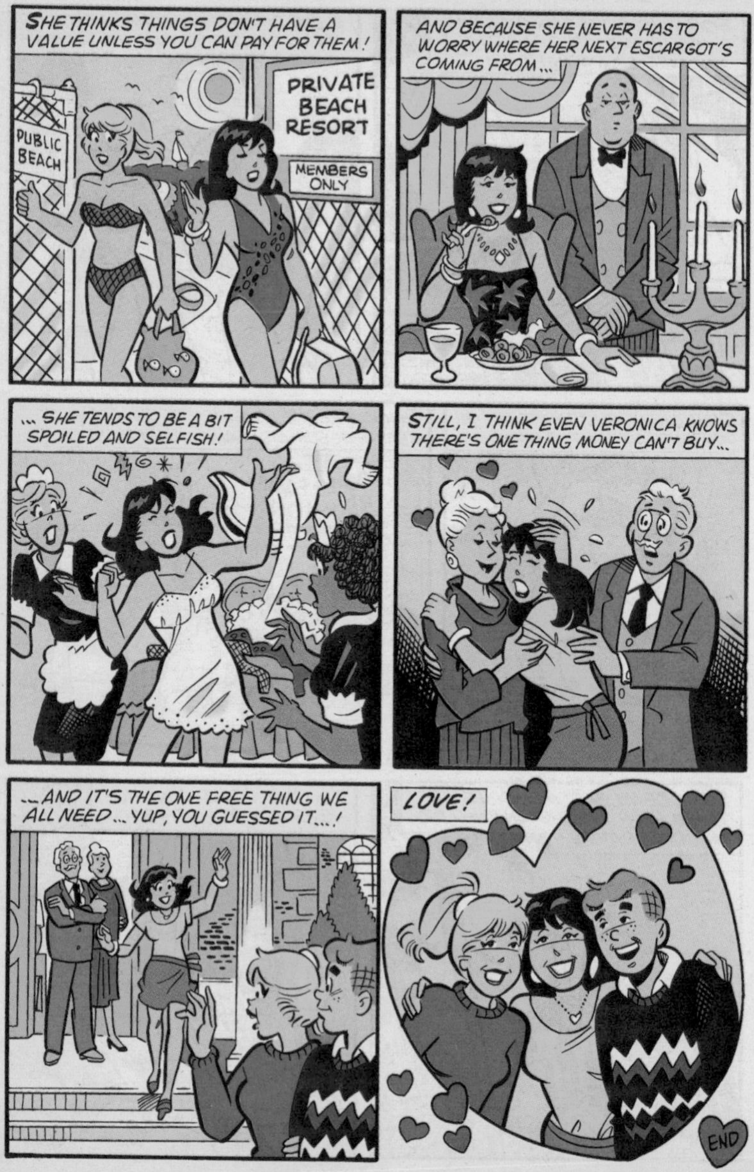
SHE THINKS THINGS DON'T HAVE A VALUE UNLESS YOU CAN PAY FOR THEM!
PUBLIC BEACH
PRIVATE BEACH RESORT
MEMBERS ONLY
AND BECAUSE SHE NEVER HAS TO WORRY WHERE HER NEXT ESCARGOT'S COMING FROM...
... SHE TENDS TO BE A BIT SPOILED AND SELFISH!
STILL, I THINK EVEN VERONICA KNOWS THERE'S ONE THING MONEY CAN'T BUY...
... AND IT'S THE ONE FREE THING WE ALL NEED... YUP, YOU GUESSED IT...!
LOVE!
END

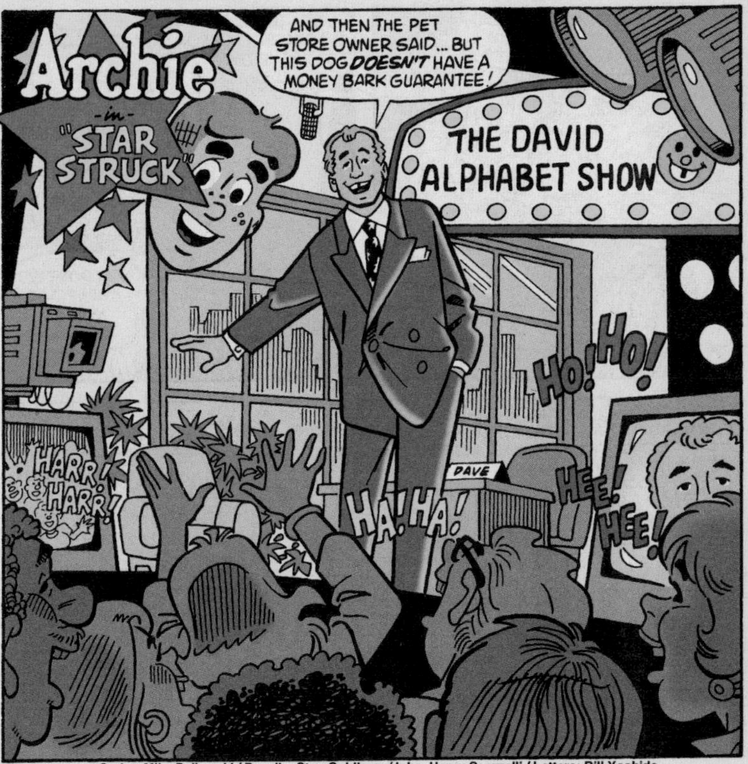
Archie
-in-
"STAR STRUCK"
AND THEN THE PET STORE OWNER SAID... BUT THIS DOG DOESN'T HAVE A MONEY BARK GUARANTEE!
THE DAVID ALPHABET SHOW
HO! HO!
HARR! HARR!
DAVE
HA! HA!
HEE! HEE!

Script: Mike Pellowski / Pencils: Stan Goldberg / Inks: Henry Scarpelli / Letters: Bill Yoshida

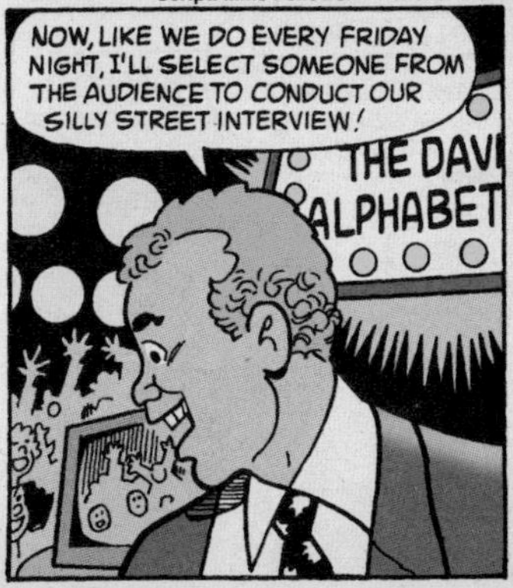
NOW, LIKE WE DO EVERY FRIDAY NIGHT, I'LL SELECT SOMEONE FROM THE AUDIENCE TO CONDUCT OUR SILLY STREET INTERVIEW!
THE DAVI
ALPHABET

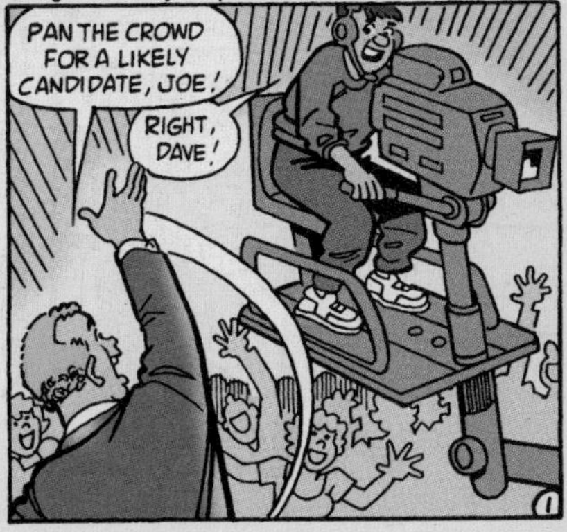
PAN THE CROWD FOR A LIKELY CANDIDATE, JOE!
RIGHT, DAVE!

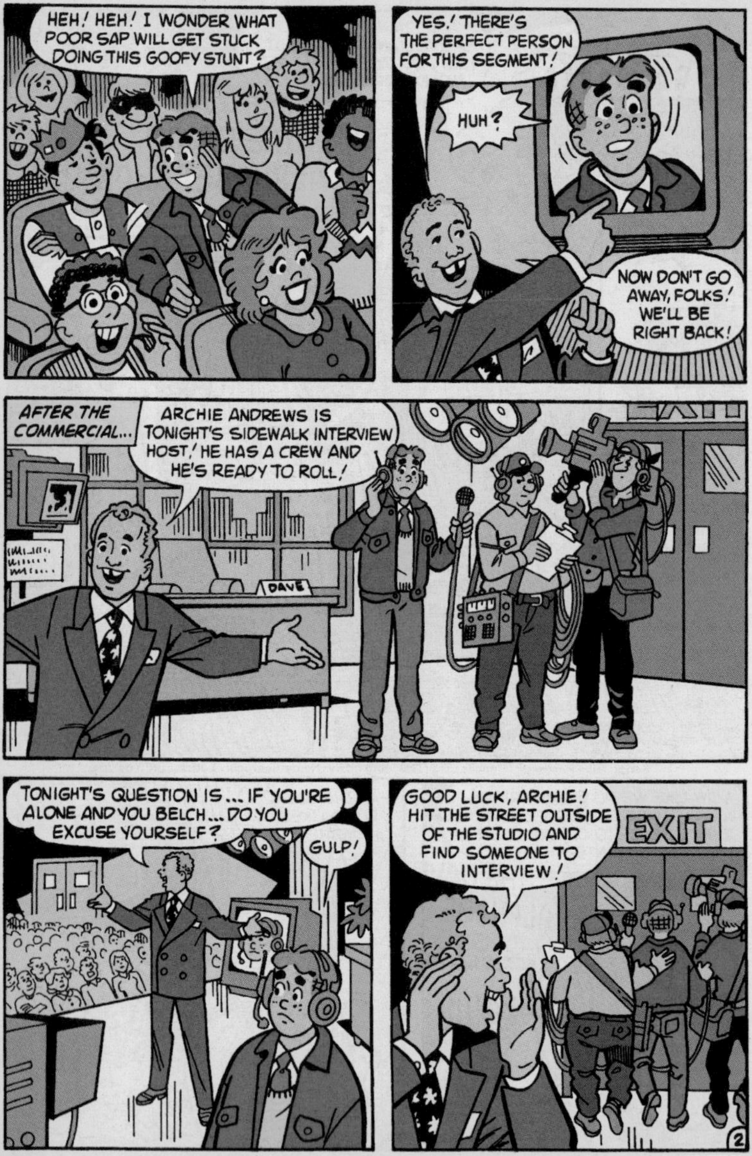
HEH! HEH! I WONDER WHAT POOR SAP WILL GET STUCK DOING THIS GOOFY STUNT?
YES! THERE'S THE PERFECT PERSON FOR THIS SEGMENT!
HUH?
NOW DON'T GO AWAY, FOLKS! WE'LL BE RIGHT BACK!
AFTER THE COMMERCIAL...
ARCHIE ANDREWS IS TONIGHT'S SIDEWALK INTERVIEW HOST! HE HAS A CREW AND HE'S READY TO ROLL!
DAVE
TONIGHT'S QUESTION IS... IF YOU'RE ALONE AND YOU BELCH... DO YOU EXCUSE YOURSELF?
GULP!
GOOD LUCK, ARCHIE! HIT THE STREET OUTSIDE OF THE STUDIO AND FIND SOMEONE TO INTERVIEW!
EXIT
2

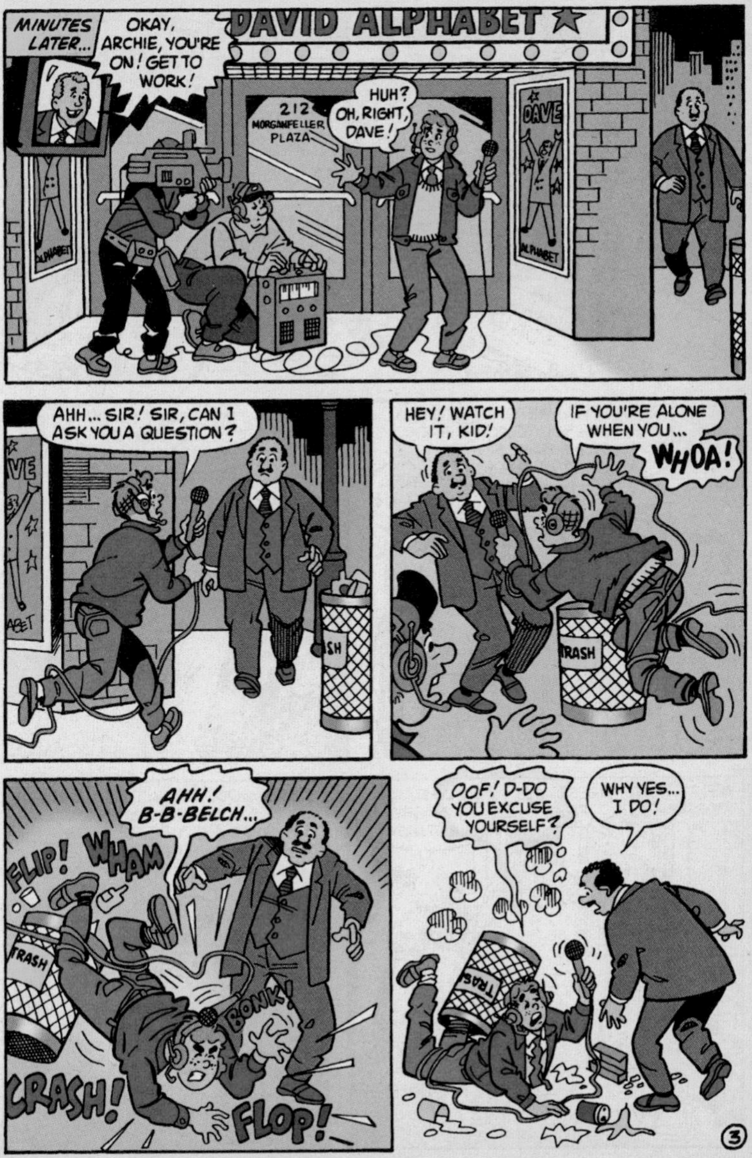

MINUTES LATER...
OKAY, ARCHIE, YOU'RE ON! GET TO WORK!
DAVID ALPHABET
212 MORGANFELLER PLAZA
HUH? OH, RIGHT, DAVE!
DAVE
ALPHABET
AHH... SIR! SIR, CAN I ASK YOU A QUESTION?
HEY! WATCH IT, KID!
IF YOU'RE ALONE WHEN YOU...
WHOA!
TRASH
AHH! B-B-BELCH...
FLIP! WHAM
TRASH
BONK!
CRASH!
FLOP!
OOF! D-DO YOU EXCUSE YOURSELF?
WHY YES... I DO!
3

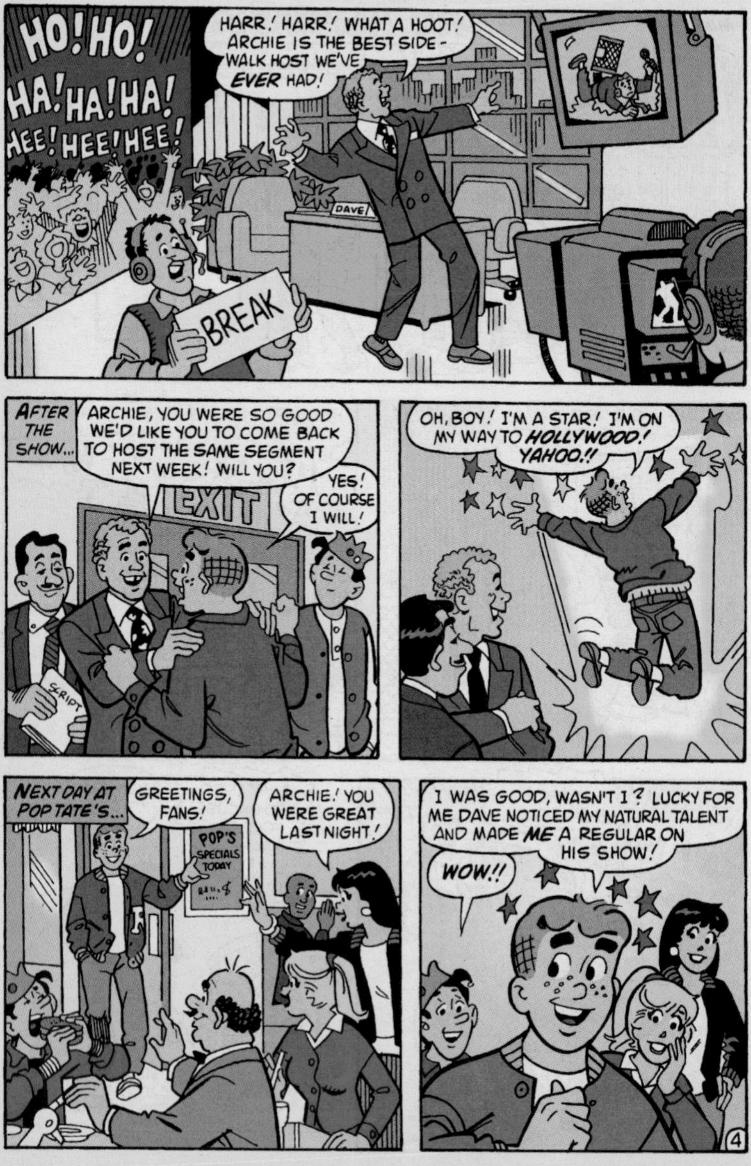
HO! HO!
HA! HA! HA!
HEE! HEE! HEE!
HARR! HARR! WHAT A HOOT! ARCHIE IS THE BEST SIDE-WALK HOST WE'VE EVER HAD!
DAVE
BREAK
AFTER THE SHOW...
ARCHIE, YOU WERE SO GOOD WE'D LIKE YOU TO COME BACK TO HOST THE SAME SEGMENT NEXT WEEK! WILL YOU?
EXIT
YES! OF COURSE I WILL!
SCRIPT
OH, BOY! I'M A STAR! I'M ON MY WAY TO HOLLYWOOD! YAHOO!!
NEXT DAY AT POP TATE'S...
GREETINGS, FANS!
POP'S SPECIALS TODAY
ARCHIE! YOU WERE GREAT LAST NIGHT!
I WAS GOOD, WASN'T I? LUCKY FOR ME DAVE NOTICED MY NATURAL TALENT AND MADE ME A REGULAR ON HIS SHOW!
WOW!!
4

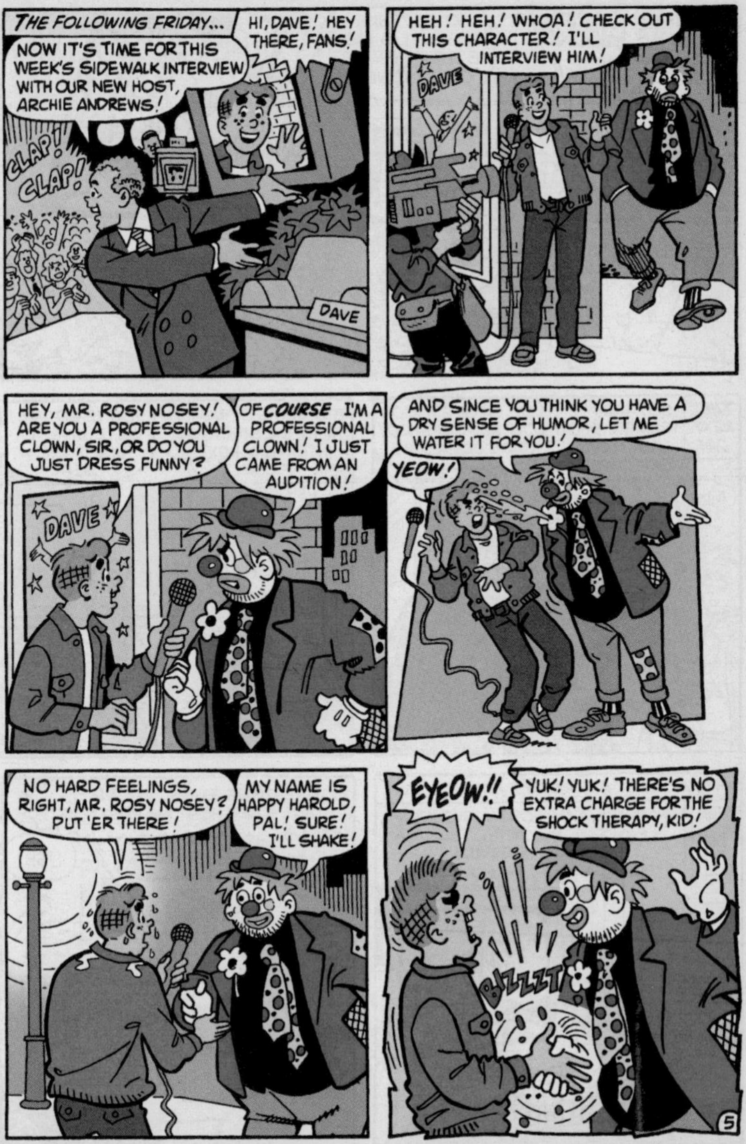
THE FOLLOWING FRIDAY...
NOW IT'S TIME FOR THIS WEEK'S SIDEWALK INTERVIEW WITH OUR NEW HOST, ARCHIE ANDREWS!
HI, DAVE! HEY THERE, FANS!
CLAP! CLAP!
DAVE
HEH! HEH! WHOA! CHECK OUT THIS CHARACTER! I'LL INTERVIEW HIM!
DAVE
HEY, MR. ROSY NOSEY! ARE YOU A PROFESSIONAL CLOWN, SIR, OR DO YOU JUST DRESS FUNNY?
OF COURSE I'M A PROFESSIONAL CLOWN! I JUST CAME FROM AN AUDITION!
DAVE
AND SINCE YOU THINK YOU HAVE A DRY SENSE OF HUMOR, LET ME WATER IT FOR YOU!
YEOW!
NO HARD FEELINGS, RIGHT, MR. ROSY NOSEY? PUT 'ER THERE!
MY NAME IS HAPPY HAROLD, PAL! SURE! I'LL SHAKE!
EYEOW!!
YUK! YUK! THERE'S NO EXTRA CHARGE FOR THE SHOCK THERAPY, KID!
BZZZZT
5

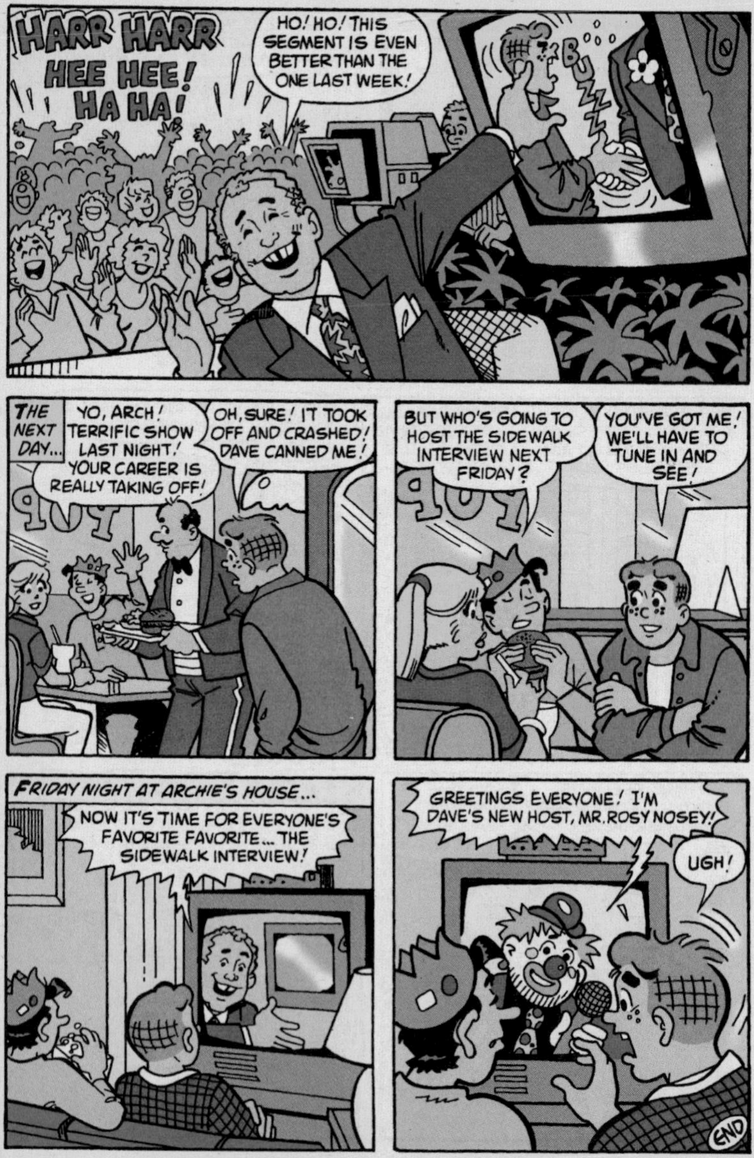

HARR HARR HEE HEE! HA HA!
HO! HO! THIS SEGMENT IS EVEN BETTER THAN THE ONE LAST WEEK!
BUZZZ
THE NEXT DAY...
YO, ARCH! TERRIFIC SHOW LAST NIGHT! YOUR CAREER IS REALLY TAKING OFF!
OH, SURE! IT TOOK OFF AND CRASHED! DAVE CANNED ME!
BUT WHO'S GOING TO HOST THE SIDEWALK INTERVIEW NEXT FRIDAY?
YOU'VE GOT ME! WE'LL HAVE TO TUNE IN AND SEE!
FRIDAY NIGHT AT ARCHIE'S HOUSE...
NOW IT'S TIME FOR EVERYONE'S FAVORITE FAVORITE... THE SIDEWALK INTERVIEW!
GREETINGS EVERYONE! I'M DAVE'S NEW HOST, MR. ROSY NOSEY!
UGH!
END

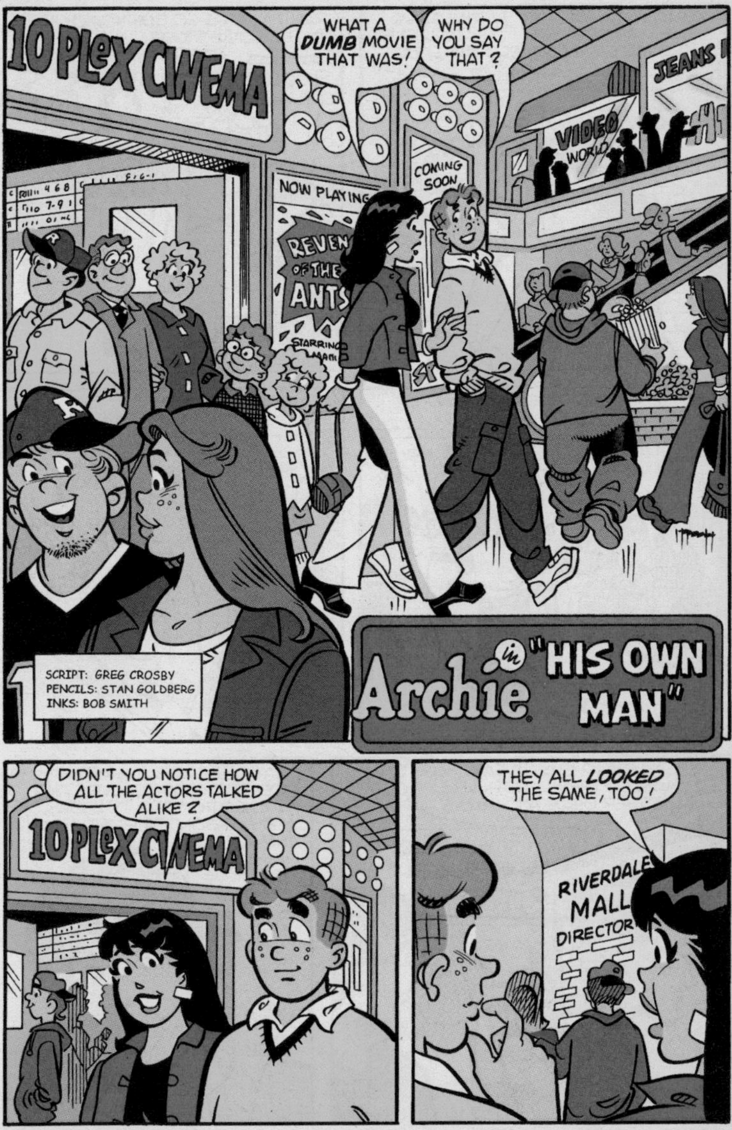
10 PLeX CINEMA
WHAT A *DUMB* MOVIE THAT WAS!
WHY DO YOU SAY THAT?
JEANS
VIDEO WORLD
NOW PLAYING
COMING SOON
STARRING
Archie in "HIS OWN MAN"
SCRIPT: GREG CROSBY
PENCILS: STAN GOLDBERG
INKS: BOB SMITH
DIDN'T YOU NOTICE HOW ALL THE ACTORS TALKED ALIKE?
10 PLeX CINEMA
THEY ALL *LOOKED* THE SAME, TOO!
RIVERDALE MALL

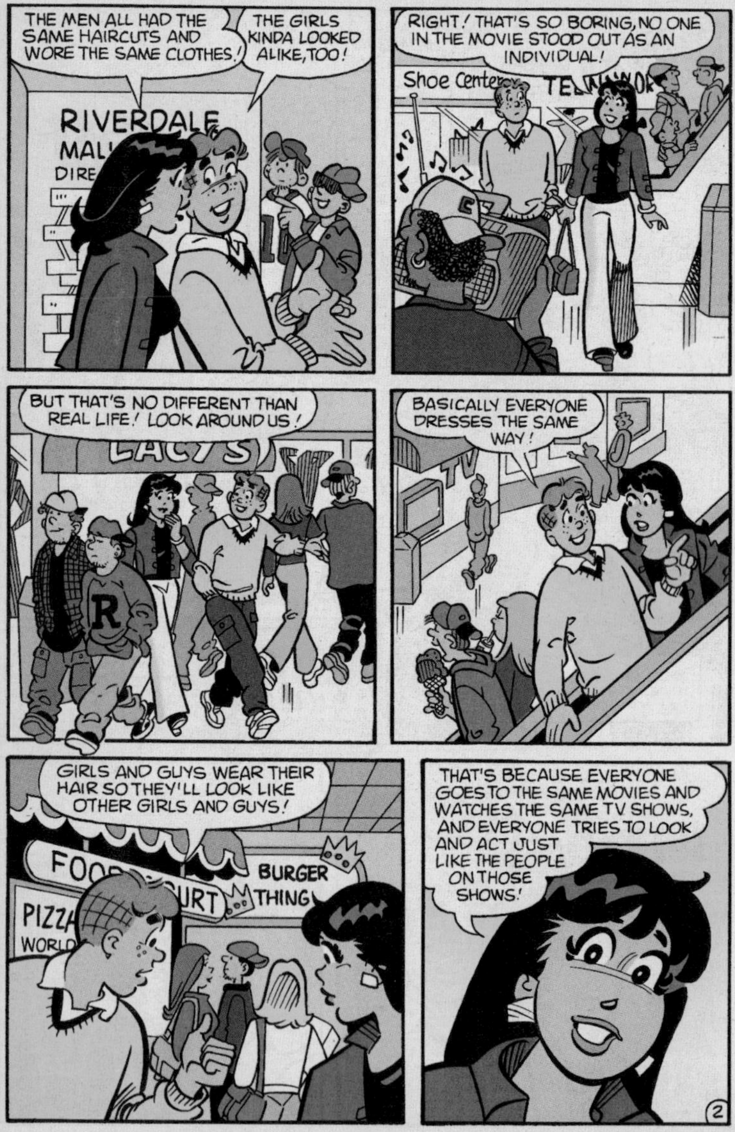
THE MEN ALL HAD THE SAME HAIRCUTS AND WORE THE SAME CLOTHES!
THE GIRLS KINDA LOOKED ALIKE, TOO!
RIVERDALE MALL
RIGHT! THAT'S SO BORING, NO ONE IN THE MOVIE STOOD OUT AS AN INDIVIDUAL!
Shoe Center
BUT THAT'S NO DIFFERENT THAN REAL LIFE! LOOK AROUND US!
BASICALLY EVERYONE DRESSES THE SAME WAY!
TV
GIRLS AND GUYS WEAR THEIR HAIR SO THEY'LL LOOK LIKE OTHER GIRLS AND GUYS!
BURGER THING
PIZZA WORLD
THAT'S BECAUSE EVERYONE GOES TO THE SAME MOVIES AND WATCHES THE SAME TV SHOWS, AND EVERYONE TRIES TO LOOK AND ACT JUST LIKE THE PEOPLE ON THOSE SHOWS!
2

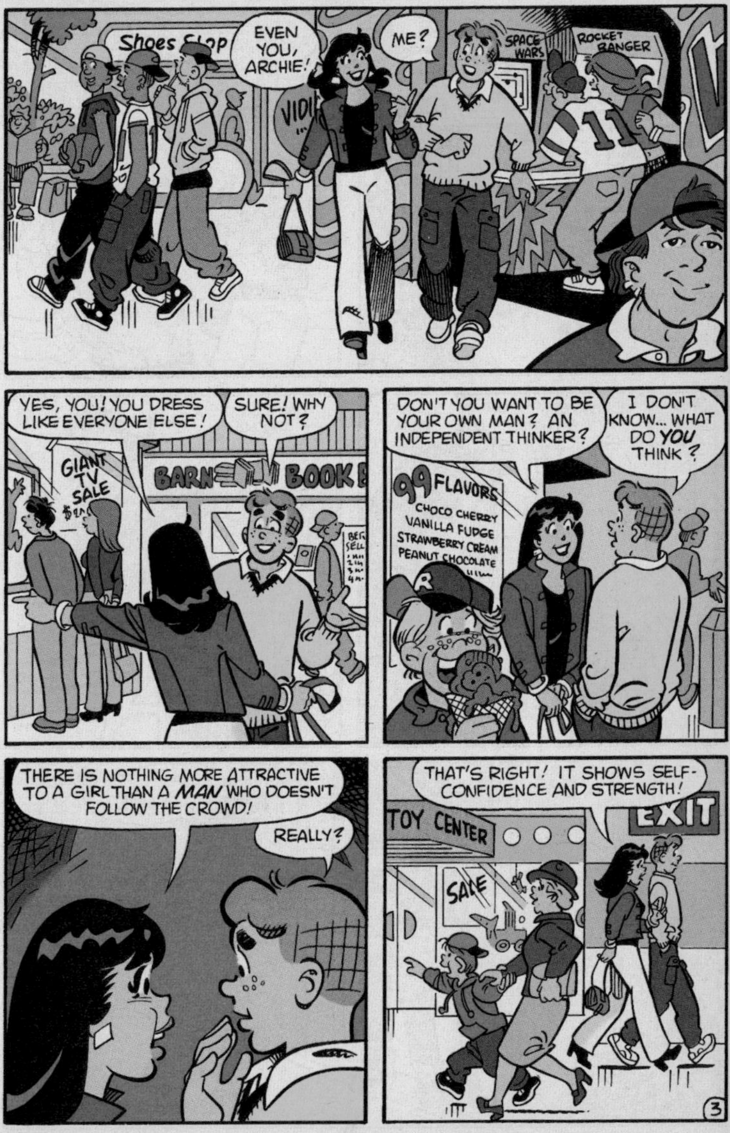
Shoes Stop
EVEN YOU, ARCHIE!
ME?
SPACE WARS
ROCKET RANGER
YES, YOU! YOU DRESS LIKE EVERYONE ELSE!
SURE! WHY NOT?
GIANT TV SALE
BARN BOOK
DON'T YOU WANT TO BE YOUR OWN MAN? AN INDEPENDENT THINKER?
I DON'T KNOW... WHAT DO YOU THINK?
99 FLAVORS
CHOCO CHERRY
VANILLA FUDGE
STRAWBERRY CREAM
PEANUT CHOCOLATE
THERE IS NOTHING MORE ATTRACTIVE TO A GIRL THAN A MAN WHO DOESN'T FOLLOW THE CROWD!
REALLY?
THAT'S RIGHT! IT SHOWS SELF-CONFIDENCE AND STRENGTH!
TOY CENTER
EXIT
SALE
3

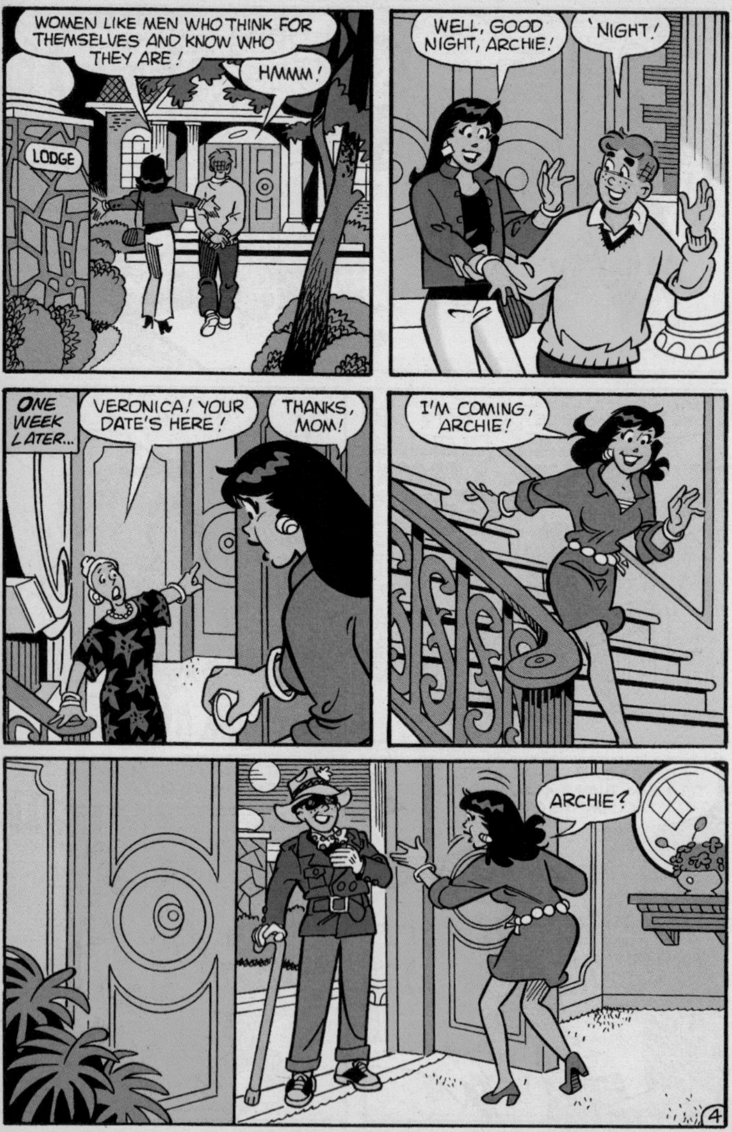
WOMEN LIKE MEN WHO THINK FOR THEMSELVES AND KNOW WHO THEY ARE!
HMMM!
LODGE
WELL, GOOD NIGHT, ARCHIE!
'NIGHT!
ONE WEEK LATER...
VERONICA! YOUR DATE'S HERE!
THANKS, MOM!
I'M COMING, ARCHIE!
ARCHIE?
4

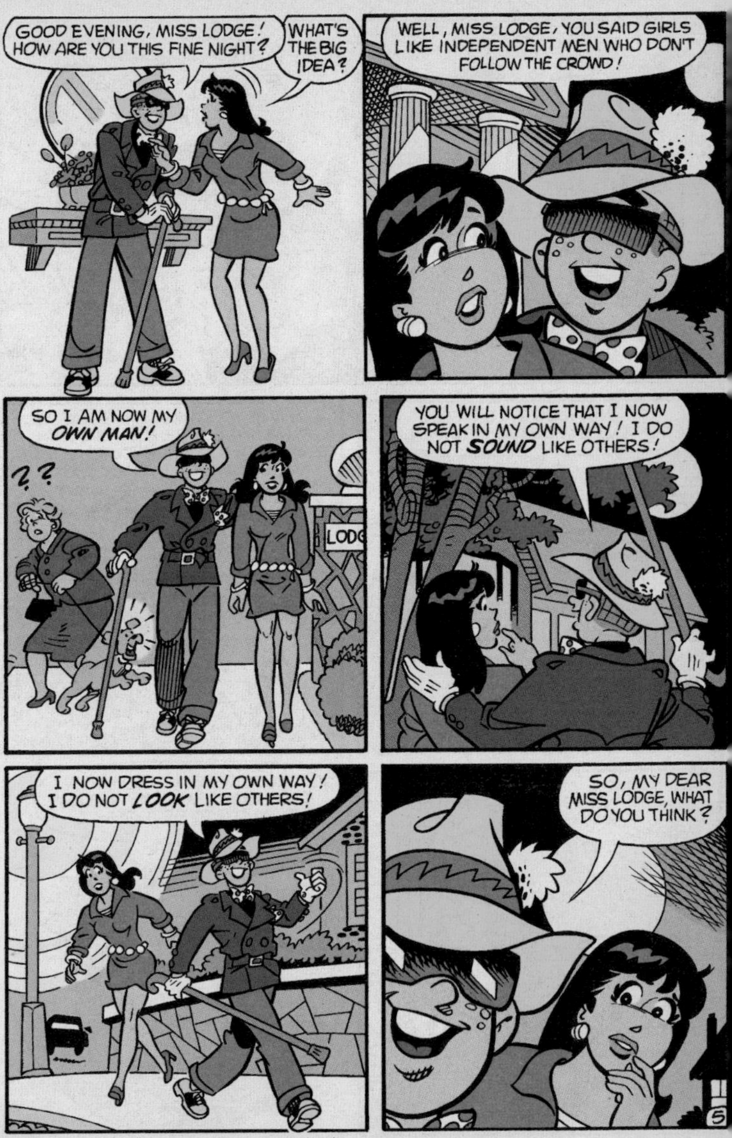
GOOD EVENING, MISS LODGE! HOW ARE YOU THIS FINE NIGHT?
WHAT'S THE BIG IDEA?
WELL, MISS LODGE, YOU SAID GIRLS LIKE INDEPENDENT MEN WHO DON'T FOLLOW THE CROWD!
SO I AM NOW MY OWN MAN!
??
LODG
YOU WILL NOTICE THAT I NOW SPEAK IN MY OWN WAY! I DO NOT SOUND LIKE OTHERS!
I NOW DRESS IN MY OWN WAY! I DO NOT LOOK LIKE OTHERS!
SO, MY DEAR MISS LODGE, WHAT DO YOU THINK?
5

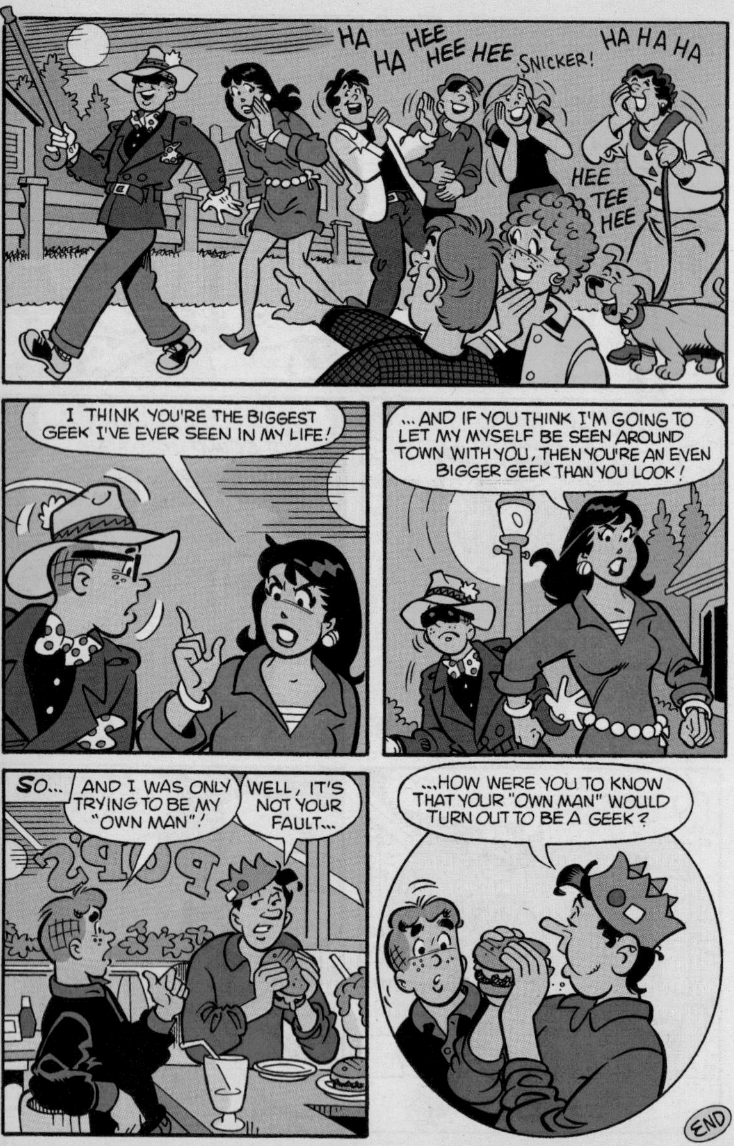
HA HA
HEE HEE HEE
SNICKER!
HA HA HA HA
HEE TEE HEE
I THINK YOU'RE THE BIGGEST GEEK I'VE EVER SEEN IN MY LIFE!
...AND IF YOU THINK I'M GOING TO LET MY MYSELF BE SEEN AROUND TOWN WITH YOU, THEN YOU'RE AN EVEN BIGGER GEEK THAN YOU LOOK!
SO...
AND I WAS ONLY TRYING TO BE MY "OWN MAN"!
WELL, IT'S NOT YOUR FAULT...
POP'S
...HOW WERE YOU TO KNOW THAT YOUR "OWN MAN" WOULD TURN OUT TO BE A GEEK?
END

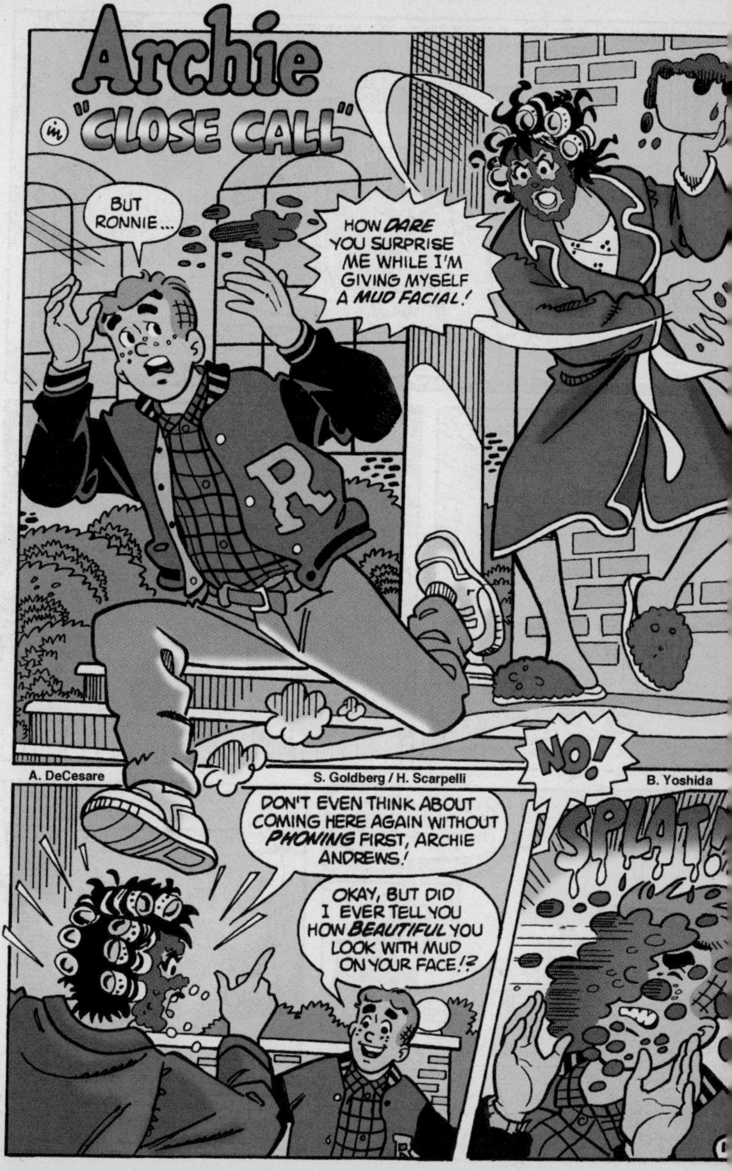
Archie
in "CLOSE CALL"
BUT RONNIE...
HOW DARE YOU SURPRISE ME WHILE I'M GIVING MYSELF A MUD FACIAL!
A. DeCesare
S. Goldberg / H. Scarpelli
B. Yoshida
DON'T EVEN THINK ABOUT COMING HERE AGAIN WITHOUT PHONING FIRST, ARCHIE ANDREWS!
OKAY, BUT DID I EVER TELL YOU HOW BEAUTIFUL YOU LOOK WITH MUD ON YOUR FACE!?
NO!
SPLAT!

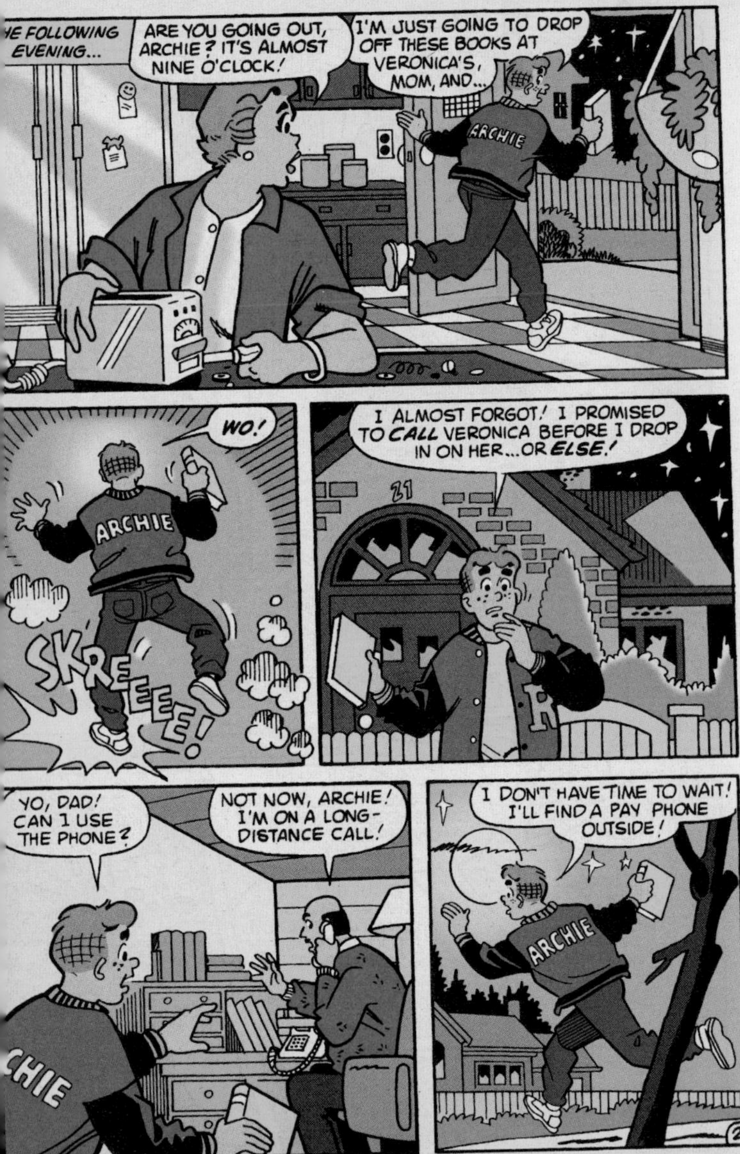

HE FOLLOWING EVENING...
ARE YOU GOING OUT, ARCHIE? IT'S ALMOST NINE O'CLOCK!
I'M JUST GOING TO DROP OFF THESE BOOKS AT VERONICA'S, MOM, AND...
ARCHIE
WO!
ARCHIE
SKREEEEE!
I ALMOST FORGOT! I PROMISED TO CALL VERONICA BEFORE I DROP IN ON HER...OR ELSE!
21
YO, DAD! CAN I USE THE PHONE?
NOT NOW, ARCHIE! I'M ON A LONG-DISTANCE CALL!
CHIE
I DON'T HAVE TIME TO WAIT! I'LL FIND A PAY PHONE OUTSIDE!
ARCHIE
2

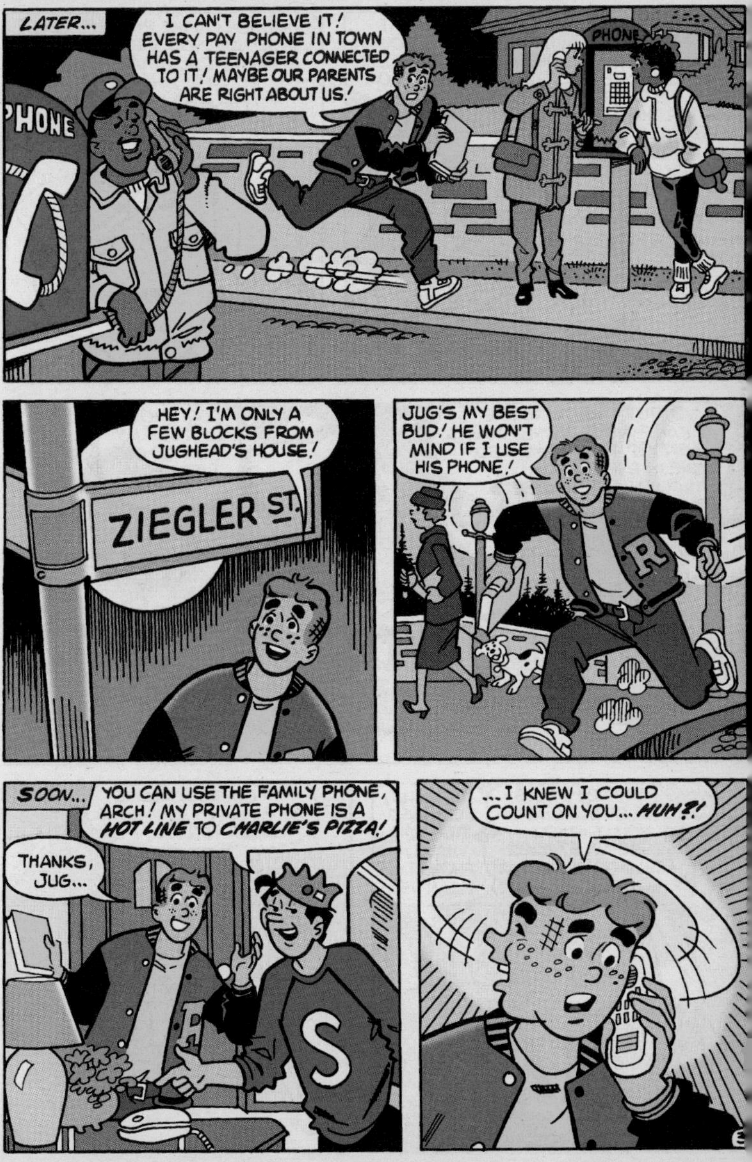
LATER...
I CAN'T BELIEVE IT! EVERY PAY PHONE IN TOWN HAS A TEENAGER CONNECTED TO IT! MAYBE OUR PARENTS ARE RIGHT ABOUT US!
PHONE
PHONE
HEY! I'M ONLY A FEW BLOCKS FROM JUGHEAD'S HOUSE!
ZIEGLER ST.
JUG'S MY BEST BUD! HE WON'T MIND IF I USE HIS PHONE!
SOON...
YOU CAN USE THE FAMILY PHONE, ARCH! MY PRIVATE PHONE IS A HOT LINE TO CHARLIE'S PIZZA!
THANKS, JUG...
...I KNEW I COULD COUNT ON YOU... HUH?!

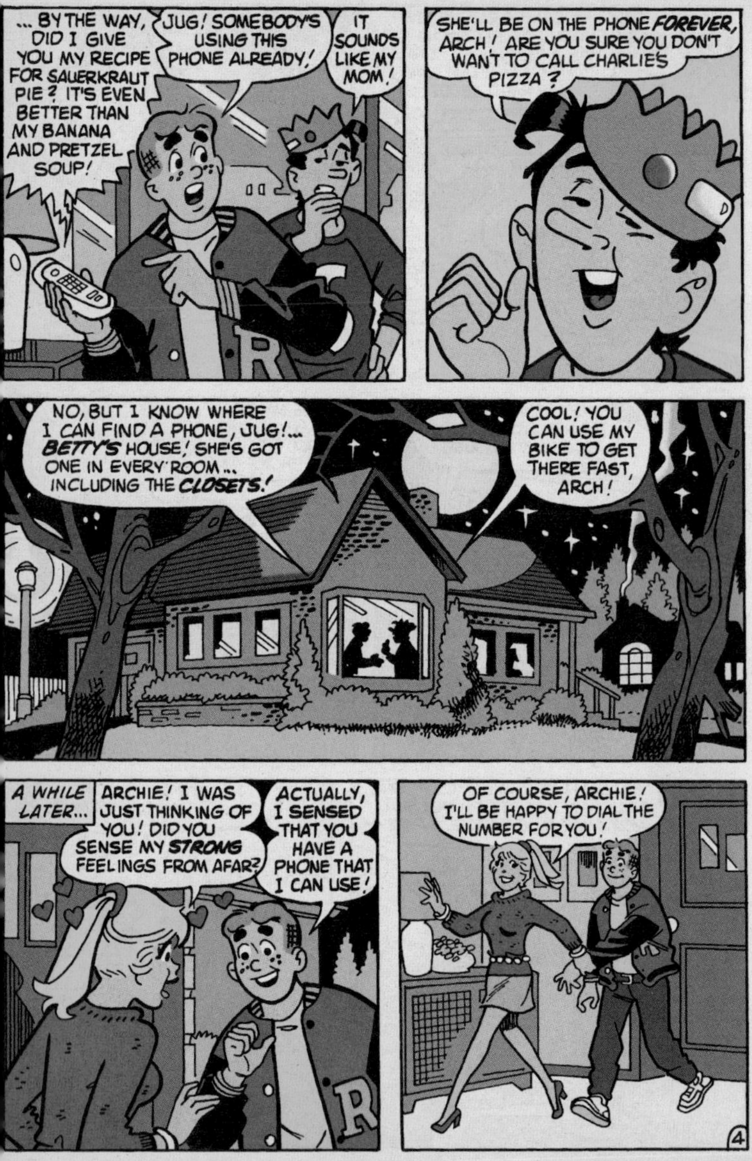
... BY THE WAY, DID I GIVE YOU MY RECIPE FOR SAUERKRAUT PIE? IT'S EVEN BETTER THAN MY BANANA AND PRETZEL SOUP!
JUG! SOMEBODY'S USING THIS PHONE ALREADY!
IT SOUNDS LIKE MY MOM!
SHE'LL BE ON THE PHONE FOREVER, ARCH! ARE YOU SURE YOU DON'T WANT TO CALL CHARLIE'S PIZZA?
NO, BUT I KNOW WHERE I CAN FIND A PHONE, JUG!... BETTY'S HOUSE! SHE'S GOT ONE IN EVERY ROOM... INCLUDING THE CLOSETS!
COOL! YOU CAN USE MY BIKE TO GET THERE FAST, ARCH!
A WHILE LATER...
ARCHIE! I WAS JUST THINKING OF YOU! DID YOU SENSE MY STRONG FEELINGS FROM AFAR?
ACTUALLY, I SENSED THAT YOU HAVE A PHONE THAT I CAN USE!
OF COURSE, ARCHIE! I'LL BE HAPPY TO DIAL THE NUMBER FOR YOU!
4

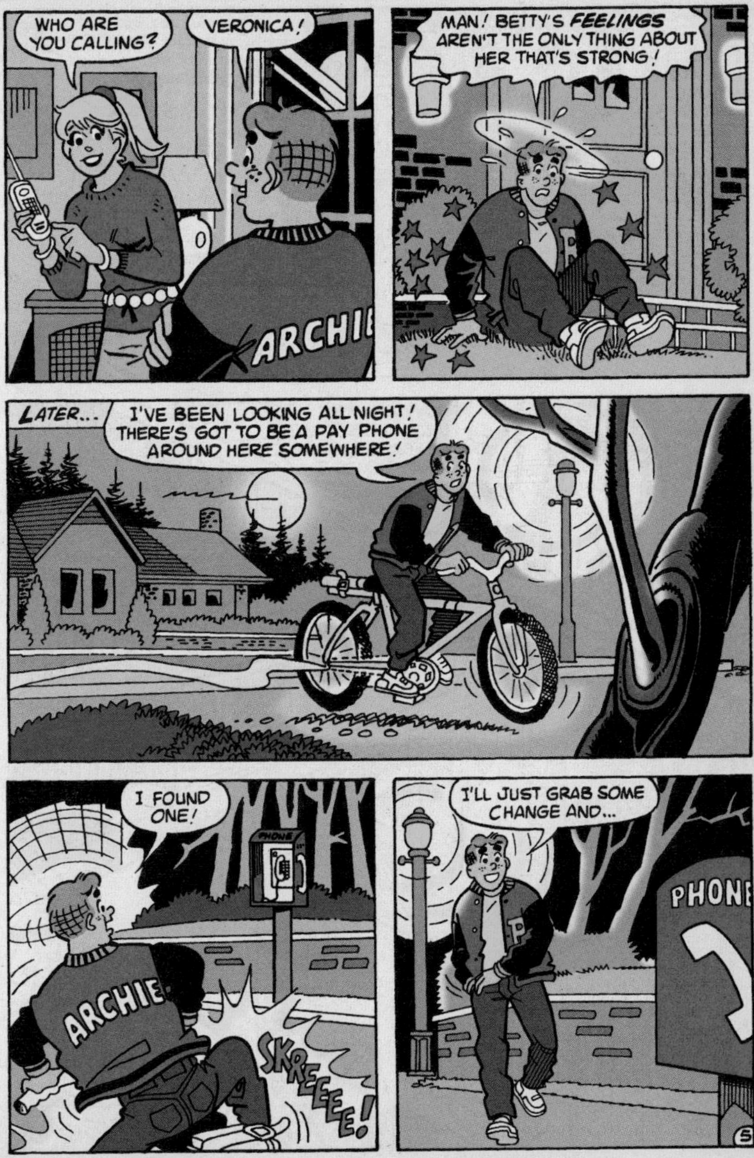

WHO ARE YOU CALLING?
VERONICA!
ARCHIE
MAN! BETTY'S FEELINGS AREN'T THE ONLY THING ABOUT HER THAT'S STRONG!
LATER...
I'VE BEEN LOOKING ALL NIGHT! THERE'S GOT TO BE A PAY PHONE AROUND HERE SOMEWHERE!
I FOUND ONE!
PHONE
ARCHIE
SKREEEEE!
I'LL JUST GRAB SOME CHANGE AND...
PHONE
5

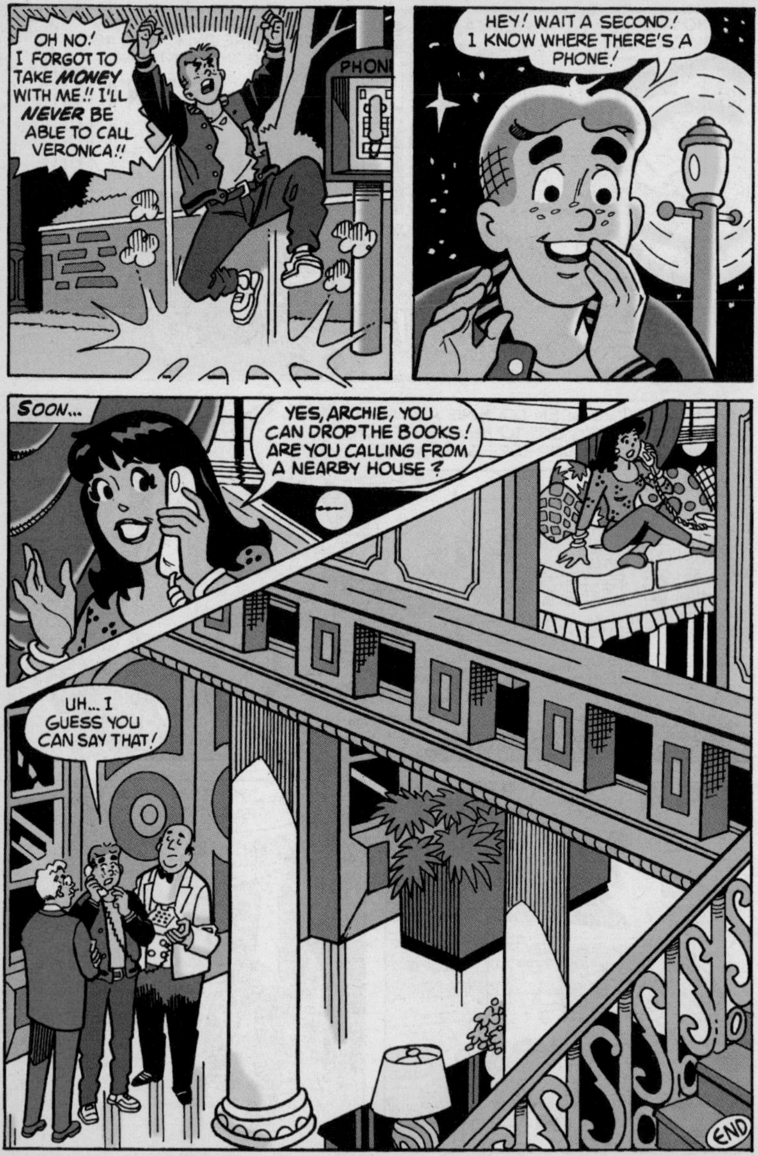
OH NO! I FORGOT TO TAKE MONEY WITH ME!! I'LL NEVER BE ABLE TO CALL VERONICA!!
PHONE
HEY! WAIT A SECOND! I KNOW WHERE THERE'S A PHONE!
SOON...
YES, ARCHIE, YOU CAN DROP THE BOOKS! ARE YOU CALLING FROM A NEARBY HOUSE?
UH... I GUESS YOU CAN SAY THAT!
END

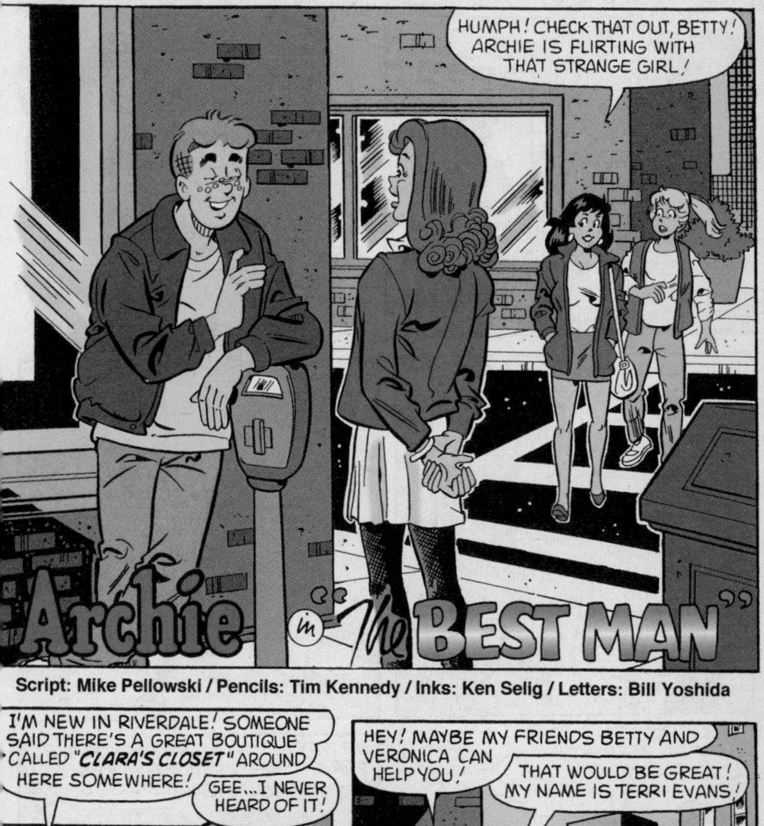
HUMPH! CHECK THAT OUT, BETTY! ARCHIE IS FLIRTING WITH THAT STRANGE GIRL!
Archie in "The BEST MAN"

Script: Mike Pellowski / Pencils: Tim Kennedy / Inks: Ken Selig / Letters: Bill Yoshida

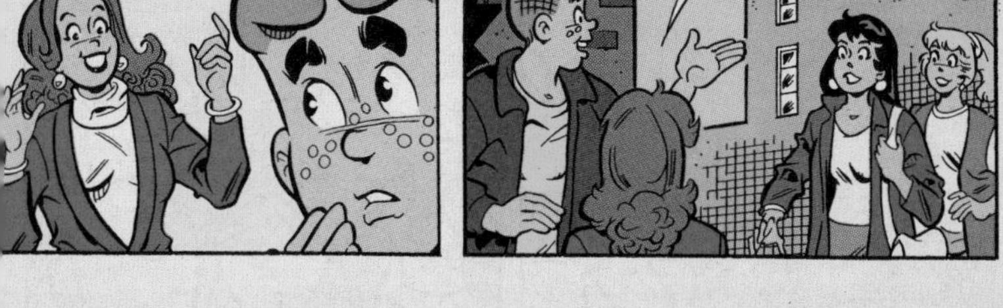
I'M NEW IN RIVERDALE! SOMEONE SAID THERE'S A GREAT BOUTIQUE CALLED "CLARA'S CLOSET" AROUND HERE SOMEWHERE!
GEE...I NEVER HEARD OF IT!
HEY! MAYBE MY FRIENDS BETTY AND VERONICA CAN HELP YOU!
THAT WOULD BE GREAT! MY NAME IS TERRI EVANS!

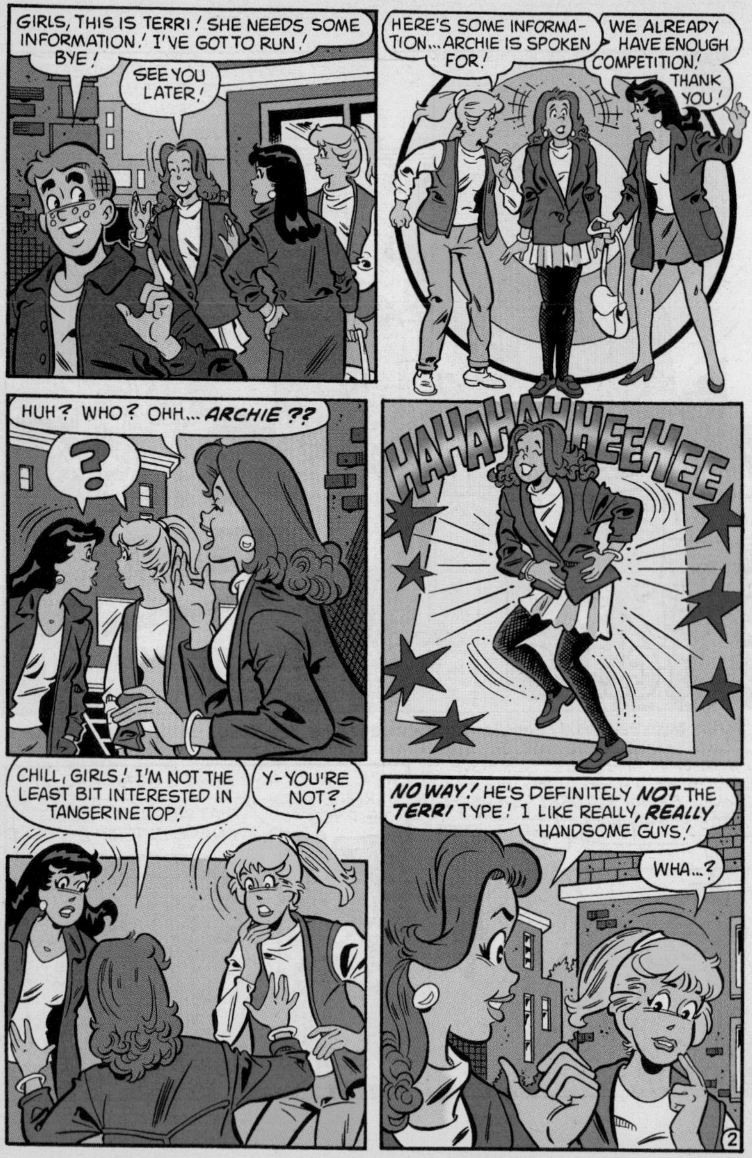
GIRLS, THIS IS TERRI! SHE NEEDS SOME INFORMATION! I'VE GOT TO RUN! BYE!
SEE YOU LATER!
HERE'S SOME INFORMATION... ARCHIE IS SPOKEN FOR!
WE ALREADY HAVE ENOUGH COMPETITION! THANK YOU!
HUH? WHO? OHH... ARCHIE??
?
HAHAHAHHEEHEE
CHILL, GIRLS! I'M NOT THE LEAST BIT INTERESTED IN TANGERINE TOP!
Y-YOU'RE NOT?
NO WAY! HE'S DEFINITELY NOT THE TERRI TYPE! I LIKE REALLY, REALLY HANDSOME GUYS!
WHA...?
2

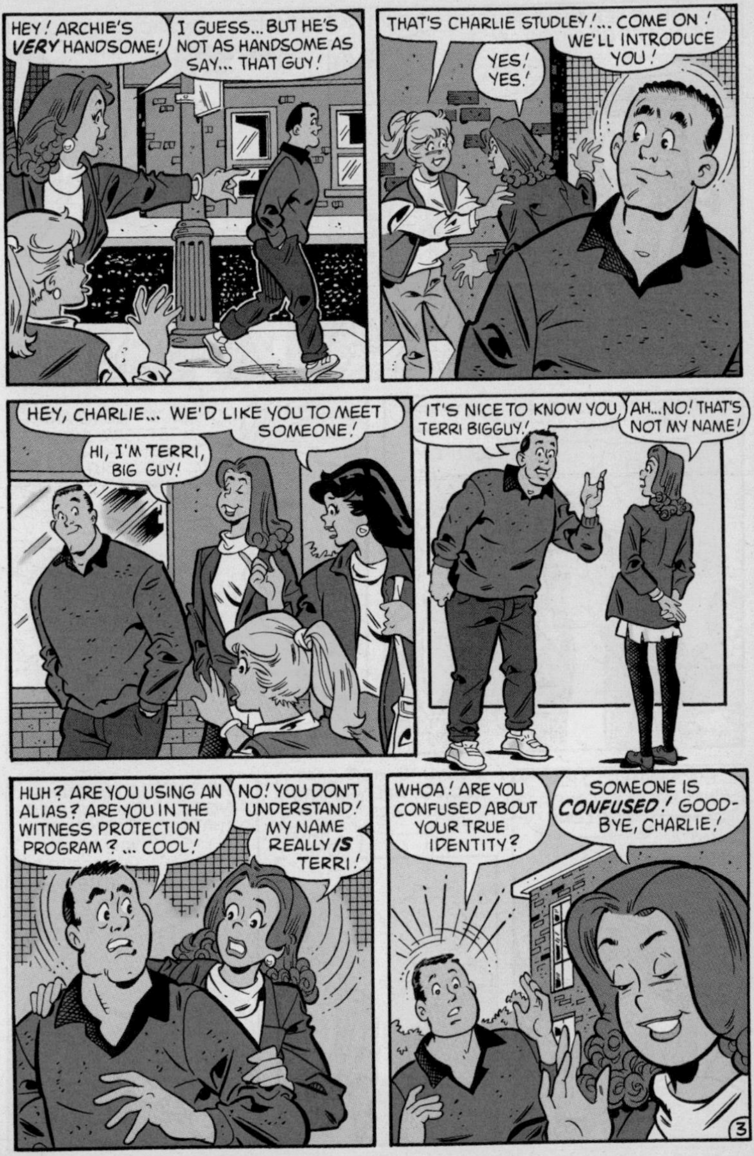
HEY! ARCHIE'S VERY HANDSOME!
I GUESS... BUT HE'S NOT AS HANDSOME AS SAY... THAT GUY!
THAT'S CHARLIE STUDLEY!... COME ON! WE'LL INTRODUCE YOU!
YES! YES!
HEY, CHARLIE... WE'D LIKE YOU TO MEET SOMEONE!
HI, I'M TERRI, BIG GUY!
IT'S NICE TO KNOW YOU, TERRI BIGGUY!
AH...NO! THAT'S NOT MY NAME!
HUH? ARE YOU USING AN ALIAS? ARE YOU IN THE WITNESS PROTECTION PROGRAM? ... COOL!
NO! YOU DON'T UNDERSTAND! MY NAME REALLY IS TERRI!
WHOA! ARE YOU CONFUSED ABOUT YOUR TRUE IDENTITY?
SOMEONE IS CONFUSED! GOOD-BYE, CHARLIE!

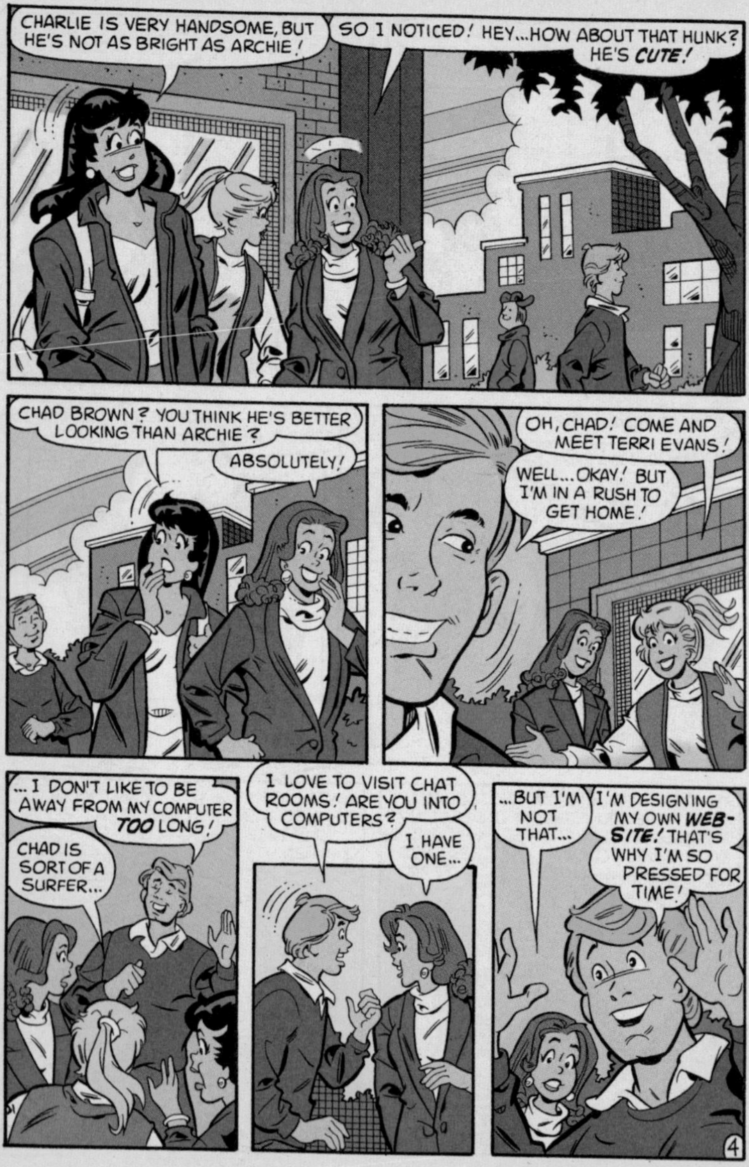
CHARLIE IS VERY HANDSOME, BUT HE'S NOT AS BRIGHT AS ARCHIE!
SO I NOTICED! HEY...HOW ABOUT THAT HUNK? HE'S CUTE!
CHAD BROWN? YOU THINK HE'S BETTER LOOKING THAN ARCHIE?
ABSOLUTELY!
OH, CHAD! COME AND MEET TERRI EVANS!
WELL...OKAY! BUT I'M IN A RUSH TO GET HOME!
...I DON'T LIKE TO BE AWAY FROM MY COMPUTER TOO LONG!
CHAD IS SORT OF A SURFER...
I LOVE TO VISIT CHAT ROOMS! ARE YOU INTO COMPUTERS?
I HAVE ONE...
...BUT I'M NOT THAT...
I'M DESIGNING MY OWN WEB-SITE! THAT'S WHY I'M SO PRESSED FOR TIME!
4

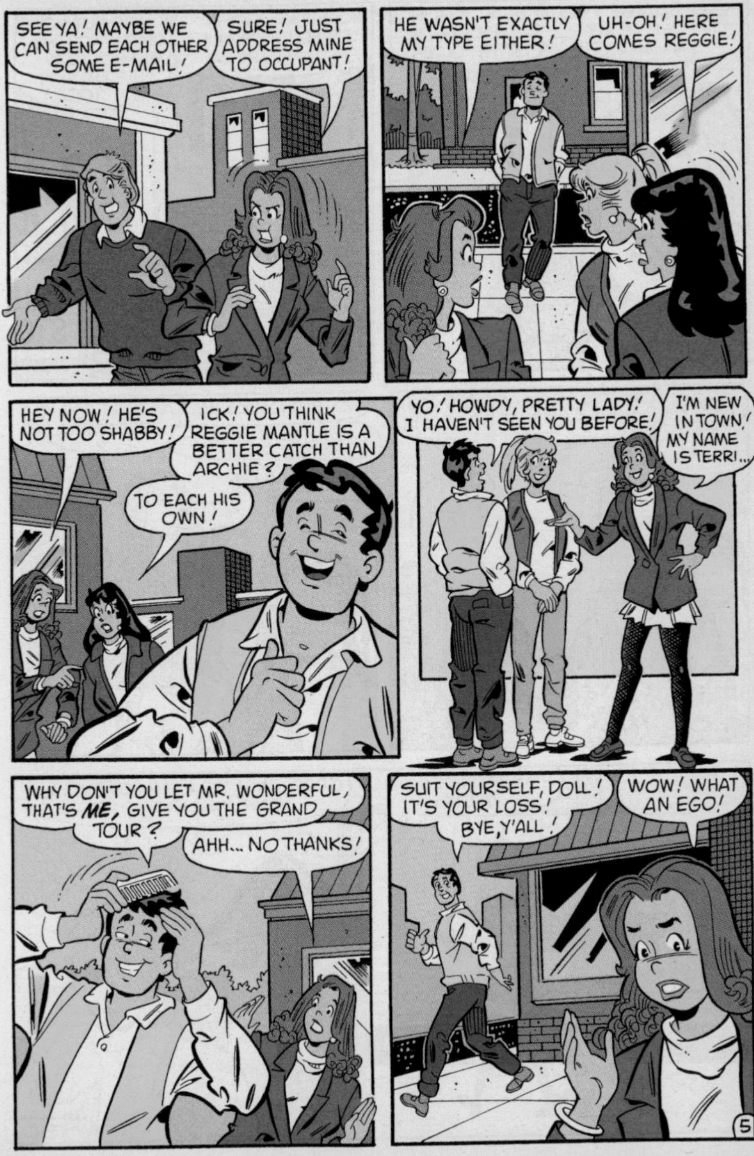
SEE YA! MAYBE WE CAN SEND EACH OTHER SOME E-MAIL!
SURE! JUST ADDRESS MINE TO OCCUPANT!
HE WASN'T EXACTLY MY TYPE EITHER!
UH-OH! HERE COMES REGGIE!
HEY NOW! HE'S NOT TOO SHABBY!
ICK! YOU THINK REGGIE MANTLE IS A BETTER CATCH THAN ARCHIE?
TO EACH HIS OWN!
YO! HOWDY, PRETTY LADY! I HAVEN'T SEEN YOU BEFORE!
I'M NEW IN TOWN! MY NAME IS TERRI...
WHY DON'T YOU LET MR. WONDERFUL, THAT'S ME, GIVE YOU THE GRAND TOUR?
AHH... NO THANKS!
SUIT YOURSELF, DOLL! IT'S YOUR LOSS! BYE, Y'ALL!
WOW! WHAT AN EGO!
5

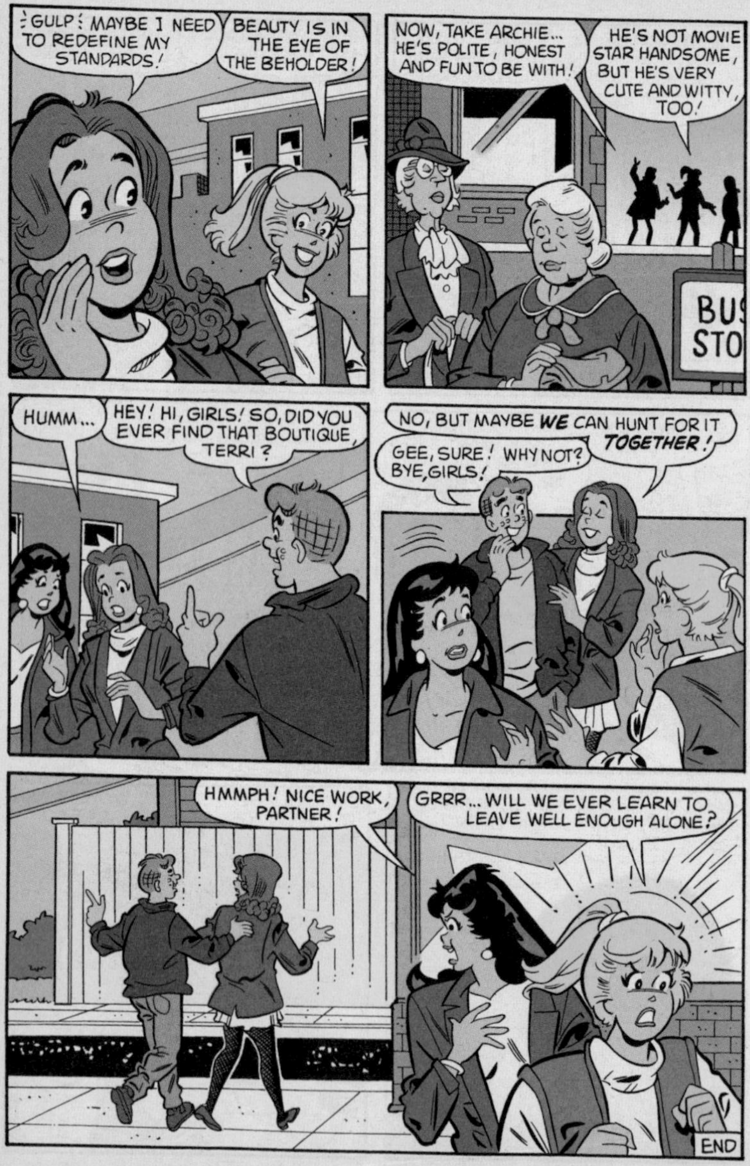

GULP! MAYBE I NEED TO REDEFINE MY STANDARDS!
BEAUTY IS IN THE EYE OF THE BEHOLDER!
NOW, TAKE ARCHIE... HE'S POLITE, HONEST AND FUN TO BE WITH!
HE'S NOT MOVIE STAR HANDSOME, BUT HE'S VERY CUTE AND WITTY, TOO!
BUS STO
HUMM...
HEY! HI, GIRLS! SO, DID YOU EVER FIND THAT BOUTIQUE, TERRI?
NO, BUT MAYBE WE CAN HUNT FOR IT TOGETHER!
GEE, SURE! WHY NOT? BYE, GIRLS!
HMMPH! NICE WORK, PARTNER!
GRRR... WILL WE EVER LEARN TO LEAVE WELL ENOUGH ALONE?
END

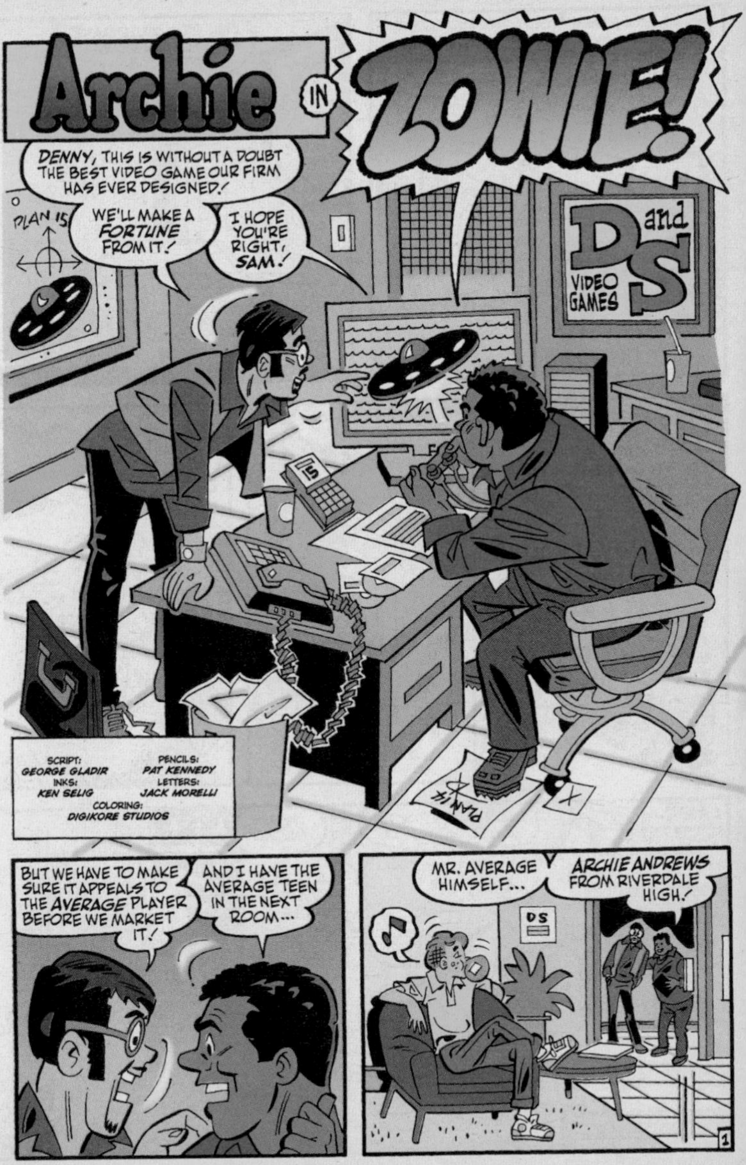
Archie
IN
ZOWIE!
DENNY, THIS IS WITHOUT A DOUBT THE BEST VIDEO GAME OUR FIRM HAS EVER DESIGNED!
WE'LL MAKE A FORTUNE FROM IT!
I HOPE YOU'RE RIGHT, SAM!
PLAN 15
D and S VIDEO GAMES
SCRIPT: GEORGE GLADIR
PENCILS: PAT KENNEDY
INKS: KEN SELIG
LETTERS: JACK MORELLI
COLORING: DIGIKORE STUDIOS
PLAN 14
BUT WE HAVE TO MAKE SURE IT APPEALS TO THE AVERAGE PLAYER BEFORE WE MARKET IT!
AND I HAVE THE AVERAGE TEEN IN THE NEXT ROOM...
MR. AVERAGE HIMSELF...
ARCHIE ANDREWS FROM RIVERDALE HIGH!
DS
1

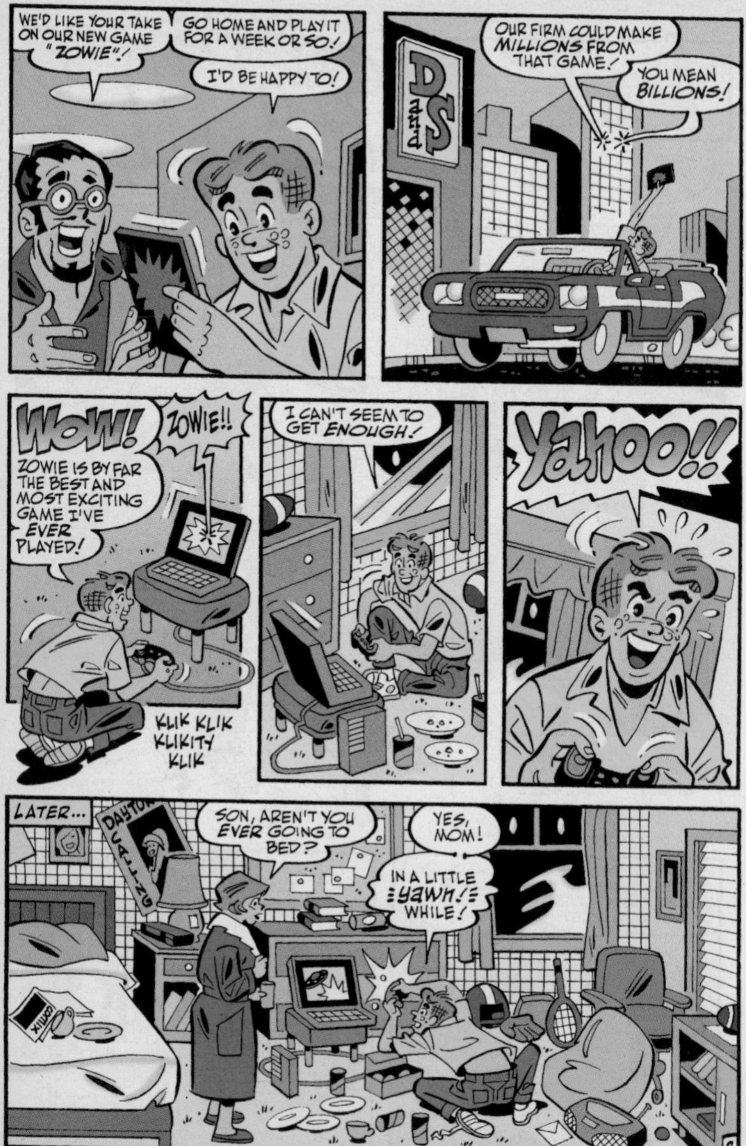
WE'D LIKE YOUR TAKE ON OUR NEW GAME "ZOWIE"!
GO HOME AND PLAY IT FOR A WEEK OR SO!
I'D BE HAPPY TO!
OUR FIRM COULD MAKE MILLIONS FROM THAT GAME!
YOU MEAN BILLIONS!
WOW!
ZOWIE!!
ZOWIE IS BY FAR THE BEST AND MOST EXCITING GAME I'VE EVER PLAYED!
KLIK KLIK KLIKITY KLIK
I CAN'T SEEM TO GET ENOUGH!
YAHOO!!
LATER...
SON, AREN'T YOU EVER GOING TO BED?
YES, MOM!
IN A LITTLE =YAWN!= WHILE!
2

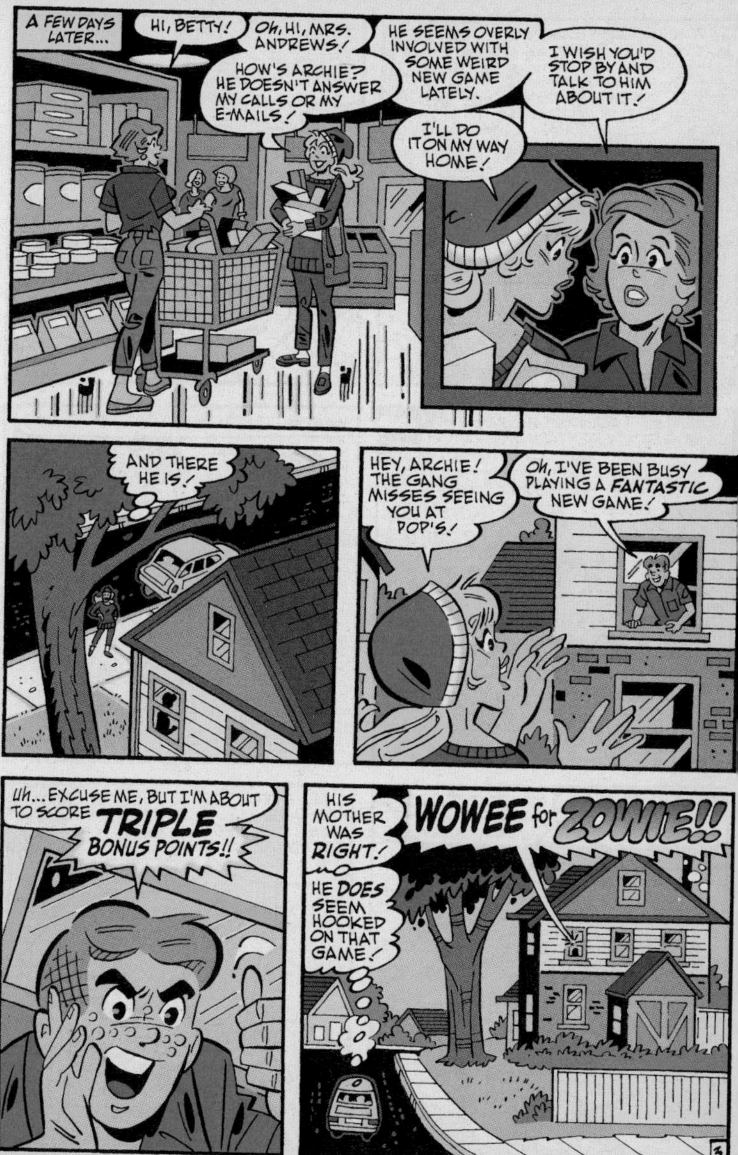
A FEW DAYS LATER...
HI, BETTY!
Oh, HI, MRS. ANDREWS!
HOW'S ARCHIE? HE DOESN'T ANSWER MY CALLS OR MY E-MAILS!
HE SEEMS OVERLY INVOLVED WITH SOME WEIRD NEW GAME LATELY.
I WISH YOU'D STOP BY AND TALK TO HIM ABOUT IT!
I'LL DO IT ON MY WAY HOME!
AND THERE HE IS!
HEY, ARCHIE! THE GANG MISSES SEEING YOU AT POP'S!
Oh, I'VE BEEN BUSY PLAYING A FANTASTIC NEW GAME!
Uh... EXCUSE ME, BUT I'M ABOUT TO SCORE TRIPLE BONUS POINTS!!
HIS MOTHER WAS RIGHT!
WOWEE for ZOWIE!!
HE DOES SEEM HOOKED ON THAT GAME!
3

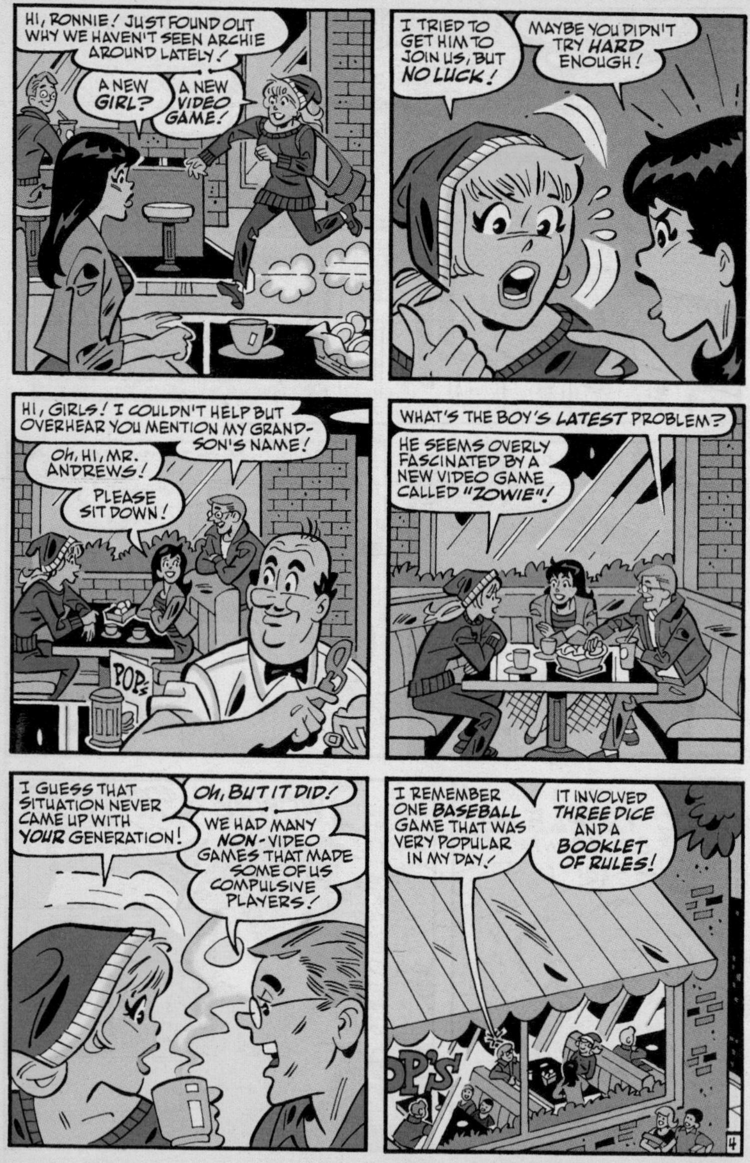

HI, RONNIE! JUST FOUND OUT WHY WE HAVEN'T SEEN ARCHIE AROUND LATELY!
A NEW GIRL?
A NEW VIDEO GAME!
I TRIED TO GET HIM TO JOIN US, BUT NO LUCK!
MAYBE YOU DIDN'T TRY HARD ENOUGH!
HI, GIRLS! I COULDN'T HELP BUT OVERHEAR YOU MENTION MY GRAND-SON'S NAME!
Oh, HI, MR. ANDREWS!
PLEASE SIT DOWN!
POP'S
WHAT'S THE BOY'S LATEST PROBLEM?
HE SEEMS OVERLY FASCINATED BY A NEW VIDEO GAME CALLED "ZOWIE"!
I GUESS THAT SITUATION NEVER CAME UP WITH YOUR GENERATION!
Oh, BUT IT DID!
WE HAD MANY NON-VIDEO GAMES THAT MADE SOME OF US COMPULSIVE PLAYERS!
I REMEMBER ONE BASEBALL GAME THAT WAS VERY POPULAR IN MY DAY!
IT INVOLVED THREE DICE AND A BOOKLET OF RULES!
4

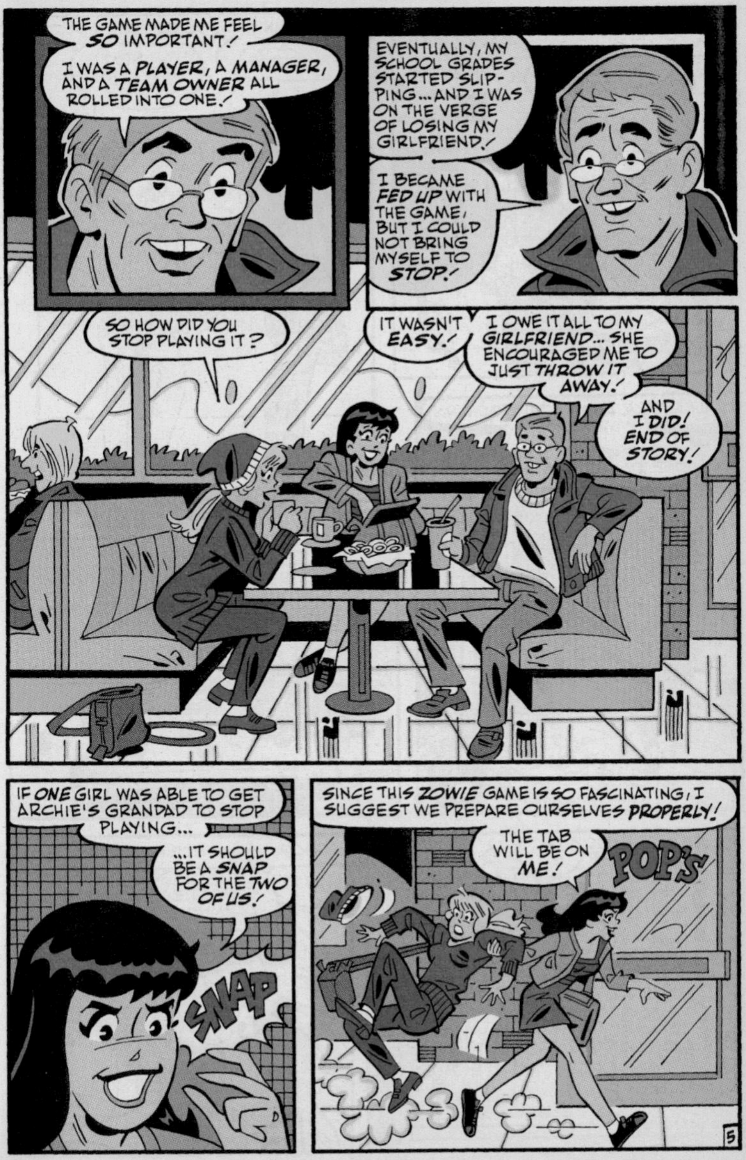
THE GAME MADE ME FEEL SO IMPORTANT!
I WAS A PLAYER, A MANAGER, AND A TEAM OWNER ALL ROLLED INTO ONE!
EVENTUALLY, MY SCHOOL GRADES STARTED SLIPPING... AND I WAS ON THE VERGE OF LOSING MY GIRLFRIEND!
I BECAME FED UP WITH THE GAME, BUT I COULD NOT BRING MYSELF TO STOP!
SO HOW DID YOU STOP PLAYING IT?
IT WASN'T EASY!
I OWE IT ALL TO MY GIRLFRIEND... SHE ENCOURAGED ME TO JUST THROW IT AWAY!
AND I DID! END OF STORY!
IF ONE GIRL WAS ABLE TO GET ARCHIE'S GRANDAD TO STOP PLAYING...
...IT SHOULD BE A SNAP FOR THE TWO OF US!
SNAP
SINCE THIS ZOWIE GAME IS SO FASCINATING, I SUGGEST WE PREPARE OURSELVES PROPERLY!
THE TAB WILL BE ON ME!
POP'S
5

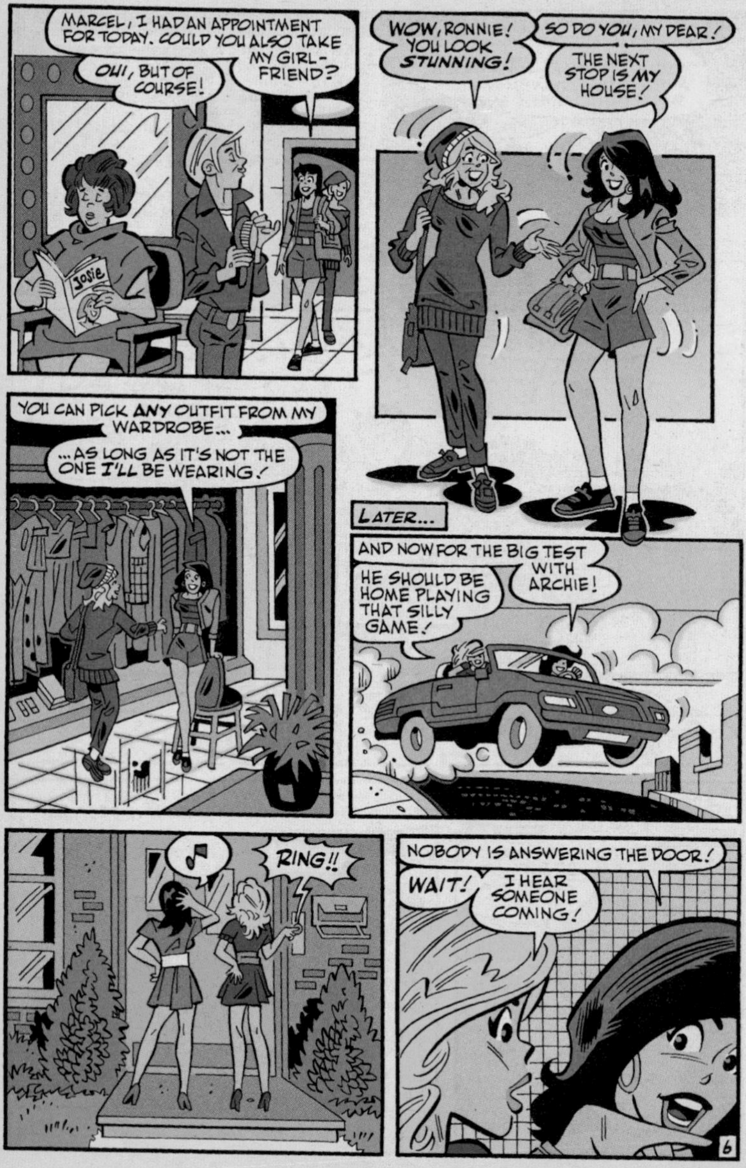
MARCEL, I HAD AN APPOINTMENT FOR TODAY. COULD YOU ALSO TAKE MY GIRL-FRIEND?
OUI, BUT OF COURSE!
JOSIE
WOW, RONNIE! YOU LOOK STUNNING!
SO DO YOU, MY DEAR!
THE NEXT STOP IS MY HOUSE!
YOU CAN PICK ANY OUTFIT FROM MY WARDROBE...
...AS LONG AS IT'S NOT THE ONE I'LL BE WEARING!
LATER...
AND NOW FOR THE BIG TEST WITH ARCHIE!
HE SHOULD BE HOME PLAYING THAT SILLY GAME!
RING!!
NOBODY IS ANSWERING THE DOOR!
WAIT!
I HEAR SOMEONE COMING!
6

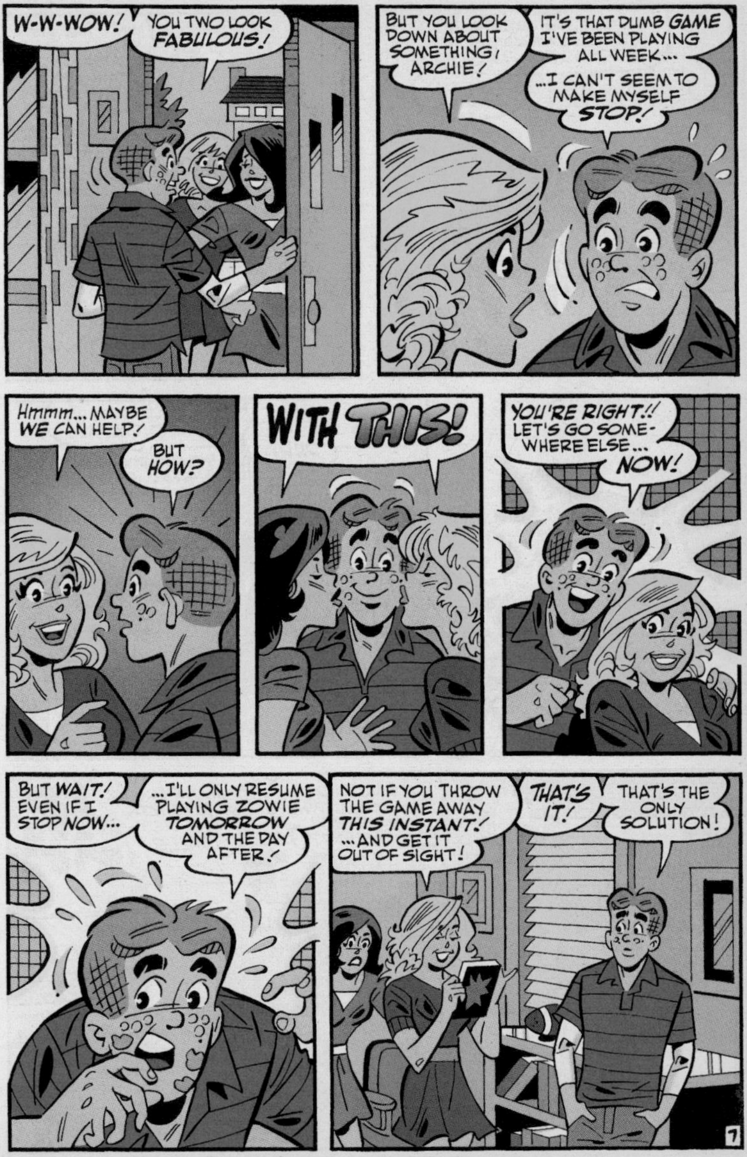
W-W-WOW!
YOU TWO LOOK FABULOUS!
BUT YOU LOOK DOWN ABOUT SOMETHING, ARCHIE!
IT'S THAT DUMB GAME I'VE BEEN PLAYING ALL WEEK...
...I CAN'T SEEM TO MAKE MYSELF STOP!
Hmmm... MAYBE WE CAN HELP!
BUT HOW?
WITH THIS!
YOU'RE RIGHT!! LET'S GO SOME-WHERE ELSE... NOW!
BUT WAIT! EVEN IF I STOP NOW...
...I'LL ONLY RESUME PLAYING ZOWIE TOMORROW AND THE DAY AFTER!
NOT IF YOU THROW THE GAME AWAY THIS INSTANT! ...AND GET IT OUT OF SIGHT!
THAT'S IT!
THAT'S THE ONLY SOLUTION!

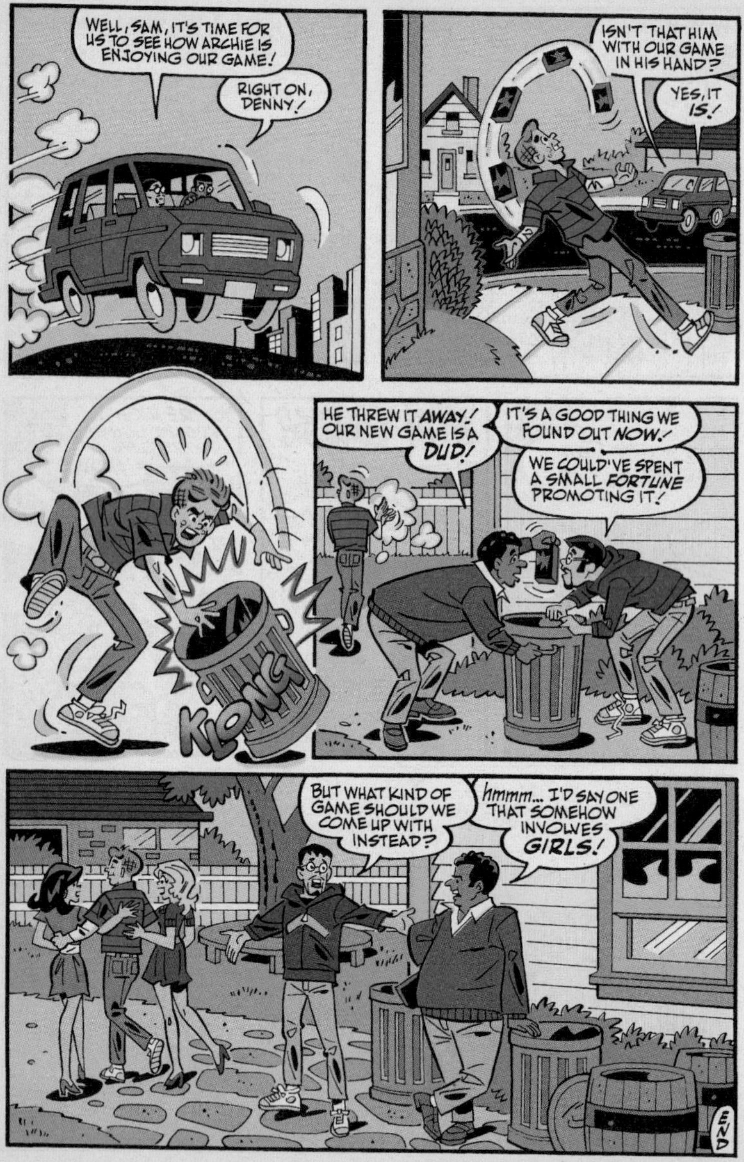
WELL, SAM, IT'S TIME FOR US TO SEE HOW ARCHIE IS ENJOYING OUR GAME!
RIGHT ON, DENNY!
ISN'T THAT HIM WITH OUR GAME IN HIS HAND?
YES, IT IS!
KLONG
HE THREW IT AWAY! OUR NEW GAME IS A DUD!
IT'S A GOOD THING WE FOUND OUT NOW!
WE COULD'VE SPENT A SMALL FORTUNE PROMOTING IT!
BUT WHAT KIND OF GAME SHOULD WE COME UP WITH INSTEAD?
hmmm... I'D SAY ONE THAT SOMEHOW INVOLVES GIRLS!
END

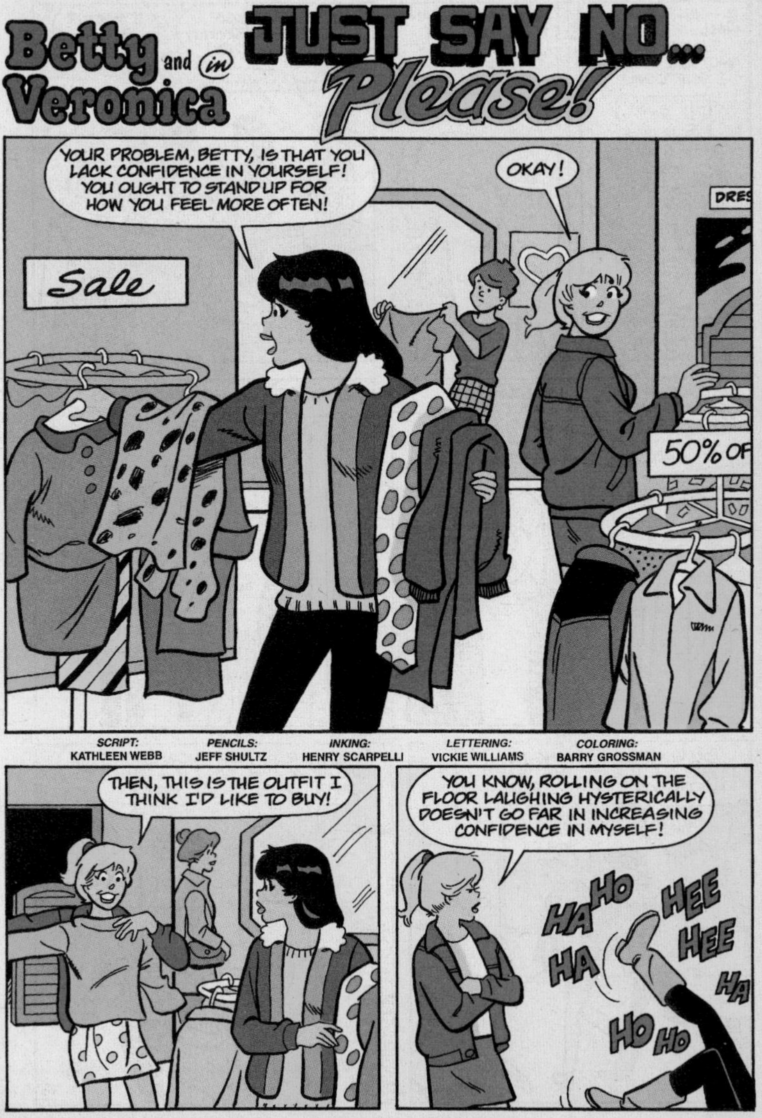
Betty and Veronica in
JUST SAY NO... Please!
YOUR PROBLEM, BETTY, IS THAT YOU LACK CONFIDENCE IN YOURSELF! YOU OUGHT TO STAND UP FOR HOW YOU FEEL MORE OFTEN!
OKAY!
Sale
50% OF
SCRIPT: KATHLEEN WEBB
PENCILS: JEFF SHULTZ
INKING: HENRY SCARPELLI
LETTERING: VICKIE WILLIAMS
COLORING: BARRY GROSSMAN
THEN, THIS IS THE OUTFIT I THINK I'D LIKE TO BUY!
YOU KNOW, ROLLING ON THE FLOOR LAUGHING HYSTERICALLY DOESN'T GO FAR IN INCREASING CONFIDENCE IN MYSELF!
HA HO HEE HA HEE HA HO HO

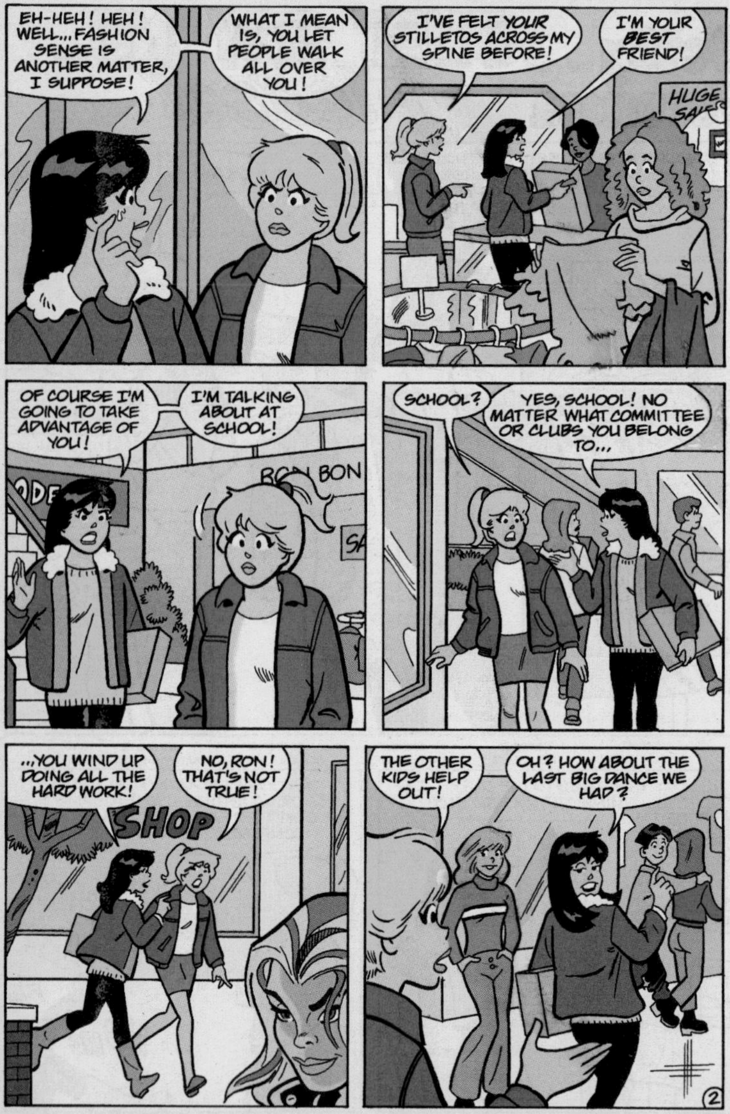
EH-HEH! HEH! WELL... FASHION SENSE IS ANOTHER MATTER, I SUPPOSE!
WHAT I MEAN IS, YOU LET PEOPLE WALK ALL OVER YOU!
I'VE FELT YOUR STILLETOS ACROSS MY SPINE BEFORE!
I'M YOUR BEST FRIEND!
HUGE
OF COURSE I'M GOING TO TAKE ADVANTAGE OF YOU!
I'M TALKING ABOUT AT SCHOOL!
BON
SCHOOL?
YES, SCHOOL! NO MATTER WHAT COMMITTEE OR CLUBS YOU BELONG TO...
...YOU WIND UP DOING ALL THE HARD WORK!
NO, RON! THAT'S NOT TRUE!
SHOP
THE OTHER KIDS HELP OUT!
OH? HOW ABOUT THE LAST BIG DANCE WE HAD?
2

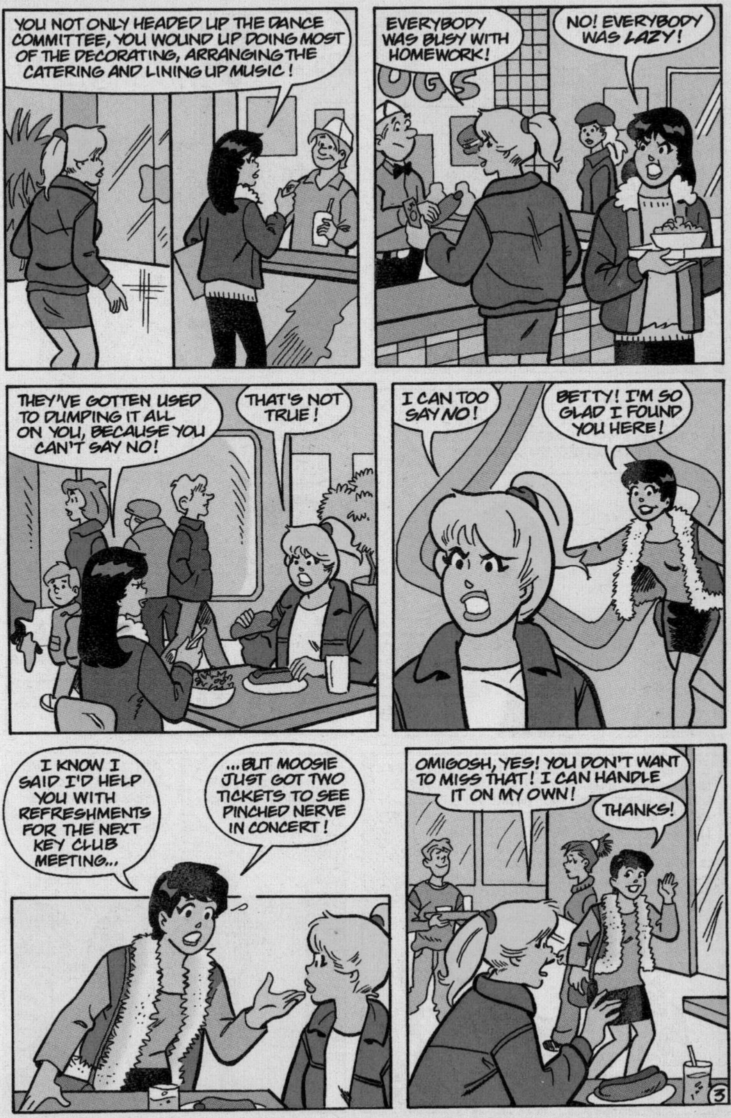

YOU NOT ONLY HEADED UP THE DANCE COMMITTEE, YOU WOUND UP DOING MOST OF THE DECORATING, ARRANGING THE CATERING AND LINING UP MUSIC!
EVERYBODY WAS BUSY WITH HOMEWORK!
NO! EVERYBODY WAS LAZY!
THEY'VE GOTTEN USED TO DUMPING IT ALL ON YOU, BECAUSE YOU CAN'T SAY NO!
THAT'S NOT TRUE!
I CAN TOO SAY NO!
BETTY! I'M SO GLAD I FOUND YOU HERE!
I KNOW I SAID I'D HELP YOU WITH REFRESHMENTS FOR THE NEXT KEY CLUB MEETING...
...BUT MOOSIE JUST GOT TWO TICKETS TO SEE PINCHED NERVE IN CONCERT!
OMIGOSH, YES! YOU DON'T WANT TO MISS THAT! I CAN HANDLE IT ON MY OWN!
THANKS!
3

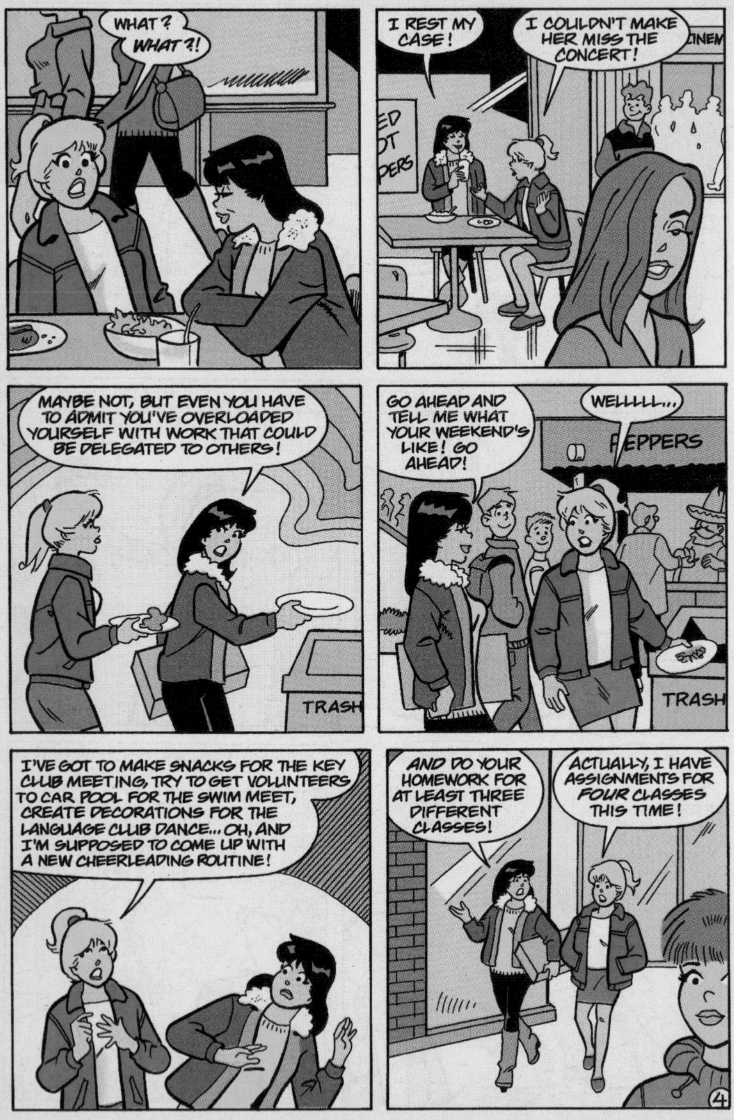
WHAT? WHAT?!
I REST MY CASE!
I COULDN'T MAKE HER MISS THE CONCERT!
CINEM
ED OT PERS
MAYBE NOT, BUT EVEN YOU HAVE TO ADMIT YOU'VE OVERLOADED YOURSELF WITH WORK THAT COULD BE DELEGATED TO OTHERS!
TRASH
GO AHEAD AND TELL ME WHAT YOUR WEEKEND'S LIKE! GO AHEAD!
WELLLLL...
PEPPERS
TRASH
I'VE GOT TO MAKE SNACKS FOR THE KEY CLUB MEETING, TRY TO GET VOLUNTEERS TO CAR POOL FOR THE SWIM MEET, CREATE DECORATIONS FOR THE LANGUAGE CLUB DANCE... OH, AND I'M SUPPOSED TO COME UP WITH A NEW CHEERLEADING ROUTINE!
AND DO YOUR HOMEWORK FOR AT LEAST THREE DIFFERENT CLASSES!
ACTUALLY, I HAVE ASSIGNMENTS FOR FOUR CLASSES THIS TIME!
4

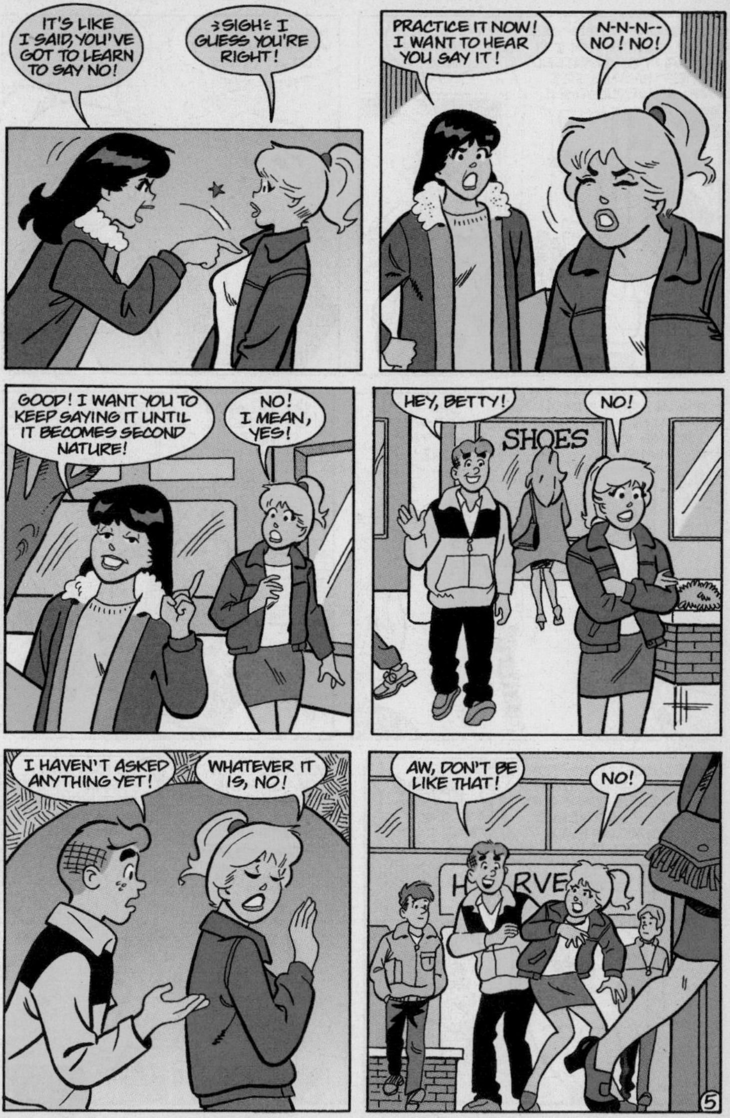
IT'S LIKE I SAID, YOU'VE GOT TO LEARN TO SAY NO!
SIGH I GUESS YOU'RE RIGHT!
PRACTICE IT NOW! I WANT TO HEAR YOU SAY IT!
N-N-N-- NO! NO!
GOOD! I WANT YOU TO KEEP SAYING IT UNTIL IT BECOMES SECOND NATURE!
NO! I MEAN, YES!
HEY, BETTY!
NO!
SHOES
I HAVEN'T ASKED ANYTHING YET!
WHATEVER IT IS, NO!
AW, DON'T BE LIKE THAT!
NO!
5

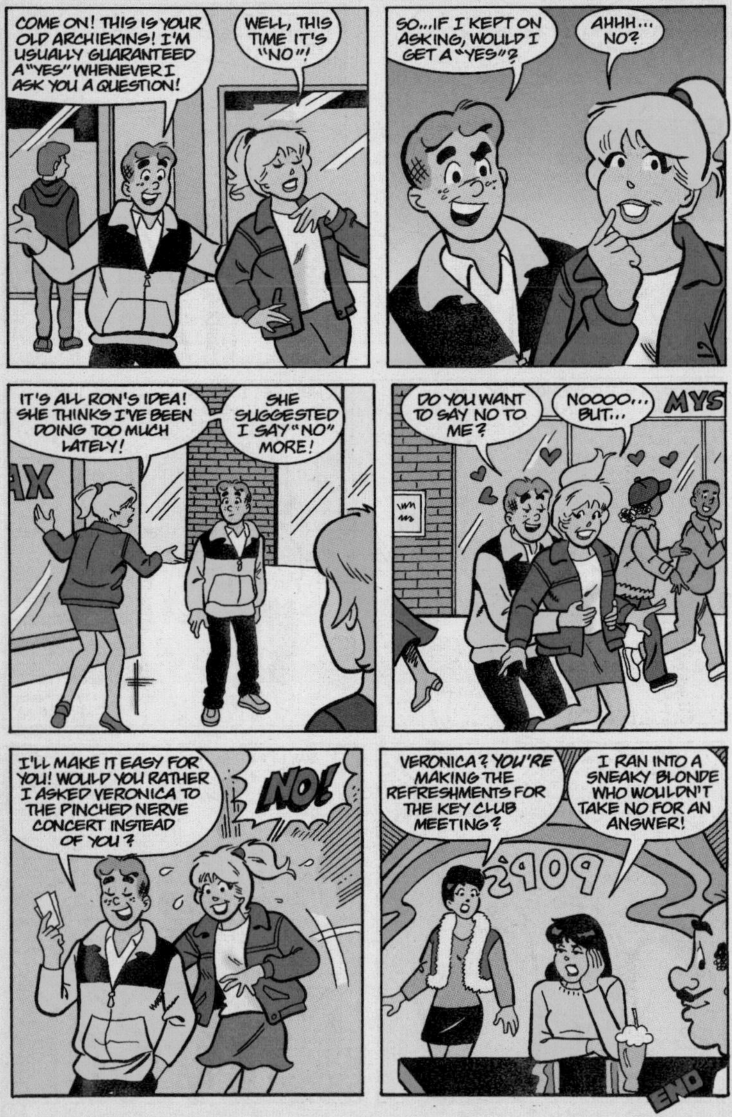
COME ON! THIS IS YOUR OLD ARCHIEKINS! I'M USUALLY GUARANTEED A "YES" WHENEVER I ASK YOU A QUESTION!
WELL, THIS TIME IT'S "NO"!
SO...IF I KEPT ON ASKING, WOULD I GET A "YES"?
AHHH... NO?
IT'S ALL RON'S IDEA! SHE THINKS I'VE BEEN DOING TOO MUCH LATELY!
SHE SUGGESTED I SAY "NO" MORE!
DO YOU WANT TO SAY NO TO ME?
NOOOO... BUT...
MYS
I'LL MAKE IT EASY FOR YOU! WOULD YOU RATHER I ASKED VERONICA TO THE PINCHED NERVE CONCERT INSTEAD OF YOU?
NO!
VERONICA? YOU'RE MAKING THE REFRESHMENTS FOR THE KEY CLUB MEETING?
I RAN INTO A SNEAKY BLONDE WHO WOULDN'T TAKE NO FOR AN ANSWER!
POP'S
END

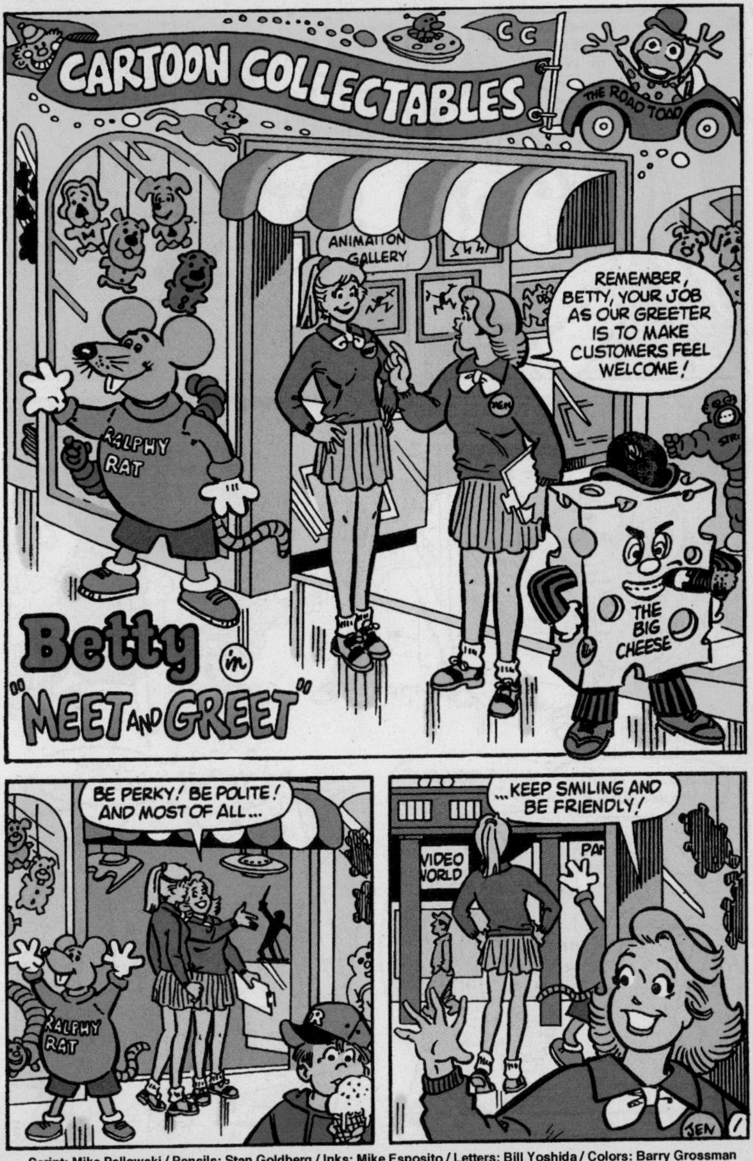
CARTOON COLLECTABLES
CC
THE ROAD TOAD
ANIMATION GALLERY
RALPHY RAT
REMEMBER, BETTY, YOUR JOB AS OUR GREETER IS TO MAKE CUSTOMERS FEEL WELCOME!
THE BIG CHEESE
Betty in "MEET AND GREET"
BE PERKY! BE POLITE! AND MOST OF ALL...
RALPHY RAT
...KEEP SMILING AND BE FRIENDLY!
VIDEO WORLD
JEN
1

Script: Mike Pellowski / Pencils: Stan Goldberg / Inks: Mike Esposito / Letters: Bill Yoshida / Colors: Barry Grossman

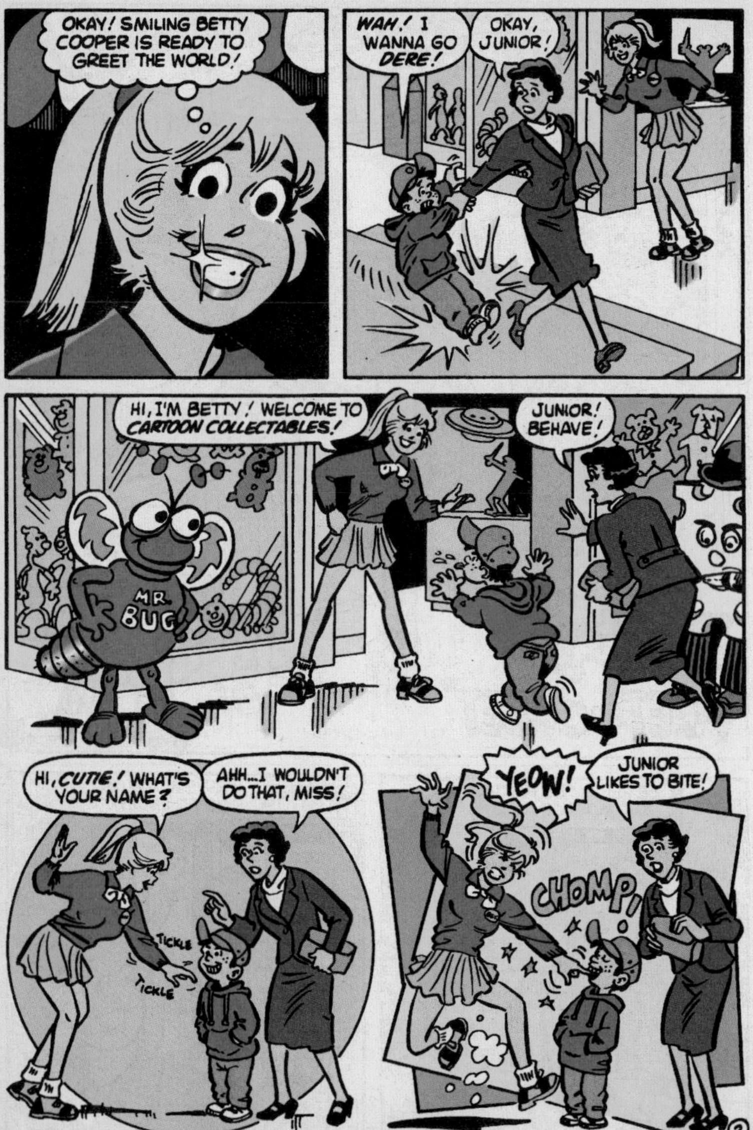
OKAY! SMILING BETTY COOPER IS READY TO GREET THE WORLD!
WAH! I WANNA GO DERE!
OKAY, JUNIOR!
HI, I'M BETTY! WELCOME TO CARTOON COLLECTABLES!
JUNIOR! BEHAVE!
MR. BUG
HI, CUTIE! WHAT'S YOUR NAME?
AHH...I WOULDN'T DO THAT, MISS!
TICKLE
TICKLE
YEOW!
JUNIOR LIKES TO BITE!
CHOMP!
2

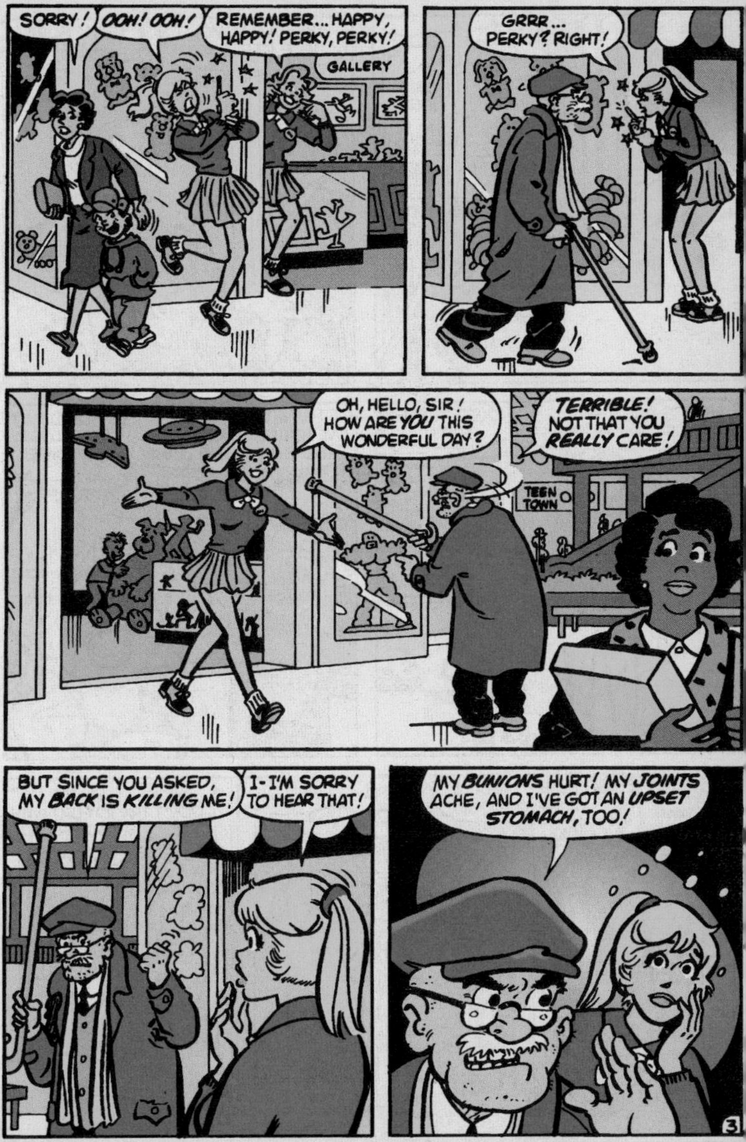

SORRY!
OOH! OOH!
REMEMBER... HAPPY, HAPPY! PERKY, PERKY!
GALLERY
GRRR... PERKY? RIGHT!
OH, HELLO, SIR! HOW ARE YOU THIS WONDERFUL DAY?
TERRIBLE! NOT THAT YOU REALLY CARE!
TEEN TOWN
BUT SINCE YOU ASKED, MY BACK IS KILLING ME!
I-I'M SORRY TO HEAR THAT!
MY BUNIONS HURT! MY JOINTS ACHE, AND I'VE GOT AN UPSET STOMACH, TOO!
3

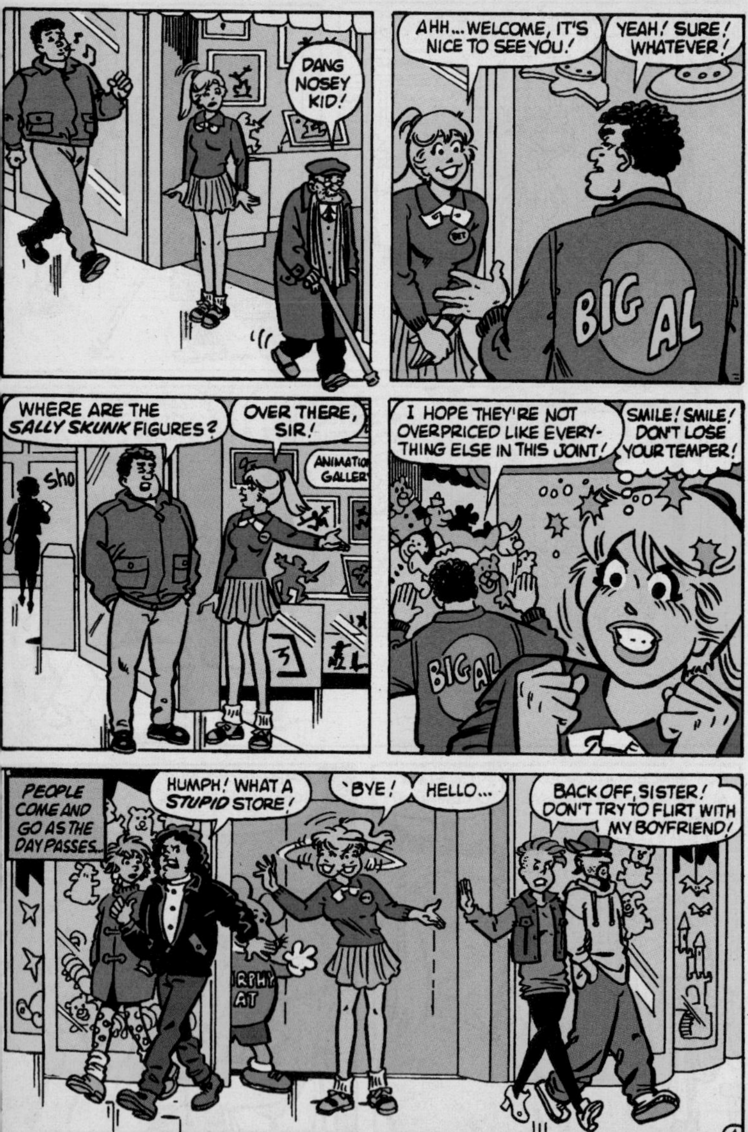
DANG NOSEY KID!
AHH... WELCOME, IT'S NICE TO SEE YOU!
YEAH! SURE! WHATEVER!
BIG AL
WHERE ARE THE SALLY SKUNK FIGURES?
OVER THERE, SIR!
ANIMATION GALLERY
I HOPE THEY'RE NOT OVERPRICED LIKE EVERYTHING ELSE IN THIS JOINT!
SMILE! SMILE! DON'T LOSE YOUR TEMPER!
BIG AL
PEOPLE COME AND GO AS THE DAY PASSES...
HUMPH! WHAT A STUPID STORE!
'BYE!
HELLO...
BACK OFF, SISTER! DON'T TRY TO FLIRT WITH MY BOYFRIEND!

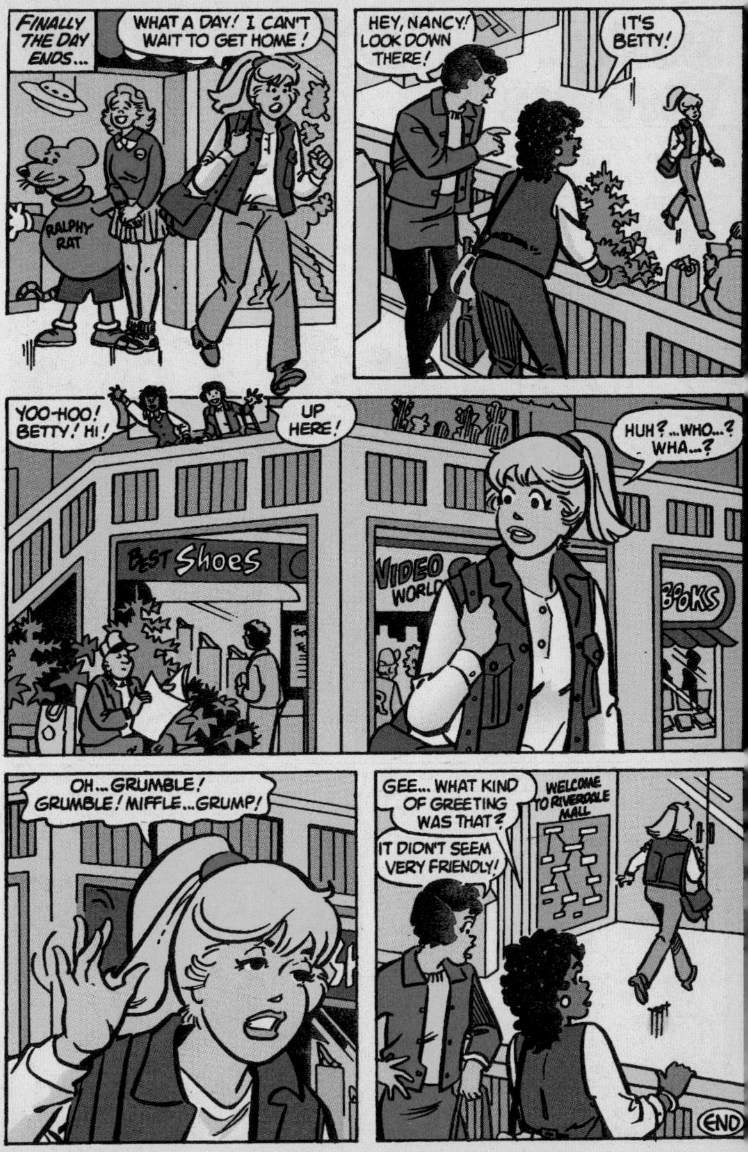
FINALLY THE DAY ENDS...
WHAT A DAY! I CAN'T WAIT TO GET HOME!
RALPHY RAT
HEY, NANCY! LOOK DOWN THERE!
IT'S BETTY!
YOO-HOO! BETTY! HI!
UP HERE!
HUH?...WHO...? WHA...?
BEST Shoes
VIDEO WORLD
BOOKS
OH...GRUMBLE! GRUMBLE! MIFFLE...GRUMP!
GEE... WHAT KIND OF GREETING WAS THAT?
IT DIDN'T SEEM VERY FRIENDLY!
WELCOME TO RIVERDALE MALL
END

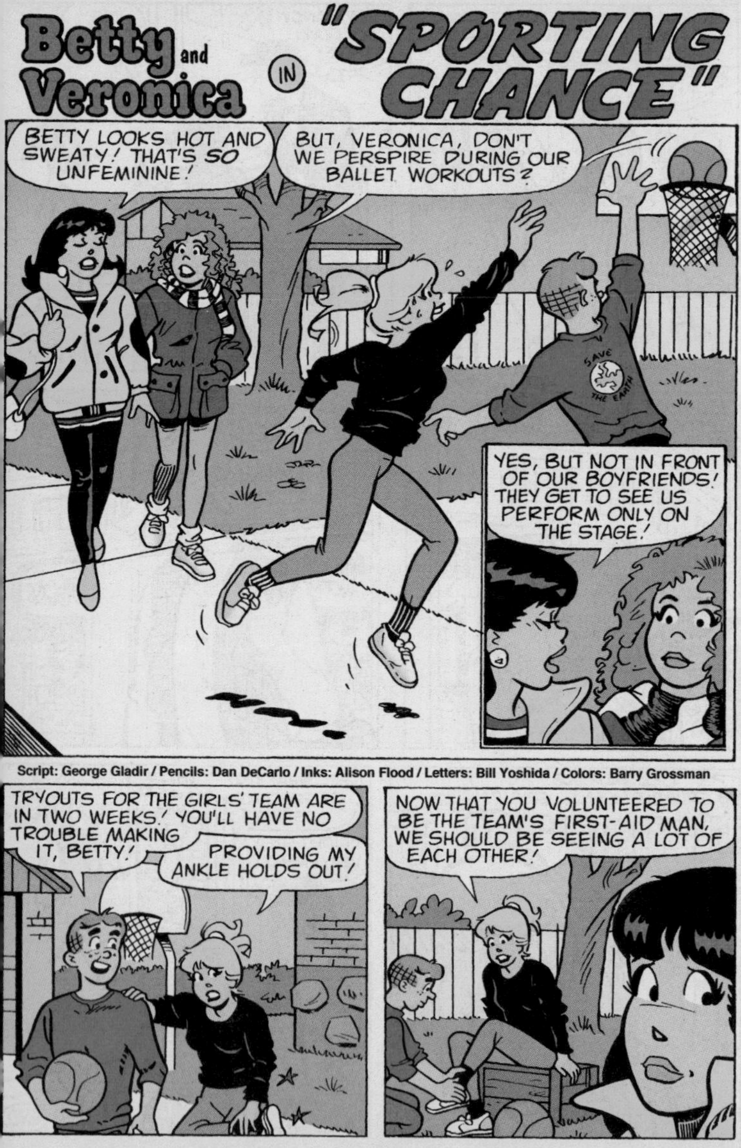
Betty and Veronica IN "SPORTING CHANCE"
BETTY LOOKS HOT AND SWEATY! THAT'S SO UNFEMININE!
BUT, VERONICA, DON'T WE PERSPIRE DURING OUR BALLET WORKOUTS?
SAVE THE EARTH
YES, BUT NOT IN FRONT OF OUR BOYFRIENDS! THEY GET TO SEE US PERFORM ONLY ON THE STAGE!
TRYOUTS FOR THE GIRLS' TEAM ARE IN TWO WEEKS! YOU'LL HAVE NO TROUBLE MAKING IT, BETTY!
PROVIDING MY ANKLE HOLDS OUT!
NOW THAT YOU VOLUNTEERED TO BE THE TEAM'S FIRST-AID MAN, WE SHOULD BE SEEING A LOT OF EACH OTHER!

Script: George Gladir / Pencils: Dan DeCarlo / Inks: Alison Flood / Letters: Bill Yoshida / Colors: Barry Grossman

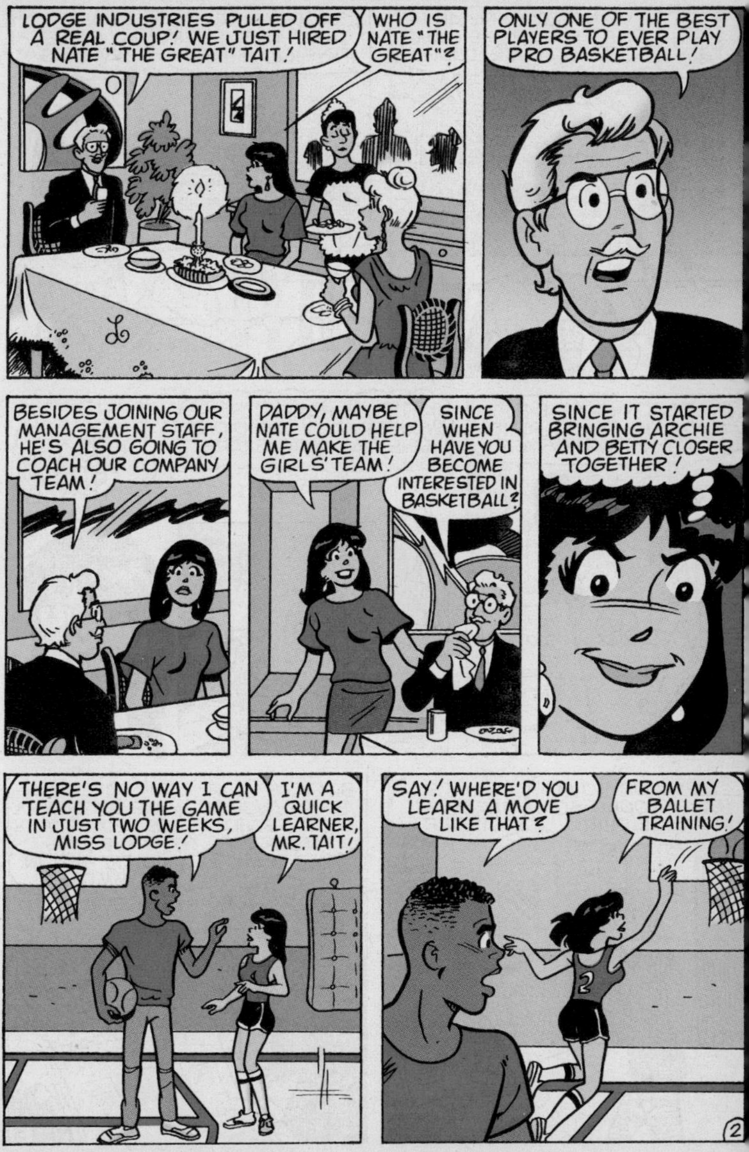

LODGE INDUSTRIES PULLED OFF A REAL COUP! WE JUST HIRED NATE "THE GREAT" TAIT!
WHO IS NATE "THE GREAT"?
ONLY ONE OF THE BEST PLAYERS TO EVER PLAY PRO BASKETBALL!
BESIDES JOINING OUR MANAGEMENT STAFF, HE'S ALSO GOING TO COACH OUR COMPANY TEAM!
DADDY, MAYBE NATE COULD HELP ME MAKE THE GIRLS' TEAM!
SINCE WHEN HAVE YOU BECOME INTERESTED IN BASKETBALL?
SINCE IT STARTED BRINGING ARCHIE AND BETTY CLOSER TOGETHER!
THERE'S NO WAY I CAN TEACH YOU THE GAME IN JUST TWO WEEKS, MISS LODGE!
I'M A QUICK LEARNER, MR. TAIT!
SAY! WHERE'D YOU LEARN A MOVE LIKE THAT?
FROM MY BALLET TRAINING!

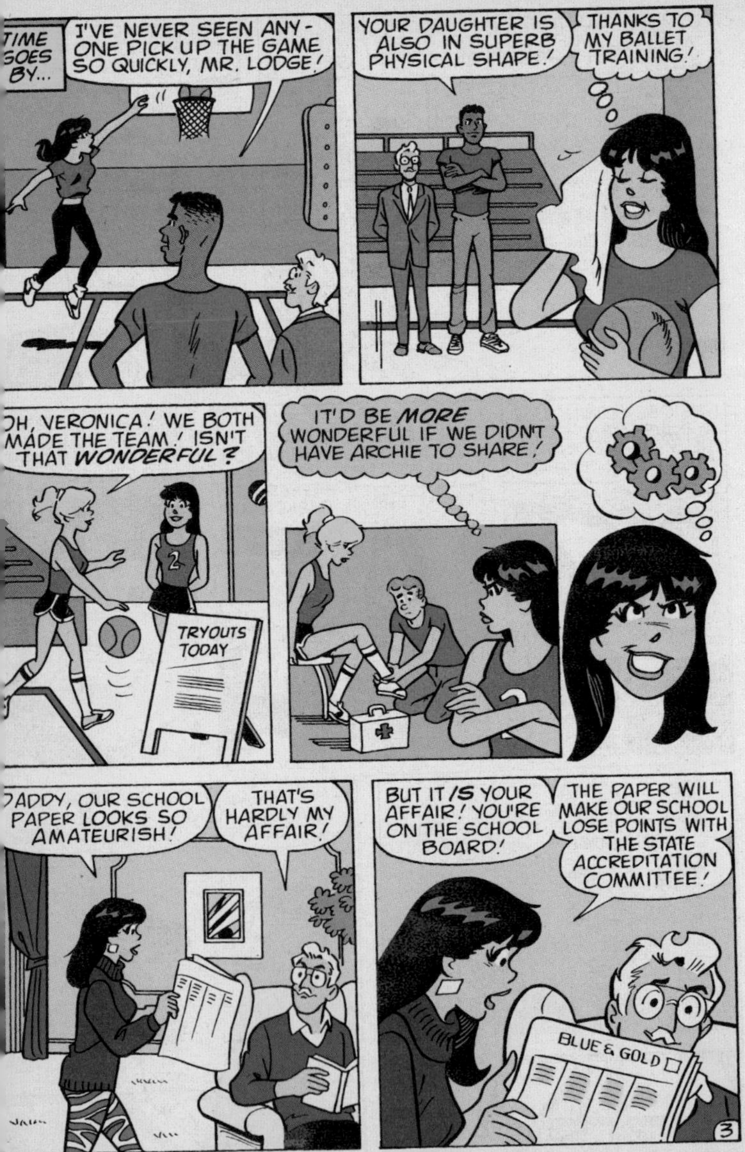
TIME GOES BY...
I'VE NEVER SEEN ANYONE PICK UP THE GAME SO QUICKLY, MR. LODGE!
YOUR DAUGHTER IS ALSO IN SUPERB PHYSICAL SHAPE!
THANKS TO MY BALLET TRAINING!
OH, VERONICA! WE BOTH MADE THE TEAM! ISN'T THAT WONDERFUL?
TRYOUTS TODAY
IT'D BE MORE WONDERFUL IF WE DIDN'T HAVE ARCHIE TO SHARE!
DADDY, OUR SCHOOL PAPER LOOKS SO AMATEURISH!
THAT'S HARDLY MY AFFAIR!
BUT IT IS YOUR AFFAIR! YOU'RE ON THE SCHOOL BOARD!
THE PAPER WILL MAKE OUR SCHOOL LOSE POINTS WITH THE STATE ACCREDITATION COMMITTEE!
BLUE & GOLD
3

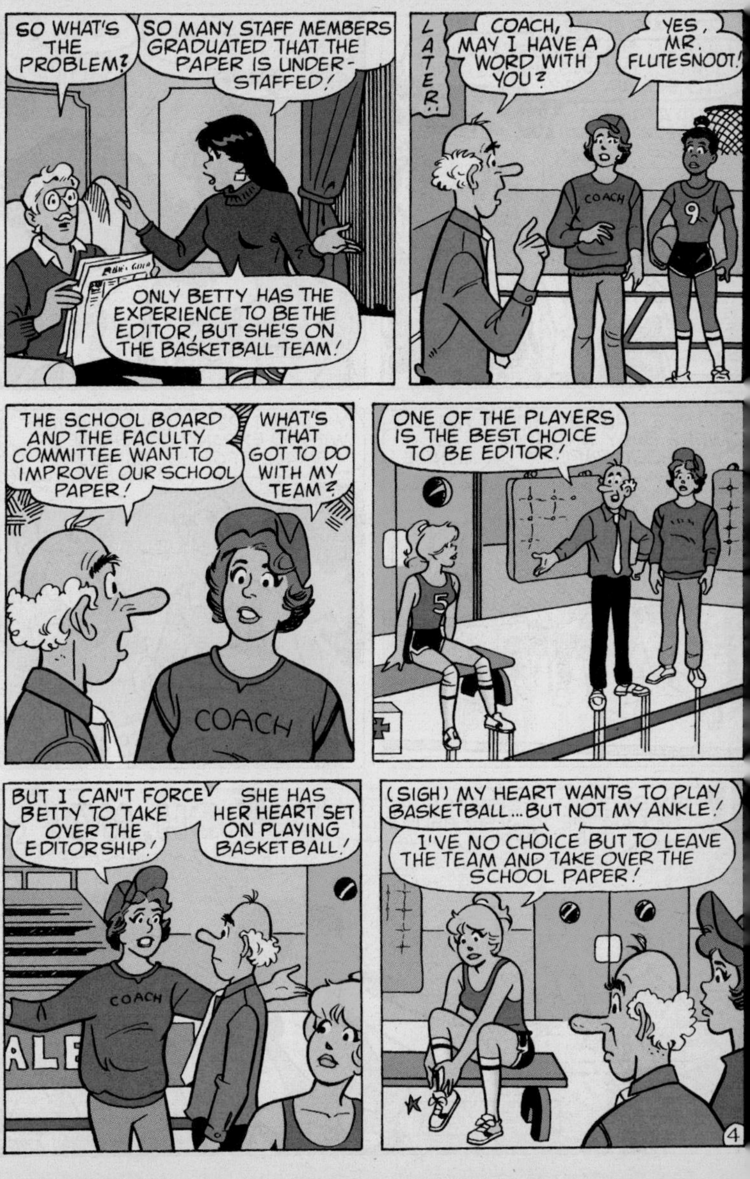
SO WHAT'S THE PROBLEM?
SO MANY STAFF MEMBERS GRADUATED THAT THE PAPER IS UNDER-STAFFED!
ONLY BETTY HAS THE EXPERIENCE TO BE THE EDITOR, BUT SHE'S ON THE BASKETBALL TEAM!
LATER..
COACH, MAY I HAVE A WORD WITH YOU?
YES, MR. FLUTESNOOT!
COACH
THE SCHOOL BOARD AND THE FACULTY COMMITTEE WANT TO IMPROVE OUR SCHOOL PAPER!
WHAT'S THAT GOT TO DO WITH MY TEAM?
COACH
ONE OF THE PLAYERS IS THE BEST CHOICE TO BE EDITOR!
BUT I CAN'T FORCE BETTY TO TAKE OVER THE EDITORSHIP!
SHE HAS HER HEART SET ON PLAYING BASKETBALL!
COACH
(SIGH) MY HEART WANTS TO PLAY BASKETBALL... BUT NOT MY ANKLE!
I'VE NO CHOICE BUT TO LEAVE THE TEAM AND TAKE OVER THE SCHOOL PAPER!
4

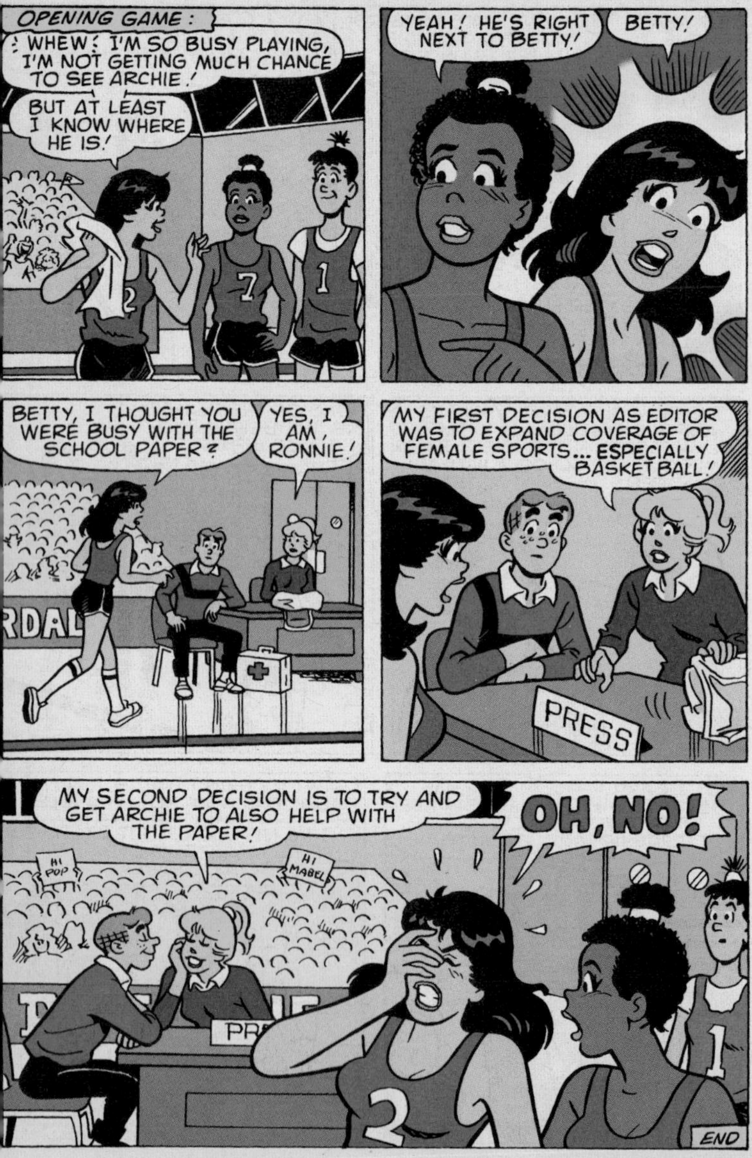
OPENING GAME:
WHEW! I'M SO BUSY PLAYING, I'M NOT GETTING MUCH CHANCE TO SEE ARCHIE!
BUT AT LEAST I KNOW WHERE HE IS!
YEAH! HE'S RIGHT NEXT TO BETTY!
BETTY!
BETTY, I THOUGHT YOU WERE BUSY WITH THE SCHOOL PAPER?
YES, I AM, RONNIE!
MY FIRST DECISION AS EDITOR WAS TO EXPAND COVERAGE OF FEMALE SPORTS... ESPECIALLY BASKETBALL!
PRESS
MY SECOND DECISION IS TO TRY AND GET ARCHIE TO ALSO HELP WITH THE PAPER!
HI POP
HI MABEL
OH, NO!
END

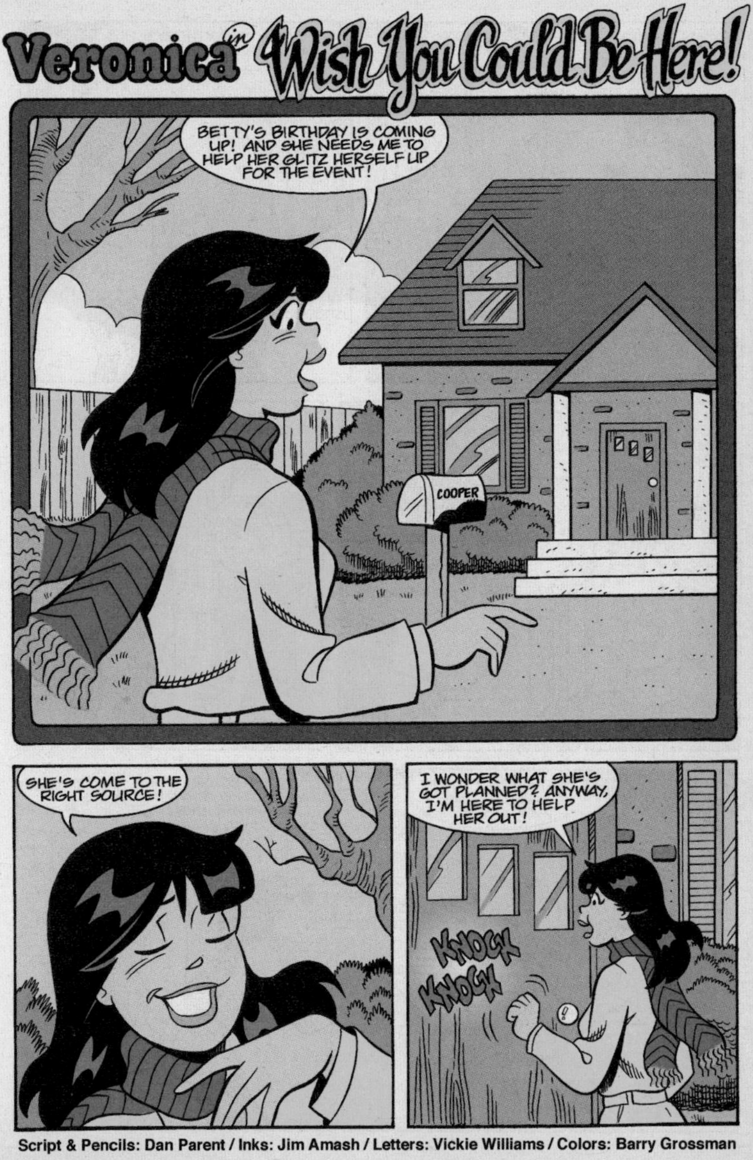
Veronica in Wish You Could Be Here!
BETTY'S BIRTHDAY IS COMING UP! AND SHE NEEDS ME TO HELP HER GLITZ HERSELF UP FOR THE EVENT!
COOPER
SHE'S COME TO THE RIGHT SOURCE!
I WONDER WHAT SHE'S GOT PLANNED? ANYWAY, I'M HERE TO HELP HER OUT!
KNOCK KNOCK

Script & Pencils: Dan Parent / Inks: Jim Amash / Letters: Vickie Williams / Colors: Barry Grossman

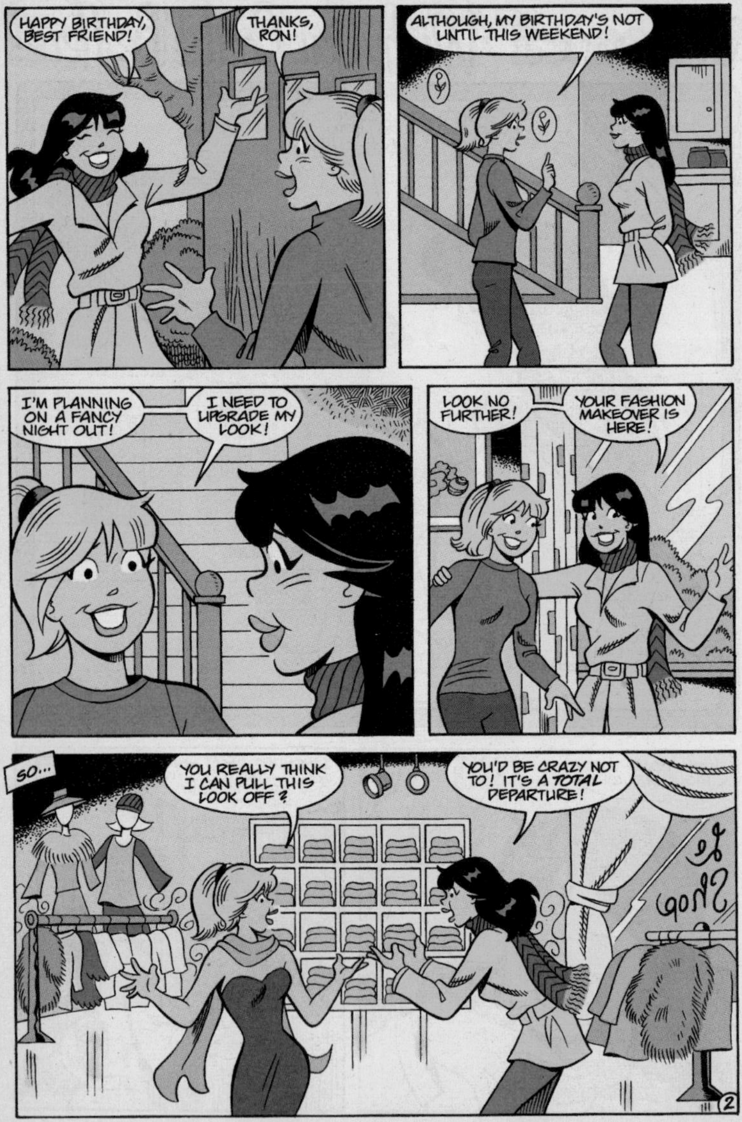
HAPPY BIRTHDAY, BEST FRIEND!
THANKS, RON!
ALTHOUGH, MY BIRTHDAY'S NOT UNTIL THIS WEEKEND!
I'M PLANNING ON A FANCY NIGHT OUT!
I NEED TO UPGRADE MY LOOK!
LOOK NO FURTHER!
YOUR FASHION MAKEOVER IS HERE!
SO...
YOU REALLY THINK I CAN PULL THIS LOOK OFF?
YOU'D BE CRAZY NOT TO! IT'S A TOTAL DEPARTURE!

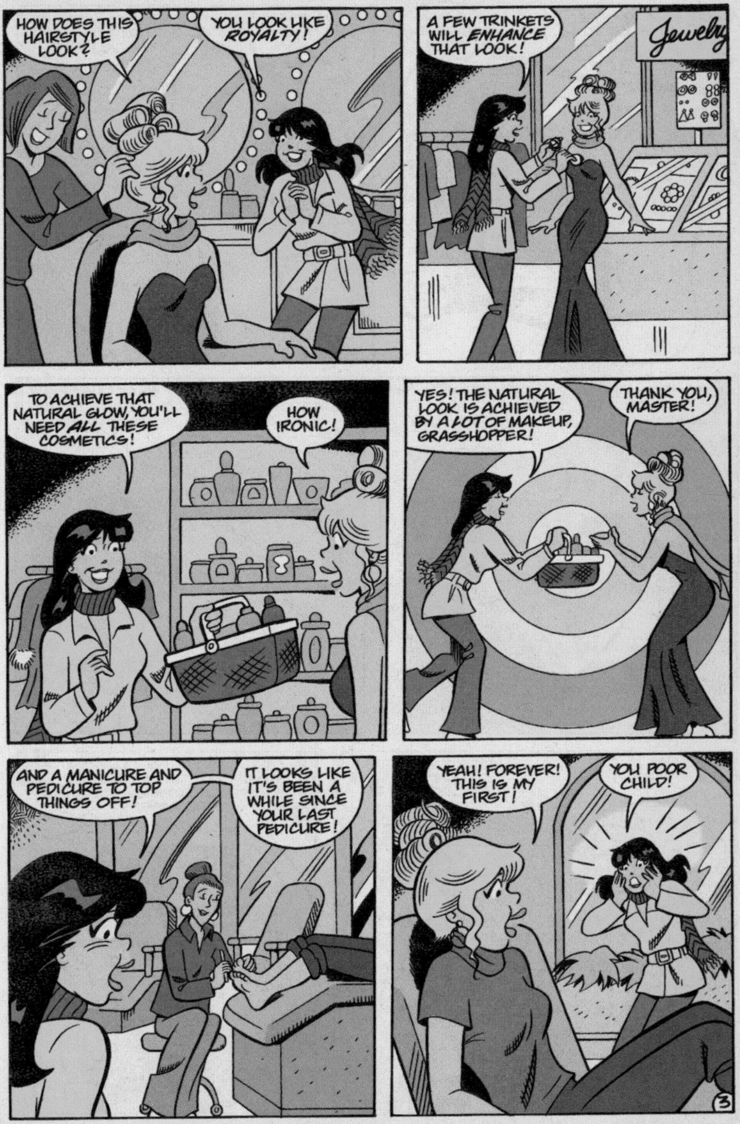
HOW DOES THIS HAIRSTYLE LOOK?
YOU LOOK LIKE ROYALTY!
A FEW TRINKETS WILL ENHANCE THAT LOOK!
Jewelry
TO ACHIEVE THAT NATURAL GLOW, YOU'LL NEED ALL THESE COSMETICS!
HOW IRONIC!
YES! THE NATURAL LOOK IS ACHIEVED BY A LOT OF MAKEUP, GRASSHOPPER!
THANK YOU, MASTER!
AND A MANICURE AND PEDICURE TO TOP THINGS OFF!
IT LOOKS LIKE IT'S BEEN A WHILE SINCE YOUR LAST PEDICURE!
YEAH! FOREVER! THIS IS MY FIRST!
YOU POOR CHILD!
3

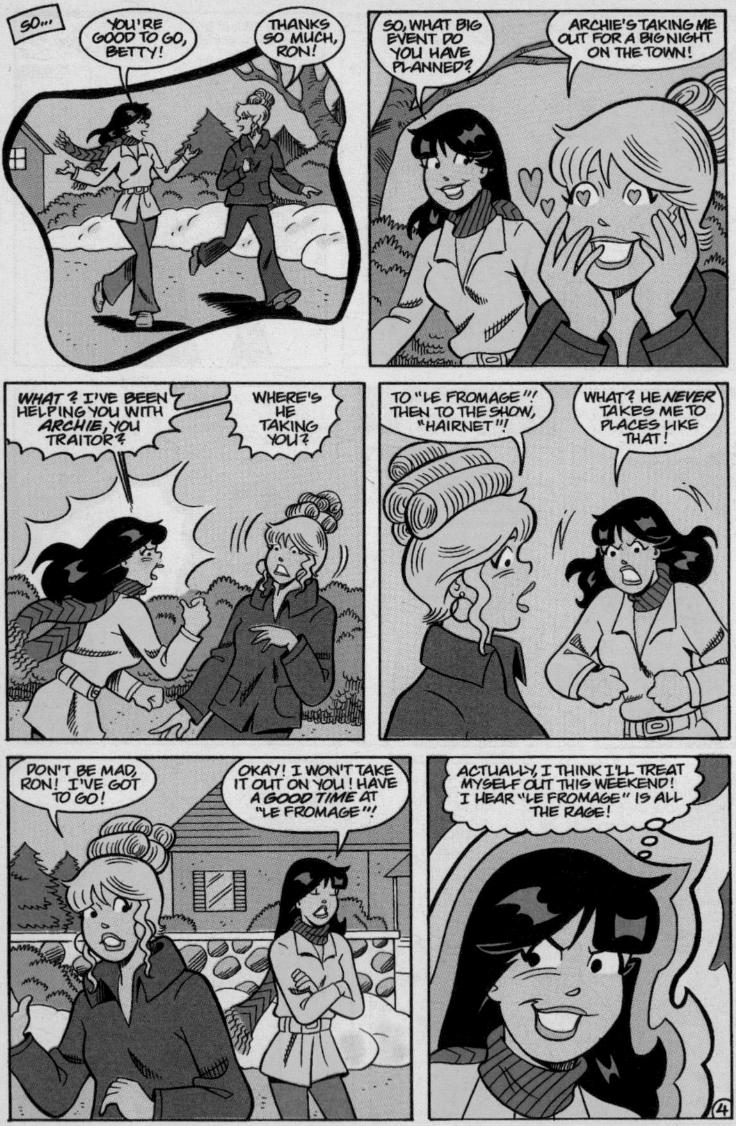
SO...
YOU'RE GOOD TO GO, BETTY!
THANKS SO MUCH, RON!
SO, WHAT BIG EVENT DO YOU HAVE PLANNED?
ARCHIE'S TAKING ME OUT FOR A BIG NIGHT ON THE TOWN!
WHAT? I'VE BEEN HELPING YOU WITH ARCHIE, YOU TRAITOR?
WHERE'S HE TAKING YOU?
TO "LE FROMAGE"! THEN TO THE SHOW, "HAIRNET"!
WHAT? HE NEVER TAKES ME TO PLACES LIKE THAT!
DON'T BE MAD, RON! I'VE GOT TO GO!
OKAY! I WON'T TAKE IT OUT ON YOU! HAVE A GOOD TIME AT "LE FROMAGE"!
ACTUALLY, I THINK I'LL TREAT MYSELF OUT THIS WEEKEND! I HEAR "LE FROMAGE" IS ALL THE RAGE!
4

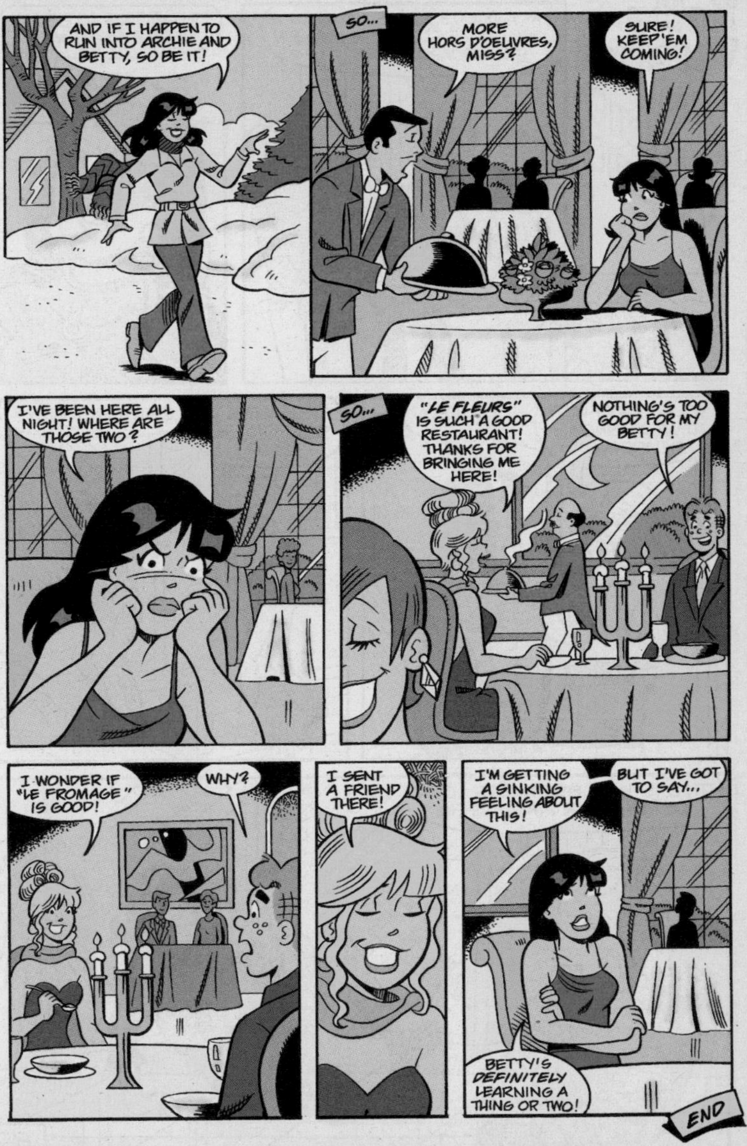
AND IF I HAPPEN TO RUN INTO ARCHIE AND BETTY, SO BE IT!
SO...
MORE HORS D'OEUVRES, MISS?
SURE! KEEP'EM COMING!
I'VE BEEN HERE ALL NIGHT! WHERE ARE THOSE TWO?
SO...
"LE FLEURS" IS SUCH A GOOD RESTAURANT! THANKS FOR BRINGING ME HERE!
NOTHING'S TOO GOOD FOR MY BETTY!
I WONDER IF "LE FROMAGE" IS GOOD!
WHY?
I SENT A FRIEND THERE!
I'M GETTING A SINKING FEELING ABOUT THIS!
BUT I'VE GOT TO SAY...
BETTY'S DEFINITELY LEARNING A THING OR TWO!
END

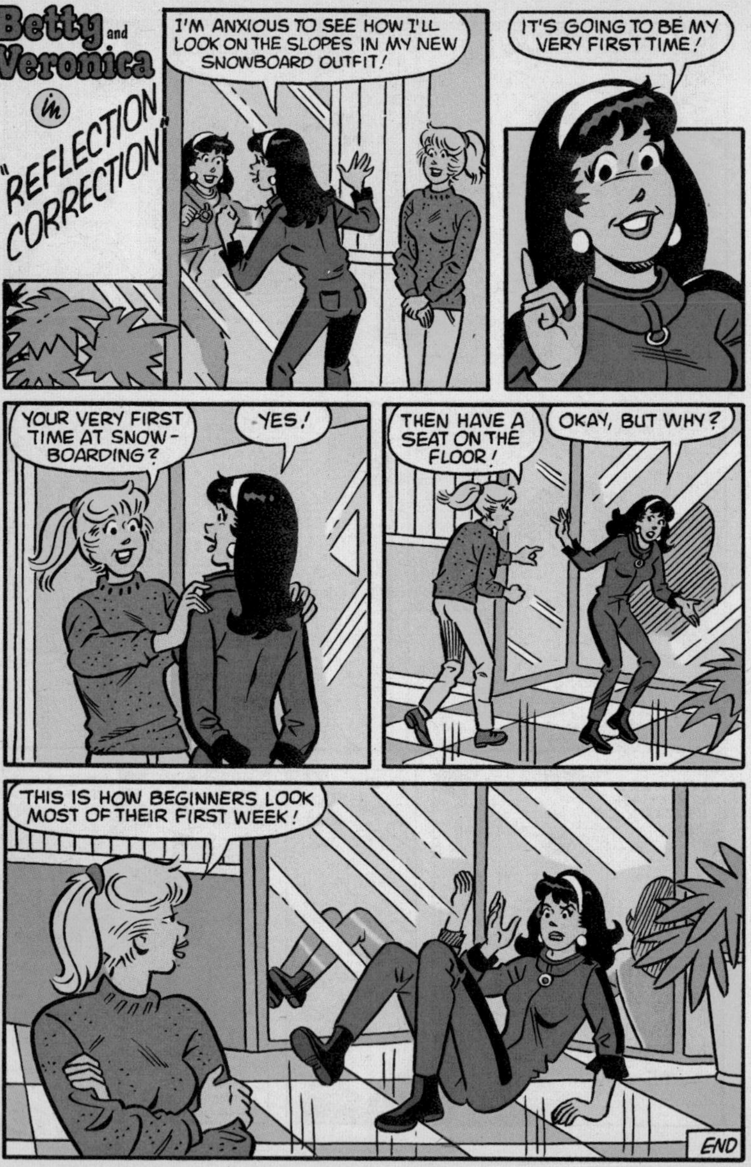
Betty and Veronica
in
"REFLECTION CORRECTION"
I'M ANXIOUS TO SEE HOW I'LL LOOK ON THE SLOPES IN MY NEW SNOWBOARD OUTFIT!
IT'S GOING TO BE MY VERY FIRST TIME!
YOUR VERY FIRST TIME AT SNOW-BOARDING?
YES!
THEN HAVE A SEAT ON THE FLOOR!
OKAY, BUT WHY?
THIS IS HOW BEGINNERS LOOK MOST OF THEIR FIRST WEEK!
END

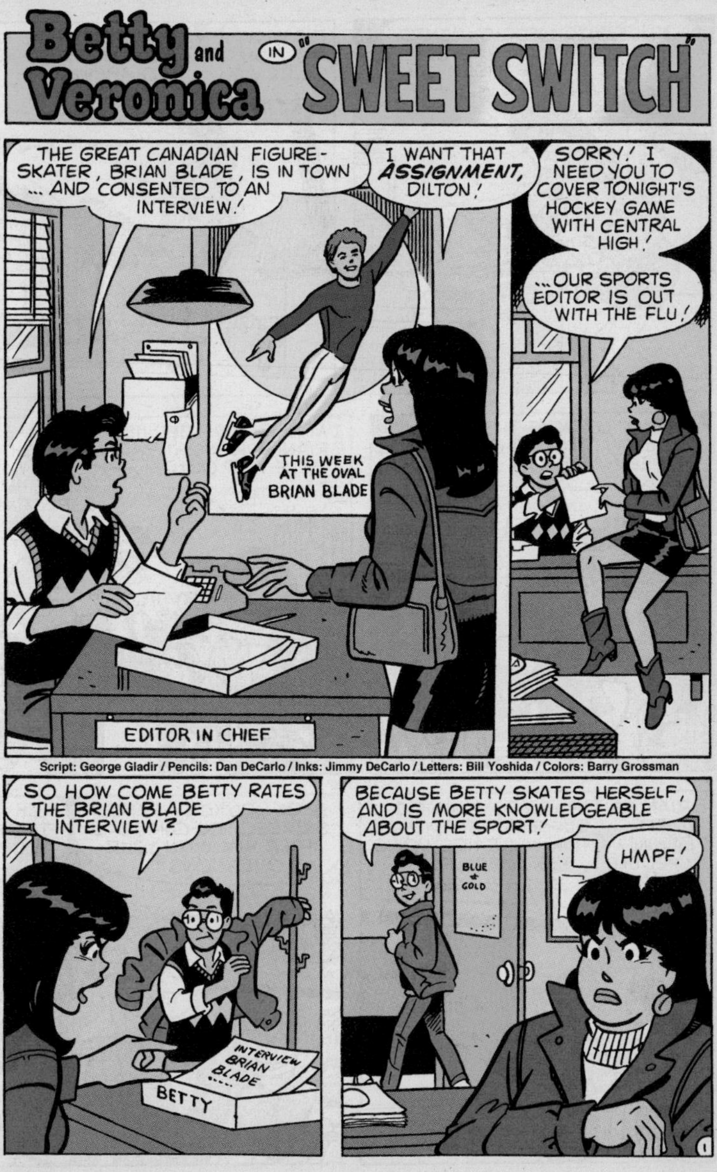
Betty and Veronica IN "SWEET SWITCH"
THE GREAT CANADIAN FIGURE-SKATER, BRIAN BLADE, IS IN TOWN ... AND CONSENTED TO AN INTERVIEW!
I WANT THAT ASSIGNMENT, DILTON!
THIS WEEK AT THE OVAL BRIAN BLADE
EDITOR IN CHIEF
SORRY! I NEED YOU TO COVER TONIGHT'S HOCKEY GAME WITH CENTRAL HIGH!
...OUR SPORTS EDITOR IS OUT WITH THE FLU!
Script: George Gladir / Pencils: Dan DeCarlo / Inks: Jimmy DeCarlo / Letters: Bill Yoshida / Colors: Barry Grossman
SO HOW COME BETTY RATES THE BRIAN BLADE INTERVIEW?
INTERVIEW BRIAN BLADE
BETTY
BECAUSE BETTY SKATES HERSELF, AND IS MORE KNOWLEDGEABLE ABOUT THE SPORT!
BLUE & GOLD
HMPF!
1

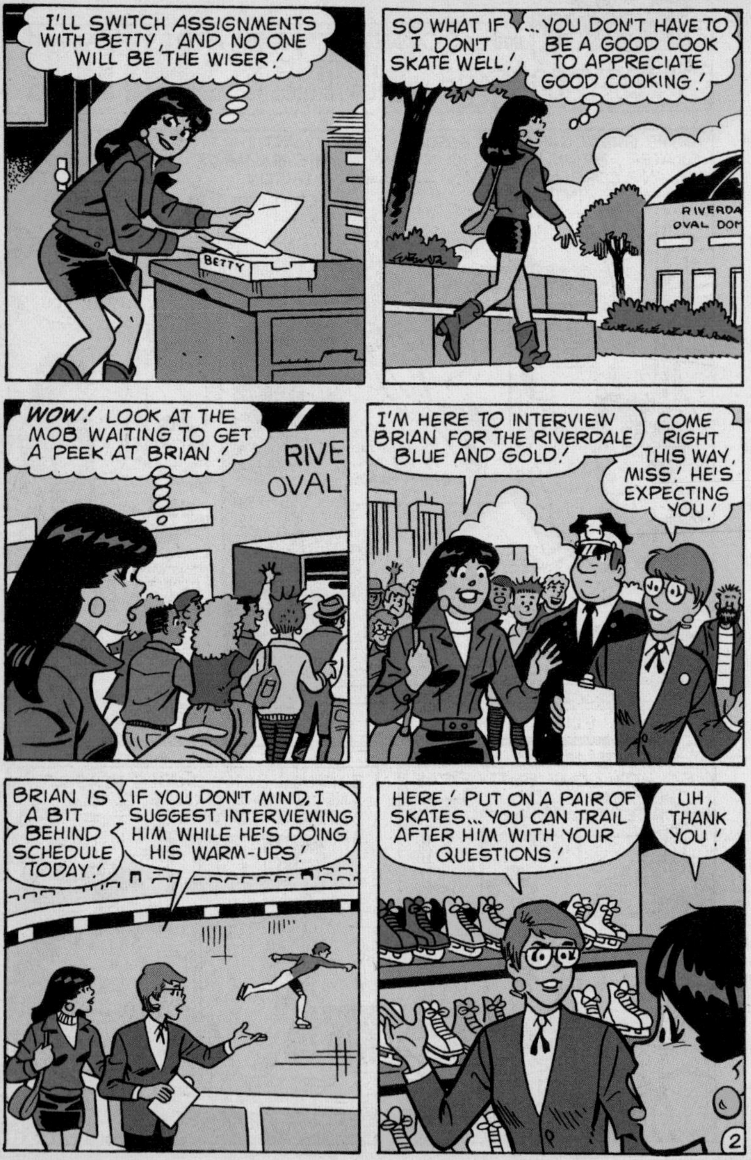
I'LL SWITCH ASSIGNMENTS WITH BETTY, AND NO ONE WILL BE THE WISER!
BETTY
SO WHAT IF I DON'T SKATE WELL!
...YOU DON'T HAVE TO BE A GOOD COOK TO APPRECIATE GOOD COOKING!
RIVERDA OVAL DOM
WOW! LOOK AT THE MOB WAITING TO GET A PEEK AT BRIAN!
RIVE OVAL
I'M HERE TO INTERVIEW BRIAN FOR THE RIVERDALE BLUE AND GOLD!
COME RIGHT THIS WAY, MISS! HE'S EXPECTING YOU!
BRIAN IS A BIT BEHIND SCHEDULE TODAY!
IF YOU DON'T MIND, I SUGGEST INTERVIEWING HIM WHILE HE'S DOING HIS WARM-UPS!
HERE! PUT ON A PAIR OF SKATES... YOU CAN TRAIL AFTER HIM WITH YOUR QUESTIONS!
UH, THANK YOU!
2

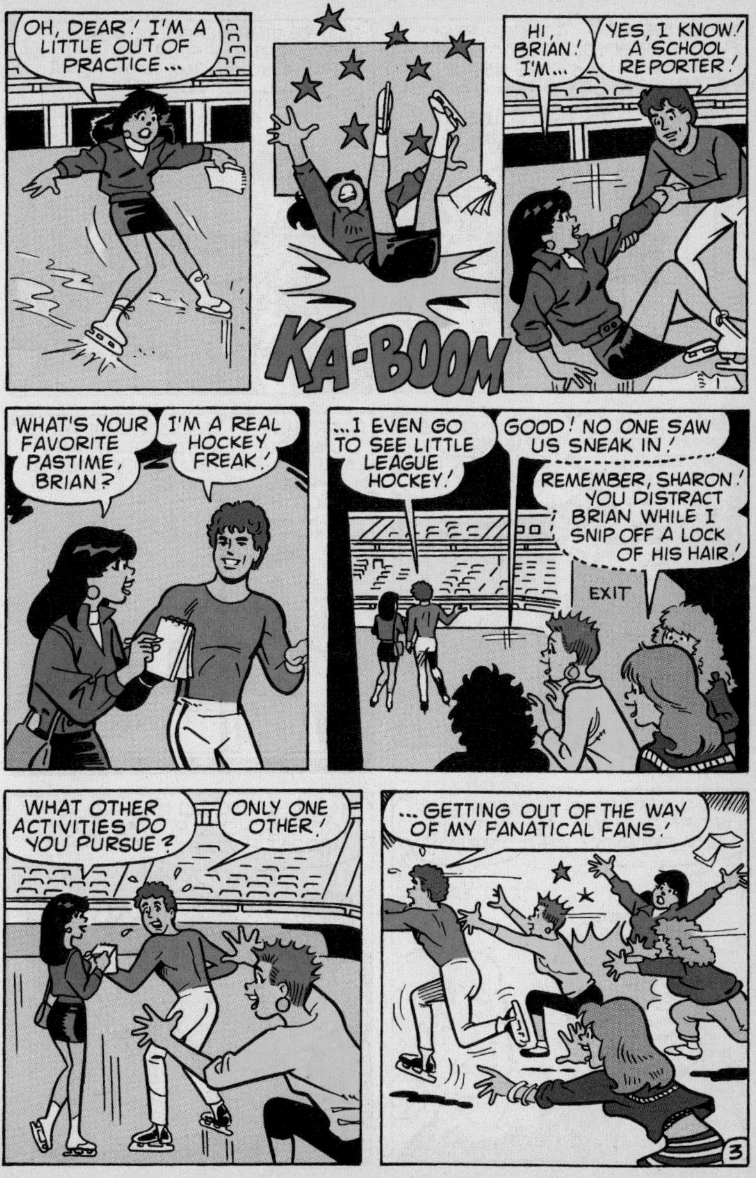
OH, DEAR! I'M A LITTLE OUT OF PRACTICE...
KA-BOOM
HI, BRIAN! I'M...
YES, I KNOW! A SCHOOL REPORTER!
WHAT'S YOUR FAVORITE PASTIME, BRIAN?
I'M A REAL HOCKEY FREAK!
...I EVEN GO TO SEE LITTLE LEAGUE HOCKEY!
GOOD! NO ONE SAW US SNEAK IN!
REMEMBER, SHARON! YOU DISTRACT BRIAN WHILE I SNIP OFF A LOCK OF HIS HAIR!
EXIT
WHAT OTHER ACTIVITIES DO YOU PURSUE?
ONLY ONE OTHER!
...GETTING OUT OF THE WAY OF MY FANATICAL FANS!
3

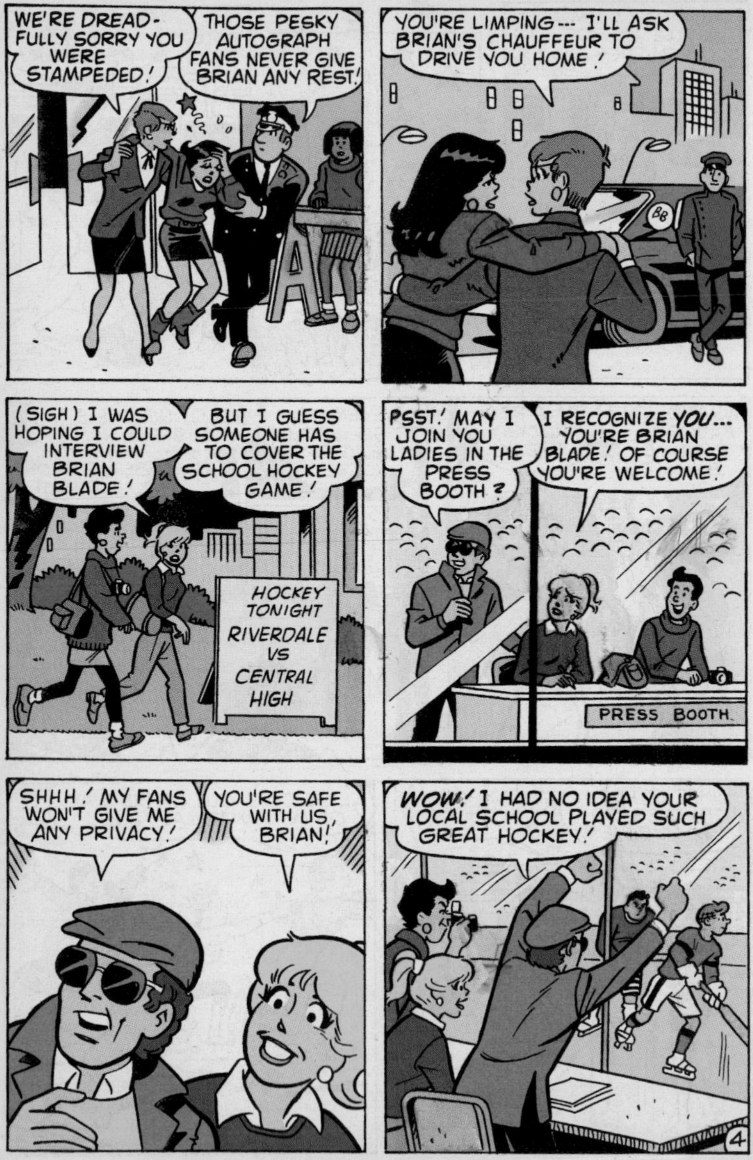
WE'RE DREAD-FULLY SORRY YOU WERE STAMPEDED!
THOSE PESKY AUTOGRAPH FANS NEVER GIVE BRIAN ANY REST!
YOU'RE LIMPING--- I'LL ASK BRIAN'S CHAUFFEUR TO DRIVE YOU HOME!
BB
(SIGH) I WAS HOPING I COULD INTERVIEW BRIAN BLADE!
BUT I GUESS SOMEONE HAS TO COVER THE SCHOOL HOCKEY GAME!
HOCKEY TONIGHT RIVERDALE VS CENTRAL HIGH
PSST! MAY I JOIN YOU LADIES IN THE PRESS BOOTH?
I RECOGNIZE YOU... YOU'RE BRIAN BLADE! OF COURSE YOU'RE WELCOME!
PRESS BOOTH
SHHH! MY FANS WON'T GIVE ME ANY PRIVACY!
YOU'RE SAFE WITH US, BRIAN!
WOW! I HAD NO IDEA YOUR LOCAL SCHOOL PLAYED SUCH GREAT HOCKEY!
4

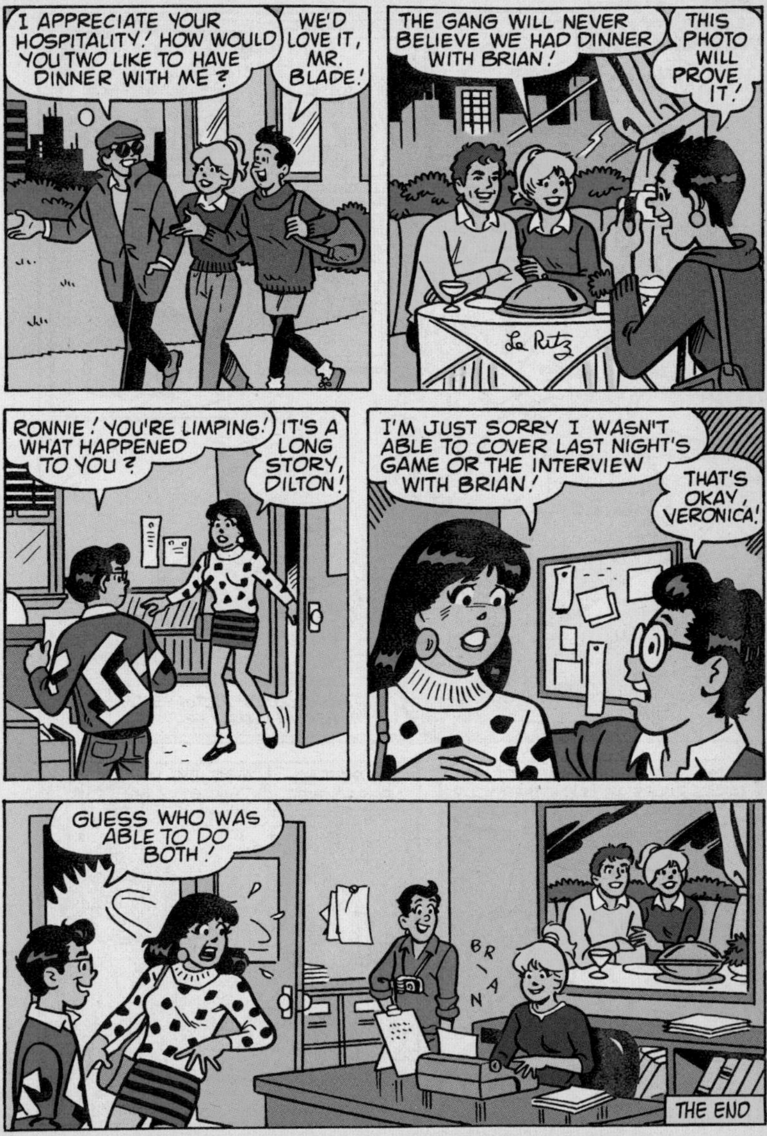
I APPRECIATE YOUR HOSPITALITY! HOW WOULD YOU TWO LIKE TO HAVE DINNER WITH ME?
WE'D LOVE IT, MR. BLADE!
THE GANG WILL NEVER BELIEVE WE HAD DINNER WITH BRIAN!
THIS PHOTO WILL PROVE IT!
Le Ritz
RONNIE! YOU'RE LIMPING! WHAT HAPPENED TO YOU?
IT'S A LONG STORY, DILTON!
I'M JUST SORRY I WASN'T ABLE TO COVER LAST NIGHT'S GAME OR THE INTERVIEW WITH BRIAN!
THAT'S OKAY, VERONICA!
GUESS WHO WAS ABLE TO DO BOTH!
BRIAN
THE END

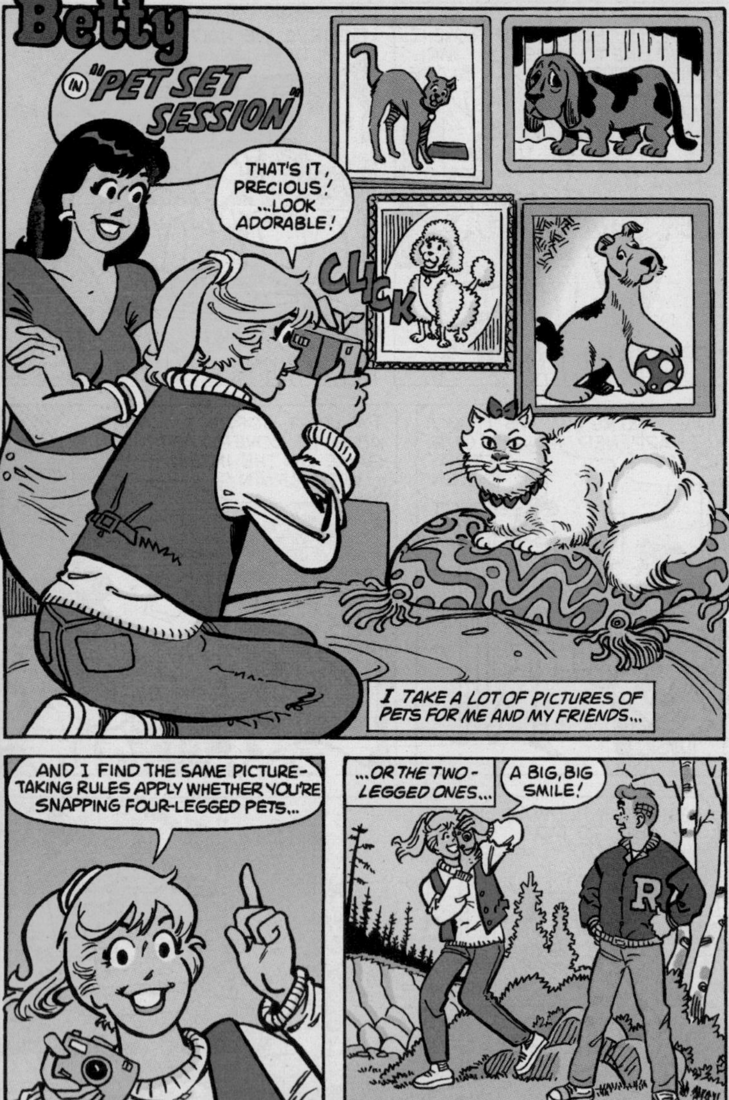

Betty
IN "PET SET SESSION"
THAT'S IT, PRECIOUS! ...LOOK ADORABLE!
CLICK
I TAKE A LOT OF PICTURES OF PETS FOR ME AND MY FRIENDS...
AND I FIND THE SAME PICTURE-TAKING RULES APPLY WHETHER YOU'RE SNAPPING FOUR-LEGGED PETS...
...OR THE TWO-LEGGED ONES...
A BIG, BIG SMILE!
R

Script: George Gladir / Pencils: Stan Goldberg / Inks: Mike Esposito / Letters: Bill Yoshida

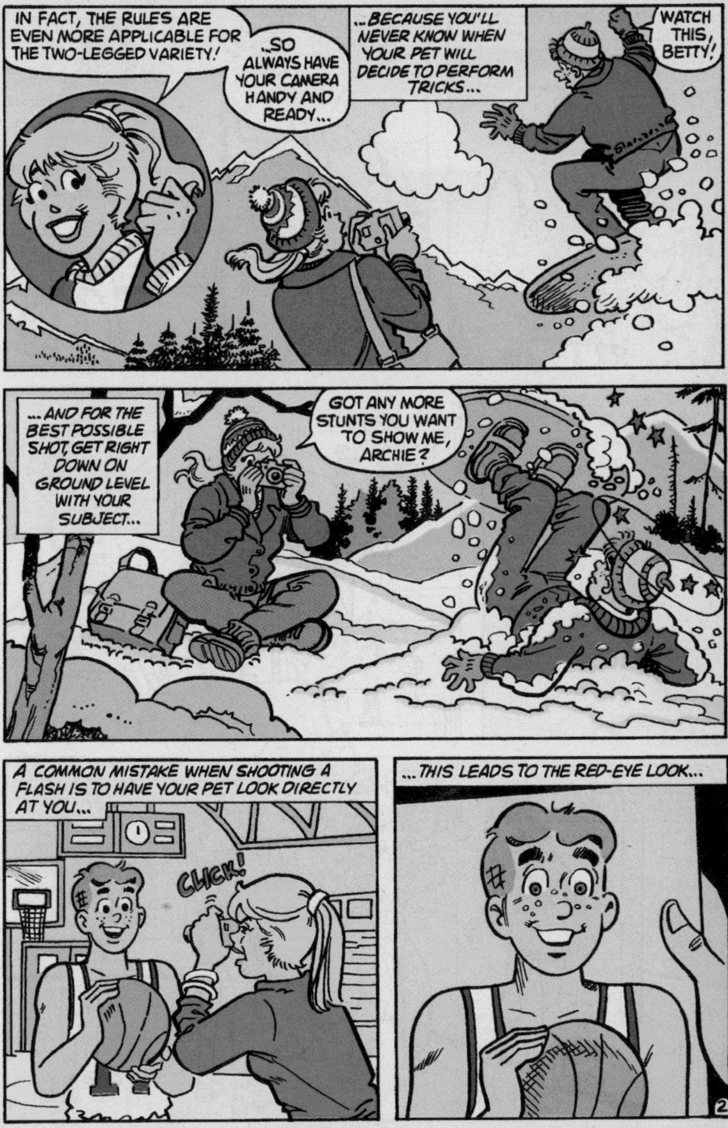

IN FACT, THE RULES ARE EVEN MORE APPLICABLE FOR THE TWO-LEGGED VARIETY!
...SO ALWAYS HAVE YOUR CAMERA HANDY AND READY...
...BECAUSE YOU'LL NEVER KNOW WHEN YOUR PET WILL DECIDE TO PERFORM TRICKS...
WATCH THIS, BETTY!
...AND FOR THE BEST POSSIBLE SHOT, GET RIGHT DOWN ON GROUND LEVEL WITH YOUR SUBJECT...
GOT ANY MORE STUNTS YOU WANT TO SHOW ME, ARCHIE?
A COMMON MISTAKE WHEN SHOOTING A FLASH IS TO HAVE YOUR PET LOOK DIRECTLY AT YOU...
CLICK!
...THIS LEADS TO THE RED-EYE LOOK...
2

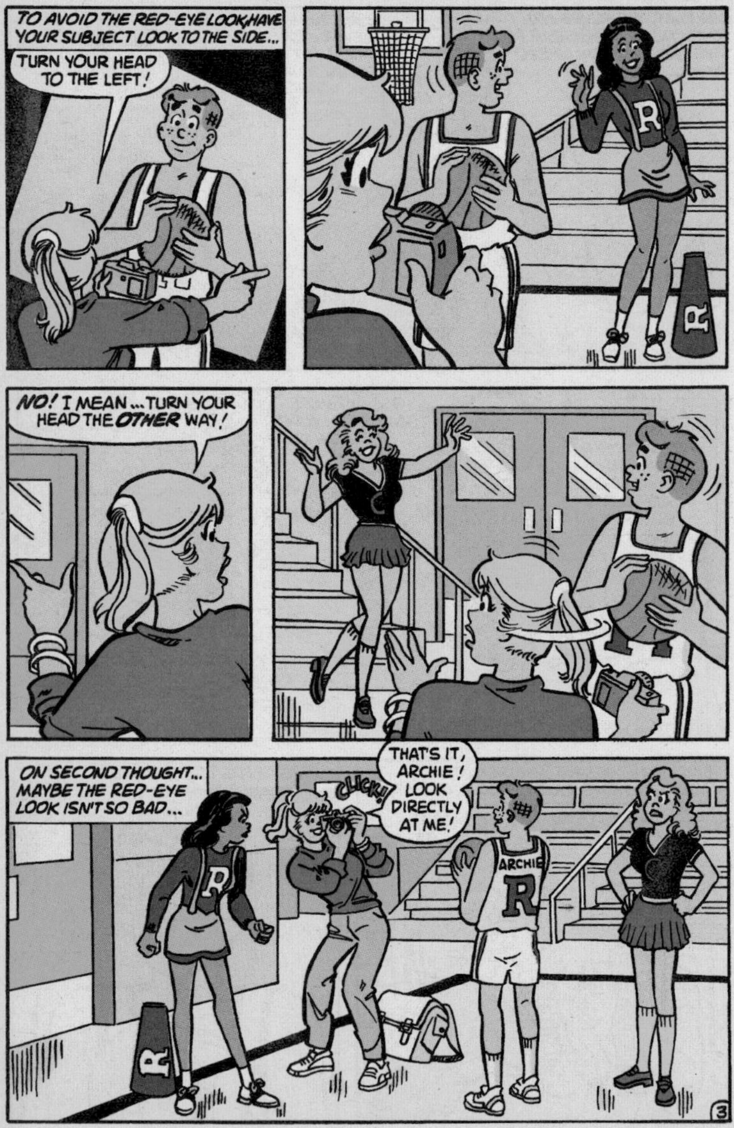
TO AVOID THE RED-EYE LOOK, HAVE YOUR SUBJECT LOOK TO THE SIDE...
TURN YOUR HEAD TO THE LEFT!
NO! I MEAN ...TURN YOUR HEAD THE OTHER WAY!
ON SECOND THOUGHT... MAYBE THE RED-EYE LOOK ISN'T SO BAD...
CLICK!
THAT'S IT, ARCHIE! LOOK DIRECTLY AT ME!
ARCHIE
3

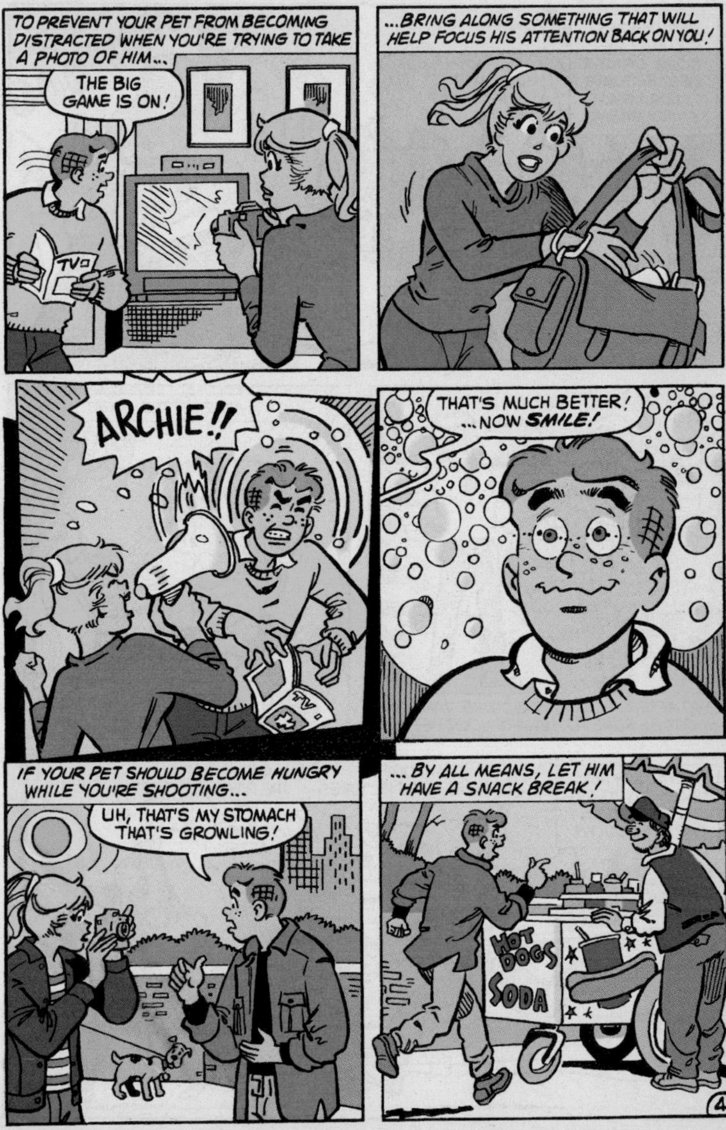
TO PREVENT YOUR PET FROM BECOMING DISTRACTED WHEN YOU'RE TRYING TO TAKE A PHOTO OF HIM...
THE BIG GAME IS ON!
TV
...BRING ALONG SOMETHING THAT WILL HELP FOCUS HIS ATTENTION BACK ON YOU!
ARCHIE!!
THAT'S MUCH BETTER! ...NOW SMILE!
IF YOUR PET SHOULD BECOME HUNGRY WHILE YOU'RE SHOOTING...
UH, THAT'S MY STOMACH THAT'S GROWLING!
... BY ALL MEANS, LET HIM HAVE A SNACK BREAK!
HOT DOGS
SODA
4

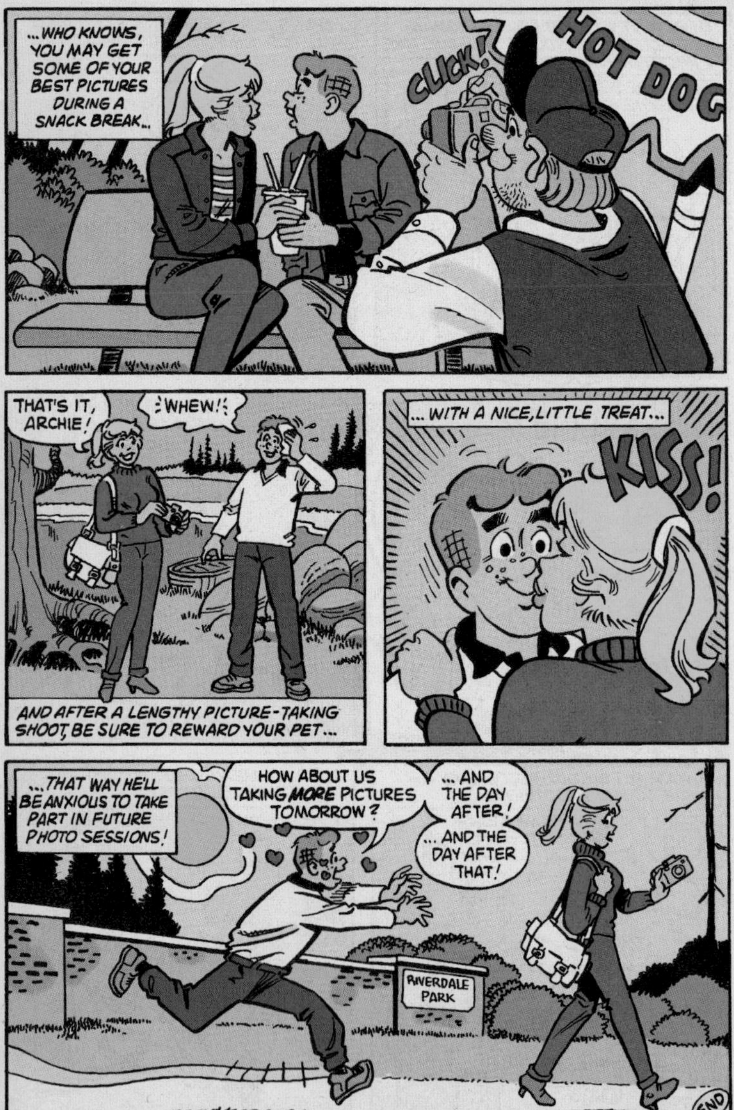
...WHO KNOWS, YOU MAY GET SOME OF YOUR BEST PICTURES DURING A SNACK BREAK...
CLICK!
HOT DOG
THAT'S IT, ARCHIE!
WHEW!
AND AFTER A LENGTHY PICTURE-TAKING SHOOT, BE SURE TO REWARD YOUR PET...
... WITH A NICE, LITTLE TREAT...
KISS!
...THAT WAY HE'LL BE ANXIOUS TO TAKE PART IN FUTURE PHOTO SESSIONS!
HOW ABOUT US TAKING MORE PICTURES TOMORROW?
... AND THE DAY AFTER!
... AND THE DAY AFTER THAT!
RIVERDALE PARK
END

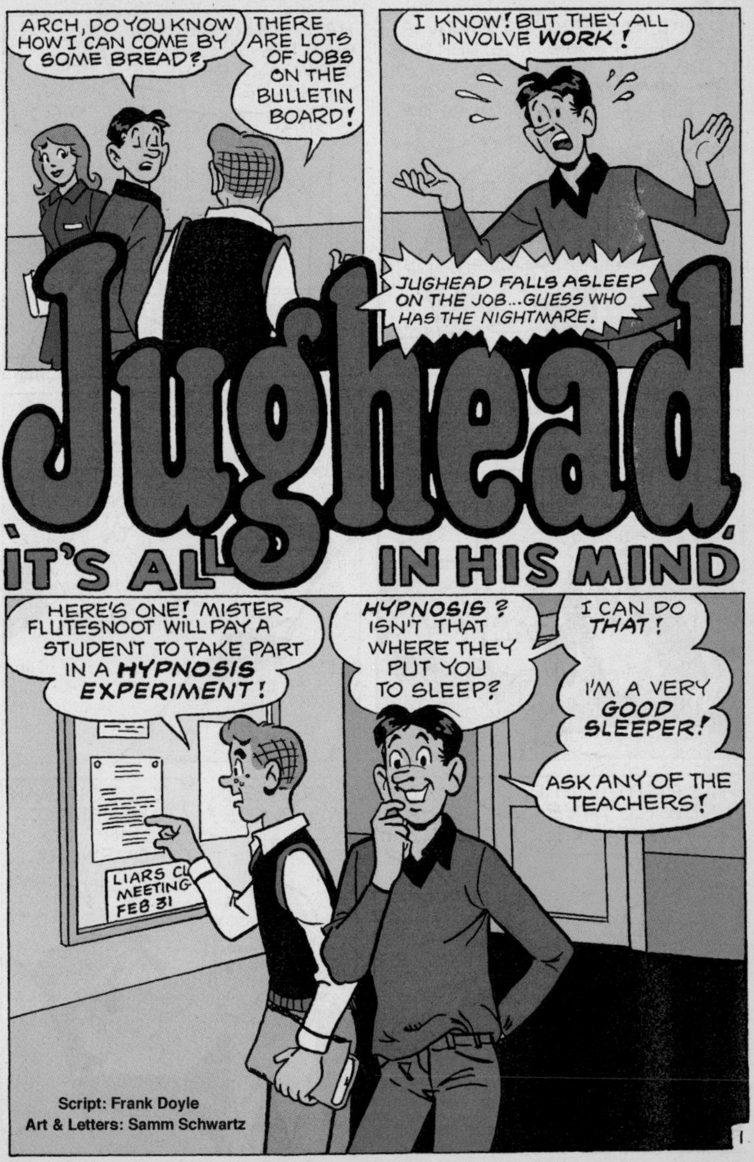
ARCH, DO YOU KNOW HOW I CAN COME BY SOME BREAD?
THERE ARE LOTS OF JOBS ON THE BULLETIN BOARD!
I KNOW! BUT THEY ALL INVOLVE WORK!
JUGHEAD FALLS ASLEEP ON THE JOB...GUESS WHO HAS THE NIGHTMARE.
Jughead
IT'S ALL IN HIS MIND
HERE'S ONE! MISTER FLUTESNOOT WILL PAY A STUDENT TO TAKE PART IN A HYPNOSIS EXPERIMENT!
HYPNOSIS? ISN'T THAT WHERE THEY PUT YOU TO SLEEP?
I CAN DO THAT!
I'M A VERY GOOD SLEEPER!
ASK ANY OF THE TEACHERS!
LIARS CL
MEETING
FEB 31
Script: Frank Doyle
Art & Letters: Samm Schwartz

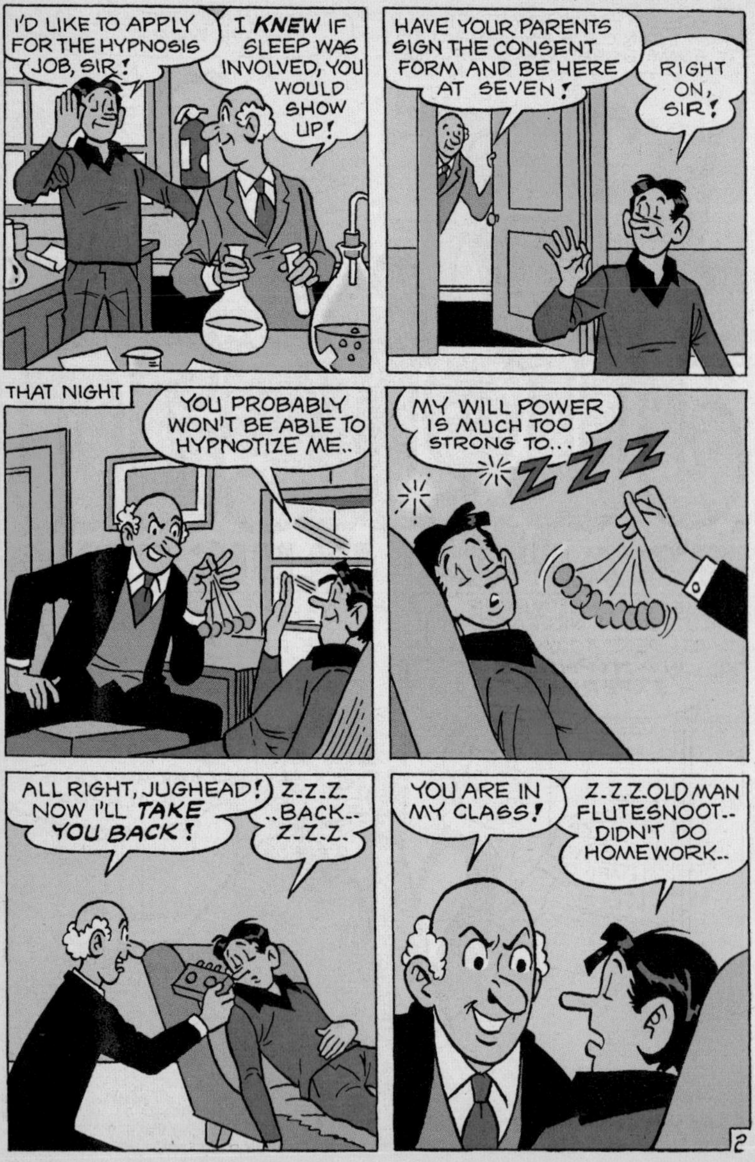

I'D LIKE TO APPLY FOR THE HYPNOSIS JOB, SIR!
I KNEW IF SLEEP WAS INVOLVED, YOU WOULD SHOW UP!
HAVE YOUR PARENTS SIGN THE CONSENT FORM AND BE HERE AT SEVEN!
RIGHT ON, SIR!
THAT NIGHT
YOU PROBABLY WON'T BE ABLE TO HYPNOTIZE ME..
MY WILL POWER IS MUCH TOO STRONG TO...
ZZZ
ALL RIGHT, JUGHEAD! NOW I'LL TAKE YOU BACK!
Z.Z.Z. ..BACK.. Z.Z.Z.
YOU ARE IN MY CLASS!
Z.Z.Z.OLD MAN FLUTESNOOT.. DIDN'T DO HOMEWORK..
2

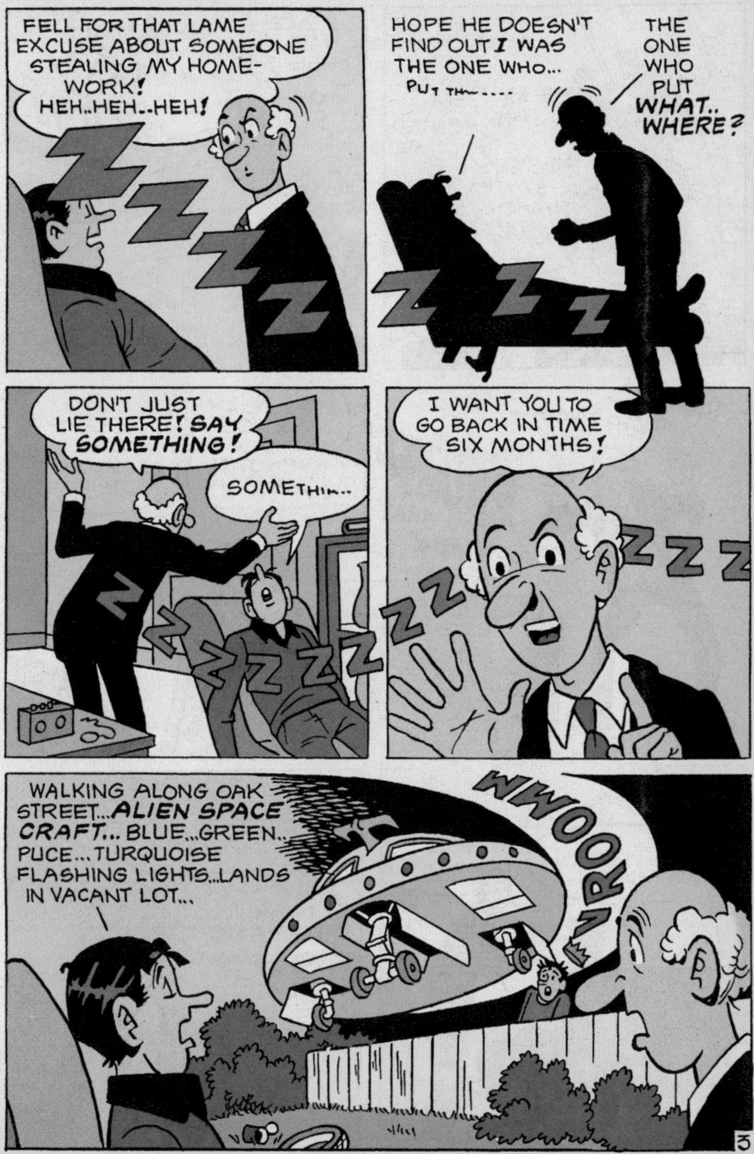

FELL FOR THAT LAME EXCUSE ABOUT SOMEONE STEALING MY HOME-WORK! HEH..HEH..HEH!
HOPE HE DOESN'T FIND OUT **I** WAS THE ONE WHO...
PUT THE....
THE ONE WHO PUT **WHAT.. WHERE?**
DON'T JUST LIE THERE! **SAY SOMETHING!**
SOMETHIN...
I WANT YOU TO GO BACK IN TIME SIX MONTHS!
WALKING ALONG OAK STREET... **ALIEN SPACE CRAFT...** BLUE...GREEN... PUCE... TURQUOISE FLASHING LIGHTS...LANDS IN VACANT LOT...
VROOOMM

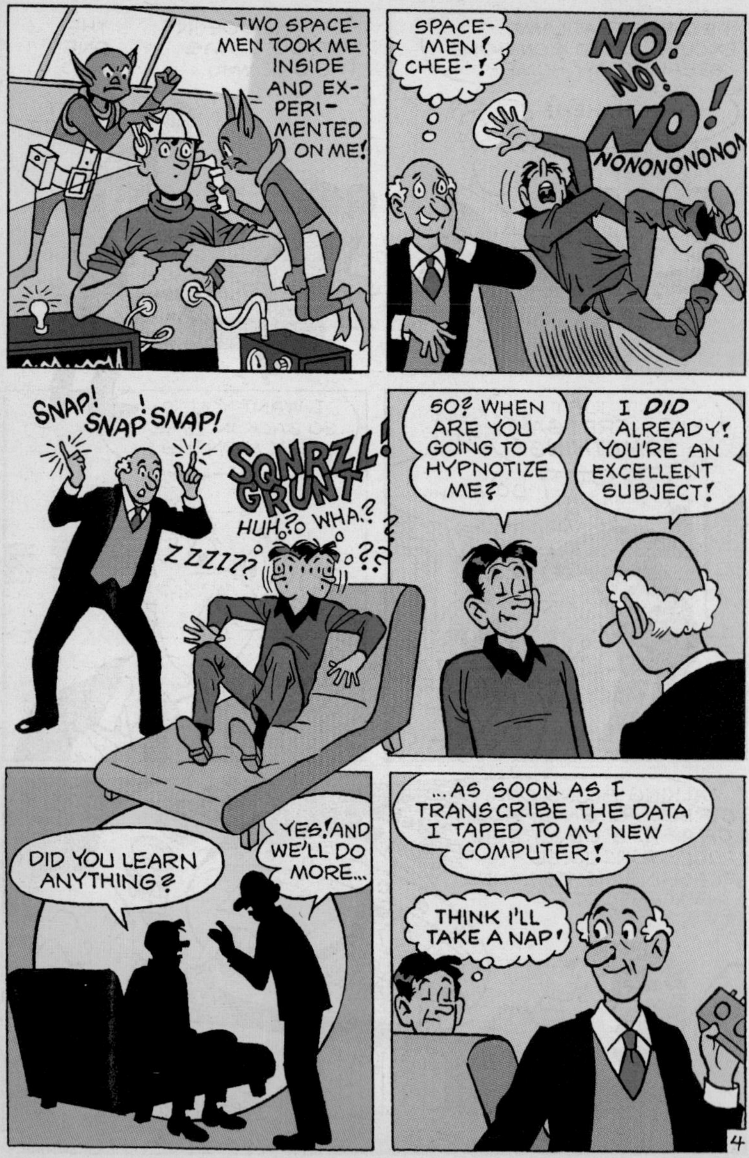
TWO SPACE-MEN TOOK ME INSIDE AND EX-PERI-MENTED ON ME!
SPACE-MEN! CHEE-!
NO! NO! NO!
NONONONONONO
SNAP! SNAP! SNAP!
SQNRZLL! GRUNT
HUH?? WHA??
ZZZZZ??
SO? WHEN ARE YOU GOING TO HYPNOTIZE ME?
I DID ALREADY! YOU'RE AN EXCELLENT SUBJECT!
DID YOU LEARN ANYTHING?
YES! AND WE'LL DO MORE...
...AS SOON AS I TRANSCRIBE THE DATA I TAPED TO MY NEW COMPUTER!
THINK I'LL TAKE A NAP!
4

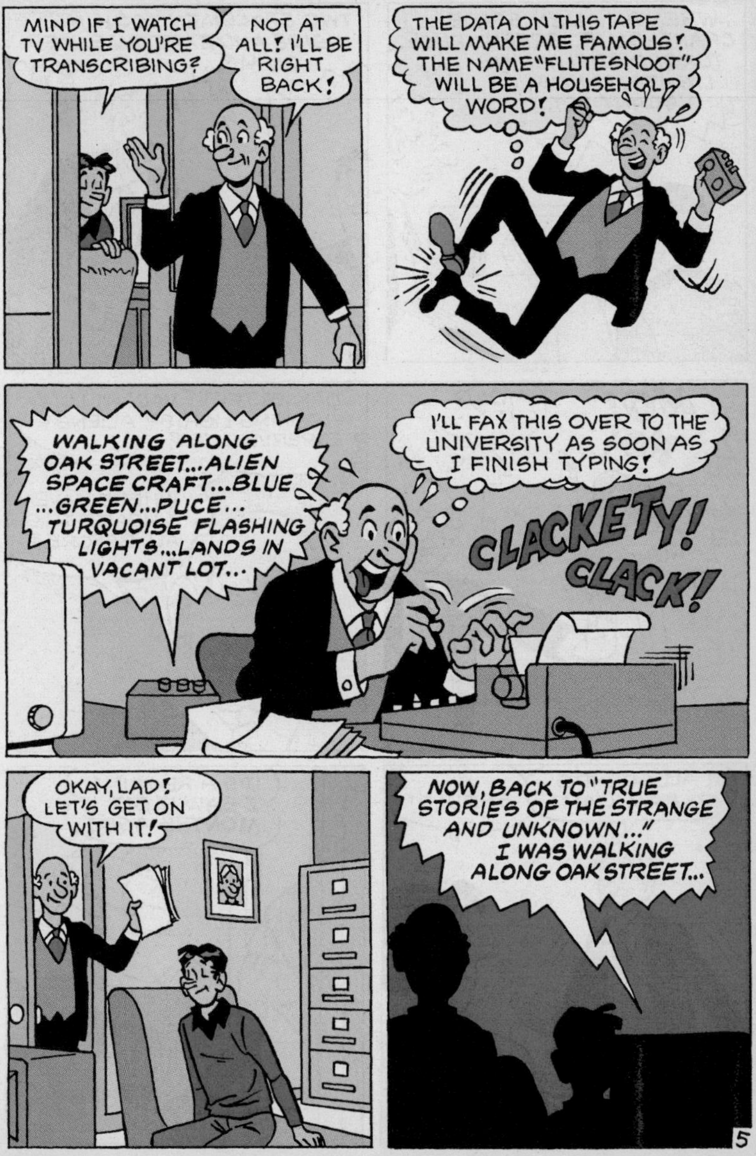
MIND IF I WATCH TV WHILE YOU'RE TRANSCRIBING?
NOT AT ALL! I'LL BE RIGHT BACK!
THE DATA ON THIS TAPE WILL MAKE ME FAMOUS! THE NAME "FLUTESNOOT" WILL BE A HOUSEHOLD WORD!
WALKING ALONG OAK STREET...ALIEN SPACE CRAFT...BLUE ...GREEN...PUCE... TURQUOISE FLASHING LIGHTS...LANDS IN VACANT LOT...
I'LL FAX THIS OVER TO THE UNIVERSITY AS SOON AS I FINISH TYPING!
CLACKETY! CLACK!
OKAY, LAD! LET'S GET ON WITH IT!
NOW, BACK TO "TRUE STORIES OF THE STRANGE AND UNKNOWN..." I WAS WALKING ALONG OAK STREET...

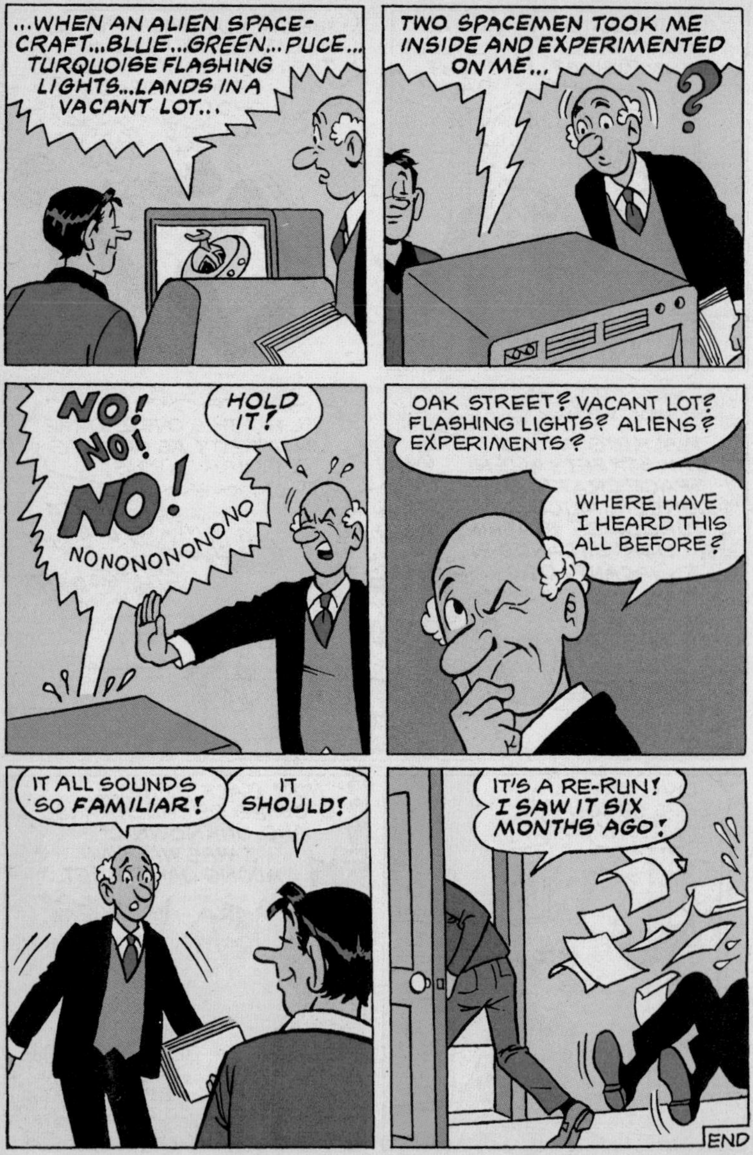

...WHEN AN ALIEN SPACE-CRAFT...BLUE...GREEN...PUCE...TURQUOISE FLASHING LIGHTS...LANDS IN A VACANT LOT...
TWO SPACEMEN TOOK ME INSIDE AND EXPERIMENTED ON ME...
?
NO! NO! NO! NONONONONONONO
HOLD IT!
OAK STREET? VACANT LOT? FLASHING LIGHTS? ALIENS? EXPERIMENTS?
WHERE HAVE I HEARD THIS ALL BEFORE?
IT ALL SOUNDS SO FAMILIAR!
IT SHOULD!
IT'S A RE-RUN! I SAW IT SIX MONTHS AGO!
END

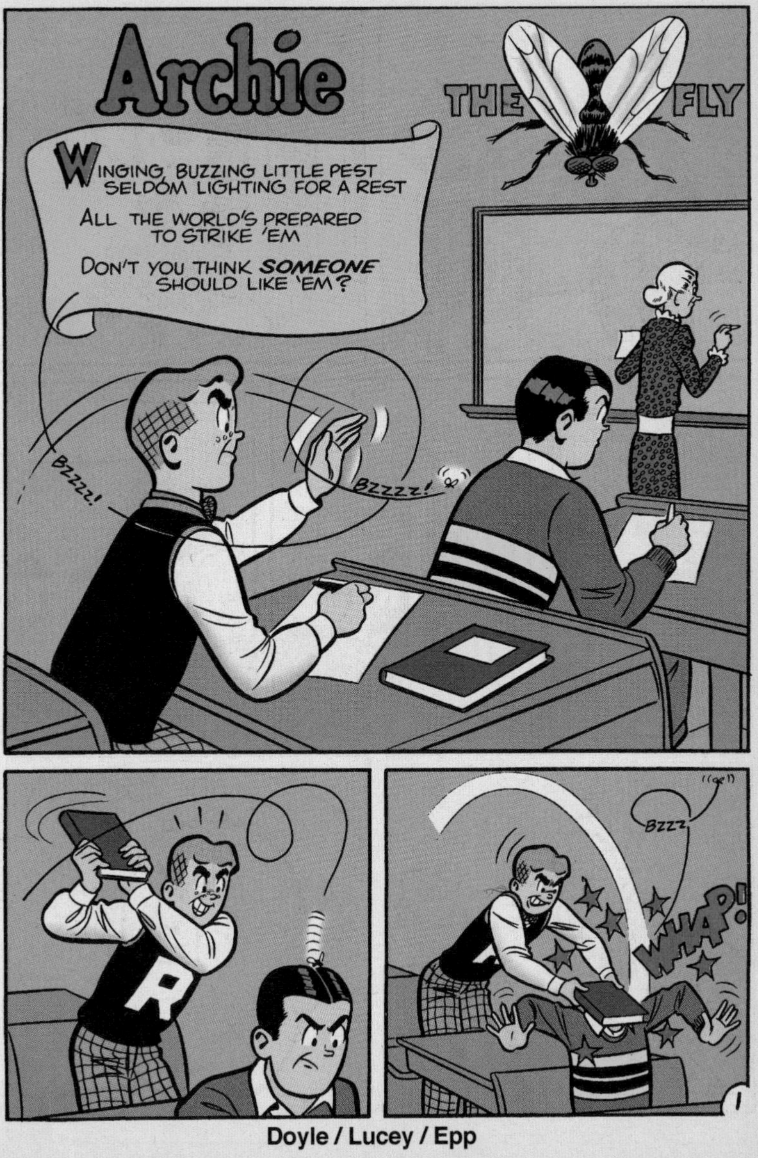
Archie
THE FLY
WINGING, BUZZING LITTLE PEST SELDOM LIGHTING FOR A REST
ALL THE WORLD'S PREPARED TO STRIKE 'EM
DON'T YOU THINK SOMEONE SHOULD LIKE 'EM?
BZZZZZ!
BZZZZ!
BZZZ
WHAP!
1

Doyle / Lucey / Epp

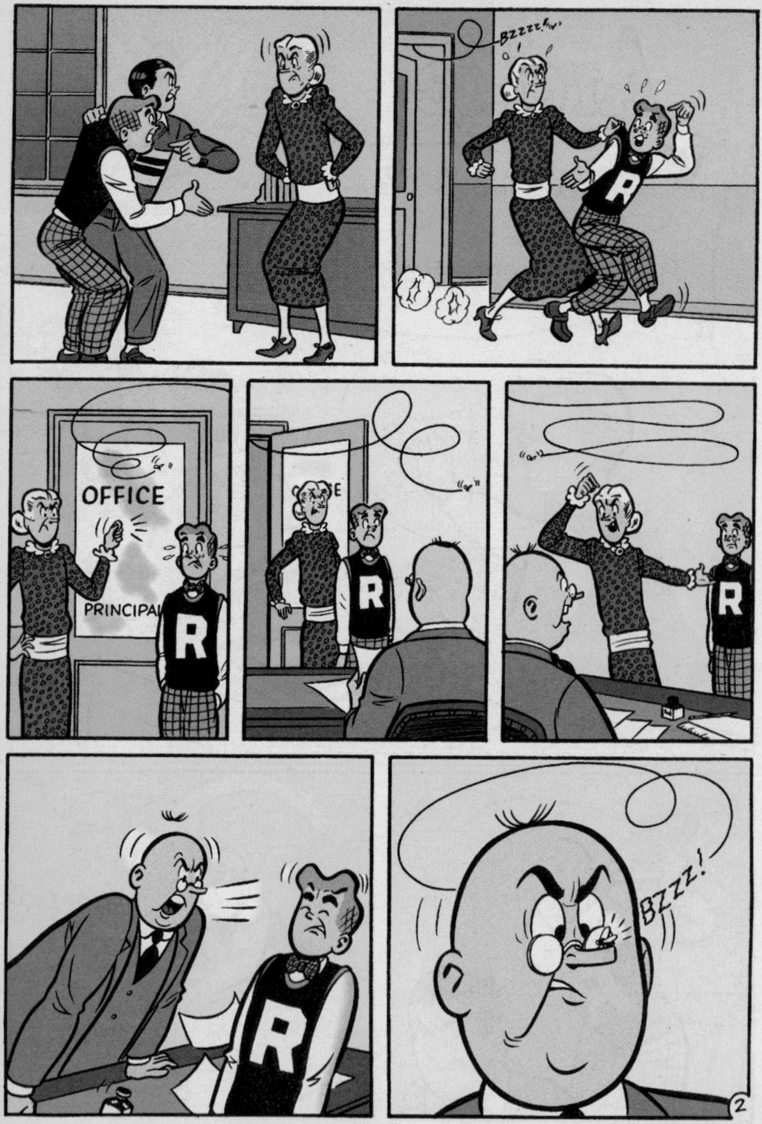
BZZZZ!
OFFICE
PRINCIPAL
BZZZ!
2

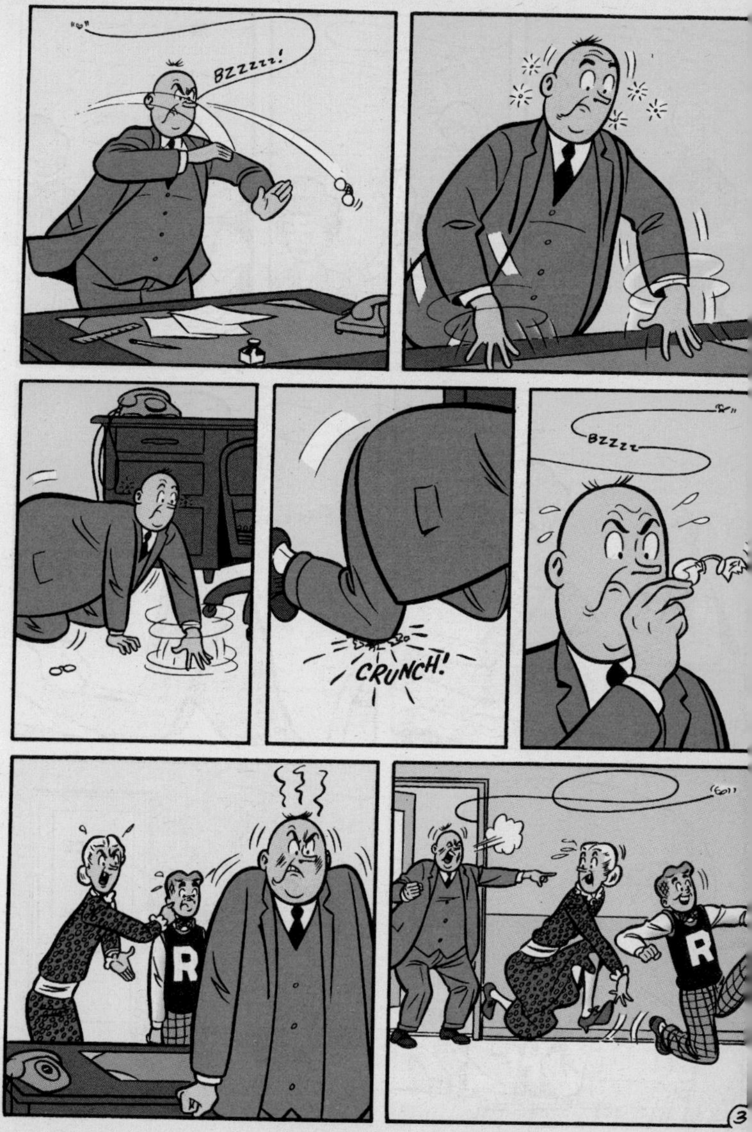
BZZZZZ!
CRUNCH!
BZZZZ

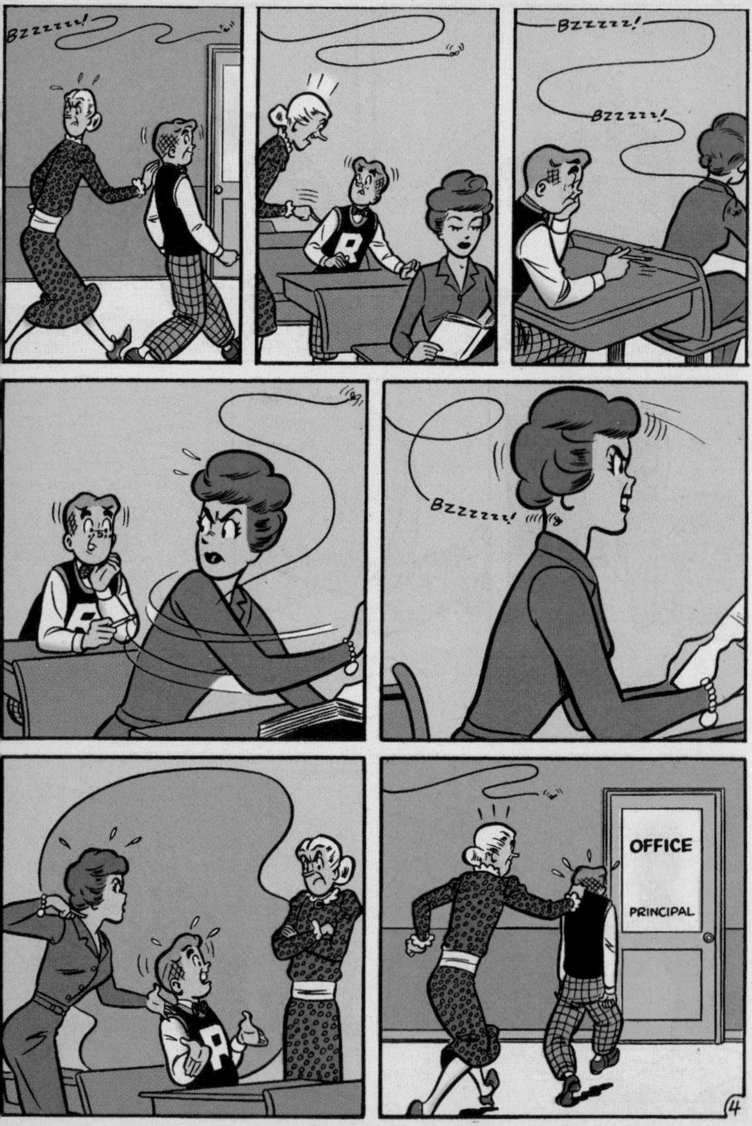
BZZZZZZ!
BZZZZZ!
BZZZZZ!
BZZZZZZZ!
OFFICE
PRINCIPAL
4

Bzzzz

Bzzzz

Bzzzzzz

Bzzzzzz

BZZZZZZZZ

Bzzzzz

THIS, DEAR READER, IS A GIMMICK! ...WATCH IT.

Bzzzzzz

5

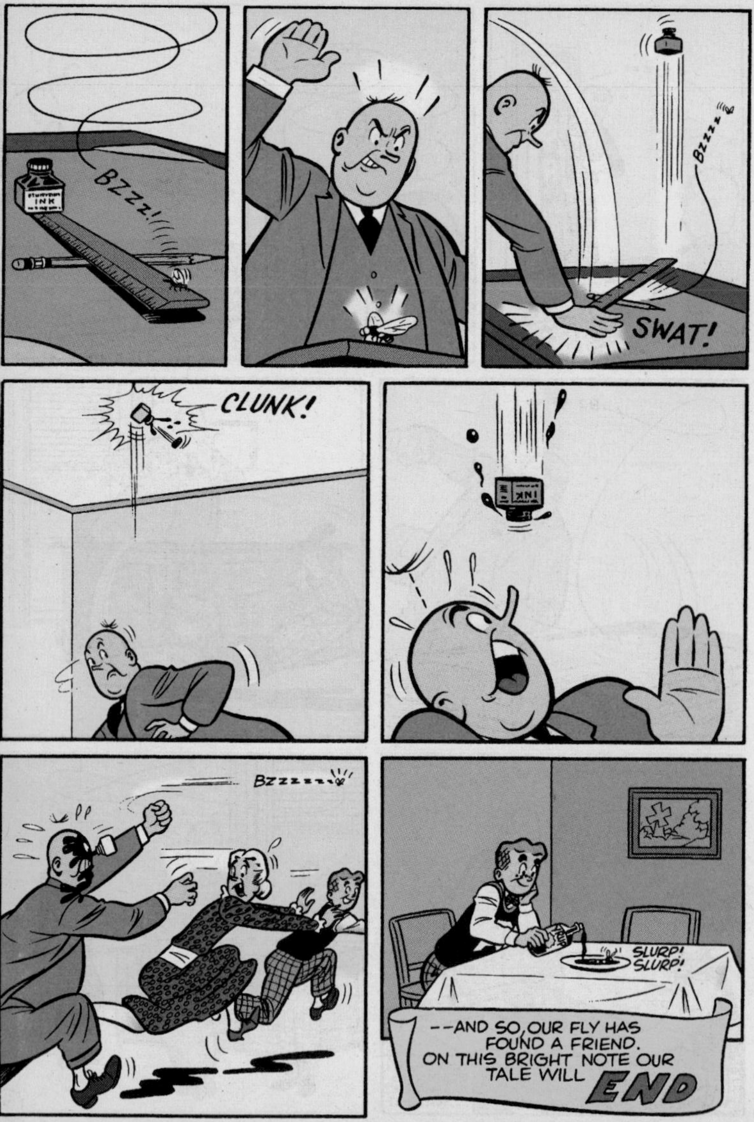
BZZZz!
INK
SWAT!
BZZZZ
CLUNK!
INK
BZZZZZZ
SLURP!
SLURP!
--AND SO, OUR FLY HAS FOUND A FRIEND.
ON THIS BRIGHT NOTE OUR TALE WILL
END

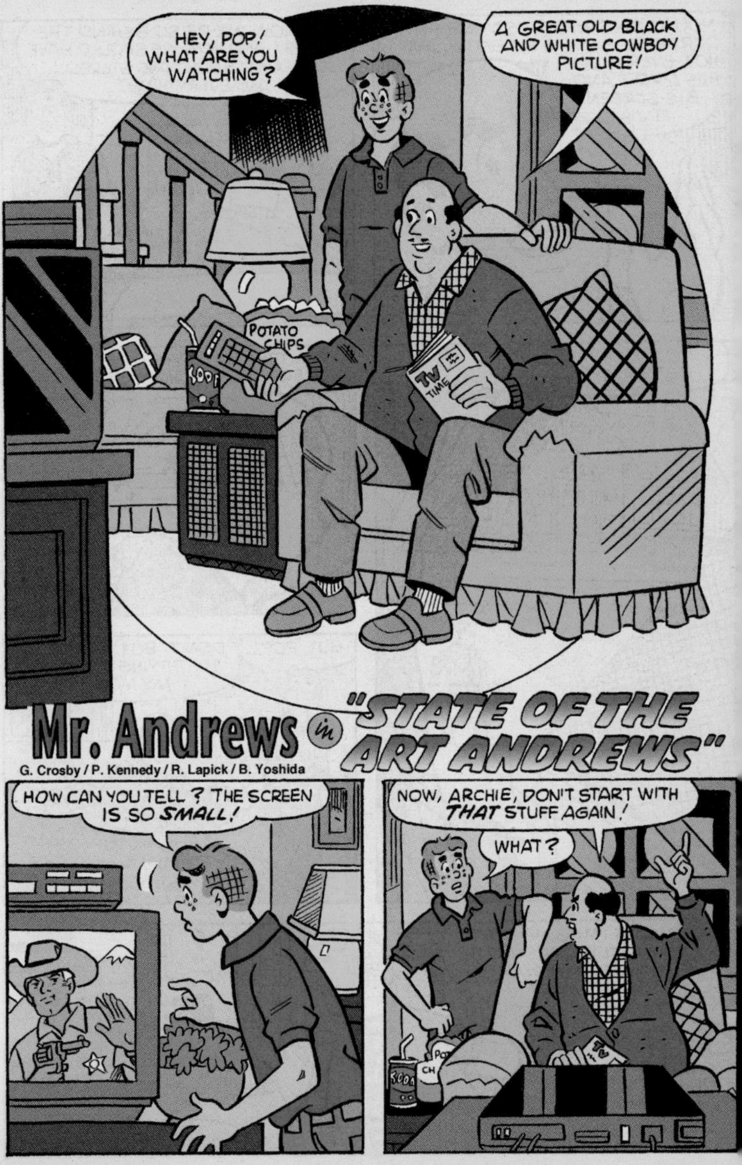
HEY, POP! WHAT ARE YOU WATCHING?
A GREAT OLD BLACK AND WHITE COWBOY PICTURE!
POTATO CHIPS
SODA
TV TIME
Mr. Andrews in "STATE OF THE ART ANDREWS"
G. Crosby / P. Kennedy / R. Lapick / B. Yoshida
HOW CAN YOU TELL? THE SCREEN IS SO SMALL!
NOW, ARCHIE, DON'T START WITH THAT STUFF AGAIN!
WHAT?

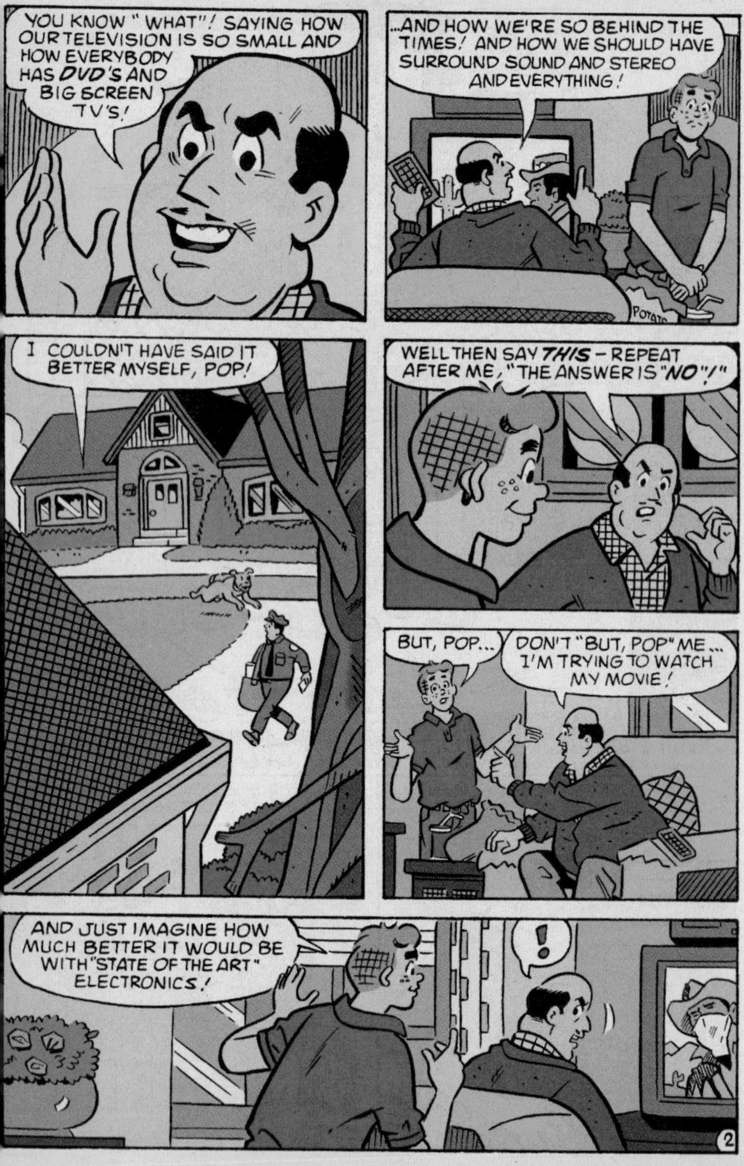
YOU KNOW "WHAT"! SAYING HOW OUR TELEVISION IS SO SMALL AND HOW EVERYBODY HAS DVD'S AND BIG SCREEN TV'S!
...AND HOW WE'RE SO BEHIND THE TIMES! AND HOW WE SHOULD HAVE SURROUND SOUND AND STEREO AND EVERYTHING!
POTATO
I COULDN'T HAVE SAID IT BETTER MYSELF, POP!
WELL THEN SAY THIS – REPEAT AFTER ME, "THE ANSWER IS "NO"!"
BUT, POP...
DON'T "BUT, POP" ME... I'M TRYING TO WATCH MY MOVIE!
AND JUST IMAGINE HOW MUCH BETTER IT WOULD BE WITH "STATE OF THE ART" ELECTRONICS!
!
2

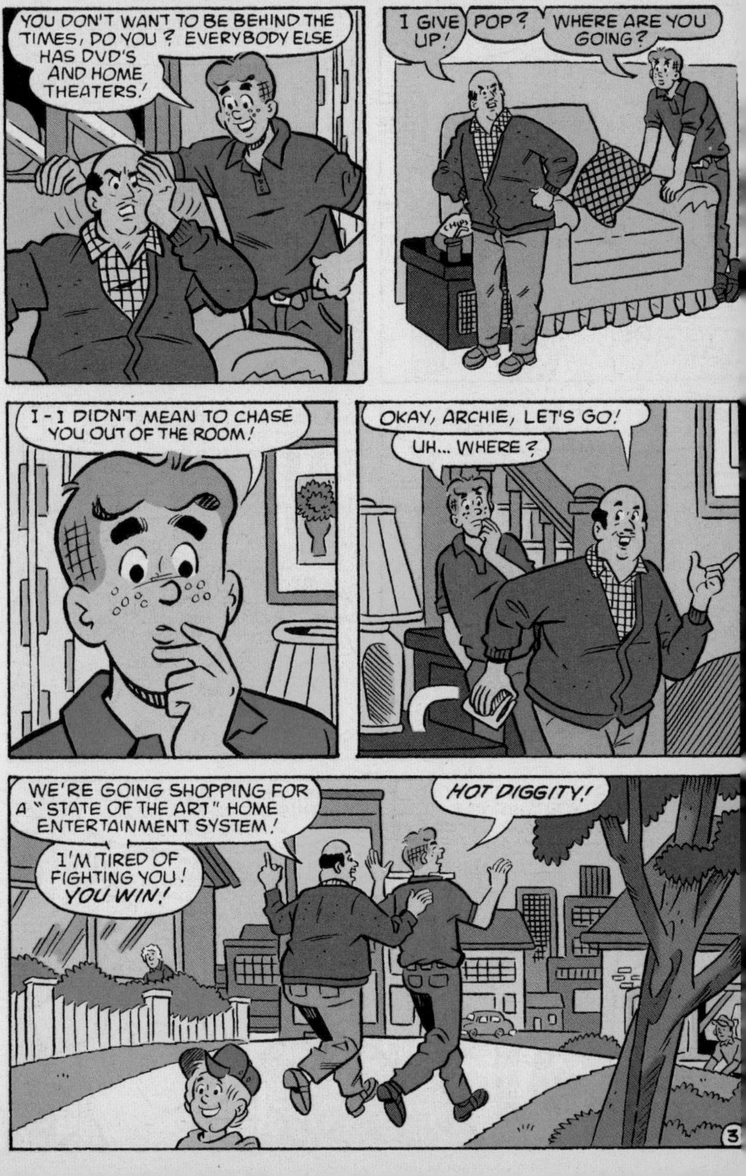
YOU DON'T WANT TO BE BEHIND THE TIMES, DO YOU? EVERYBODY ELSE HAS DVD'S AND HOME THEATERS!
I GIVE UP!
POP?
WHERE ARE YOU GOING?
I-I DIDN'T MEAN TO CHASE YOU OUT OF THE ROOM!
OKAY, ARCHIE, LET'S GO!
UH... WHERE?
WE'RE GOING SHOPPING FOR A "STATE OF THE ART" HOME ENTERTAINMENT SYSTEM!
I'M TIRED OF FIGHTING YOU! YOU WIN!
HOT DIGGITY!
CHIPS
3

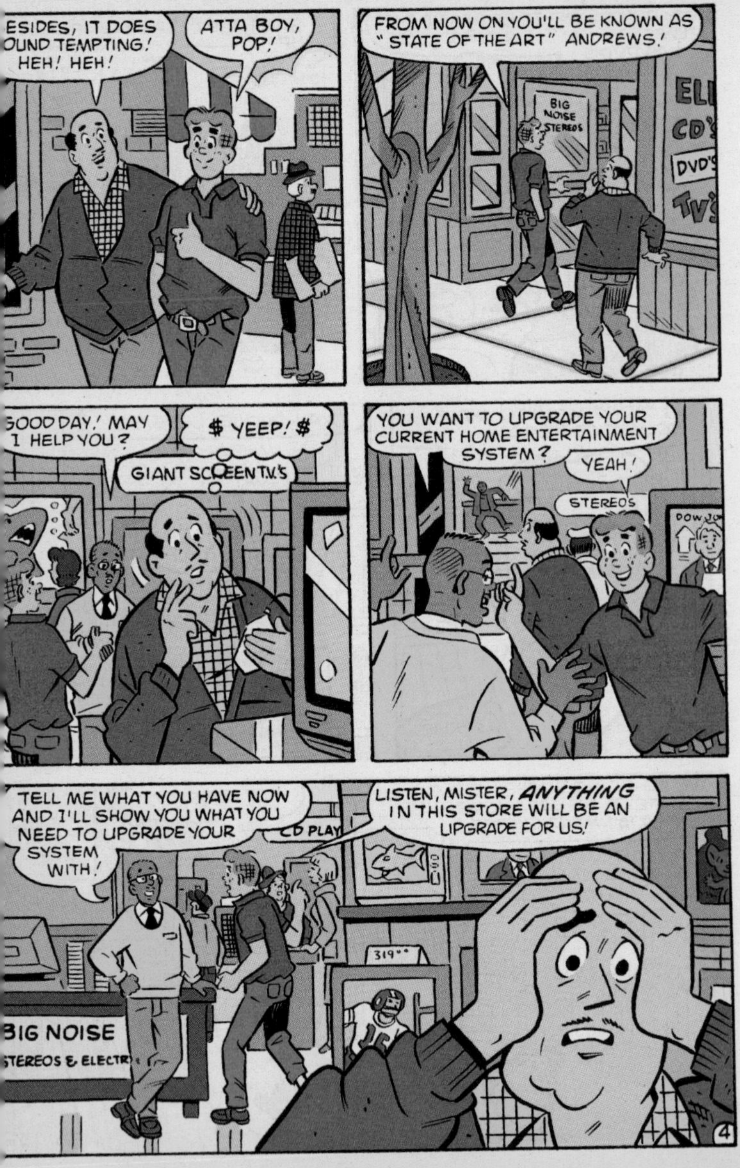
ESIDES, IT DOES OUND TEMPTING! HEH! HEH!
ATTA BOY, POP!
FROM NOW ON YOU'LL BE KNOWN AS "STATE OF THE ART" ANDREWS!
BIG NOISE STEREOS
CD'S
DVD'S
TV'S
GOOD DAY! MAY I HELP YOU?
$ YEEP! $
GIANT SCREEN T.V.'S
YOU WANT TO UPGRADE YOUR CURRENT HOME ENTERTAINMENT SYSTEM?
YEAH!
STEREOS
TELL ME WHAT YOU HAVE NOW AND I'LL SHOW YOU WHAT YOU NEED TO UPGRADE YOUR SYSTEM WITH!
LISTEN, MISTER, ANYTHING IN THIS STORE WILL BE AN UPGRADE FOR US!
CD PLAY
319
BIG NOISE
STEREOS & ELECTR
4

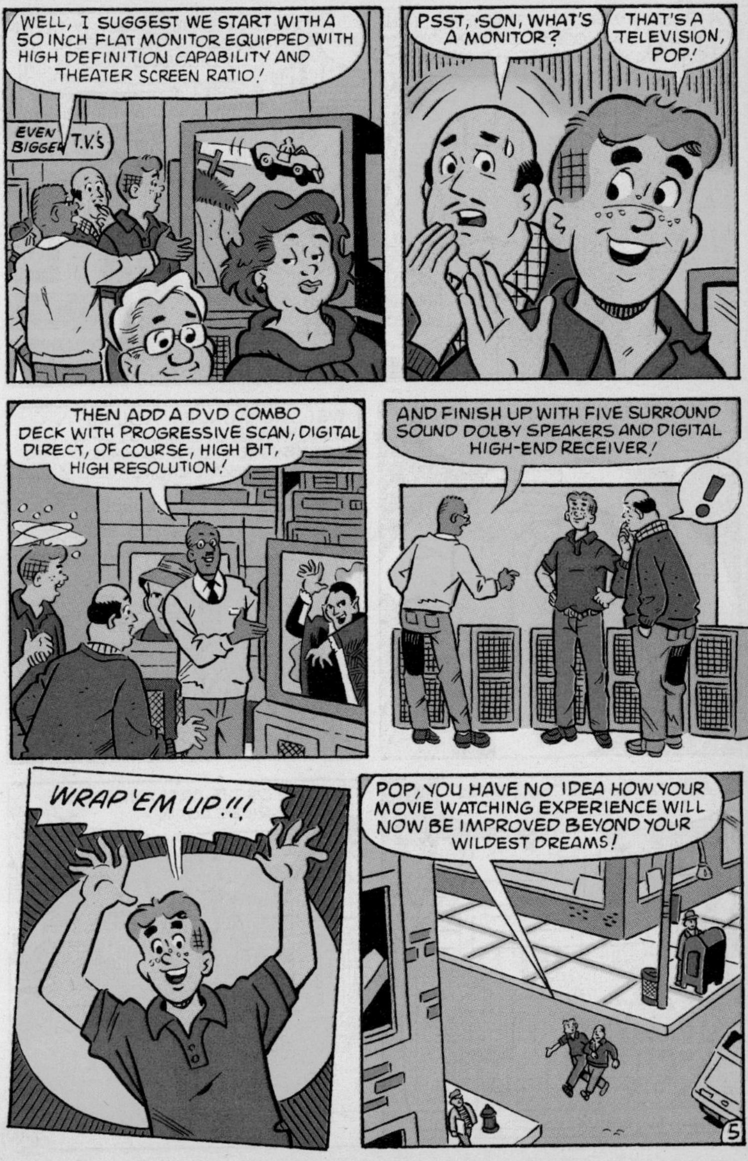
WELL, I SUGGEST WE START WITH A 50 INCH FLAT MONITOR EQUIPPED WITH HIGH DEFINITION CAPABILITY AND THEATER SCREEN RATIO!
EVEN BIGGER T.V.'S
PSST, SON, WHAT'S A MONITOR?
THAT'S A TELEVISION, POP!
THEN ADD A DVD COMBO DECK WITH PROGRESSIVE SCAN, DIGITAL DIRECT, OF COURSE, HIGH BIT, HIGH RESOLUTION!
AND FINISH UP WITH FIVE SURROUND SOUND DOLBY SPEAKERS AND DIGITAL HIGH-END RECEIVER!
!
WRAP 'EM UP!!!
POP, YOU HAVE NO IDEA HOW YOUR MOVIE WATCHING EXPERIENCE WILL NOW BE IMPROVED BEYOND YOUR WILDEST DREAMS!
5

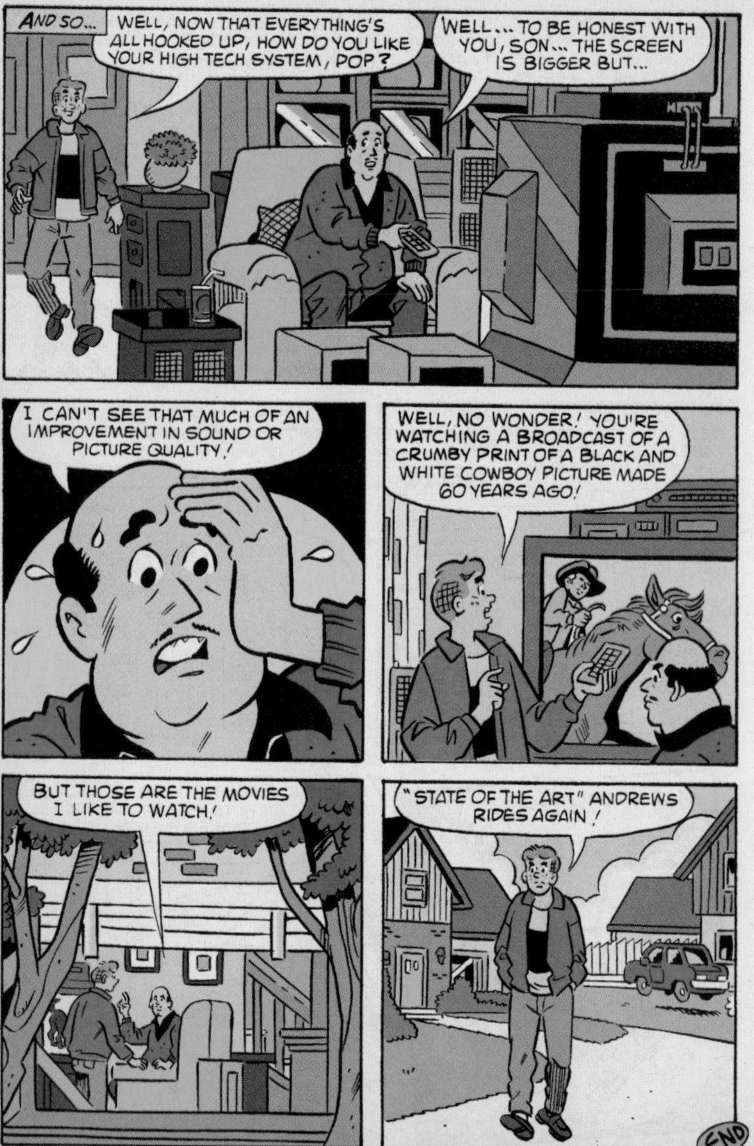
AND SO...
WELL, NOW THAT EVERYTHING'S ALL HOOKED UP, HOW DO YOU LIKE YOUR HIGH TECH SYSTEM, POP?
WELL... TO BE HONEST WITH YOU, SON... THE SCREEN IS BIGGER BUT...
I CAN'T SEE THAT MUCH OF AN IMPROVEMENT IN SOUND OR PICTURE QUALITY!
WELL, NO WONDER! YOU'RE WATCHING A BROADCAST OF A CRUMBY PRINT OF A BLACK AND WHITE COWBOY PICTURE MADE 60 YEARS AGO!
BUT THOSE ARE THE MOVIES I LIKE TO WATCH!
"STATE OF THE ART" ANDREWS RIDES AGAIN!
END

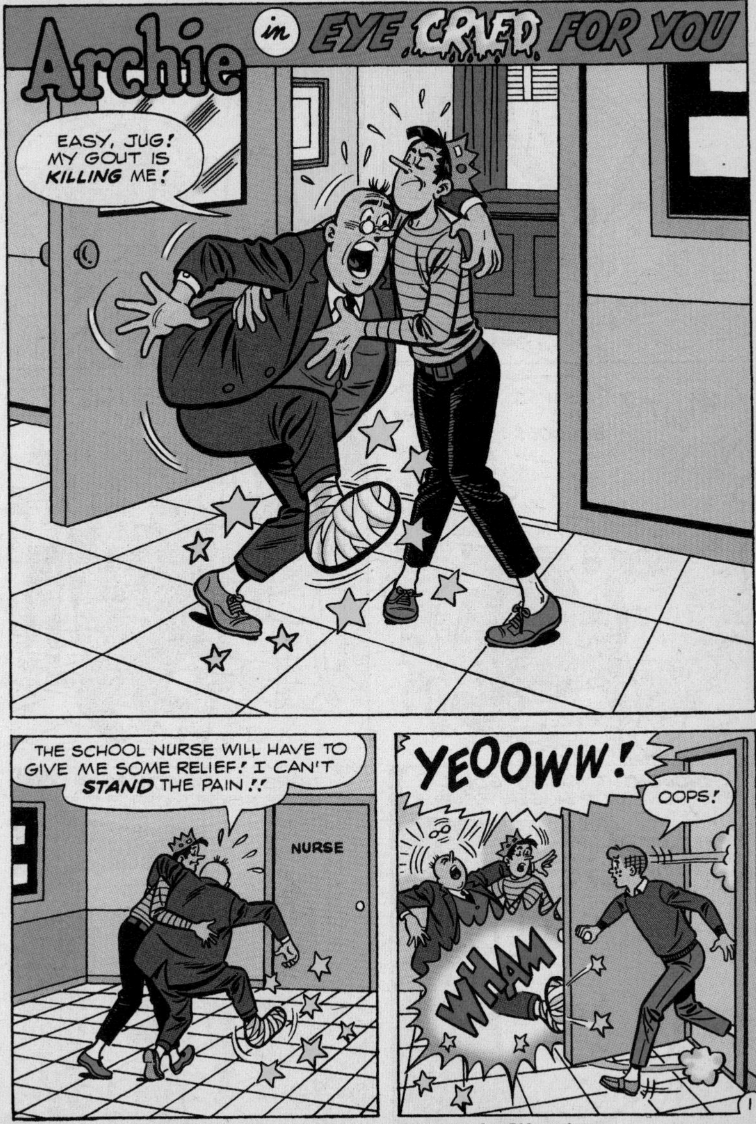
Archie
in
EYE CRIED FOR YOU
EASY, JUG! MY GOUT IS KILLING ME!
THE SCHOOL NURSE WILL HAVE TO GIVE ME SOME RELIEF! I CAN'T STAND THE PAIN!!
NURSE
YEOOWW!
OOPS!
WHAM
1

Script & Pencils: Al Hartley / Inks & Letters: Jon D'Agostino

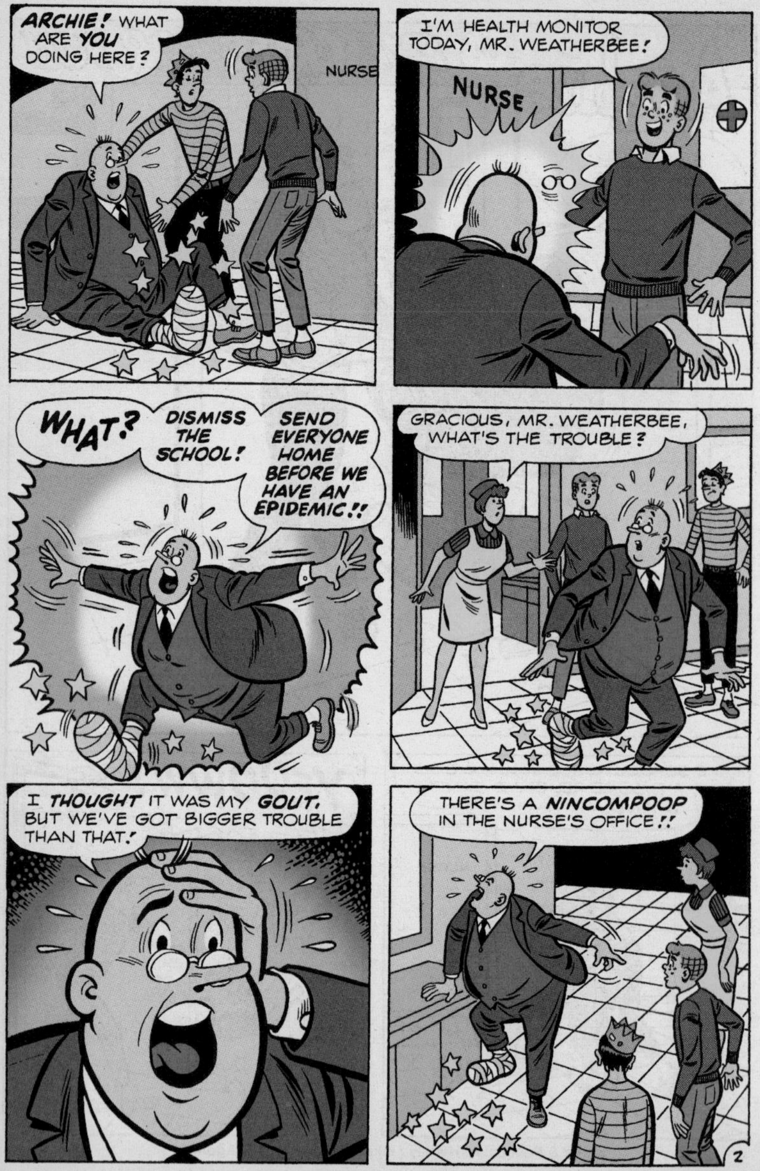
ARCHIE! WHAT ARE YOU DOING HERE?
NURSE
I'M HEALTH MONITOR TODAY, MR. WEATHERBEE!
NURSE
WHAT?
DISMISS THE SCHOOL!
SEND EVERYONE HOME BEFORE WE HAVE AN EPIDEMIC!!
GRACIOUS, MR. WEATHERBEE, WHAT'S THE TROUBLE?
I THOUGHT IT WAS MY GOUT, BUT WE'VE GOT BIGGER TROUBLE THAN THAT!
THERE'S A NINCOMPOOP IN THE NURSE'S OFFICE!!
2

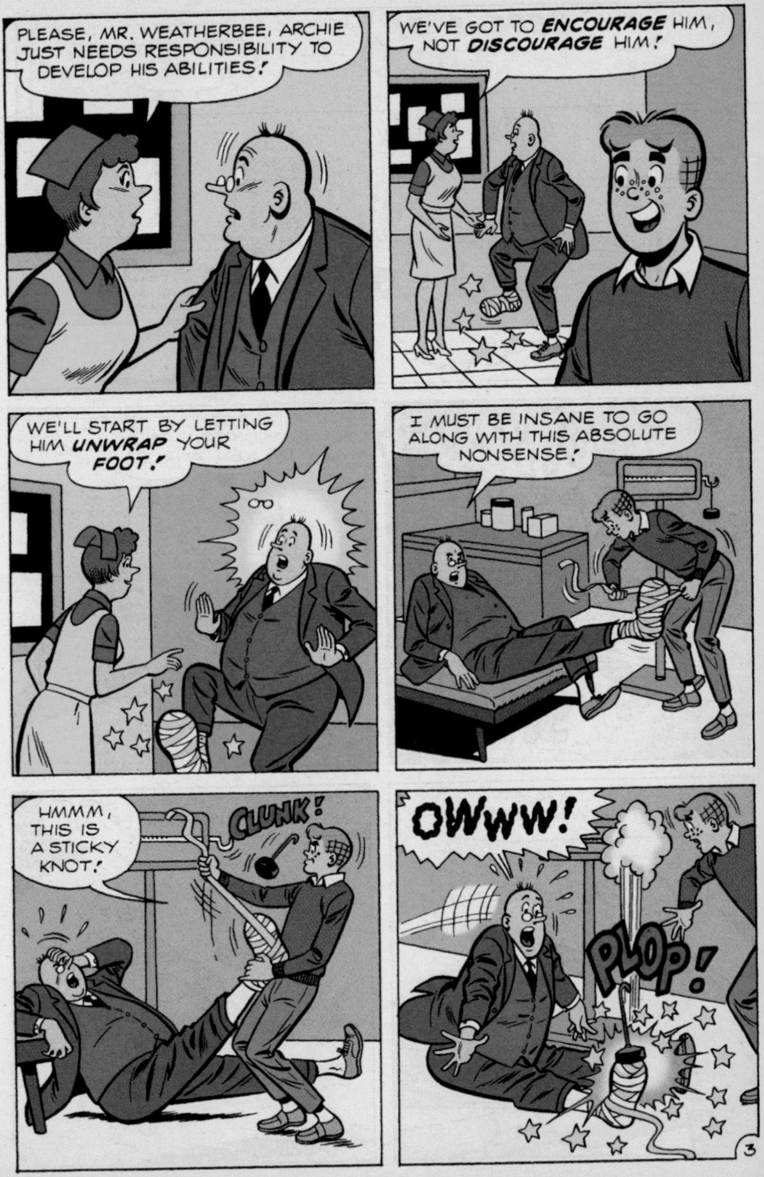
PLEASE, MR. WEATHERBEE, ARCHIE JUST NEEDS RESPONSIBILITY TO DEVELOP HIS ABILITIES!
WE'VE GOT TO ENCOURAGE HIM, NOT DISCOURAGE HIM!
WE'LL START BY LETTING HIM UNWRAP YOUR FOOT!
I MUST BE INSANE TO GO ALONG WITH THIS ABSOLUTE NONSENSE!
HMMM, THIS IS A STICKY KNOT!
CLUNK!
OWWW!
PLOP!
3

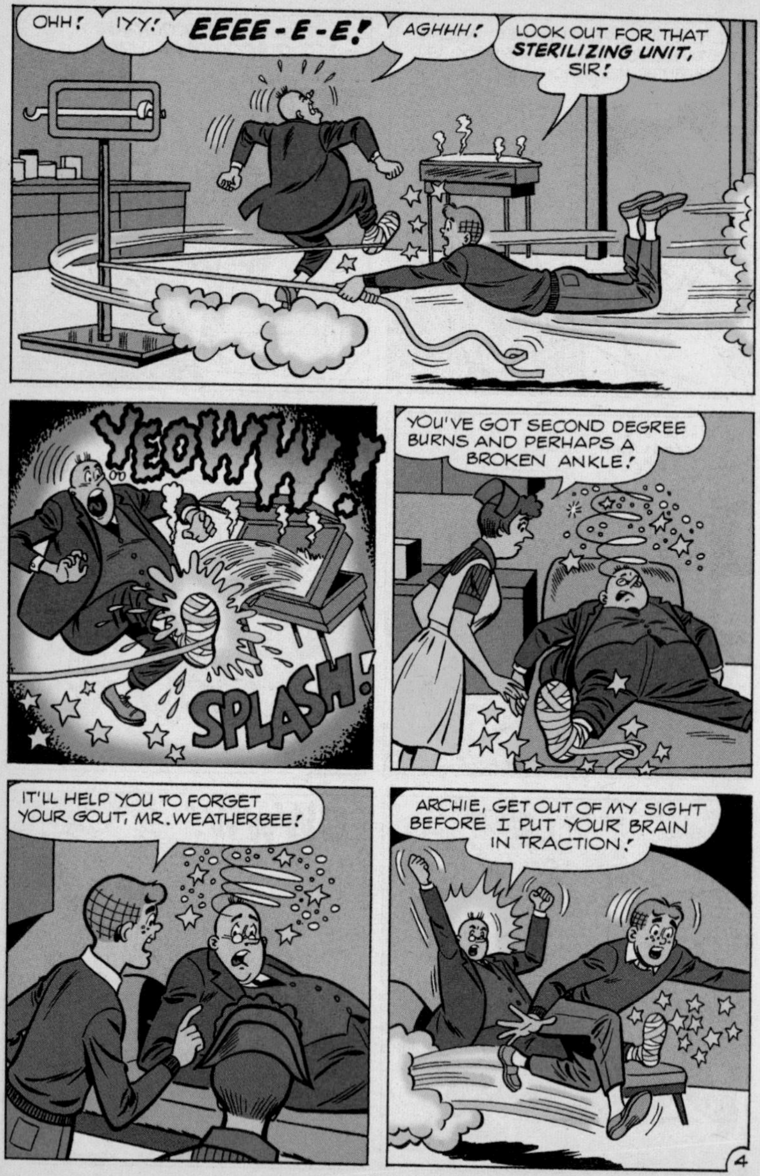
OHH!
IYY!
EEEE-E-E!
AGHHH!
LOOK OUT FOR THAT STERILIZING UNIT, SIR!
YEOWW!
SPLASH!
YOU'VE GOT SECOND DEGREE BURNS AND PERHAPS A BROKEN ANKLE!
IT'LL HELP YOU TO FORGET YOUR GOUT, MR. WEATHERBEE!
ARCHIE, GET OUT OF MY SIGHT BEFORE I PUT YOUR BRAIN IN TRACTION!
4

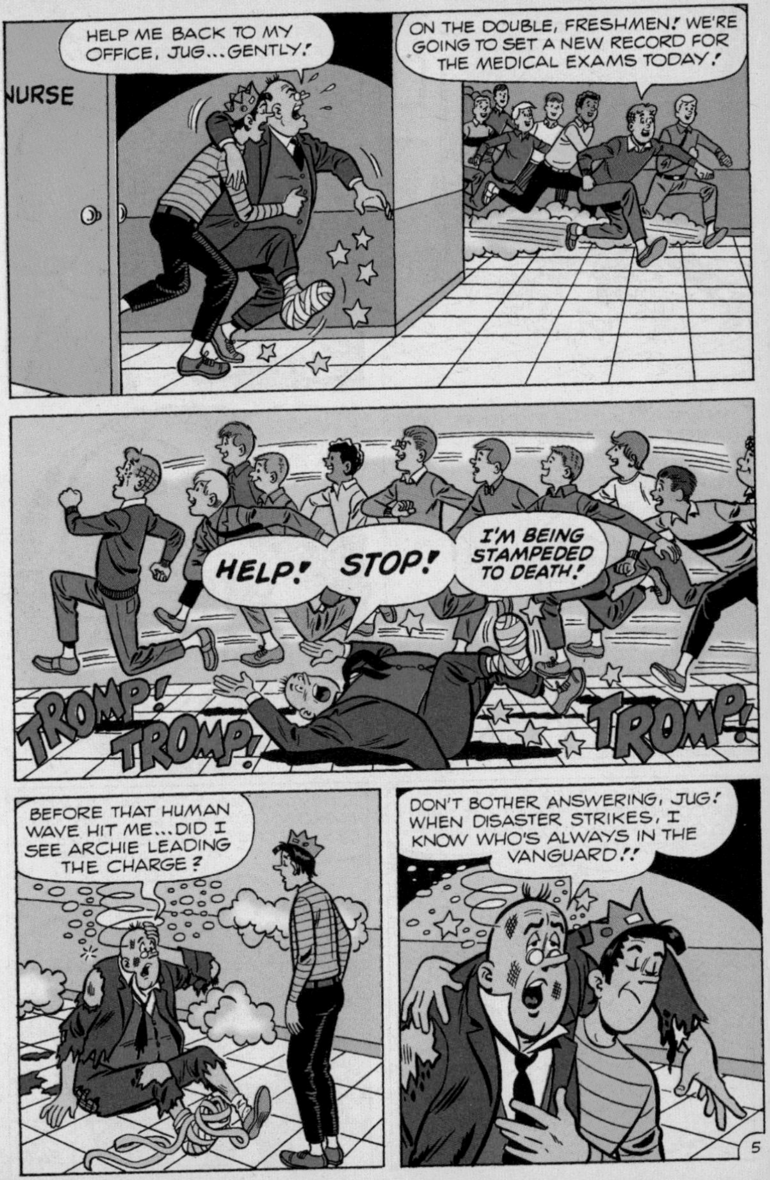
HELP ME BACK TO MY OFFICE, JUG...GENTLY!
NURSE
ON THE DOUBLE, FRESHMEN! WE'RE GOING TO SET A NEW RECORD FOR THE MEDICAL EXAMS TODAY!
HELP!
STOP!
I'M BEING STAMPEDED TO DEATH!
TROMP!
TROMP!
TROMP!
BEFORE THAT HUMAN WAVE HIT ME...DID I SEE ARCHIE LEADING THE CHARGE?
DON'T BOTHER ANSWERING, JUG! WHEN DISASTER STRIKES, I KNOW WHO'S ALWAYS IN THE VANGUARD!!

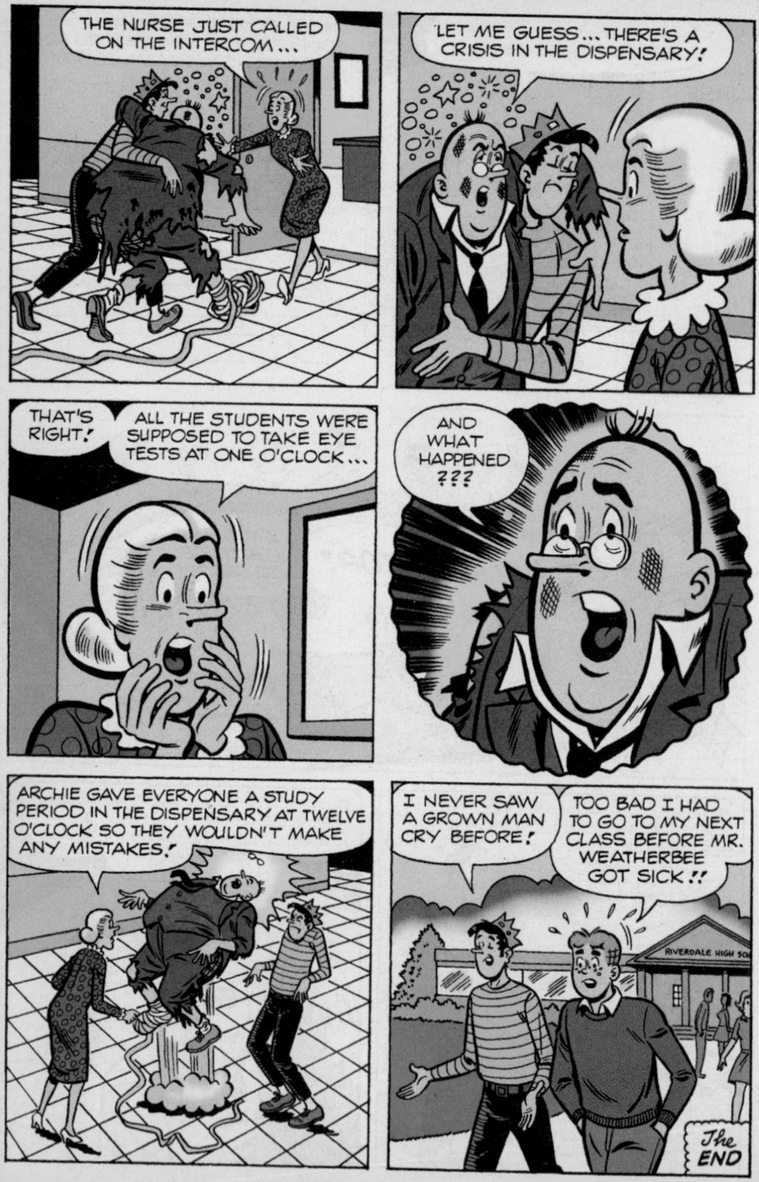
THE NURSE JUST CALLED ON THE INTERCOM...
LET ME GUESS... THERE'S A CRISIS IN THE DISPENSARY!
THAT'S RIGHT!
ALL THE STUDENTS WERE SUPPOSED TO TAKE EYE TESTS AT ONE O'CLOCK...
AND WHAT HAPPENED ???
ARCHIE GAVE EVERYONE A STUDY PERIOD IN THE DISPENSARY AT TWELVE O'CLOCK SO THEY WOULDN'T MAKE ANY MISTAKES!
I NEVER SAW A GROWN MAN CRY BEFORE!
TOO BAD I HAD TO GO TO MY NEXT CLASS BEFORE MR. WEATHERBEE GOT SICK!!
RIVERDALE HIGH SCH
The END

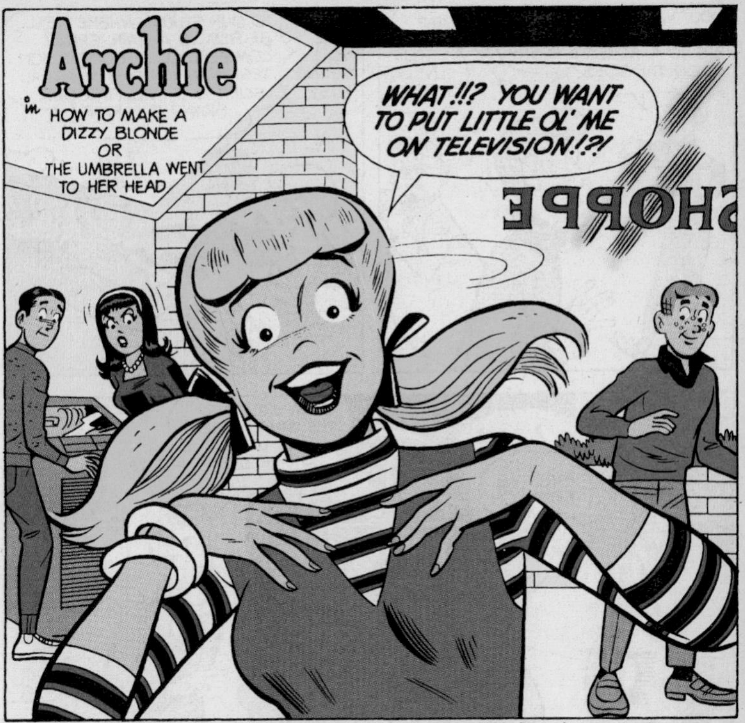
Archie
in HOW TO MAKE A DIZZY BLONDE OR THE UMBRELLA WENT TO HER HEAD
WHAT!!? YOU WANT TO PUT LITTLE OL' ME ON TELEVISION!?!

Script & Pencils: Bob Bolling / Inks & Letters: Mario Acquaviva

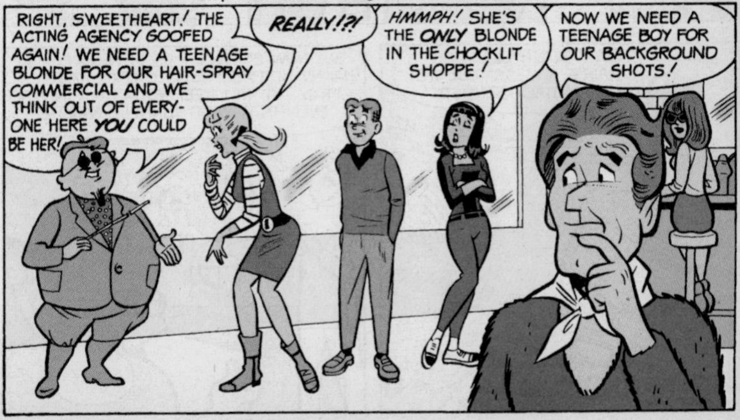
RIGHT, SWEETHEART! THE ACTING AGENCY GOOFED AGAIN! WE NEED A TEENAGE BLONDE FOR OUR HAIR-SPRAY COMMERCIAL AND WE THINK OUT OF EVERY-ONE HERE YOU COULD BE HER!
REALLY!?!
HMMPH! SHE'S THE ONLY BLONDE IN THE CHOCKLIT SHOPPE!
NOW WE NEED A TEENAGE BOY FOR OUR BACKGROUND SHOTS!

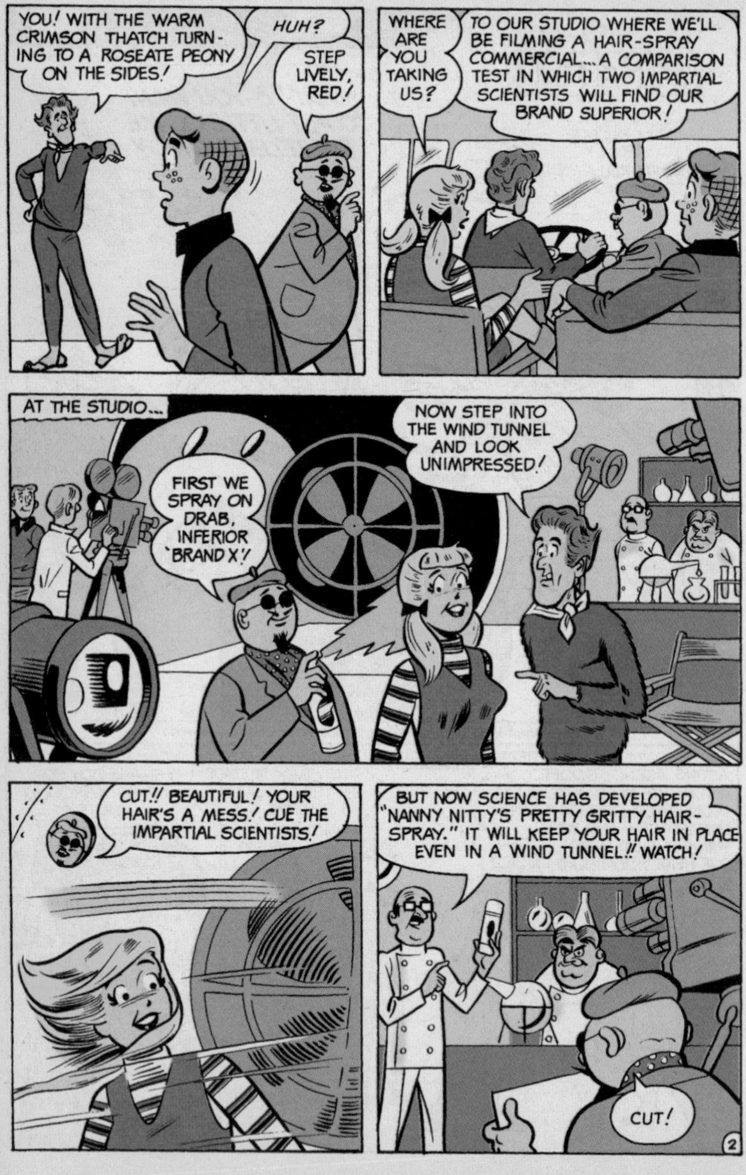

YOU! WITH THE WARM CRIMSON THATCH TURNING TO A ROSEATE PEONY ON THE SIDES!
HUH?
STEP LIVELY, RED!
WHERE ARE YOU TAKING US?
TO OUR STUDIO WHERE WE'LL BE FILMING A HAIR-SPRAY COMMERCIAL... A COMPARISON TEST IN WHICH TWO IMPARTIAL SCIENTISTS WILL FIND OUR BRAND SUPERIOR!
AT THE STUDIO...
FIRST WE SPRAY ON DRAB, INFERIOR 'BRAND X'!
NOW STEP INTO THE WIND TUNNEL AND LOOK UNIMPRESSED!
CUT!! BEAUTIFUL! YOUR HAIR'S A MESS! CUE THE IMPARTIAL SCIENTISTS!
BUT NOW SCIENCE HAS DEVELOPED "NANNY NITTY'S PRETTY GRITTY HAIR-SPRAY." IT WILL KEEP YOUR HAIR IN PLACE EVEN IN A WIND TUNNEL!! WATCH!
CUT!
2

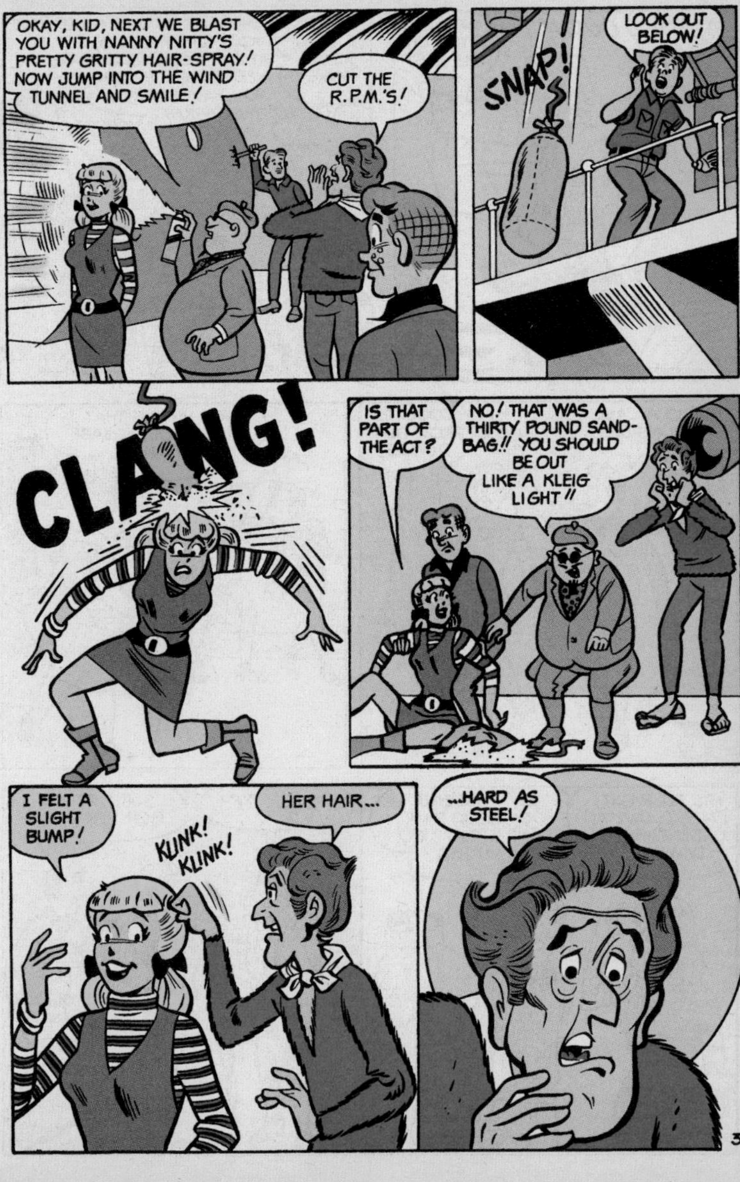
OKAY, KID, NEXT WE BLAST YOU WITH NANNY NITTY'S PRETTY GRITTY HAIR-SPRAY! NOW JUMP INTO THE WIND TUNNEL AND SMILE!
CUT THE R.P.M.'S!
LOOK OUT BELOW!
SNAP!
CLANG!
IS THAT PART OF THE ACT?
NO! THAT WAS A THIRTY POUND SAND-BAG!! YOU SHOULD BE OUT LIKE A KLEIG LIGHT!!
I FELT A SLIGHT BUMP!
HER HAIR...
KLINK! KLINK!
...HARD AS STEEL!

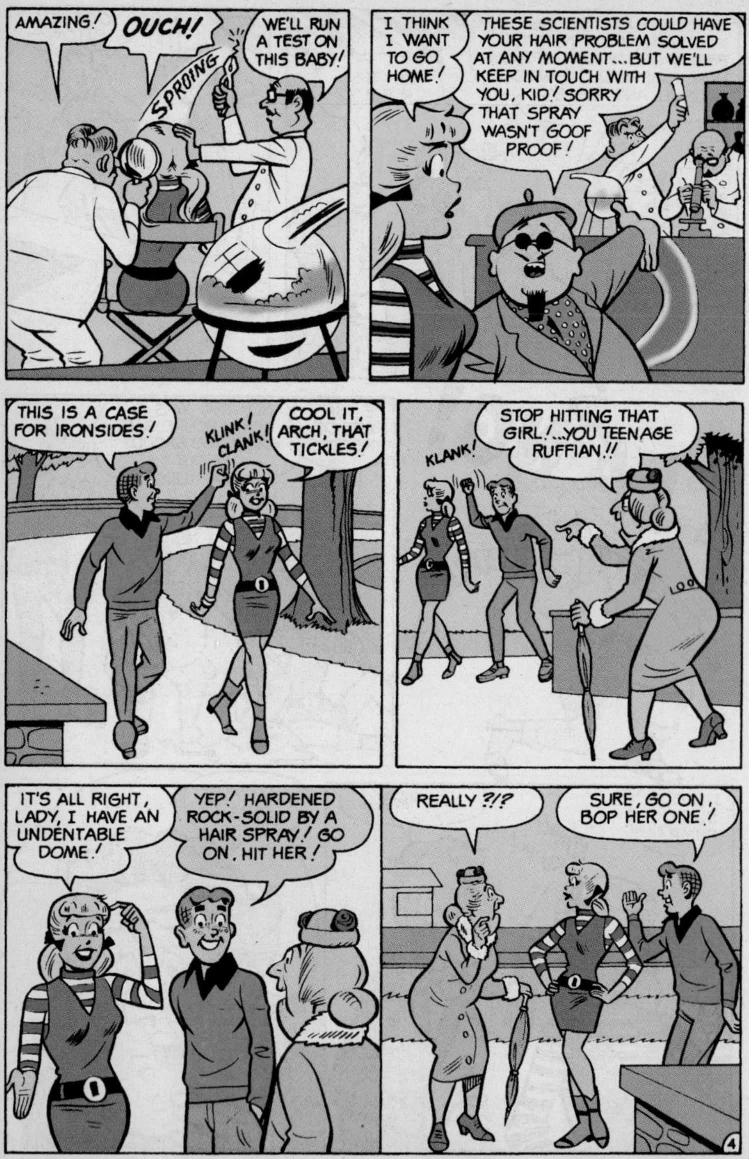
AMAZING!
OUCH!
SPROING
WE'LL RUN A TEST ON THIS BABY!
I THINK I WANT TO GO HOME!
THESE SCIENTISTS COULD HAVE YOUR HAIR PROBLEM SOLVED AT ANY MOMENT... BUT WE'LL KEEP IN TOUCH WITH YOU, KID! SORRY THAT SPRAY WASN'T GOOF PROOF!
THIS IS A CASE FOR IRONSIDES!
KLINK! CLANK!
COOL IT, ARCH, THAT TICKLES!
KLANK!
STOP HITTING THAT GIRL!...YOU TEENAGE RUFFIAN!!
IT'S ALL RIGHT, LADY, I HAVE AN UNDENTABLE DOME!
YEP! HARDENED ROCK-SOLID BY A HAIR SPRAY! GO ON, HIT HER!
REALLY?!?
SURE, GO ON, BOP HER ONE!
4

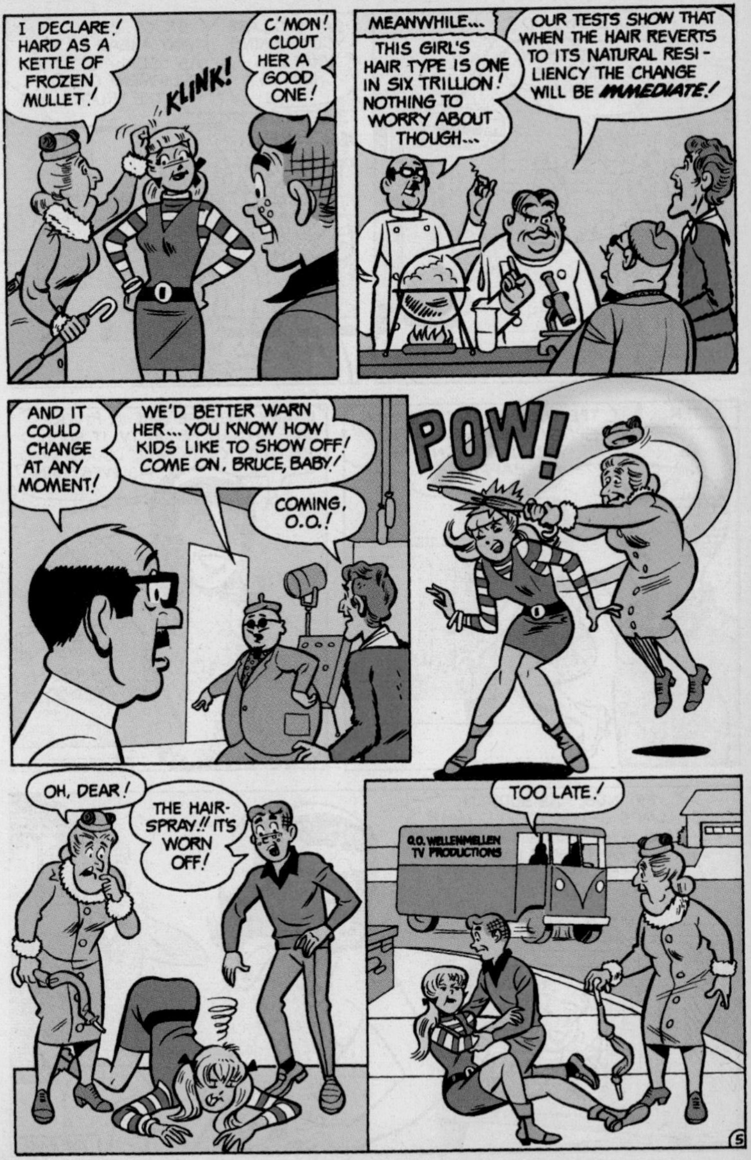

I DECLARE! HARD AS A KETTLE OF FROZEN MULLET!
KLINK!
C'MON! CLOUT HER A GOOD ONE!
MEANWHILE...
THIS GIRL'S HAIR TYPE IS ONE IN SIX TRILLION! NOTHING TO WORRY ABOUT THOUGH...
OUR TESTS SHOW THAT WHEN THE HAIR REVERTS TO ITS NATURAL RESI - LIENCY THE CHANGE WILL BE IMMEDIATE!
AND IT COULD CHANGE AT ANY MOMENT!
WE'D BETTER WARN HER... YOU KNOW HOW KIDS LIKE TO SHOW OFF! COME ON, BRUCE, BABY!
COMING, O.O.!
POW!
OH, DEAR!
THE HAIR-SPRAY!! IT'S WORN OFF!
TOO LATE!
O.O. WELLENMELLEN TV PRODUCTIONS
5

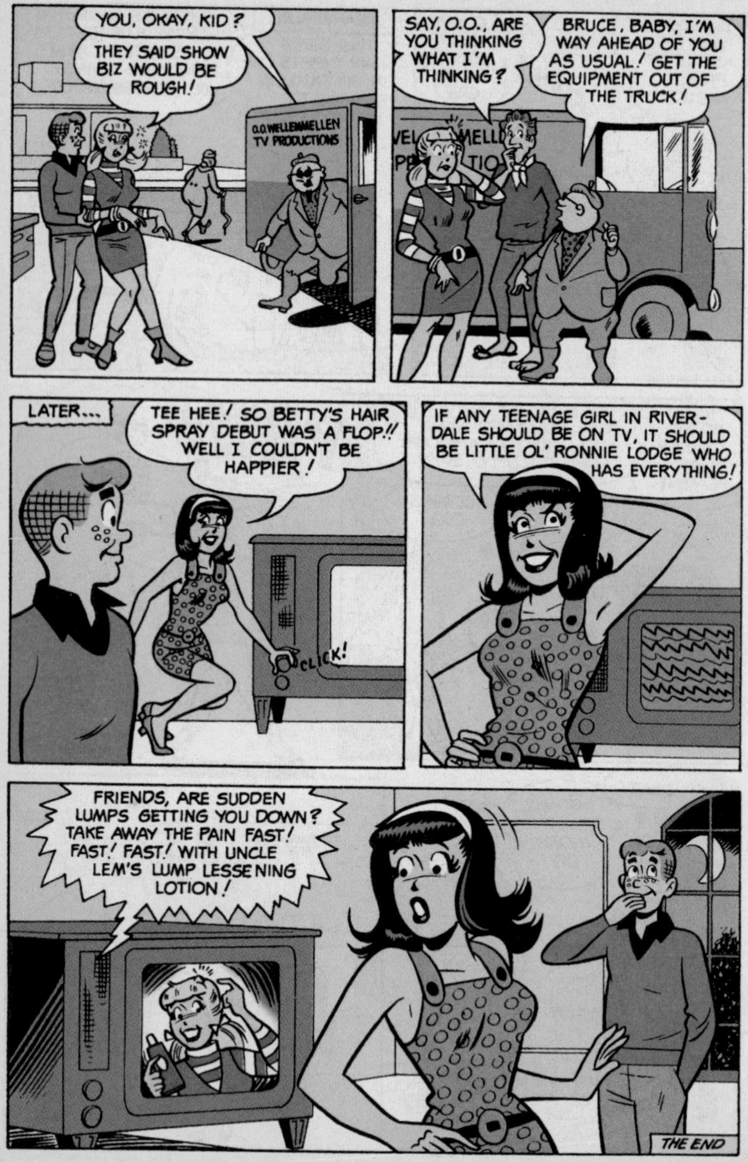
YOU, OKAY, KID?
THEY SAID SHOW BIZ WOULD BE ROUGH!
O.O. WELLEMMELLEN TV PRODUCTIONS
SAY, O.O., ARE YOU THINKING WHAT I'M THINKING?
BRUCE, BABY, I'M WAY AHEAD OF YOU AS USUAL! GET THE EQUIPMENT OUT OF THE TRUCK!
LATER...
TEE HEE! SO BETTY'S HAIR SPRAY DEBUT WAS A FLOP!! WELL I COULDN'T BE HAPPIER!
CLICK!
IF ANY TEENAGE GIRL IN RIVER-DALE SHOULD BE ON TV, IT SHOULD BE LITTLE OL' RONNIE LODGE WHO HAS EVERYTHING!
FRIENDS, ARE SUDDEN LUMPS GETTING YOU DOWN? TAKE AWAY THE PAIN FAST! FAST! FAST! WITH UNCLE LEM'S LUMP LESSENING LOTION!
THE END

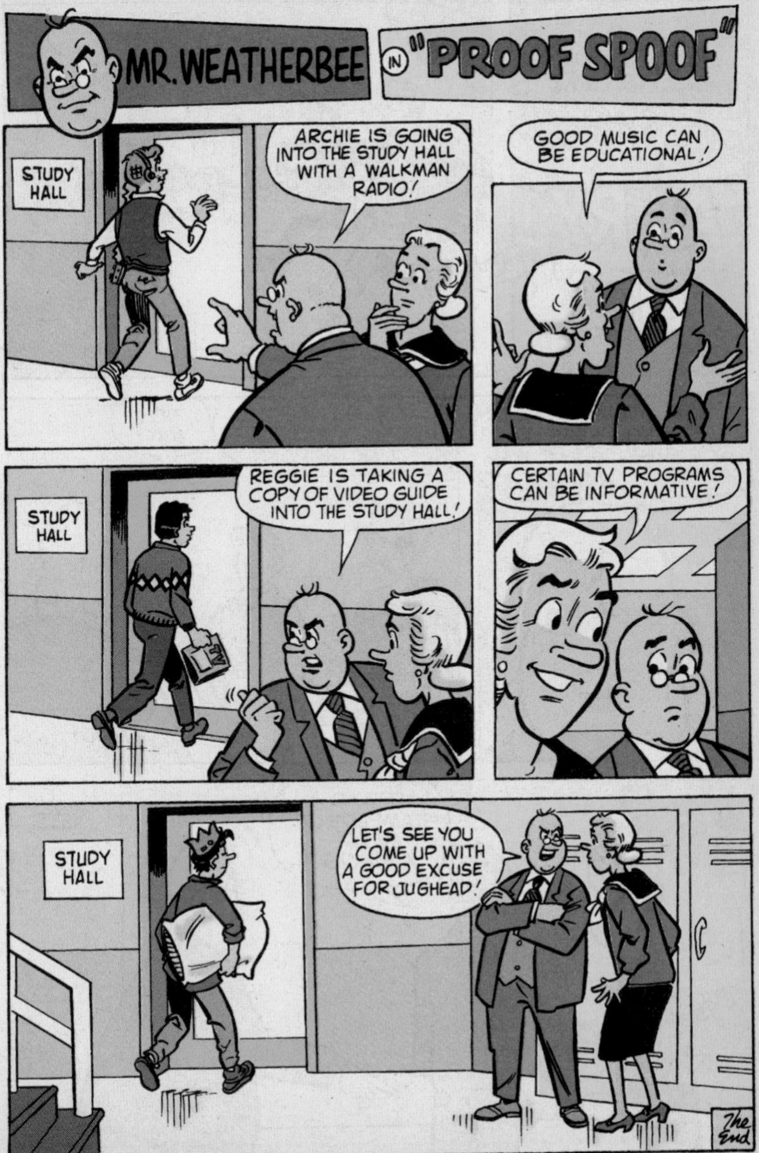
MR. WEATHERBEE IN "PROOF SPOOF"
STUDY HALL
ARCHIE IS GOING INTO THE STUDY HALL WITH A WALKMAN RADIO!
GOOD MUSIC CAN BE EDUCATIONAL!
STUDY HALL
REGGIE IS TAKING A COPY OF VIDEO GUIDE INTO THE STUDY HALL!
CERTAIN TV PROGRAMS CAN BE INFORMATIVE!
STUDY HALL
LET'S SEE YOU COME UP WITH A GOOD EXCUSE FOR JUGHEAD!
The End

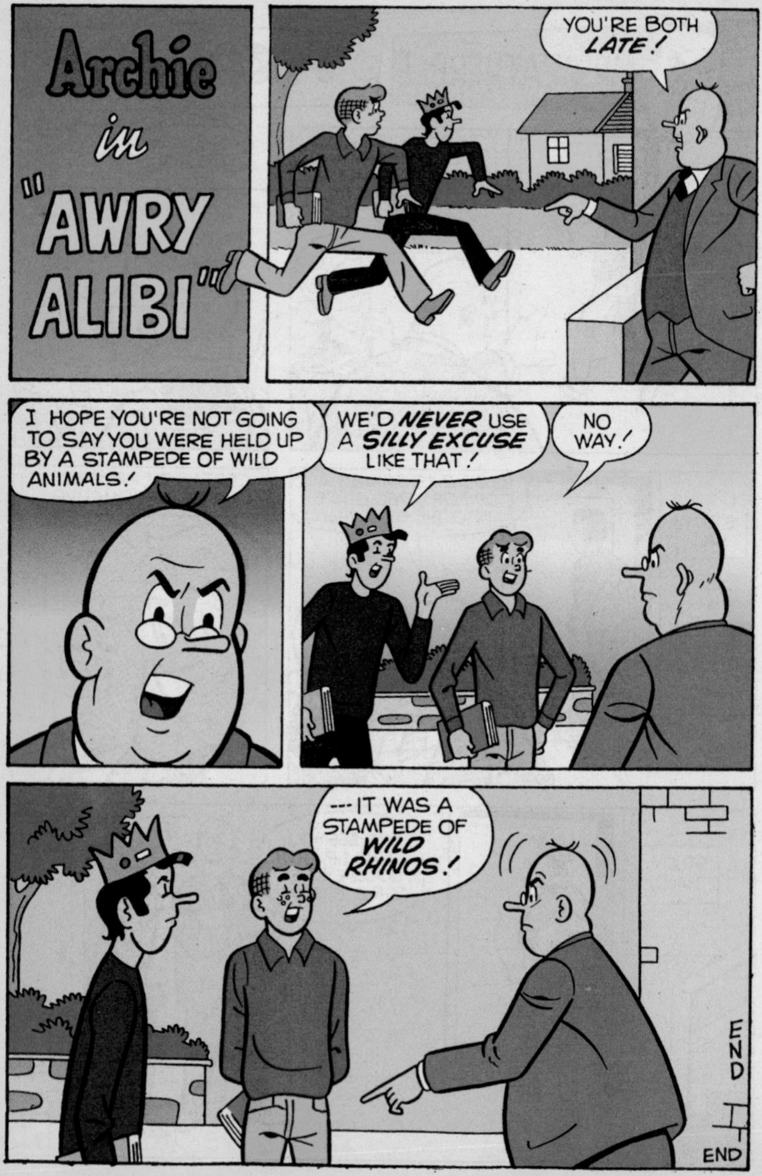
Archie
in
"AWRY ALIBI"
YOU'RE BOTH LATE!
I HOPE YOU'RE NOT GOING TO SAY YOU WERE HELD UP BY A STAMPEDE OF WILD ANIMALS!
WE'D NEVER USE A SILLY EXCUSE LIKE THAT!
NO WAY!
---IT WAS A STAMPEDE OF WILD RHINOS!
END
END

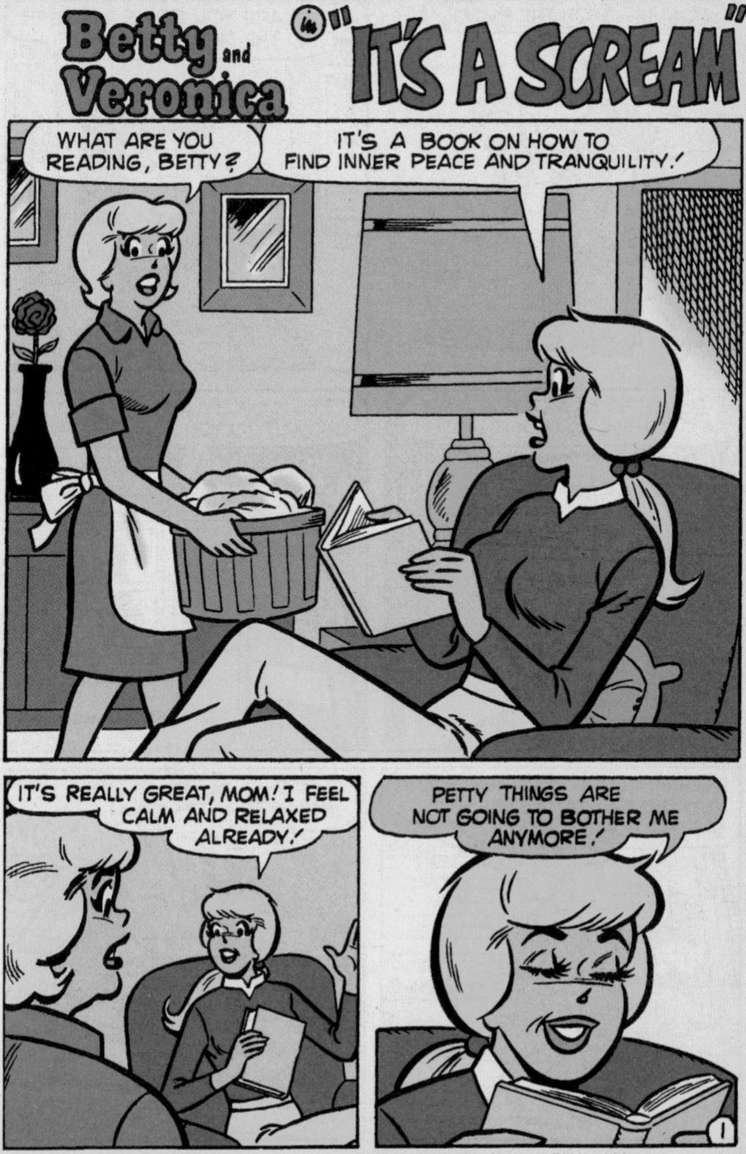
Betty and Veronica
in "IT'S A SCREAM"
WHAT ARE YOU READING, BETTY?
IT'S A BOOK ON HOW TO FIND INNER PEACE AND TRANQUILITY!
IT'S REALLY GREAT, MOM! I FEEL CALM AND RELAXED ALREADY!
PETTY THINGS ARE NOT GOING TO BOTHER ME ANYMORE!
1

Script & Pencils: Dick Malmgren / Pencils: Jon D'Agostino / Letters: Bill Yoshida

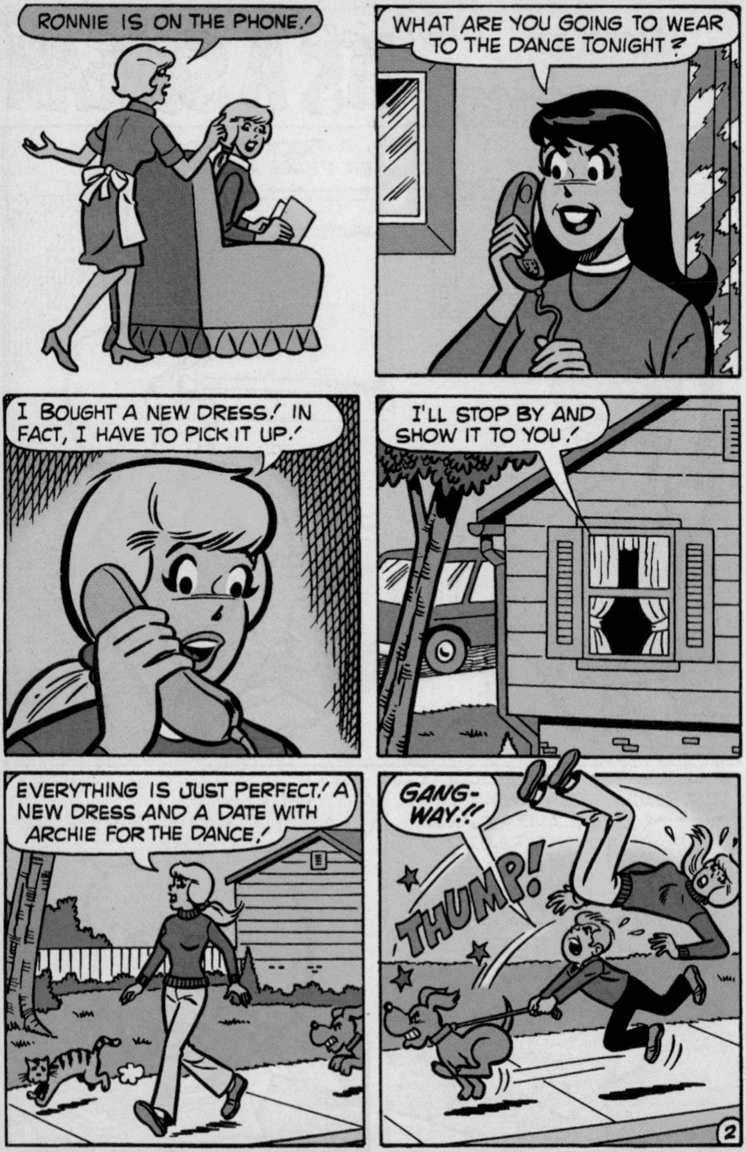
RONNIE IS ON THE PHONE!
WHAT ARE YOU GOING TO WEAR TO THE DANCE TONIGHT?
I BOUGHT A NEW DRESS! IN FACT, I HAVE TO PICK IT UP!
I'LL STOP BY AND SHOW IT TO YOU!
EVERYTHING IS JUST PERFECT! A NEW DRESS AND A DATE WITH ARCHIE FOR THE DANCE!
GANG-WAY!!
THUMP!

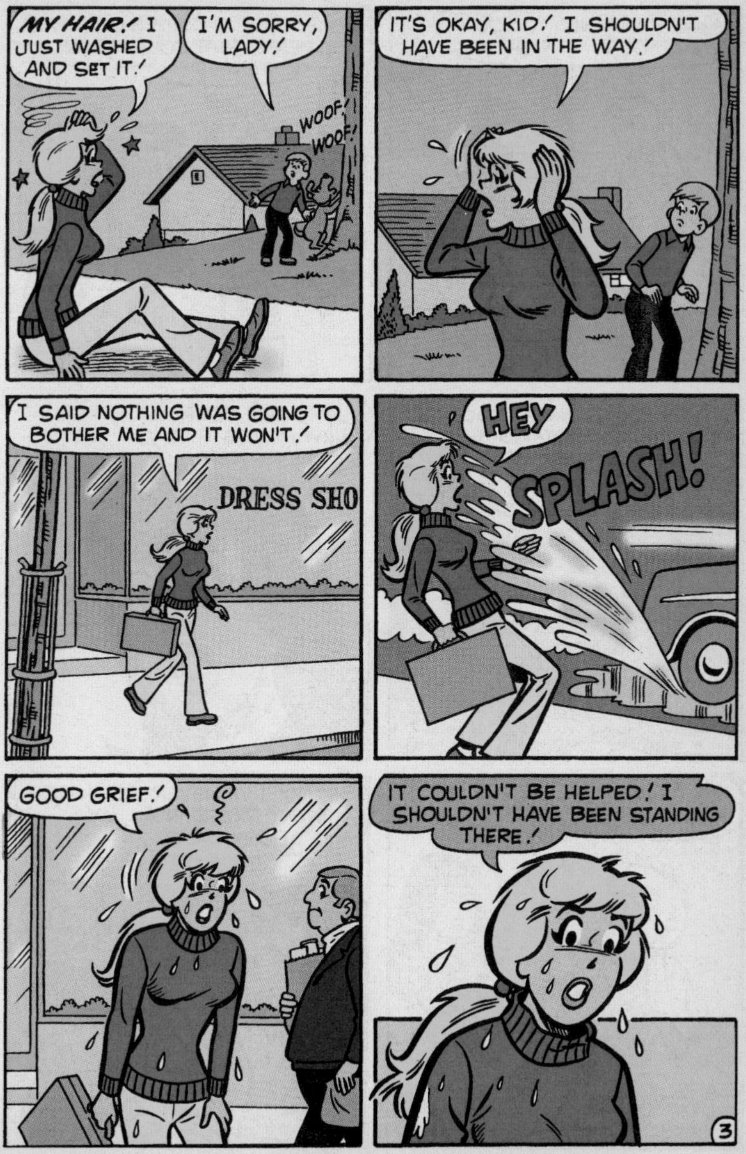
MY HAIR! I JUST WASHED AND SET IT!
I'M SORRY, LADY!
WOOF! WOOF!
IT'S OKAY, KID! I SHOULDN'T HAVE BEEN IN THE WAY!
I SAID NOTHING WAS GOING TO BOTHER ME AND IT WON'T!
DRESS SHO
HEY
SPLASH!
GOOD GRIEF!
IT COULDN'T BE HELPED! I SHOULDN'T HAVE BEEN STANDING THERE!
3

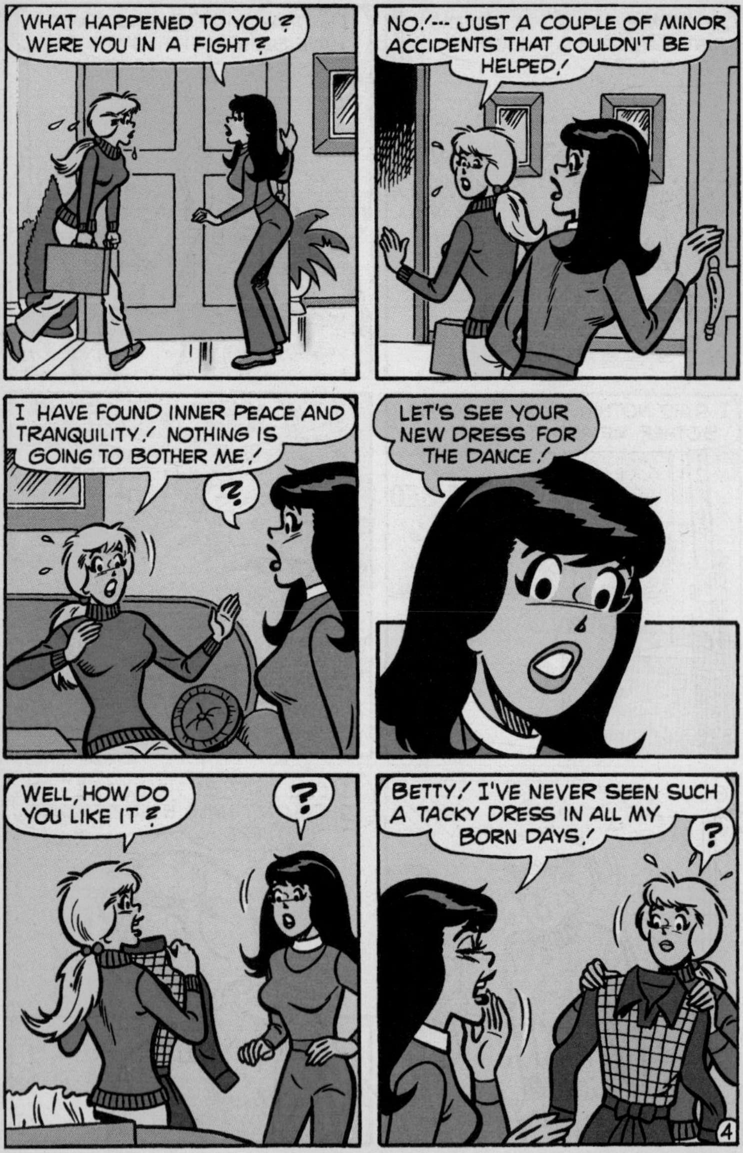
WHAT HAPPENED TO YOU? WERE YOU IN A FIGHT?
NO!--- JUST A COUPLE OF MINOR ACCIDENTS THAT COULDN'T BE HELPED!
I HAVE FOUND INNER PEACE AND TRANQUILITY! NOTHING IS GOING TO BOTHER ME!
?
LET'S SEE YOUR NEW DRESS FOR THE DANCE!
WELL, HOW DO YOU LIKE IT?
?
BETTY! I'VE NEVER SEEN SUCH A TACKY DRESS IN ALL MY BORN DAYS!
?
4

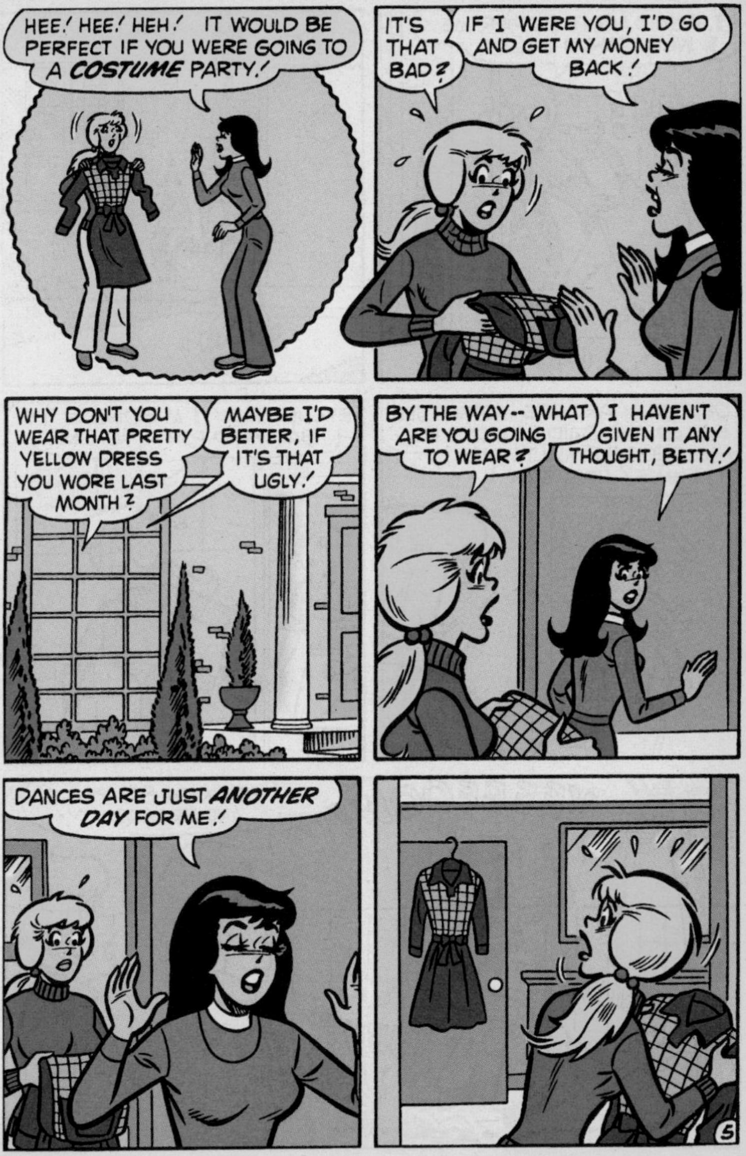
HEE! HEE! HEH! IT WOULD BE PERFECT IF YOU WERE GOING TO A COSTUME PARTY!
IT'S THAT BAD?
IF I WERE YOU, I'D GO AND GET MY MONEY BACK!
WHY DON'T YOU WEAR THAT PRETTY YELLOW DRESS YOU WORE LAST MONTH?
MAYBE I'D BETTER, IF IT'S THAT UGLY!
BY THE WAY-- WHAT ARE YOU GOING TO WEAR?
I HAVEN'T GIVEN IT ANY THOUGHT, BETTY!
DANCES ARE JUST ANOTHER DAY FOR ME!
5

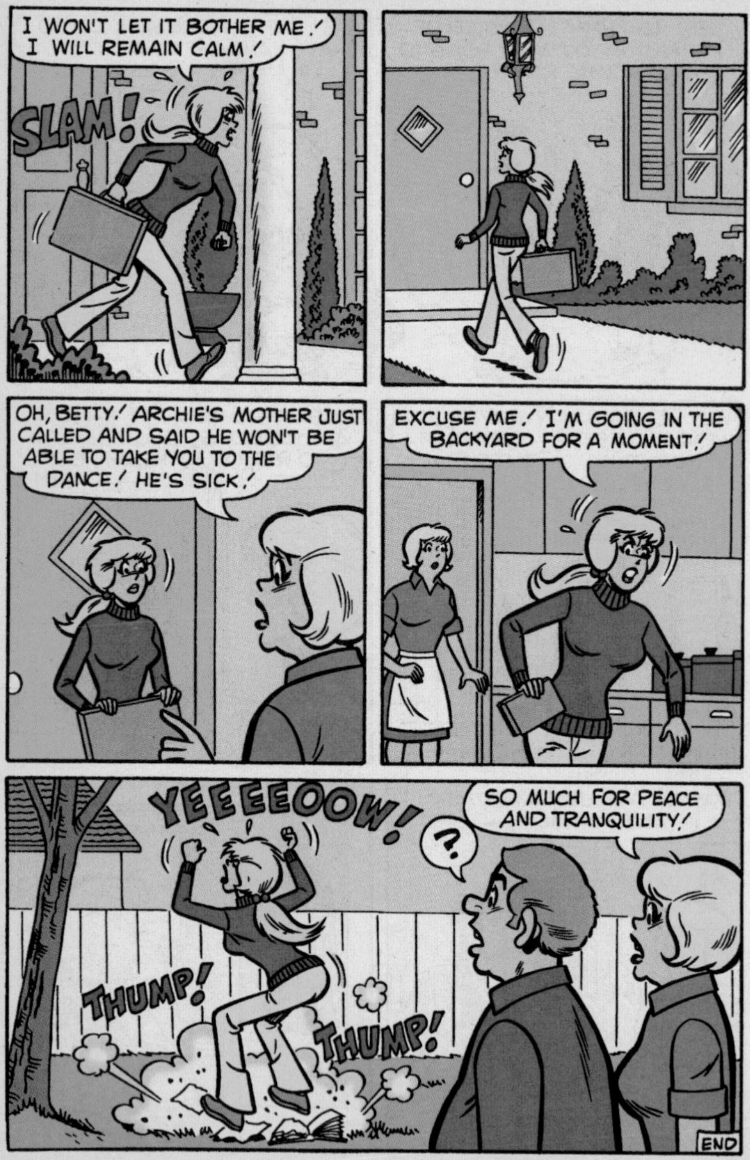
I WON'T LET IT BOTHER ME.! I WILL REMAIN CALM.!
SLAM!
OH, BETTY.! ARCHIE'S MOTHER JUST CALLED AND SAID HE WON'T BE ABLE TO TAKE YOU TO THE DANCE.! HE'S SICK.!
EXCUSE ME.! I'M GOING IN THE BACKYARD FOR A MOMENT.!
YEEEEOOOW!
?
SO MUCH FOR PEACE AND TRANQUILITY.!
THUMP!
THUMP!
END

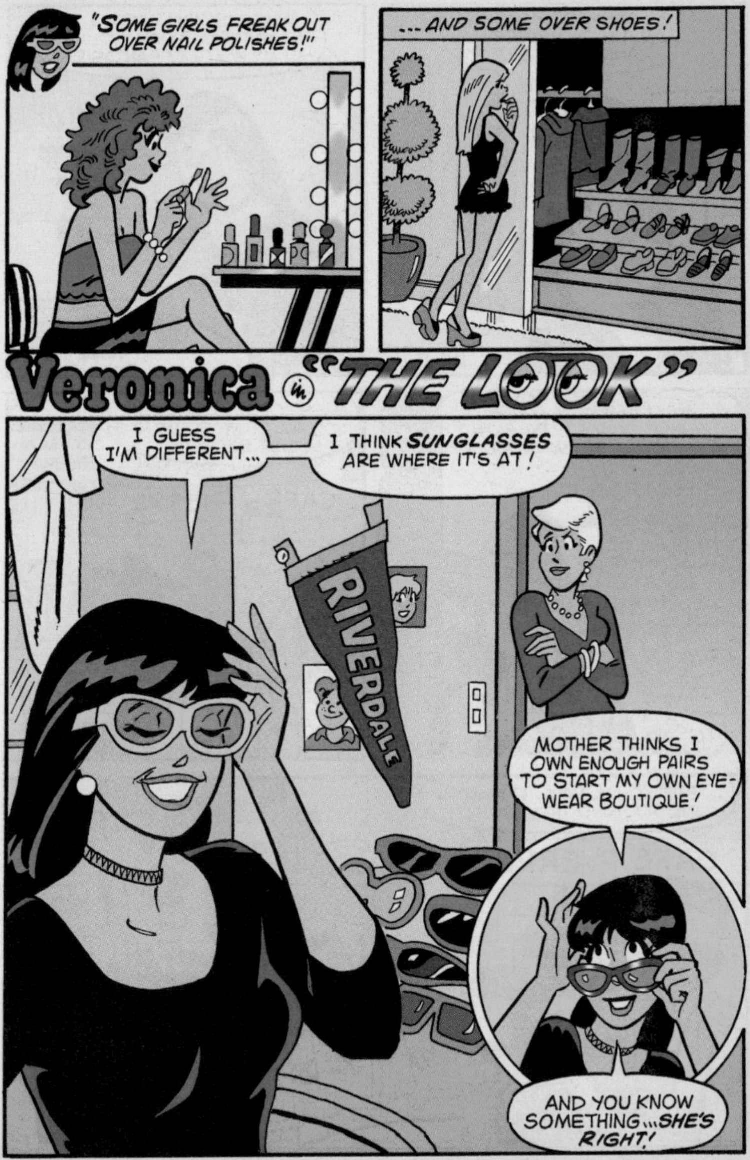
"SOME GIRLS FREAK OUT OVER NAIL POLISHES!"
... AND SOME OVER SHOES!
Veronica in "THE LOOK"
I GUESS I'M DIFFERENT...
I THINK SUNGLASSES ARE WHERE IT'S AT!
RIVERDALE
MOTHER THINKS I OWN ENOUGH PAIRS TO START MY OWN EYE-WEAR BOUTIQUE!
AND YOU KNOW SOMETHING...SHE'S RIGHT!

Script: George Gladir / Pencils: Dan DeCarlo / Inks: Henry Scarpelli / Letters: Bill Yoshida

Panel 1: I FIND SHADES GIVE OFF AN AIR OF MYSTERY AND INTRIGUE!

Panel 2: WHICH IS WHY WHEN I WEAR THEM, I CAN INDULGE IN MY *WILDEST* FANTASIES!

BELUGA CAVIAR

Panel 3: ...MEET VERONICA LODGE, FEMME FATALE IN THE WORLD OF ESPIONAGE AND INTRIGUE!

Panel 4: MISS LODGE, I BROUGHT YOU ALL OF MY COUNTRY'S LATEST SECRETS!

I APPRECIATE THAT, MON GENERAL!

CAFE PIERRE

...BUT YOU'LL HAVE TO WAIT IN LINE TO HAND THEM OVER!

CAFE PIERRE

SUPER SECRET

EXTRA SECRET

SEC

COLOSSA SECRETS

2

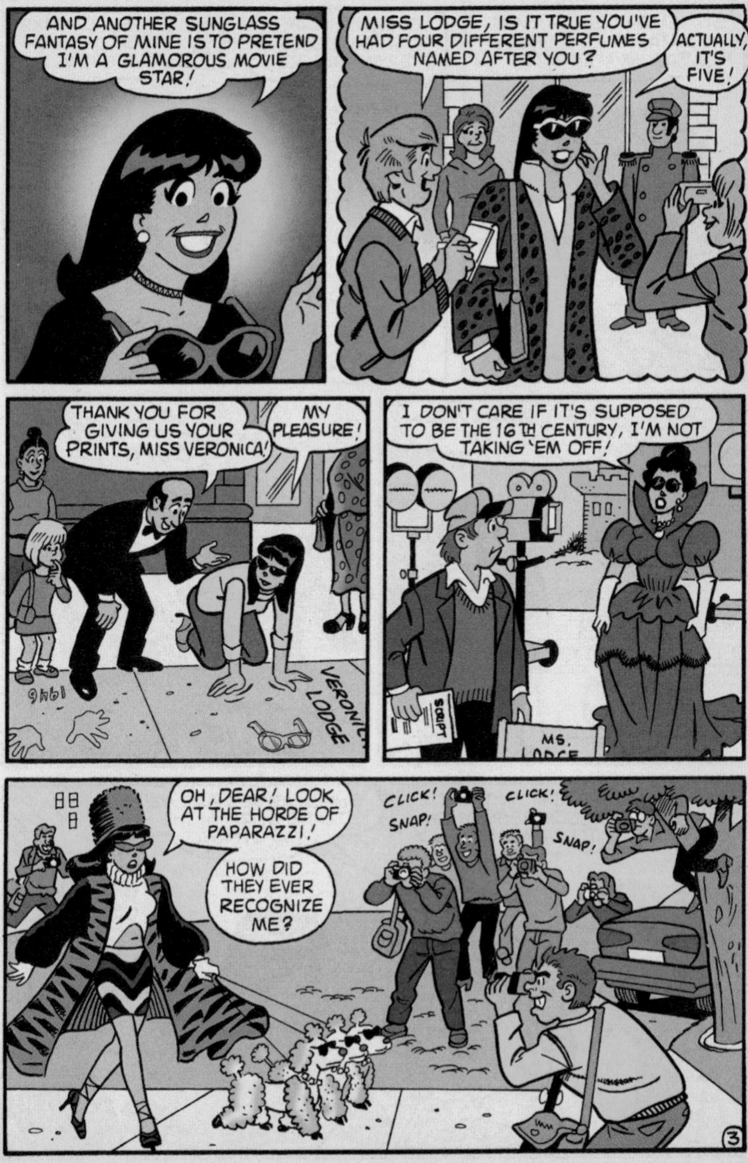
AND ANOTHER SUNGLASS FANTASY OF MINE IS TO PRETEND I'M A GLAMOROUS MOVIE STAR!
MISS LODGE, IS IT TRUE YOU'VE HAD FOUR DIFFERENT PERFUMES NAMED AFTER YOU?
ACTUALLY, IT'S FIVE!
THANK YOU FOR GIVING US YOUR PRINTS, MISS VERONICA!
MY PLEASURE!
VERONICA LODGE
I DON'T CARE IF IT'S SUPPOSED TO BE THE 16TH CENTURY, I'M NOT TAKING 'EM OFF!
SCRIPT
MS. LODGE
OH, DEAR! LOOK AT THE HORDE OF PAPARAZZI!
HOW DID THEY EVER RECOGNIZE ME?
CLICK!
CLICK!
SNAP!
SNAP!
3

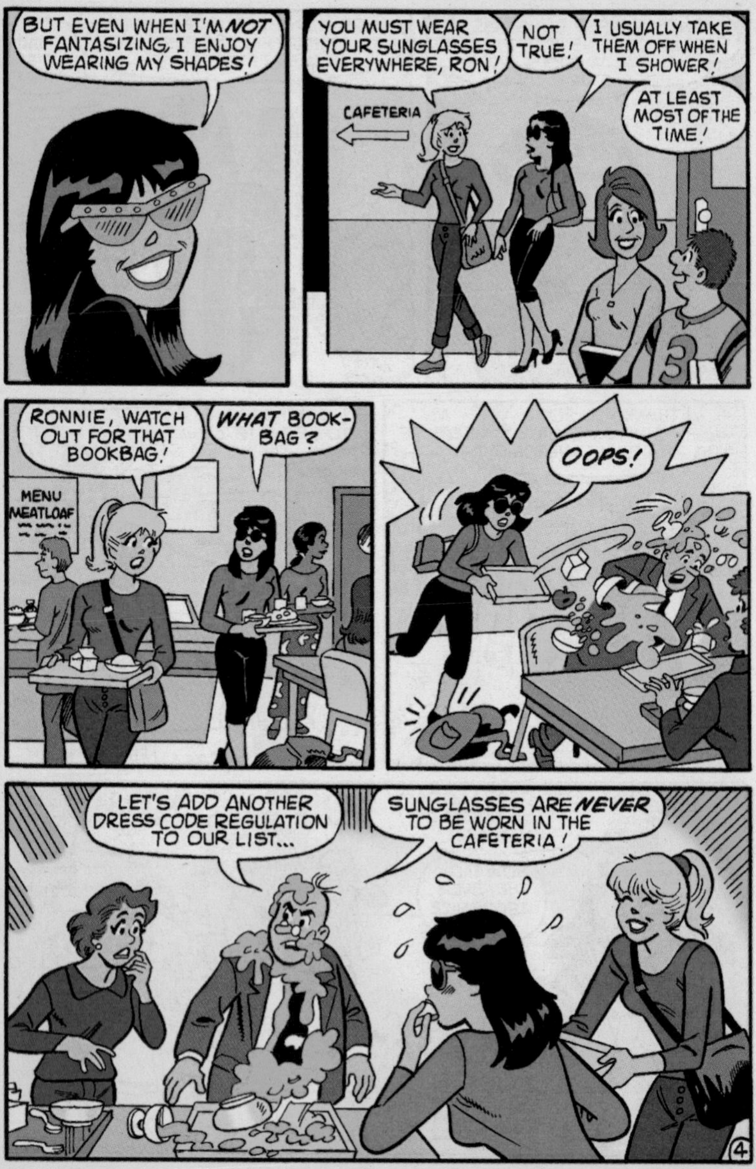

BUT EVEN WHEN I'M *NOT* FANTASIZING, I ENJOY WEARING MY SHADES!
YOU MUST WEAR YOUR SUNGLASSES EVERYWHERE, RON!
NOT TRUE!
I USUALLY TAKE THEM OFF WHEN I SHOWER!
AT LEAST MOST OF THE TIME!
CAFETERIA
RONNIE, WATCH OUT FOR THAT BOOKBAG!
WHAT BOOK-BAG?
MENU
MEATLOAF
OOPS!
LET'S ADD ANOTHER DRESS CODE REGULATION TO OUR LIST...
SUNGLASSES ARE *NEVER* TO BE WORN IN THE CAFETERIA!

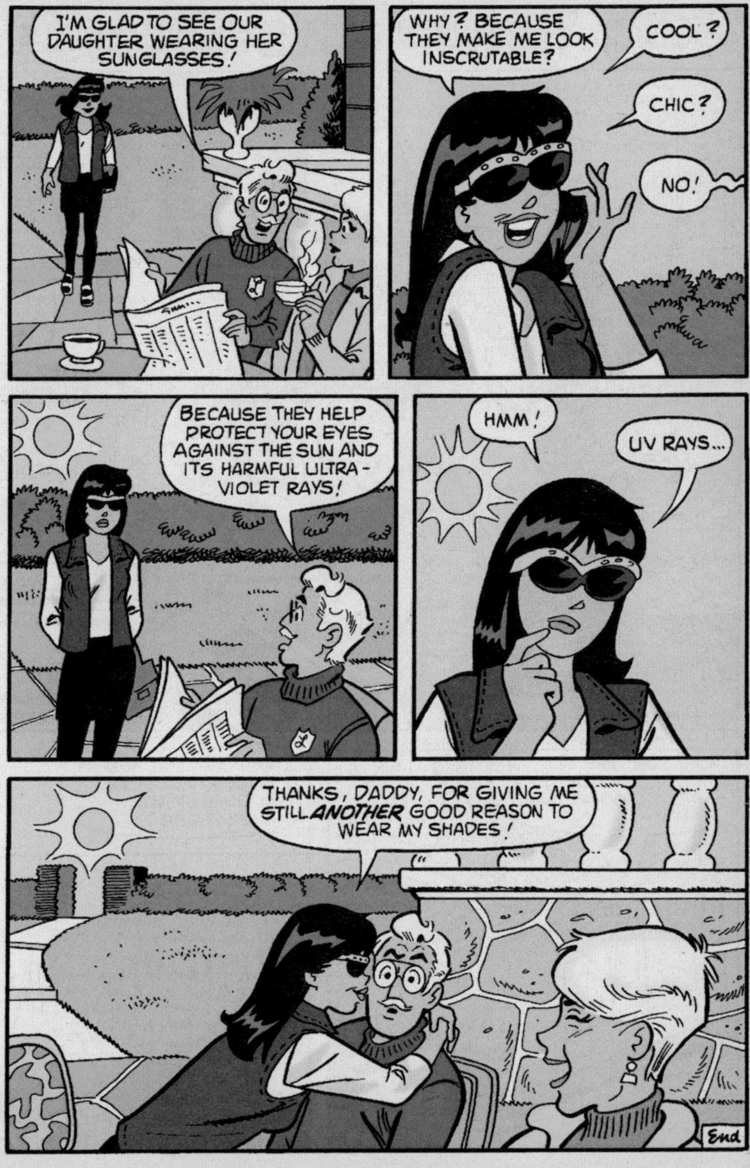
I'M GLAD TO SEE OUR DAUGHTER WEARING HER SUNGLASSES!
WHY? BECAUSE THEY MAKE ME LOOK INSCRUTABLE?
COOL?
CHIC?
NO!
BECAUSE THEY HELP PROTECT YOUR EYES AGAINST THE SUN AND ITS HARMFUL ULTRA-VIOLET RAYS!
HMM!
UV RAYS...
THANKS, DADDY, FOR GIVING ME STILL ANOTHER GOOD REASON TO WEAR MY SHADES!
End

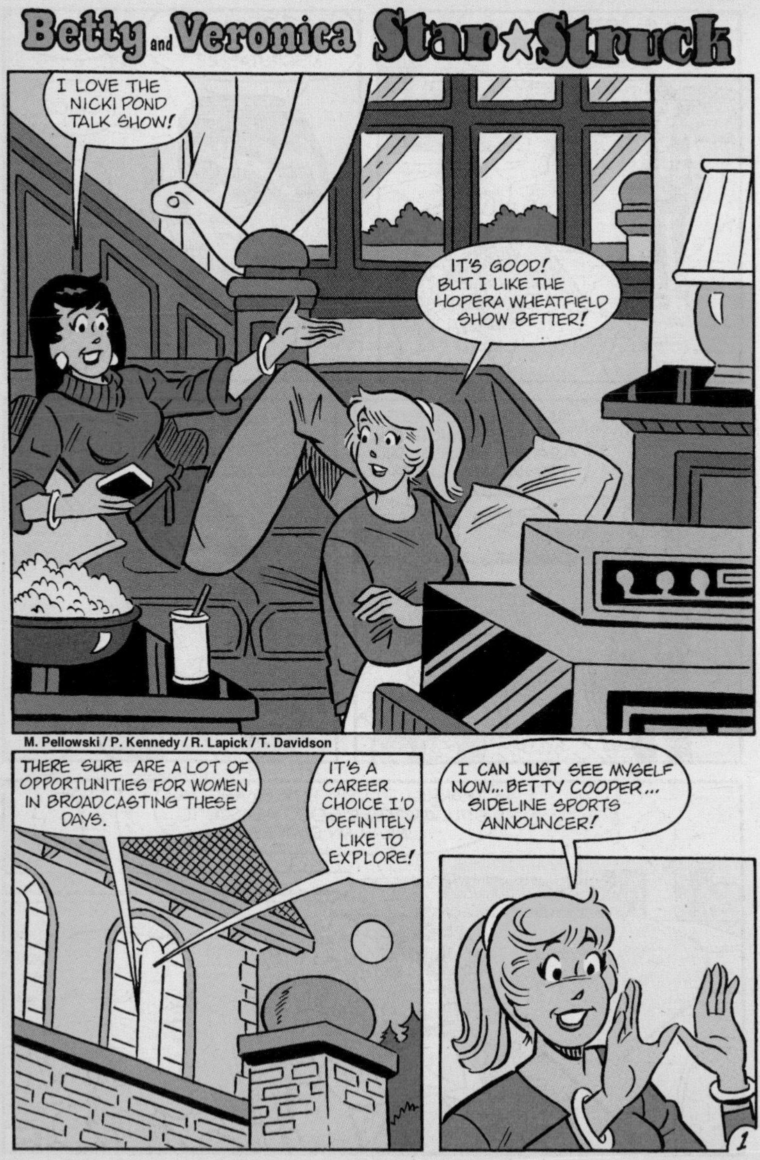
Betty and Veronica Star★Struck
I LOVE THE NICKI POND TALK SHOW!
IT'S GOOD! BUT I LIKE THE HOPERA WHEATFIELD SHOW BETTER!
M. Pellowski / P. Kennedy / R. Lapick / T. Davidson
THERE SURE ARE A LOT OF OPPORTUNITIES FOR WOMEN IN BROADCASTING THESE DAYS.
IT'S A CAREER CHOICE I'D DEFINITELY LIKE TO EXPLORE!
I CAN JUST SEE MYSELF NOW... BETTY COOPER... SIDELINE SPORTS ANNOUNCER!
1

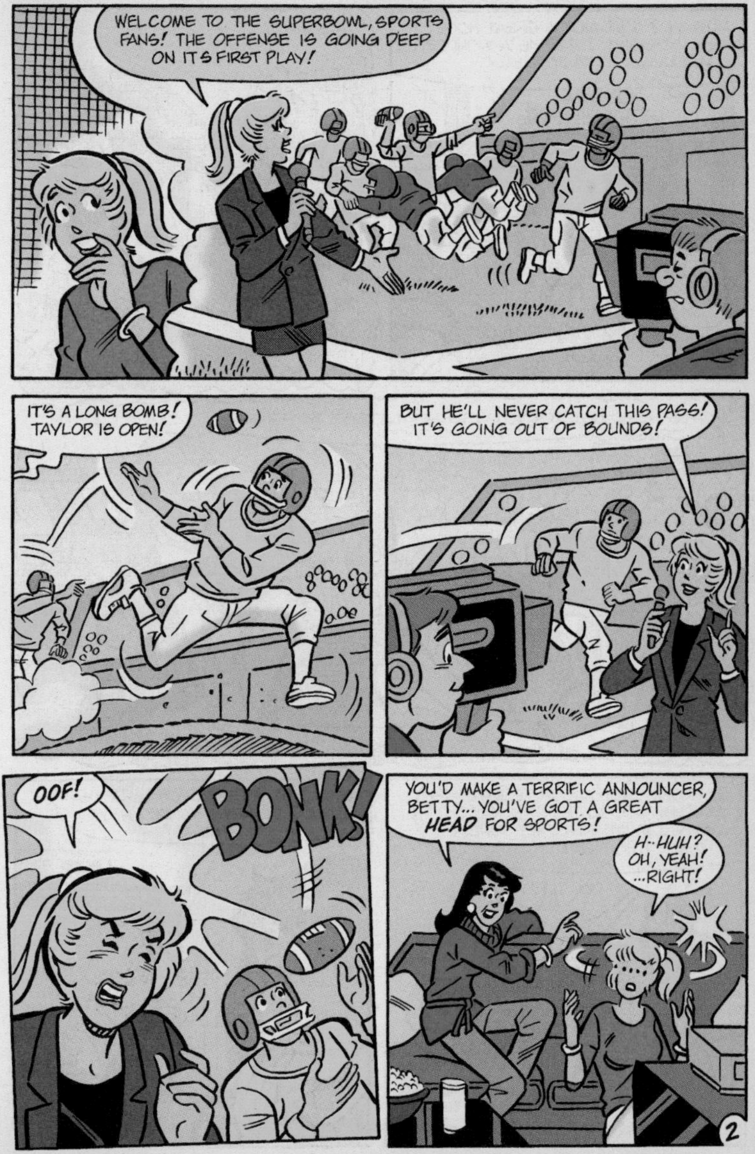
WELCOME TO THE SUPERBOWL, SPORTS FANS! THE OFFENSE IS GOING DEEP ON IT'S FIRST PLAY!
IT'S A LONG BOMB! TAYLOR IS OPEN!
BUT HE'LL NEVER CATCH THIS PASS! IT'S GOING OUT OF BOUNDS!
OOF!
BONK!
YOU'D MAKE A TERRIFIC ANNOUNCER, BETTY... YOU'VE GOT A GREAT HEAD FOR SPORTS!
H-HUH? OH, YEAH! ...RIGHT!

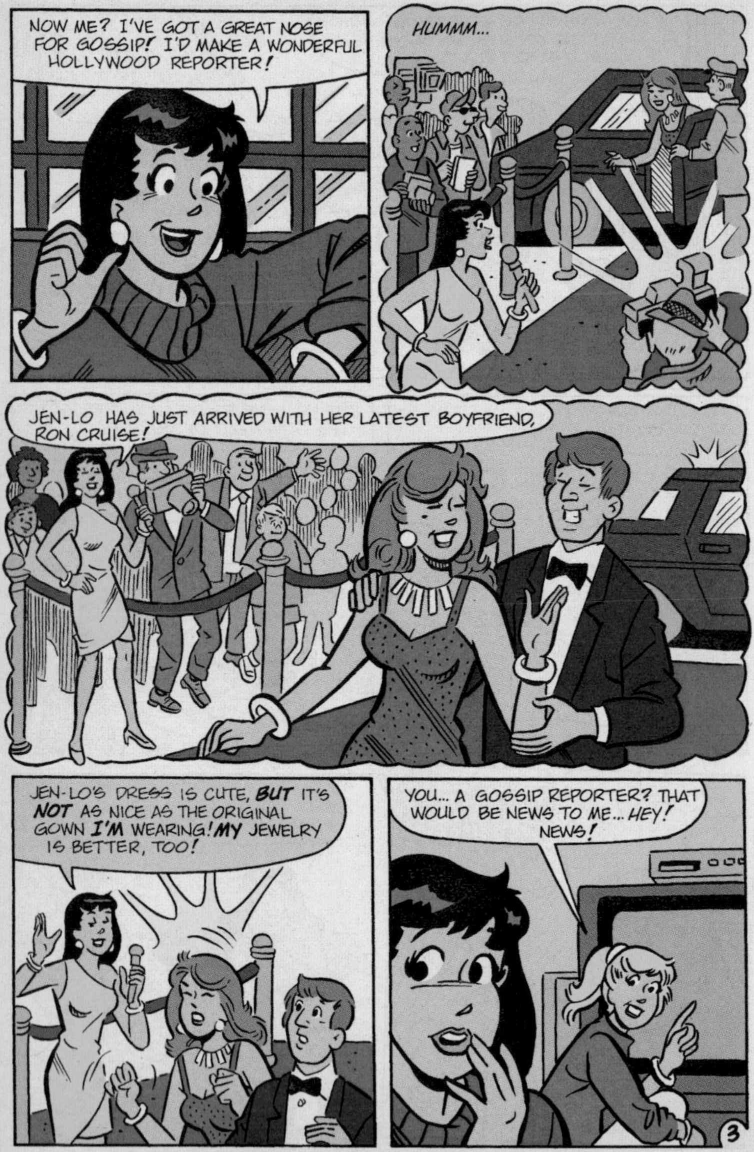
NOW ME? I'VE GOT A GREAT NOSE FOR GOSSIP! I'D MAKE A WONDERFUL HOLLYWOOD REPORTER!
HUMMM...
JEN-LO HAS JUST ARRIVED WITH HER LATEST BOYFRIEND, RON CRUISE!
JEN-LO'S DRESS IS CUTE, BUT IT'S NOT AS NICE AS THE ORIGINAL GOWN I'M WEARING! MY JEWELRY IS BETTER, TOO!
YOU... A GOSSIP REPORTER? THAT WOULD BE NEWS TO ME... HEY! NEWS!

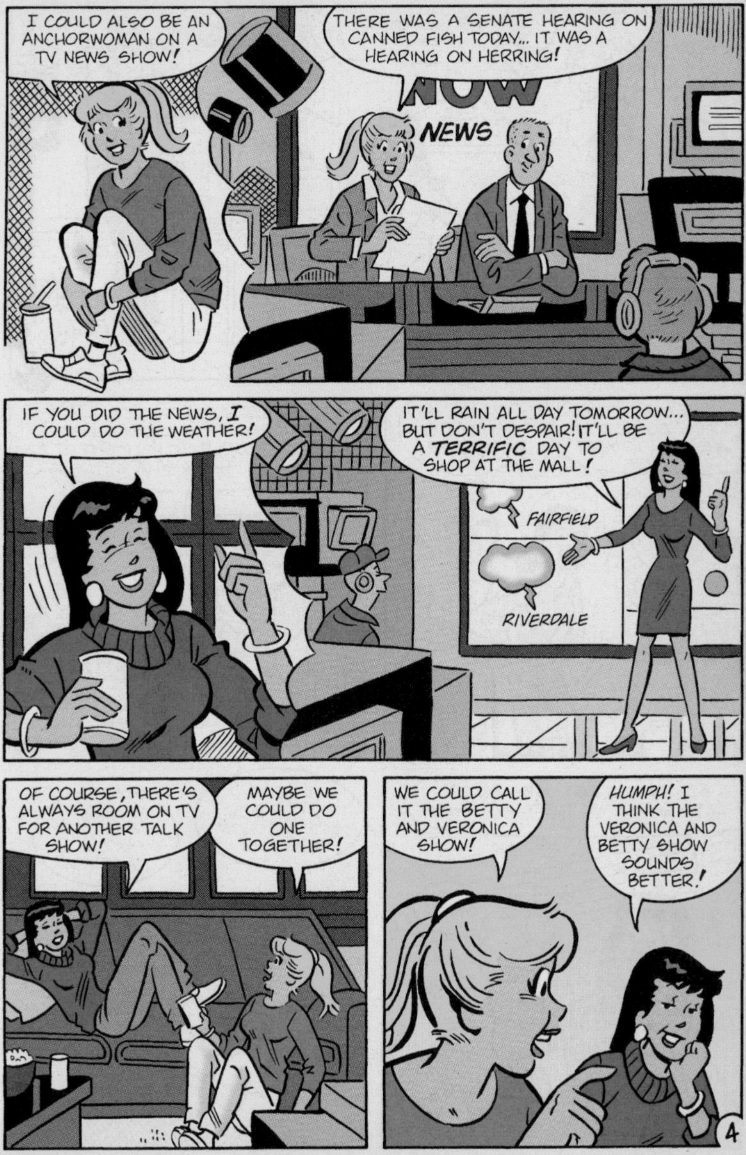
I COULD ALSO BE AN ANCHORWOMAN ON A TV NEWS SHOW!
THERE WAS A SENATE HEARING ON CANNED FISH TODAY... IT WAS A HEARING ON HERRING!
NOW
NEWS
IF YOU DID THE NEWS, I COULD DO THE WEATHER!
IT'LL RAIN ALL DAY TOMORROW... BUT DON'T DESPAIR! IT'LL BE A TERRIFIC DAY TO SHOP AT THE MALL!
FAIRFIELD
RIVERDALE
OF COURSE, THERE'S ALWAYS ROOM ON TV FOR ANOTHER TALK SHOW!
MAYBE WE COULD DO ONE TOGETHER!
WE COULD CALL IT THE BETTY AND VERONICA SHOW!
HUMPH! I THINK THE VERONICA AND BETTY SHOW SOUNDS BETTER!
4

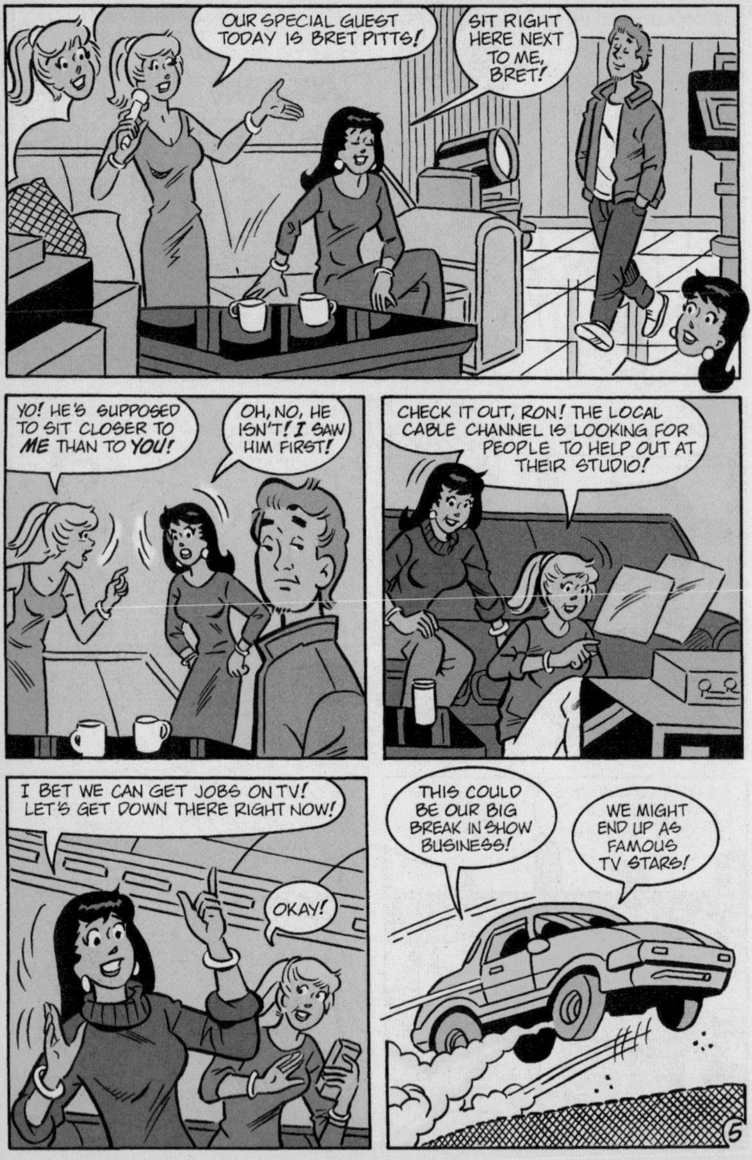

OUR SPECIAL GUEST TODAY IS BRET PITTS!
SIT RIGHT HERE NEXT TO ME, BRET!
YO! HE'S SUPPOSED TO SIT CLOSER TO ME THAN TO YOU!
OH, NO, HE ISN'T! I SAW HIM FIRST!
CHECK IT OUT, RON! THE LOCAL CABLE CHANNEL IS LOOKING FOR PEOPLE TO HELP OUT AT THEIR STUDIO!
I BET WE CAN GET JOBS ON TV! LET'S GET DOWN THERE RIGHT NOW!
OKAY!
THIS COULD BE OUR BIG BREAK IN SHOW BUSINESS!
WE MIGHT END UP AS FAMOUS TV STARS!

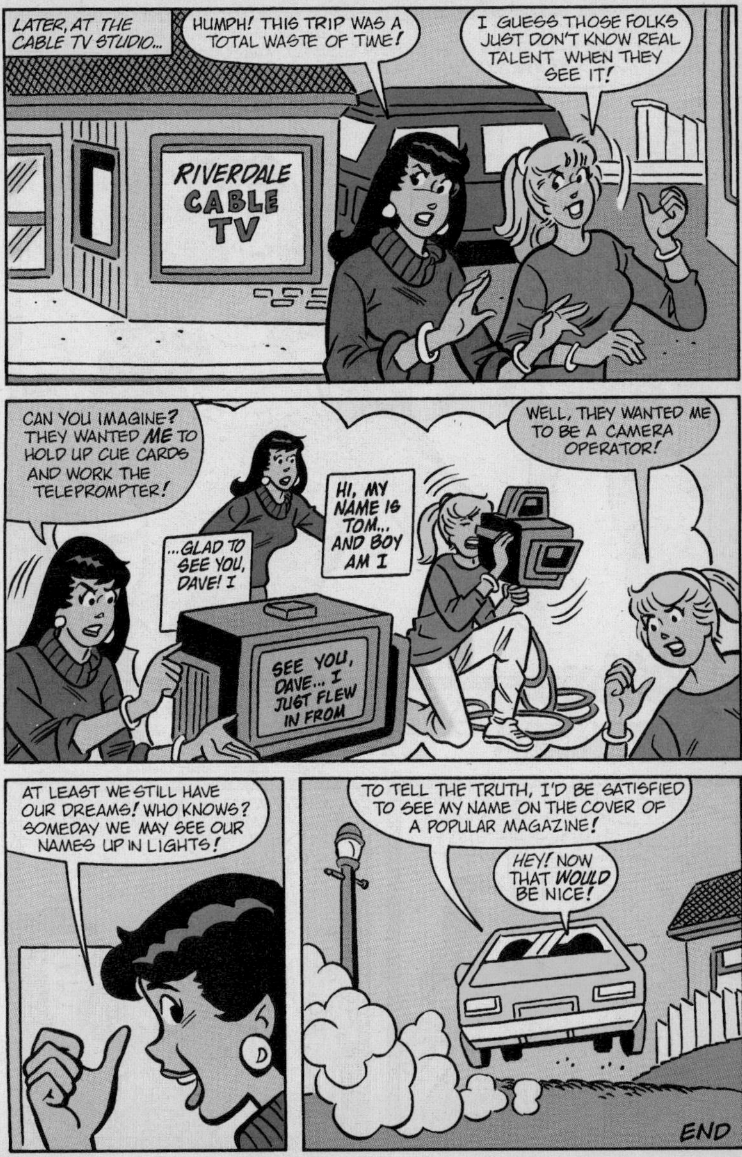

LATER, AT THE CABLE TV STUDIO...
HUMPH! THIS TRIP WAS A TOTAL WASTE OF TIME!
I GUESS THOSE FOLKS JUST DON'T KNOW REAL TALENT WHEN THEY SEE IT!
RIVERDALE CABLE TV
CAN YOU IMAGINE? THEY WANTED ME TO HOLD UP CUE CARDS AND WORK THE TELEPROMPTER!
WELL, THEY WANTED ME TO BE A CAMERA OPERATOR!
HI, MY NAME IS TOM... AND BOY AM I
...GLAD TO SEE YOU, DAVE! I
SEE YOU, DAVE... I JUST FLEW IN FROM
AT LEAST WE STILL HAVE OUR DREAMS! WHO KNOWS? SOMEDAY WE MAY SEE OUR NAMES UP IN LIGHTS!
TO TELL THE TRUTH, I'D BE SATISFIED TO SEE MY NAME ON THE COVER OF A POPULAR MAGAZINE!
HEY! NOW THAT WOULD BE NICE!
END

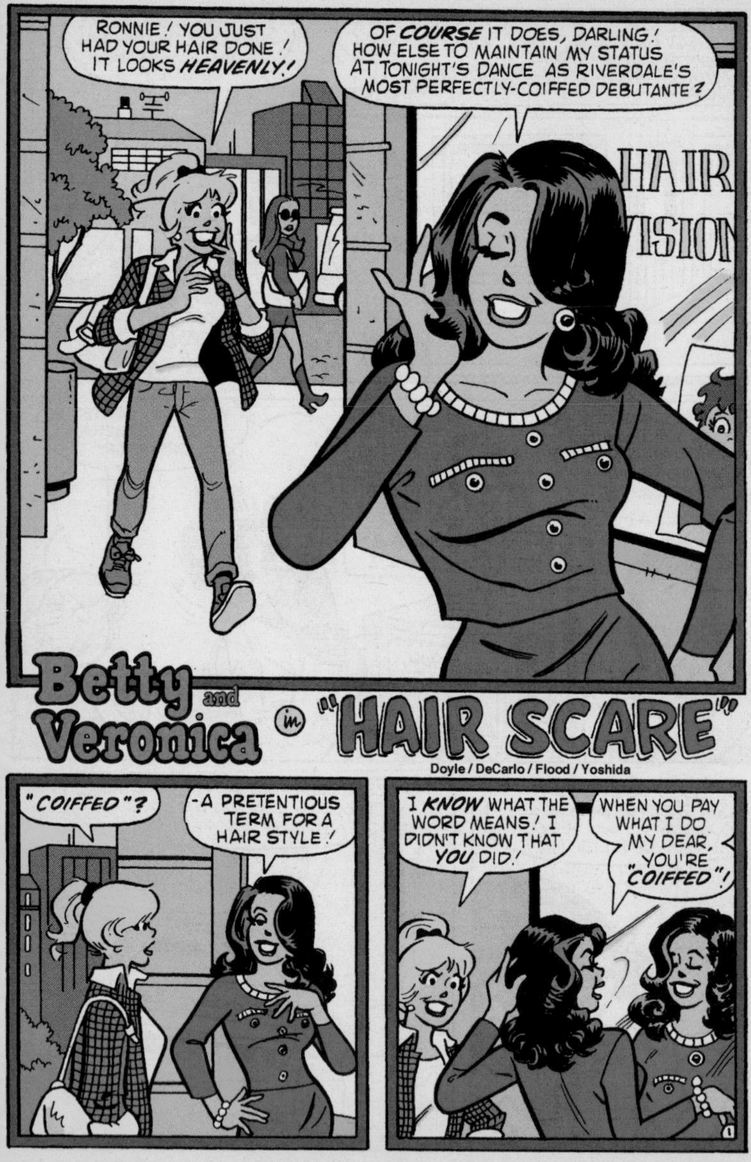
RONNIE! YOU JUST HAD YOUR HAIR DONE! IT LOOKS HEAVENLY!
OF COURSE IT DOES, DARLING! HOW ELSE TO MAINTAIN MY STATUS AT TONIGHT'S DANCE AS RIVERDALE'S MOST PERFECTLY-COIFFED DEBUTANTE?
HAIR
VISION
Betty and Veronica in "HAIR SCARE"
Doyle / DeCarlo / Flood / Yoshida
"COIFFED"?
-A PRETENTIOUS TERM FOR A HAIR STYLE!
I KNOW WHAT THE WORD MEANS! I DIDN'T KNOW THAT YOU DID!
WHEN YOU PAY WHAT I DO MY DEAR, YOU'RE "COIFFED"!
1

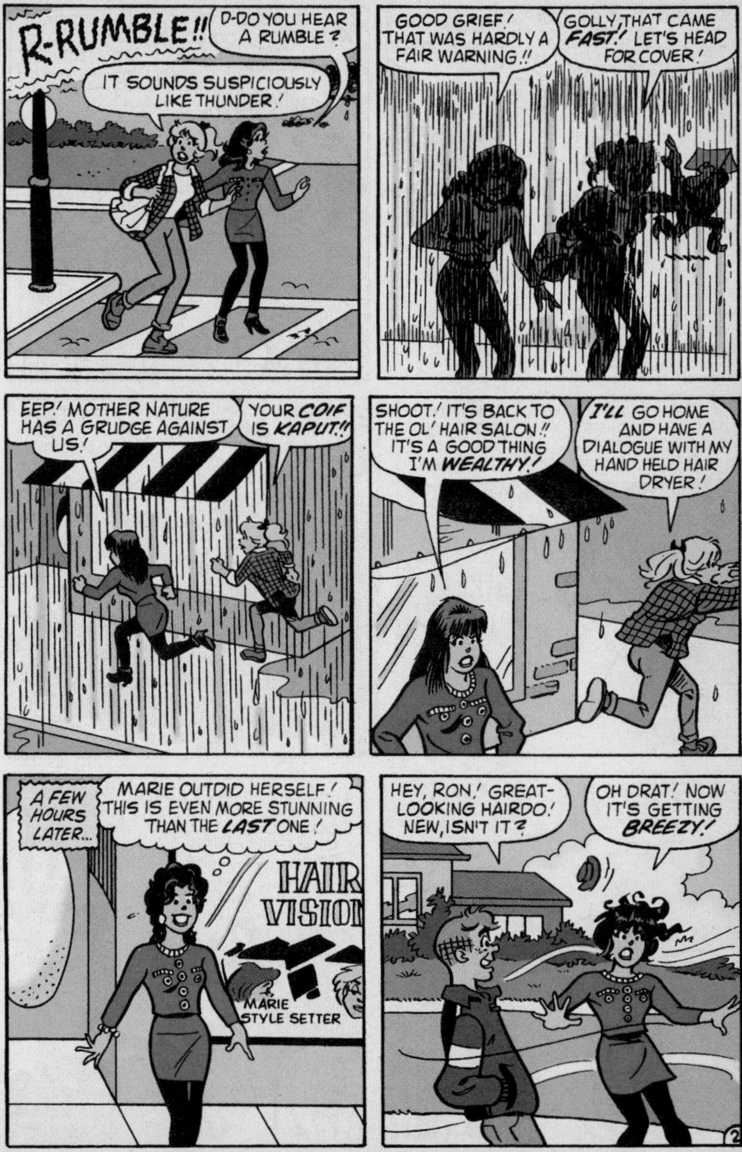
R-RUMBLE!!
D-DO YOU HEAR A RUMBLE?
IT SOUNDS SUSPICIOUSLY LIKE THUNDER!
GOOD GRIEF! THAT WAS HARDLY A FAIR WARNING!!
GOLLY, THAT CAME FAST! LET'S HEAD FOR COVER!
EEP! MOTHER NATURE HAS A GRUDGE AGAINST US!
YOUR COIF IS KAPUT!!
SHOOT! IT'S BACK TO THE OL' HAIR SALON!! IT'S A GOOD THING I'M WEALTHY!
I'LL GO HOME AND HAVE A DIALOGUE WITH MY HAND HELD HAIR DRYER!
A FEW HOURS LATER...
MARIE OUTDID HERSELF! THIS IS EVEN MORE STUNNING THAN THE LAST ONE!
HAIR VISIO
MARIE STYLE SETTER
HEY, RON! GREAT-LOOKING HAIRDO! NEW, ISN'T IT?
OH DRAT! NOW IT'S GETTING BREEZY!
2

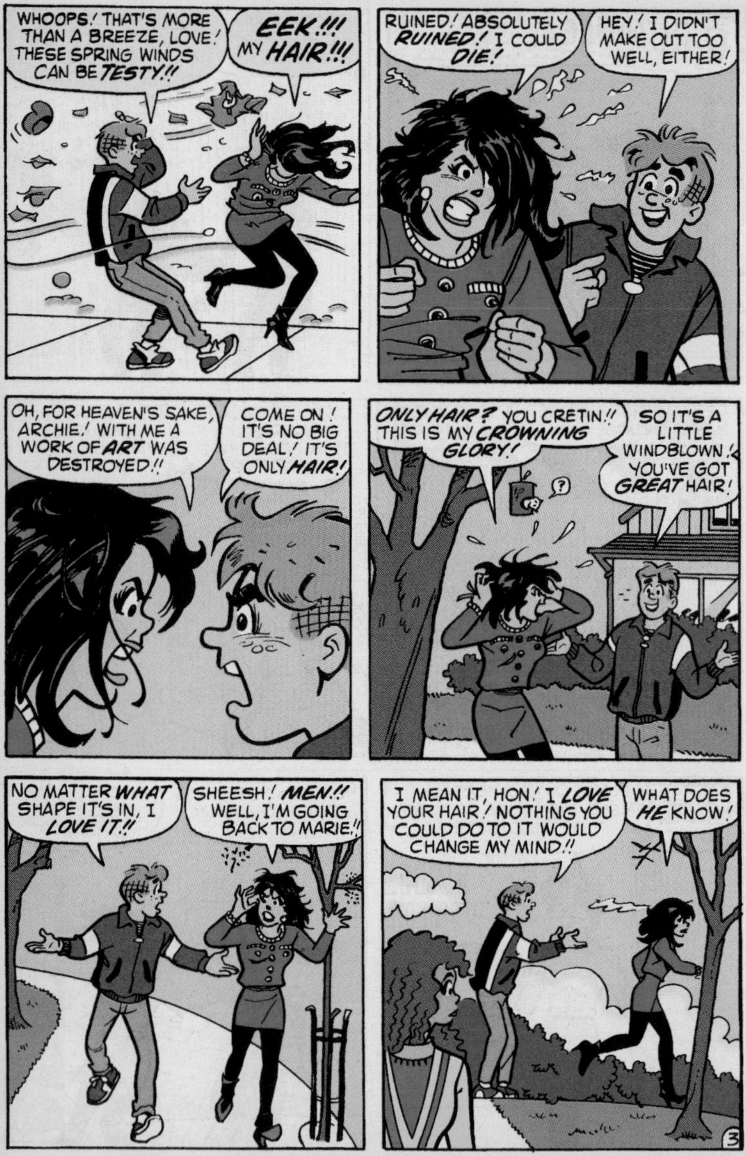
WHOOPS! THAT'S MORE THAN A BREEZE, LOVE! THESE SPRING WINDS CAN BE TESTY!!
EEK!!! MY HAIR!!!
RUINED! ABSOLUTELY RUINED! I COULD DIE!
HEY! I DIDN'T MAKE OUT TOO WELL, EITHER!
OH, FOR HEAVEN'S SAKE, ARCHIE! WITH ME A WORK OF ART WAS DESTROYED!!
COME ON! IT'S NO BIG DEAL! IT'S ONLY HAIR!
ONLY HAIR? YOU CRETIN!! THIS IS MY CROWNING GLORY!
SO IT'S A LITTLE WINDBLOWN! YOU'VE GOT GREAT HAIR!
NO MATTER WHAT SHAPE IT'S IN, I LOVE IT!!
SHEESH! MEN!! WELL, I'M GOING BACK TO MARIE!!
I MEAN IT, HON! I LOVE YOUR HAIR! NOTHING YOU COULD DO TO IT WOULD CHANGE MY MIND!!
WHAT DOES HE KNOW!
3

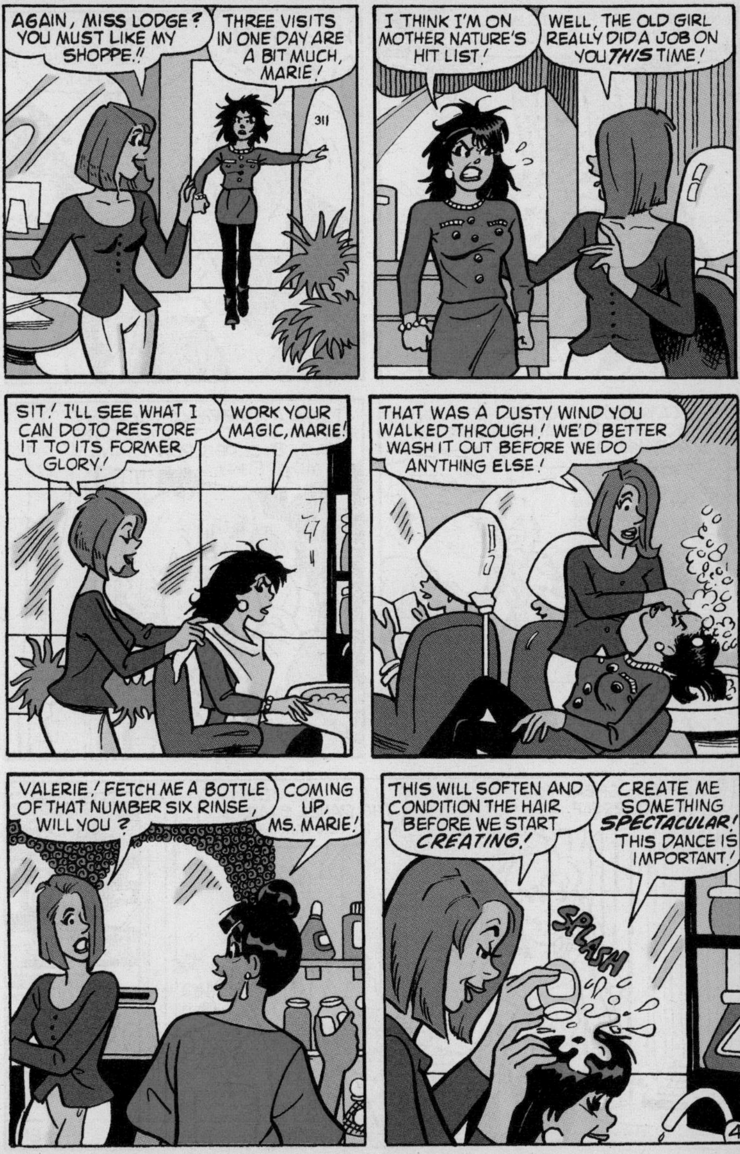
AGAIN, MISS LODGE? YOU MUST LIKE MY SHOPPE!!
THREE VISITS IN ONE DAY ARE A BIT MUCH, MARIE!
311
I THINK I'M ON MOTHER NATURE'S HIT LIST!
WELL, THE OLD GIRL REALLY DID A JOB ON YOU THIS TIME!
SIT! I'LL SEE WHAT I CAN DO TO RESTORE IT TO ITS FORMER GLORY!
WORK YOUR MAGIC, MARIE!
THAT WAS A DUSTY WIND YOU WALKED THROUGH! WE'D BETTER WASH IT OUT BEFORE WE DO ANYTHING ELSE!
VALERIE! FETCH ME A BOTTLE OF THAT NUMBER SIX RINSE, WILL YOU?
COMING UP, MS. MARIE!
THIS WILL SOFTEN AND CONDITION THE HAIR BEFORE WE START CREATING!
CREATE ME SOMETHING SPECTACULAR! THIS DANCE IS IMPORTANT!
SPLASH
4

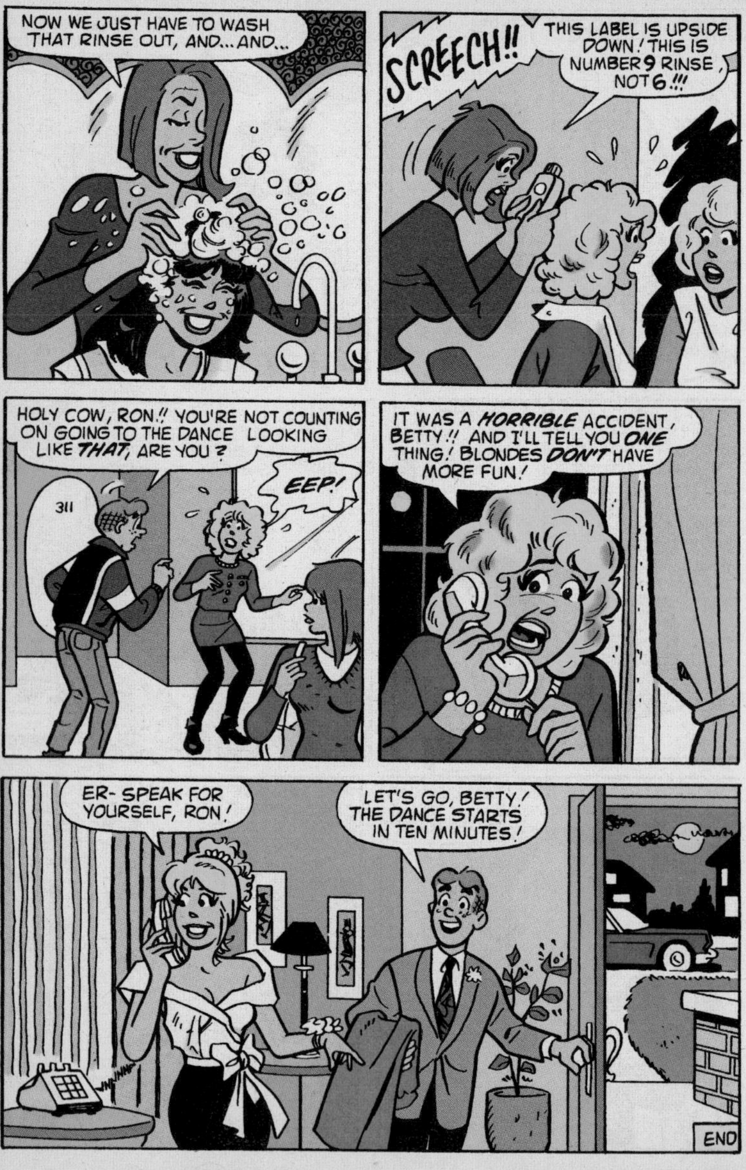

NOW WE JUST HAVE TO WASH THAT RINSE OUT, AND... AND...
SCREECH!!
THIS LABEL IS UPSIDE DOWN! THIS IS NUMBER 9 RINSE, NOT 6!!!
HOLY COW, RON!! YOU'RE NOT COUNTING ON GOING TO THE DANCE LOOKING LIKE *THAT*, ARE YOU?
311
EEP!
IT WAS A *HORRIBLE* ACCIDENT, BETTY!! AND I'LL TELL YOU *ONE* THING! BLONDES *DON'T* HAVE MORE FUN!
ER- SPEAK FOR YOURSELF, RON!
LET'S GO, BETTY! THE DANCE STARTS IN TEN MINUTES!
END

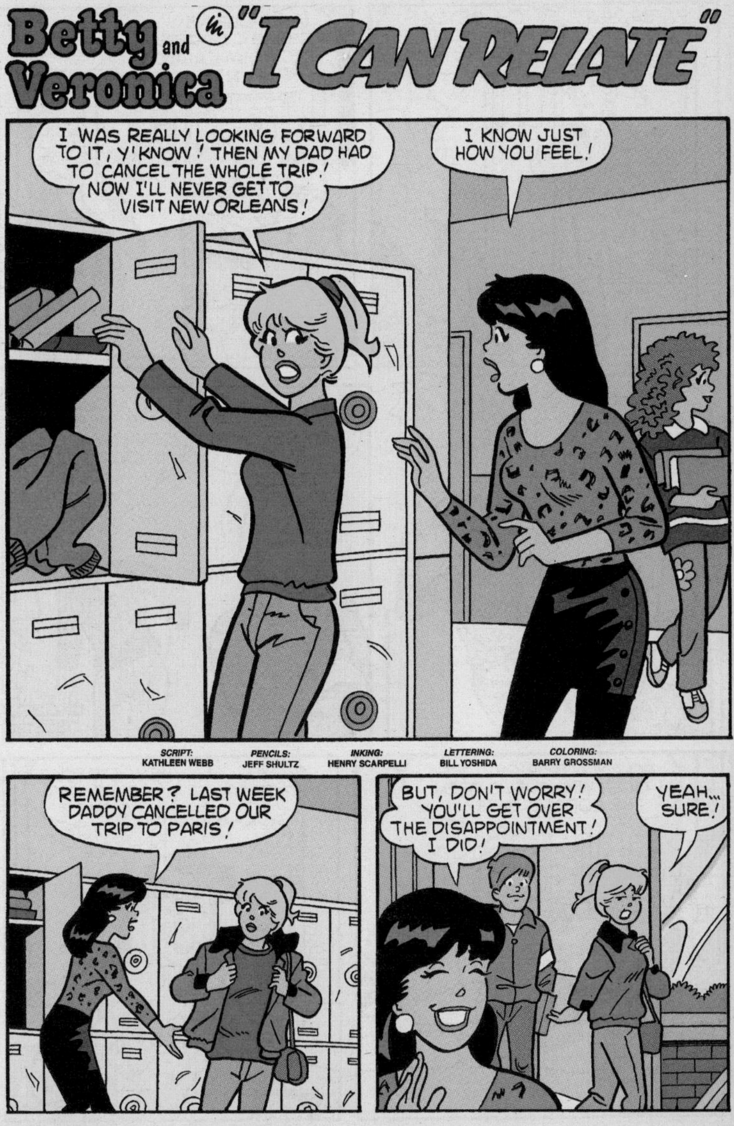
Betty and Veronica
in
"I CAN RELATE"
I WAS REALLY LOOKING FORWARD TO IT, Y'KNOW! THEN MY DAD HAD TO CANCEL THE WHOLE TRIP! NOW I'LL NEVER GET TO VISIT NEW ORLEANS!
I KNOW JUST HOW YOU FEEL!
SCRIPT: KATHLEEN WEBB
PENCILS: JEFF SHULTZ
INKING: HENRY SCARPELLI
LETTERING: BILL YOSHIDA
COLORING: BARRY GROSSMAN
REMEMBER? LAST WEEK DADDY CANCELLED OUR TRIP TO PARIS!
BUT, DON'T WORRY! YOU'LL GET OVER THE DISAPPOINTMENT! I DID!
YEAH... SURE!

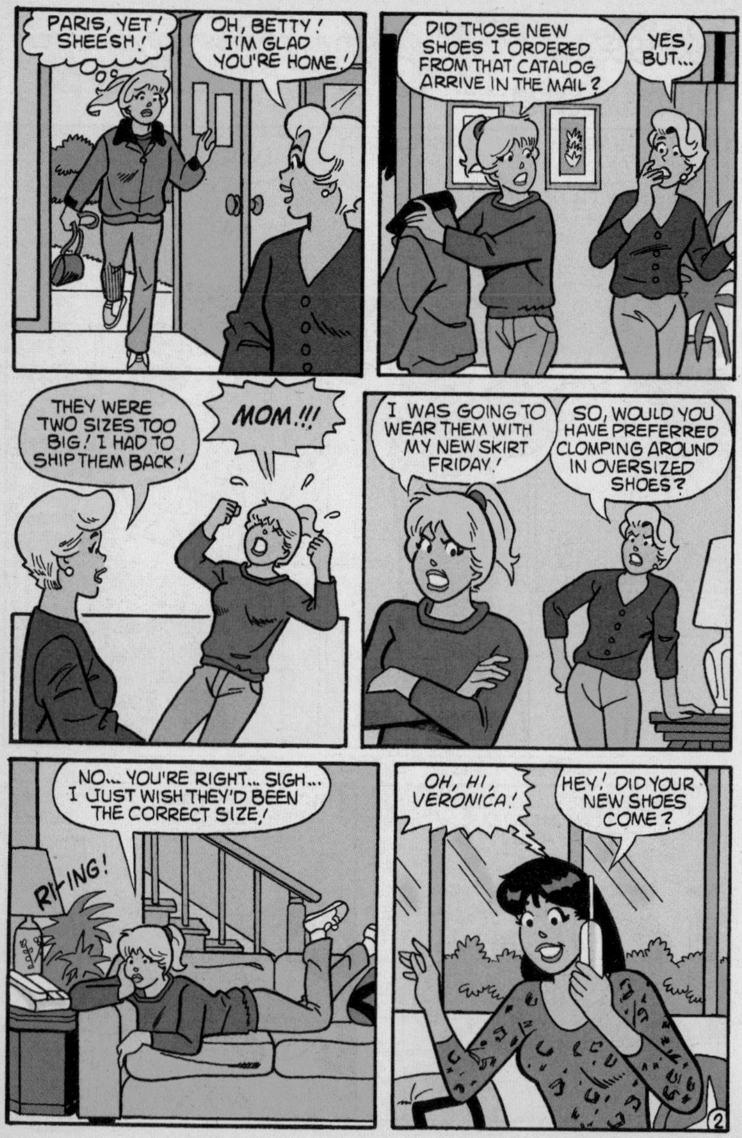
PARIS, YET! SHEESH!
OH, BETTY! I'M GLAD YOU'RE HOME!
DID THOSE NEW SHOES I ORDERED FROM THAT CATALOG ARRIVE IN THE MAIL?
YES, BUT...
THEY WERE TWO SIZES TOO BIG! I HAD TO SHIP THEM BACK!
MOM!!!
I WAS GOING TO WEAR THEM WITH MY NEW SKIRT FRIDAY!
SO, WOULD YOU HAVE PREFERRED CLOMPING AROUND IN OVERSIZED SHOES?
NO... YOU'RE RIGHT... SIGH... I JUST WISH THEY'D BEEN THE CORRECT SIZE!
RI-ING!
OH, HI, VERONICA!
HEY! DID YOUR NEW SHOES COME?
2

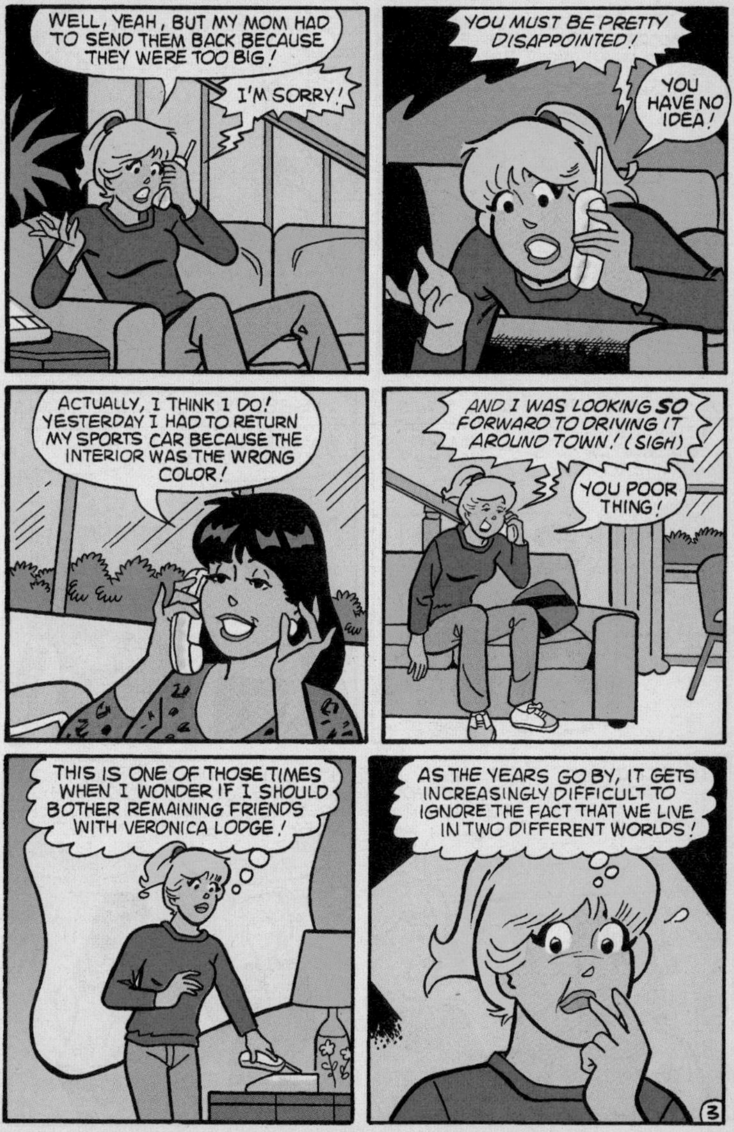
WELL, YEAH, BUT MY MOM HAD TO SEND THEM BACK BECAUSE THEY WERE TOO BIG!
I'M SORRY!
YOU MUST BE PRETTY DISAPPOINTED!
YOU HAVE NO IDEA!
ACTUALLY, I THINK I DO! YESTERDAY I HAD TO RETURN MY SPORTS CAR BECAUSE THE INTERIOR WAS THE WRONG COLOR!
AND I WAS LOOKING SO FORWARD TO DRIVING IT AROUND TOWN! (SIGH)
YOU POOR THING!
THIS IS ONE OF THOSE TIMES WHEN I WONDER IF I SHOULD BOTHER REMAINING FRIENDS WITH VERONICA LODGE!
AS THE YEARS GO BY, IT GETS INCREASINGLY DIFFICULT TO IGNORE THE FACT THAT WE LIVE IN TWO DIFFERENT WORLDS!
3

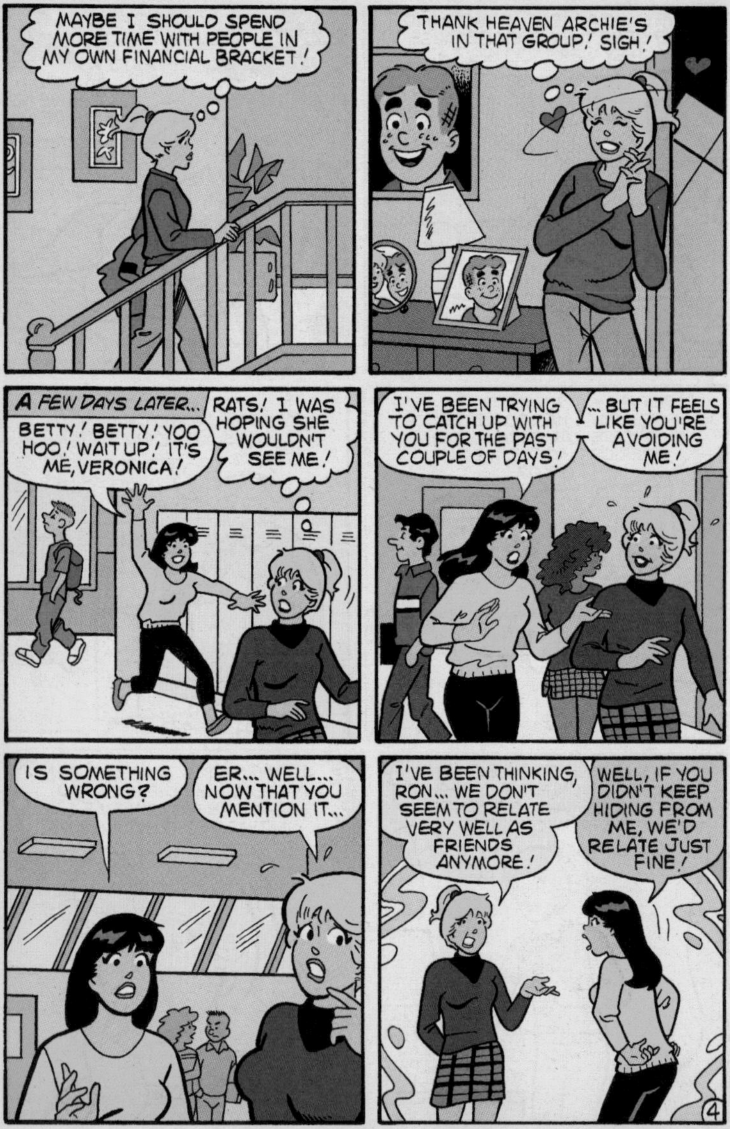
MAYBE I SHOULD SPEND MORE TIME WITH PEOPLE IN MY OWN FINANCIAL BRACKET!
THANK HEAVEN ARCHIE'S IN THAT GROUP! SIGH!
A FEW DAYS LATER...
BETTY! BETTY! YOO HOO! WAIT UP! IT'S ME, VERONICA!
RATS! I WAS HOPING SHE WOULDN'T SEE ME!
I'VE BEEN TRYING TO CATCH UP WITH YOU FOR THE PAST COUPLE OF DAYS!
... BUT IT FEELS LIKE YOU'RE AVOIDING ME!
IS SOMETHING WRONG?
ER... WELL... NOW THAT YOU MENTION IT...
I'VE BEEN THINKING, RON... WE DON'T SEEM TO RELATE VERY WELL AS FRIENDS ANYMORE!
WELL, IF YOU DIDN'T KEEP HIDING FROM ME, WE'D RELATE JUST FINE!
4

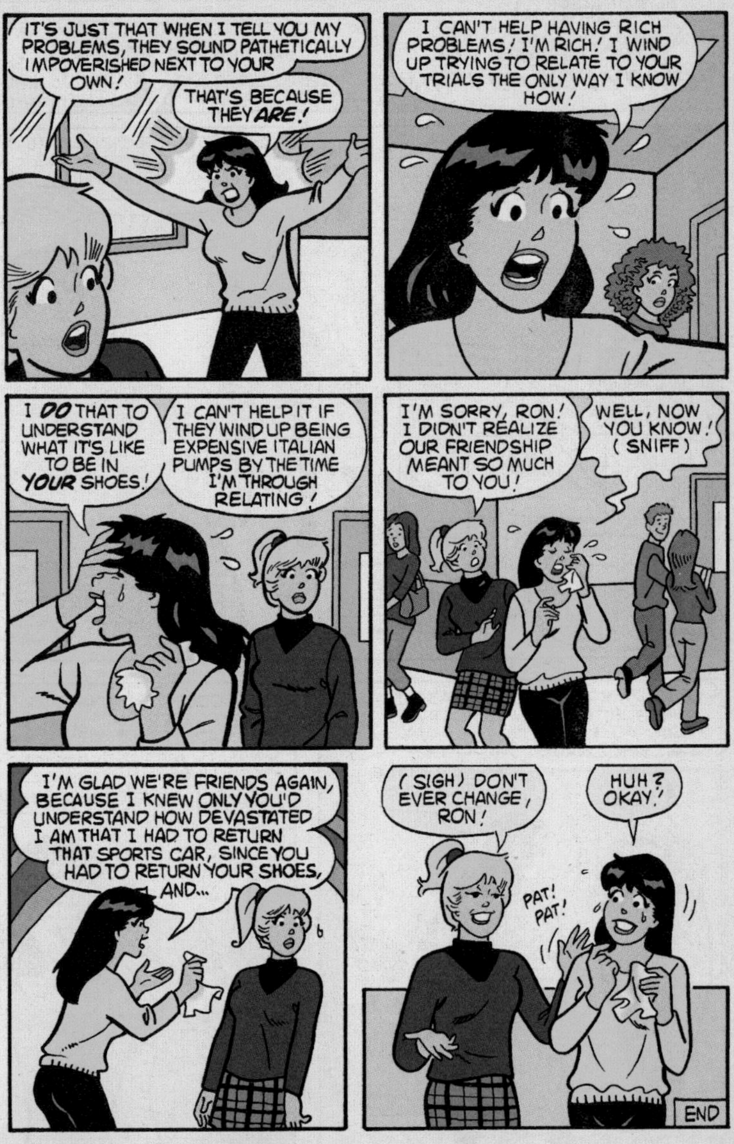
IT'S JUST THAT WHEN I TELL YOU MY PROBLEMS, THEY SOUND PATHETICALLY IMPOVERISHED NEXT TO YOUR OWN!
THAT'S BECAUSE THEY ARE!
I CAN'T HELP HAVING RICH PROBLEMS! I'M RICH! I WIND UP TRYING TO RELATE TO YOUR TRIALS THE ONLY WAY I KNOW HOW!
I DO THAT TO UNDERSTAND WHAT IT'S LIKE TO BE IN YOUR SHOES!
I CAN'T HELP IT IF THEY WIND UP BEING EXPENSIVE ITALIAN PUMPS BY THE TIME I'M THROUGH RELATING!
I'M SORRY, RON! I DIDN'T REALIZE OUR FRIENDSHIP MEANT SO MUCH TO YOU!
WELL, NOW YOU KNOW! (SNIFF)
I'M GLAD WE'RE FRIENDS AGAIN, BECAUSE I KNEW ONLY YOU'D UNDERSTAND HOW DEVASTATED I AM THAT I HAD TO RETURN THAT SPORTS CAR, SINCE YOU HAD TO RETURN YOUR SHOES, AND...
(SIGH) DON'T EVER CHANGE, RON!
HUH? OKAY!
PAT! PAT!
END

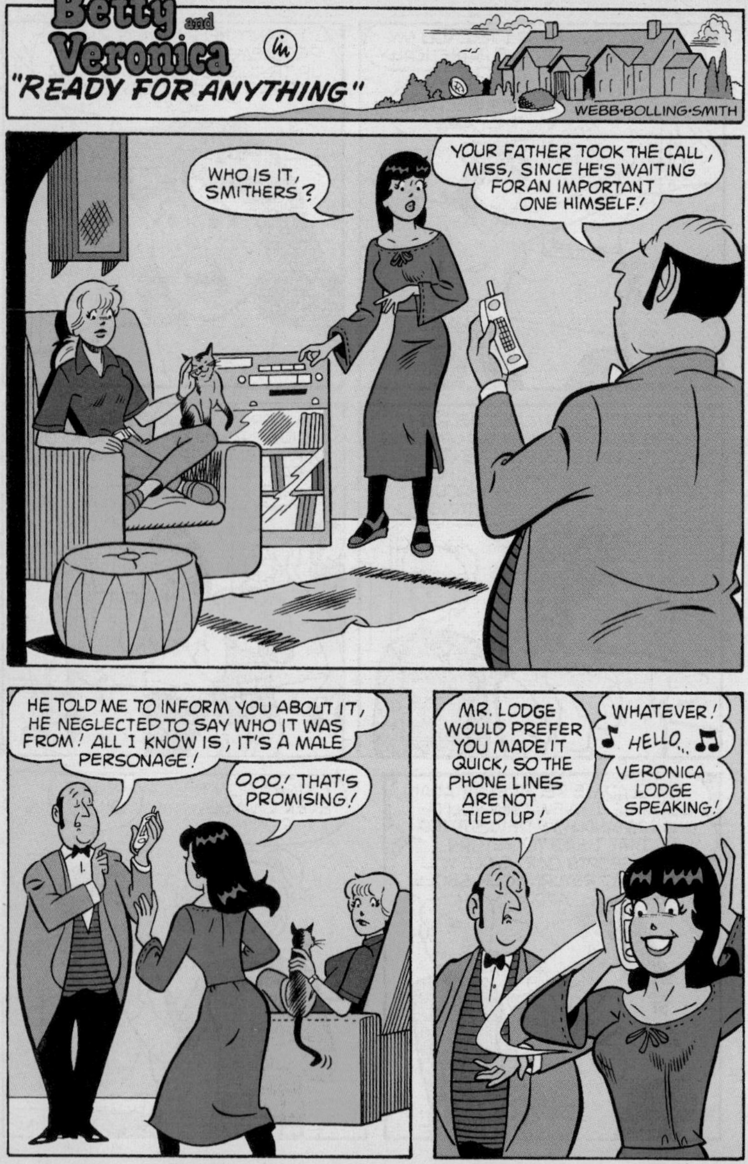
Betty and Veronica
in
"READY FOR ANYTHING"
WEBB•BOLLING•SMITH
WHO IS IT, SMITHERS?
YOUR FATHER TOOK THE CALL, MISS, SINCE HE'S WAITING FORAN IMPORTANT ONE HIMSELF!
HE TOLD ME TO INFORM YOU ABOUT IT, HE NEGLECTED TO SAY WHO IT WAS FROM! ALL I KNOW IS, IT'S A MALE PERSONAGE!
OOO! THAT'S PROMISING!
MR. LODGE WOULD PREFER YOU MADE IT QUICK, SO THE PHONE LINES ARE NOT TIED UP!
WHATEVER!
HELLO...
VERONICA LODGE SPEAKING!

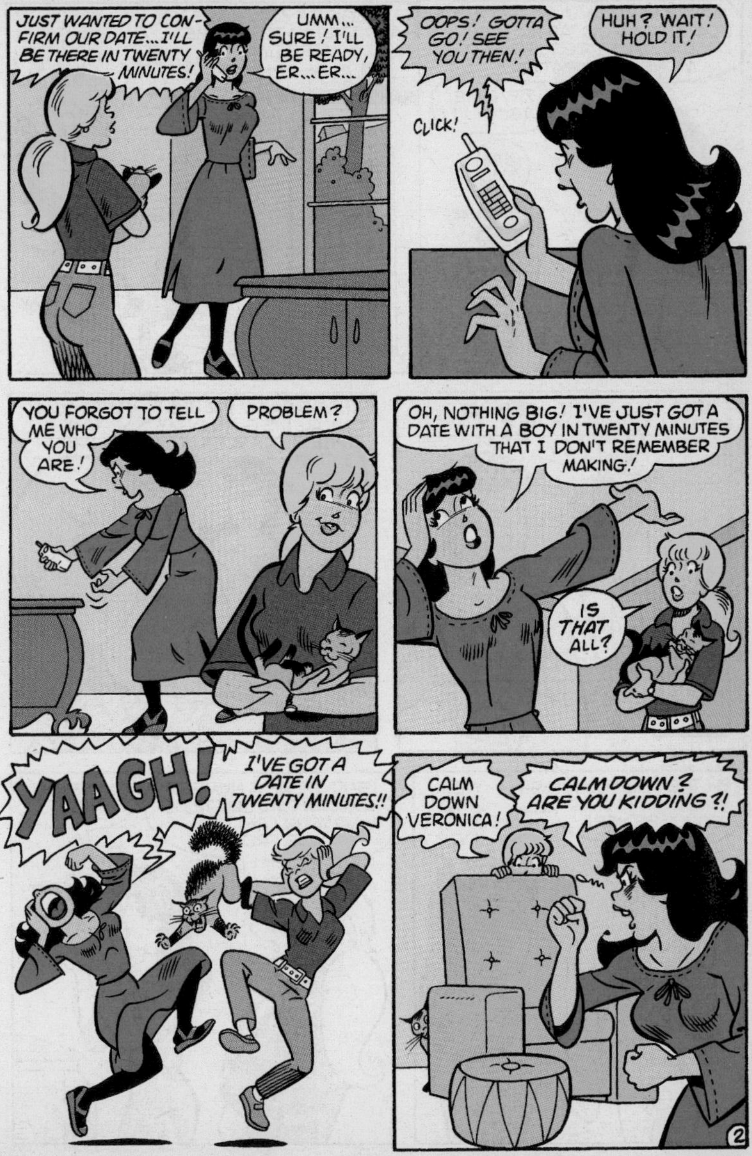
JUST WANTED TO CONFIRM OUR DATE...I'LL BE THERE IN TWENTY MINUTES!
UMM... SURE! I'LL BE READY, ER...ER...
OOPS! GOTTA GO! SEE YOU THEN!
CLICK!
HUH? WAIT! HOLD IT!
YOU FORGOT TO TELL ME WHO YOU ARE!
PROBLEM?
OH, NOTHING BIG! I'VE JUST GOT A DATE WITH A BOY IN TWENTY MINUTES THAT I DON'T REMEMBER MAKING!
IS THAT ALL?
YAAGH!
I'VE GOT A DATE IN TWENTY MINUTES!!
CALM DOWN VERONICA!
CALM DOWN? ARE YOU KIDDING?!
2

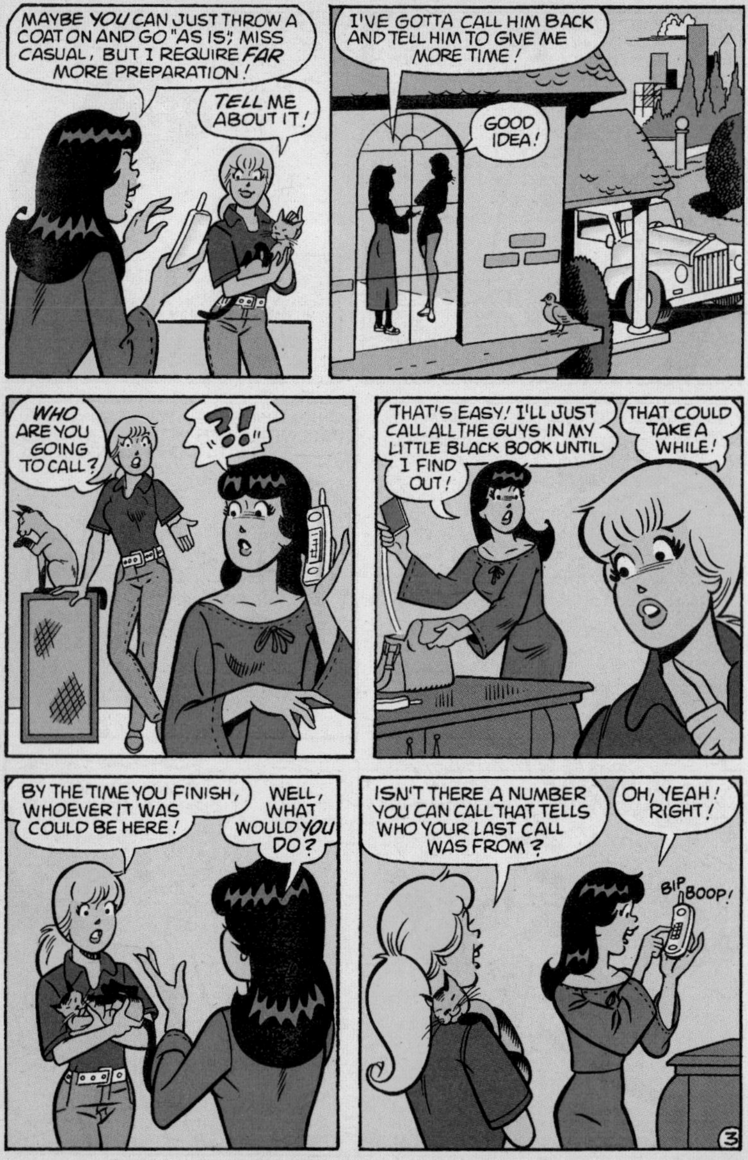

MAYBE YOU CAN JUST THROW A COAT ON AND GO "AS IS," MISS CASUAL, BUT I REQUIRE FAR MORE PREPARATION!
TELL ME ABOUT IT!
I'VE GOTTA CALL HIM BACK AND TELL HIM TO GIVE ME MORE TIME!
GOOD IDEA!
WHO ARE YOU GOING TO CALL?
?!
THAT'S EASY! I'LL JUST CALL ALL THE GUYS IN MY LITTLE BLACK BOOK UNTIL I FIND OUT!
THAT COULD TAKE A WHILE!
BY THE TIME YOU FINISH, WHOEVER IT WAS COULD BE HERE!
WELL, WHAT WOULD YOU DO?
ISN'T THERE A NUMBER YOU CAN CALL THAT TELLS WHO YOUR LAST CALL WAS FROM?
OH, YEAH! RIGHT!
BIP BOOP!

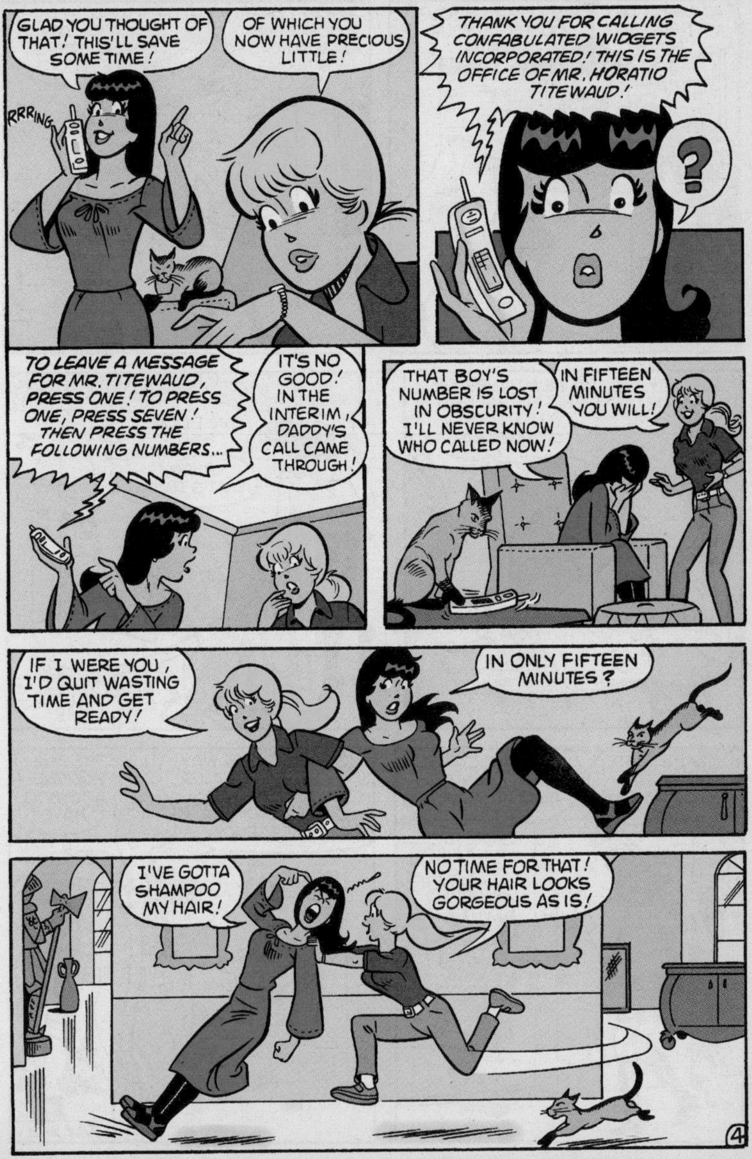
GLAD YOU THOUGHT OF THAT! THIS'LL SAVE SOME TIME!
RRRING
OF WHICH YOU NOW HAVE PRECIOUS LITTLE!
THANK YOU FOR CALLING CONFABULATED WIDGETS INCORPORATED! THIS IS THE OFFICE OF MR. HORATIO TITEWAUD!
?
TO LEAVE A MESSAGE FOR MR. TITEWAUD, PRESS ONE! TO PRESS ONE, PRESS SEVEN! THEN PRESS THE FOLLOWING NUMBERS...
IT'S NO GOOD! IN THE INTERIM, DADDY'S CALL CAME THROUGH!
THAT BOY'S NUMBER IS LOST IN OBSCURITY! I'LL NEVER KNOW WHO CALLED NOW!
IN FIFTEEN MINUTES YOU WILL!
IF I WERE YOU, I'D QUIT WASTING TIME AND GET READY!
IN ONLY FIFTEEN MINUTES?
I'VE GOTTA SHAMPOO MY HAIR!
NO TIME FOR THAT! YOUR HAIR LOOKS GORGEOUS AS IS!
4

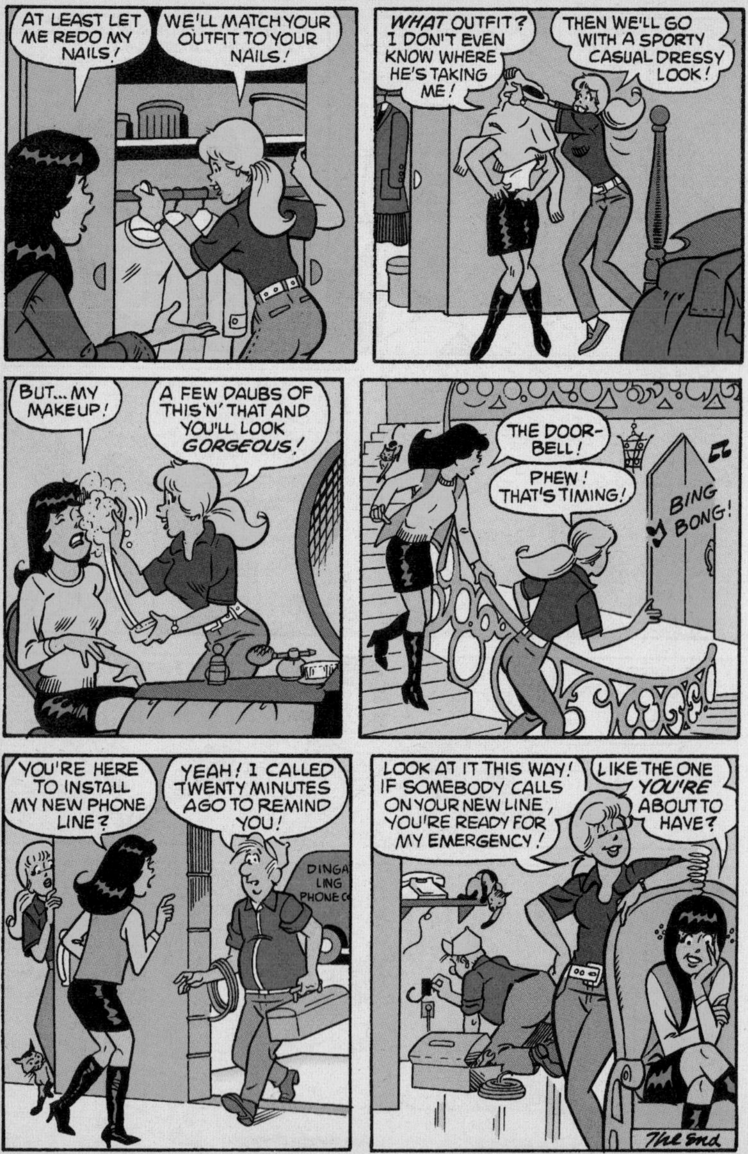
AT LEAST LET ME REDO MY NAILS!
WE'LL MATCH YOUR OUTFIT TO YOUR NAILS!
WHAT OUTFIT? I DON'T EVEN KNOW WHERE HE'S TAKING ME!
THEN WE'LL GO WITH A SPORTY CASUAL DRESSY LOOK!
BUT... MY MAKEUP!
A FEW DAUBS OF THIS 'N' THAT AND YOU'LL LOOK GORGEOUS!
THE DOOR-BELL!
PHEW! THAT'S TIMING!
BING BONG!
YOU'RE HERE TO INSTALL MY NEW PHONE LINE?
YEAH! I CALLED TWENTY MINUTES AGO TO REMIND YOU!
DINGA LING PHONE CO
LOOK AT IT THIS WAY! IF SOMEBODY CALLS ON YOUR NEW LINE, YOU'RE READY FOR MY EMERGENCY!
LIKE THE ONE YOU'RE ABOUT TO HAVE?
The End

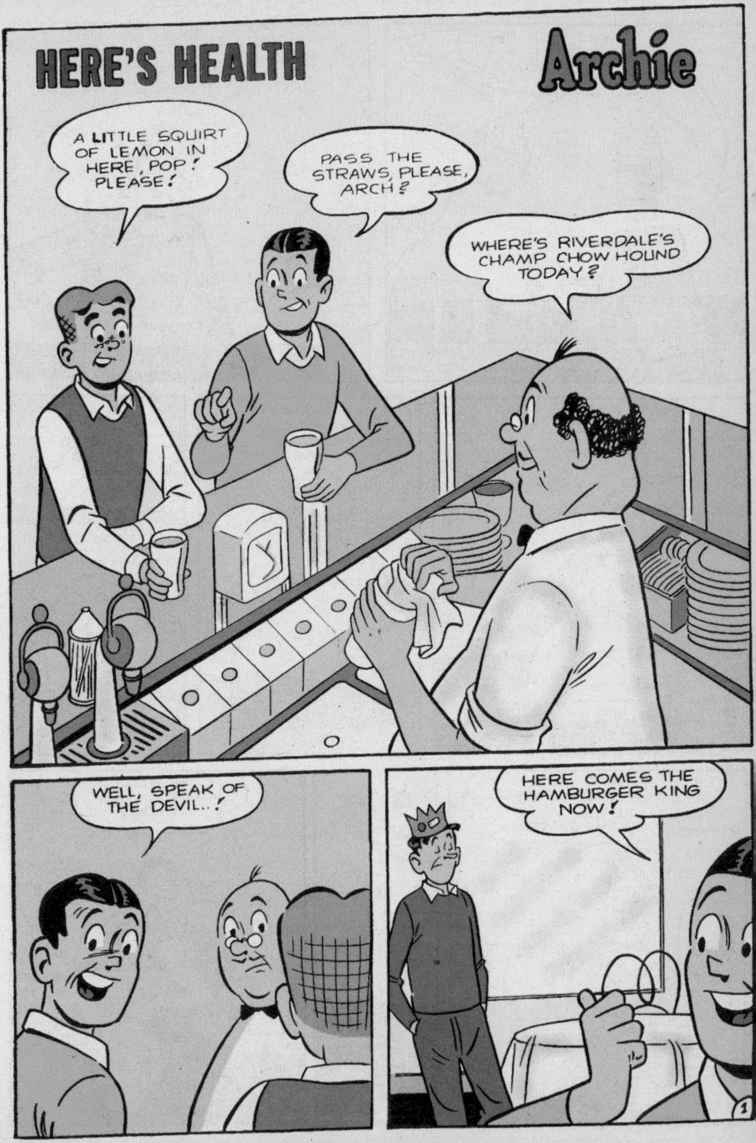
HERE'S HEALTH
Archie
A LITTLE SQUIRT OF LEMON IN HERE, POP! PLEASE!
PASS THE STRAWS, PLEASE, ARCH?
WHERE'S RIVERDALE'S CHAMP CHOW HOUND TODAY?
WELL, SPEAK OF THE DEVIL..!
HERE COMES THE HAMBURGER KING NOW!
1

Script: George Gladir / Art & Letters: Samm Schwartz

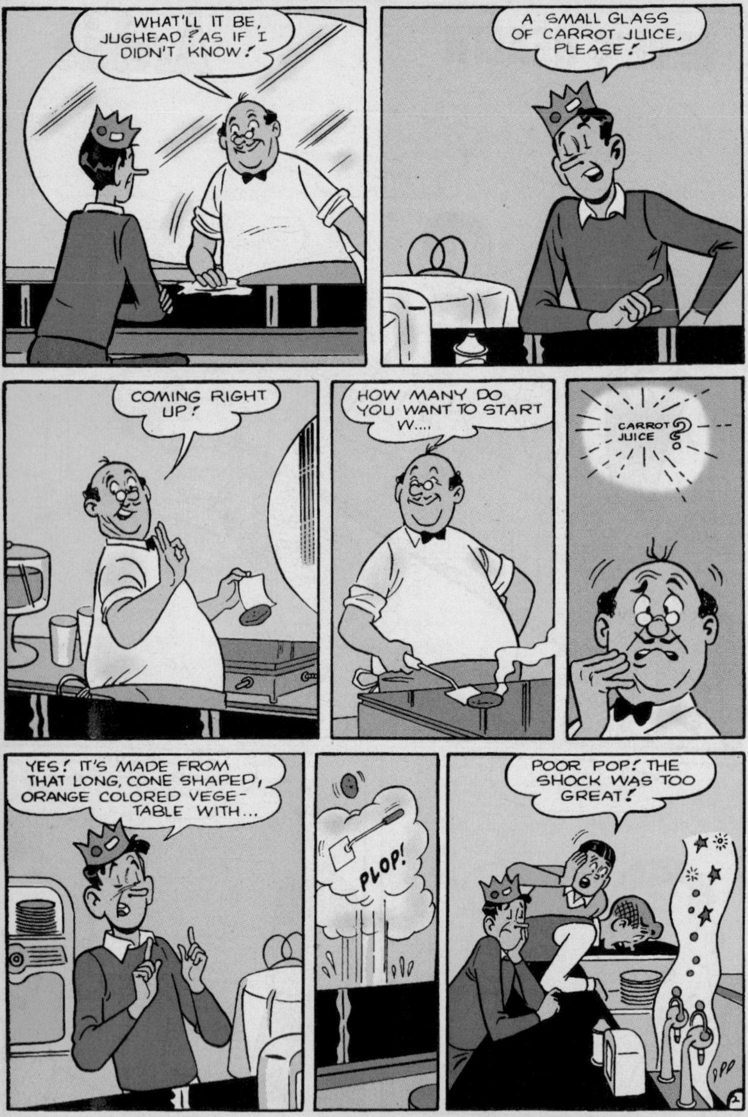
WHAT'LL IT BE, JUGHEAD? AS IF I DIDN'T KNOW!
A SMALL GLASS OF CARROT JUICE, PLEASE!
COMING RIGHT UP!
HOW MANY DO YOU WANT TO START W....
CARROT JUICE?
YES! IT'S MADE FROM THAT LONG, CONE SHAPED, ORANGE COLORED VEGE-TABLE WITH...
PLOP!
POOR POP! THE SHOCK WAS TOO GREAT!

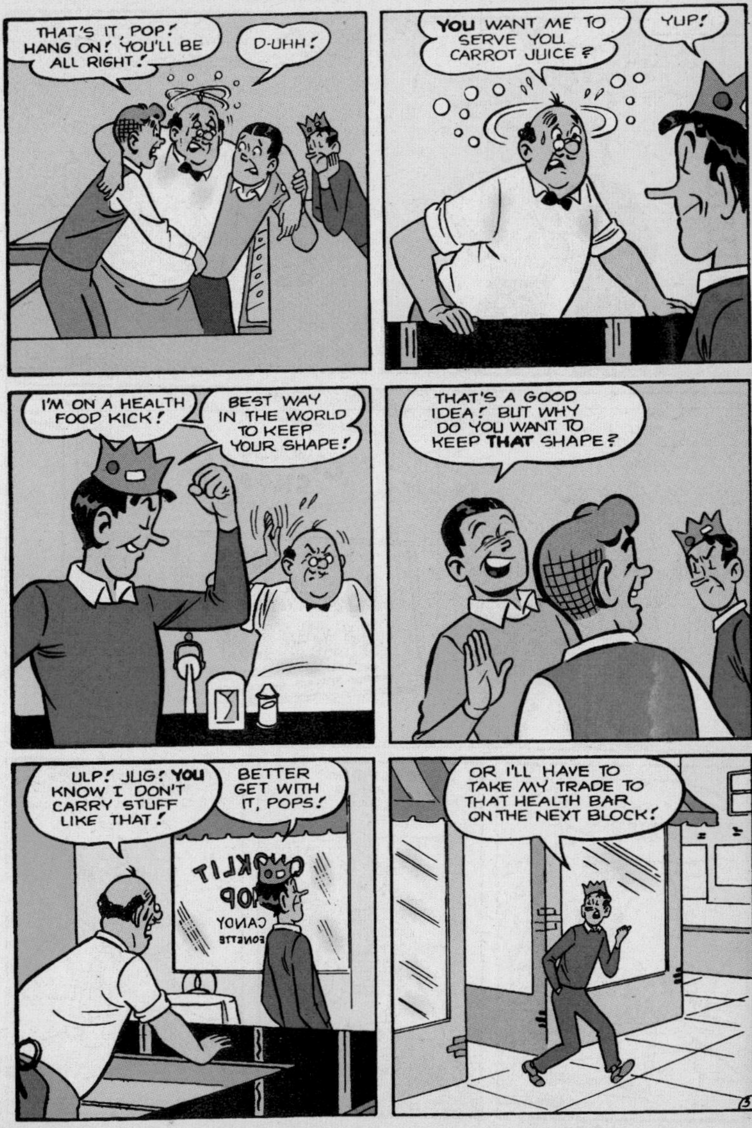
THAT'S IT, POP! HANG ON! YOU'LL BE ALL RIGHT!
D-UHH!
YOU WANT ME TO SERVE YOU CARROT JUICE?
YUP!
I'M ON A HEALTH FOOD KICK!
BEST WAY IN THE WORLD TO KEEP YOUR SHAPE!
THAT'S A GOOD IDEA! BUT WHY DO YOU WANT TO KEEP THAT SHAPE?
ULP! JUG! YOU KNOW I DON'T CARRY STUFF LIKE THAT!
BETTER GET WITH IT, POPS!
CANDY
OR I'LL HAVE TO TAKE MY TRADE TO THAT HEALTH BAR ON THE NEXT BLOCK!
3

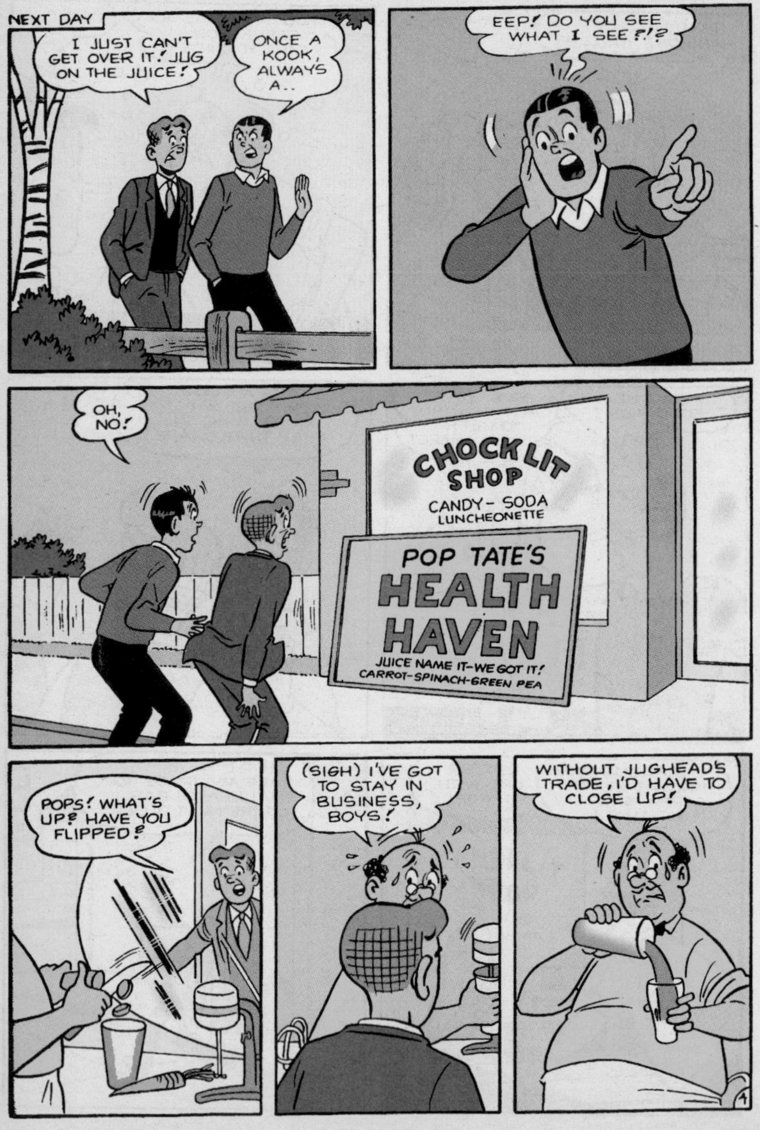
NEXT DAY
I JUST CAN'T GET OVER IT! JUG ON THE JUICE!
ONCE A KOOK, ALWAYS A..
EEP! DO YOU SEE WHAT I SEE?!?
OH, NO!
CHOCKLIT SHOP
CANDY - SODA
LUNCHEONETTE
POP TATE'S
HEALTH HAVEN
JUICE NAME IT-WE GOT IT!
CARROT-SPINACH-GREEN PEA
POPS! WHAT'S UP? HAVE YOU FLIPPED?
(SIGH) I'VE GOT TO STAY IN BUSINESS, BOYS!
WITHOUT JUGHEAD'S TRADE, I'D HAVE TO CLOSE UP!
4

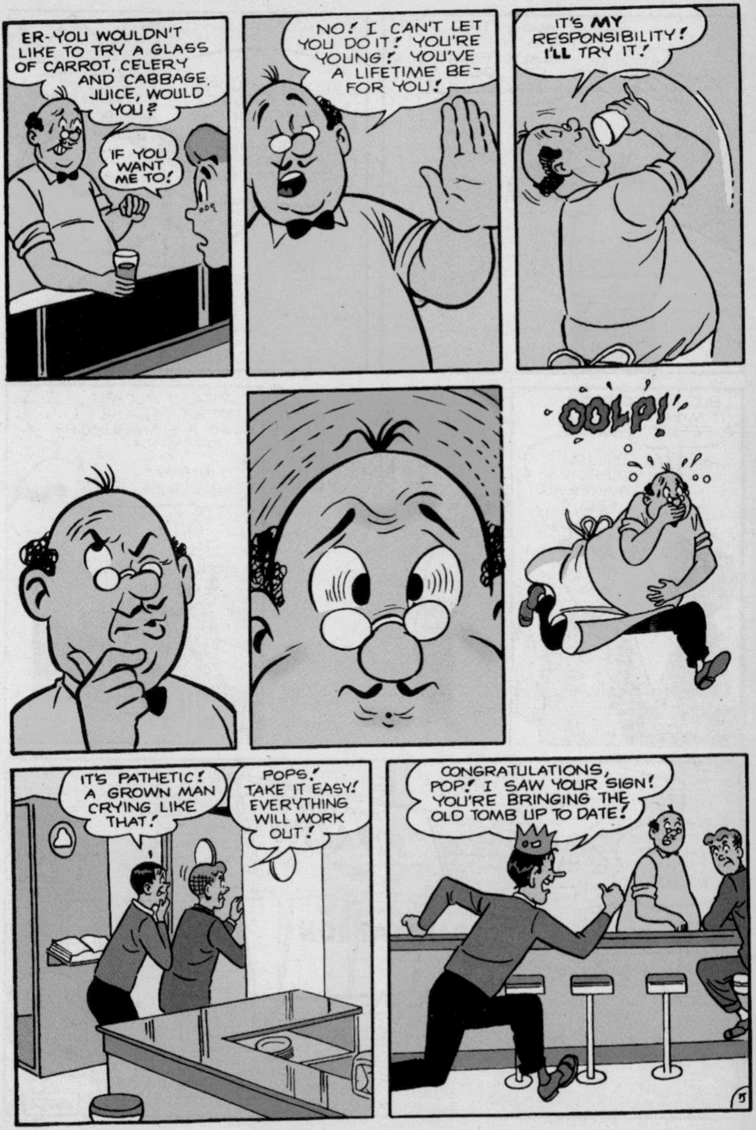
ER-YOU WOULDN'T LIKE TO TRY A GLASS OF CARROT, CELERY AND CABBAGE JUICE, WOULD YOU?
IF YOU WANT ME TO!
NO! I CAN'T LET YOU DO IT! YOU'RE YOUNG! YOU'VE A LIFETIME BE-FOR YOU!
IT'S MY RESPONSIBILITY! I'LL TRY IT!
OOLP!
IT'S PATHETIC! A GROWN MAN CRYING LIKE THAT!
POPS! TAKE IT EASY! EVERYTHING WILL WORK OUT!
CONGRATULATIONS, POP! I SAW YOUR SIGN! YOU'RE BRINGING THE OLD TOMB UP TO DATE!
5

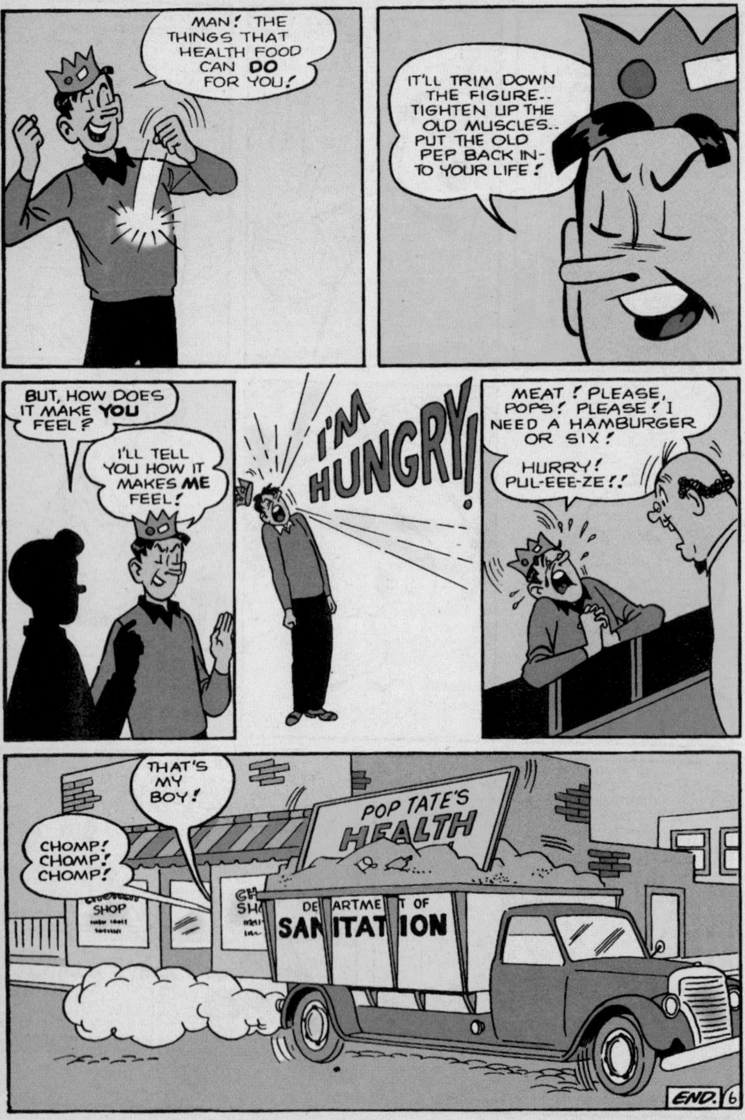
MAN! THE THINGS THAT HEALTH FOOD CAN **DO** FOR YOU!
IT'LL TRIM DOWN THE FIGURE.. TIGHTEN UP THE OLD MUSCLES.. PUT THE OLD PEP BACK IN-TO YOUR LIFE!
BUT, HOW DOES IT MAKE **YOU** FEEL?
I'LL TELL YOU HOW IT MAKES **ME** FEEL!
I'M HUNGRY!
MEAT! PLEASE, POPS! PLEASE! I NEED A HAMBURGER OR SIX!
HURRY! PUL-EEE-ZE!!
THAT'S MY BOY!
CHOMP! CHOMP! CHOMP!
SHOP
POP TATE'S HEALTH
DE ARTME T OF SAN ITAT ION
END. 6

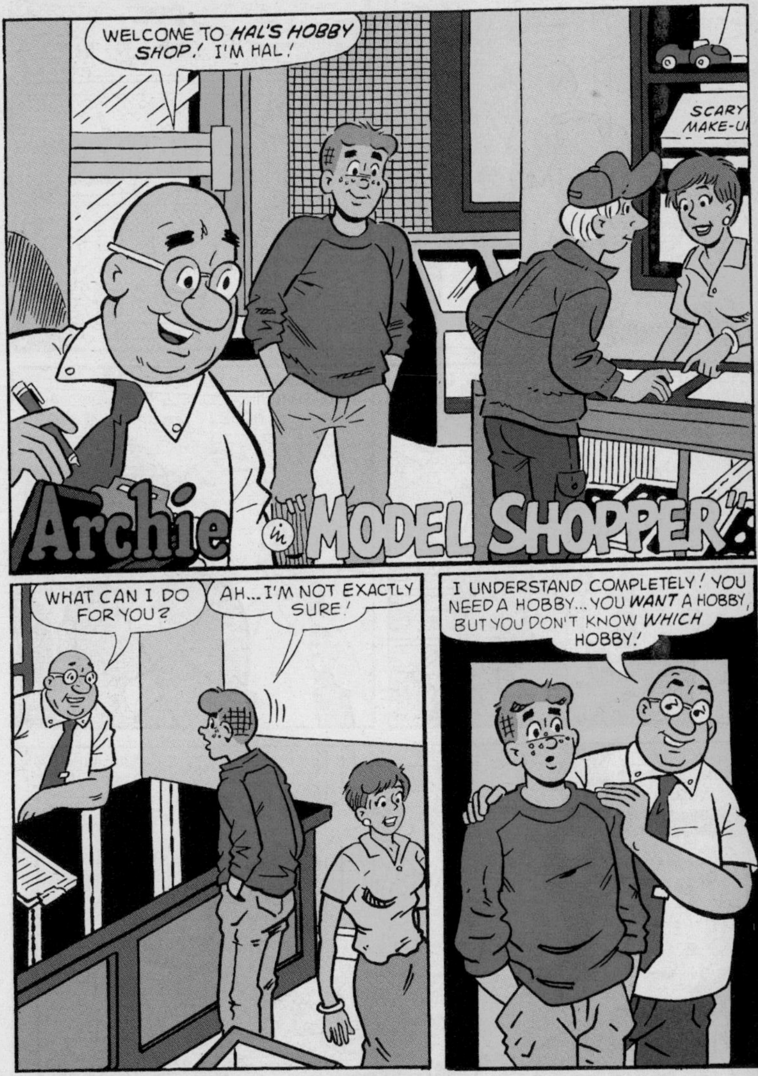
WELCOME TO HAL'S HOBBY SHOP! I'M HAL!
SCARY MAKE-U
Archie in "MODEL SHOPPER"
WHAT CAN I DO FOR YOU?
AH... I'M NOT EXACTLY SURE!
I UNDERSTAND COMPLETELY! YOU NEED A HOBBY... YOU WANT A HOBBY, BUT YOU DON'T KNOW WHICH HOBBY!

Script: George Gladir / Pencils: Tim Kennedy / Inks: Al Nickerson / Letters: Bill Yoshida

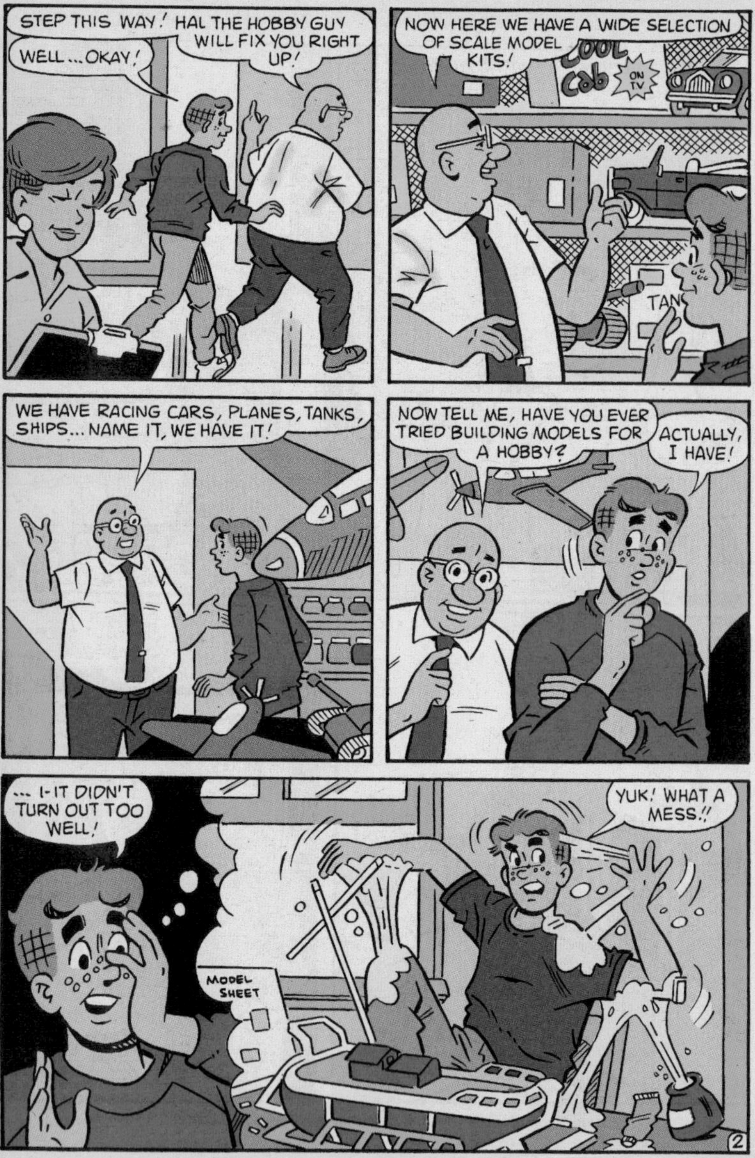
STEP THIS WAY! HAL THE HOBBY GUY WILL FIX YOU RIGHT UP!
WELL...OKAY!
NOW HERE WE HAVE A WIDE SELECTION OF SCALE MODEL KITS!
COOL Cab
ON TV
TAN
WE HAVE RACING CARS, PLANES, TANKS, SHIPS... NAME IT, WE HAVE IT!
NOW TELL ME, HAVE YOU EVER TRIED BUILDING MODELS FOR A HOBBY?
ACTUALLY, I HAVE!
... I-IT DIDN'T TURN OUT TOO WELL!
YUK! WHAT A MESS!!
MODEL SHEET
2

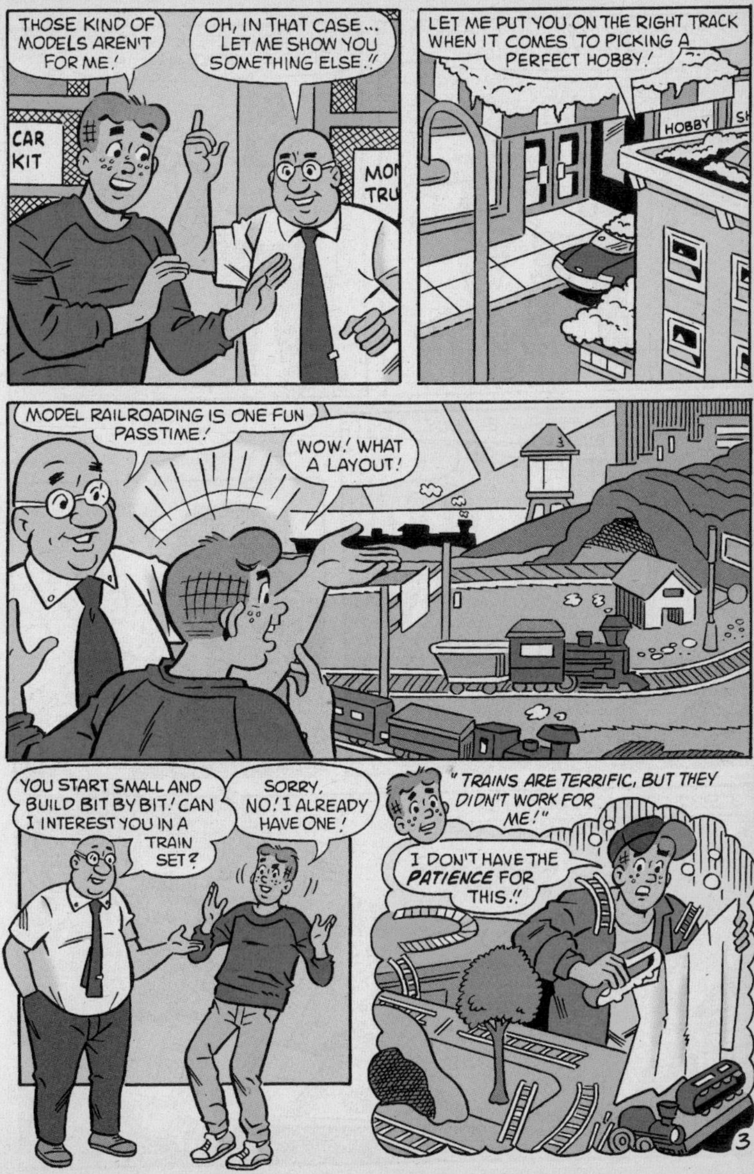

THOSE KIND OF MODELS AREN'T FOR ME!
OH, IN THAT CASE... LET ME SHOW YOU SOMETHING ELSE.!!
CAR KIT
LET ME PUT YOU ON THE RIGHT TRACK WHEN IT COMES TO PICKING A PERFECT HOBBY!
HOBBY
MODEL RAILROADING IS ONE FUN PASSTIME!
WOW! WHAT A LAYOUT!
YOU START SMALL AND BUILD BIT BY BIT! CAN I INTEREST YOU IN A TRAIN SET?
SORRY, NO! I ALREADY HAVE ONE!
"TRAINS ARE TERRIFIC, BUT THEY DIDN'T WORK FOR ME!"
I DON'T HAVE THE PATIENCE FOR THIS.!!

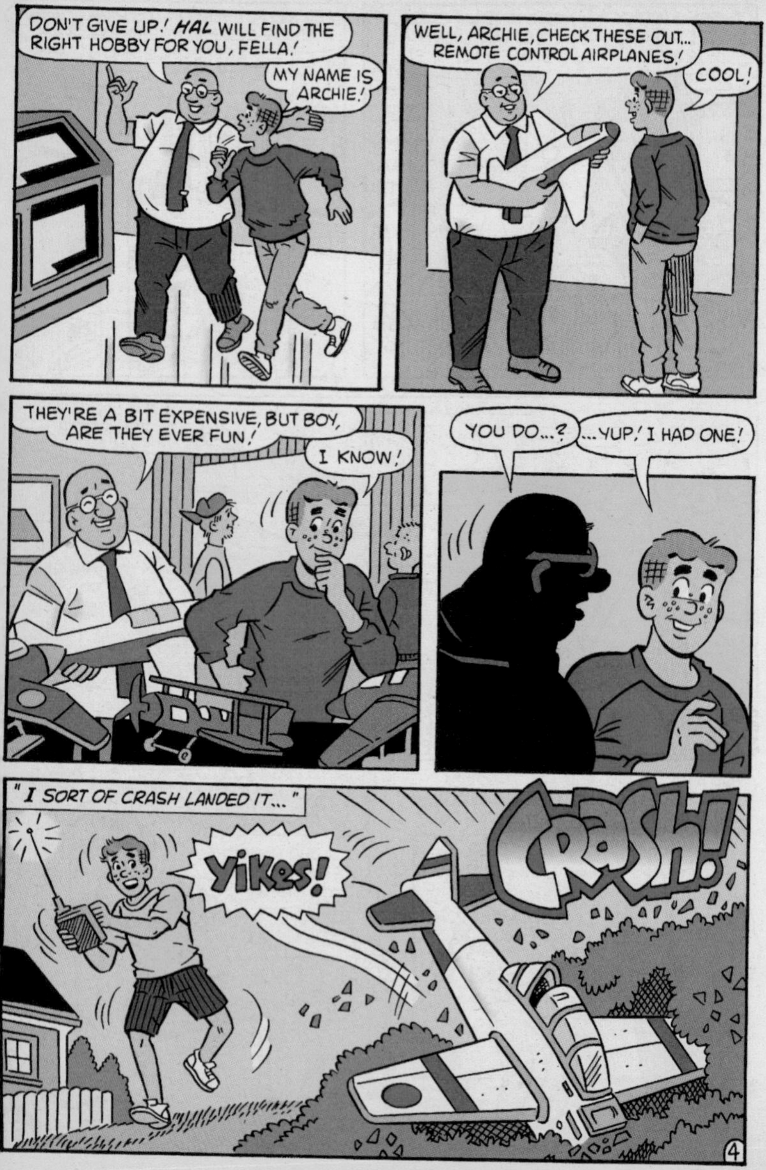
DON'T GIVE UP! HAL WILL FIND THE RIGHT HOBBY FOR YOU, FELLA!
MY NAME IS ARCHIE!
WELL, ARCHIE, CHECK THESE OUT... REMOTE CONTROL AIRPLANES!
COOL!
THEY'RE A BIT EXPENSIVE, BUT BOY, ARE THEY EVER FUN!
I KNOW!
YOU DO...?
...YUP! I HAD ONE!
"I SORT OF CRASH LANDED IT..."
YIKES!
CRASH!

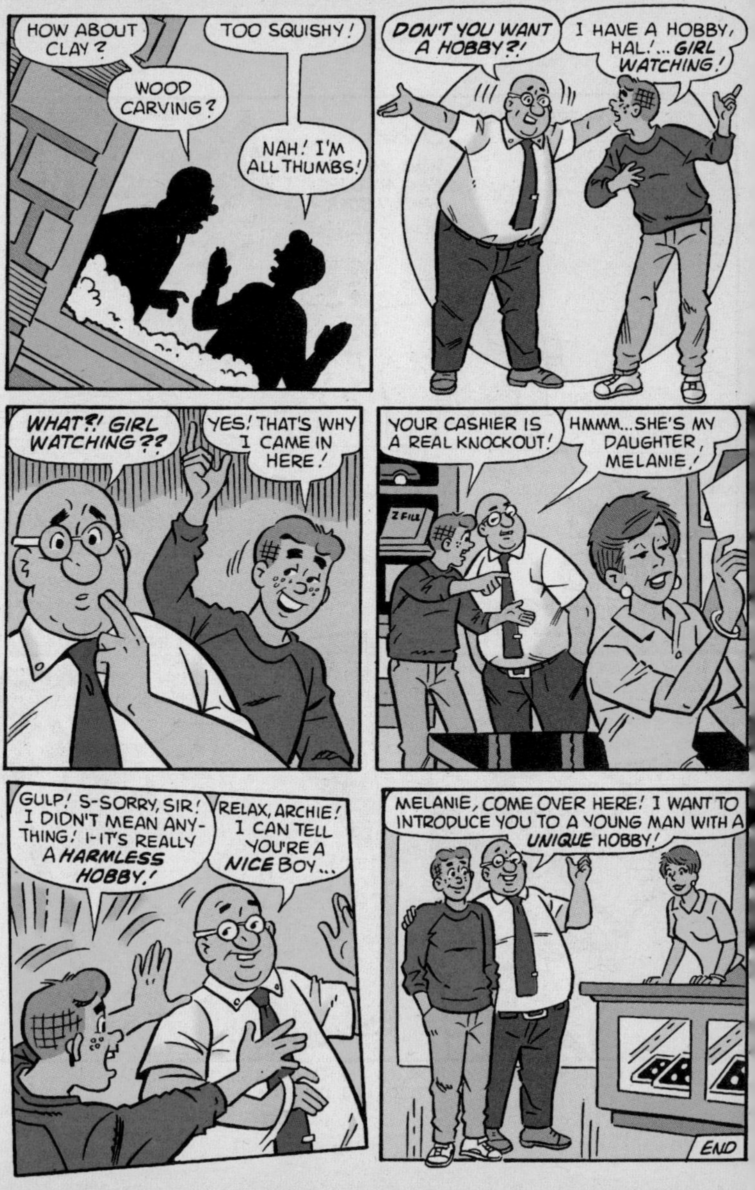
HOW ABOUT CLAY?
TOO SQUISHY!
WOOD CARVING?
NAH! I'M ALL THUMBS!
DON'T YOU WANT A HOBBY?!
I HAVE A HOBBY, HAL!... GIRL WATCHING!
WHAT?! GIRL WATCHING??
YES! THAT'S WHY I CAME IN HERE!
YOUR CASHIER IS A REAL KNOCKOUT!
HMMM...SHE'S MY DAUGHTER, MELANIE!
GULP! S-SORRY, SIR! I DIDN'T MEAN ANYTHING! I-IT'S REALLY A HARMLESS HOBBY!
RELAX, ARCHIE! I CAN TELL YOU'RE A NICE BOY...
MELANIE, COME OVER HERE! I WANT TO INTRODUCE YOU TO A YOUNG MAN WITH A UNIQUE HOBBY!
Z FILL
END

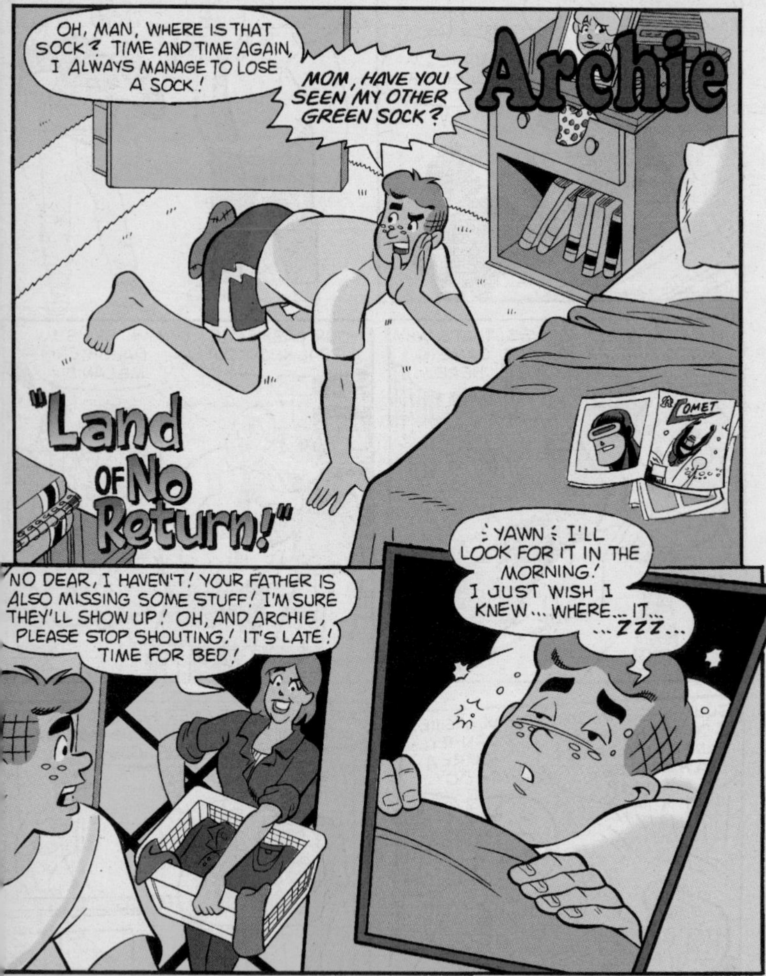
Archie
OH, MAN, WHERE IS THAT SOCK? TIME AND TIME AGAIN, I ALWAYS MANAGE TO LOSE A SOCK!
MOM, HAVE YOU SEEN MY OTHER GREEN SOCK?
"Land of No Return!"
COMET
NO DEAR, I HAVEN'T! YOUR FATHER IS ALSO MISSING SOME STUFF! I'M SURE THEY'LL SHOW UP! OH, AND ARCHIE, PLEASE STOP SHOUTING! IT'S LATE! TIME FOR BED!
:YAWN: I'LL LOOK FOR IT IN THE MORNING! I JUST WISH I KNEW... WHERE... IT... ...ZZZ...

SCRIPT: BRYAN DELGADO PENCILS: FERNANDO RUIZ INKS: JIM AMASH
LETTERS: BILL YOSHIDA

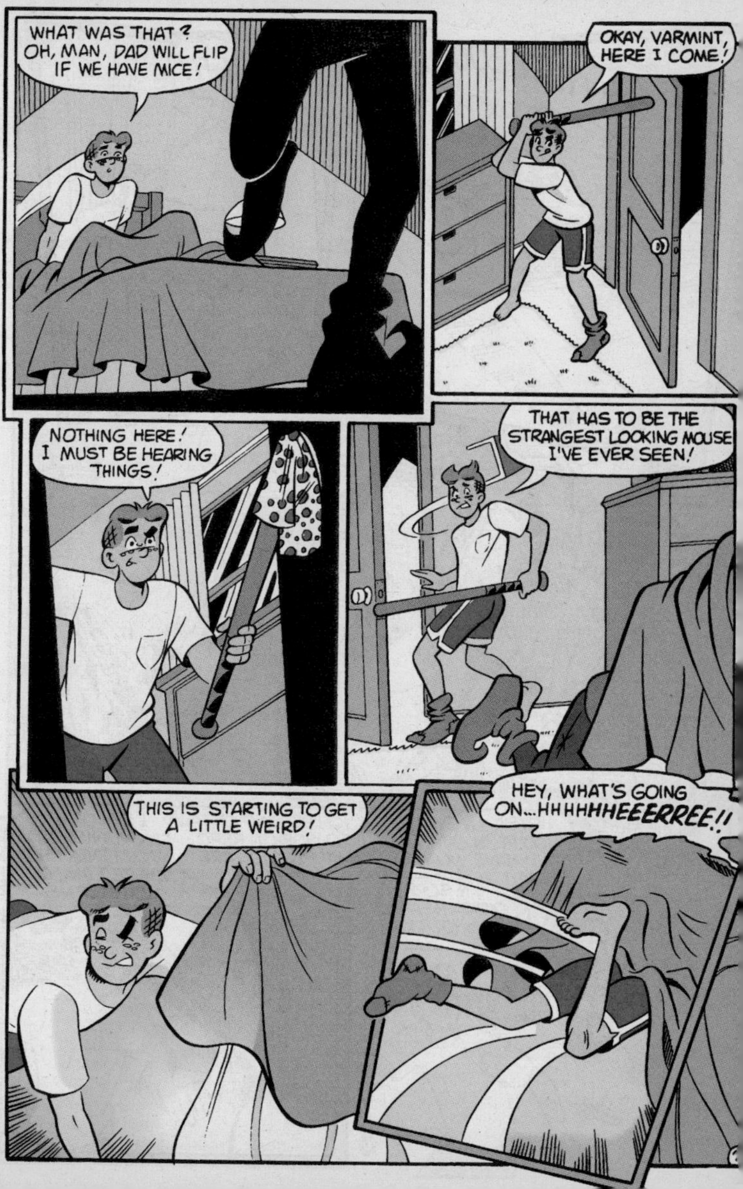
WHAT WAS THAT? OH, MAN, DAD WILL FLIP IF WE HAVE MICE!
OKAY, VARMINT, HERE I COME!
NOTHING HERE! I MUST BE HEARING THINGS!
THAT HAS TO BE THE STRANGEST LOOKING MOUSE I'VE EVER SEEN!
THIS IS STARTING TO GET A LITTLE WEIRD!
HEY, WHAT'S GOING ON...HHHHHHEEERRREE!!

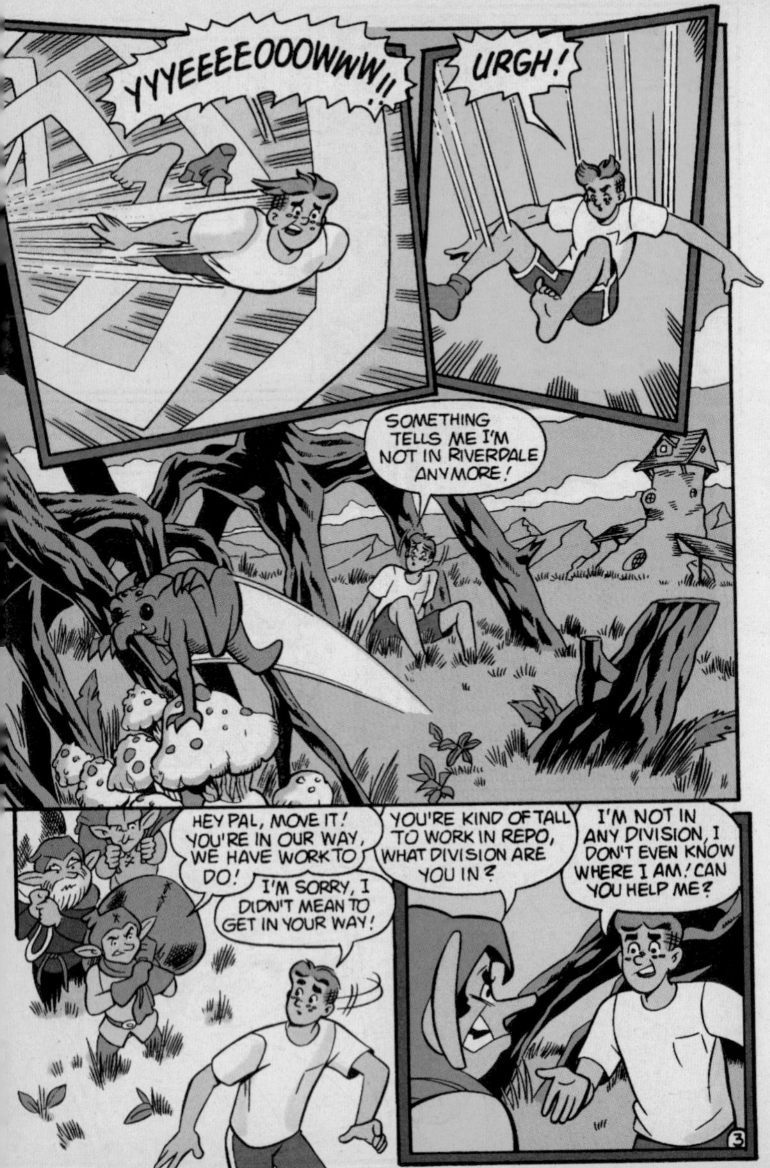

YYYEEEEOOOWWW!!
URGH!
SOMETHING TELLS ME I'M NOT IN RIVERDALE ANYMORE!
HEY PAL, MOVE IT! YOU'RE IN OUR WAY, WE HAVE WORK TO DO!
I'M SORRY, I DIDN'T MEAN TO GET IN YOUR WAY!
YOU'RE KIND OF TALL TO WORK IN REPO, WHAT DIVISION ARE YOU IN?
I'M NOT IN ANY DIVISION, I DON'T EVEN KNOW WHERE I AM! CAN YOU HELP ME?
3

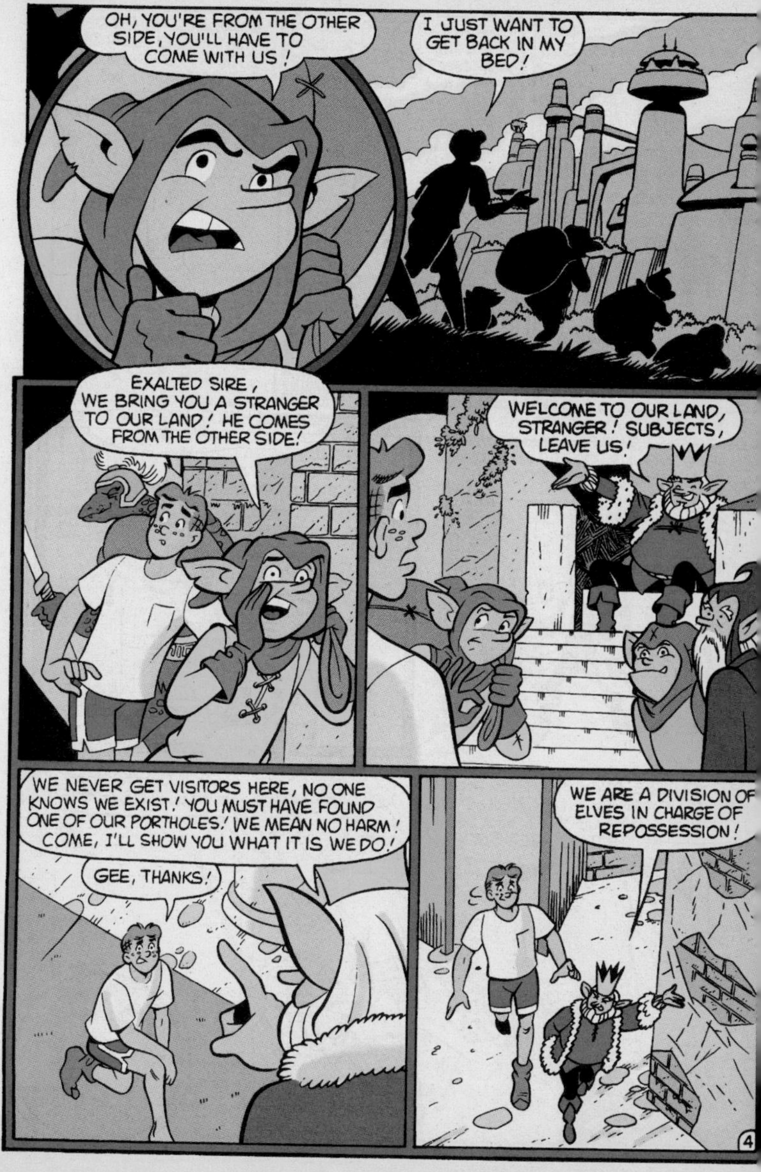
OH, YOU'RE FROM THE OTHER SIDE, YOU'LL HAVE TO COME WITH US!
I JUST WANT TO GET BACK IN MY BED!
EXALTED SIRE, WE BRING YOU A STRANGER TO OUR LAND! HE COMES FROM THE OTHER SIDE!
WELCOME TO OUR LAND, STRANGER! SUBJECTS, LEAVE US!
WE NEVER GET VISITORS HERE, NO ONE KNOWS WE EXIST! YOU MUST HAVE FOUND ONE OF OUR PORTHOLES! WE MEAN NO HARM! COME, I'LL SHOW YOU WHAT IT IS WE DO!
GEE, THANKS!
WE ARE A DIVISION OF ELVES IN CHARGE OF REPOSSESSION!
4

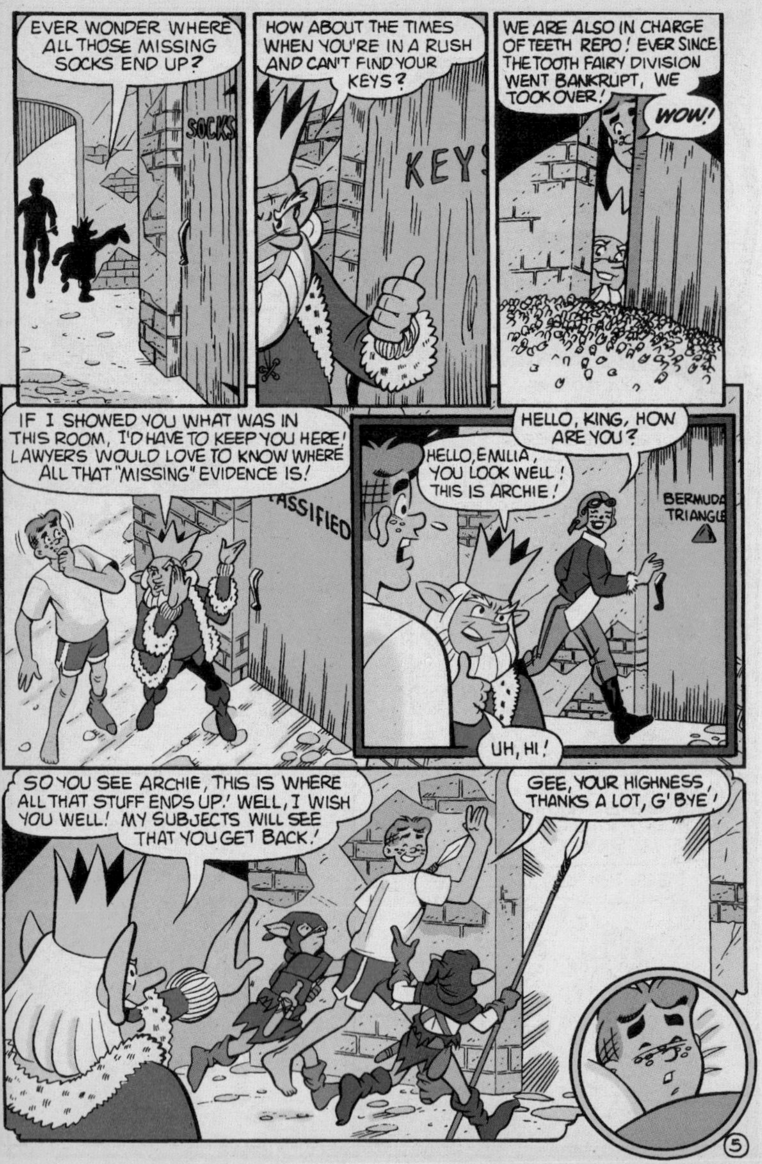
EVER WONDER WHERE ALL THOSE MISSING SOCKS END UP?
SOCKS
HOW ABOUT THE TIMES WHEN YOU'RE IN A RUSH AND CAN'T FIND YOUR KEYS?
KEYS
WE ARE ALSO IN CHARGE OF TEETH REPO! EVER SINCE THE TOOTH FAIRY DIVISION WENT BANKRUPT, WE TOOK OVER!
WOW!
IF I SHOWED YOU WHAT WAS IN THIS ROOM, I'D HAVE TO KEEP YOU HERE! LAWYERS WOULD LOVE TO KNOW WHERE ALL THAT "MISSING" EVIDENCE IS!
HELLO, KING, HOW ARE YOU?
HELLO, EMILIA, YOU LOOK WELL! THIS IS ARCHIE!
BERMUDA TRIANGLE
UH, HI!
SO YOU SEE ARCHIE, THIS IS WHERE ALL THAT STUFF ENDS UP! WELL, I WISH YOU WELL! MY SUBJECTS WILL SEE THAT YOU GET BACK!
GEE, YOUR HIGHNESS, THANKS A LOT, G'BYE!

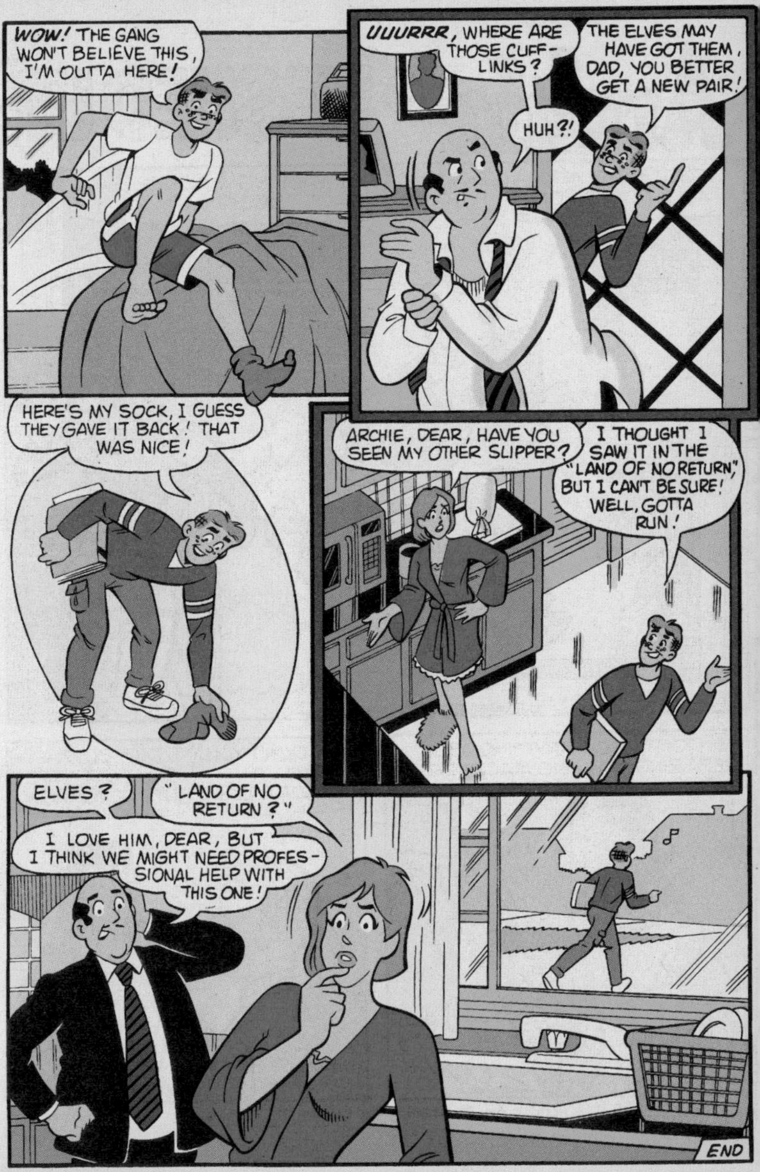

WOW! THE GANG WON'T BELIEVE THIS, I'M OUTTA HERE!
UUURRR, WHERE ARE THOSE CUFF-LINKS?
THE ELVES MAY HAVE GOT THEM, DAD, YOU BETTER GET A NEW PAIR!
HUH?!
HERE'S MY SOCK, I GUESS THEY GAVE IT BACK! THAT WAS NICE!
ARCHIE, DEAR, HAVE YOU SEEN MY OTHER SLIPPER?
I THOUGHT I SAW IT IN THE "LAND OF NO RETURN", BUT I CAN'T BE SURE! WELL, GOTTA RUN!
ELVES?
"LAND OF NO RETURN?"
I LOVE HIM, DEAR, BUT I THINK WE MIGHT NEED PROFES-SIONAL HELP WITH THIS ONE!
END

Archie in "WASHED UP"

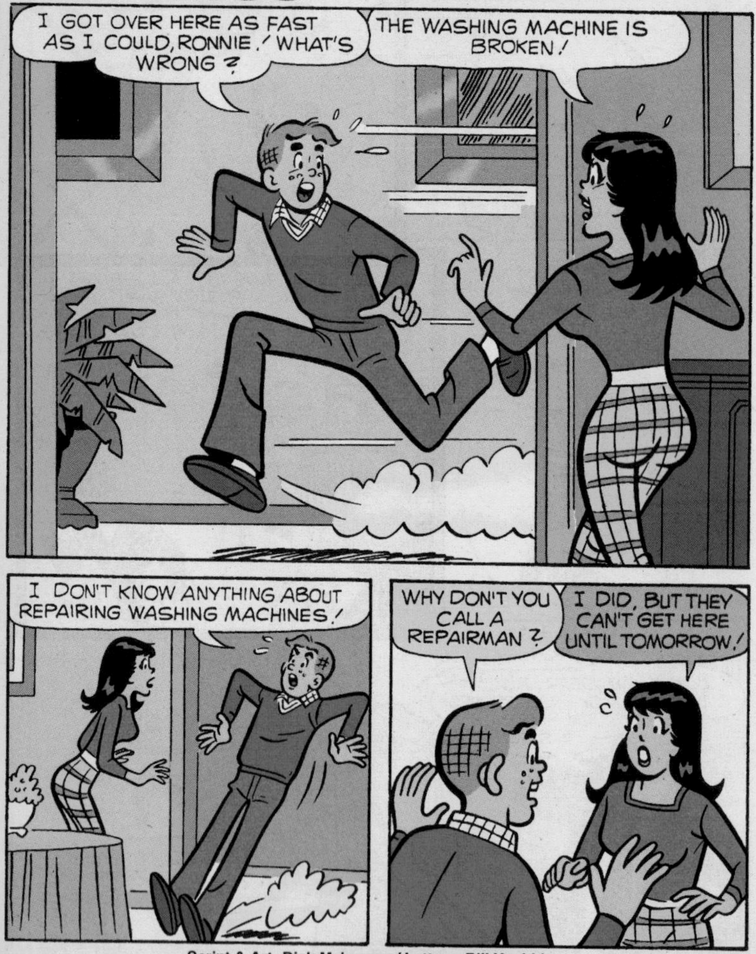
I GOT OVER HERE AS FAST AS I COULD, RONNIE! WHAT'S WRONG?
THE WASHING MACHINE IS BROKEN!
I DON'T KNOW ANYTHING ABOUT REPAIRING WASHING MACHINES!
WHY DON'T YOU CALL A REPAIRMAN?
I DID, BUT THEY CAN'T GET HERE UNTIL TOMORROW!

Script & Art: Dick Malmgren / Letters: Bill Yoshida

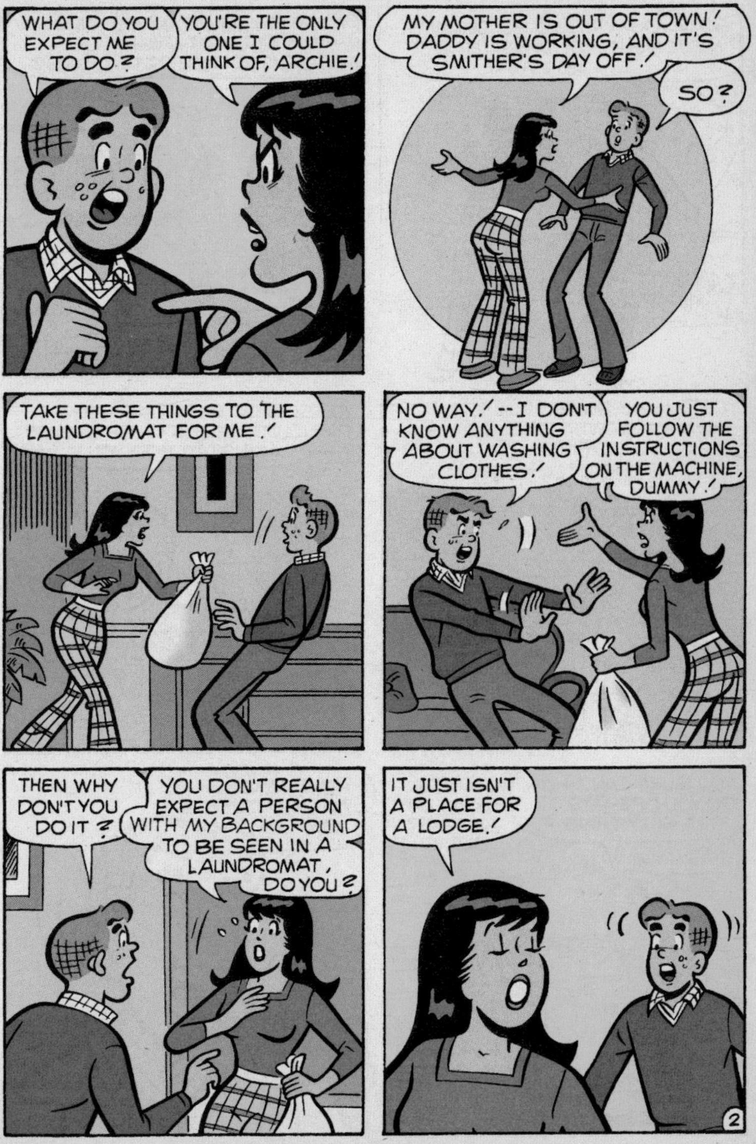

WHAT DO YOU EXPECT ME TO DO?
YOU'RE THE ONLY ONE I COULD THINK OF, ARCHIE!
MY MOTHER IS OUT OF TOWN! DADDY IS WORKING, AND IT'S SMITHER'S DAY OFF!
SO?
TAKE THESE THINGS TO THE LAUNDROMAT FOR ME!
NO WAY! -- I DON'T KNOW ANYTHING ABOUT WASHING CLOTHES!
YOU JUST FOLLOW THE INSTRUCTIONS ON THE MACHINE, DUMMY!
THEN WHY DON'T YOU DO IT?
YOU DON'T REALLY EXPECT A PERSON WITH MY BACKGROUND TO BE SEEN IN A LAUNDROMAT, DO YOU?
IT JUST ISN'T A PLACE FOR A LODGE!
2

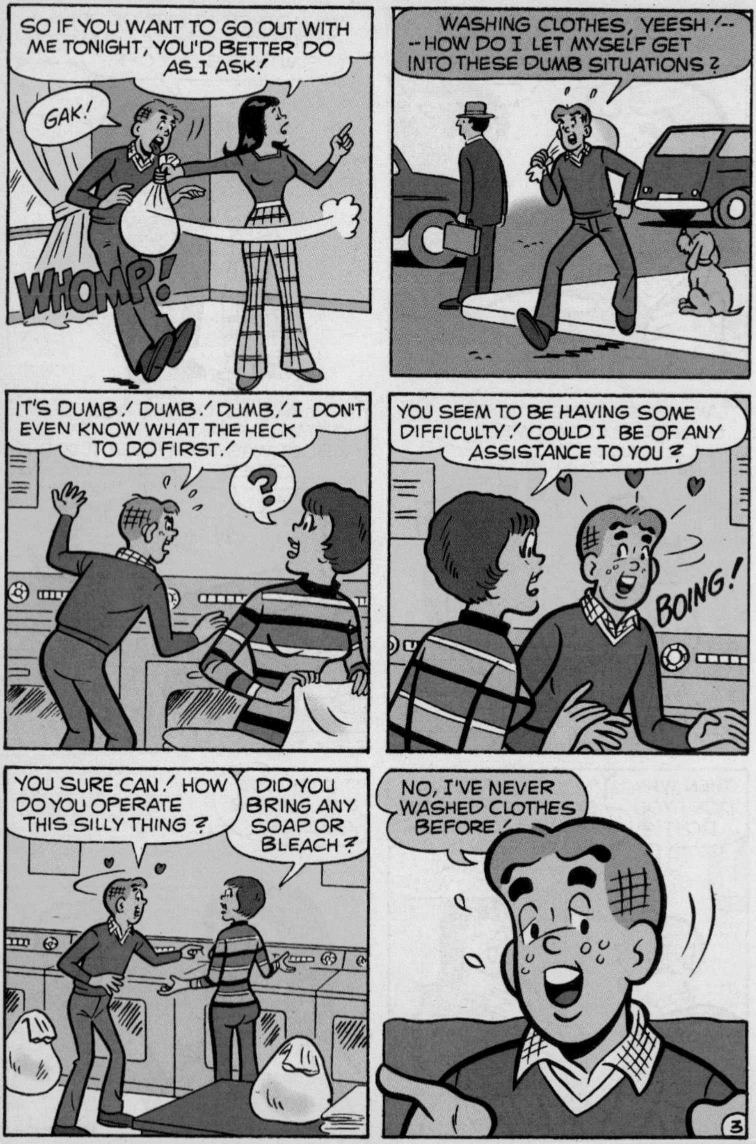
SO IF YOU WANT TO GO OUT WITH ME TONIGHT, YOU'D BETTER DO AS I ASK!
GAK!
WHOMP!
WASHING CLOTHES, YEESH!-- --HOW DO I LET MYSELF GET INTO THESE DUMB SITUATIONS?
IT'S DUMB! DUMB! DUMB! I DON'T EVEN KNOW WHAT THE HECK TO DO FIRST!
?
YOU SEEM TO BE HAVING SOME DIFFICULTY! COULD I BE OF ANY ASSISTANCE TO YOU?
BOING!
YOU SURE CAN! HOW DO YOU OPERATE THIS SILLY THING?
DID YOU BRING ANY SOAP OR BLEACH?
NO, I'VE NEVER WASHED CLOTHES BEFORE!
3

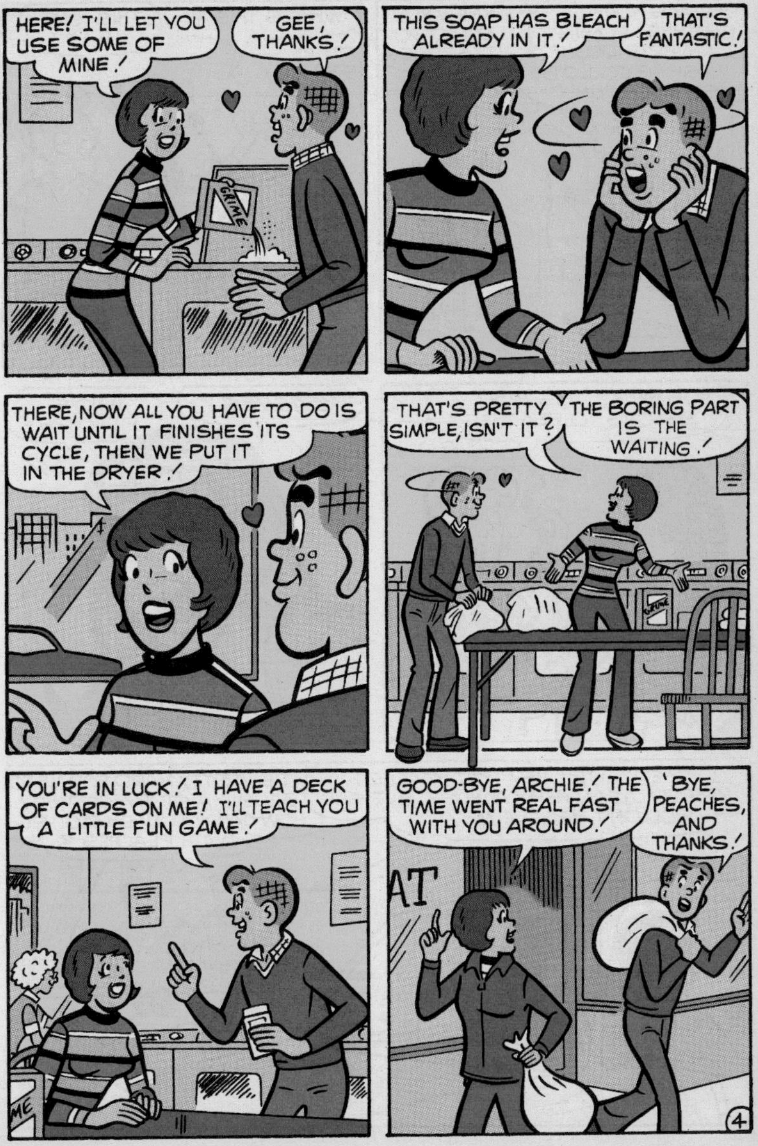

HERE! I'LL LET YOU USE SOME OF MINE!
GEE, THANKS!
GRIME
THIS SOAP HAS BLEACH ALREADY IN IT!
THAT'S FANTASTIC!
THERE, NOW ALL YOU HAVE TO DO IS WAIT UNTIL IT FINISHES ITS CYCLE, THEN WE PUT IT IN THE DRYER!
THAT'S PRETTY SIMPLE, ISN'T IT?
THE BORING PART IS THE WAITING!
YOU'RE IN LUCK! I HAVE A DECK OF CARDS ON ME! I'LL TEACH YOU A LITTLE FUN GAME!
GOOD-BYE, ARCHIE! THE TIME WENT REAL FAST WITH YOU AROUND!
'BYE, PEACHES, AND THANKS!

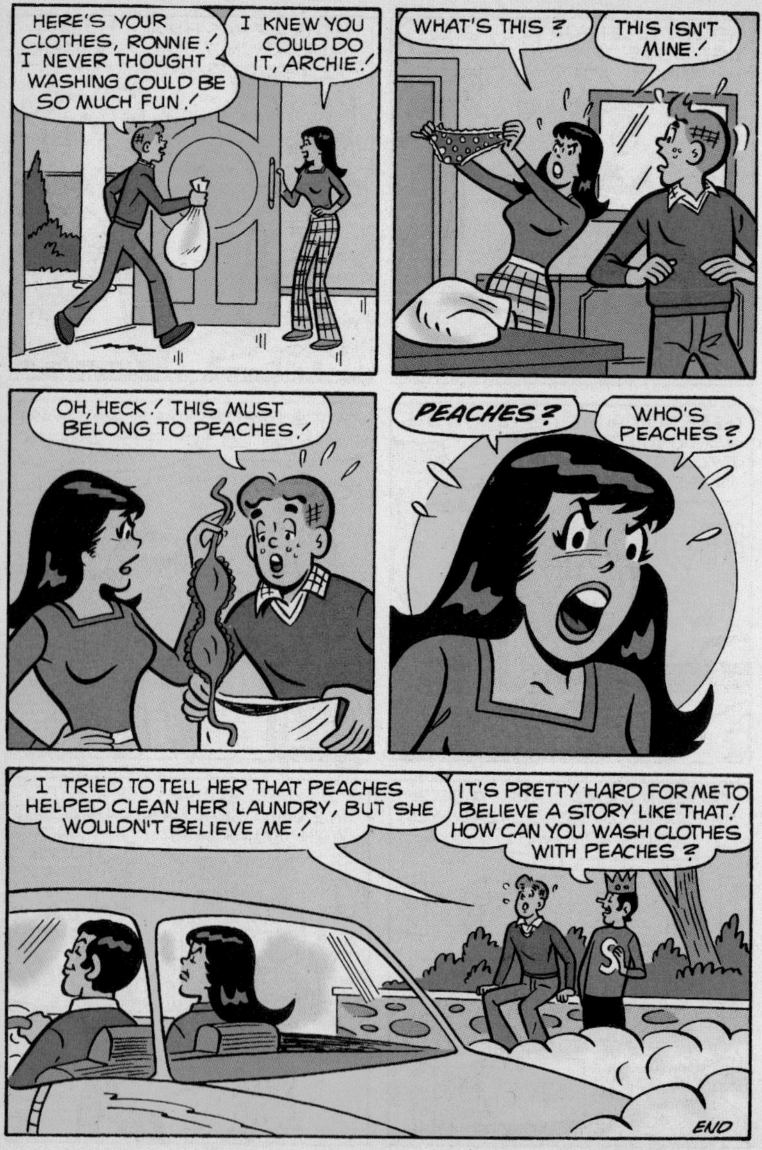
HERE'S YOUR CLOTHES, RONNIE! I NEVER THOUGHT WASHING COULD BE SO MUCH FUN!
I KNEW YOU COULD DO IT, ARCHIE!
WHAT'S THIS ?
THIS ISN'T MINE!
OH, HECK! THIS MUST BELONG TO PEACHES!
PEACHES ?
WHO'S PEACHES ?
I TRIED TO TELL HER THAT PEACHES HELPED CLEAN HER LAUNDRY, BUT SHE WOULDN'T BELIEVE ME!
IT'S PRETTY HARD FOR ME TO BELIEVE A STORY LIKE THAT! HOW CAN YOU WASH CLOTHES WITH PEACHES ?
END

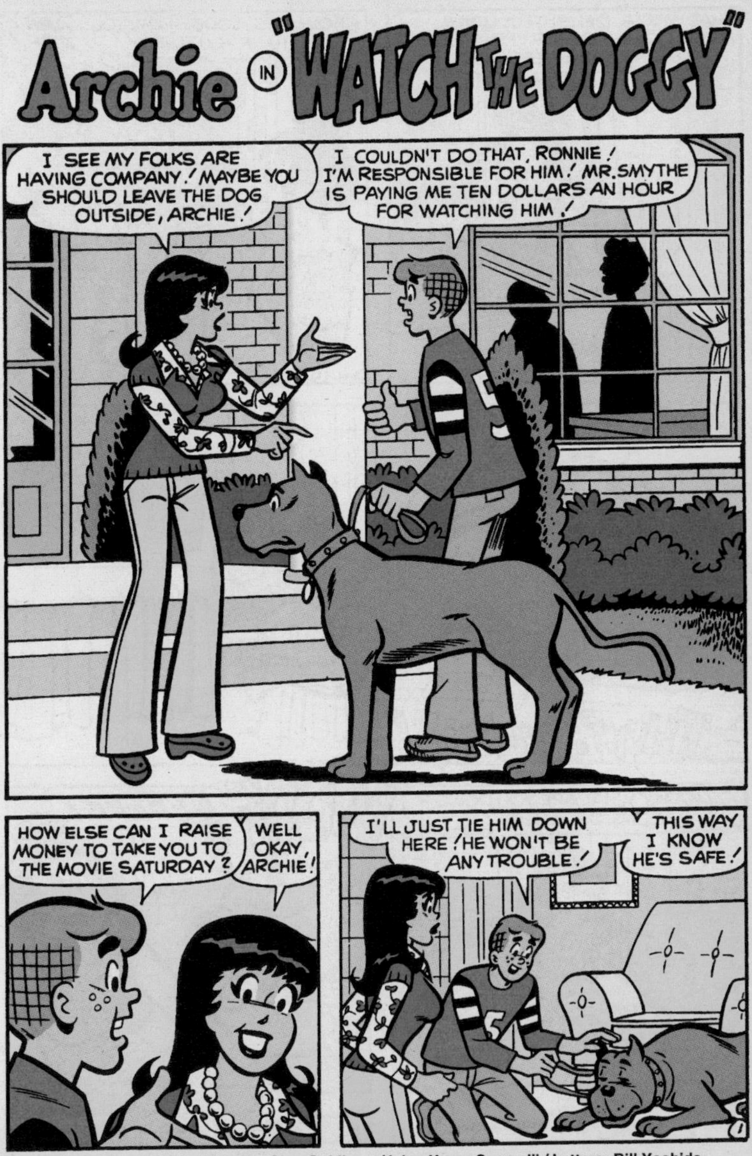
Archie IN "WATCH THE DOGGY"
I SEE MY FOLKS ARE HAVING COMPANY! MAYBE YOU SHOULD LEAVE THE DOG OUTSIDE, ARCHIE!
I COULDN'T DO THAT, RONNIE! I'M RESPONSIBLE FOR HIM! MR. SMYTHE IS PAYING ME TEN DOLLARS AN HOUR FOR WATCHING HIM!
HOW ELSE CAN I RAISE MONEY TO TAKE YOU TO THE MOVIE SATURDAY?
WELL OKAY, ARCHIE!
I'LL JUST TIE HIM DOWN HERE! HE WON'T BE ANY TROUBLE!
THIS WAY I KNOW HE'S SAFE!
1

Script: Frank Doyle / Pencils: Stan Goldberg / Inks: Henry Scarpelli / Letters: Bill Yoshida

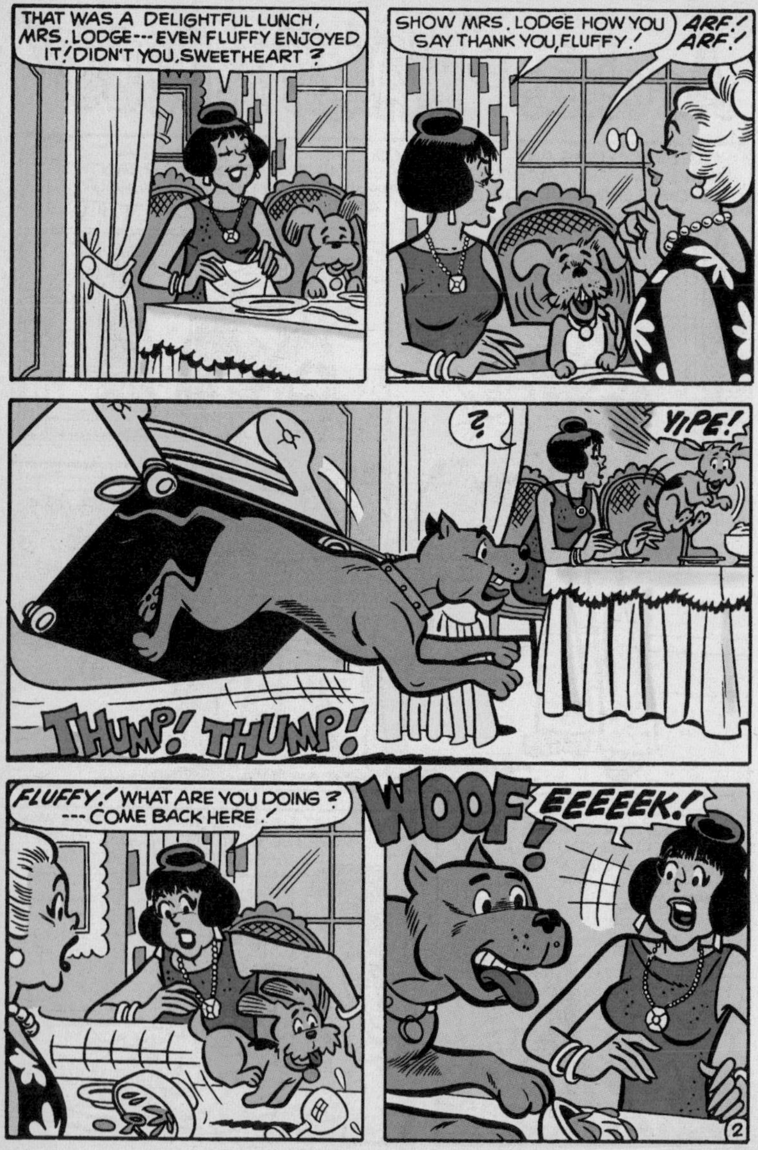
THAT WAS A DELIGHTFUL LUNCH, MRS. LODGE--- EVEN FLUFFY ENJOYED IT! DIDN'T YOU, SWEETHEART ?
SHOW MRS. LODGE HOW YOU SAY THANK YOU, FLUFFY !
ARF! ARF!
?
YIPE!
THUMP! THUMP!
FLUFFY! WHAT ARE YOU DOING ? --- COME BACK HERE !
WOOF!
EEEEEK!
2

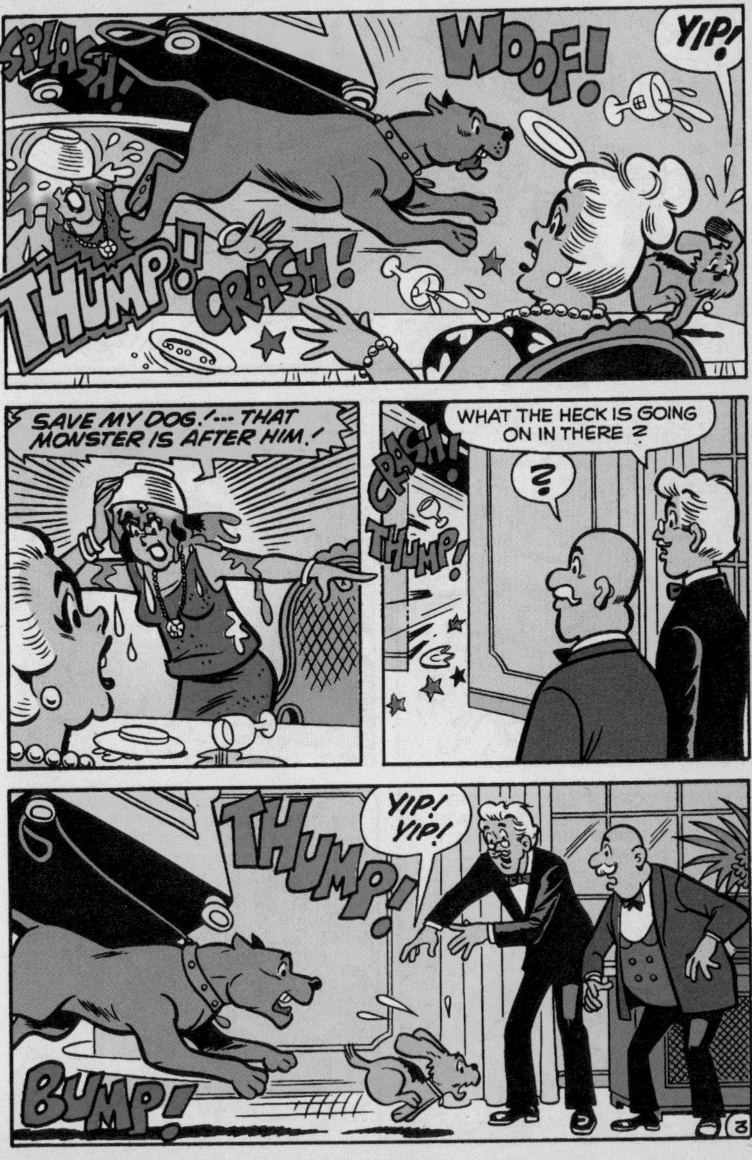
SPLASH!
WOOF!
YIP!
THUMP!
CRASH!
SAVE MY DOG!... THAT MONSTER IS AFTER HIM!
WHAT THE HECK IS GOING ON IN THERE?
?
CRASH!
THUMP!
THUMP!
YIP! YIP!
BUMP!
3

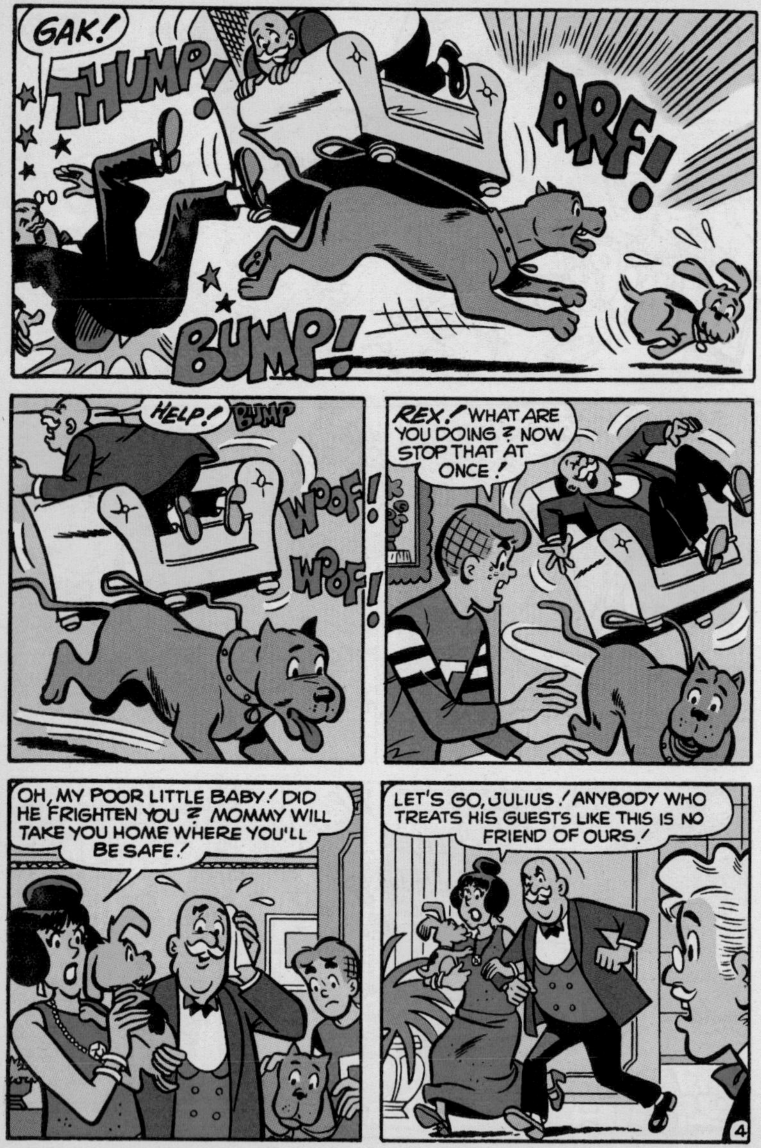
GAK!
THUMP!
ARF!
BUMP!
HELP!
BUMP
WOOF!
WOOF!
REX! WHAT ARE YOU DOING? NOW STOP THAT AT ONCE!
OH, MY POOR LITTLE BABY! DID HE FRIGHTEN YOU? MOMMY WILL TAKE YOU HOME WHERE YOU'LL BE SAFE!
LET'S GO, JULIUS! ANYBODY WHO TREATS HIS GUESTS LIKE THIS IS NO FRIEND OF OURS!
4

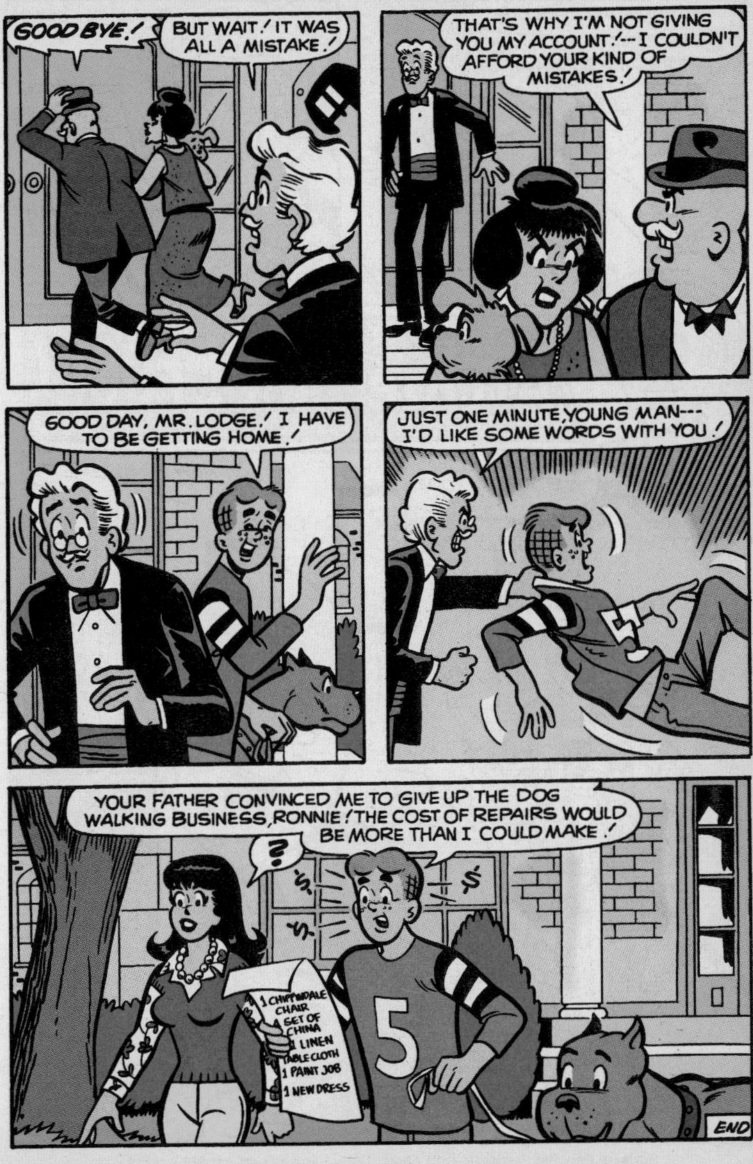
GOOD BYE!
BUT WAIT! IT WAS ALL A MISTAKE!
THAT'S WHY I'M NOT GIVING YOU MY ACCOUNT!--- I COULDN'T AFFORD YOUR KIND OF MISTAKES!
GOOD DAY, MR. LODGE! I HAVE TO BE GETTING HOME!
JUST ONE MINUTE, YOUNG MAN--- I'D LIKE SOME WORDS WITH YOU!
YOUR FATHER CONVINCED ME TO GIVE UP THE DOG WALKING BUSINESS, RONNIE! THE COST OF REPAIRS WOULD BE MORE THAN I COULD MAKE!
?
1 CHIPPENDALE CHAIR
1 SET OF CHINA
1 LINEN TABLE CLOTH
1 PAINT JOB
1 NEW DRESS
5
END

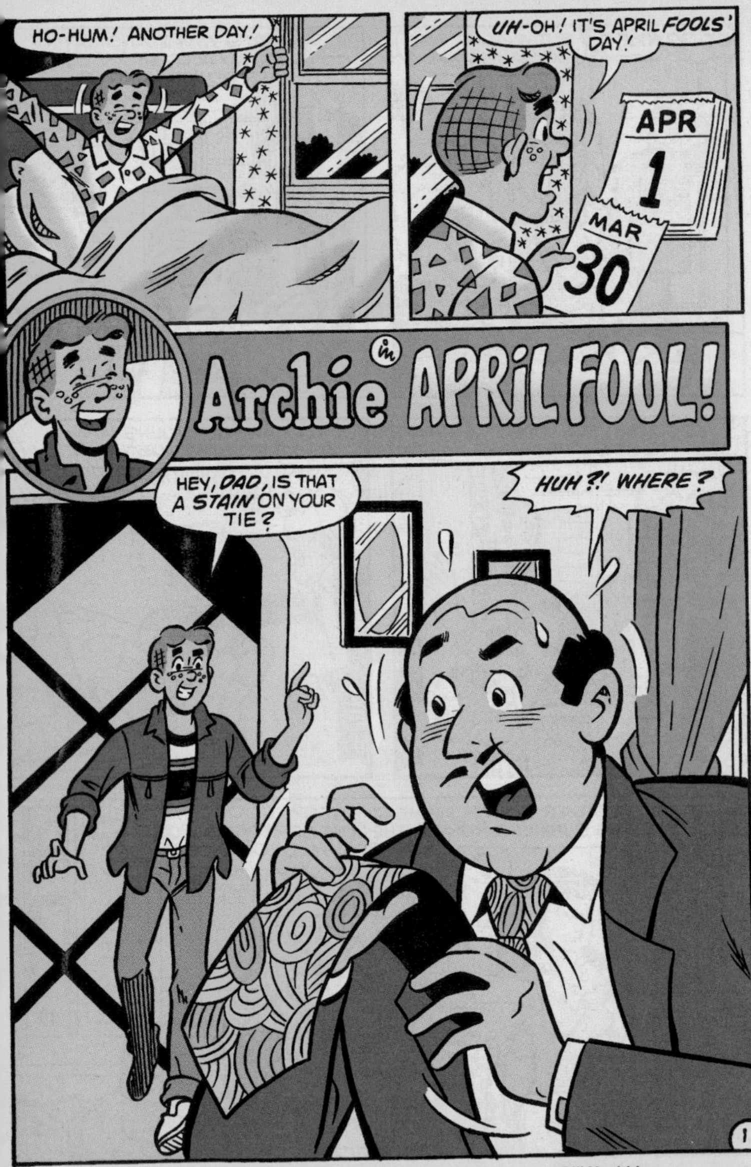
HO-HUM! ANOTHER DAY!
UH-OH! IT'S APRIL FOOLS' DAY!
APR
1
MAR
30
Archie in APRIL FOOL!
HEY, DAD, IS THAT A STAIN ON YOUR TIE?
HUH?! WHERE?
1

Script & Pencils: Fernando Ruiz / Inks: Rudy Lapick / Letters: Bill Yoshida

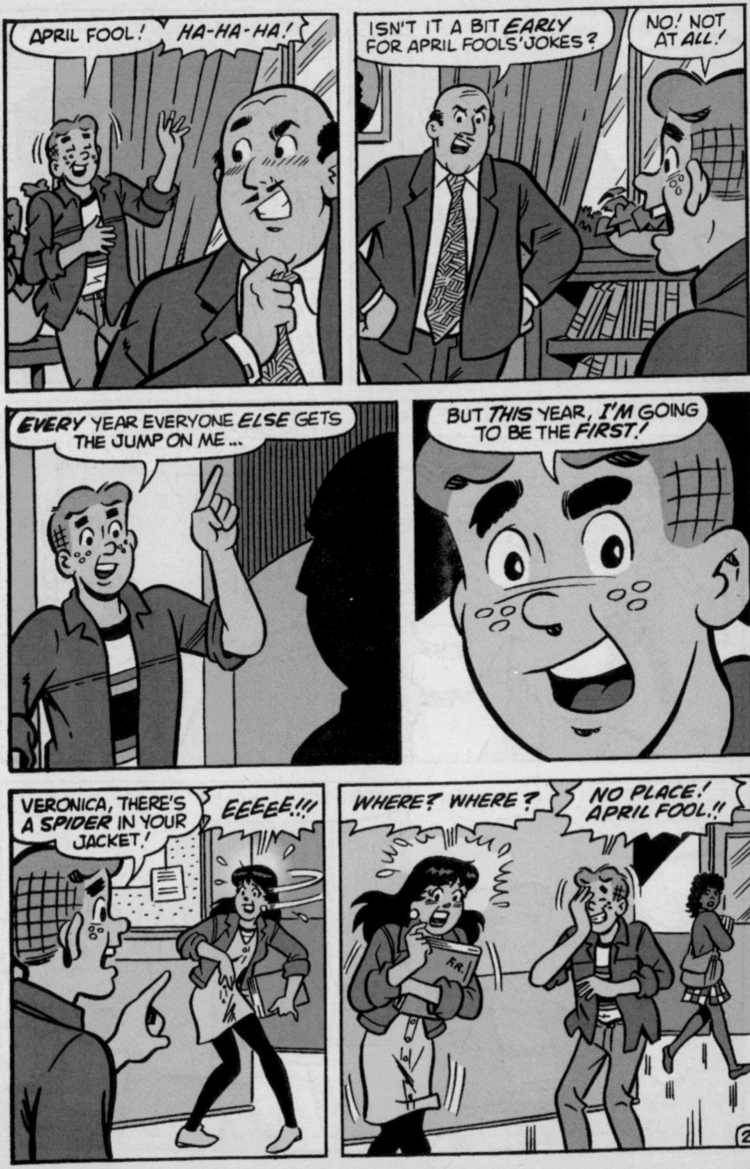
APRIL FOOL!
HA-HA-HA!
ISN'T IT A BIT EARLY FOR APRIL FOOLS' JOKES?
NO! NOT AT ALL!
EVERY YEAR EVERYONE ELSE GETS THE JUMP ON ME...
BUT THIS YEAR, I'M GOING TO BE THE FIRST!
VERONICA, THERE'S A SPIDER IN YOUR JACKET!
EEEEEE!!!
WHERE? WHERE?
NO PLACE! APRIL FOOL!!
FR.
2

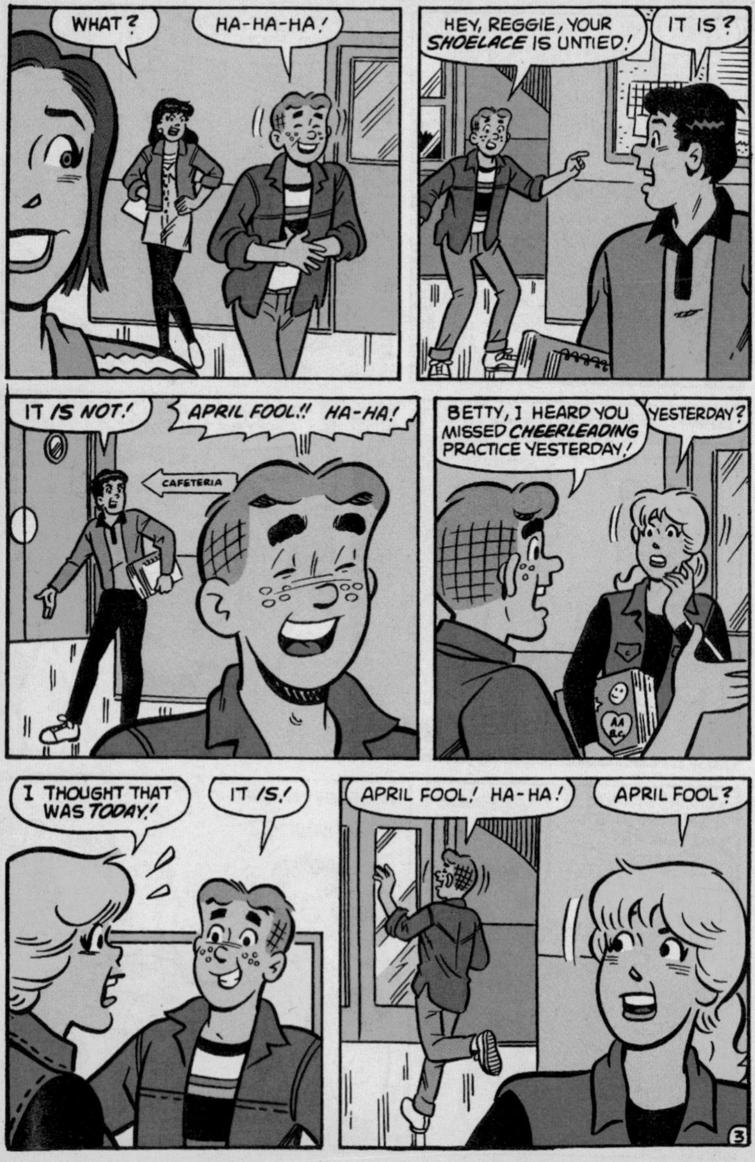
WHAT?
HA-HA-HA!
HEY, REGGIE, YOUR SHOELACE IS UNTIED!
IT IS?
IT IS NOT!
APRIL FOOL!! HA-HA!
CAFETERIA
BETTY, I HEARD YOU MISSED CHEERLEADING PRACTICE YESTERDAY!
YESTERDAY?
I THOUGHT THAT WAS TODAY!
IT IS!
APRIL FOOL! HA-HA!
APRIL FOOL?

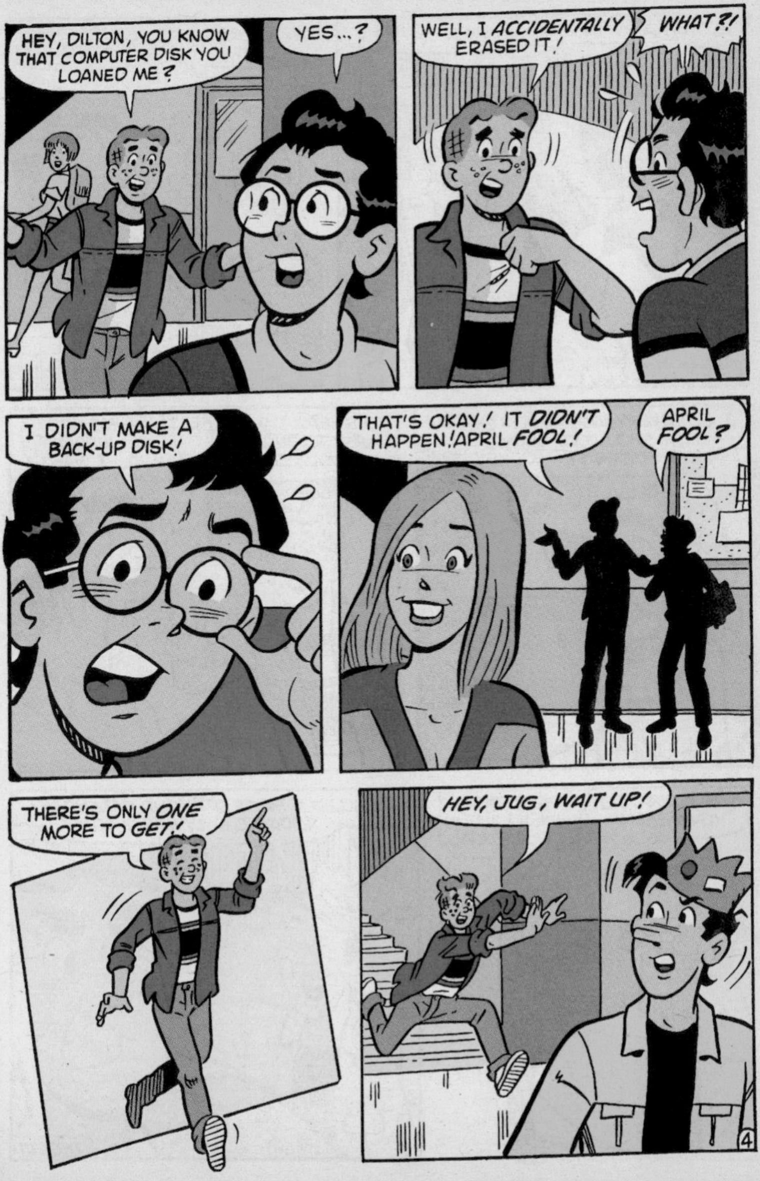
HEY, DILTON, YOU KNOW THAT COMPUTER DISK YOU LOANED ME?
YES...?
WELL, I ACCIDENTALLY ERASED IT!
WHAT?!
I DIDN'T MAKE A BACK-UP DISK!
THAT'S OKAY! IT DIDN'T HAPPEN! APRIL FOOL!
APRIL FOOL?
THERE'S ONLY ONE MORE TO GET!
HEY, JUG, WAIT UP!
4

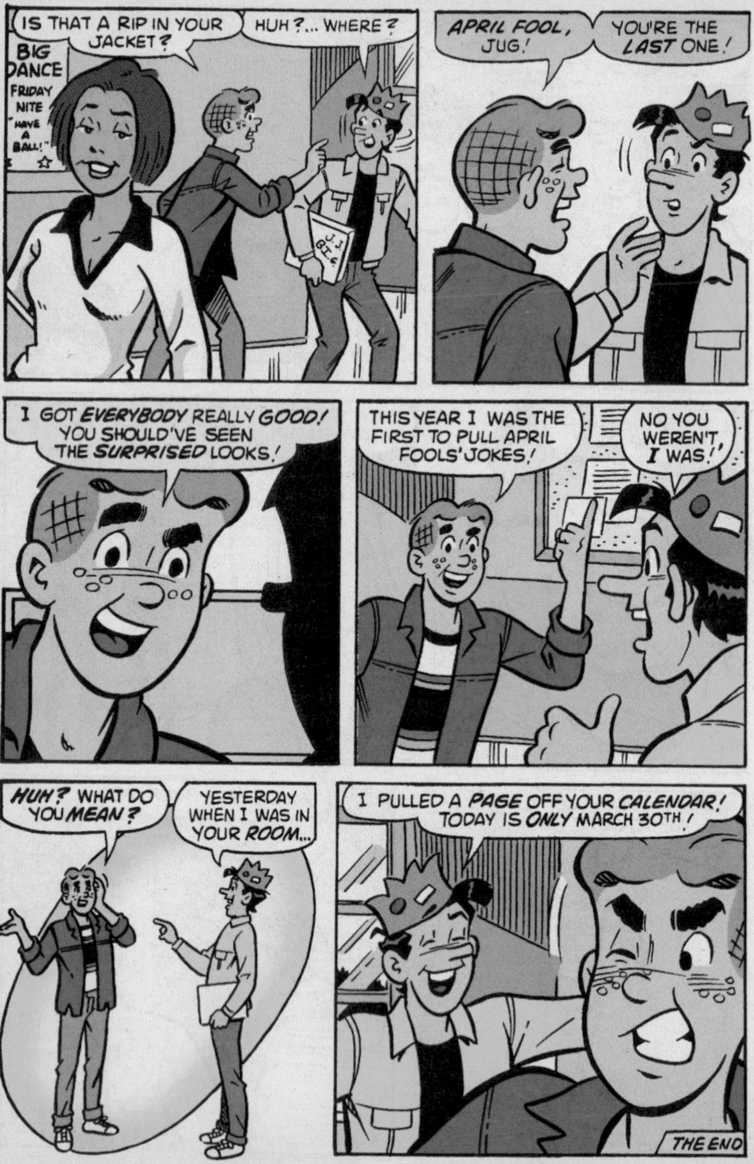
IS THAT A RIP IN YOUR JACKET?
BIG DANCE FRIDAY NITE "HAVE A BALL!"
HUH?... WHERE?
APRIL FOOL, JUG!
YOU'RE THE LAST ONE!
I GOT EVERYBODY REALLY GOOD! YOU SHOULD'VE SEEN THE SURPRISED LOOKS!
THIS YEAR I WAS THE FIRST TO PULL APRIL FOOLS' JOKES!
NO YOU WEREN'T, I WAS!
HUH? WHAT DO YOU MEAN?
YESTERDAY WHEN I WAS IN YOUR ROOM...
I PULLED A PAGE OFF YOUR CALENDAR! TODAY IS ONLY MARCH 30TH!
THE END

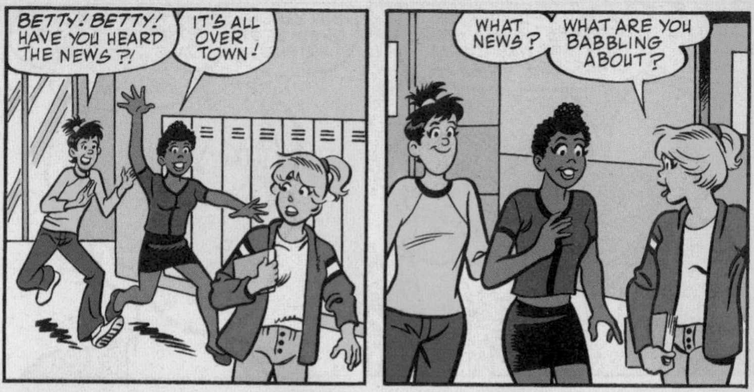
BETTY! BETTY! HAVE YOU HEARD THE NEWS?!
IT'S ALL OVER TOWN!
WHAT NEWS?
WHAT ARE YOU BABBLING ABOUT?

Betty and Veronica in Best Friends

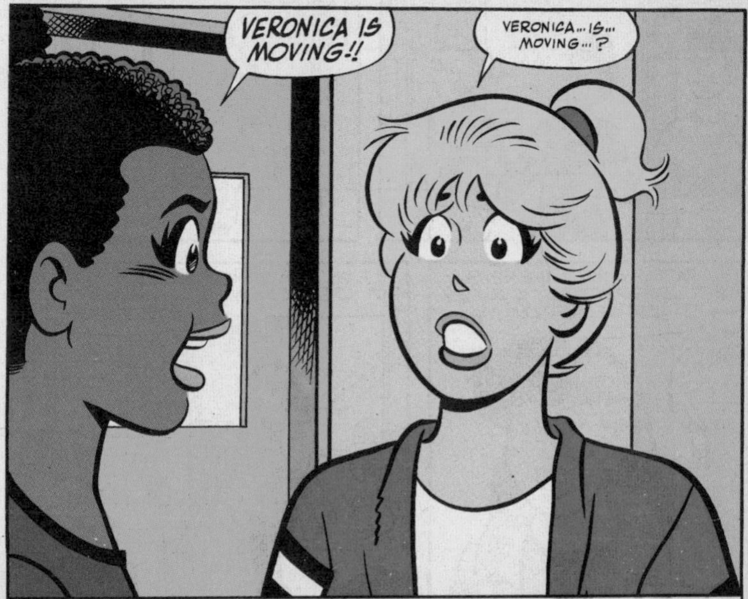
VERONICA IS MOVING!!
VERONICA... IS... MOVING...?

SCRIPT: GEORGE GLADIR PENCILS: JEFF SHULTZ INKING: AL MILGROM LETTERING: JACK MORELLI COLORING: BARRY GROSSMAN

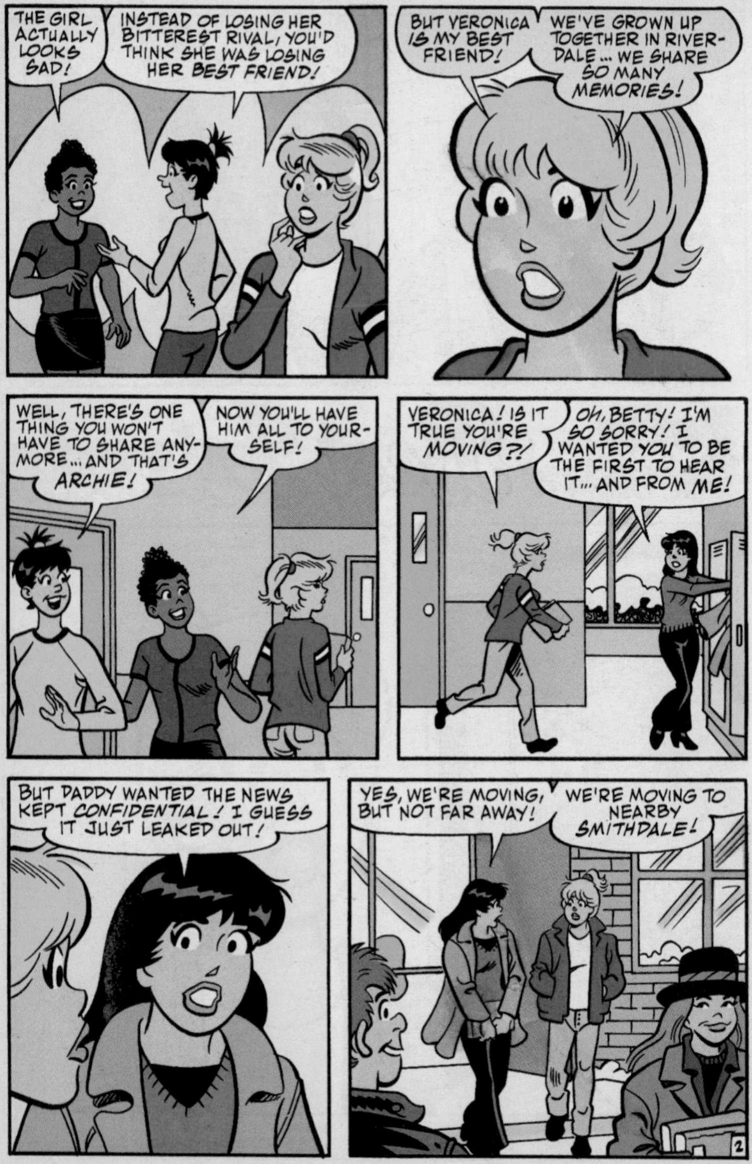
THE GIRL ACTUALLY LOOKS SAD!
INSTEAD OF LOSING HER BITTEREST RIVAL, YOU'D THINK SHE WAS LOSING HER BEST FRIEND!
BUT VERONICA IS MY BEST FRIEND!
WE'VE GROWN UP TOGETHER IN RIVER-DALE ... WE SHARE SO MANY MEMORIES!
WELL, THERE'S ONE THING YOU WON'T HAVE TO SHARE ANY-MORE... AND THAT'S ARCHIE!
NOW YOU'LL HAVE HIM ALL TO YOUR-SELF!
VERONICA! IS IT TRUE YOU'RE MOVING?!
OH, BETTY! I'M SO SORRY! I WANTED YOU TO BE THE FIRST TO HEAR IT... AND FROM ME!
BUT DADDY WANTED THE NEWS KEPT CONFIDENTIAL! I GUESS IT JUST LEAKED OUT!
YES, WE'RE MOVING, BUT NOT FAR AWAY!
WE'RE MOVING TO NEARBY SMITHDALE!
2

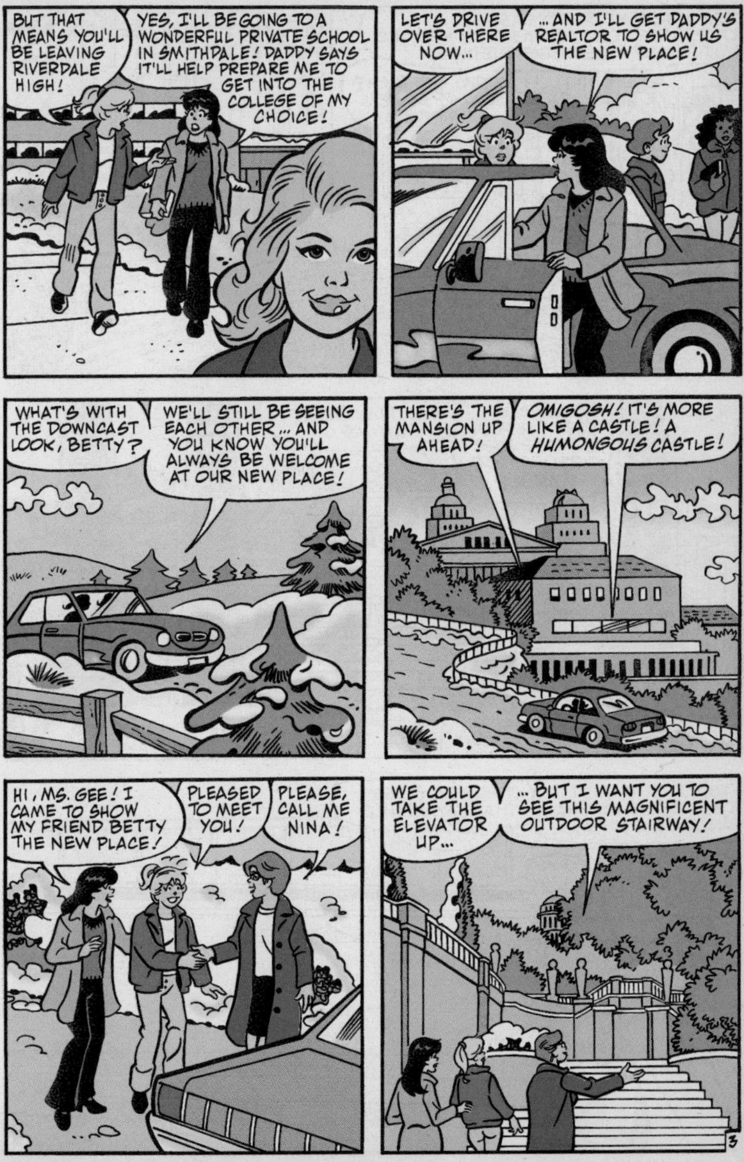

BUT THAT MEANS YOU'LL BE LEAVING RIVERDALE HIGH!
YES, I'LL BE GOING TO A WONDERFUL PRIVATE SCHOOL IN SMITHDALE! DADDY SAYS IT'LL HELP PREPARE ME TO GET INTO THE COLLEGE OF MY CHOICE!
LET'S DRIVE OVER THERE NOW...
... AND I'LL GET DADDY'S REALTOR TO SHOW US THE NEW PLACE!
WHAT'S WITH THE DOWNCAST LOOK, BETTY?
WE'LL STILL BE SEEING EACH OTHER ... AND YOU KNOW YOU'LL ALWAYS BE WELCOME AT OUR NEW PLACE!
THERE'S THE MANSION UP AHEAD!
OMIGOSH! IT'S MORE LIKE A CASTLE! A HUMONGOUS CASTLE!
HI, MS. GEE! I CAME TO SHOW MY FRIEND BETTY THE NEW PLACE!
PLEASED TO MEET YOU!
PLEASE, CALL ME NINA!
WE COULD TAKE THE ELEVATOR UP...
... BUT I WANT YOU TO SEE THIS MAGNIFICENT OUTDOOR STAIRWAY!
3

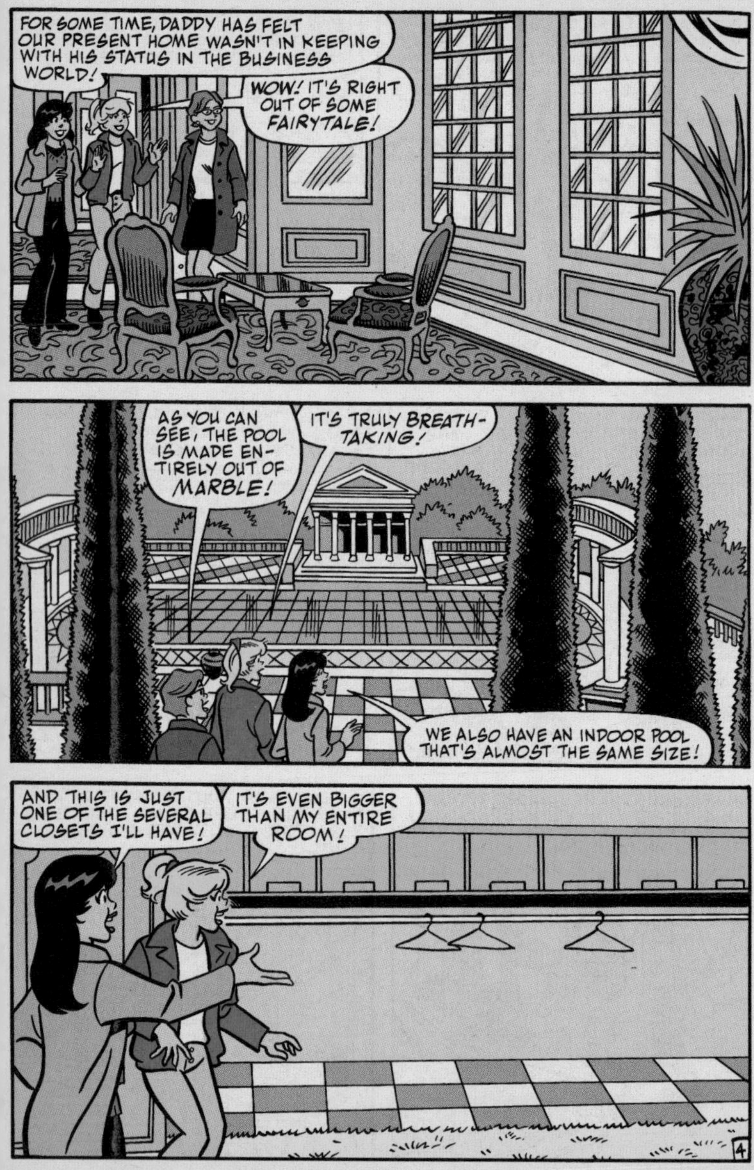
FOR SOME TIME, DADDY HAS FELT OUR PRESENT HOME WASN'T IN KEEPING WITH HIS STATUS IN THE BUSINESS WORLD!
WOW! IT'S RIGHT OUT OF SOME FAIRYTALE!
AS YOU CAN SEE, THE POOL IS MADE EN-TIRELY OUT OF MARBLE!
IT'S TRULY BREATH-TAKING!
WE ALSO HAVE AN INDOOR POOL THAT'S ALMOST THE SAME SIZE!
AND THIS IS JUST ONE OF THE SEVERAL CLOSETS I'LL HAVE!
IT'S EVEN BIGGER THAN MY ENTIRE ROOM!
4

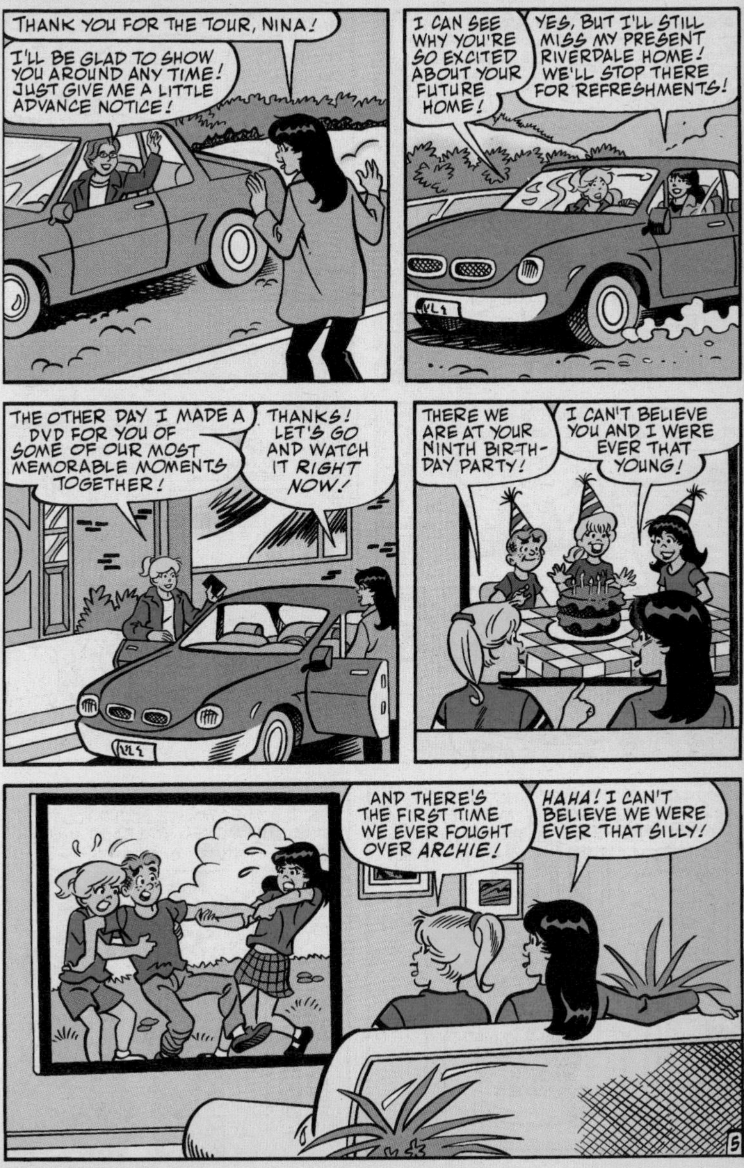
THANK YOU FOR THE TOUR, NINA!
I'LL BE GLAD TO SHOW YOU AROUND ANY TIME! JUST GIVE ME A LITTLE ADVANCE NOTICE!
I CAN SEE WHY YOU'RE SO EXCITED ABOUT YOUR FUTURE HOME!
YES, BUT I'LL STILL MISS MY PRESENT RIVERDALE HOME! WE'LL STOP THERE FOR REFRESHMENTS!
THE OTHER DAY I MADE A DVD FOR YOU OF SOME OF OUR MOST MEMORABLE MOMENTS TOGETHER!
THANKS! LET'S GO AND WATCH IT RIGHT NOW!
THERE WE ARE AT YOUR NINTH BIRTH-DAY PARTY!
I CAN'T BELIEVE YOU AND I WERE EVER THAT YOUNG!
AND THERE'S THE FIRST TIME WE EVER FOUGHT OVER ARCHIE!
HAHA! I CAN'T BELIEVE WE WERE EVER THAT SILLY!
5

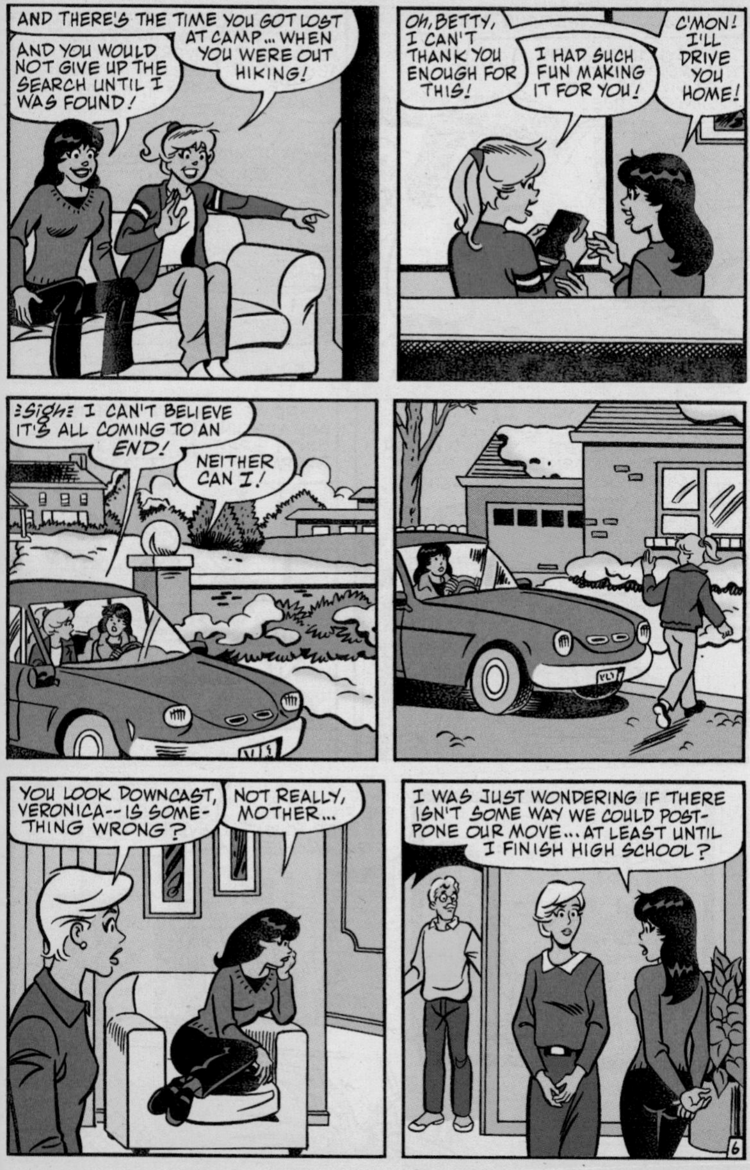
AND THERE'S THE TIME YOU GOT LOST AT CAMP... WHEN YOU WERE OUT HIKING!
AND YOU WOULD NOT GIVE UP THE SEARCH UNTIL I WAS FOUND!
Oh, BETTY, I CAN'T THANK YOU ENOUGH FOR THIS!
I HAD SUCH FUN MAKING IT FOR YOU!
C'MON! I'LL DRIVE YOU HOME!
=Sigh= I CAN'T BELIEVE IT'S ALL COMING TO AN END!
NEITHER CAN I!
YOU LOOK DOWNCAST, VERONICA--IS SOMETHING WRONG?
NOT REALLY, MOTHER...
I WAS JUST WONDERING IF THERE ISN'T SOME WAY WE COULD POSTPONE OUR MOVE... AT LEAST UNTIL I FINISH HIGH SCHOOL?
6

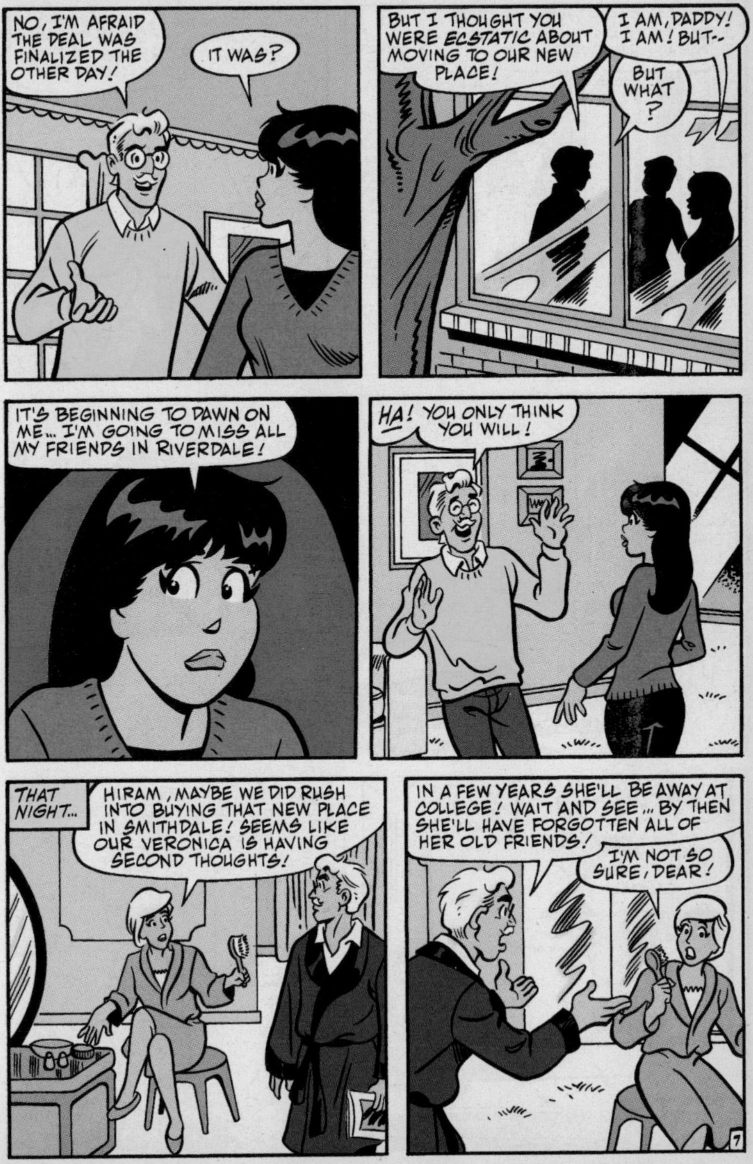

NO, I'M AFRAID THE DEAL WAS FINALIZED THE OTHER DAY!
IT WAS?
BUT I THOUGHT YOU WERE *ECSTATIC* ABOUT MOVING TO OUR NEW PLACE!
I AM, DADDY! I AM! BUT--
BUT WHAT?
IT'S BEGINNING TO DAWN ON ME... I'M GOING TO MISS ALL MY FRIENDS IN RIVERDALE!
HA! YOU ONLY THINK YOU WILL!
THAT NIGHT...
HIRAM, MAYBE WE DID RUSH INTO BUYING THAT NEW PLACE IN SMITHDALE! SEEMS LIKE OUR VERONICA IS HAVING SECOND THOUGHTS!
IN A FEW YEARS SHE'LL BE AWAY AT COLLEGE! WAIT AND SEE ... BY THEN SHE'LL HAVE FORGOTTEN ALL OF HER OLD FRIENDS!
I'M NOT SO SURE, DEAR!
7

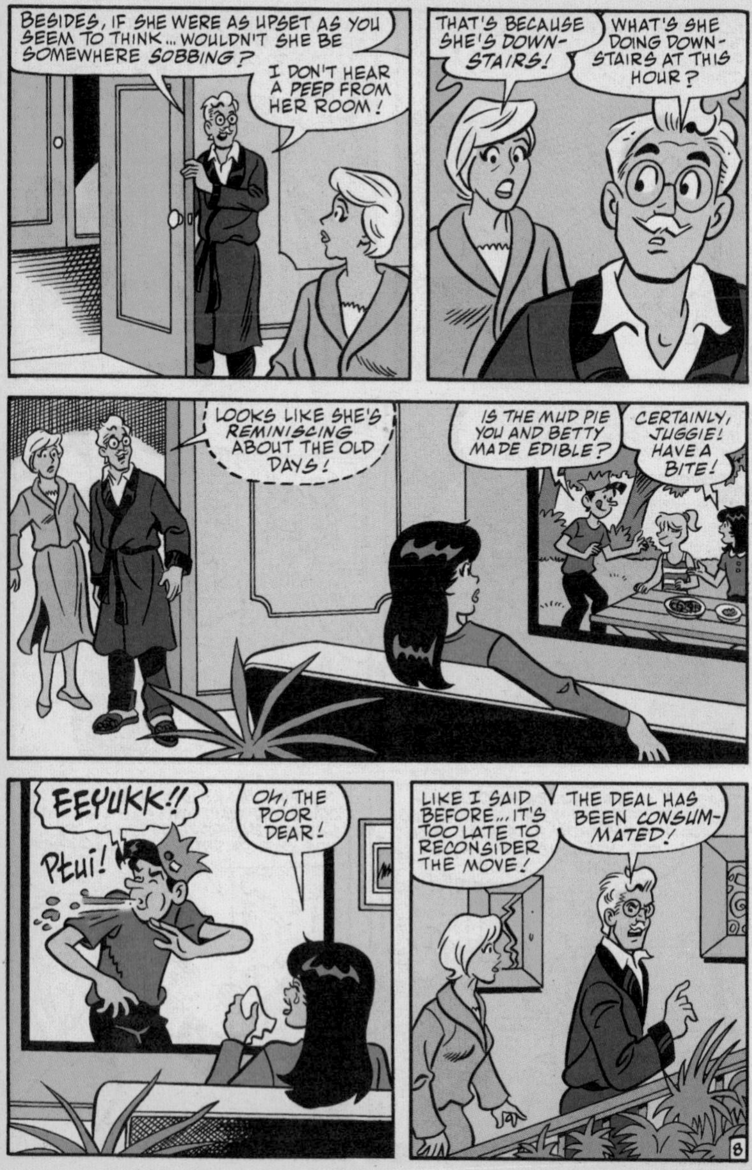
BESIDES, IF SHE WERE AS UPSET AS YOU SEEM TO THINK... WOULDN'T SHE BE SOMEWHERE SOBBING?
I DON'T HEAR A PEEP FROM HER ROOM!
THAT'S BECAUSE SHE'S DOWN-STAIRS!
WHAT'S SHE DOING DOWN-STAIRS AT THIS HOUR?
LOOKS LIKE SHE'S REMINISCING ABOUT THE OLD DAYS!
IS THE MUD PIE YOU AND BETTY MADE EDIBLE?
CERTAINLY, JUGGIE! HAVE A BITE!
EEYUKK!!
Ptui!
Oh, THE POOR DEAR!
LIKE I SAID BEFORE... IT'S TOO LATE TO RECONSIDER THE MOVE!
THE DEAL HAS BEEN CONSUM-MATED!
8

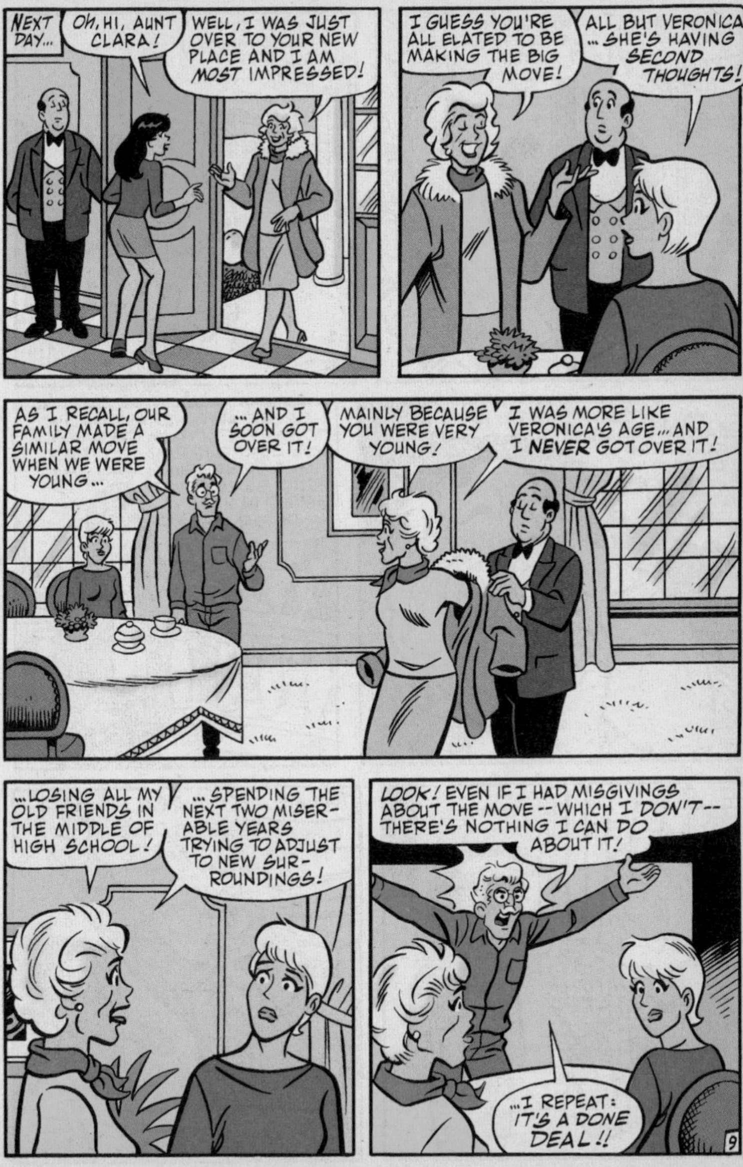
NEXT DAY...
Oh, HI, AUNT CLARA!
WELL, I WAS JUST OVER TO YOUR NEW PLACE AND I AM MOST IMPRESSED!
I GUESS YOU'RE ALL ELATED TO BE MAKING THE BIG MOVE!
ALL BUT VERONICA ... SHE'S HAVING SECOND THOUGHTS!
AS I RECALL, OUR FAMILY MADE A SIMILAR MOVE WHEN WE WERE YOUNG...
...AND I SOON GOT OVER IT!
MAINLY BECAUSE YOU WERE VERY YOUNG!
I WAS MORE LIKE VERONICA'S AGE... AND I NEVER GOT OVER IT!
...LOSING ALL MY OLD FRIENDS IN THE MIDDLE OF HIGH SCHOOL!
...SPENDING THE NEXT TWO MISER-ABLE YEARS TRYING TO ADJUST TO NEW SUR-ROUNDINGS!
LOOK! EVEN IF I HAD MISGIVINGS ABOUT THE MOVE -- WHICH I DON'T -- THERE'S NOTHING I CAN DO ABOUT IT!
...I REPEAT: IT'S A DONE DEAL!!
9

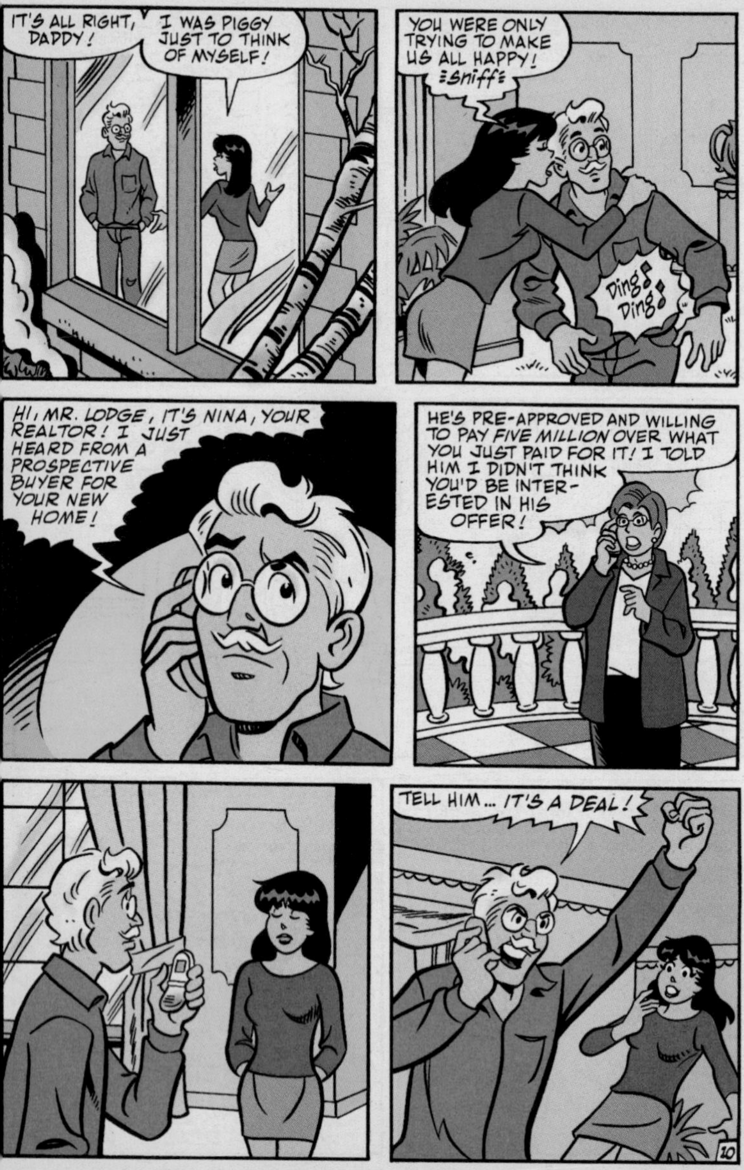
IT'S ALL RIGHT, DADDY!
I WAS PIGGY JUST TO THINK OF MYSELF!
YOU WERE ONLY TRYING TO MAKE US ALL HAPPY! *sniff*
Ding! Ding!
HI, MR. LODGE, IT'S NINA, YOUR REALTOR! I JUST HEARD FROM A PROSPECTIVE BUYER FOR YOUR NEW HOME!
HE'S PRE-APPROVED AND WILLING TO PAY FIVE MILLION OVER WHAT YOU JUST PAID FOR IT! I TOLD HIM I DIDN'T THINK YOU'D BE INTERESTED IN HIS OFFER!
TELL HIM... IT'S A DEAL!
10

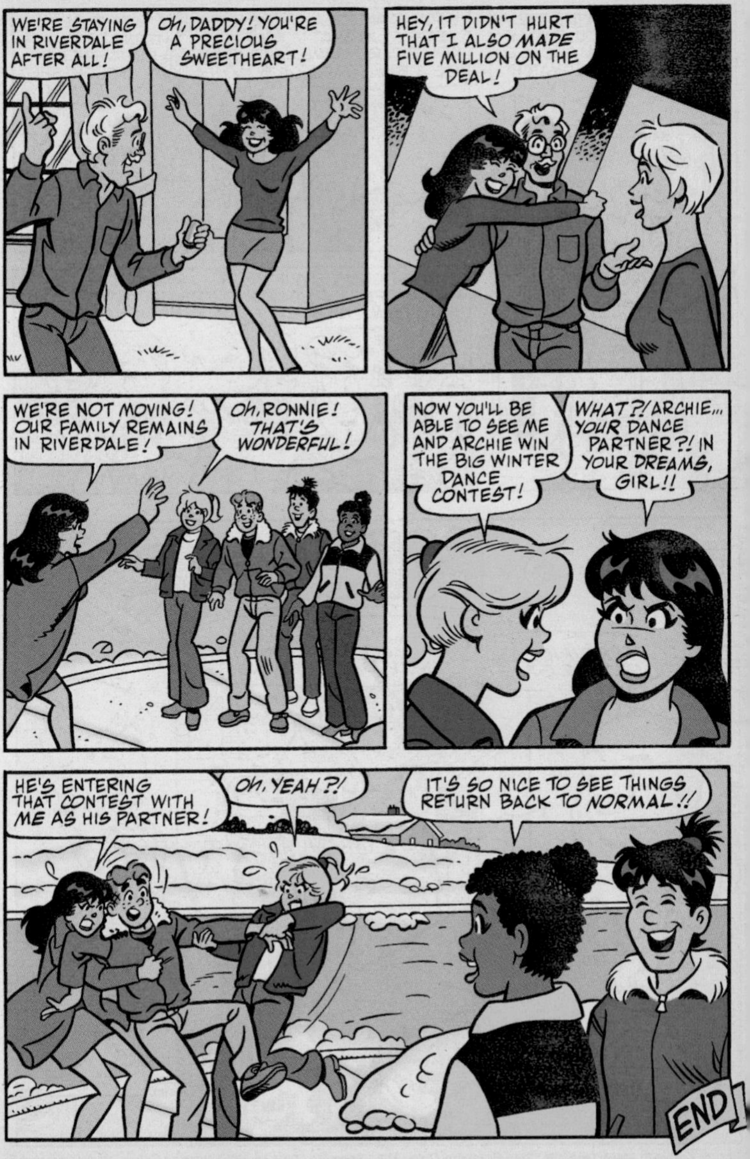
WE'RE STAYING IN RIVERDALE AFTER ALL!
Oh, DADDY! YOU'RE A PRECIOUS SWEETHEART!
HEY, IT DIDN'T HURT THAT I ALSO MADE FIVE MILLION ON THE DEAL!
WE'RE NOT MOVING! OUR FAMILY REMAINS IN RIVERDALE!
Oh, RONNIE! THAT'S WONDERFUL!
NOW YOU'LL BE ABLE TO SEE ME AND ARCHIE WIN THE BIG WINTER DANCE CONTEST!
WHAT?! ARCHIE... YOUR DANCE PARTNER?! IN YOUR DREAMS, GIRL!!
HE'S ENTERING THAT CONTEST WITH ME AS HIS PARTNER!
Oh, YEAH?!
IT'S SO NICE TO SEE THINGS RETURN BACK TO NORMAL!!
END

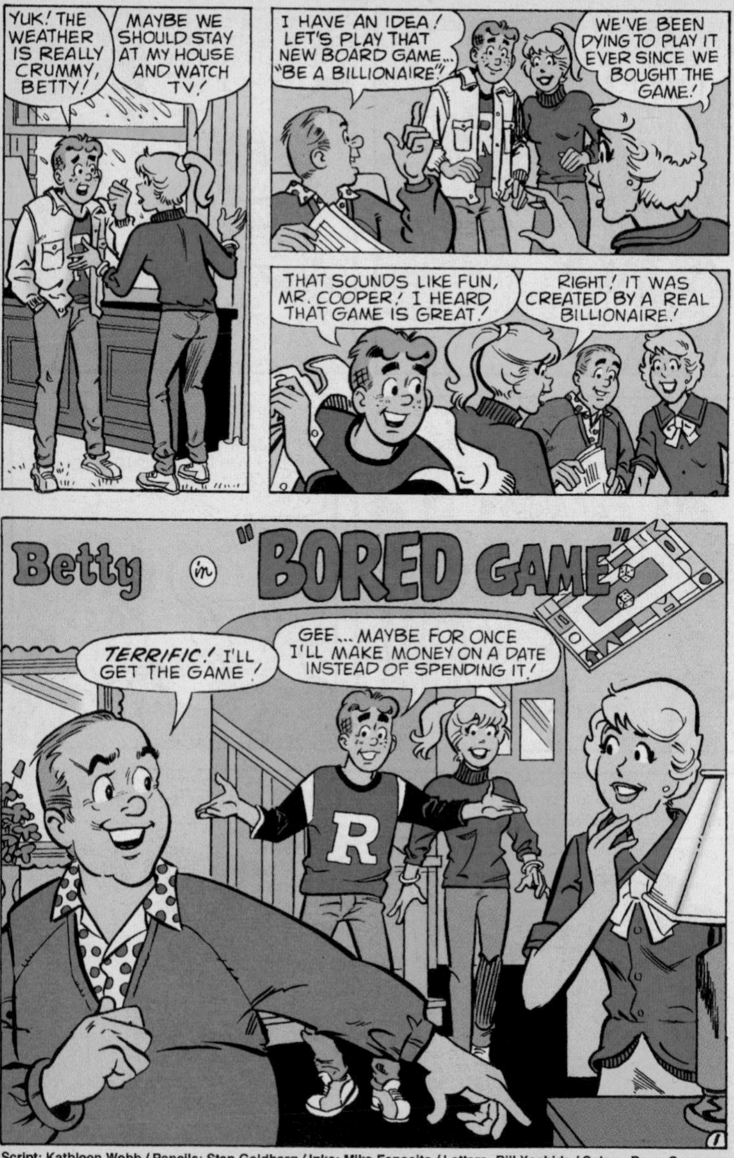
YUK! THE WEATHER IS REALLY CRUMMY, BETTY!
MAYBE WE SHOULD STAY AT MY HOUSE AND WATCH TV!
I HAVE AN IDEA! LET'S PLAY THAT NEW BOARD GAME... "BE A BILLIONAIRE"!
WE'VE BEEN DYING TO PLAY IT EVER SINCE WE BOUGHT THE GAME!
THAT SOUNDS LIKE FUN, MR. COOPER! I HEARD THAT GAME IS GREAT!
RIGHT! IT WAS CREATED BY A REAL BILLIONAIRE!
Betty in "BORED GAME"
TERRIFIC! I'LL GET THE GAME!
GEE... MAYBE FOR ONCE I'LL MAKE MONEY ON A DATE INSTEAD OF SPENDING IT!
1

Script: Kathleen Webb / Pencils: Stan Goldberg / Inks: Mike Esposito / Letters: Bill Yoshida / Colors: Barry Grossman

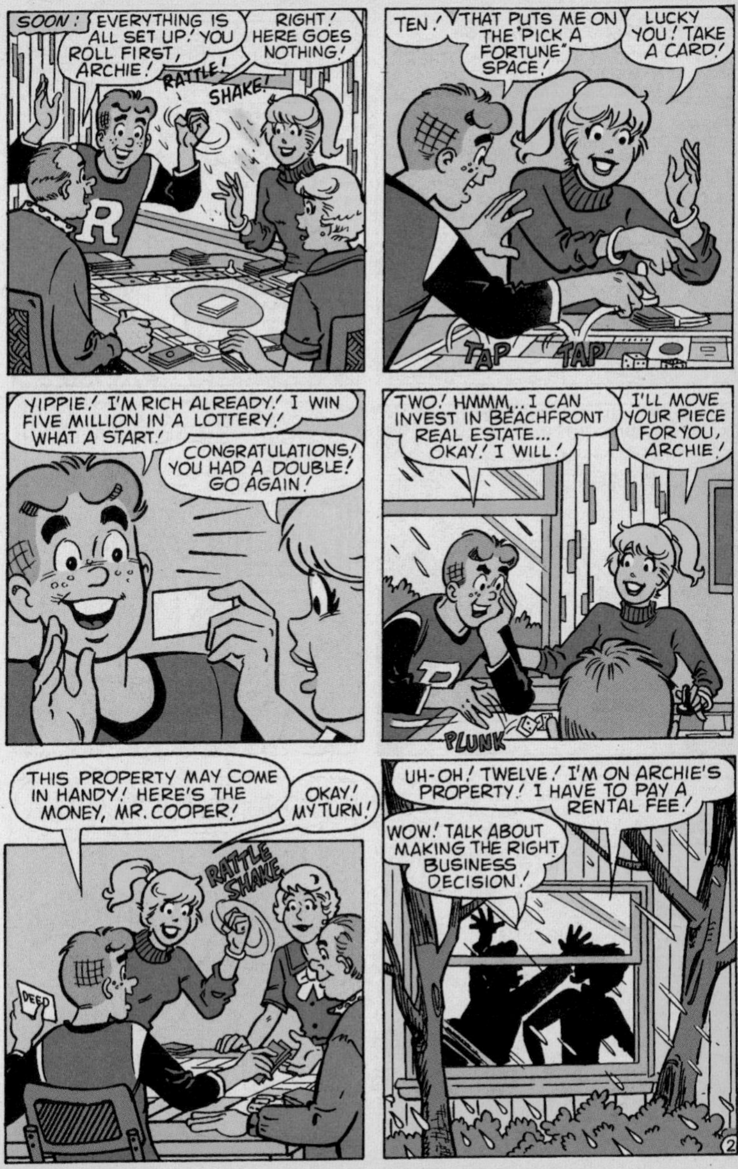
SOON:
EVERYTHING IS ALL SET UP! YOU ROLL FIRST, ARCHIE!
RIGHT! HERE GOES NOTHING!
RATTLE!
SHAKE!
TEN!
THAT PUTS ME ON THE "PICK A FORTUNE" SPACE!
LUCKY YOU! TAKE A CARD!
TAP
TAP
YIPPIE! I'M RICH ALREADY! I WIN FIVE MILLION IN A LOTTERY! WHAT A START!
CONGRATULATIONS! YOU HAD A DOUBLE! GO AGAIN!
TWO! HMMM... I CAN INVEST IN BEACHFRONT REAL ESTATE... OKAY! I WILL!
I'LL MOVE YOUR PIECE FOR YOU, ARCHIE!
PLUNK
THIS PROPERTY MAY COME IN HANDY! HERE'S THE MONEY, MR. COOPER!
OKAY! MY TURN!
RATTLE SHAKE
DEED
UH-OH! TWELVE! I'M ON ARCHIE'S PROPERTY! I HAVE TO PAY A RENTAL FEE!
WOW! TALK ABOUT MAKING THE RIGHT BUSINESS DECISION!
2

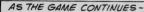
AS THE GAME CONTINUES—

YAHOO! I EARNED ANOTHER TEN MILLION IN THE STOCK MARKET! I'M RICH! *RICH!*

HMMM...YOU'RE THE ONLY ONE WHO IS DOING WELL IN THIS GAME, ARCHIE!

YOU KNOW...THEY SAY THIS GAME MIRRORS REAL LIFE BUSINESS OPPORTUNITIES!

MAYBE ARCHIE *WILL* BE A REAL TYCOON SOMEDAY!

HMMM....ME? A BILLIONAIRE? YEAH! WHY NOT? OH YEAH!

A MOVIE PRODUCER IS ON LINE ONE, SIR! YOUR BROKER IS ON LINE TWO! AND WASHINGTON IS ON LINE THREE!

MY FIRST MILLION

THANK YOU, MIDGE! HOLD ALL CALLS! I'M TAKING THE DAY OFF TO GO YACHTING!

YES, SIR, A.A.!

CEO

OUR FOUNDER

D-UH... HI, MR. ANDREWS! DOWN, SIR?

YES, REGGIE!

GOOD DAY, SIR!

3

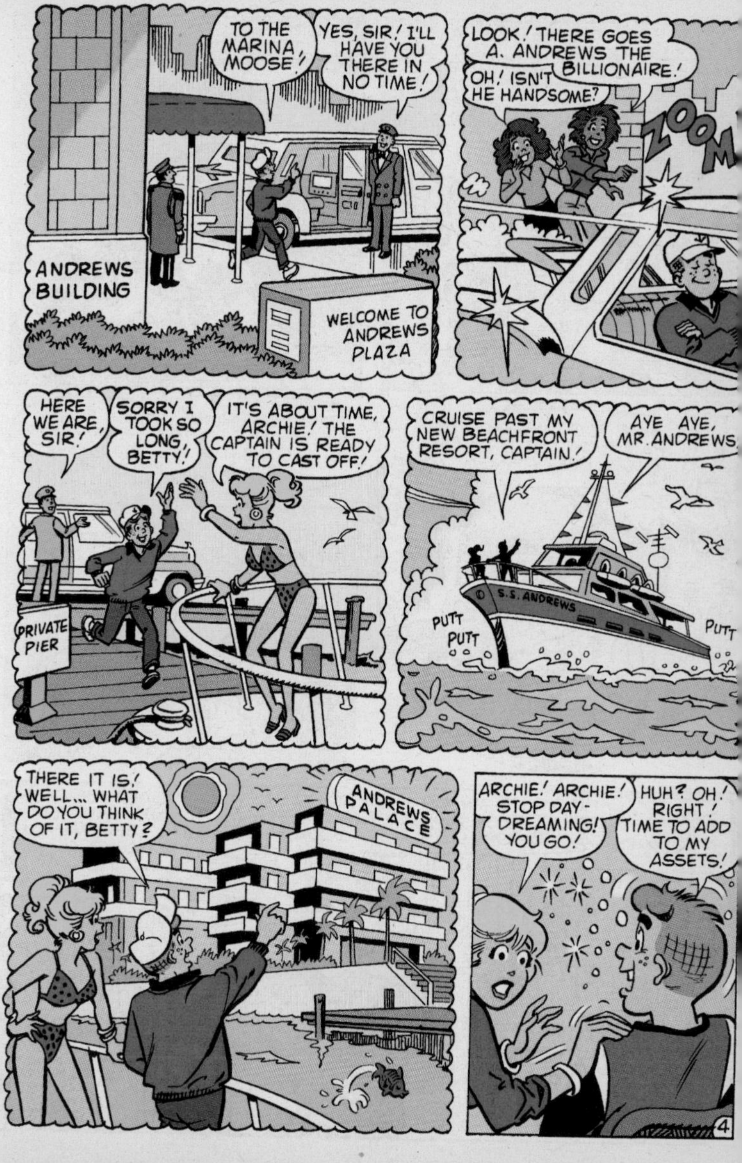
TO THE MARINA, MOOSE!
YES, SIR! I'LL HAVE YOU THERE IN NO TIME!
ANDREWS BUILDING
WELCOME TO ANDREWS PLAZA
LOOK! THERE GOES A. ANDREWS THE BILLIONAIRE!
OH! ISN'T HE HANDSOME?
ZOOM
HERE WE ARE, SIR!
SORRY I TOOK SO LONG, BETTY!
IT'S ABOUT TIME, ARCHIE! THE CAPTAIN IS READY TO CAST OFF!
PRIVATE PIER
CRUISE PAST MY NEW BEACHFRONT RESORT, CAPTAIN!
AYE AYE, MR. ANDREWS
S.S. ANDREWS
PUTT PUTT
PUTT
THERE IT IS! WELL... WHAT DO YOU THINK OF IT, BETTY?
ANDREWS PALACE
ARCHIE! ARCHIE! STOP DAY-DREAMING! YOU GO!
HUH? OH! RIGHT! TIME TO ADD TO MY ASSETS!

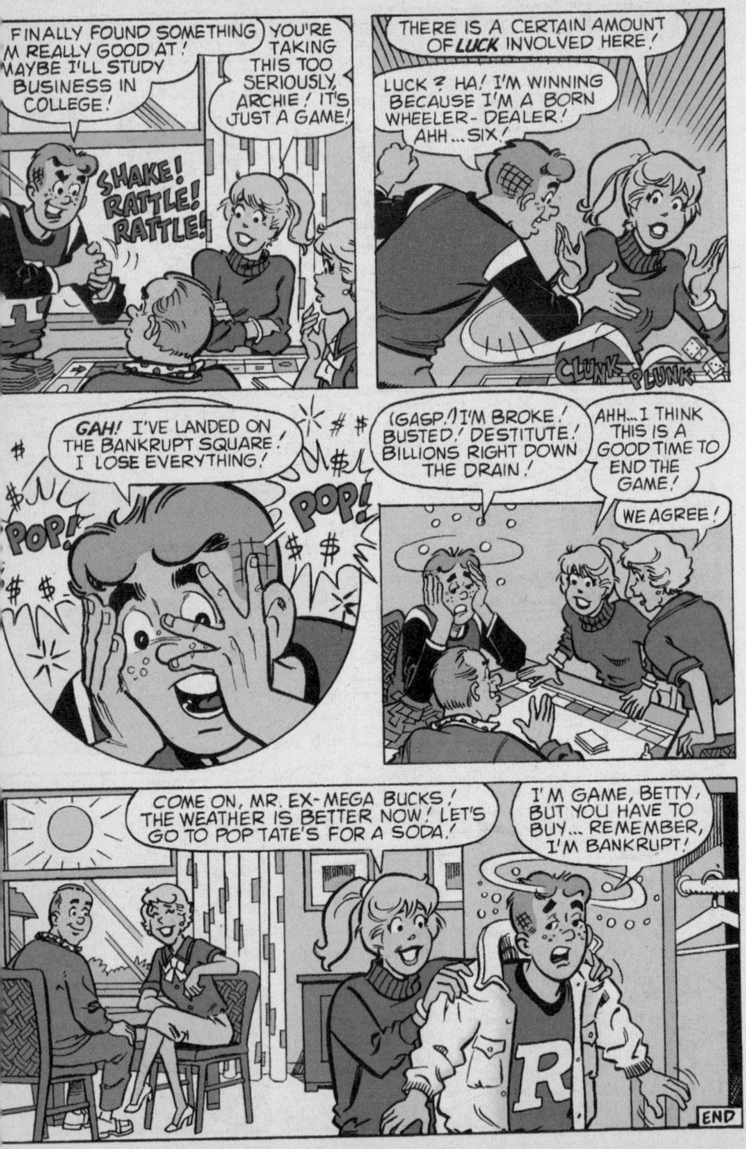

FINALLY FOUND SOMETHING M REALLY GOOD AT! MAYBE I'LL STUDY BUSINESS IN COLLEGE!
YOU'RE TAKING THIS TOO SERIOUSLY, ARCHIE! IT'S JUST A GAME!
SHAKE! RATTLE! RATTLE!
THERE IS A CERTAIN AMOUNT OF LUCK INVOLVED HERE!
LUCK? HA! I'M WINNING BECAUSE I'M A BORN WHEELER-DEALER! AHH...SIX!
CLUNK PLUNK
GAH! I'VE LANDED ON THE BANKRUPT SQUARE! I LOSE EVERYTHING!
POP! POP!
(GASP!) I'M BROKE! BUSTED! DESTITUTE! BILLIONS RIGHT DOWN THE DRAIN!
AHH...I THINK THIS IS A GOOD TIME TO END THE GAME!
WE AGREE!
COME ON, MR. EX-MEGA BUCKS! THE WEATHER IS BETTER NOW! LET'S GO TO POP TATE'S FOR A SODA!
I'M GAME, BETTY, BUT YOU HAVE TO BUY... REMEMBER, I'M BANKRUPT!
END

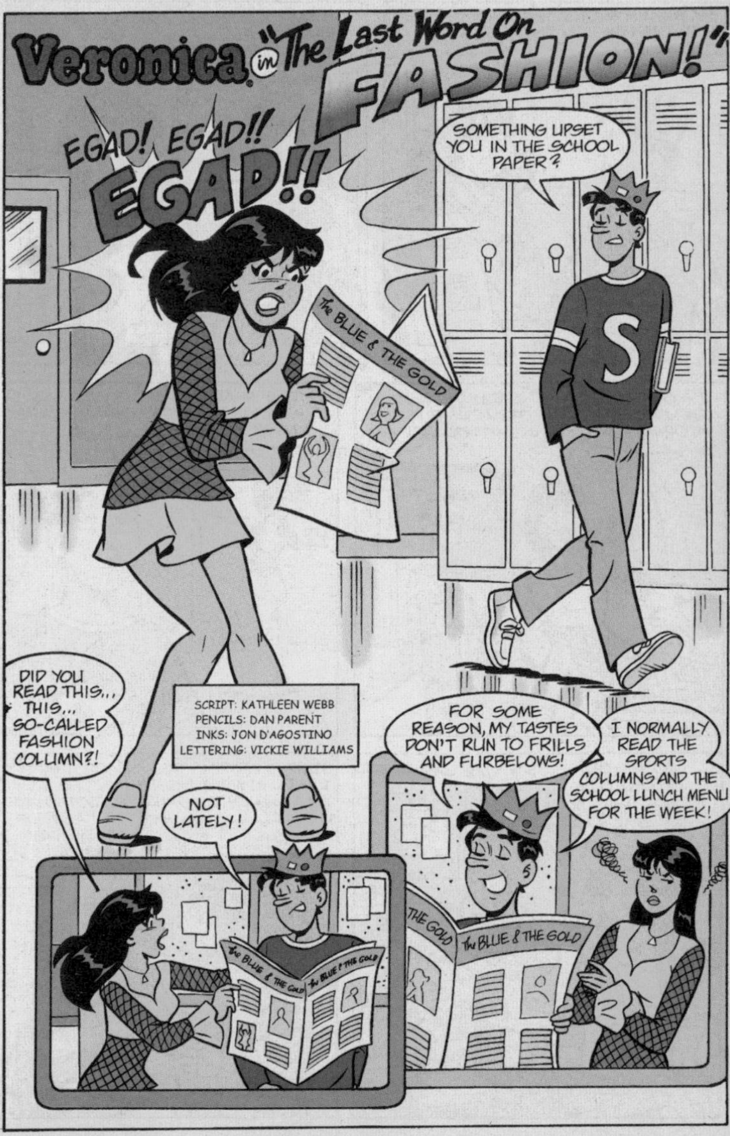
Veronica in "The Last Word On FASHION!"
EGAD! EGAD!!
EGAD!!
SOMETHING UPSET YOU IN THE SCHOOL PAPER?
The BLUE & THE GOLD
S
DID YOU READ THIS... THIS... SO-CALLED FASHION COLUMN?!
SCRIPT: KATHLEEN WEBB
PENCILS: DAN PARENT
INKS: JON D'AGOSTINO
LETTERING: VICKIE WILLIAMS
NOT LATELY!
The BLUE & THE GOLD
FOR SOME REASON, MY TASTES DON'T RUN TO FRILLS AND FURBELOWS!
I NORMALLY READ THE SPORTS COLUMNS AND THE SCHOOL LUNCH MENU FOR THE WEEK!
THE GOLD
The BLUE & THE GOLD

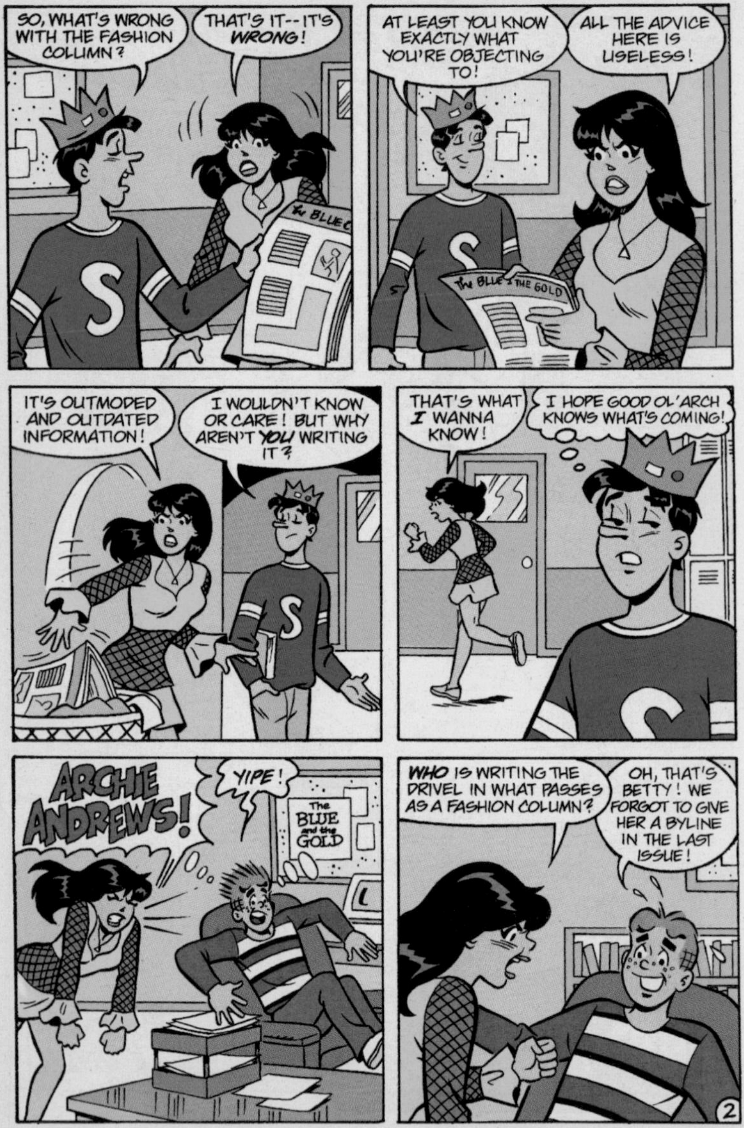
SO, WHAT'S WRONG WITH THE FASHION COLUMN?
THAT'S IT-- IT'S WRONG!
The BLUE
AT LEAST YOU KNOW EXACTLY WHAT YOU'RE OBJECTING TO!
ALL THE ADVICE HERE IS USELESS!
The BLUE & THE GOLD
IT'S OUTMODED AND OUTDATED INFORMATION!
I WOULDN'T KNOW OR CARE! BUT WHY AREN'T YOU WRITING IT?
THAT'S WHAT I WANNA KNOW!
I HOPE GOOD OL' ARCH KNOWS WHAT'S COMING!
ARCHIE ANDREWS!
YIPE!
The BLUE and the GOLD
WHO IS WRITING THE DRIVEL IN WHAT PASSES AS A FASHION COLUMN?
OH, THAT'S BETTY! WE FORGOT TO GIVE HER A BYLINE IN THE LAST ISSUE!
2

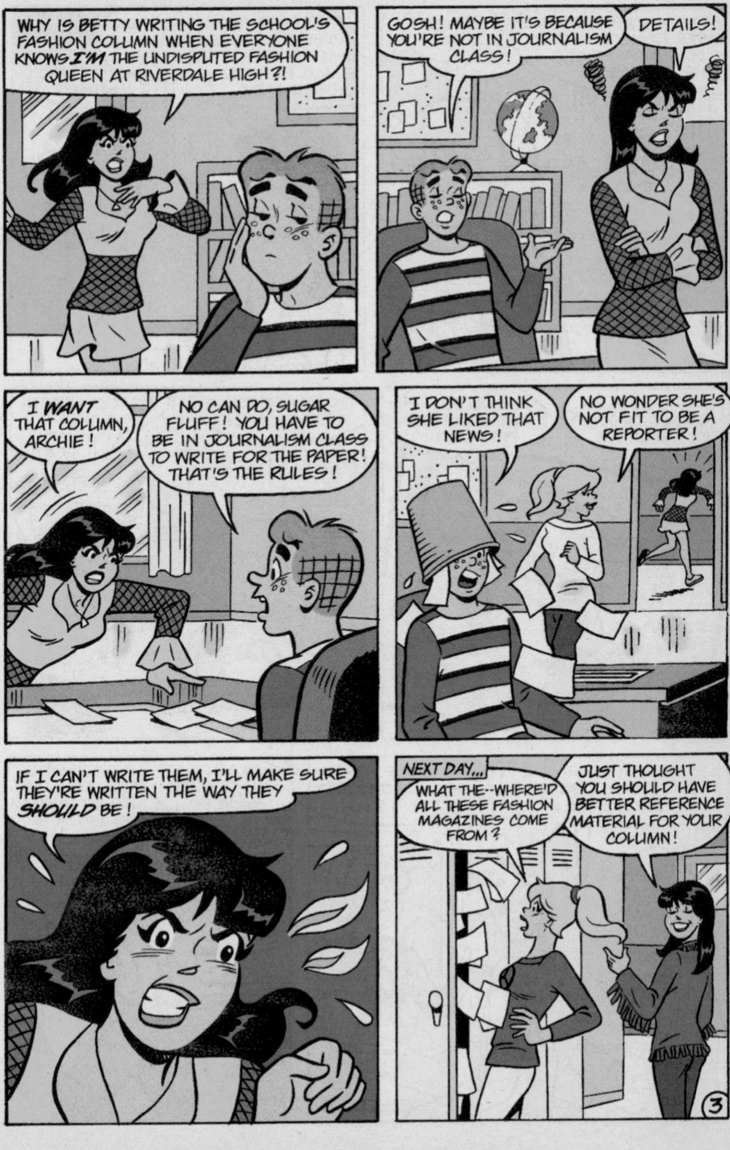
WHY IS BETTY WRITING THE SCHOOL'S FASHION COLUMN WHEN EVERYONE KNOWS I'M THE UNDISPUTED FASHION QUEEN AT RIVERDALE HIGH?!
GOSH! MAYBE IT'S BECAUSE YOU'RE NOT IN JOURNALISM CLASS!
DETAILS!
I WANT THAT COLUMN, ARCHIE!
NO CAN DO, SUGAR FLUFF! YOU HAVE TO BE IN JOURNALISM CLASS TO WRITE FOR THE PAPER! THAT'S THE RULES!
I DON'T THINK SHE LIKED THAT NEWS!
NO WONDER SHE'S NOT FIT TO BE A REPORTER!
IF I CAN'T WRITE THEM, I'LL MAKE SURE THEY'RE WRITTEN THE WAY THEY SHOULD BE!
NEXT DAY...
WHAT THE--WHERE'D ALL THESE FASHION MAGAZINES COME FROM?
JUST THOUGHT YOU SHOULD HAVE BETTER REFERENCE MATERIAL FOR YOUR COLUMN!
3

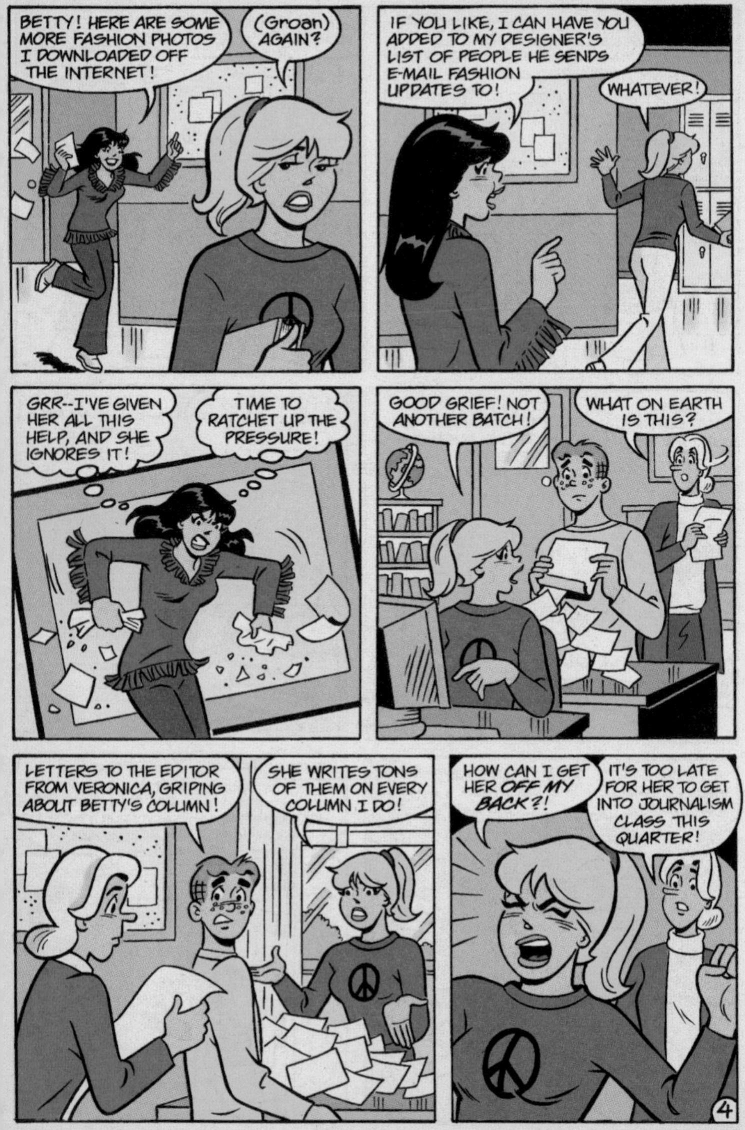
BETTY! HERE ARE SOME MORE FASHION PHOTOS I DOWNLOADED OFF THE INTERNET!
(Groan) AGAIN?
IF YOU LIKE, I CAN HAVE YOU ADDED TO MY DESIGNER'S LIST OF PEOPLE HE SENDS E-MAIL FASHION UPDATES TO!
WHATEVER!
GRR--I'VE GIVEN HER ALL THIS HELP, AND SHE IGNORES IT!
TIME TO RATCHET UP THE PRESSURE!
GOOD GRIEF! NOT ANOTHER BATCH!
WHAT ON EARTH IS THIS?
LETTERS TO THE EDITOR FROM VERONICA, GRIPING ABOUT BETTY'S COLUMN!
SHE WRITES TONS OF THEM ON EVERY COLUMN I DO!
HOW CAN I GET HER *OFF MY BACK*?!
IT'S TOO LATE FOR HER TO GET INTO JOURNALISM CLASS THIS QUARTER!
4

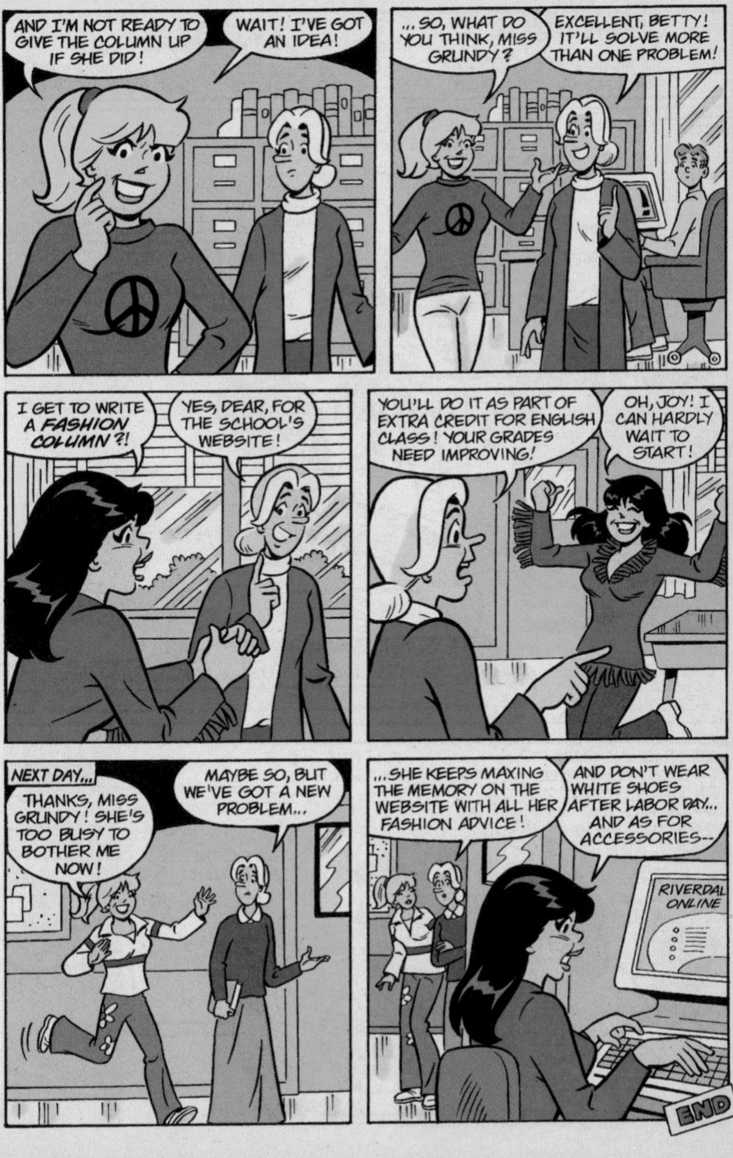
AND I'M NOT READY TO GIVE THE COLUMN UP IF SHE DID!
WAIT! I'VE GOT AN IDEA!
...SO, WHAT DO YOU THINK, MISS GRUNDY?
EXCELLENT, BETTY! IT'LL SOLVE MORE THAN ONE PROBLEM!
I GET TO WRITE A FASHION COLUMN?!
YES, DEAR, FOR THE SCHOOL'S WEBSITE!
YOU'LL DO IT AS PART OF EXTRA CREDIT FOR ENGLISH CLASS! YOUR GRADES NEED IMPROVING!
OH, JOY! I CAN HARDLY WAIT TO START!
NEXT DAY...
THANKS, MISS GRUNDY! SHE'S TOO BUSY TO BOTHER ME NOW!
MAYBE SO, BUT WE'VE GOT A NEW PROBLEM...
...SHE KEEPS MAXING THE MEMORY ON THE WEBSITE WITH ALL HER FASHION ADVICE!
AND DON'T WEAR WHITE SHOES AFTER LABOR DAY... AND AS FOR ACCESSORIES--
RIVERDAL ONLINE
END

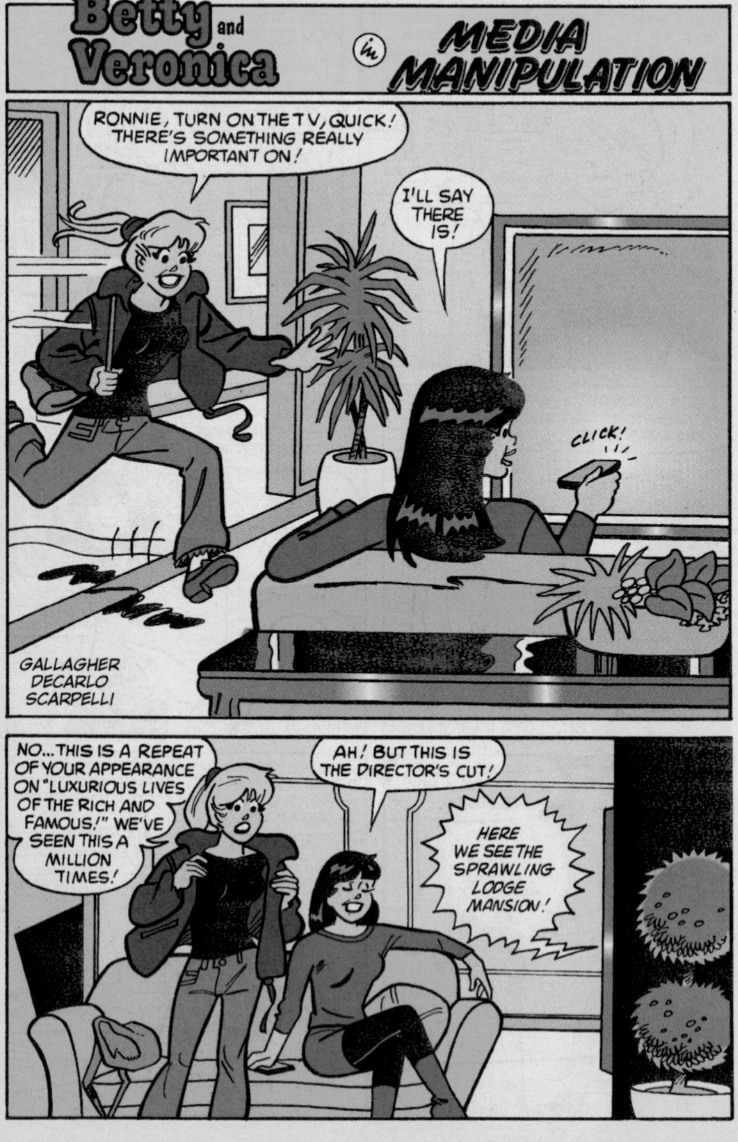
Betty and Veronica in
MEDIA MANIPULATION
RONNIE, TURN ON THE TV, QUICK! THERE'S SOMETHING REALLY IMPORTANT ON!
I'LL SAY THERE IS!
CLICK!
GALLAGHER
DECARLO
SCARPELLI
NO... THIS IS A REPEAT OF YOUR APPEARANCE ON "LUXURIOUS LIVES OF THE RICH AND FAMOUS!" WE'VE SEEN THIS A MILLION TIMES!
AH! BUT THIS IS THE DIRECTOR'S CUT!
HERE WE SEE THE SPRAWLING LODGE MANSION!

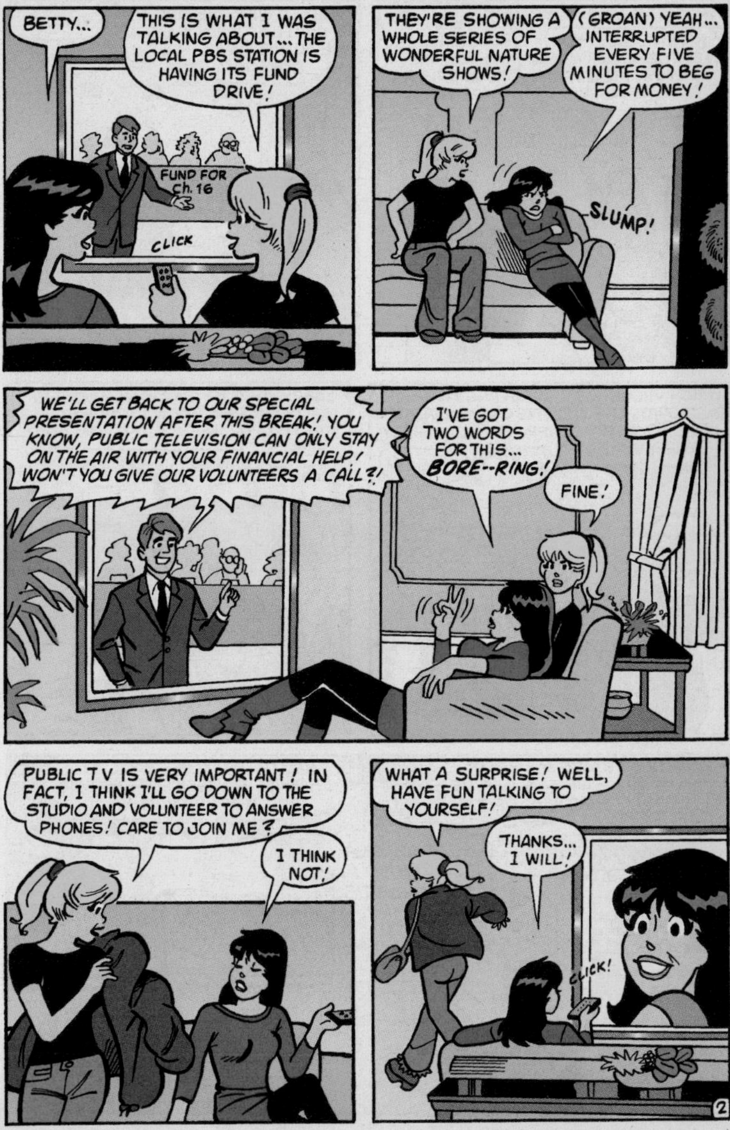
BETTY...
THIS IS WHAT I WAS TALKING ABOUT... THE LOCAL PBS STATION IS HAVING ITS FUND DRIVE!
FUND FOR Ch. 16
CLICK
THEY'RE SHOWING A WHOLE SERIES OF WONDERFUL NATURE SHOWS!
(GROAN) YEAH... INTERRUPTED EVERY FIVE MINUTES TO BEG FOR MONEY!
SLUMP!
WE'LL GET BACK TO OUR SPECIAL PRESENTATION AFTER THIS BREAK! YOU KNOW, PUBLIC TELEVISION CAN ONLY STAY ON THE AIR WITH YOUR FINANCIAL HELP! WON'T YOU GIVE OUR VOLUNTEERS A CALL?!
I'VE GOT TWO WORDS FOR THIS... BORE--RING!
FINE!
PUBLIC TV IS VERY IMPORTANT! IN FACT, I THINK I'LL GO DOWN TO THE STUDIO AND VOLUNTEER TO ANSWER PHONES! CARE TO JOIN ME?
I THINK NOT!
WHAT A SURPRISE! WELL, HAVE FUN TALKING TO YOURSELF!
THANKS... I WILL!
CLICK!
2

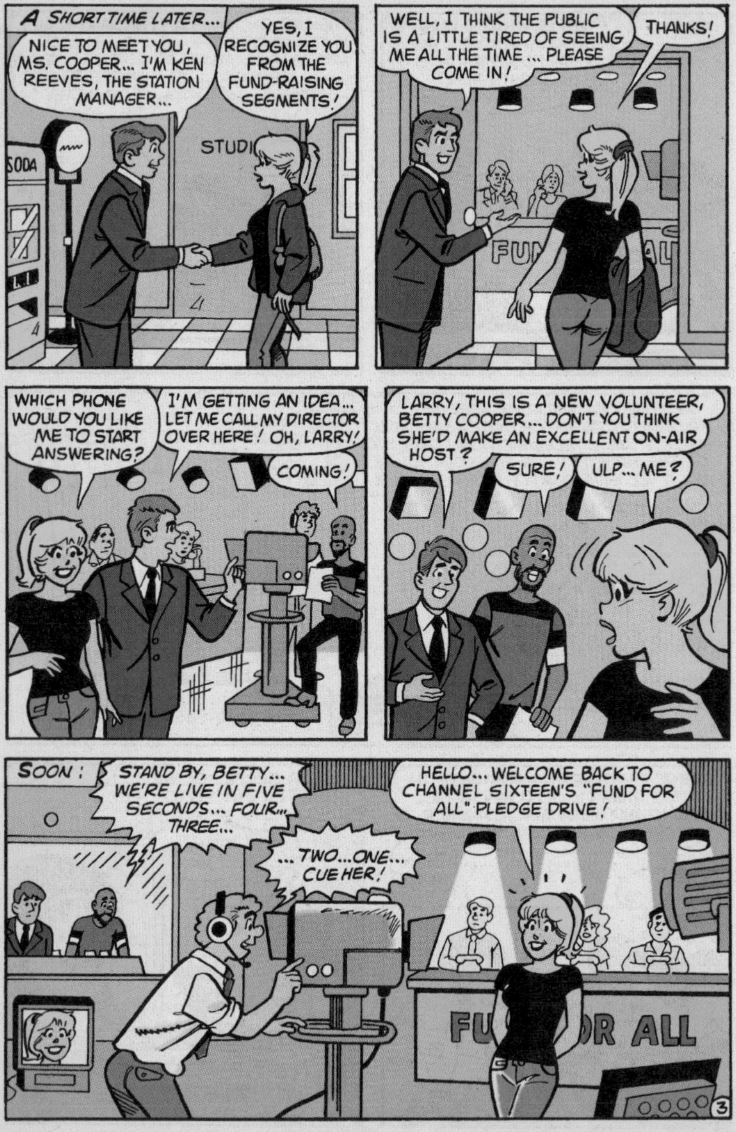
A SHORT TIME LATER...
NICE TO MEET YOU, MS. COOPER... I'M KEN REEVES, THE STATION MANAGER...
YES, I RECOGNIZE YOU FROM THE FUND-RAISING SEGMENTS!
SODA
STUDI
WELL, I THINK THE PUBLIC IS A LITTLE TIRED OF SEEING ME ALL THE TIME... PLEASE COME IN!
THANKS!
WHICH PHONE WOULD YOU LIKE ME TO START ANSWERING?
I'M GETTING AN IDEA... LET ME CALL MY DIRECTOR OVER HERE! OH, LARRY!
COMING!
LARRY, THIS IS A NEW VOLUNTEER, BETTY COOPER... DON'T YOU THINK SHE'D MAKE AN EXCELLENT ON-AIR HOST?
SURE!
ULP... ME?
SOON:
STAND BY, BETTY... WE'RE LIVE IN FIVE SECONDS... FOUR... THREE...
...TWO...ONE... CUE HER!
HELLO... WELCOME BACK TO CHANNEL SIXTEEN'S "FUND FOR ALL" PLEDGE DRIVE!
FU OR ALL
3

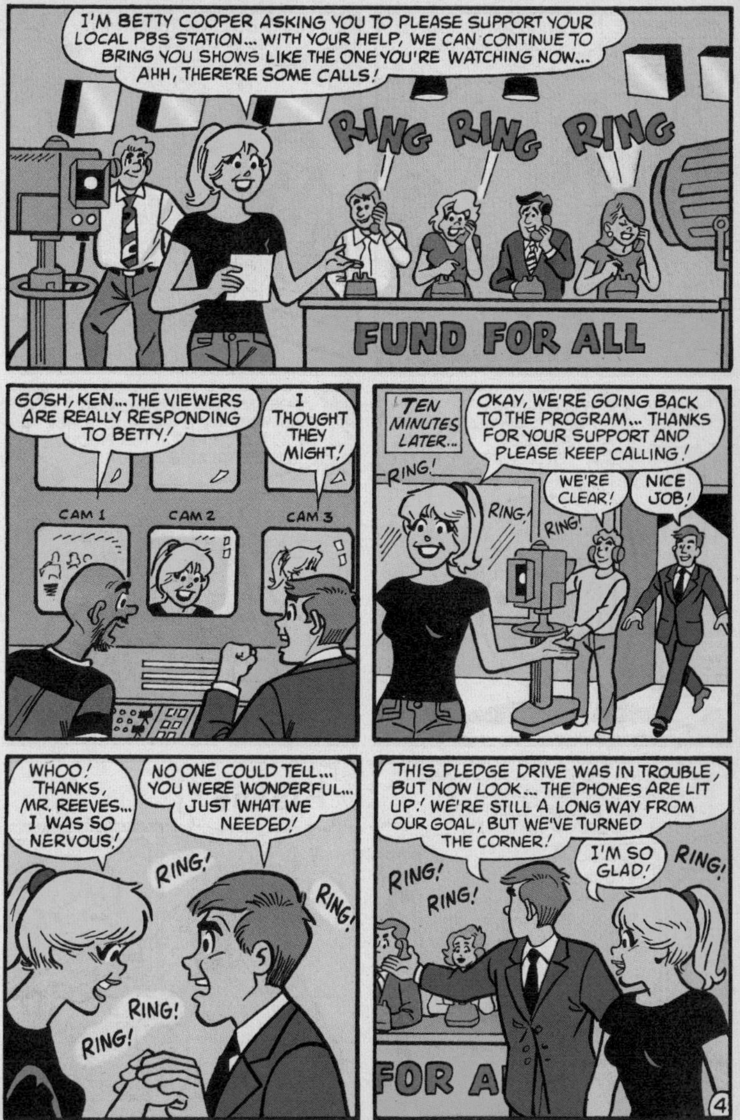
I'M BETTY COOPER ASKING YOU TO PLEASE SUPPORT YOUR LOCAL PBS STATION... WITH YOUR HELP, WE CAN CONTINUE TO BRING YOU SHOWS LIKE THE ONE YOU'RE WATCHING NOW... AHH, THERE'RE SOME CALLS!
RING RING RING
FUND FOR ALL
GOSH, KEN...THE VIEWERS ARE REALLY RESPONDING TO BETTY!
I THOUGHT THEY MIGHT!
CAM 1
CAM 2
CAM 3
TEN MINUTES LATER...
OKAY, WE'RE GOING BACK TO THE PROGRAM... THANKS FOR YOUR SUPPORT AND PLEASE KEEP CALLING!
RING!
RING!
RING!
WE'RE CLEAR!
NICE JOB!
WHOO! THANKS, MR. REEVES... I WAS SO NERVOUS!
NO ONE COULD TELL... YOU WERE WONDERFUL... JUST WHAT WE NEEDED!
RING!
RING!
RING!
RING!
THIS PLEDGE DRIVE WAS IN TROUBLE, BUT NOW LOOK... THE PHONES ARE LIT UP! WE'RE STILL A LONG WAY FROM OUR GOAL, BUT WE'VE TURNED THE CORNER!
I'M SO GLAD!
RING!
RING!
RING!
FOR A

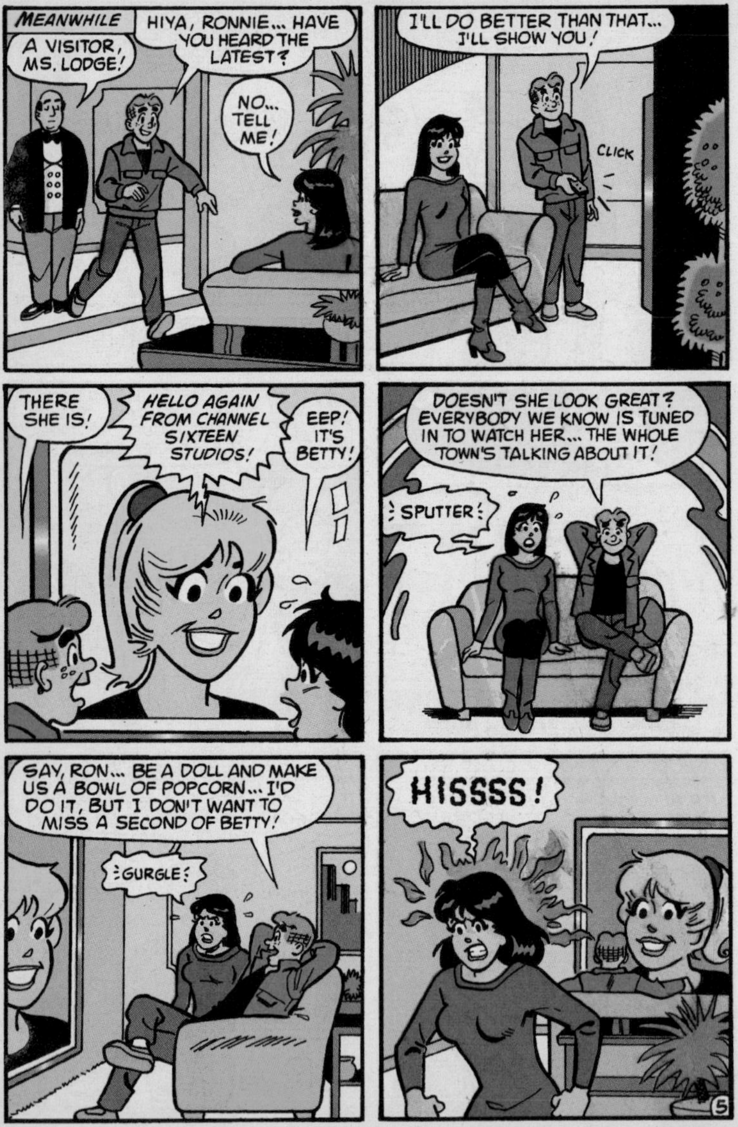
MEANWHILE
A VISITOR, MS. LODGE!
HIYA, RONNIE... HAVE YOU HEARD THE LATEST?
NO... TELL ME!
I'LL DO BETTER THAN THAT... I'LL SHOW YOU!
CLICK
THERE SHE IS!
HELLO AGAIN FROM CHANNEL SIXTEEN STUDIOS!
EEP! IT'S BETTY!
DOESN'T SHE LOOK GREAT? EVERYBODY WE KNOW IS TUNED IN TO WATCH HER... THE WHOLE TOWN'S TALKING ABOUT IT!
SPUTTER
SAY, RON... BE A DOLL AND MAKE US A BOWL OF POPCORN... I'D DO IT, BUT I DON'T WANT TO MISS A SECOND OF BETTY!
GURGLE
HISSSS!
5

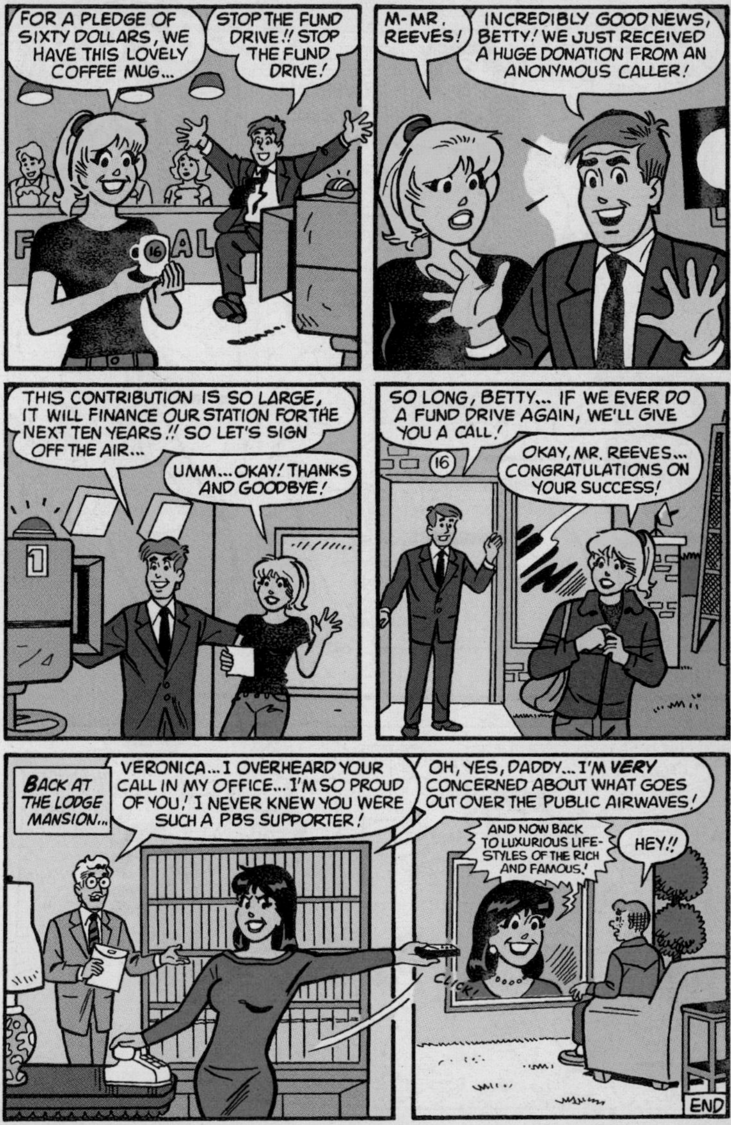

FOR A PLEDGE OF SIXTY DOLLARS, WE HAVE THIS LOVELY COFFEE MUG...
STOP THE FUND DRIVE!! STOP THE FUND DRIVE!
M-MR. REEVES!
INCREDIBLY GOOD NEWS, BETTY! WE JUST RECEIVED A HUGE DONATION FROM AN ANONYMOUS CALLER!
THIS CONTRIBUTION IS SO LARGE, IT WILL FINANCE OUR STATION FOR THE NEXT TEN YEARS!! SO LET'S SIGN OFF THE AIR...
UMM...OKAY! THANKS AND GOODBYE!
SO LONG, BETTY... IF WE EVER DO A FUND DRIVE AGAIN, WE'LL GIVE YOU A CALL!
OKAY, MR. REEVES... CONGRATULATIONS ON YOUR SUCCESS!
BACK AT THE LODGE MANSION...
VERONICA...I OVERHEARD YOUR CALL IN MY OFFICE... I'M SO PROUD OF YOU! I NEVER KNEW YOU WERE SUCH A PBS SUPPORTER!
OH, YES, DADDY... I'M VERY CONCERNED ABOUT WHAT GOES OUT OVER THE PUBLIC AIRWAVES!
AND NOW BACK TO LUXURIOUS LIFE-STYLES OF THE RICH AND FAMOUS!
HEY!!
CLICK!
END

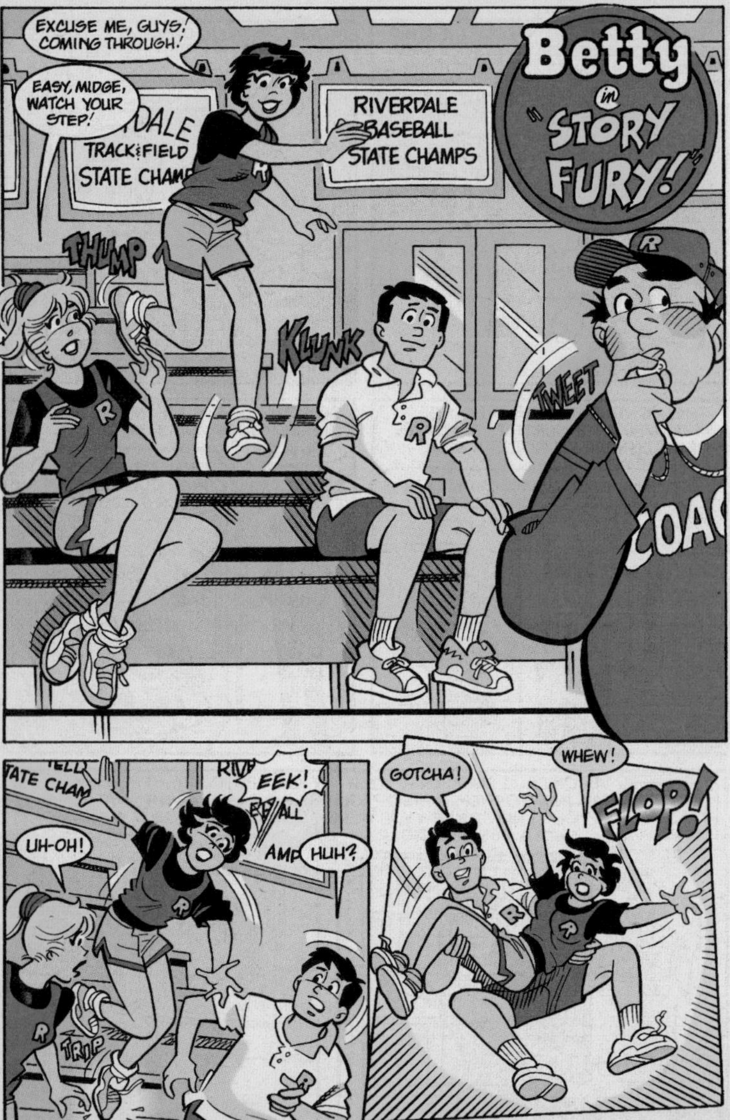

EXCUSE ME, GUYS! COMING THROUGH!
EASY, MIDGE, WATCH YOUR STEP!
RIVERDALE BASEBALL STATE CHAMPS
TRACK & FIELD STATE CHAM
Betty in "STORY FURY!"
THUMP
KLUNK
TWEET
COAC
UH-OH!
EEK!
HUH?
TRIP
GOTCHA!
WHEW!
FLOP!

Script: Mike Pellowski / Pencils: Stan Goldberg / Inks: John Lowe / Letters: Bill Yoshida / Colors: Barry Grossman

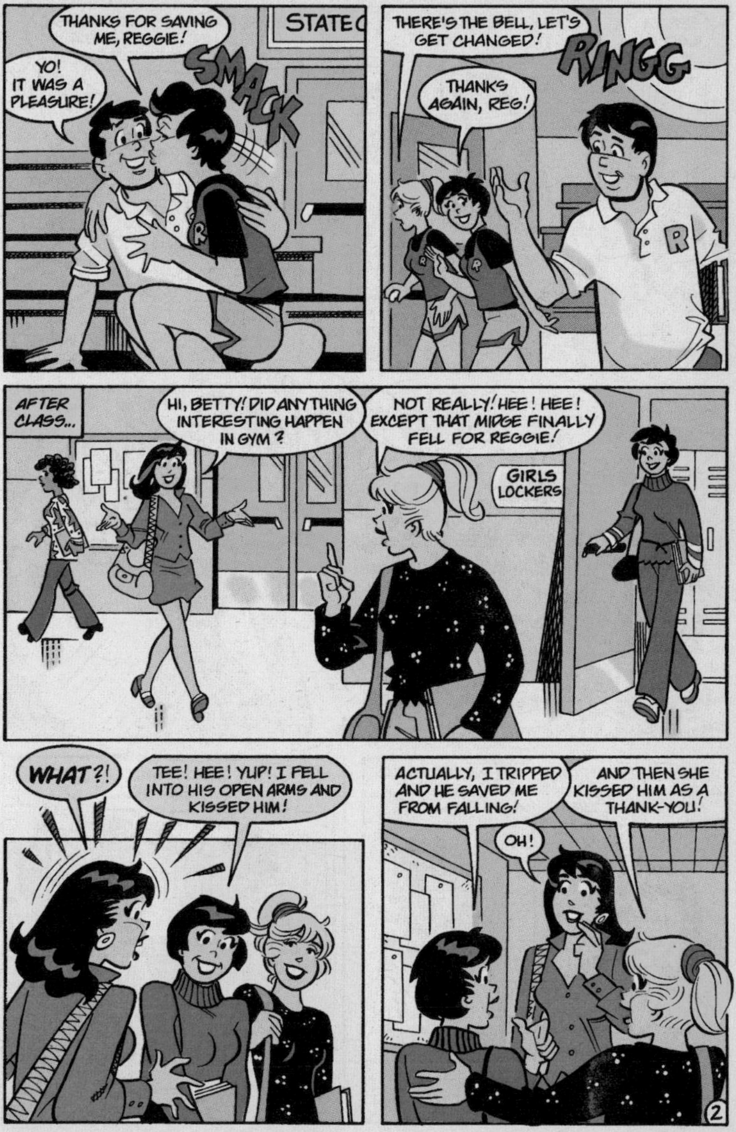

THANKS FOR SAVING ME, REGGIE!
YO! IT WAS A PLEASURE!
SMACK
STATE
THERE'S THE BELL, LET'S GET CHANGED!
RINGG
THANKS AGAIN, REG!
AFTER CLASS...
HI, BETTY! DID ANYTHING INTERESTING HAPPEN IN GYM?
NOT REALLY! HEE! HEE! EXCEPT THAT MIDGE FINALLY FELL FOR REGGIE!
GIRLS LOCKERS
WHAT?!
TEE! HEE! YUP! I FELL INTO HIS OPEN ARMS AND KISSED HIM!
ACTUALLY, I TRIPPED AND HE SAVED ME FROM FALLING!
AND THEN SHE KISSED HIM AS A THANK-YOU!
OH!
2

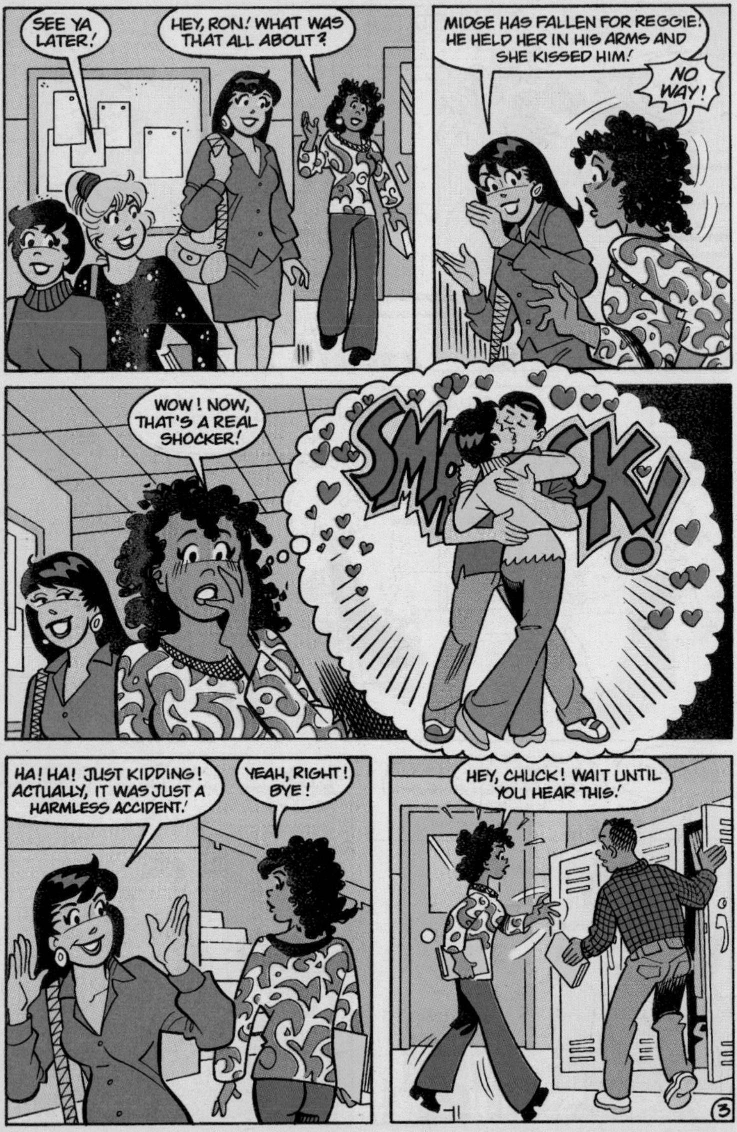
SEE YA LATER!
HEY, RON! WHAT WAS THAT ALL ABOUT?
MIDGE HAS FALLEN FOR REGGIE! HE HELD HER IN HIS ARMS AND SHE KISSED HIM!
NO WAY!
WOW! NOW, THAT'S A REAL SHOCKER!
SMACK!
HA! HA! JUST KIDDING! ACTUALLY, IT WAS JUST A HARMLESS ACCIDENT!
YEAH, RIGHT! BYE!
HEY, CHUCK! WAIT UNTIL YOU HEAR THIS!
3

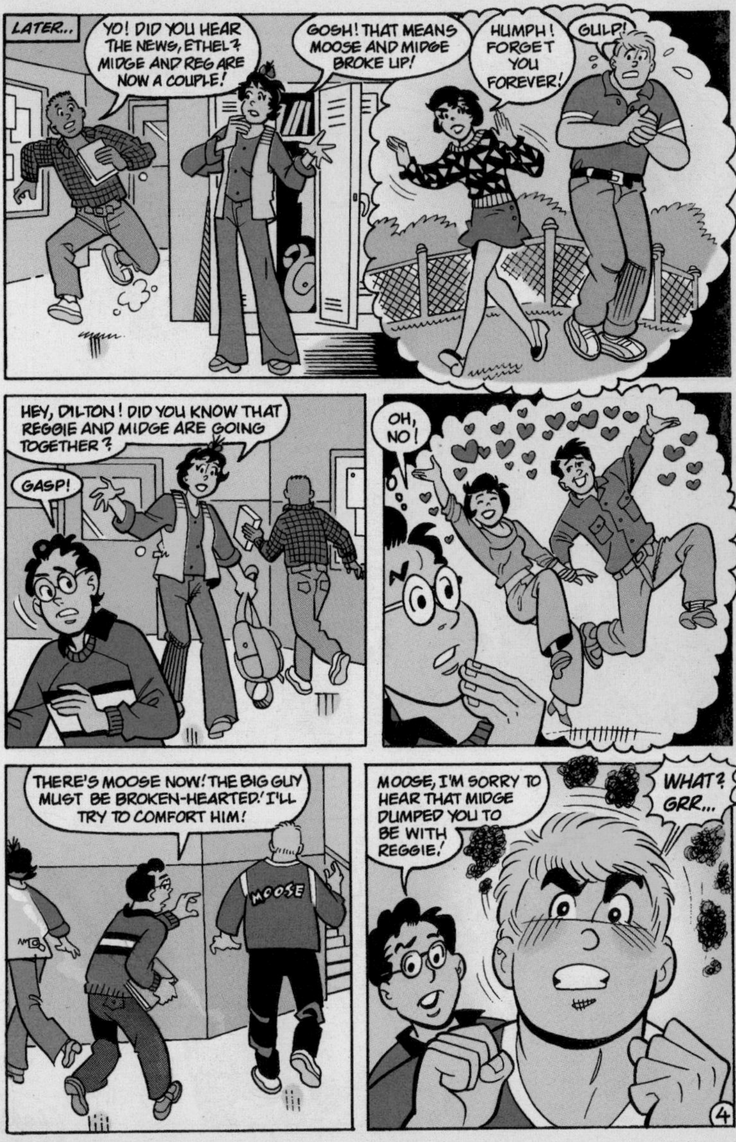
LATER...
YO! DID YOU HEAR THE NEWS, ETHEL? MIDGE AND REG ARE NOW A COUPLE!
GOSH! THAT MEANS MOOSE AND MIDGE BROKE UP!
HUMPH! FORGET YOU FOREVER!
GULP!
HEY, DILTON! DID YOU KNOW THAT REGGIE AND MIDGE ARE GOING TOGETHER?
GASP!
OH, NO!
THERE'S MOOSE NOW! THE BIG GUY MUST BE BROKEN-HEARTED! I'LL TRY TO COMFORT HIM!
MOOSE
MOOSE, I'M SORRY TO HEAR THAT MIDGE DUMPED YOU TO BE WITH REGGIE!
WHAT? GRR...
4

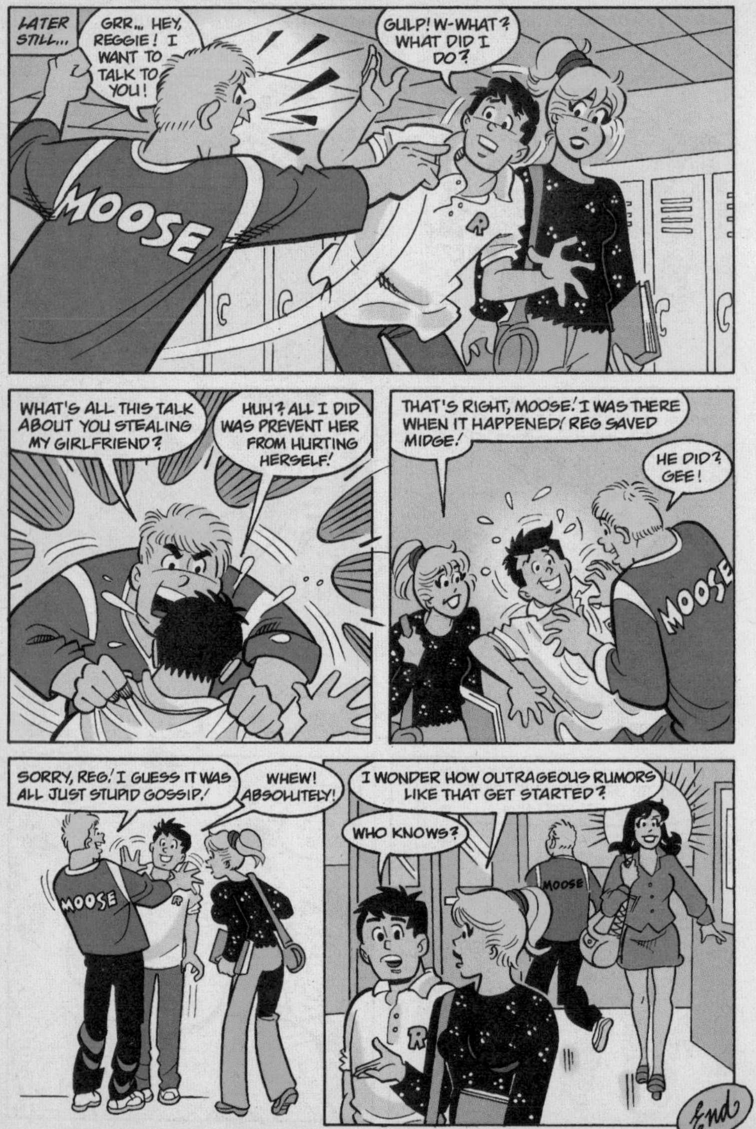
LATER STILL...
GRR... HEY, REGGIE! I WANT TO TALK TO YOU!
GULP! W-WHAT? WHAT DID I DO?
WHAT'S ALL THIS TALK ABOUT YOU STEALING MY GIRLFRIEND?
HUH? ALL I DID WAS PREVENT HER FROM HURTING HERSELF!
THAT'S RIGHT, MOOSE! I WAS THERE WHEN IT HAPPENED! REG SAVED MIDGE!
HE DID? GEE!
SORRY, REG! I GUESS IT WAS ALL JUST STUPID GOSSIP!
WHEW! ABSOLUTELY!
I WONDER HOW OUTRAGEOUS RUMORS LIKE THAT GET STARTED?
WHO KNOWS?
End

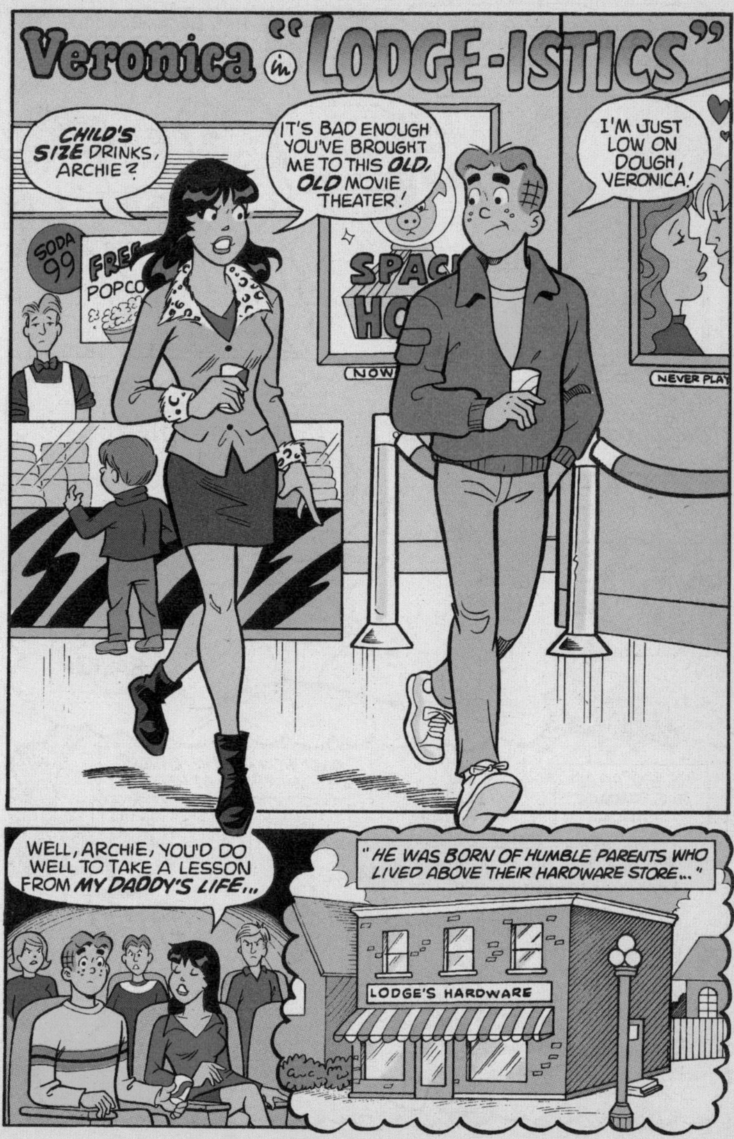
Veronica in "LODGE-ISTICS"
CHILD'S SIZE DRINKS, ARCHIE?
IT'S BAD ENOUGH YOU'VE BROUGHT ME TO THIS OLD, OLD MOVIE THEATER!
I'M JUST LOW ON DOUGH, VERONICA!
SODA 99
WELL, ARCHIE, YOU'D DO WELL TO TAKE A LESSON FROM MY DADDY'S LIFE...
"HE WAS BORN OF HUMBLE PARENTS WHO LIVED ABOVE THEIR HARDWARE STORE..."
LODGE'S HARDWARE

Script: Vic Lockman / Pencils: Dan Parent / Inks: Rich Koslowski

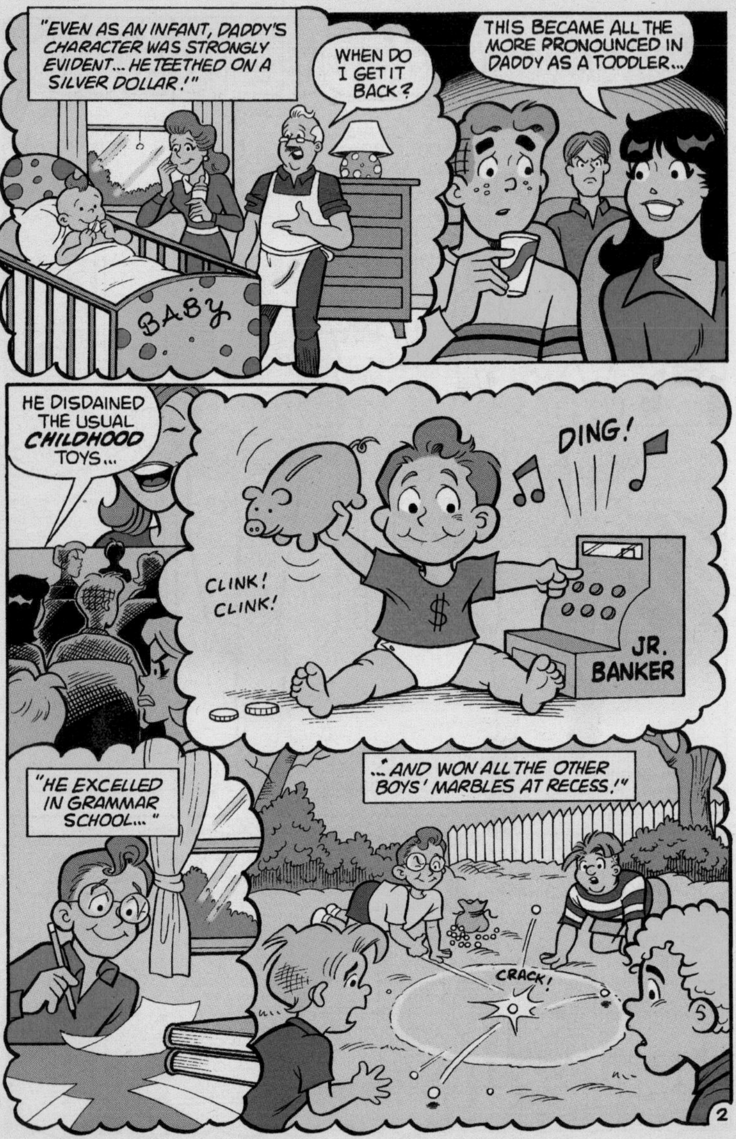
"EVEN AS AN INFANT, DADDY'S CHARACTER WAS STRONGLY EVIDENT... HE TEETHED ON A SILVER DOLLAR!"
WHEN DO I GET IT BACK?
BABY
THIS BECAME ALL THE MORE PRONOUNCED IN DADDY AS A TODDLER...
HE DISDAINED THE USUAL CHILDHOOD TOYS...
DING!
CLINK! CLINK!
$
JR. BANKER
"HE EXCELLED IN GRAMMAR SCHOOL..."
..."AND WON ALL THE OTHER BOYS' MARBLES AT RECESS!"
CRACK!

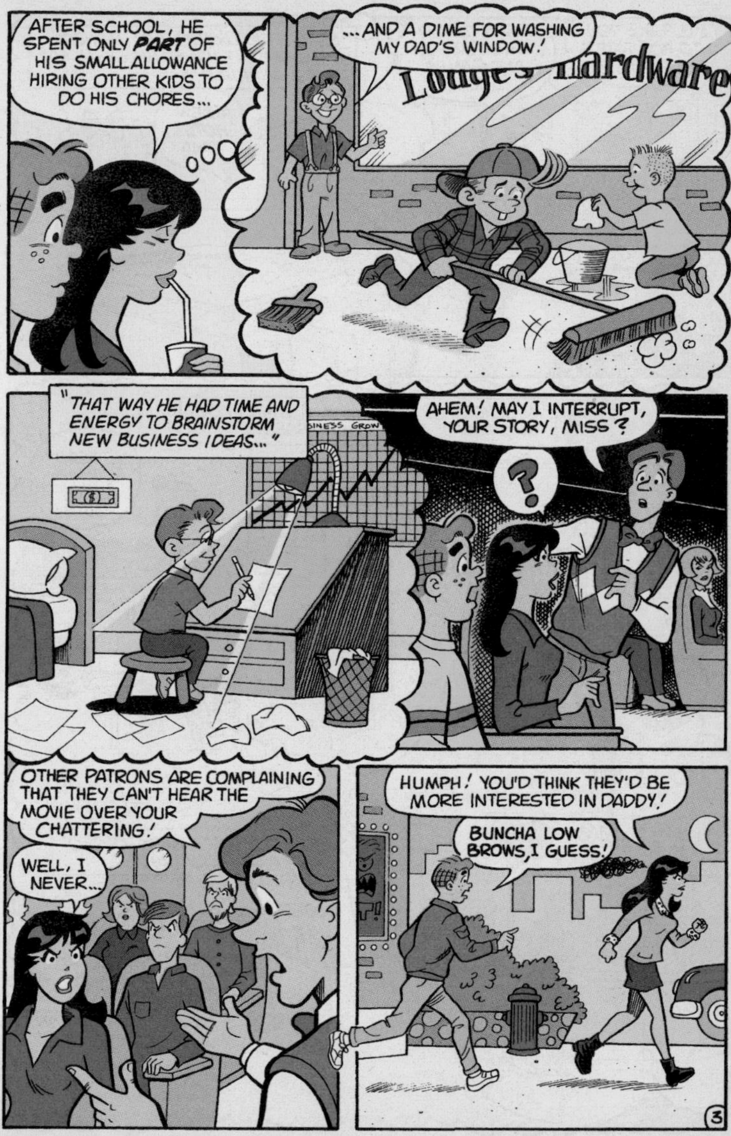
AFTER SCHOOL, HE SPENT ONLY PART OF HIS SMALL ALLOWANCE HIRING OTHER KIDS TO DO HIS CHORES...
...AND A DIME FOR WASHING MY DAD'S WINDOW!
Lodge's Hardware
"THAT WAY HE HAD TIME AND ENERGY TO BRAINSTORM NEW BUSINESS IDEAS..."
AHEM! MAY I INTERRUPT, YOUR STORY, MISS?
?
OTHER PATRONS ARE COMPLAINING THAT THEY CAN'T HEAR THE MOVIE OVER YOUR CHATTERING!
WELL, I NEVER...
HUMPH! YOU'D THINK THEY'D BE MORE INTERESTED IN DADDY!
BUNCHA LOW BROWS, I GUESS!

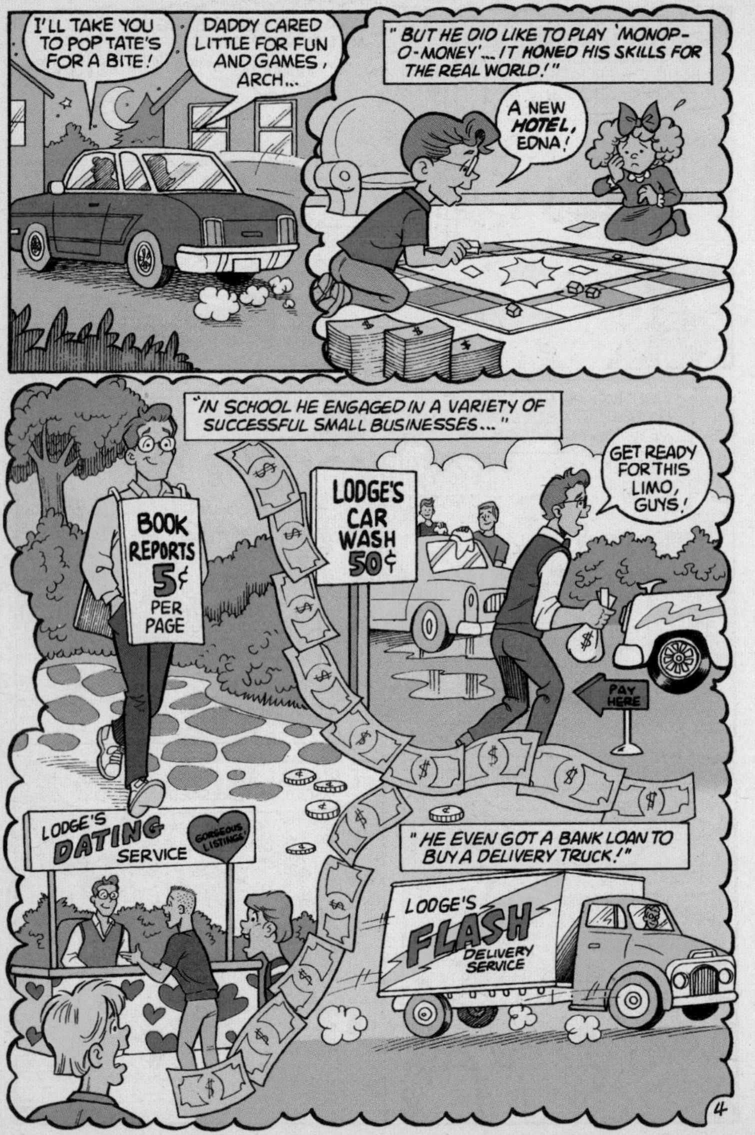
I'LL TAKE YOU TO POP TATE'S FOR A BITE!
DADDY CARED LITTLE FOR FUN AND GAMES, ARCH...
" BUT HE DID LIKE TO PLAY 'MONOP-O-MONEY'... IT HONED HIS SKILLS FOR THE REAL WORLD!"
A NEW HOTEL, EDNA!
"IN SCHOOL HE ENGAGED IN A VARIETY OF SUCCESSFUL SMALL BUSINESSES..."
BOOK REPORTS 5¢ PER PAGE
LODGE'S CAR WASH 50¢
GET READY FOR THIS LIMO, GUYS!
PAY HERE
LODGE'S DATING SERVICE
GORGEOUS LISTINGS!
" HE EVEN GOT A BANK LOAN TO BUY A DELIVERY TRUCK!"
LODGE'S FLASH DELIVERY SERVICE
4

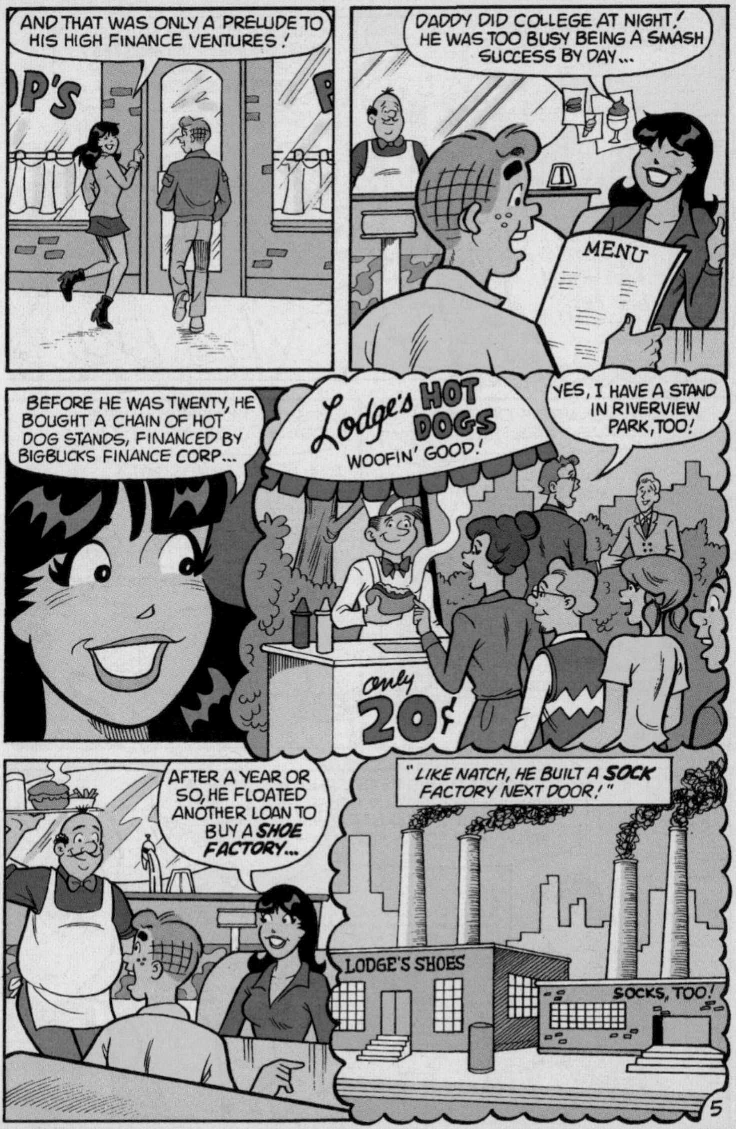
AND THAT WAS ONLY A PRELUDE TO HIS HIGH FINANCE VENTURES!
DADDY DID COLLEGE AT NIGHT! HE WAS TOO BUSY BEING A SMASH SUCCESS BY DAY...
MENU
BEFORE HE WAS TWENTY, HE BOUGHT A CHAIN OF HOT DOG STANDS, FINANCED BY BIGBUCKS FINANCE CORP...
Lodge's HOT DOGS
WOOFIN' GOOD!
YES, I HAVE A STAND IN RIVERVIEW PARK, TOO!
only 20¢
AFTER A YEAR OR SO, HE FLOATED ANOTHER LOAN TO BUY A SHOE FACTORY...
"LIKE NATCH, HE BUILT A SOCK FACTORY NEXT DOOR!"
LODGE'S SHOES
SOCKS, TOO!

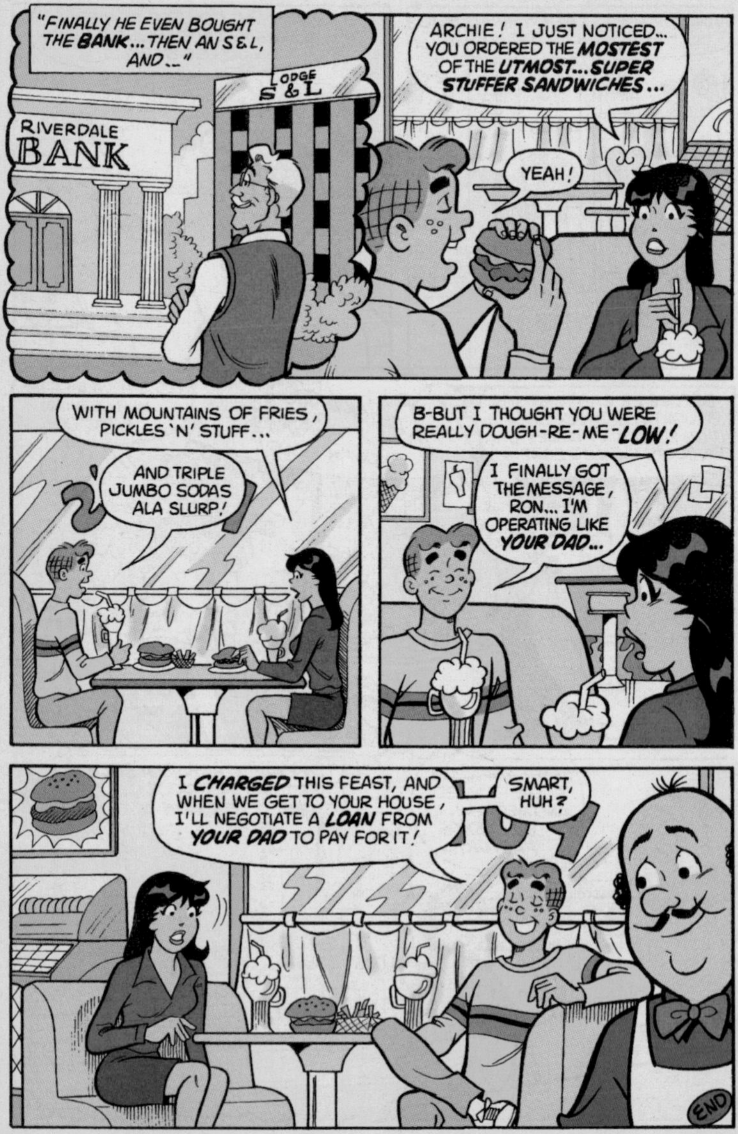
"FINALLY HE EVEN BOUGHT THE BANK... THEN AN S&L, AND..."
LODGE S&L
RIVERDALE BANK
ARCHIE! I JUST NOTICED... YOU ORDERED THE MOSTEST OF THE UTMOST... SUPER STUFFER SANDWICHES...
YEAH!
WITH MOUNTAINS OF FRIES, PICKLES 'N' STUFF...
AND TRIPLE JUMBO SODAS ALA SLURP!
B-BUT I THOUGHT YOU WERE REALLY DOUGH-RE-ME-LOW!
I FINALLY GOT THE MESSAGE, RON... I'M OPERATING LIKE YOUR DAD...
I CHARGED THIS FEAST, AND WHEN WE GET TO YOUR HOUSE, I'LL NEGOTIATE A LOAN FROM YOUR DAD TO PAY FOR IT!
SMART, HUH?
END

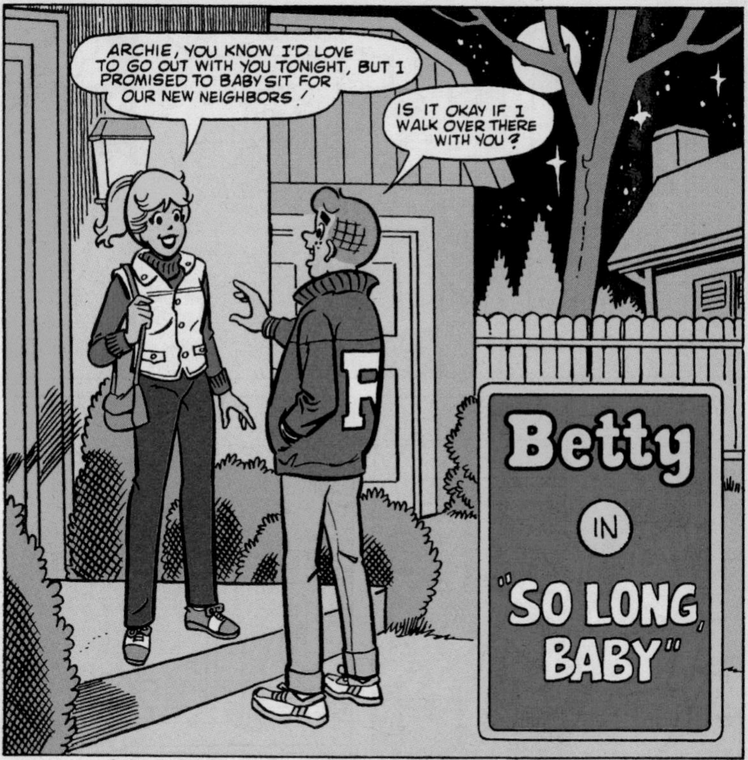
ARCHIE, YOU KNOW I'D LOVE TO GO OUT WITH YOU TONIGHT, BUT I PROMISED TO BABY SIT FOR OUR NEW NEIGHBORS!
IS IT OKAY IF I WALK OVER THERE WITH YOU?
Betty
IN
"SO LONG, BABY"

Script: Jim Ruth / Pencils: Stan Goldberg / Inks: Mike Esposito / Letters: Bill Yoshida

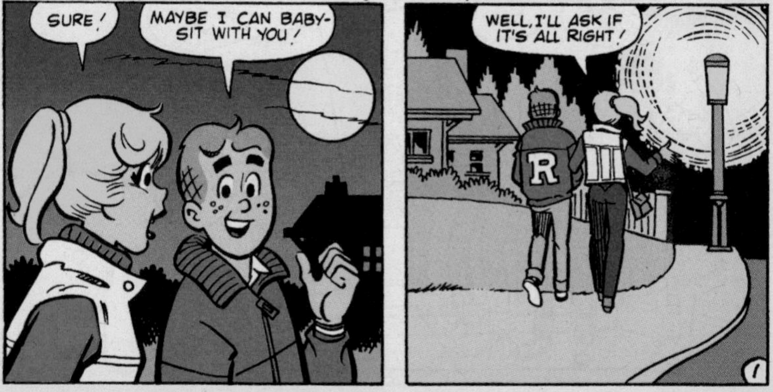
SURE!
MAYBE I CAN BABY-SIT WITH YOU!
WELL, I'LL ASK IF IT'S ALL RIGHT!

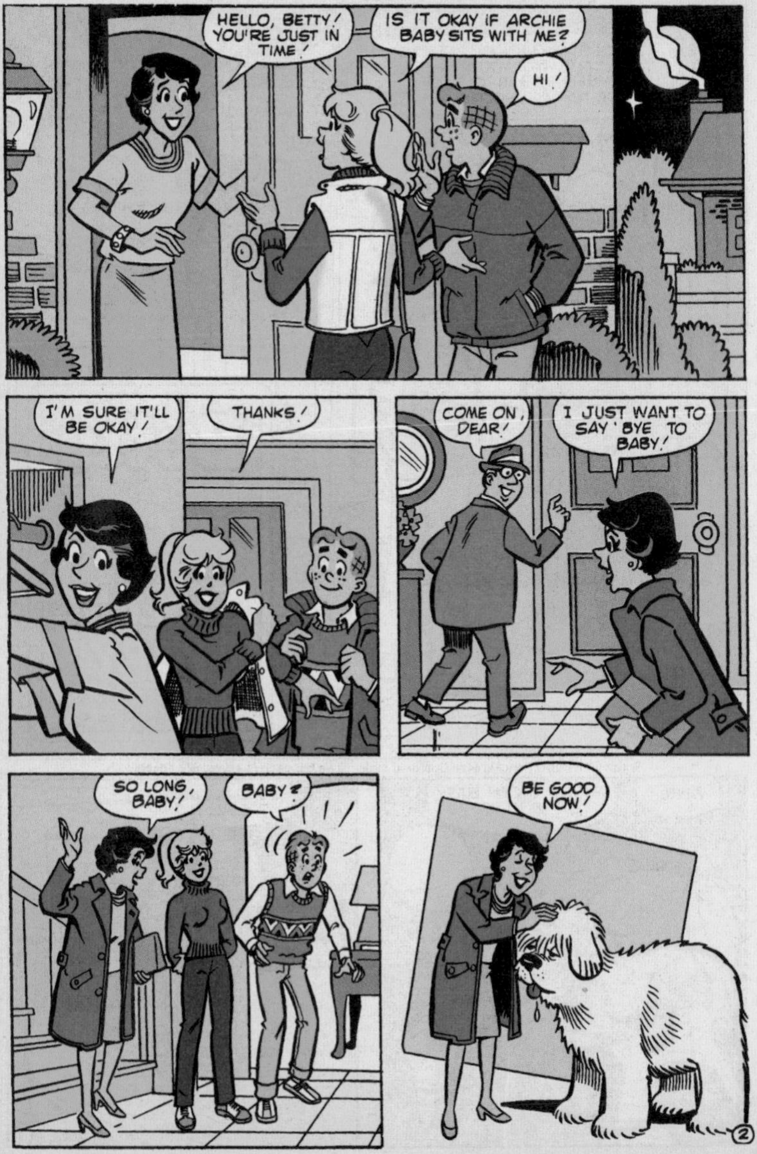
HELLO, BETTY! YOU'RE JUST IN TIME!
IS IT OKAY IF ARCHIE BABY SITS WITH ME?
HI!
I'M SURE IT'LL BE OKAY!
THANKS!
COME ON, DEAR!
I JUST WANT TO SAY 'BYE TO BABY!
SO LONG, BABY!
BABY?
BE GOOD NOW!
2

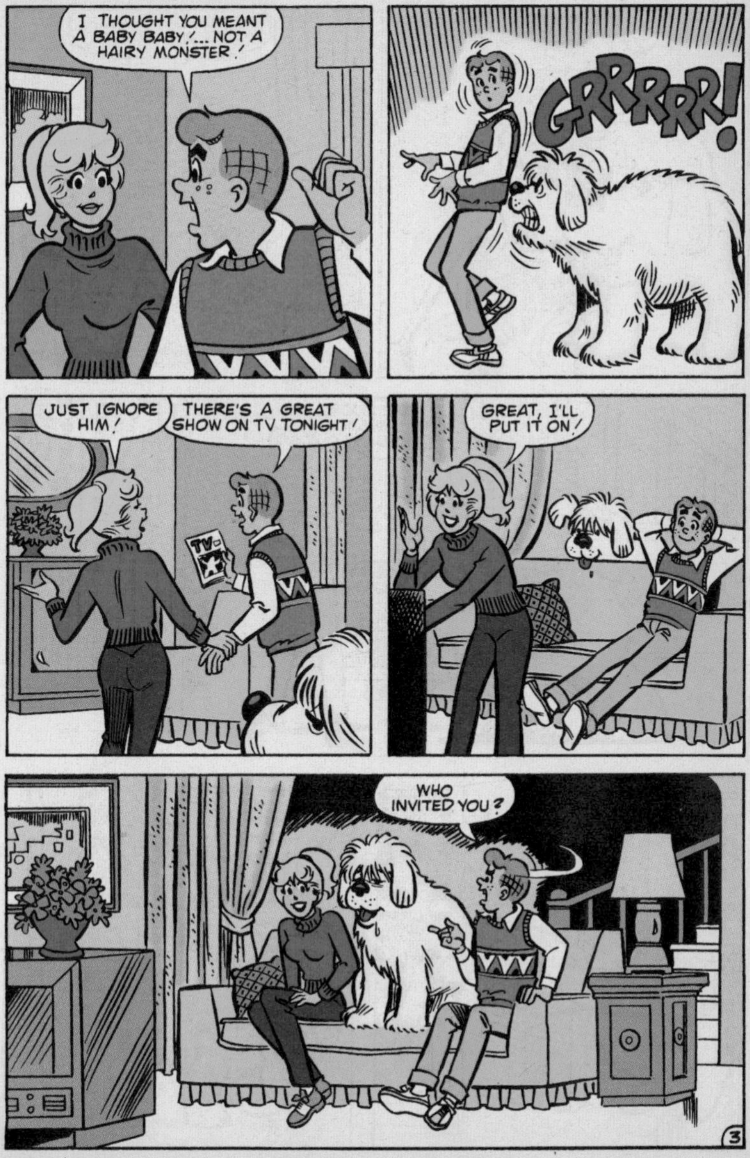
I THOUGHT YOU MEANT A BABY BABY!... NOT A HAIRY MONSTER!
GRRRRR!
JUST IGNORE HIM!
THERE'S A GREAT SHOW ON TV TONIGHT!
TV
GREAT, I'LL PUT IT ON!
WHO INVITED YOU?
3

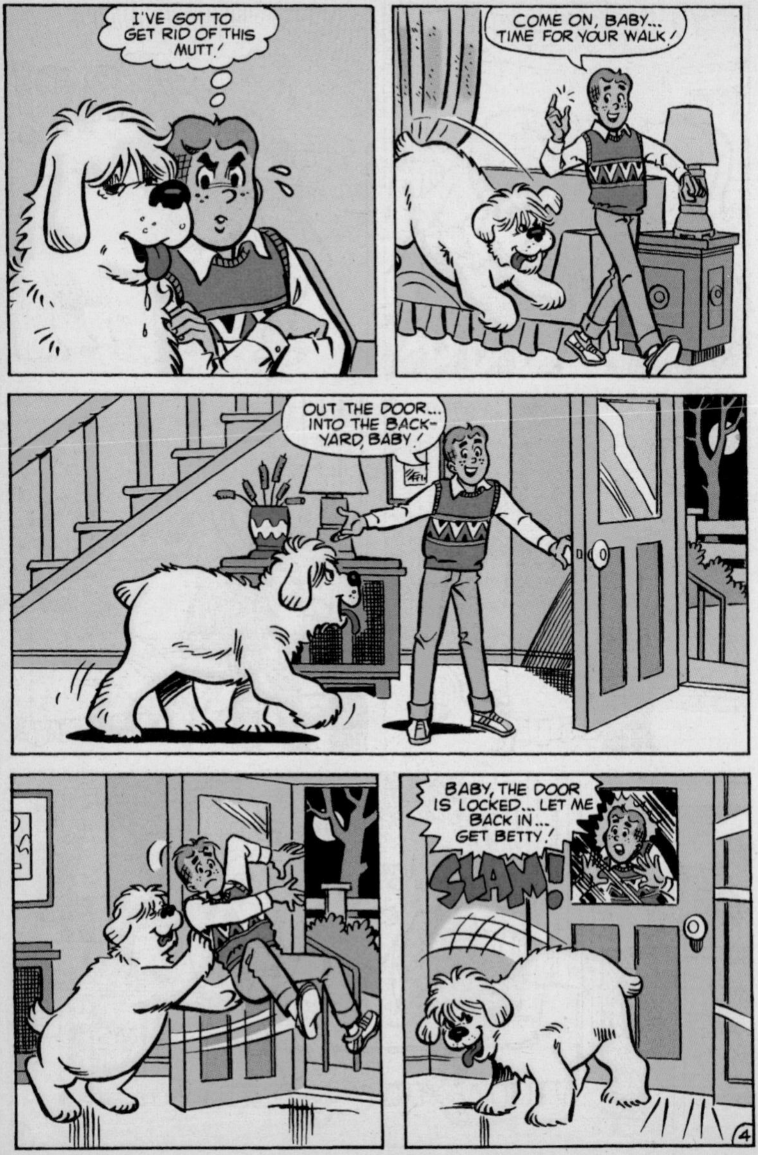

I'VE GOT TO GET RID OF THIS MUTT!
COME ON, BABY... TIME FOR YOUR WALK!
OUT THE DOOR... INTO THE BACK-YARD, BABY!
BABY, THE DOOR IS LOCKED... LET ME BACK IN... GET BETTY!
SLAM!

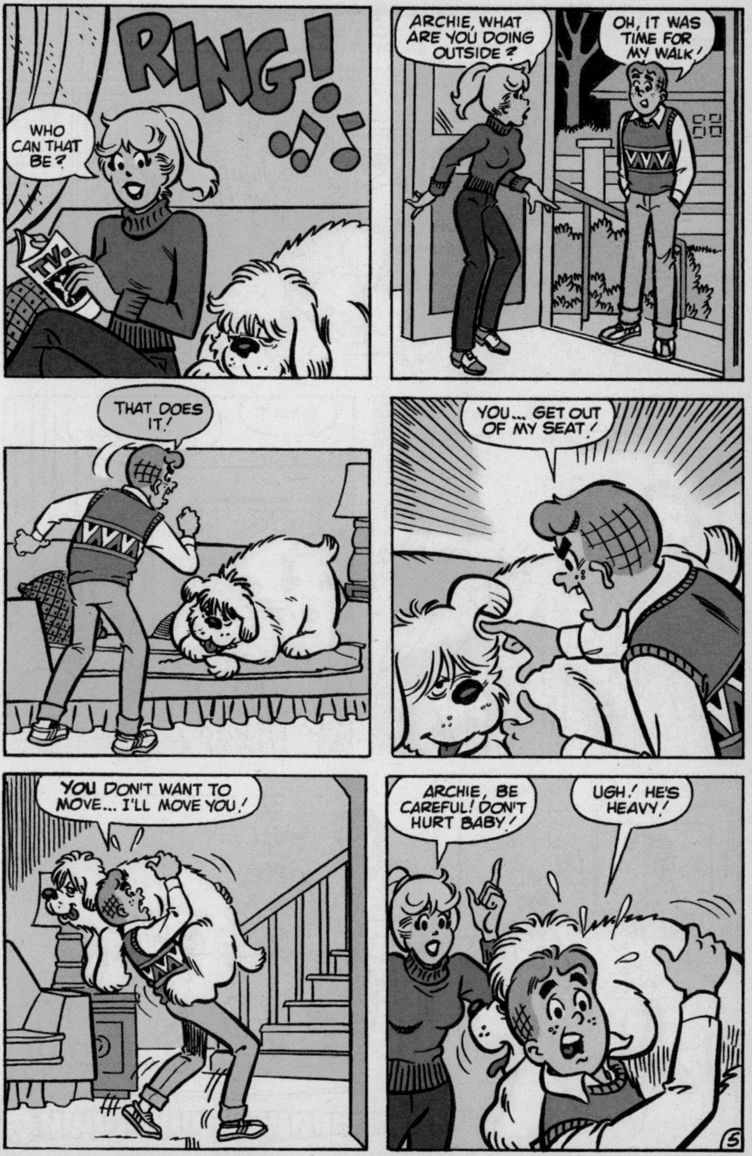
RING!
WHO CAN THAT BE?
TV
ARCHIE, WHAT ARE YOU DOING OUTSIDE?
OH, IT WAS TIME FOR MY WALK!
THAT DOES IT!
YOU... GET OUT OF MY SEAT!
YOU DON'T WANT TO MOVE... I'LL MOVE YOU!
ARCHIE, BE CAREFUL! DON'T HURT BABY!
UGH! HE'S HEAVY!

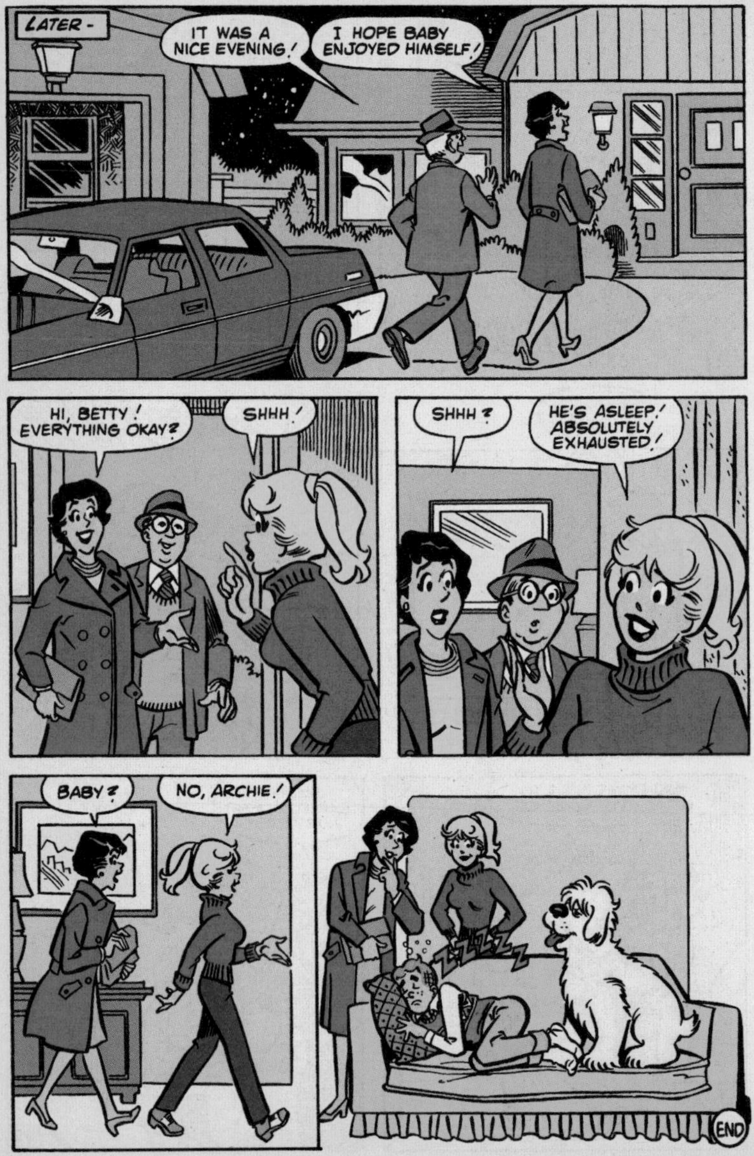
LATER -
IT WAS A NICE EVENING!
I HOPE BABY ENJOYED HIMSELF!
HI, BETTY! EVERYTHING OKAY?
SHHH!
SHHH?
HE'S ASLEEP! ABSOLUTELY EXHAUSTED!
BABY?
NO, ARCHIE!
END

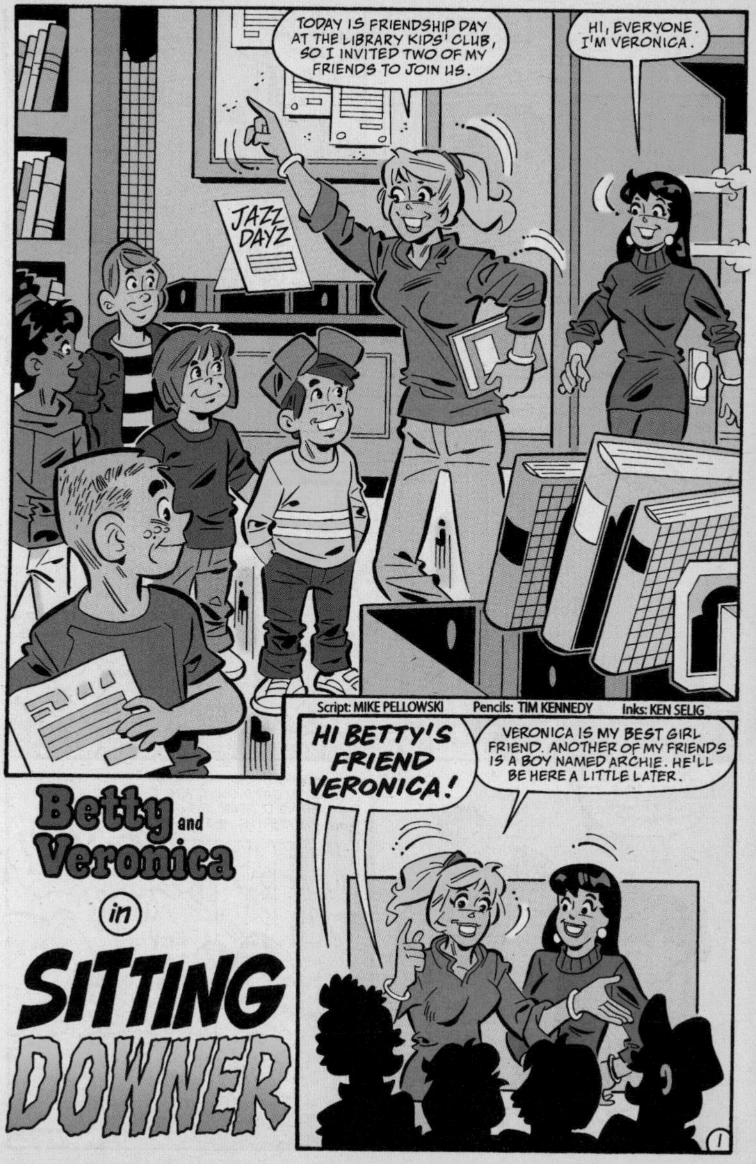
TODAY IS FRIENDSHIP DAY AT THE LIBRARY KIDS' CLUB, SO I INVITED TWO OF MY FRIENDS TO JOIN US.
HI, EVERYONE. I'M VERONICA.
JAZZ DAYZ
Script: MIKE PELLOWSKI Pencils: TIM KENNEDY Inks: KEN SELIG
HI BETTY'S FRIEND VERONICA!
VERONICA IS MY BEST GIRL FRIEND. ANOTHER OF MY FRIENDS IS A BOY NAMED ARCHIE. HE'LL BE HERE A LITTLE LATER.
Betty and Veronica in
SITTING DOWNER
1

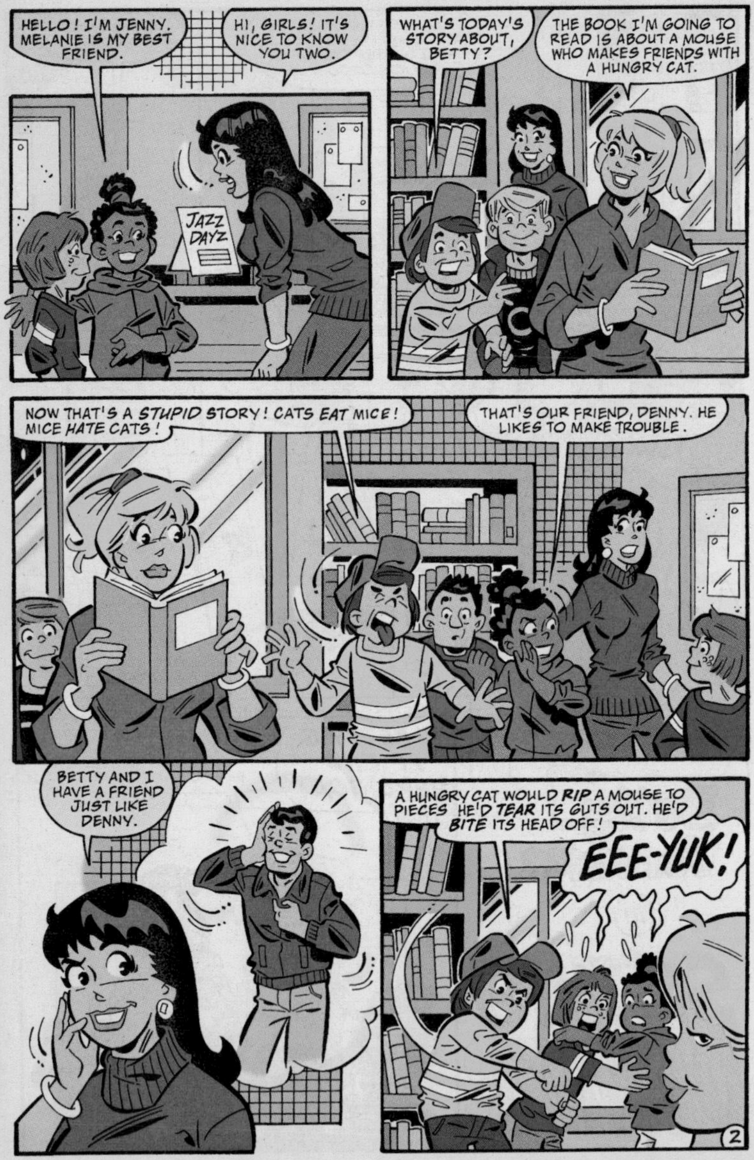

HELLO! I'M JENNY. MELANIE IS MY BEST FRIEND.
HI, GIRLS! IT'S NICE TO KNOW YOU TWO.
JAZZ DAYZ
WHAT'S TODAY'S STORY ABOUT, BETTY?
THE BOOK I'M GOING TO READ IS ABOUT A MOUSE WHO MAKES FRIENDS WITH A HUNGRY CAT.
NOW THAT'S A STUPID STORY! CATS EAT MICE! MICE HATE CATS!
THAT'S OUR FRIEND, DENNY. HE LIKES TO MAKE TROUBLE.
BETTY AND I HAVE A FRIEND JUST LIKE DENNY.
A HUNGRY CAT WOULD RIP A MOUSE TO PIECES HE'D TEAR ITS GUTS OUT. HE'D BITE ITS HEAD OFF!
EEE-YUK!
2

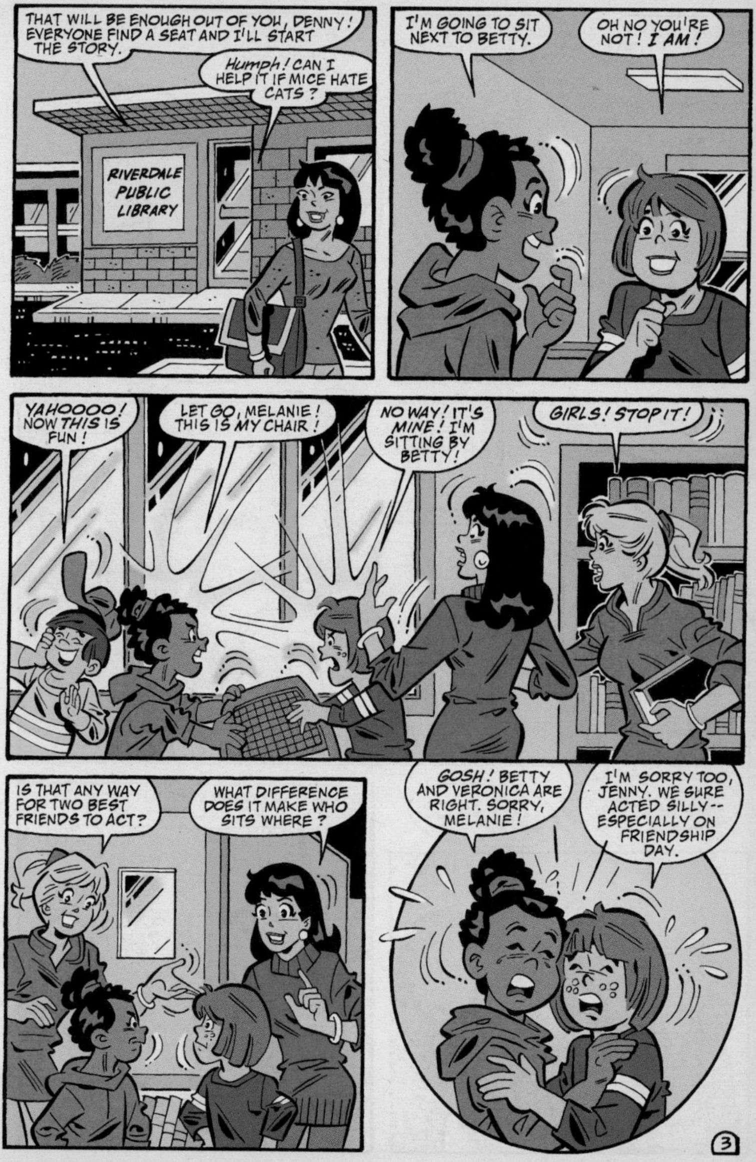
THAT WILL BE ENOUGH OUT OF YOU, DENNY! EVERYONE FIND A SEAT AND I'LL START THE STORY.
Humph! CAN I HELP IT IF MICE HATE CATS?
RIVERDALE PUBLIC LIBRARY
I'M GOING TO SIT NEXT TO BETTY.
OH NO YOU'RE NOT! I AM!
YAHOOOO! NOW THIS IS FUN!
LET GO, MELANIE! THIS IS MY CHAIR!
NO WAY! IT'S MINE! I'M SITTING BY BETTY!
GIRLS! STOP IT!
IS THAT ANY WAY FOR TWO BEST FRIENDS TO ACT?
WHAT DIFFERENCE DOES IT MAKE WHO SITS WHERE?
GOSH! BETTY AND VERONICA ARE RIGHT. SORRY, MELANIE!
I'M SORRY TOO, JENNY. WE SURE ACTED SILLY -- ESPECIALLY ON FRIENDSHIP DAY.

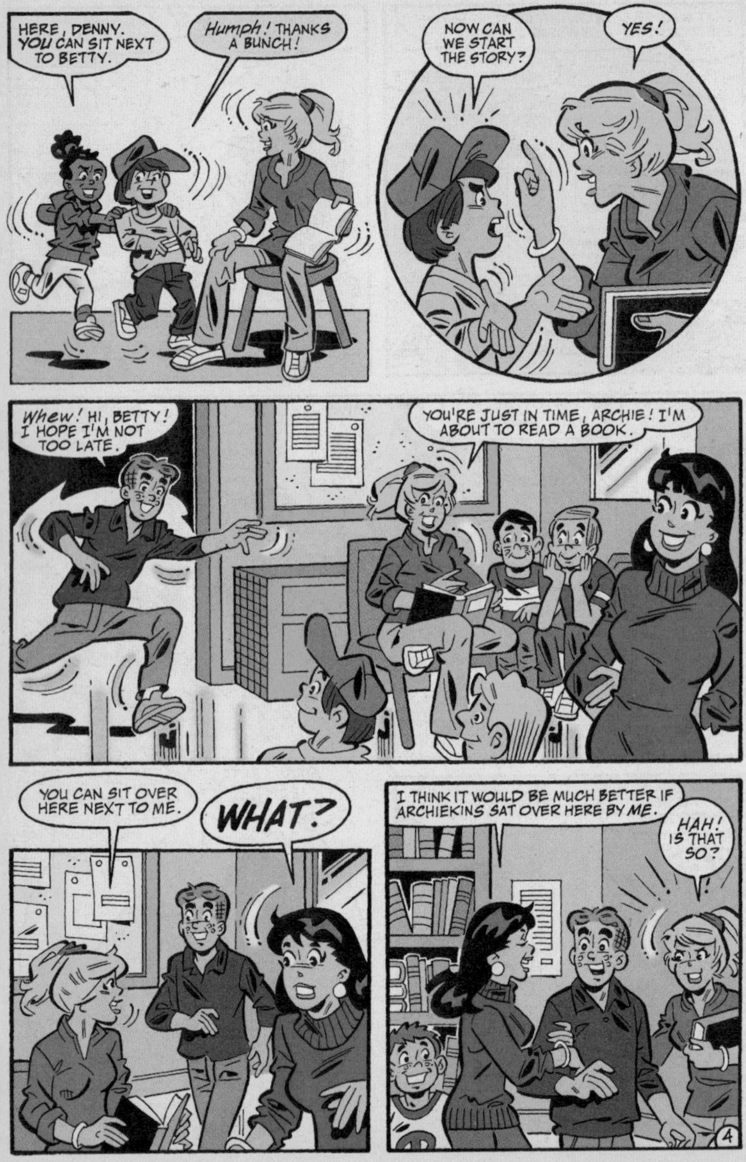
HERE, DENNY. YOU CAN SIT NEXT TO BETTY.
Humph! THANKS A BUNCH!
NOW CAN WE START THE STORY?
YES!
Whew! HI, BETTY! I HOPE I'M NOT TOO LATE.
YOU'RE JUST IN TIME, ARCHIE! I'M ABOUT TO READ A BOOK.
YOU CAN SIT OVER HERE NEXT TO ME.
WHAT?
I THINK IT WOULD BE MUCH BETTER IF ARCHIEKINS SAT OVER HERE BY ME.
HAH! IS THAT SO?
4

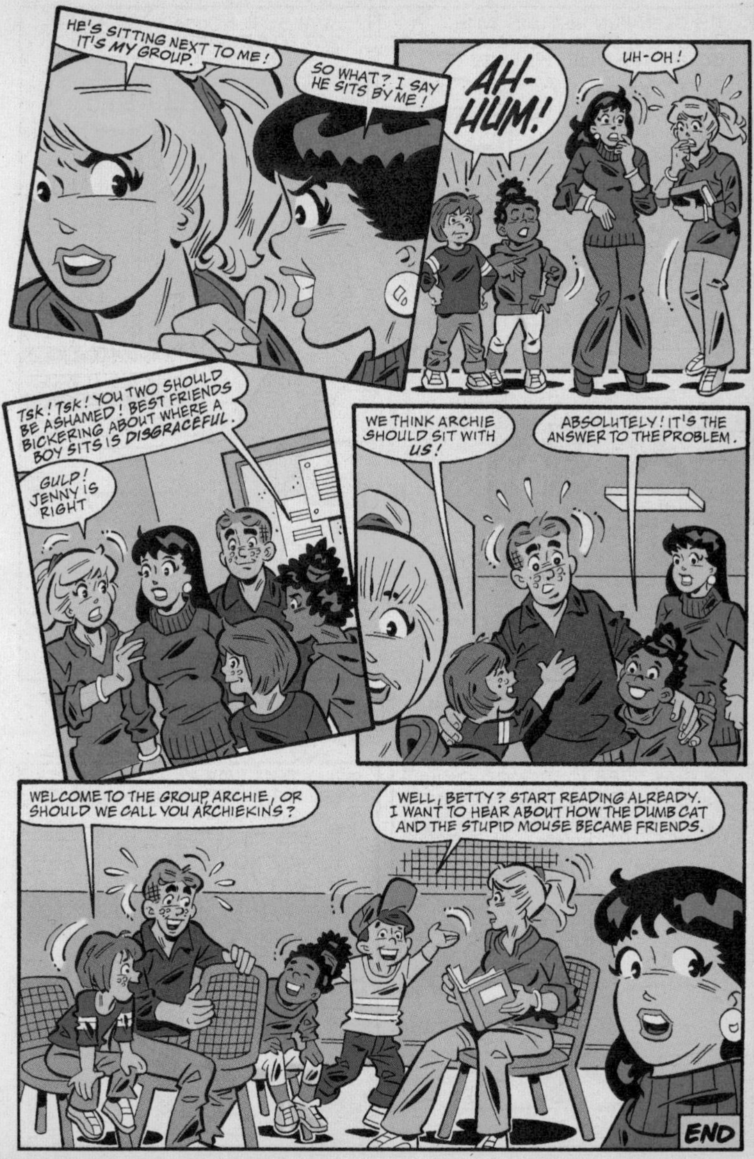

HE'S SITTING NEXT TO ME! IT'S MY GROUP.
SO WHAT? I SAY HE SITS BY ME!
AH-HUM!
UH-OH!
Tsk! Tsk! YOU TWO SHOULD BE ASHAMED! BEST FRIENDS BICKERING ABOUT WHERE A BOY SITS IS DISGRACEFUL.
GULP! JENNY IS RIGHT
WE THINK ARCHIE SHOULD SIT WITH US!
ABSOLUTELY! IT'S THE ANSWER TO THE PROBLEM.
WELCOME TO THE GROUP ARCHIE, OR SHOULD WE CALL YOU ARCHIEKINS?
WELL, BETTY? START READING ALREADY. I WANT TO HEAR ABOUT HOW THE DUMB CAT AND THE STUPID MOUSE BECAME FRIENDS.
END

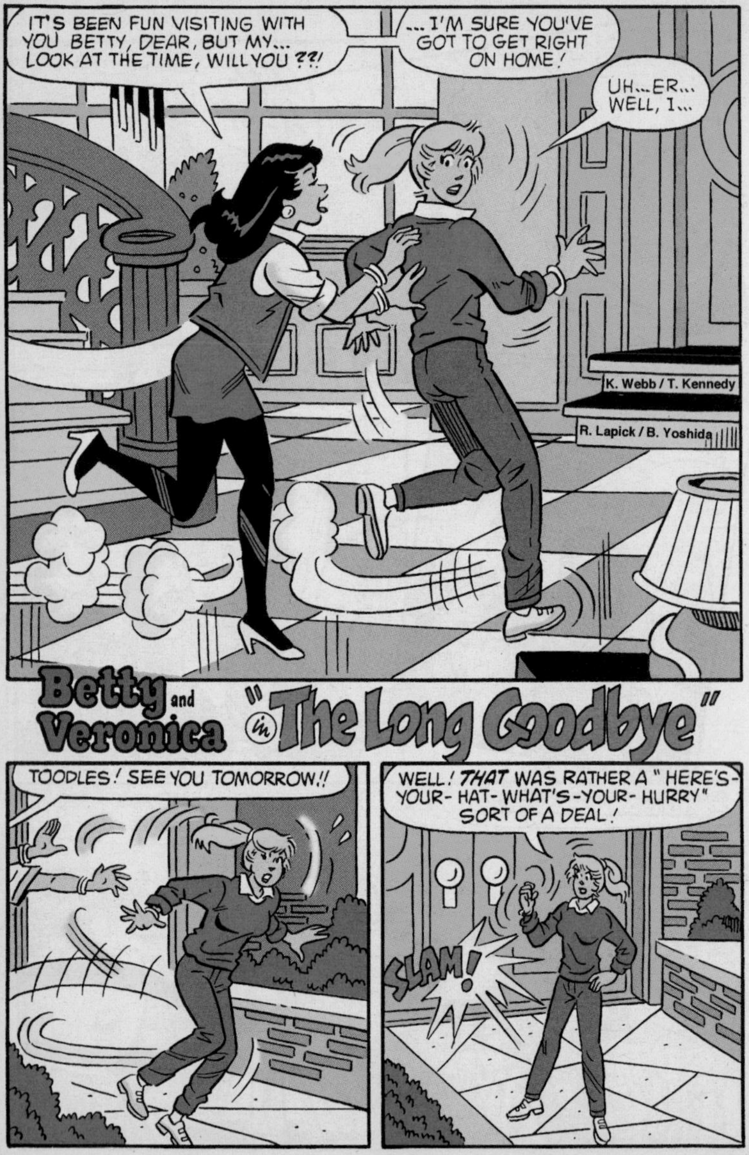

IT'S BEEN FUN VISITING WITH YOU BETTY, DEAR, BUT MY... LOOK AT THE TIME, WILL YOU ??!
... I'M SURE YOU'VE GOT TO GET RIGHT ON HOME!
UH...ER... WELL, I...
K. Webb / T. Kennedy
R. Lapick / B. Yoshida
Betty and Veronica in "The Long Goodbye"
TOODLES! SEE YOU TOMORROW!!
WELL! THAT WAS RATHER A "HERE'S-YOUR-HAT-WHAT'S-YOUR-HURRY" SORT OF A DEAL!
SLAM!

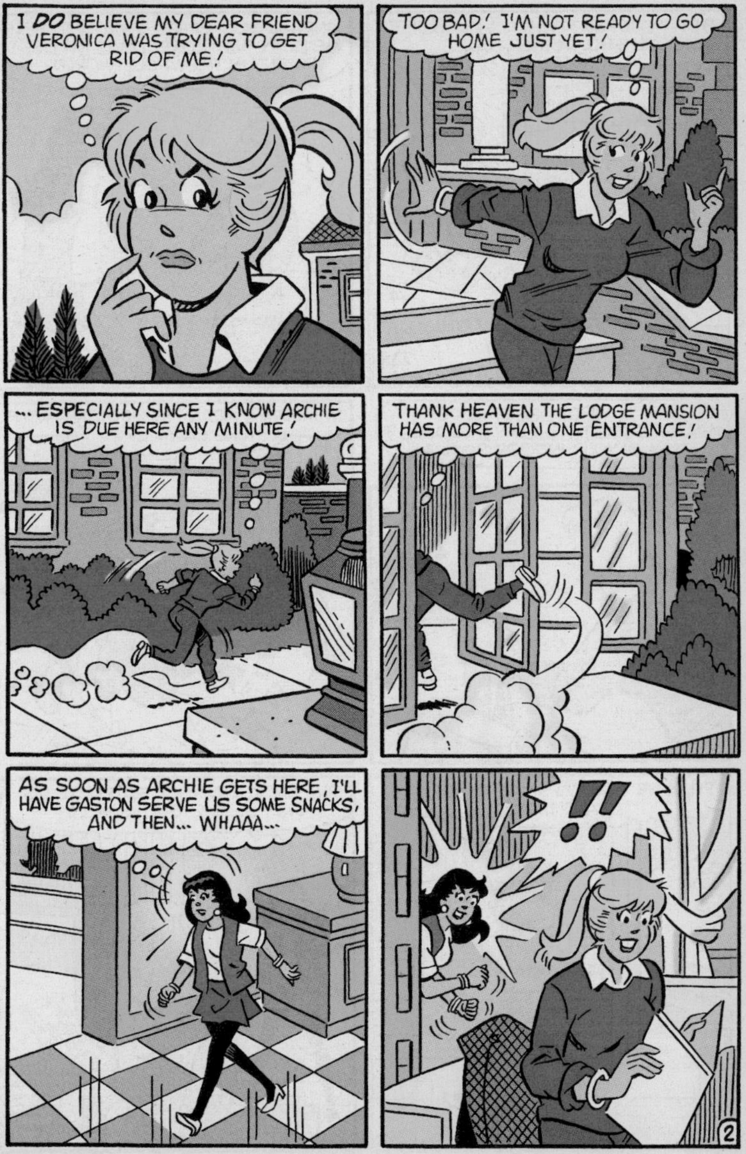
I DO BELIEVE MY DEAR FRIEND VERONICA WAS TRYING TO GET RID OF ME!
TOO BAD! I'M NOT READY TO GO HOME JUST YET!
... ESPECIALLY SINCE I KNOW ARCHIE IS DUE HERE ANY MINUTE!
THANK HEAVEN THE LODGE MANSION HAS MORE THAN ONE ENTRANCE!
AS SOON AS ARCHIE GETS HERE, I'LL HAVE GASTON SERVE US SOME SNACKS, AND THEN... WHAAA...
!!
2

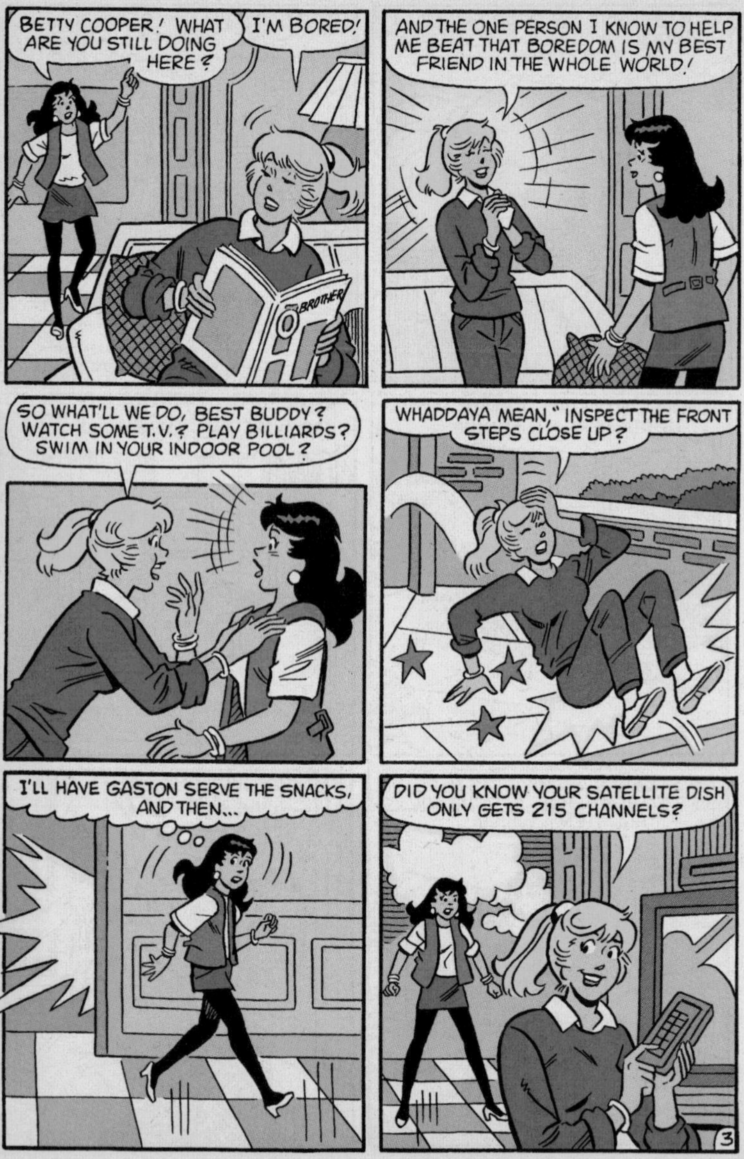
BETTY COOPER! WHAT ARE YOU STILL DOING HERE?
I'M BORED!
BROTHER
AND THE ONE PERSON I KNOW TO HELP ME BEAT THAT BOREDOM IS MY BEST FRIEND IN THE WHOLE WORLD!
SO WHAT'LL WE DO, BEST BUDDY? WATCH SOME T.V.? PLAY BILLIARDS? SWIM IN YOUR INDOOR POOL?
WHADDAYA MEAN, "INSPECT THE FRONT STEPS CLOSE UP?
I'LL HAVE GASTON SERVE THE SNACKS, AND THEN...
DID YOU KNOW YOUR SATELLITE DISH ONLY GETS 215 CHANNELS?
3

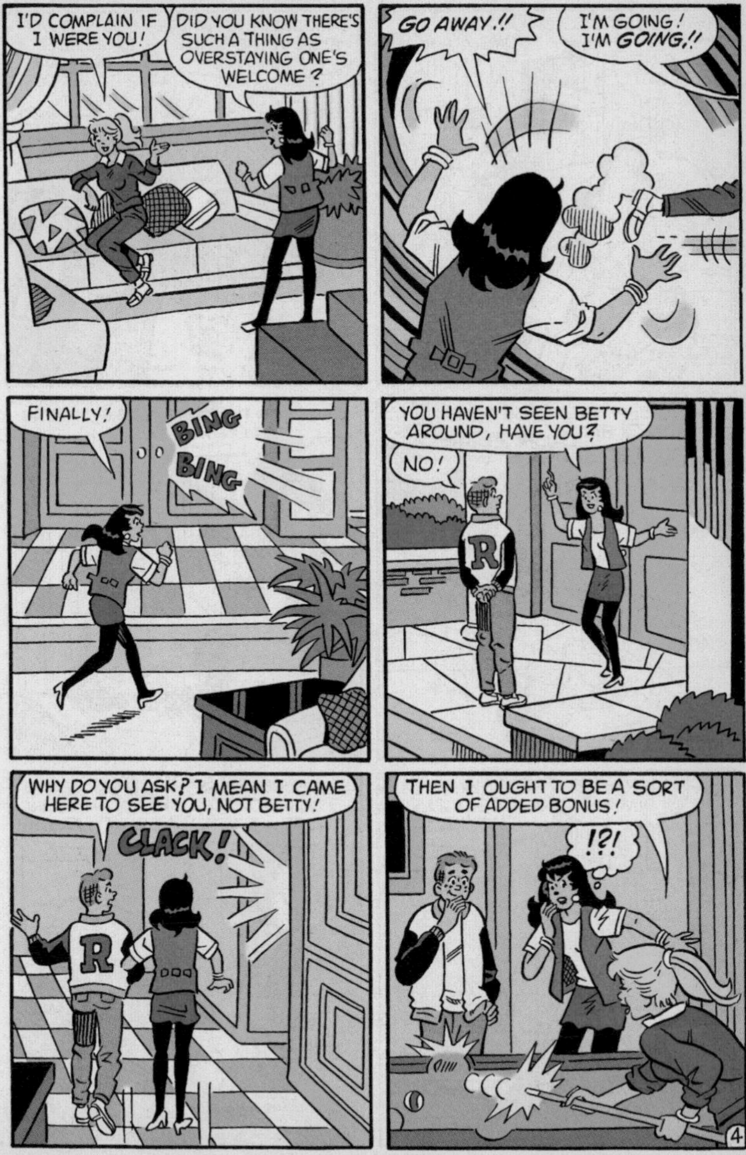

I'D COMPLAIN IF I WERE YOU!
DID YOU KNOW THERE'S SUCH A THING AS OVERSTAYING ONE'S WELCOME?
GO AWAY.!!
I'M GOING! I'M GOING.!!
FINALLY!
BING
BING
YOU HAVEN'T SEEN BETTY AROUND, HAVE YOU?
NO!
WHY DO YOU ASK? I MEAN I CAME HERE TO SEE YOU, NOT BETTY!
CLACK!
THEN I OUGHT TO BE A SORT OF ADDED BONUS!
!?!
4

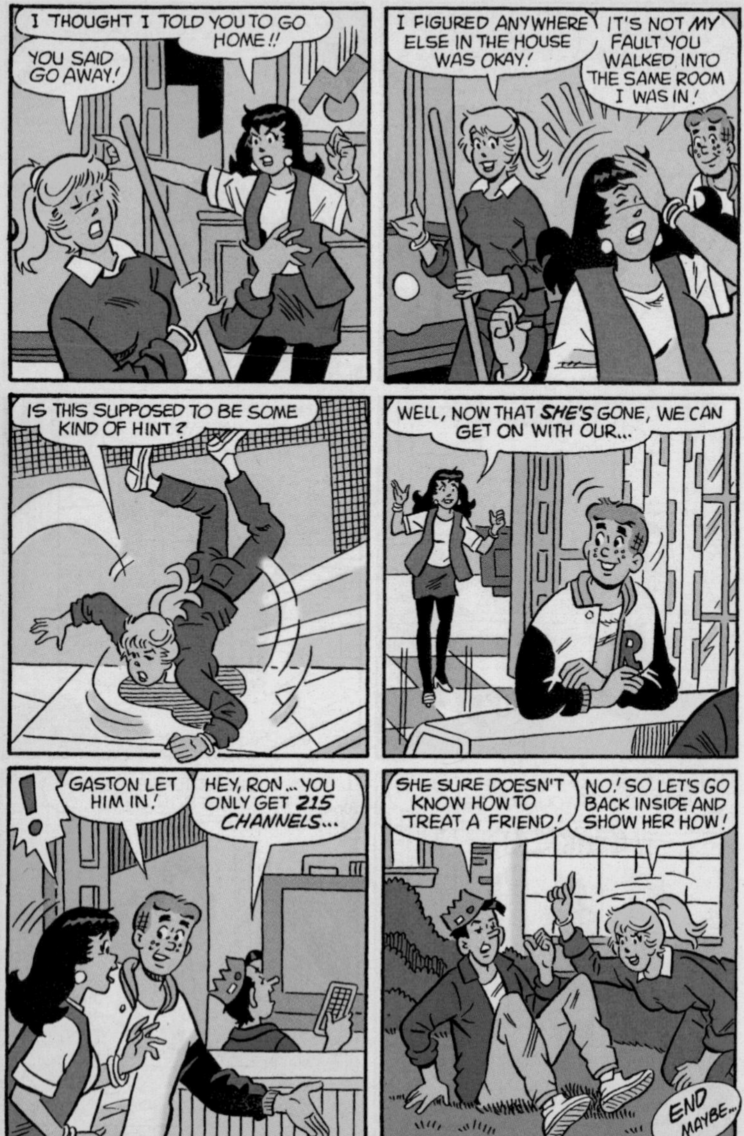
I THOUGHT I TOLD YOU TO GO HOME!!
YOU SAID GO AWAY!
I FIGURED ANYWHERE ELSE IN THE HOUSE WAS OKAY!
IT'S NOT MY FAULT YOU WALKED INTO THE SAME ROOM I WAS IN!
IS THIS SUPPOSED TO BE SOME KIND OF HINT?
WELL, NOW THAT SHE'S GONE, WE CAN GET ON WITH OUR...
!
GASTON LET HIM IN!
HEY, RON... YOU ONLY GET 215 CHANNELS...
SHE SURE DOESN'T KNOW HOW TO TREAT A FRIEND!
NO! SO LET'S GO BACK INSIDE AND SHOW HER HOW!
END ...MAYBE...

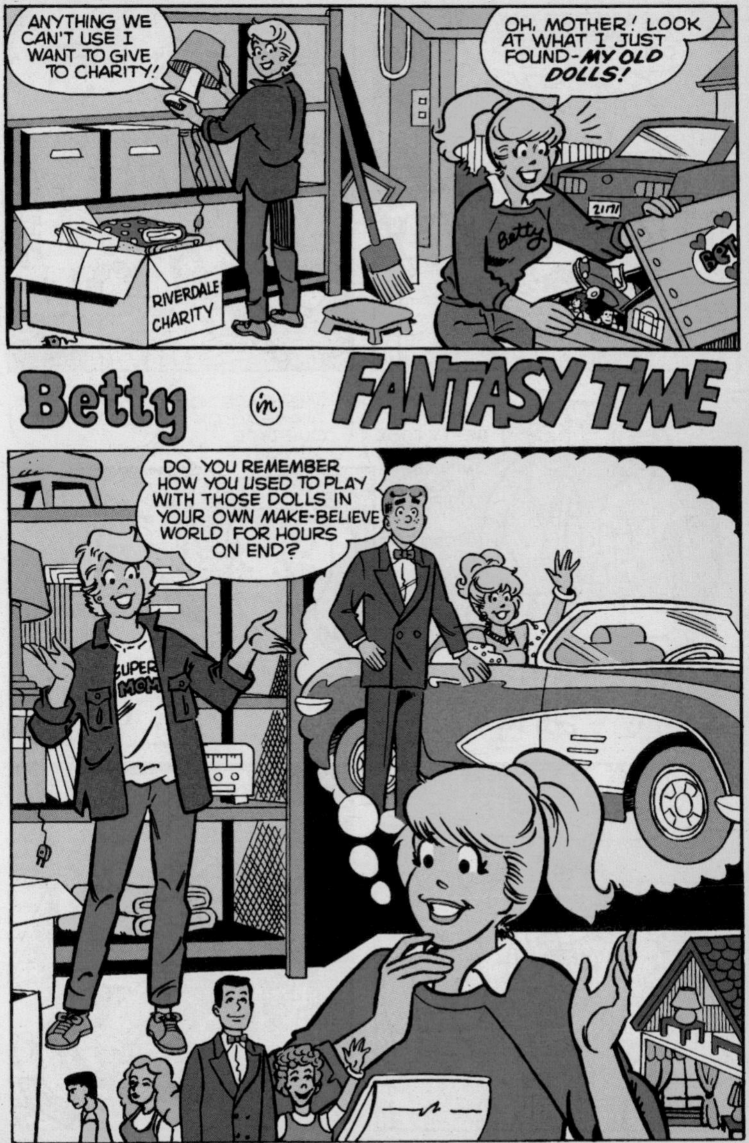
ANYTHING WE CAN'T USE I WANT TO GIVE TO CHARITY!
OH, MOTHER! LOOK AT WHAT I JUST FOUND-MY OLD DOLLS!
RIVERDALE CHARITY
Betty
Betty in FANTASY TIME
DO YOU REMEMBER HOW YOU USED TO PLAY WITH THOSE DOLLS IN YOUR OWN MAKE-BELIEVE WORLD FOR HOURS ON END?
SUPER MOM

Script: George Gladir / Pencils: Stan Goldberg / Inks: Mike Esposito / Letters: Bill Yoshida

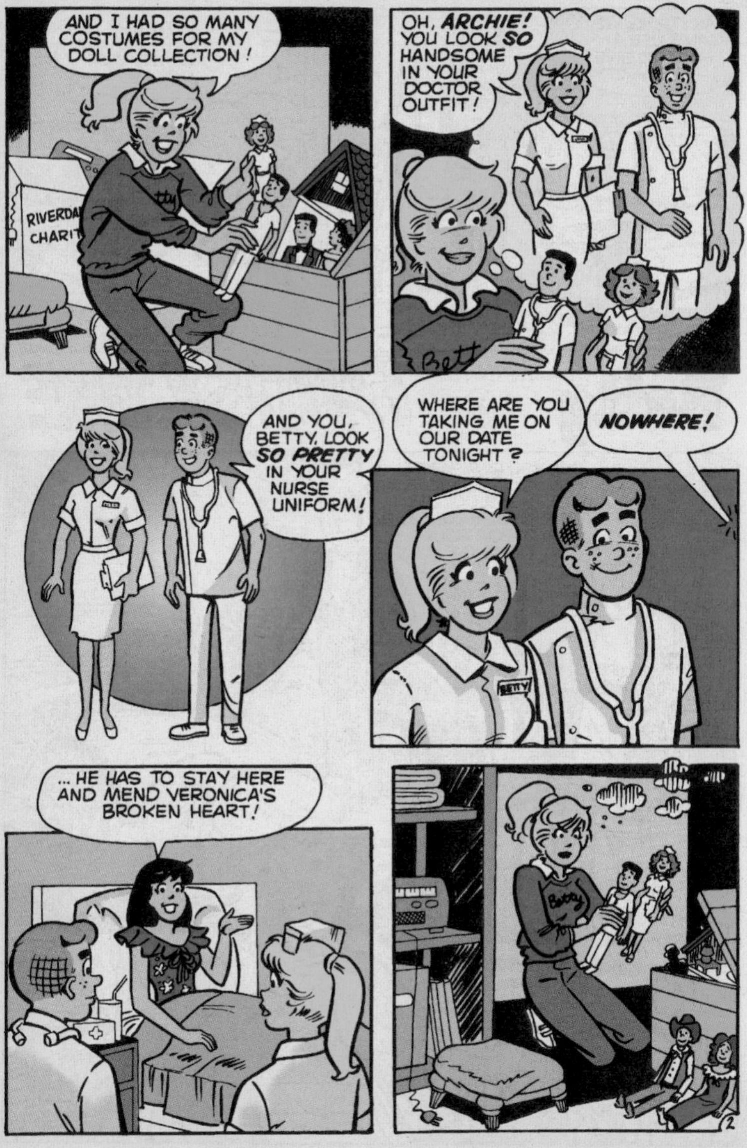
AND I HAD SO MANY COSTUMES FOR MY DOLL COLLECTION!
RIVERDA
CHARIT
OH, ARCHIE! YOU LOOK SO HANDSOME IN YOUR DOCTOR OUTFIT!
AND YOU, BETTY, LOOK SO PRETTY IN YOUR NURSE UNIFORM!
WHERE ARE YOU TAKING ME ON OUR DATE TONIGHT?
NOWHERE!
BETTY
...HE HAS TO STAY HERE AND MEND VERONICA'S BROKEN HEART!
Betty
2

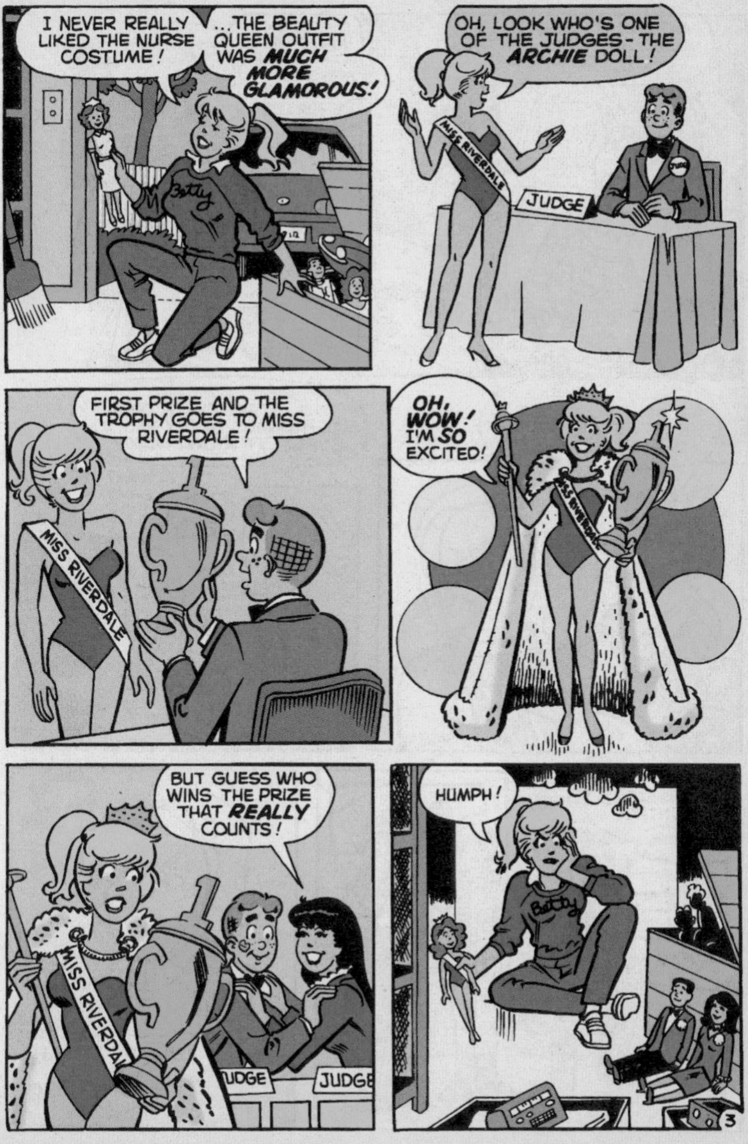
I NEVER REALLY LIKED THE NURSE COSTUME!
...THE BEAUTY QUEEN OUTFIT WAS MUCH MORE GLAMOROUS!
Betty
OH, LOOK WHO'S ONE OF THE JUDGES- THE ARCHIE DOLL!
MISS RIVERDALE
JUDGE
FIRST PRIZE AND THE TROPHY GOES TO MISS RIVERDALE!
MISS RIVERDALE
OH, WOW! I'M SO EXCITED!
MISS RIVERDALE
BUT GUESS WHO WINS THE PRIZE THAT REALLY COUNTS!
MISS RIVERDAL
JUDGE
JUDGE
HUMPH!
Betty

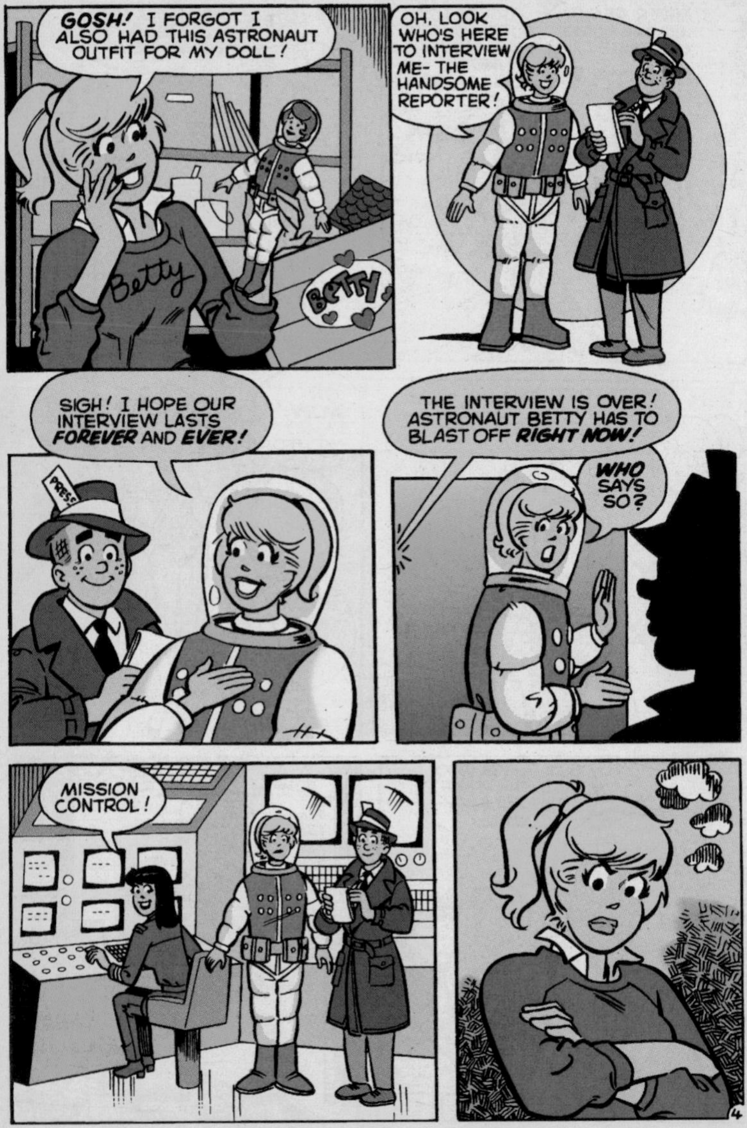
GOSH! I FORGOT I ALSO HAD THIS ASTRONAUT OUTFIT FOR MY DOLL!
Betty
BETTY
OH, LOOK WHO'S HERE TO INTERVIEW ME- THE HANDSOME REPORTER!
SIGH! I HOPE OUR INTERVIEW LASTS FOREVER AND EVER!
PRESS
THE INTERVIEW IS OVER! ASTRONAUT BETTY HAS TO BLAST OFF RIGHT NOW!
WHO SAYS SO?
MISSION CONTROL!
4

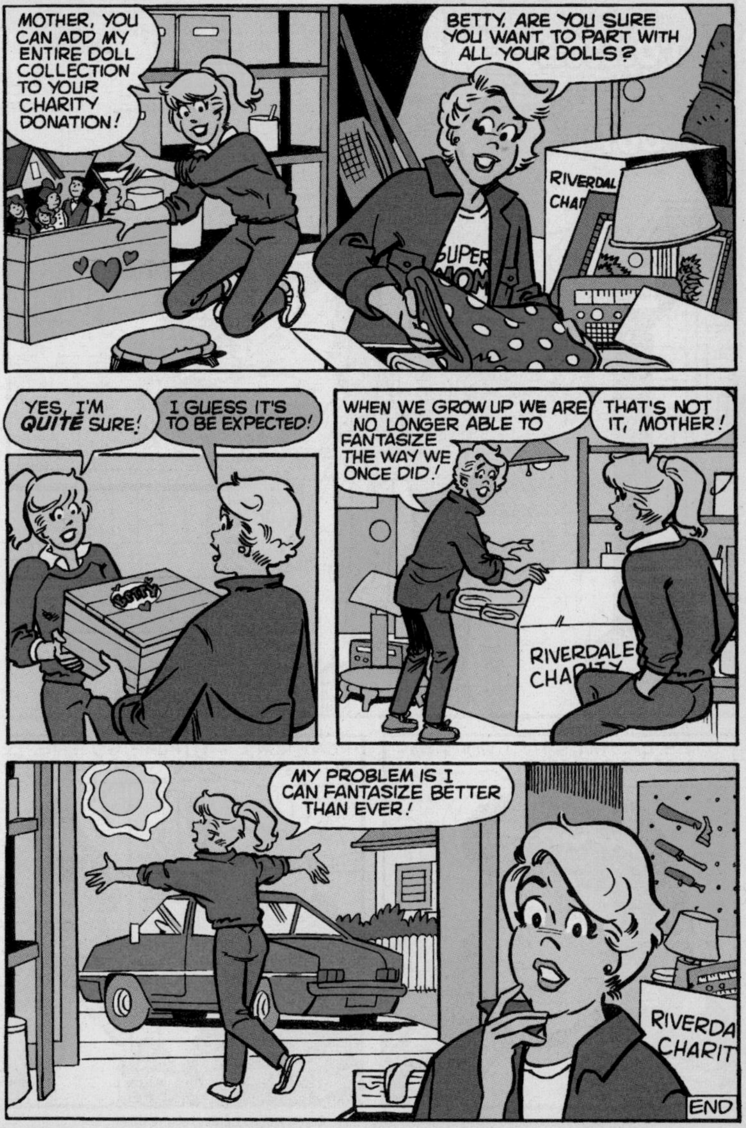
MOTHER, YOU CAN ADD MY ENTIRE DOLL COLLECTION TO YOUR CHARITY DONATION!
BETTY, ARE YOU SURE YOU WANT TO PART WITH ALL YOUR DOLLS?
RIVERDAL
CHA
SUPER MOM
YES, I'M *QUITE* SURE!
I GUESS IT'S TO BE EXPECTED!
BETTY
WHEN WE GROW UP WE ARE NO LONGER ABLE TO FANTASIZE THE WAY WE ONCE DID!
THAT'S NOT IT, MOTHER!
RIVERDALE
CHA
MY PROBLEM IS I CAN FANTASIZE BETTER THAN EVER!
RIVERDA
CHARIT
END

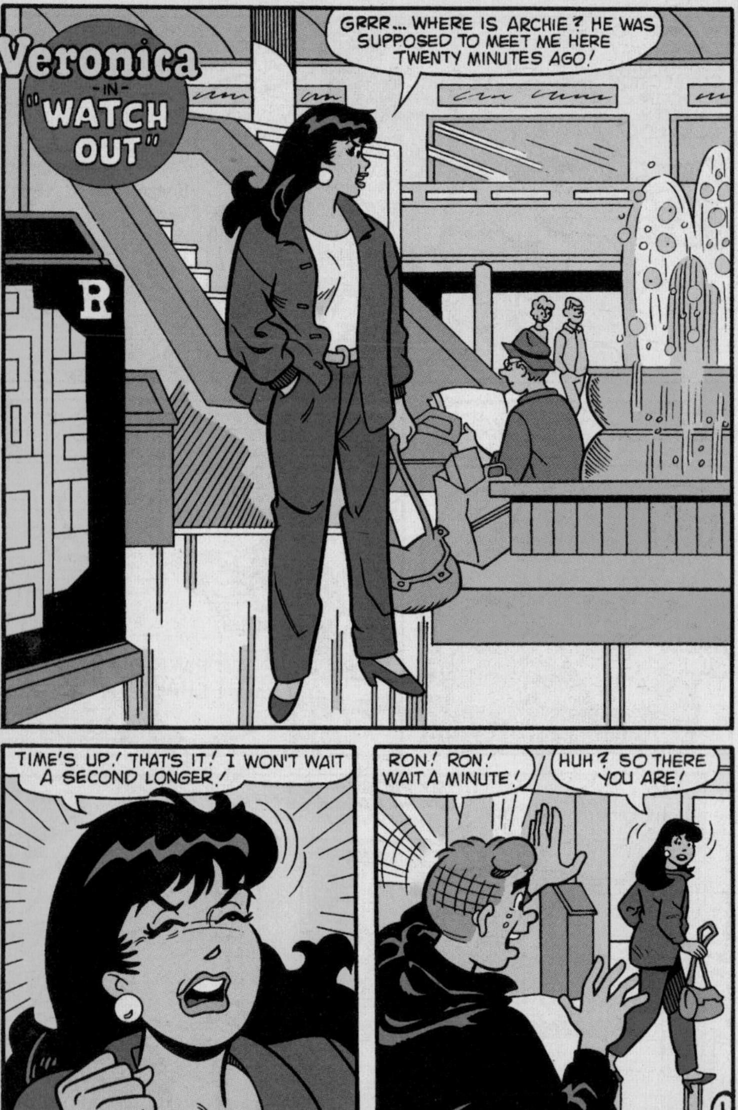
Veronica
-IN-
"WATCH OUT"
GRRR... WHERE IS ARCHIE? HE WAS SUPPOSED TO MEET ME HERE TWENTY MINUTES AGO!
R
TIME'S UP! THAT'S IT! I WON'T WAIT A SECOND LONGER!
RON! RON! WAIT A MINUTE!
HUH? SO THERE YOU ARE!
1

Script: Mike Pellowski / Pencils: Tim Kennedy / Inks: Alison Flood / Letters: Bill Yoshida

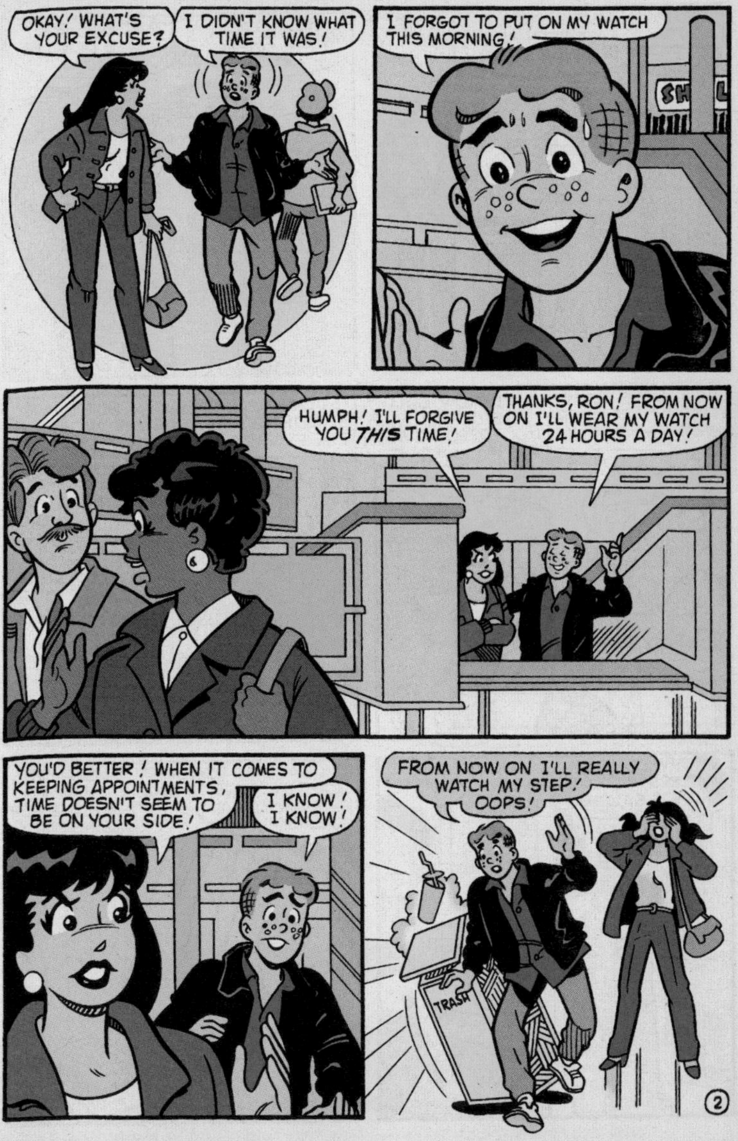
OKAY! WHAT'S YOUR EXCUSE?
I DIDN'T KNOW WHAT TIME IT WAS!
I FORGOT TO PUT ON MY WATCH THIS MORNING!
HUMPH! I'LL FORGIVE YOU THIS TIME!
THANKS, RON! FROM NOW ON I'LL WEAR MY WATCH 24 HOURS A DAY!
YOU'D BETTER! WHEN IT COMES TO KEEPING APPOINTMENTS, TIME DOESN'T SEEM TO BE ON YOUR SIDE!
I KNOW! I KNOW!
FROM NOW ON I'LL REALLY WATCH MY STEP! OOPS!
TRASH
2

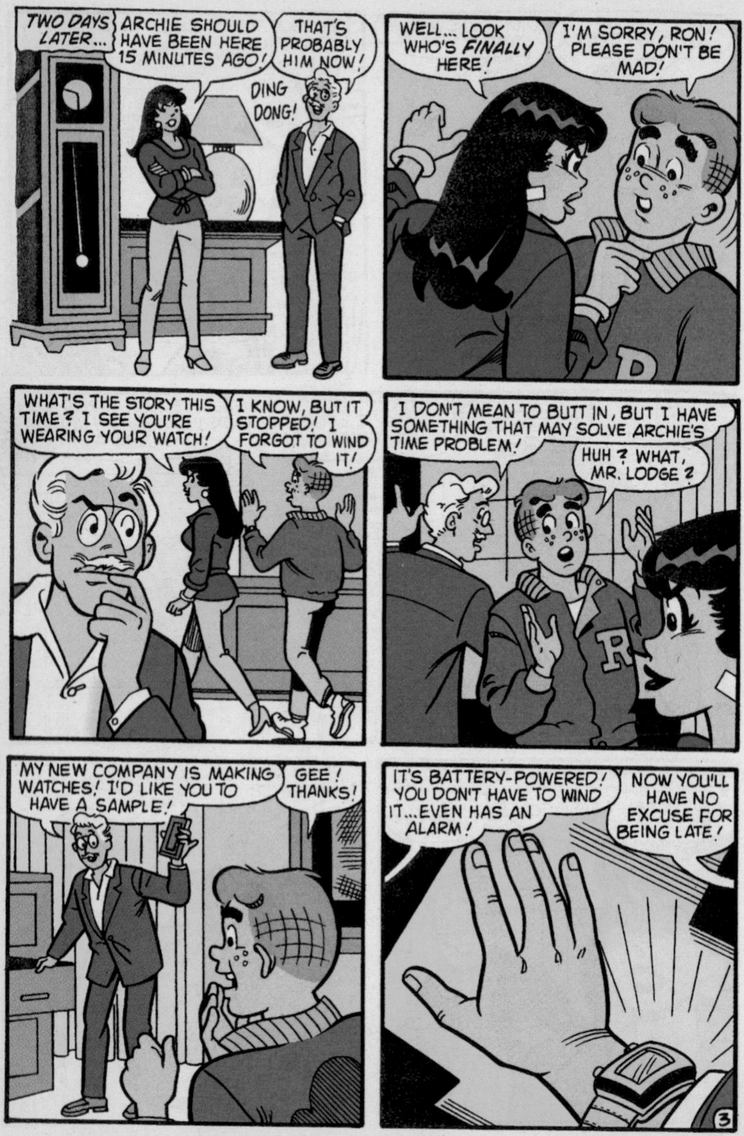
TWO DAYS LATER...
ARCHIE SHOULD HAVE BEEN HERE 15 MINUTES AGO!
THAT'S PROBABLY HIM NOW!
DING DONG!
WELL... LOOK WHO'S FINALLY HERE!
I'M SORRY, RON! PLEASE DON'T BE MAD!
WHAT'S THE STORY THIS TIME? I SEE YOU'RE WEARING YOUR WATCH!
I KNOW, BUT IT STOPPED! I FORGOT TO WIND IT!
I DON'T MEAN TO BUTT IN, BUT I HAVE SOMETHING THAT MAY SOLVE ARCHIE'S TIME PROBLEM!
HUH? WHAT, MR. LODGE?
MY NEW COMPANY IS MAKING WATCHES! I'D LIKE YOU TO HAVE A SAMPLE!
GEE! THANKS!
IT'S BATTERY-POWERED! YOU DON'T HAVE TO WIND IT...EVEN HAS AN ALARM!
NOW YOU'LL HAVE NO EXCUSE FOR BEING LATE!
3

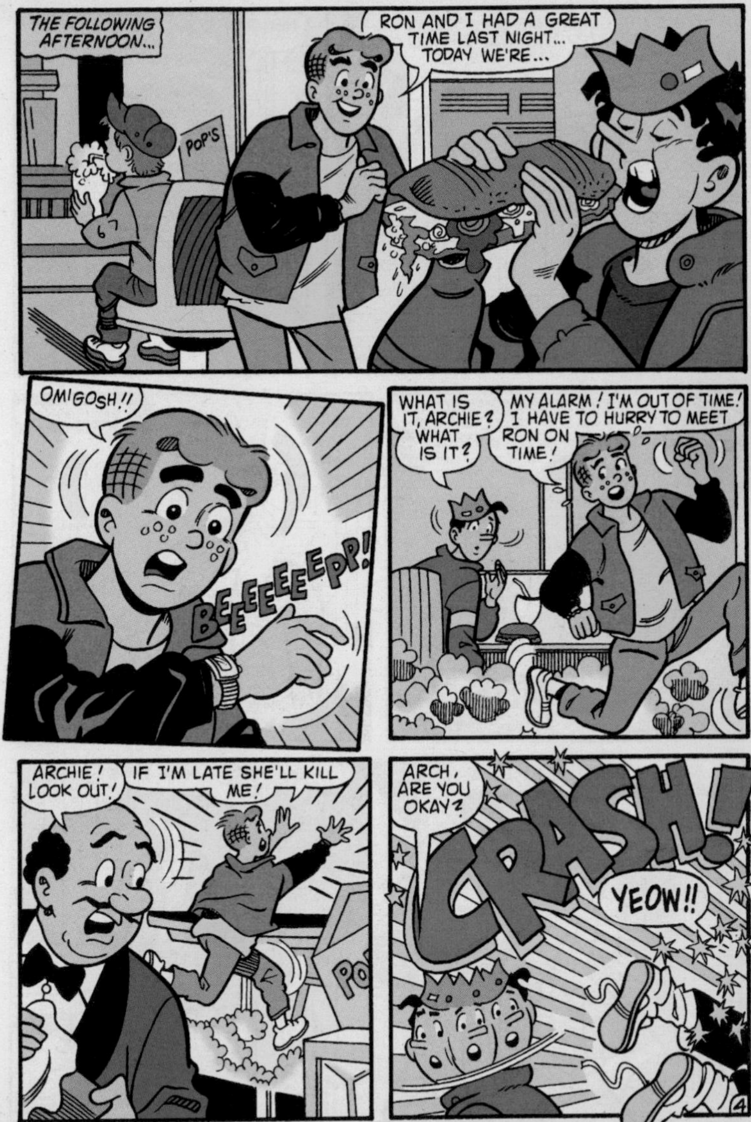
THE FOLLOWING AFTERNOON...
POP'S
RON AND I HAD A GREAT TIME LAST NIGHT... TODAY WE'RE...
OMIGOSH!!
BEEEEEEEPP!
WHAT IS IT, ARCHIE? WHAT IS IT?
MY ALARM! I'M OUT OF TIME! I HAVE TO HURRY TO MEET RON ON TIME!
ARCHIE! LOOK OUT!
IF I'M LATE SHE'LL KILL ME!
ARCH, ARE YOU OKAY?
CRASH!
YEOW!!
4

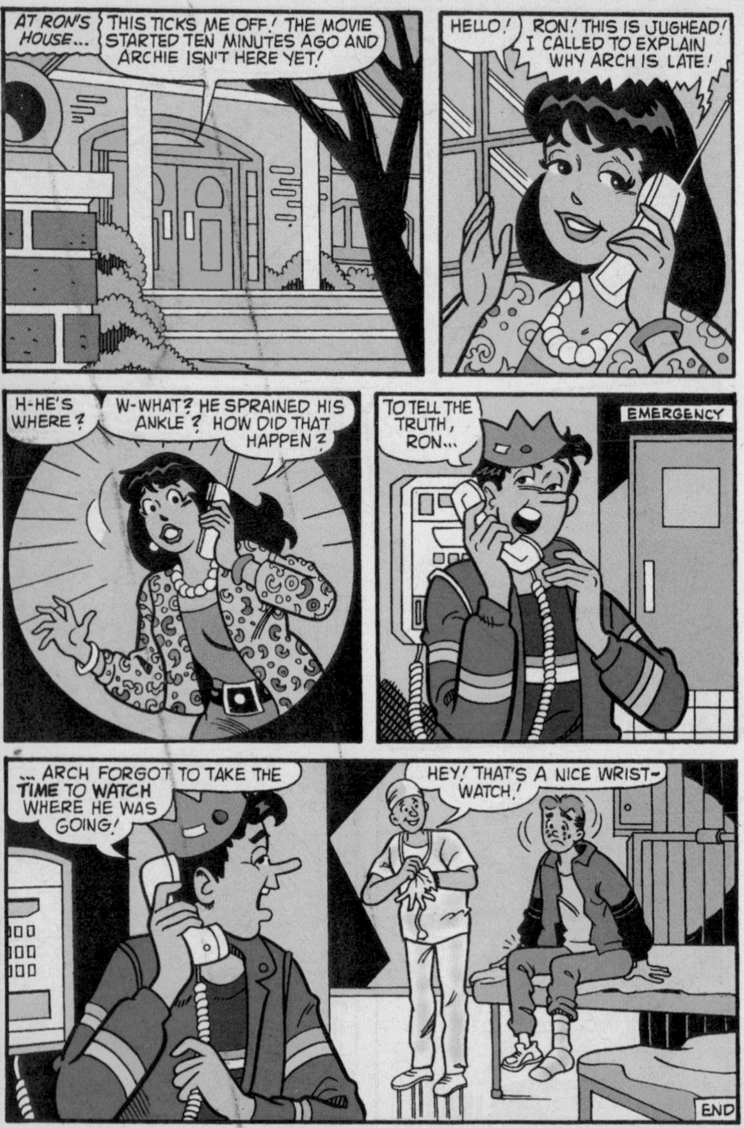
AT RON'S HOUSE...
THIS TICKS ME OFF! THE MOVIE STARTED TEN MINUTES AGO AND ARCHIE ISN'T HERE YET!
HELLO!
RON! THIS IS JUGHEAD! I CALLED TO EXPLAIN WHY ARCH IS LATE!
H-HE'S WHERE?
W-WHAT? HE SPRAINED HIS ANKLE? HOW DID THAT HAPPEN?
TO TELL THE TRUTH, RON...
EMERGENCY
... ARCH FORGOT TO TAKE THE TIME TO WATCH WHERE HE WAS GOING!
HEY! THAT'S A NICE WRIST-WATCH!
END